THE ARTIST AND THE ORC

A MONSTER FANTASY ROMANCE

FINLEY FENN

Editing: Eris Adderly
Proofreading: Emmy from @brabedrebelt
Botanical science and art consultant: Linda Ann Vorobik, PhD
Icelandic (Aelakesh) translation: Þórey H.
Cover artwork: Skadior Art
Cover design: Sylvia at The Book Brander
Supported by the generous members of the Orc Sworn Patreon

~

The Artist and the Orc

~

Sign up at www.finleyfenn.com for bonus stories and epilogues, delicious orc artwork, complete content guidance, news about upcoming books, and more!

ALSO BY FINLEY FENN

ORC SWORN

The Lady and the Orc

The Heiress and the Orc

The Librarian and the Orc

The Duchess and the Orc

The Midwife and the Orc

The Maid and the Orcs

The Governess and the Orc

The Beauty and the Orcs

The Widow and the Orcs

The Artist and the Orc

Offered by the Orc

Tryggred by the Orc

Yuled by the Orcs

Tales of Orc Sworn

ORC FORGED

The Sins of the Orc

The Fall of the Orc

THE MAGES

The Mage's Maid

The Mage's Match

The Mage's Master

The Mage's Groom

1

Daisy Carlyle's partner had another woman in their bed.

Daisy froze in the doorway of their small rented apartment, her eyes snapped wide and unseeing, her heart battering against her ribs. While her ears desperately strained to listen, to catch the warmth in Lew's low muffled laughter, and—yes, oh gods—the tinkling trill of a woman's laugh in return.

"Oh, Lewie," came the woman's distant, teasing voice. "That feels so—*eep!*"

Lew laughed again, the sound easy and genuine and painfully familiar, scraping like sharp vicious quills up Daisy's back. And she only distantly noticed her hands were shaking, and she thrust down her bag of food onto the counter just in time, before it dropped and smashed all over the floor.

Because—Lew had *known* she was coming back before sundown. Right? He'd *known*. And not bringing third parties home into their bed was one of the most fundamental rules they'd agreed upon. One of the rules *Lew* had agreed upon, when they'd first decided to open up their relationship the year before.

It's the civilized thing to do these days, Daisy, Lew had told her, with his usual authority ringing through his voice. *Humans were never meant to be tied down to one partner for our entire lives, were we? But this way, we can benefit from the best of both worlds. A committed partnership, and a bit of variety on the side.*

Of course, it had been far easier for Lew to blithely propose such an arrangement, since he was the one with the coin. He was the one with the prestigious position at the realm's most renowned university. He was the one who published the books and papers, who led all the latest botanical research, who had all the colleagues and contracts, while Daisy was...

Lew's illustrator. His quiet, awkward illustrator, with middling education and prospects. And being hired to illustrate *the* Lewis Wallace's first published botanical compendium—a critically acclaimed triumph—had utterly transformed Daisy's previously mundane life, hurling into her a world of light and wonder and possibility. Especially once the handsome botanist's interest had begun to extend in a more... personal direction.

You're absolutely brilliant, Daisy, Lew had told her late one night, after she'd spent hours drawing a rare amaranth just the way he'd wanted it. *Brilliant, and beautiful.*

No one had ever called Daisy beautiful before, what with her average build, baggy secondhand wardrobe, and messy, brassy hair. But that fateful night, as she'd gasped and begged in Lew Wallace's strong, capable arms, she'd almost, *almost,* believed it. Almost believed she was a beautiful, desirable creative, an artist of skill and talent, worthy of attention and devotion.

And in the four years since, with that dazzling dream still dangling before her, Daisy had gone on to become Lew

Wallace's constant companion in life, in bed, and in work. Researching with him, learning with him, travelling around the realm with him. Including this particular weeks-long sojourn in Dusbury, staying in this small rented apartment, and...

And listening to Lew make love to another woman in their bed.

"Lewie!" came the woman's squeal, twisting in Daisy's gut. "Oh, no, no, no—ohhhh, yes—"

Daisy gritted her teeth, squeezed her eyes shut, and willed her trampling heartbeat to slow. This didn't have to mean anything, or change anything. Lew cared for *her*. He'd chosen *her*. And he'd reminded her of that again and again, holding her gaze with his beautiful brown eyes.

You're still my partner, Daisy, he would say. *I chose you, remember? My heart is forever yours.*

Daisy silently repeated that marginally comforting thought as she groped for her sketchbook, and then for the little bouquet of bright, colourful wildflowers she'd picked on her way home. Red trillium, purple coneflower, buttercups, even a few daisies. The kind of banal, in-your-face flora Lew always rolled his eyes at, but they were still lovely to look at, and fun to draw. And Daisy needed a distraction, needed something, anything, to block out those warm, intimate sounds still emanating from her bedroom.

But once she'd arranged the flowers, and plunked herself down at the small table with her sketchbook and pencils, she soon found that her hand wouldn't stop trembling, or streaking sweat on the paper. And she couldn't even get the coneflower's simple stem right, couldn't draw a single straight line, the perspective was wrong and everything, everything was wrong—

She flipped the page, began anew on a fresh sheet—but this time it seemed even harder, her lines stiff and flat, the flowers' cheerful, vivid beauty gone dull and lifeless on the paper. And the more she kept at it, trying to fix it, to salvage it, the more hideous it became, as if in dreadful competition with the sounds still grating into her ears.

"Oh, *yes*, darling," Lew was groaning now, over the rhythmic creaks of the heavy wooden bed. "That's good. Just like that. *Mmmm*."

Daisy's heartbeat spiked, her breaths sharp and shallow—and before she'd even realized it, she slammed down her pencil, and stalked toward the bedroom door. Rapping on it with a loud, echoing knock, even as her hand kept shaking, and fresh misery roared and raged in her chest.

"Lew, I'm home," she called out, as steadily as she could. "And I need to—talk to you. *Now*, please."

Her voice was followed by a sudden, stilted silence, broken only by the thunder of her galloping heartbeat—and then, finally, a cough, low and discreet. Lew's cough.

"Yes, of course," his familiar voice called back, though it sounded distinctly breathless. "Just a moment."

For an awful, agonizing instant, Daisy thought he was going to make her listen while he finished, while he emptied himself out into this laughing, moaning stranger in her bed—but then, thank all the gods, she could soon hear the rustle of clothing, and the sound of footsteps. Until finally, finally, the bedroom door swept open.

And there, standing before her, was Daisy's tall, handsome partner. His eyes sparkling, his cheeks flushed, his short brown hair falling in becoming curls over his forehead. The sight of him still enough to catch Daisy's breath, except for... the woman. The woman standing just behind him, her hand curving light and easy around his arm.

And this woman was—beautiful. Truly stunning, with shiny, raven-black hair, high cheekbones, and large, long-lashed eyes. And her dress, while obviously thrown on with haste, was sleek, stylish, and perfectly fitted to her graceful, willowy form.

"Ah... hello," she said to Daisy, in a low, pleasing voice, before angling a wary glance toward Lew. "And this is...?"

There was another instant's horrible, scraping silence, but then Lew coughed again. "This is Daisy," he replied, his voice creditably smooth. "Daisy Carlyle."

The new woman's eyes cleared at once, and a bright smile flashed across her lovely face. "Oh, your *artist!*" she said, in tones of deep relief. "Your work is absolutely stunning, Miss Carlyle. I was just telling Lewie earlier, I've pored over every one of your publications until they're all dog-eared and tattered. No one brings flowers to life the way you do! You even make *vegetables* look interesting."

What? In the midst of the clamouring confusion now screaming through her brain, Daisy somehow refrained from making the irrelevant, irrational point that plant organs weren't *vegetables*—an amateur error that Lew had always considered an unpardonable offense. But Daisy's narrow glance at Lew found him smiling warmly back toward this woman, without even a glimmer of judgement in his eyes.

It left Daisy standing there slack-jawed and staring, while the furious disbelief churned ever higher in her chest, and a dozen possible responses spewed across her thoughts at once. *How dare you. That bedroom is supposed to be mine. I'm not just his artist, I'm his partner. I don't want empty compliments. Stop touching him. Stop looking at me. Get the hell out.*

But none of them would come. Not a single word. And instead, Daisy's face was burning hot, and something was stinging behind her eyes—and suddenly she was sharply, horribly aware of how she must look, standing here silent and plain and unstylish, gaping at Lew and this beautiful, graceful woman. This woman who Lew had just touched, and kissed, and made love to. The woman who'd just had Lew *inside* her.

"Why don't we say goodnight for now, Sybil," Lew finally

said, around another quiet, subtle cough. "I'll see you out, and we'll talk tomorrow."

The churning chaos screamed even louder through Daisy's skull, because of course this lovely woman was named *Sybil*, rather than being named after a common, over-rated herbaceous plant that Lew would never deign to include in any of his books. And what the hell did Lew mean, he was talking to this Sybil again tomorrow? After she'd apparently read all his books, and yet still called plant organs *vegetables*?!

This Sybil looked perplexed, but she allowed Lew to guide her toward the door, and usher her out into the hall-way—now with his hand on her back, damn him. And when Lew finally came back in and shut the door, Daisy found that she still hadn't moved from beside the bedroom, and she still couldn't breathe properly, and her heart was still thundering in her ears.

"There was no need to be so rude, Daisy," Lew said, as he strode past her toward the counter, and began unpacking the supper she'd bought at the market. "I only lost track of time, that's all."

That's all. He spoke so calmly, so rationally, even coolly raising his brows toward Daisy, as if in full expectation of an immediate and profuse apology. While Daisy still couldn't think, couldn't find air, couldn't even feel her furiously trem-bling fingers.

"It's against our rule, Lew," she finally ground out, in a hoarse, ugly croak. "We agreed on the rules. No one else in our bedroom."

Lew's brows snapped higher, his expression radiating frank, surprised innocence. "But this isn't our house, Daisy," he countered, as though this fact might have somehow slipped her notice. "This is an entirely unrelated rented apartment, provided by *my* employer."

There was a faint stress on the *my*, just a subtle reminder to Daisy of who was footing the bill for all this. And while it usually worked—she knew very well who held the purse-strings in their relationship—this time it only launched her miserable rage higher, kindling like rotten, oily tinder in her belly.

"It doesn't matter, Lew," she snapped back. "I don't want other people in my—in the bed I'm sleeping in. The bed that's supposed to be *ours*. And I made that very, *very* clear to you when I agreed to all this!"

Lew kept looking at Daisy with that cool disapproval, even as he continued calmly unpacking her bag. "Well, forgive me for not understanding your unilaterally revised definition of 'your' bed," he said curtly. "I'll refrain from bringing Sybil here, going forward."

From bringing Sybil here. As if he was fully planning upon seeing Sybil again—of course he was—and Daisy's miserable fury surged even higher, so strong she could taste bile in her throat. "Does she even know who I am?" she demanded. "Does she know I'm your partner and lover of four years, and not just your *artist*?"

Lew's answering shrug was just a shade too nonchalant, his eyes fixed on his unpacking. "She knows it's not exclusive," he said smoothly, as he turned toward the icebox. "But I don't feel the need to go around announcing all the details to everyone I meet, either. I thought keeping our outside encounters impersonal was another one of your *rules*?"

Daisy's mouth fell open—they'd created those rules *together*, Lew had written out the damned list himself—and she dragged down a long, bracing breath. "I want you to tell Sybil the truth about me," she replied, too quickly. "And actually"—was she going to say it, she *was*—"actually, I want you to break it off with her. Permanently."

Lew betrayed a brief, almost imperceptible twitch, and his eyes sharpened, narrowing on Daisy's face. But he wasn't speaking, and she drew down another breath, deeper this time. "I want you to stop seeing Sybil," she repeated—and yes, even the thought of it was settling the frantic chaos in her chest, just a little. "As per those rules we made—*together*—either of us has the right to veto the other's... *attachments*. At any time, for any reason."

Her voice came out sounding too loud, almost triumphant, because that particular rule had been what had finally swayed her into this whole arrangement in the first place. Not because she'd wanted to inspect or approve of Lew's bed-partners—in truth, she wanted to know as little about them as possible—but because of the position it had given her. It had meant she was still the most important, that she still occupied an inviolable place of honour—or even power—in Lew's life, and his bed. *My heart is forever yours.*

But the expression on Lew's face had turned decidedly sour, his mouth pinched and thin. "Good gods, Daisy," he snapped back. "What possible reason do you have for disapproving of her? She was polite, she left without a fuss, she even praised your work! It was a *very* generous compliment, and one that *you* returned with entirely unwarranted rudeness!"

The misery curdled deeper in Daisy's belly—someone praising her work was a *very generous compliment*, now?—and Lew lifted his chin, his lovely eyes gone cold, condescending, imperious. "We've discussed this at length, Daisy," he added. "I've offered you countless solutions and reassurances. I even gave you that ring as a sign of my affections, though it seems you can scarcely be bothered to remember it, let alone actually wear it!"

Daisy grimaced and glanced downwards, toward the familiar large, glittering ring on her left hand. A gift she'd badly wanted, yes, and she knew it had been costly and custom made—but it was also heavy and cumbersome to work around, and often ended up spattered with paints and ink. And on days like this, it almost felt like a mockery, like a shiny toy tossed to distract an annoying, misbehaving pet.

"Yes, because I'm your *partner*, Lew," Daisy insisted, too shaky, too late. "And as your partner, I don't want you to see Sybil anymore."

Lew's mouth twisted, and he slammed down a loaf of bread onto the counter. "Why are you doing this, Daisy?" he demanded. "Because you're jealous?"

Jealous. Daisy's throat spasmed, and it took far too much effort to keep breathing, to hold herself upright. Yes, yes, she was jealous. She was so jealous she felt sick with it. She'd been able to handle their arrangement when she couldn't see it, when Lew had been discreet about it—but he'd been less and less discreet lately, hadn't he? Less often at home with her, and more often out with... whoever. And Daisy had just kept going, fighting to keep her focus on that shimmering vision of magic, of the dream. On her work, on her art, on their next book. On this free eight-week stay in Dusbury, entirely paid for by...

"You *are* jealous, Daisy," Lew's implacable voice continued, his eyes glinting with cold certainty. "Which is foolish and immature behaviour, and you know it. We're all consenting adults here, and we should be capable of managing our emotions without resorting to childish manipulations and ultimatums like this. Did I work myself into a jealous frenzy when you went off with that grimy painter? Or that *geologist*?"

He couldn't hide that familiar curl of his lip—he'd always nursed a deep dislike of geologists—and Daisy fought down the sudden, irrational urge to break into high-pitched laughter. She'd seen two other people since the start of this last year—*two*—and while they'd both been nice enough, with intriguing careers, Daisy could admit they'd also been... uninspiring, especially in the bedroom. And while she knew she should have gone and sought out other partners instead, the entire ordeal had been tedious and exhausting, and Lew had still been there. And he'd always been confident and compelling in bed, generous with his coin and collaboration, and excellent at managing all the tiresome schedules and deadlines Daisy often struggled with. And until now, it had still been enough. Until...

"Look, it's not just that I'm jealous," Daisy managed, over the ever-rising din in her thoughts. "It's also—how do you know this Sybil? Are you working with her on the project? She looks... familiar."

That distant nagging felt more certain, now—Daisy had always had a very good memory for faces—and Lew's shifty sidelong look confirmed it. "Yes, she's from the city, too," he said, a little too blandly. "She's also here on the project."

Oh, of *course*. So not only was this Sybil sharing Lew's bed, but she knew about the damned top-secret project. The project that had brought Lew and Daisy all the way down here to Dusbury, which was deep in Sakkin, the most south-western province in the realm. And while Sakkin did boast some intriguing flora and fauna—not to mention the huge, highly notorious Orc Mountain, only a day's journey to the south—most of it had already been thoroughly catalogued, and a trip here didn't align with Lew's previous research interests in the slightest. It had made no sense, but Lew had told Daisy nothing, and now—now this?

"I thought we were supposed to keep these things casual, Lew," Daisy shot back, too late. "Professional colleagues should be entirely off-limits. Although, wait"—something new surged in her rioting belly—"how the hell is this Sybil a colleague of yours, if she thinks I draw *vegetables*?!"

Lew couldn't quite hide his wince, but shook his head. "Sybil's not a botanist," he snapped back. "And *you* were my colleague at first too, weren't you, Daisy? Which apparently was perfectly fine and acceptable for *you*, but now that it's someone else, it's suddenly a problem?"

Daisy fought another wild urge to laugh, because in no world had she been anywhere near Lew's level, when they'd first met. He'd been a well-born, well-established academic, educated at the realm's finest university, while she'd been a poor, orphaned, nineteen-year-old artist, living in a tolerant painter friend's cellar, and sinking ever deeper into debt. She'd only been scraping by on commissions—usually of wealthy women's children or pets—when Lew had seen one of her commissions at a party, and had taken particular note not of the plump-faced baby, but the detailed philodendron she'd drawn in the foreground.

You have some true potential in this field, he'd told Daisy, when he'd first shown up at her door, like a beautiful rescuing angel from on high. *You must come and do some sketches for me.*

But that glorious day suddenly felt very far away, and Daisy swallowed down the lurking lump in her throat. "It wasn't the same, Lew," she replied, her voice thick. "And it's petty and self-serving of you to pretend that it is. Especially"—she drew in a shaky breath—"when you're apparently able to share the top-secret details of this project with your new woman, and not with me!"

And if she was honest with herself, maybe that was what hurt the most about all this. No matter how many other people Lew had shared his body with over the past year, Daisy had always had exclusive access to his mind, and his work. She'd eagerly embraced his academic world, his enthusiasm for his field—perhaps because it had so closely echoed her devotion to her own chosen discipline, her commitment to applying and improving her art to the best of her ability. And Lew had seen that, and recognized that, and rewarded it by intimately involving Daisy in his projects, his passions, his research—until these past few months. Until... this.

"So how about this, Lew," Daisy added, her voice harder,

steadier than before. "You can either stop seeing this Sybil—permanently—or you can tell me everything you've been keeping from me about this project. Who hired you. What you're researching. What outcomes you're supposed to achieve. And"—she raised her chin, clenched her teeth—"why you need to be down here in the backwoods of the realm for eight weeks to do it!"

Her voice rang through the small apartment, shrill and demanding—but Lew didn't immediately reply. Instead, he just kept gazing at her, while his throat betrayed an almost imperceptible swallow, his jaw flexing in his cheek.

And as Daisy stared at him, waiting, waiting, it slowly, distantly occurred to her that Lew was... refusing. He was... saying no.

He... *wanted* this Sybil. He *wanted* this secret project. More than he wanted Daisy. More than he wanted their partnership, their shared passions, their successful books, their four years working and living together.

And how long had Lew felt this way? At least for a year, surely, back when he'd first proposed they open their relationship? And why hadn't he just dumped Daisy, why hadn't she dumped him, why had he kept stringing her along, what had he wanted...

But then Daisy's blinking, stinging eyes dropped to the table. To her sketchbook. Which was still lying open and abandoned, with those empty, ugly flowers still shouting at her from the page.

Oh. *Oh.* Of course.

She'd been a fool. Such a stupid, stupid fool.

And before either of them could say it, before the water started streaming down her cheeks, Daisy silently, frantically snatched for her sketchbook, and left.

2

Daisy rushed through Dusbury's quieting streets as quickly as she could, her head down, her sketchbook clutched tightly to her chest.

Gods, she'd been so stupid. To ignore all those doubts and whispers and warnings, flashing in front of her face. To just keep floating along like a merry little seed on the wind, lost in the world she'd so desperately wanted to be true. The world where she was beautiful and desired, a true qualified artist, renowned and acclaimed and beloved. Rather than a mediocre, lucky amateur, clinging to a famous man's coattails…

Daisy's breath choked out in a loud, broken groan, a sound which drew an uneasy frown from a respectable-looking man on the opposite side of the road, and she rubbed at her eyes, and walked faster. Curse her, had Lew even cared about her at all, all this time? Or had it all been about keeping exclusive access to her, to her work? Keeping her close and available, ready to follow him across the realm, to jump to obey his every whim?

Daisy groaned again, earning a disapproving glance from a passing woman this time, but she kept walking, shaking her head. Because damn it, Lew's career was everything to him—and of course he had wanted a dedicated artist, committed only to him and his goals. An artist with plenty of debt, perhaps, and no stable home or employment, who would willingly accept modest payments in exchange for guaranteed room and board and travel and exposure. An artist who would keep offering up her loyalty, her support, and her very best work, on the altar of a handsome commanding lover in her bed, and a bright, tantalizing dream.

You're absolutely brilliant, Daisy. Beautiful. My heart is forever yours.

Daisy didn't care who heard her laugh this time, the sound scraping bitter and broken through the street. She'd been such a fool. Such a typical, brainless, oblivious *fool*.

The water had at some point begun escaping her eyes, trickling in hot tracks down her cheeks, and she impatiently swiped it away as she finally strode through Dusbury's town gate, and turned off the main road. Tromping across a farmer's hayfield, and making straight for the nearby line of trees beyond.

It was early evening now, but there was still a little daylight left, and Daisy's frantic, distracted brain only had one location in mind. A place she'd found a few days before, when she'd been seeking out wild *Cascabela thevetia* to draw, in preparation for its inclusion in Lew's next book.

She groaned and picked up speed, now nearly jogging into the ever-thickening forest. Deeper and deeper, past that cluster of pines, following the sandstone shelf as it gradually grew from the earth. And there, tucked deep inside that jagged rock cliff, was the narrow, hidden opening to the cave.

Daisy had always loved caves—they were another entire world, a secret upside-down reality, bursting with bizarre, highly intriguing flora and rock formations. And as far as she had ever seen, there were very few well-drawn depictions of cave flora and formations in the current literature, and drawing them always felt like an exploration. An adventure. Like something that was only hers.

And gods, Daisy needed something to be only hers right now. Needed to find the weirdest, ugliest stalagmite in this cave, and fill entire pages with drawings of it from every possible angle. Needed to imagine Lew looking at it, wrinkling his nose, making some snide comment about arrogant geologists, and—

Daisy groaned again as she fumbled in her pocket for a candle—her last one—and lit it with a match. And then, holding the candle high, she stumbled through the long, narrow tunnel at the cave's entrance. Taking the left fork, nearly tripping on some large loose stones, and then down further, through the narrow chasm. And then...

Her breath caught, her lips parting, her candle trembling in her fingers. Because yes, the cave was just as incredible as she remembered. Impossibly large, almost circular, with a smooth, high stone ceiling, and a spectacular variety of jagged rocks and boulders studded about, casting intriguing shadows in the flickering light of Daisy's candle.

Daisy's eyes swept across these untold riches with ever-increasing eagerness, and for a brief, wonderful moment, she almost forgot about Lew, about her stupidity, her ruined relationship, her ruined life. Because there was only this, only stark, powerful beauty reigning rampant all around her, offering itself to her, ready to be revealed anew upon a fresh clean page.

Daisy took a slow breath, inhaling as deeply as she could, drinking up the distinctive scents of stone and earth around her. Feeling it fill her lungs, her awareness, strong enough to drown out the distant drumming of her heartbeat.

She still had this. She always, always had this.

She wedged her candle into a rock beside the entrance, high enough to cast its faint flickering light throughout most of the cave—and then she fumbled to open her sketchbook, to flip past the page with the flat ugly flowers. To find that new page, waiting bright and free, ready to begin whispering of the wonder shimmering alive all around it.

Daisy's pencil was already in her hand, fished out of her dress pocket, and now sketching out smooth, sweeping strokes across the page. Not focusing on one single peculiarity, as she'd initially intended, but instead just capturing the cave's elegant shape, its inherent architecture, its wild, chaotic beauty. Almost as if it had been a grand greatroom, once, before it had fallen to ruin, overrun by the very earth itself.

And the more Daisy drew, the stronger that strange certainty felt. The ceiling was too smooth, too round, the floor beneath the rioting rubble far too flat and even. And the floor looked almost checkered in that section, as though its builder had originally alternated the colours of the rock, creating an intricate repeating pattern. A pattern Daisy could barely begin to extrapolate, but she was somehow already making the attempt. Extending the line of that tile, and drawing it over to there, where—yes, yes—it narrowed as it curved into there. And if that mass of rock hadn't fallen in, it would keep going to there, and now Daisy's feet were following it, her steps turning and tripping and meandering as they sought out the middle, the heart...

Her own heart thudded as she found it, her shaky foot sliding aside a wash of rubble to reveal... a circle. A perfect, polished stone circle, embedded in the floor. Not unlike a gleaming black eye, looking up at her from beneath her worn, muddy boots. Watching her, *weighing* her, the sensation sharp enough to send a strange, shimmering quiver up her spine. As if... as if...

Daisy whirled around, her heartbeat shouting through the silent room—because there, by the cave's entrance, near where she'd stuck the candle, there was...

A figure. A tall, lean figure, faintly illuminated by the candlelight.

And yes, it was a him. It had to be, with the height, the sharp square shoulders, the flat bare chest. But he was too tall, too gaunt and bony and strange, his head smooth and entirely hairless, his skin oddly pale in the dim light.

And his skin looked like it was marked with... patterns. Patterns printed in deep, inky black, over his bare head, down his forearms, and even... on his hands. His long-fingered, sharp-tipped hands, held facing out toward Daisy, with... black circles in his palms. Black circles, black *eyes*, just like the one on the floor, just like the ones in his stark, staring, skull-like face...

"What... what are you?" Daisy whispered, over her surging, screeching heartbeat. "Is this"—her eyes darted around the ruined room, the staring eye on the floor—"is this *yours*?"

The man—the creature—didn't move, didn't respond, didn't even blink. And for a fraught, shuddering breath, Daisy was sure she'd imagined him, conjured him up from the very earth itself. And perhaps it was a sign, some cruel omen from the gods that she wasn't supposed to be here. She wasn't wanted, she wasn't a real artist, she wasn't—

But then, the creature... moved. Stepped forward into the cave, the movement slow, sinuous, controlled. His eyes sinking into unreadable black hollows as he moved past her candle, and his face grew even more shadowed, more like a hard empty skull. And one of those hovering hands finally turned away from Daisy, its hidden black eye now pressing flat against the wall, long fingers spreading wide...

And as Daisy stared, the terror flashing white and desperate behind her eyes, the tunnel behind him... fell. Crashed. *Collapsed,* into pure, utter blackness, beneath a thundering crush of stone.

3

Daisy screamed.

The sound rang and echoed, far too loud in the sudden suffocating darkness. But louder still was Daisy's rioting heartbeat, pummelling in her ears, crushing all rational thought beneath the charging horrified terror.

She was trapped. In a pitch-black cave. Alone. With... with *that*.

She had to run. Escape. *Now*.

Her sketchbook and pencil clattered to the floor, and she whirled around in the darkness, staggering, unseeing. Frantically flailing her hands before her, groping for walls, for stone, for—for anything. Maybe there was another way out, maybe she could find a place to hide, maybe she could dig out her candle or find a sharp deadly rock and throw it at the—the *thing*—

But the dark was so complete, so thick and heavy and utterly disorienting, with not even a single pinprick of light, no matter where she looked. And the ground beneath her feet was rocky and uneven, a treacherous foreign wasteland, conspiring with the *thing* to keep her here, and—

She tripped. Tripped over a hard, unmoving solidness—some kind of boulder, curse it. And even as she flailed, caught herself, her other foot tripped, too. And suddenly she was flying, falling through the blackness toward the ground, no, no, *no*—

The impact juddered through her hands, her elbows, snapping her head forward, striking her cheek against something sharp and grating. And with the shock was the sudden surging pain, blooming vicious and eyewatering through her face, her skull. So stunning she couldn't breathe, couldn't think, oh gods what was this, what had she done, what was she supposed to do, how badly was she hurt, was she going to *die*—

"*Róleg*," came a voice, low and rasping and far too close. "*Stopp! Vertu kyrr.*"

Daisy's heartbeat pummelled louder, screaming in her ears, because it was—the *thing*. It was *him*, he was *right here*—

She yelped as she scrabbled and staggered upwards, backwards, away. She had to run, had to escape him or fight him or kill him, but everything hurt, and she still couldn't fucking *see*. And then her foot tripped *again*, and she pitched backwards, flailing and shrieking, trapped, lost, doomed...

When something—caught her. Something warm. Strong. Solid. Bracing close and firm against her back, drawing her upright, holding her steady. Waiting for her to find her footing again.

It was—him. The thing. Touching her. *Touching* her.

Daisy gasped and lurched sideways, shoving him away, away, away—but then her foot caught again. Tripping over yet another rock, curse it, *curse* it. She couldn't even move in here, she was going to *die* in here—

And then—that touch again. An *arm*. Circling swiftly around Daisy's back, yanking her forward against solid unyielding heat, as something warm and powerful snapped tight around—her *neck*.

His *hand*. Around her *neck*.

Daisy froze, her scream stoppered in her throat—*no*—as her shaky hands flailed upwards, clutching and scratching at that hand around her neck. And gods it was big, its fingers impossibly long, and tipped at the ends with—*sharpness*. With multiple painful prodding points, sinking into her soft skin, oh gods, oh please, what was this, what was happening, he was going to force her and kill her and—

"*Gott*," the voice said again, low and decisive, so close his breath stirred against her hair. "*Vertu kyrr.*"

Daisy flinched and shuddered all over, as more wild disjointed panic screeched through her head. She was lost, she was dead, she was doomed. Because this *thing* had her trapped, clutched close against his chest, with his hand—his claws—squeezing her throat. And now, now he was going to—to—

Pat her?

Wait, yes, what the hell? He was—*patting* her. His hand tapping brief and approving against her back, as if Daisy was an obedient puppy who'd properly performed a new trick. While his other hand stayed clamped close and deadly around her neck, its claws still gently digging into her skin. A command. A threat.

Daisy shuddered again, gulping desperately for air, and oh, hell, that was another pat, another certain sign of approval. And the grip around her neck even softened a little, though the sharpness was still very much there, still silently shouting its threat into her skin.

"*Gott*," the low voice said, sounding distinctly satisfied this time. "*Bíddu.*"

What? Daisy couldn't stop shuddering, shivering beneath his implacable grip, her heartbeat still clanging, her breaths gasping in the silence. She was caught, trapped, in a dark treacherous cave, with—with—

"W-what the hell," she finally gasped, her voice strained and wavering. "Who are you? What is this? What do you want from me?!"

There was another little pat to her back, a caress of that sharpness against her throat. "*Bíddu hér*," he replied, his voice firm. "*Vertu örugg.*"

It felt both commanding and approving, almost as if Daisy had... pleased him, somehow. But how? What was she doing now that she hadn't done before, and...

Oh. She was standing still. Not moving. Not... falling.

And—wait. Did that mean—was he—was this—was he—

Was he just trying to *help* her?

Daisy shook her head, and desperately gulped for air, for sensible thought. "I can't—understand you," she choked. "Can't you—speak common-tongue?"

There was an instant's silence, and then a heavy exhale, a drum of sharp fingers against her back. "*Nei*," he replied. "*Aðeins Aelakesh.*"

Daisy squeezed her eyes shut, her heart thudding in her ears, because *nei* sounded a hell of a lot like *no*, didn't it? And nearly everyone in the realm spoke at least some common-tongue, and what did that mean, what was this—*creature*, where had he come from, he was—

Her clattering thoughts flashed back to that moment when she'd first seen him, in the light of her candle. How tall he'd been. How thin and gaunt and pale. And how he'd been hairless, bare-chested, with all those stark black patterns printed across his skin... and how he'd had those black marks on his hands that had looked like *eyes*. And both his hands were still touching her, those eyes now pressing flat against her, as if *seeing* her...

But wait. *Wait.* Surely he could see in the dark, too—

because he'd somehow gotten all the way from the cave's entrance over to here, despite all the chaotic rubble of this destroyed room. And he'd done it without so much as an audible footstep, let alone a crunch or a crack or a fall, when Daisy couldn't even move two steps in here without falling over.

A suspicion had begun whispering, too futile, too foolish, too late. And without thinking, Daisy groped again for the hand still circled around her neck, and—felt it. Felt the warm callused skin, the long slim fingers, and...

The *claws*. The long, curved claws, extending sharp and dangerous from his fingertips. And no human had claws like that, Daisy had seen illustrations of claws like that, and they belonged to—to—

He was... an *orc*.

$$4$$

Daisy was trapped in a cave with an orc. An *orc*.

Her body had begun wildly trembling, shuddering hard and uncontrollable against the orc's solid, relentless grip. Gods, how stupid had she been? Of course he was an orc. They were in orc country, Orc Mountain was barely a day's journey away from Dusbury. And here she'd gone and wandered off all alone, late in the day, into an isolated cave. A cave that clearly hadn't occurred naturally, and she'd stayed in it anyway, and hadn't even once thought about who might have made it. Who might still live there.

Daisy's breaths heaved faster, her body shivering harder, because even if she'd never personally met an orc before, she knew all the tales, didn't she? Orcs were vicious, heartless, warmongering monsters, with huge, powerful bodies, and deadly claws and teeth. They could see in the dark, they could sniff out blood and fear and death, and there were even rumours that some orcs could wield dark, terrible magic to gain their evil ends.

And worst of all, the orcs wanted human women. They would do anything to entrap and kidnap hapless unsuspecting women, to rut and swive upon them again and again, until the women bore their massive, monstrous sons. Because it was always sons with orcs, never daughters, and Daisy could distinctly recall Lew bitterly complaining about that, pointing out that orcs were nothing more than overly fecund, ill-adapted obligate parasites, who should have gone extinct millennia ago.

But nothing had gotten rid of the orcs, not even a bloody, centuries-long war against them—and finally, a few years before, the realm's human lords had gone and signed a comprehensive peace-treaty with the orcs. A treaty that had bound the orcs to stop the raids and kidnapping, and to honour human laws, and...

And—wait. Those laws most certainly included things like attacking and murdering women in dark caves... right? Not that this orc would need to care, because no one would ever find Daisy in here—but it was still something. Something to cling to, in this wheeling quaking nightmare.

"Let go of me," Daisy managed, into the dark silence. "Let *go*, orc!"

She wrenched backwards again, away from the orc's firm grip—and to her surprise, he easily released her. His warm sharp hands dropping from her neck and her waist, leaving her feeling strangely... cold, somehow. Untouched. With a strange tingling where his hands had been...

And now, without the all-consuming distraction of his touch, there was—pain. Pain radiating through Daisy's cheek, where she'd smashed it against what must have been a rock—and even worse pain in her hands, which both felt scraped and bloody and raw. And a tentative touch to her palm found it sticky and stinging, and she hissed through her teeth, whipping her head back and forth. No, *no*, how could this horrible day get any worse—

"*Biddu*," the voice said, the *orc* said, and when Daisy flinched backwards, she again felt—his hand. His callused palm, his long sharp fingers, circling tightly around her wrist, drawing her own hand out toward him. And then he carefully turned her injured palm upwards, almost as if—as if he could *see* it. But of course he could see it, he was truly a gods-damned *orc*, and she was trapped in this dark cave with him, so stupid, stupid, *stupid*—

And then—something warm. Soft. Wet. Touching against Daisy's torn, stinging skin. Something—*alive.*

The orc's *tongue.*

Daisy gasped and fought to yank her hand away, but the orc's grip held it tight and firm, in strange, peculiar contrast to his soft, slick tongue. Easing so gently against her skin, lapping at the bloody wounds, foreign and filthy and— utterly *riveting*, and—

Daisy quivered, her hand spasming in his grip—but she wasn't pulling away now, either. And she should be pulling away, she should be yelling at him, slapping him, hurling something toward him. She should be doing whatever it took to escape this, whatever the hell it was—

But instead, she just kept standing there, hushed, caught. Trapped in the eerie, silent certainty of those strong sharp fingers around her wrist, the bizarre gentleness of that slick licking tongue...

And in how the pain had somehow... lessened. Faded. Slipping away, weaker and weaker, beneath every soft wet stroke, every shudder of her breath.

It didn't make sense, it didn't, but Daisy still hadn't pulled away, and her distant, disjointed thoughts pointed out that this orc still wasn't actually hurting her—not yet, at least. And again, maybe... maybe he was even trying to *help* her. Though it was probably his fault that they were even trapped here in the first place, even if Daisy couldn't quite follow how, because he couldn't possibly have caused this... right?

"*Betra?*" the orc said, sounding distinctly like a question, as his hand circling her wrist shifted, into something almost like a caress. "*Gott?*"

Daisy swallowed, and gave a surreptitious flex of her hand in his grip—and again, impossibly, it did feel... better. Only stinging a little, now, and the sticky blood was entirely gone, because he'd licked it all away. And she really should be disgusted by that, terrified, she should be running and screaming and finding sharp rocks to throw at him, and instead, she just kept...

Standing here. Waiting, her heart thudding in her chest, as she felt the orc's hand now closing around her other wrist, and drawing it up. So he could start licking that palm, too, his tongue stroking just as soft, just as slick and smooth. Warmth tingling and flickering, easing the pain away, settling Daisy's shoulders, exhaling her breath...

Because maybe—maybe it really was helping. And it wasn't out of the realm of possibility that orc saliva could have analgesic effects, was it? She'd read a paper last year theorizing about various properties of mammalian saliva, and it had seemed at least somewhat plausible... and was that why she was still allowing this? Letting a dangerous orc touch her, and *lick* her?

She finally yanked her hand free, out of the orc's solid grip, away from his tongue's wet warmth. And again, he didn't fight it, didn't protest—at least, until she felt his warm callused fingers settling against her *face*.

Daisy yelped and jerked backwards, stumbling over more loose rocks behind her—and that was a loud, exasperated-sounding groan from the orc as his arm again caught her, snapping swift and firm around her back. Pressing her tightly into him this time, trapping her trembling body close against tall steady leanness, smooth warm skin over hard muscle and bone, oh *gods*—

Daisy gasped and shivered all over, but the orc didn't seem to notice. Instead, his fingers settled back to her face, firmly gripping her jaw, tilting it up and sideways. So he could...

Oh. Lick her *cheek*. His slick warm tongue trailing against that stinging wound, caressing so soft and gentle, stroking again and again. Feeling unreasonably close, intimate, his breath hot against her skin, his body so hard and steady against hers, his skin scenting of something rich and sweet. And as he licked her, his hand's grip slowly softened on her face—and then it even began patting her cheek. Again as if praising her, conveying that he approved of this, he was pleased by this.

Daisy shivered again, but she didn't feel nearly as revolted as she should have, even when the orc's arm drew her a little closer. Folding her even tighter into his lean powerful warmth, his firm embrace, his strangely appealing scent. And Daisy really, really should still be pushing against it, trying to escape, something...

"We need to get out of here," she finally said into the darkness. "Is there another way out?"

There was a beat of silence, a heavy huff of the orc's breath against her skin. "*Hvað sagðiru?*" came his reply. "*Ég skil ekki.*"

Daisy hauled in a deep breath, and twisted to give a shaky wave toward the exit—or at least, what she hoped was the exit. "We need to get out of here," she said again, louder this time, and she wrenched out of his arms, and attempted a careful step toward where she'd come in. "Out. Out! Escape!"

She could almost feel the orc's attention, maybe his confusion, as his strong arm drew her back into his warm embrace, fitting her easily against him. "*Bíddu,*" he replied. "*Örugg.*"

Daisy groaned, and rapidly shook her head. "We will *die* in here, orc," she snapped. "We have no water, and no food, and gods only know how long the air will be safe. We need to find a way out!"

The panic was beginning to simmer again, because even if this orc wasn't going to kill her—he wasn't going to kill her, was he?—this was still so dangerous. So stupid. And why the hell wasn't the orc moving, why was he still holding her like this, why didn't he seem alarmed in the slightest?

"*Bíddu,*" he said again, with another one of those pats to her back. "*Örugg.*"

Daisy's groan was sharp and disbelieving this time, and she again yanked away from him, toward the exit. But he didn't let go of her, and instead, he moved *with* her. His arm circling tighter around her waist, his warm body easing close beside her, and now—*guiding* her. Walking with slow, purposeful steps through the darkness toward the door, weaving them both back and forth around what must have been rocks and rubble. He even helped Daisy climb over what felt like a mess of fallen boulders, communicating through more pats of his hands, and the occasional low murmur of his voice.

When he finally drew them to a halt, near what must have been the cave's exit, he said something else, firm and decisive. Something that felt like an order, but again, Daisy couldn't even begin to follow what he meant.

"I don't understand," she said helplessly, toward where his face might have been. "Does this mean we can get out now?"

She mimed a walking gesture with her fingers, earning in return a sharp, disapproving growl from the orc—and then, after an instant's silence, he grasped her hand, and drew it forward in the darkness. Until her fingers met something cool and solid, standing here vertically before them. Rock. A wall.

For an instant, Daisy's only thought was that her hand didn't hurt at all, when it really still should have—but then her stomach plunged, as comprehension flashed through her brain. This was surely the exit. The tunnel. But now it was only a sheer wall of rock, dusty and gritty and rough, blocking them in, trapping them here.

And the more she ran her hand over the wall, the more alarming it felt. It was all boulders, big and sharp-edged, and they seemed thoroughly wedged together. And when she tried tugging at one of the craggy edges, she only succeeded in scraping her hand again—a development which drew another disapproving growl from the orc, who then snatched her hand up, and began licking it again.

This time, Daisy didn't even flinch, and she slowly exhaled as that soft, slick warmth trailed against her skin. Tending her, caressing her, fading the pain into a strange, shivery prickle. Until even that had eased away, too, and now it was only his slick supple tongue, his hot hitching breath, a brush of something that felt almost like lips…

Too late, Daisy snatched her hand away, and jabbed purposefully toward the blocked tunnel. "We still need to get out, orc," she told him, as steadily as she could. "Out. *Out!*"

The orc's sigh was heavy, almost a growl, and his claws drummed against her back with distinct irritation. "*Nei,*" he replied, his voice flat. "*Ekki strax.*"

Daisy should have wrenched away from his touch—how did he have his arm around her again?—but instead she frowned up toward the sound of his voice, and again waved toward the wall. "We could *die* in here, orc," she hissed. "Help me dig us out!"

The orc sighed again, and gave another annoyed drum of his claws against her. "*Nei,*" he said again. "*Nei. Bíddu eftir sólinni.*"

Whatever it meant, he was clearly refusing, saying no— and with a desperate groan, Daisy wrenched away from him again, and groped wildly for the wall of fallen stone. Pushing at it, pulling at it, there had to be something, they were going to *die*—

"*Nei!*" snarled the orc, close and sharp in Daisy's ear, as strong clawed hands circled both her wrists, and yanked them away. "*Nei, blómið mitt! Bíddu!*"

Gods curse him, and when Daisy struggled and hissed at him, fighting to yank her wrists away, he only gripped them tighter, jerked her closer, and then—

He *roared* at her. The sound deep and harsh and menacing, shuddering up her shivering spine. Saying—*no*. Or else.

Daisy would have yelled back, shoved away—if not for how his warm clever hands had curved around her again, stroking up and down her back with something between reassurance and urgency. As if trying to comfort her, while also trying to communicate something. Something—important.

"*Nei*," came his voice again, softer this time—and then he kept speaking, low and swift and unintelligible. Again explaining something, perhaps why Daisy couldn't dig like that, or why they couldn't go out that way.

But whatever it was, there was no denying the utter certainty in his voice. The determination, the eloquence, the refusal. The conviction, somehow, that there *was* a reason they couldn't leave. And the reason wasn't just that this orc wanted to keep her trapped here, where he could next force her to his bed, or kill her.

When he finished speaking, it felt almost expectant, like he was waiting for her reply. And finally Daisy sighed, her shoulders sagging, her eyes fluttering closed.

"Oh, fine," she said, heavy and resigned. "Is there another way out, then? Another exit out the back, or something?"

She drew up one of her hands, and then waved purposefully around the room, before making another walking gesture with her fingers. "Another way?" she asked, foolishly, because of course he couldn't understand it. "Another exit, then?"

But in return, the orc made an approving sound, and patted at her back. Saying—yes. *Yes.*

Really? Daisy's heart leapt, and she shot a swift, delighted grin toward him—or toward where he must have been in the darkness—before lurching forward, back into the room. They would find another way out, she could still escape, run away, go home to... to...

But then—the orc again. Here again. His body blocking Daisy's path, his hand again gripping tight against her wrist. "*Nei*," he said again. "*Ekki strax. Bíddu.*"

What? Was he saying—no? No leaving? But he'd just suggested they could still escape—hadn't he? So Daisy shook her head, and stepped forward—and again found herself held, caught, against the orc's tall, solid body. As if he did want to trap her here after all, as if this was all some kind of nefarious orc trick...

"Let me go!" she hissed at him. "I want to get out!"

But the orc didn't let go, and huffed another low, irritated groan. And when Daisy kept glaring upwards in the darkness, he drew in a deep breath, and again began speaking. The words tangled and foreign, swift and certain, a stream of urgent fluent conviction in his low, velvety voice.

But again, there was no hope of understanding it, and Daisy could only stand there and listen to it, hear the rise and fall of it. Catching the distinct patterns in it, the deft twists and turns of it, as his fingers stroked and skittered against her back, his rich scent again flitting through her breath...

And for a strange, stilted instant, his voice felt almost like music, like a dance, like... *art*. Like smooth, thick dark lines, scraping on a fresh page, drawing something unknown, something new...

When he finished speaking, Daisy kept blinking for a breath, caught in the bizarre, vivid image of it—but then she grimaced, and shook her head. And in return the orc growled, harsh and heavy with frustration, as if he wanted her to understand, needed her to understand, and...

With a sudden movement, his hand dropped her wrist, and slipped down Daisy's front, settling against—her *belly*. And gods, what was he doing now, was he going to grope her, was he going to attack her or force her after all, what was he—

Oh. His claw. A single soft, gentle point, touching her. And it wasn't caressing, wasn't taking advantage, because it was—*drawing*?

But yes, *yes*, it was drawing. Drawing a circle, again and again, tracing it smooth and careful against the loose fabric of Daisy's shabby dress. And then that claw drew sideways, tracing straight lines out from the circle's edge, like spokes on a wheel, or—or—petals on a flower. Like...

A daisy.

Daisy froze, even as a brief, convulsive shiver rippled out from her belly. From where the orc had started it all over again, his sharp claw circling smoothly around her navel, and then drawing those lines out again. A daisy. A flower. A wheel. A birth, a light, something new...

Daisy shivered again, her heart skipping a beat in her chest, but the orc just kept drawing, his touch ringing and jangling, like a clear, piercing call, a song in the dark. A light. A flower. A daisy. An eye. A sun...

"*Sól*," he murmured, a note of shimmering light in the song. "*Sól*."

Sól. Light. *Sun*.

The certainty struck deep into Daisy's gut, staggering her on her feet, because yes, of course, he was drawing a sun. The kind of sun every child drew, with the circle in the middle, the rays streaming out from all sides. Sun.

"*Sól*," he said again, softer, as his claw kept touching, kept drawing. "*Sól. Morgun.*"

Sun. *Morgun*. Morning? As if he was saying—he needed sun? Needed... morning?

But maybe—maybe that could make sense, couldn't it?

Because surely the sun had set by now, it had already been late when Daisy had come here... but maybe the light would help them find another way out, somehow. Maybe it would shine through the rocks, show them a new way forward...

But—no. No. Daisy couldn't honestly be considering giving up, abandoning her quest to escape... right? Relenting to this, and spending an entire night trapped in here in the dark with him? With an *orc*?

But the orc was still drawing, still marking that sun-daisy-song onto her skin, and Daisy wasn't even pretending to resist it, to protest or escape. And instead, she was shivering again, reverberating against him, as her jolting thoughts whispered strange, surreal justifications, or maybe even temptations...

She'd run away from Lew. She'd found this ruined, beautiful cave. It had trapped her here with this orc, this creature with a voice like music, with his rich scent, his healing tongue, his sharp deadly fingers that drew suns and daisies against her skin. And now he was speaking with her like this, communicating with her through art, through light in the darkness...

Gods, it was ridiculous, and gods, how Lew would laugh at her. He would accuse her of being flighty and foolish, irrational and unscientific, falling prey to her emotions, mistaking silly anecdotal hunches for actual provable hypotheses.

But maybe it was Lew's voice, Lew's judgement, that drew in Daisy's breath, expanded her belly against the orc's still-drawing finger. One night. One night, until the sun. Until morning. Until she would escape here, for good.

"Fine," she told the orc, with only a slight waver in her voice. "I'll stay. Until the *sól*."

5

She would stay.

Daisy's breath was heaving, now, her eyes foolishly searching in the blackness, as if she could somehow find the orc's face. As if she was seeking his gratitude, or even his... his *approval*.

It was so stupid, so ludicrous, and Daisy should not—*not*—have shivered at the feel of his hand, finally halting its sun-drawing against her waist, so it could give her a light, approving pat instead.

"*Gott*," he said, with distinct satisfaction. "*Gott, blómið mitt.*"

Gott almost sounded like *good*, maybe, and Daisy's shoulders sagged as she twitched a brief, furtive nod in return. To which the orc huffed a bright, triumphant sound, almost like a laugh, as his warm arm again circled around her.

"*Gott*," he said again, tilting her body toward him, drawing her close. "*Þú ert mín.*"

It was truly ridiculous, that he already felt so entitled to touch her like this, spreading his long fingers so easily against her back, fitting her even closer against his tall, lean body. As if he had every right to guide her and hold and caress her, to lightly tickle his sharp claws against her spine.

And even more ridiculous was how Daisy was—allowing it. Sinking into the strength of his touch, his warmth, his embrace. His... certainty, maybe, his absolute lack of fear or unease over being trapped in here, in facing down the very real possibility of his own impending death.

"You should be scared," Daisy muttered, halfheartedly, into his solid bare chest. "This is an appalling situation. We could *die* in here."

But the orc huffed another laugh, his head shaking against Daisy's hair, and his claw on her back drew the sun again. "*Sól*," he said again, lightly this time. "*Sólin kemur upp í fyrramálið, og þá förum við.*"

Whatever it was, he again sounded very, very certain, and Daisy couldn't seem to find the will to argue, or even to pull away. And she should be pulling away, she should, he was a stranger, he was terrifying, he was an *orc*...

But he still just felt so certain, so sure of himself, so... safe, somehow. And he clearly wanted to keep touching Daisy, wanted to keep holding her like this, now drawing that slow circle of his sun into her back. The sharpness of his claw still such a bizarre contrast to the lightness of his touch, and the word it kept silently speaking to her. His sun, his flower, his light...

And then... something new. His hand shifting sideways from his sun, and drawing a rounded, scalloped shape against Daisy's shoulder. "*Sól*," he murmured, as he first tapped at the sun, and then slid to the shape. "*Og ský.*"

Daisy blinked, and twitched at the feeling of him drawing another scalloped shape, on her other shoulder—and then one slightly covering the sun, too. As if—oh. He was drawing a sky. With *clouds*.

Despite herself, Daisy huffed a short little laugh, and then twitched a nod. "*Sól*," she repeated, as she slipped her own hand up behind the orc's back, and drew her own sun against his smooth bare skin. "*Og ský.*"

She made her clouds light and gauzy, drawing with four fingers across his shoulder blade, and she didn't miss the brief quiver of his lean body against her, his own breath of laughter rustling her hair.

"*Ach,*" he murmured. "*Og stjörnur.*"

Stjörnur were multiple little dots, tapped by his claws across the sky of her back, as if—of course. *Stars.* So Daisy did the same to him, sprinkling her own light taps of stars across his shoulders, her fingers skating over firm muscle and hard protruding bone. "*Stjörnur,*" she repeated. "Stars."

There was an instant's silence, an audible swallow from the orc—and then he exhaled, and again flickered his own clawed fingertips across her back. "*Stars,*" he repeated, in common-tongue, the word sounding flat and strange on his voice. "*Stars.*"

Daisy flashed a brief, surprised smile up toward the sound of his voice, and her hand might have tightened a little against his back. Touching him, she was willingly touching an *orc*—and oh, he was still touching her, too. His hands spreading wider against her, his clawed fingers gently prodding against the fabric of her dress, and she should not have shivered like that, vibrating her body closer against him. Against his touch, his warmth, his sweet hovering scent, his solid stubborn strength...

But he certainly didn't seem to mind, and she could even feel his head bending down toward hers, his breath inhaling against her hair. "*Stjarnan mín,*" he murmured. "*Sólin mín.*"

What? It almost sounded like he was saying *she* was those things—but no, no, of course not, that was ridiculous. And Daisy really should be pulling away now, away from whatever this was, from the orc's hands now slowly caressing against her back, his lean chest shuddering with his slow, deep inhale...

But instead, she kept standing there. Breathing, waiting, feeling his hands stroking her. His touch already feeling almost familiar, even as one of those hands ventured a little further down her back, spreading slow and careful. Almost as if seeking, testing, asking…

But Daisy only shivered again, squeezed her eyes shut, and somehow her own fingers had spread wider against his back, too. Because yes, she'd still been touching him, after going and *drawing* on him like that, but it seemed strangely difficult to stop. To pull away from the feel of his warm smooth skin, the hard ridges of his ribs beneath it…

And now, before she'd even caught it, it was her own hand sliding. Seeking. Feeling the long hard curves of his ribs, so sharp and distinct beneath his skin. Far more prominent than she'd felt on any man before, and that wasn't typical orc anatomy, was it? Weren't orcs supposed to be big, muscular, powerful? Not gaunt and bony and starved?

But there was no way to ask, and maybe Daisy didn't want to, either. Didn't want to break this hushed, hitching moment, touching this orc, while he touched her. His hands both steadily stroking, circling, as that one on her back kept sliding lower. And then lower, oh gods, until it was spreading wide and possessive against her arse, hitching her tighter against him, and suddenly Daisy could feel—

Oh. Oh, hell. *That.* That other highly notorious bit of orc anatomy, swelling out against the front of his trousers, thick and hard and hungry.

It was just as shocking, just as impossible as all the books and rumours had said—and Daisy should be pulling away now. She should be screaming, escaping, running for her life. Damn the sun and the morning and his damned claw-drawing, what was she thinking, he was an orc, an *orc*—

But curse her, she still wasn't moving. Wasn't escaping. And instead, she might have even gasped too, gripping tighter at the orc's hard straining back. And suddenly he felt so hard all over, somehow, rigid and taut and strained and quivering. As if...

As if he was holding himself in place. Locking himself here. Desperately fighting himself, as if he might... he might...

"What?" Daisy whispered, breathless, as her own audacious, impossible hand slipped further down his back, to the hard curve of his own arse. Feeling it, spreading against it, maybe—maybe even guiding his hips closer, grinding that shocking length tighter, oh—

And then the orc—snapped. His powerful body flashing into movement against her, his breath moaning harsh and low, his strong hands gripping tight. Dragging Daisy sideways, skittering the rough rubble beneath her feet, and then spinning her around and away from him. Shoving her hands firmly against something—a hard flat stone, about waist-height—so he could yank her hips out and back toward him, and kick her ankles apart...

Oh, gods. Oh *gods*. Because it left Daisy bent double, facing away from him, her hands on a rock, her legs spread wide. And what the hell, what the fuck, and why wasn't she fighting him, did she even want to fight him, were they really doing this—

"Ach?" came his voice, his harsh breathless demand, and Daisy arched and quivered in the darkness—and *still* didn't try to run. Didn't even speak, or protest. Not even when she felt the orc's sharp-tipped hand slipping down again, palming brazenly at her jutting arse through the fabric of her dress, squeezing it tight, like he had every right...

And then that hand gave her a brief, demanding *slap*. Quaking her all over, firing desperate heat up her spine, and... and then...

He stopped. Waiting. Wanting.

"*Ach*?" he rasped. "*Ach, eða nei?*"

Ach, or *nei*. Yes, or no. Asking her. *Asking* her. For... this.

It was chaos, it was madness, and Daisy didn't want this... did she? No, not with him, not here, not like this. Not with an orc who could see in the dark, who had a voice like music, who drew suns on her skin. An orc who kept her from falling, and licked her wounds, and held her tight amidst her fear...

And an orc who now wanted this. From her.

Unbelievable, Daisy, Lew would have said, curling his lip with distaste. *Irrational. This is ridiculous and immature behaviour, appallingly unscientific, foolish, dangerous, what if you spawn offspring from this...*

But Lew had been the one to research all those pregnancy prevention herbs, hadn't he? He'd been the one to make damned sure Daisy was taking the strongest available protections in the realm, with powerful doses that lasted for well over a month. Because he'd always been very adamant about not wanting children, and—more bitter awareness flickered through Daisy's thoughts—of course he hadn't wanted to risk losing her to a pregnancy, either. Let alone to some other man's child.

But even the thought of it flared more strange sudden recklessness through Daisy's shouting brain, because what would Lew say, if he knew she'd done this with an orc? Orcs weren't against the rules they'd agreed upon, because of course Lew had never once imagined a moment like this, with his mousy unwanted *illustrator* bent double in a dark cave, while an orc's deadly clawed hand again slapped hungry and firm against her arse.

"Ach?" the orc's voice demanded again, sounding shaky and strained this time, as his other hand gripped Daisy's hip, caressed it, tilted her upper body down lower. "*Langar þig?*"

Daisy still couldn't understand his question, but his meaning was vividly clear, rippling another hard shiver up her back. Did she want this? With an orc? With him? Like this? Here? Now?

"Gods, I don't even *know* you," Daisy choked, but it came out sounding needy, almost plaintive. "And you don't know me."

But the orc's hands had begun stroking now, sliding up and down her flanks over her dress, and—oh—drawing the dress up as he went. "*Mig langar,*" he breathed, husky now. "*Ég vil sól. Mín. Sólin mín.*"

Sól. Mín. Sólin mín. Almost as if it meant... *sun. Mine. Sun mine. My sun.*

It shouldn't have felt like an answer, but somehow... it did. He wanted her. He wanted this. Here. Now.

And again, the certainty of that, the utter lack of fear in that, said something. Changed something. Something strange and new, shimmering all through Daisy's body. Flaring up a wild, furious yearning, even as the orc lifted her dress all the way, bared her most secret places toward him...

For a breath, there was only stillness, shuddering hard between them—and then, oh gods, a touch. Not brazen or demanding this time, but instead light, gentle, a barest skim of a claw against Daisy's bare hip. And it was drawing again, drawing the sun again, firing out sharp tingles of light with every gentle stroke. Asking again, speaking again, did she want this, she did, she did...

"Ach?" he asked again. "*Sannlega, sólin mín.*"

His sun. Daisy quaked all over, swallowed hard, dragged in a desperate breath. And then—

Nodded.

Yes. Yes, she did want this. Here, with him, now.

Yes.

And oh, now she could feel a distinct, slick hardness, bobbing hot and heavy between her bare parted thighs. Nudging, stroking, showing her what this meant, what he was going to do...

"*Ertu viss?*" he gasped, as his claw slipped downwards, and began drawing another slow, careful circle. Drawing around *there*, oh gods, around the sight he'd exposed, the place he wanted to use, to fill. That taunting sharpness blatantly trailing over wet skin, over quivering thighs, over puckering clenching heat...

And then, again, he drew the lines out. Like a sun, like light, like life and fire and blooming unfurling petals. And Daisy wasn't thinking about what that might mean, she wasn't, because suddenly she just needed it, needed it so much it was pain, please yes, please...

"Ach," she croaked. "Ach, orc. Yes!"

And—a laugh. A growl. One more scrape of claws, harder this time, drawing the sun, the flower, the life...

And then his hot, seeking cock found its flower, its daisy, its home, and plunged in hard and deep.

6

Daisy's shout echoed through the cave, sharp and shrill and helpless.

The orc was inside her. *Inside* her.

And gods, how he felt. So hard. So smooth. So hot and silken and demanding and alive, pulsing and quivering and sputtering within her. Feeling like strength, like certainty, like *him*—

And suddenly, it felt—right. Stunning. *Perfect.* After all the mess of today, after everything, Daisy needed this. Needed it so damned much. Needed to be filled, held, *wanted.*

"*Ach, sólin mín,*" the orc hissed behind her, the words crackling in his voice. "*Almáttugur.*"

Daisy gasped and nodded, and then shivered all over as he slowly began drawing back again. Pulling himself out breath by breath, making it slow and agonizing, just as it should be, because oh, the loss of this was no small thing, it was *everything.* And when he fell fully free of her, Daisy couldn't bite back her whimper, mingling with his own low groan of displeasure. His own disapproval at not having this, with her.

But then—yes. Yes. Relief. His slick head seeking again, prodding again, opening her soft, willing heat around it. And then he slowly plunged in again, filling her again, as they both groaned aloud—and then they quaked together, too, as their hips met, their bodies locked snug and deep. And his strong hands on Daisy's hips ground her even tighter, as she arched and pushed back to meet him, gripping him as tightly as she could. Just needing more, needing to make him hold and stay like this, yes, oh gods, *yes.*

"*Gott?*" he breathed, close and hot into her ear, and Daisy fervently nodded, and reached back to grip at his hand. Prodding those sharp claws a little deeper into her tingling trembling hip, needing more of those too, that perfect mingled strength and pain, *oh.*

The orc's laugh was low and husky as he obliged, digging his claws harder—and now his other hand was scraping, too. Drawing long straight lines down her bare quivering flank, and yes that was good too, so good, *fuck.*

Daisy again felt the orc's laughing approval, close against her ear—followed by a soft, experimental scrape of sharp teeth to her earlobe. Firing yet more fierce flashing sensation through her entire body, still impaled tight and helpless on where he was holding himself there, keeping himself buried there, feeling her squirm and seize upon him.

"*Gott, sólin mín,*" he breathed again, another flare of furious heat, and oh, now he was drawing out again, taking himself away again, no—and then plunging back inside. Filling her swift and hard and smooth, again making her gasp and writhe for it, as his claws kept scraping, his teeth nipping her ear, and slipping down toward her neck. And when he softly bit down against her throat, it flared out another surge of devastating hunger, of utter overwhelming need, *please*—

He chuckled again, low and soft and approving, as he brought up—his hand. Curving it gentle but hungry around the front of Daisy's throat, his fingers long and supple and greedy, and her thoughts flashed back to when he'd done that earlier, when he'd been trying to keep her from moving. And had he wanted it then too, had he known, how had she betrayed it, oh gods...

But she was definitely betraying it now, moaning harsh and shaky as his hand circled tighter around her neck, as his claws scraped her skin. As his sharp teeth nipped close beside it, his other hand's claws still scoring lines against her hip, his hard cock now pumping in and out, moving faster and faster. Flooding her all over with pain and pleasure, even better than that time Lew had used the quills on her, and she couldn't stop gasping, trembling, begging—

"Oh gods, orc," she gulped, as she arched and writhed upon him, pressed back as hard as she could. "Oh, don't stop, I beg you, *please*, orc."

His answering grunt was low and satisfied, his teeth biting sharper at her ear. "*Nei* orc," he replied, a hot breathless demand, accompanied by a light, thrilling slap to her arse. "*Filak. Eg er Filak.*"

Filak? Daisy blinked, hesitated, and the orc's hand shifted to clutch at her wrist, drawing her hand down and around and backwards. Until it was touching against—his chest. His bare, sweaty chest, with his breath and his voice heaving through it. "*Filak,*" he said again. "*Ég er Filak.*"

The comprehension flared through Daisy's juddering thoughts, and she inhaled, nodded, arched harder against his onslaught. "Filak," she gasped. "Don't stop, Filak."

He groaned at the sound of it, ramming himself harder and deeper inside her, oh—so Daisy kept saying it, kept babbling and begging for it, as he kept driving faster, his hips and bollocks slapping hard, his claws and teeth scraping more sweet perfect pain into her skin. One of those deadly hands still gripping her neck, while the other one slowly slipped down and around her front, dragging against her belly, her coarse hair, down to where he was plunging himself inside her. Feeling this, feeling himself doing this, stroking and grinding and pounding, the ecstasy reeling closer, tighter, bright and breathless and brilliant, until—

Daisy screamed as it swallowed her, consumed her, flooding her all through with its blinding searing light. Pummelling her again and again, wrenching and seizing her—until behind her, the orc shouted too, his voice raw and ragged in her ear, as his hard invading strength bucked, and exploded. Bursting out wild and forceful inside her, spraying sharp and stunning and utterly overwhelming, filling her with heat and power and certainty. She was his, his, claimed, consumed, marked inside and out, painted all over with his claws and his seed and his sun.

When it finally ended, Daisy was trembling all over, groping uselessly at the hard rock before her, while the orc slowly drew free of her with a wet, obscene-sounding squelch. Releasing a surge of thick, rich-scented fluid from inside her, streaking hot down her thighs, splashing out onto the stone below. While Daisy gasped and shook and felt it, and squeezed her eyes shut. What was happening, what was this, what had she done...

But the orc was murmuring behind her, speaking soft and reassuring, giving a light, approving nip at her neck. And then, in a whirl of movement, he swept her shaky body entirely off her feet, and up into his arms.

Daisy choked and quivered, but his arms were strong and steady and safe, his chest solid and warm. And already he'd begun moving in the darkness, carrying her across the messy cave, his steps astonishingly smooth and swift. Until he finally hesitated again, and set her down on something flat and hard. Not the ground, no, but some kind of... of platform, perhaps. A table, or maybe even a bed.

But it was uneven and cold, not like any bed Daisy had ever known—at least, until the orc sank down beside her, and then drew her up into his arms. So she was now lying half on top of him, her limp arm and leg sprawled over his lean body. And with more quick, efficient movements, he tucked her face into his neck, and then hitched her leg fully over his. So he could firmly settle his solid thigh between her legs, raising it up, pressing flat against her quivering, tender heat. Which was still liberally leaking hot thick fluid, smearing it against the fabric of his trousers—but if he cared, he didn't show it. Instead, his hands began stroking her again, slower and lazier than before, his claws not feeling nearly as sharp as they had been.

"*Gott, sólin mín,*" he murmured, and in Daisy's whirling thoughts, it made perfect, beautiful sense. "*Stjarnan mín.*"

His star. Daisy shivered and settled closer, inhaling that rich, sweet scent of his warm neck. "It's actually—Daisy," she said, her voice a strange rasping scrape, tainted with sadness, with shame. It wasn't a sun or a star, it was a common, boring name, a name Lew had never liked, and...

"Daisy," she said again, harder this time, and her hand even fluttered up, and drew a daisy against the orc's bare chest. Starting with the disc at the centre, and then sketching out the long ray florets, with their curved oval shape, their fluted ends. While the orc stayed perfectly still beneath it, perhaps not even breathing, as she finally drew the straight stem down his belly, and a few simple lobed leaves.

She couldn't seem to speak once she'd finished, just blinking down toward her hand in the darkness. Feeling the strength of his silence, was he judging her too, or perhaps he hadn't understood her at all...

"Daisy," he finally said, hushed, as his hand found hers, and pressed it back flat against his warm skin. "Daisy. *Eins og sól. Stjarna.*"

Oh. It felt like he was saying—was he saying a daisy was like a sun? A star? And yes, perhaps the shape was similar, and the colours, and even the daisy's white "petals" were actually called rays too, just like a sun's. But...

"*Það er gott*," he said now, with a reassuring squeeze to Daisy's hand, as his other hand slipped to her back, and drew another sun against her. "*Gott. Sólin mín. Daisy mín.*"

Oh. It was so certain, so approving, so reassuring. And it didn't make sense, none of it, it was all utterly absurd, and what would Lew say...

But Lew suddenly felt very, very far away, and this orc—Filak—was so close. So powerful. So... safe.

"*Bíddu nú hér*," he said firmly. "*Þangað til í fyrramálið. Þangað til á morgun.*"

Morgun. Until morning, he surely meant.

And yes. Yes, Daisy could do that, nodding into his sweet-scented neck, sinking into his warm reassuring strength. She would stay. Until the sun.

7

Daisy shouldn't have slept like that. On a hard rock, trapped in a dark cave, with an orc. With... *Filak.*

But somehow, she did. And it didn't feel nearly as uncomfortable or unnerving as it should have, not with Filak's warm solid safety beneath her, his hands spread against her, his breaths rising and falling steady through his chest.

At one point, Daisy vaguely registered him easing away, leaving her alone on the cold hard stone—but before the alarm could swallow her, he slipped back beside her again, and gathered her into his side. And when his claw gently eased down the front of her dress, and began drawing suns against her heart, she only shivered and settled closer, slipping back into soft, swirling dreams.

When she finally awoke again, she was somehow fully sprawled on top of Filak's warm body, her face buried in his rich-scented neck. And his long arms were wrapped close around her, his long legs tangled with hers, his slow breaths tickling against her hair. All of it surrounding her, cocooning her quiet and drowsy and safe, and gods, she wanted to never move again, she wanted to stay here forever...

But then—a noise. A scattering crumbling sound, in the direction of what might have been the exit. Enough to flare up Daisy's heartbeat, rapid and pattering and strange, because did it mean—was it morning? Could they get out?

She shoved up on her shaky arms, twisting to frown toward the exit, but she still couldn't find even a pinprick of light in the dark. And beneath her, Filak shifted too, and his warm familiar hands were already caressing her back, speaking that silent reassurance Daisy already knew far too well.

"*Þetta er ekkert*," he said, husky. "*Bara meindýr*."

Whatever it was, it meant not to worry, that everything was fine—but even as Daisy sank her head back to his shoulder, it occurred to her that she was thirsty, and hungry, and in rapidly increasing need of a latrine, especially with that distinct feel of wetness pooling between her legs. And was it really morning, now? It had felt like a long time sleeping, right?

"Is it morning?" she asked him, hoarse. "Or—er—*morgun*? *Sól*?"

She didn't miss Filak's sudden stiffness beneath her, or the hitching exhale of his breath. "Ach," he said, clipped. "*Morgun. Sól*."

Oh. Well. And that meant they should get up, and he was going to find them another way out—right? But he hadn't yet moved, and if anything, his hands had tightened a little more against her. And one of those hands had begun slowly slipping down her back, further and further, until it gently curved over her arse, settling her closer against him. Against where—Daisy's breath caught—he was already hard and ready in his trousers, his hips smoothly rocking up, oh gods...

Daisy couldn't deny her reflexive rock back, or the pooling heat in her belly—but the movement uncomfortably jostled her overfull bladder, too. And gods damn it, she was thirsty, and hungry, and her head was beginning to ache, pulsing quietly behind her eyes.

"Sorry, but I need a drink first," she told Filak, with a wince. "And a latrine. Can we just—get out first? And then..."

She bit her lip, frowning, because then... what? What happened, after that? Would Filak find her food and water and a latrine? Did he live somewhere near here? Or was he perhaps just... passing through? Heading somewhere else, where she would never see him again?

Daisy swallowed, glanced toward his face in the darkness—but of course there was nothing to see, and no answers, either. Because how—how would she ever find out where he lived? Or how to find him again? Because there was no way to find out anything about him, not really, not even the most fundamental things like his work, his background, his family?

And wait—what if he *did* have a family? What if he had a wife, or even children? Was he someone who regularly went outside his relationship for pleasure, just like Lew? Could he carry any contagious orc infections? Would his furious jealous wife show up at any moment? How—how the hell would Daisy ever know?

Daisy's heart raced faster, her eyes rapidly blinking in the darkness, and she shoved herself up and away from Filak, away from his safe solid warmth. "I—I really need food, and water," she stammered, as she raised her shaky hand, and mimed drinking from a cup. "I need out. *Sól. Morgun.* Please."

There was a beat of silence, followed by his slow exhale—and then his hand, slipping around her back, guiding her up to her feet. And despite the sudden, shocking sensation of more hot fluid, seeping sticky down her thighs beneath her baggy dress, Daisy could still have sobbed with the dizzying relief of it. If nothing else, it was morning. He was going to keep his word, and find them a way outside. Now.

So she took a deep breath, and eased close into Filak's side. Feeling that steady strength of him, the firm grip of his hand on her waist, the certainty of his steps as he guided her across the room. But it wasn't toward the way they'd come in, the place where the tunnel had collapsed, right? No, no, he was taking her in the opposite direction, leading her over grit and gravel and rubble, toward... a wall. Or no, wait, into a passage in the wall, a tunnel, a chasm—and he gently drew her hands to touch both sides of it, showing her, as his steady hand on her back kept leading her forward, through the tunnel after him in the darkness.

The ground felt rougher with every step, rocky and slippery and uneven, but Filak held Daisy steady, and waited as she found her footing again and again. And when she almost slid sideways into the rough stone wall, he was instantly there, his strong arm holding her up, gripping her close and safe into his side.

But he hadn't spoken again, and Daisy hadn't, either. Because he wouldn't understand her anyway, would he? And all she could think of were questions, hopeless miserable questions, bubbling and boiling hotter with every halting step. *What comes after this? Will I ever see you again? What the hell am I supposed to do now?*

And that, perhaps, was the worst one of all, because gods curse her, Daisy had entirely lost sight of reality last night, between the cave and the darkness and—and *him*. But now, with morning looming before them, and last night's whirling trance scattered away into dust and regret, where did that leave her? Hungry, thirsty, stuck here in the backwoods of the realm, with no coin, no contacts, no way home. With only this orc who couldn't understand a word she said, and with...

With *Lew*. Lew's project. Lew's work. Lew's food and coin and shelter.

A low, frustrated groan escaped Daisy's mouth, and in return, Filak briefly stilled, his breath exhaling—and then he drew her along faster. Maybe thinking her groan had been meant for him, but there was no way to communicate that, either. And Daisy would have reached for him, tucked herself closer into his warm safety, even for a moment—but then he lurched away, his hand briefly squeezing her shoulder.

"*Vertu hér*," came his flat voice. "*Bíddu*."

It meant nothing, again, but when Daisy tried to fumble after where he'd gone, his hand again caught her shoulder, held her still. "*Nei*," he said firmly. "*Bíddu, sólin mín*."

His sun. It shivered something deep in Daisy's belly, and she held herself still, breathing fast and shallow, as Filak stepped away. His footsteps slightly crunching, moving over there, the sound of something scraping, of his voice hissing sharp and deep, and—

A crash. A crash of screeching shattering stone, tumbling, rumbling through Daisy's belly, her chest, her pounding skull. And then—

Then, there was light. Burning, blazing, blinding, pouring into the dark. Filling up this narrow, rocky tunnel with pure dazzling white, so bright Daisy had to shrink away, and cover her eyes. And for an instant, there was a bizarre, desperate urge to run back down the tunnel, to hide back in the quiet safe darkness, to feel Filak's warm hands on her skin, Filak's hard strength sliding inside her...

But—Filak. Filak was here. There. Before her. And for the first time, Daisy could finally fully see him. His hands, his body, his skin, his... *face*...

And Filak wasn't just an orc.

He was... a wraith. A skeleton. A *monster*.

8

Daisy froze all over, seized on the sight before her. On... Filak.

He was impossibly tall, and unnaturally thin. His bare chest was ridged with the bones of his ribs, his belly a hollowed concave below. And his bare arms looked far too stringy and slim, ending in big, gangly hands, with impossibly long, sharp fingers. Fingers that—Daisy's breath caught—were tipped with curved, deadly black talons. Talons like a crow would have, maybe, or a bear, or a—a *demon*.

But even more alarming was his skin. In all the diagrams and illustrations Daisy had ever seen of orcs, their skin was grey or green, or somewhere in between. But Filak's skin was chalk-white, far paler than Daisy's own—and making it look even harsher were the black marks stamped liberally across it. And yes, Daisy had caught sight of those marks, on her first glimpse of him in the tunnel—but she'd never once imagined a living creature being marked like this. Down his arms, up his neck, his jaw, over his smooth hairless head, even his tall pointed ears.

And the marks weren't simple drawings, or designs, like

the various tattoos Daisy had seen on humans before. No, they almost looked like—script. Like writing. Like someone had taken a brush and a bucket of ink, and written out an entire book's worth of stories or blessings or curses all over his paper-white skin.

But none of it was anything Daisy could read, the script stark and strange and entirely unfamiliar. Just like the rest of him, with the bones and the claws and his sunken skeleton face...

And then, for perhaps the first time, Daisy's eyes held on his face. His hard, ravenous face, with sharp cheekbones, a strong hooked nose, and thick, slashing black brows. And his eyes, oh gods, his eyes were sunken black coals, glittering deep in those hollow sockets, and—seeing her. Staring at her.

Daisy couldn't move, couldn't breathe, caught, trapped, doomed. Hanging like a fly in a web, waiting for the attack, the bite, those killer claws clutching around her throat...

But it was that vision, suddenly, that seemed to—stutter. Catching, stilling, shifting upside-down. Because this—this was still... *him*. Filak. This was the orc—surely still the orc?— she'd spent last night with. The orc who'd touched her, caressed her, curled those long fingers so carefully around her throat.

But—how? How hadn't he cut her, or wounded her? Because yes, she'd felt those claws, she'd known they were long and sharp, but he hadn't once drawn her blood... had he? He hadn't once hurt her.

And yes, she'd felt his ribs too, she'd felt how gaunt he was—but she'd also felt the lean strength in his tall body, the warmth of it, that rich heady scent of it. She'd felt his hunger when he'd taken her, and filled her—and when her stunned gaze flicked down to his trousers, yes, that was familiar too. That hard, thick ridge, ready and waiting behind the coarse black fabric.

Daisy's cheeks heated, and she dragged her gaze back up to his face. To where the orc—Filak—was still looking back toward her, unblinking, unmoving. As if he was coiled, taut, waiting, maybe expecting her to scream or run or...

"Filak?" she finally whispered—and in return, his long-fingered hand spasmed, while one of the rocks beneath him clattered away.

"Ach," he replied, low. And yes, yes, the voice was right too—but not the flash of sharp white fangs as he spoke, the hard little curl of his lip. "*Ég er enn Filak.*"

Oh. Daisy swallowed hard, opened her mouth—and then shut it again, because gods, what was the point, and what was she even going to say? *Are you still an orc? Are you ill? Why did someone write all over you? Where is your hair? Do you realize you look like a corpse?*

And worst of all, *Did I really do that with you last night? Did I touch you? Beg for you? Welcome your cock and your seed inside me? What the fuck was I thinking?!*

"So—er—what now, then?" Daisy finally croaked, into the dangling silence. "G-goodbye, I suppose?"

There was another instant's silence, and then a sharp, fluid gesture of Filak's long-fingered hand toward the light. Toward the exit. Toward... toward what Daisy had wanted.

"*Sól,*" he replied, his voice flat. "*Morgun.*"

Right. Yes. Daisy shot a look toward the light, toward where—she squinted her still-adjusting eyes—she could now see greenery, a forest. Another exit, just like she'd wanted, and now she was free to go. Free to find water, food, a latrine, and then...

Daisy stepped toward the light, her foot crunching against fresh rubble and stone—and then she stopped, and turned back toward Filak. Who was still standing there unmoving, still watching her with those sunken unnerving eyes.

"Er, I don't suppose," she began, hoarse, "you might want to—to come?"

And gods, what was she saying? What was she thinking? She couldn't go anywhere with him, she couldn't take him out in public, he would start a clamouring riot in the middle of the street—

And more importantly, she didn't actually *want* to keep seeing him, did she? This... wraith? This *corpse*?

But she didn't take it back, either. And gods curse her, crush her, but she even raised her shaky hand, and gestured it between him, and the light. Saying, *come*.

"Come?" she asked aloud, her voice wavering now. "Come with me, Filak?"

She couldn't at all read that strange twitch of his hand, the staring flat emptiness of his sunken black eyes as they looked toward the sun, and then back to her face again. And though Daisy didn't see his foot move, he must have kicked a rock beneath him, because another one rolled away, tumbling toward the waiting light.

"*Ég get það ekki*," he finally said, his mouth twisting. "*Ekki núna. Nei.*"

And though Daisy again couldn't follow the depth of it, he was saying—no. No.

He wouldn't. No.

Daisy's stomach plummeted, her prickling eyes dropping, because gods, what the hell else had she expected? It had been a ridiculous, reckless night, she'd lost herself in the frenzy and the fantasy, and—yes, she could admit—she'd wanted to strike back at Lew. She'd needed an escape, and some relief, and this orc had seen it, and offered it, and that—that was all.

And surely it was for the best, because they didn't even speak the same language, Daisy still knew nothing about him, he probably wasn't even from here. And of course she shouldn't want to continue this, right? To keep seeing this skeletal, desiccated wraith? To make *love* to him? Good gods, how desperate was she?!

So she nodded, curt and jerky toward the rubble at their feet, and lurched toward the exit. Keeping her eyes on her staggering feet, because she couldn't bear to look at him, to again face his refusal, his rejection. Just like Lew, Filak didn't want her, she wasn't desirable, she wasn't interesting or creative, this wasn't a whirling magical dream, it *wasn't*. It had just been stupid, foolish, a fantasy. And she was going to break down sobbing, oh gods—

When something—caught her. Something warm, supple, familiar, curling around her wrist. His hand. Filak's familiar callused hand, with those long gaunt fingers, the sharp talons so black and deadly against her skin.

"Daisy," he said, low. "*Ég finn þig í kvöld. Ach?*"

But again it meant nothing, nothing—and Daisy jerked a shrug, barked out a laugh. Whatever it was, it didn't matter, he was saying no, no, no...

But then—his other hand, on her face. His warm, sharp fingers spreading, tilting her chin up. The feeling so familiar, so right—but now it came with the jarring sight of his pale sunken face, his hollow unblinking eyes. And Daisy couldn't even begin to read those eyes, to follow what he was thinking, what he was trying to say...

But gods, the feel of his hand. So gentle. So warm and familiar and capable. Those deadly talons only slightly scraping, taking care not to mar her skin.

"Daisy," he said again. "*Þú ert enn mín. Sólin mín. Daisy mín.*"

His sun. His Daisy. Surely empty words, the kind of words Lew always said, too—and Daisy should look away, pull away. Escape this entire ludicrous situation, with this ludicrous orc, and go back to... to...

"*Mín,*" he murmured, his eyes held fixed to hers, as if waiting for her agreement. But Daisy could only swallow, bite her lip, because she wasn't, he wasn't. It had been one stupid, irresponsible night, and she just needed to leave...

Filak's breath hitched out, his mouth grimacing, his hand dropping from her cheek. Because yes, he knew that too, of course he did. They would say farewell and never see each other again...

But then—he grasped her hand. Brought it up to his mouth. As if—as if he was going to kiss her hand, or propose, or—or—

Smell it? Or wait, no—he was smelling her *ring*. Lew's big, expensive, custom-made ring, with the gold band, the heavy glittering diamond.

Daisy winced, her fingers twitching in Filak's grip, and suddenly the ring looked even more wrong than usual, more hideous, like a gaudy screeching bauble stuck into a pig's snuffling nose. Like it was meant for that foolish fantasy version of Daisy, the beautiful brilliant creative version, and not at all for the real one. The one who was dirty and dusty all over, who'd willingly spent the night in a cave with a corpse, who still had said corpse's sticky spunk seeping down her thighs.

And maybe Filak saw it too, because his lip curled even higher, his hooked nose wrinkling with clear contempt. And his sharp claws had caught on the ring, plucking it off Daisy's finger entirely, so he could draw it up and glare at it, his breath exhaling in a harsh, mocking little scoff.

And then, with a sharp flick of his claws, he... *crushed* it. Crushed the gold, that bright solid *diamond*, into a crumpled glittering tangle in his fingers.

Daisy yelped and stared—what the hell, no one could crush *diamonds*—not even orcs, right?! But Filak's lip curled higher, into something starkly, bitterly pleased. And then he brushed off his hands, scattering glittering dust all over the rubble-strewn ground at their feet.

A choked sound escaped Daisy's mouth—she could have

sold that ring, could have used it to buy passage back home to the city—but before she could fall to her knees, start sifting for pieces, Filak caught her hand, and shook his head. As more dangerous contempt curled on his lip, and something hard and bleak flared in his sunken eyes.

"*Nei*," he hissed. "*Nei, Daisy. Mín.*"

No. No, Daisy. Mine. And what the hell was this, what the hell had he done, what had Daisy done? And staring at his vicious, sunken white face, at the foreign black marks etched into his skin, Daisy felt the first true trickle of fear, skittering up her spine. He was dangerous. He was deadly. He could— he could break *diamonds*. He could so easily break her...

Daisy flinched and wrenched away, staggering backwards over the rubble and stone, into the streaming light. And this time, Filak didn't come for her, didn't try to stop her. Only held himself still, his eyes so bleak and empty on hers, his claws dangling sharp and deadly at his sides. Again looking impossibly alarming, like darkness, like death.

And as Daisy stumbled out into the sun, into the fresh bright morning, Filak spread out his sharp skeleton hands, one of them splaying against the rocky wall beside him. And then he tilted his face back, his hollow eyes fixed on the cave ceiling above. As if opening himself wide for his gods, for their destruction, their devastation...

And with another deep, shuddering rumble, the cave's opening before him collapsed, crashing into dust and rock and ruin.

He was gone.

9

Daisy trudged back to Dusbury with her head ducked low, her trembling arms tightly folded over her chest.

What the hell. What the *hell*.

Had *Filak* collapsed that cave? Had he done it... on purpose?

Of course it wasn't possible, of course—but then again, Daisy had watched him crush that diamond, too. Her diamond, her expensive valuable property, that she could have used to fund her escape back home. To help her run away from here, run away from Lew, forever.

But instead, Filak had just taken the ring, and destroyed it. Maybe just like he'd decided to take her, and destroy her, too.

The vision of that first tunnel's sudden collapse swarmed again through Daisy's thoughts, bright and clear and menacing. How that pale, marked, mysterious figure had appeared in the shadows, put his hand to the wall, and...

Crash.

Daisy shivered all over, wrapping her arms tighter around her chest. No. Filak couldn't have done all that on purpose. He couldn't have *chosen* to trap her with him like that. It was impossible. Magic wasn't *real*. Right?

Of course orcs don't have magic, Daisy, Lew had said, rolling his eyes, when Daisy had mentioned all those tales to him. *They only have overdeveloped auditory and olfactory processing, likely due to their extreme consanguinity. It's a miracle they're even still able to reproduce, let alone as excessively as they do.*

Daisy shivered again, and gritted her teeth as she walked through Dusbury's town gates, and headed for their apartment's street. Because curse it, whatever the hell last night had been, it was over now. Finished. She'd been reckless and foolish, and she'd even gone and thoroughly humiliated herself, at the end. Asking an orc to come with her. An *orc*. An orc with a face like that, who'd behaved like that, and possibly trapped her like that. An orc who, for the horrible finishing touch, had carelessly ruined her ring, her one way to escape this disastrous mess for good.

And now? Now, Daisy was stuck. Stuck here in Dusbury, with no coin, no food, nowhere to stay, and no way home… except for Lew. She had no choice but to go back to Lew, who had lied to her, and let her believe she was special. Beautiful. Brilliant. *My heart is forever yours.*

Daisy groaned, and let out a shaky breath as she halted before their rented apartment's door. On her way here, she'd at least found a stream to drink from and wash up in, and she'd emptied her bladder in a protective thicket, too. But she was still painfully hungry, her head badly aching, and she just wanted to curl up alone and sleep for days. *Nei, Daisy. Nei. My heart is forever yours.*

She yanked the door open with a trembling hand, and plodded down the narrow hallway toward the apartment. Maybe Lew wouldn't even be here. Maybe he would be off with Sybil, or some other beautiful woman, working on the top-secret project. Maybe Daisy could eat and sleep in peace, and then sort out some kind of plan…

So of course, the instant she opened the door, there was Lew. Whirling around to stare at her, from where he'd been pacing back and forth across the room.

"Daisy!" he exclaimed, his voice something between relieved and furious. "Where the hell have you been?"

Daisy's stomach twisted—as if he had a right to ask, now?—and she shoved her ringless left hand into her pocket, and shut the door behind her. "Out," she replied, as steadily as she could. "Busy."

Lew stared at her for a long, jolting moment, as strange red blotches rose on his handsome face. "You could have *said*," he snapped. "I was *worried* about you."

Daisy blinked at him, because yes, he did look worried, and still even angry, too—but then his narrow eyes flicked, brief but unmistakable, over toward the table. Toward where Daisy had been working on inking pages for their next book, and one of them was still lying half-finished on top. The rare *Aconitum napellus* she'd spent days studying and sketching, until she'd been certain she'd captured every lobe, every hooded flower.

A sudden tightness spasmed in Daisy's throat, and she clutched her hand to a fist in her pocket, and dropped her eyes. Gods, she couldn't do this right now, she couldn't handle a fight with him, she needed to eat, to think, *nei, Daisy, nei...*

"Well, I hope you feel vindicated, at least," came Lew's voice, a little flatter this time. "Now that you've made your point?"

Daisy attempted a shrug, and choked down the sudden, irrational urge to laugh. Of course Lew would think she'd run off just to get back at him. And now that she'd finished her petty little tantrum, things could instantly return to normal, and she would go back to work at once.

"Though the marks are really a bit juvenile, don't you

think?" Lew added, his voice clipped. "I hope to gods that's not permanent."

What? Daisy blinked at him, and followed his frowning eyes downward. Toward her chest, where her increasingly grubby dress was still pulled low, revealing her collarbone, and—

A mark. A *sun.*

It was inked in thick, vivid black, directly over Daisy's heart. A circle, with long straight lines radiating out from its edges.

Sólin mín. Daisy mín.

Daisy's heartbeat skipped, and then wrenched into a wild thundering drum, banging against her ribs. *Filak* had done that, last night. Filak had marked her. Tattooed her, to match himself.

But—when? How? How had he possibly done such a thing, without her even noticing? Why had she not felt it? Surely she would have—

But then the vision swirled up, hard enough to sway her on her feet. During the night, when Filak had gotten up, gone away, and then come back. When she'd felt his claw gently drawing that sun on her, just there, again and again and again.

And it hadn't hurt, had it? And real tattoos were supposed to hurt, supposed to prick their ink deep into the skin. Which meant it wasn't permanent, it couldn't be permanent, and Daisy certainly wouldn't have ever wanted it to be... would she?

But she couldn't seem to stop blinking down at it, and despite the weight of Lew's watching judging eyes, she brought up a trembling finger to touch at it. To stroke her finger against that deep black sun, so strong and striking against her pale skin.

But it didn't feel any different, and it didn't smear, either. It just stayed there, solid and stubborn, as steady as Filak's stroking hands, his unblinking black eyes. *Sólin mín. Daisy mín.*

Daisy fought down her convulsive shiver, and blinked back up at Lew's face. "No," she said, with surprising steadiness. "It's not permanent."

Lew's eyes flared with unmistakable relief, even as they flicked up to—to Daisy's throat. "Those bite-marks had better not scar, either," he snapped. "Gods, did you go find someone *feral*?"

Someone feral. And gods curse her, but Daisy's face suddenly flushed hot, and something tugged at her mouth. Because yes, Filak had been completely and utterly feral, like a vicious starved wildcat trapped alone in a cellar for too long. And that sharp twist in Daisy's chest felt too much like longing, like loss, like... grief.

"Who was it, then?" Lew demanded, sharper than before. "Anyone I should know about?"

Daisy swallowed hard, shook her head. "No," she replied, hollow. "I won't be seeing him again."

There was an instant's silence, and then Lew harrumphed, and turned away. "I've brought you a new specimen of *Cascabela thevetia*," he said, with a curt nod toward the table. "It should give you more to work with than the last one, I hope."

Daisy followed his eyes toward the new specimen, its root ball carefully wrapped in thick brown paper. The *cascabela's* distinctive yellow flowers had been fairly straightforward to draw, but she'd been struggling with the dense, prickly lobed leaves, and she'd asked Lew if he could find another one. And of course he had, pretending as though nothing had happened at all, as though a wild orc hadn't trapped and ravaged Daisy last night, and marked his sun on her skin.

Thankfully, Lew didn't speak again, or demand a reply— and instead he stalked for the bedroom, and shut the door loudly behind him. Maybe expecting Daisy to follow him, to try to apologize, or even to caress and taste him, to make it up to him in all the ways she knew he liked best.

But even the thought of touching Lew churned up bile in Daisy's empty stomach, and she sagged back against the nearest wall, and buried her face in her hands. Gods, what was she going to do? How could she get back home to the city? To where she at least still had some connections, contacts, clear paths toward finding other work?

But there were no answers, and she was so tired, so hungry, so muddled and overwhelmed. And finally she dug out some food from the icebox—bread and an apple—and staggered over to the table, and swiped for her pencils, her sketchbook...

But the sketchbook was gone. And Daisy stared at where it should have been for far too long, her thoughts bumping and floundering, because—she'd taken it to the cave. She'd left it there. Lost it.

She groaned aloud, dragging her hands down her face, because sketchbooks were expensive, and that one had not only included multiple studies and preliminary drawings for Lew's next book, but it had also included her own work. Her own drawings of funny plants and insects, of cave flora and mushrooms, of fascinating people in striking outfits, whatever had caught her eye that day. And while most of the sketches were staunchly mediocre, there were a few she'd been rather proud of, and she would even flip back to look at them, drink them in like air, like hope.

But now—now they were gone forever, too. Just like her relationship, her pride, her diamond ring. And she was damned lucky Lew hadn't thought to look for the ring, to ask for it, what was she going to do?

But there was still nothing, nothing, and finally Daisy scrounged up some loose paper, and sank down at the table. And then just started drawing the *Cascabela thevetia,* because it was there, and what the hell else was she supposed to do?

What kinds of other clients would she find down here in this backwood? What kinds of jobs could she do? How could she prove her history and references? Where would she stay, how would she eat? Could she steal coin from Lew, and run? Or do it slowly, over the course of weeks? Grit her teeth and pretend until then, keep sharing his bed, try to forget Filak had ever existed?

It made for an endless, miserable day, and of course the *cascabela* still seemed impossible to draw, no matter how Daisy arranged it. And when Lew finally stalked out of the bedroom again, late in the afternoon, Daisy almost flinched at the sight of him, at the cold satisfaction in his eyes. Even if she wasn't fawning over him in bed and begging for his forgiveness, she was at least still drawing. Doing exactly what he'd wanted her to do.

"It's getting late," he said, without preamble. "You still haven't finished that yet?"

Daisy couldn't even bear to look at him, because of course he still expected her to perform on his schedule, too. "No," she said, toward her hideous *cascabela*. "I'm not feeling well."

Lew didn't even pretend to be sympathetic, and instead grasped for his coat, and muttered something about the club. And then he strode out, slamming the door behind him, leaving Daisy alone with the *cascabela*, and her grief.

The tears finally began squeezing from her eyes, streaking hot and shameful down her cheeks, and finally she went and curled up on the small couch, and sobbed into her hands. What was she going to do. What had she done.

She must have slept like that, because she twitched awake to the sound of the apartment door thudding closed, and Lew's steps stomping off to the bedroom. And when she rubbed at her bleary eyes, the room was cool and quiet and dark, illuminated only by a faint, silvery stream of moonlight from the window.

And maybe it was the exhaustion, or the overwhelming mess this day had been, but something... prickled, on Daisy's neck. Something... here. Strange. *Wrong*.

She shoved up on her hands, blinking into the darkness—but there were only shadows, looming silent and forbidding in the room's corners. Only her imagination, surely, and...

The darkness *moved*. Slipped and swept and emptied, leaving something... white. Something pale and skeletal and menacing, rising up tall before her, as a strong slim hand stabbed toward her, and curled its sharp fingers around her throat.

And even as Daisy opened her mouth to scream, her heartbeat stuttered and swayed, hurling her full of something almost like... relief.

It was Filak.

10

Filak was here. Now. In Dusbury. In Daisy and Lew's *apartment*.

Daisy gulped, quivered all over, and leapt up to her staggering feet. An irrational, unthinking movement that only lurched her closer toward the pale, deadly wraith who'd somehow invaded her apartment, and clamped his sharp hand around her neck.

But instead of impact, or pain, or judgement, there was only—warmth. Warmth, and that familiar rich scent, gathering Daisy tight and close, enveloping her in sudden, astonishing safety.

"*Sólin mín,*" murmured Filak's low voice in her ear, as one warm steady hand stroked up and down her back, and the other hand caressed its sharp claws so gently against her throat. "*Daisy mín.*"

It didn't make sense, it was ridiculous, appalling, *dangerous*—but Daisy couldn't seem to pull away. Could only stand there, trembling in an orc's strong safe arms, and finding that she'd somehow clutched her arms tightly around him, too.

"Filak," she whispered, choked, into the silken skin of his chest. "What—why? I thought—"

He murmured something back, together with more firm, proprietary strokes of his hands. And whatever it meant, Daisy knew the feel of those hands, knew their steady certain reassurance, maybe even... their possessiveness. The way they too whispered, *mine.*

A hot shiver rippled up Daisy's spine, and she drew back a little, needing to look at him, to search his face in the faint moonlight. To see if he really meant that, had he really come here for her...

But then she stilled, her breath hovering in her throat, her eyes staring, unblinking. Because somehow, here in the shadows and the moonlight, Filak looked... different. Still sharp, yes, still all hard-cut bone and striking black and white. But his pale skin beneath the black marks almost seemed to glow, like smooth burnished silver—and his hollow eyes looked far less skull-like, and more like deep shadowy pools, with light hidden and glinting inside. And even his mouth looked softer, more supple, its corner curling up in something hungry, something dangerous, something that flared heat straight to Daisy's groin.

"*Daisy mín,*" he murmured again, as his hand still on her neck slipped up beneath her jaw, tilting up her face. "*Mín. Ach?*"

His. Daisy shivered again, caught in his touch, his voice, his eyes, his bizarrely compelling face. While a distant voice valiantly nattered and chanted, dredging up dark-edged visions of the tunnel, the cave, her ring crushed in his fingers, the mark over her heart...

"But," she gulped at him, between breaths, searching his intent, shadowy eyes. "Last night. Did you—did you trap me on purpose? Mark me like this on purpose?"

She flapped her hand at the sun on her heart, and Filak's gaze instantly followed it, and held there. And then his own hand slipped up toward it, his long sharp fingers splaying wide and proprietary against her thundering heartbeat.

"Ach," he murmured, steady, utterly unrepentant. "*Mín.*"

Daisy's breath shuddered out, her throat swallowing hard. Because even if Filak hadn't understood the question, his implication was still far too clear, wasn't it? He thought he owned Daisy. He thought he could do whatever the hell he wanted with her. Even if that meant drawing on her without her permission, or destroying her valuable ring, or trapping her in a dark cave, or...

Or this. Bodily steering her around and backwards, toward the table. Moving her just as he had in the cave last night, his deft hands and his lean body silently speaking, leading her, guiding her down onto her back. Spreading her out onto the table's hard wood, all over her strewn messy drafts of the *cascabela*, oh gods—

"Filak!" Daisy hissed, but his mouth was quirking, as one of his hands returned to her neck, stroking with smooth, easy reassurance. While his other hand slipped down to her knee, sliding up her skirts to her thighs, her hips...

He was *undressing* her. Undressing her, here, in Lew's apartment, on the kitchen table. After he'd all but admitted to trapping her like that last night, on *purpose*. And Daisy should have jumped up, wrenched away, shouted at him, demanded answers, apologies, *something*...

But instead, she just kept lying there, gasping and shuddering, as Filak's steady hand slid her skirts up to her waist, and smoothly guided her knees apart. Exposing everything in between, oh gods, cool air tickling at hot swollen skin, her entire body trembling beneath his watching, glittering eyes.

The quirk on Filak's mouth had slightly faded, in place of a slick, pointed black tongue, brushing swift and hungry against his lips. And with another sharp, decisive sweep of his hand, he shoved down his own trousers, and released his hard, bobbing cock.

Oh, hell. Daisy's breath choked, her eyes snapping wide on the sight. On that long, silken cock, jutting out thick and brazen and demanding from the thatch of black hair at his groin. Its skin was just as pale as the rest of him, almost a perfect match with the pearly liquid seeping from inside that deep cleft, dangling down from him in a slowly thickening string...

But against that pale skin, again, were the marks. That same black script that was written all over the rest of his body—but here, the text was written so dense and fine that it almost looked like thick, fluid lines. Lines that weren't drawn straight down his length, no, but instead curled around it, as if encircling it, protecting it. And they grew thicker and deeper as they went, until they coalesced upon that supple sliding skin at the head of him, painting it a full, dense black. Black that would usually sheath that seeping rounded head, but now, fully peeled back like this, it framed the clear, untouched white cleft beneath, and that string of matching, dangling white fluid still oozing out the middle of it.

Good gods. It was unthinkable, utterly bizarre, unlike anything Daisy had ever imagined existing on another living creature—and it had been *inside* her, just last night. And there was a sudden, irrational urge to grope for her pencil and draw it, to put it forever to paper, where she could pull it out and look at it whenever she pleased...

But instead, there was this. Filak's lean body shifting closer between her spread legs, lining up that pale, shining head with her open, exposed heat. Until he just barely, briefly brushed against her, just *there*, oh gods—and Daisy jolted all over, her breath seizing, her swollen body help-lessly quivering and clenching back against him, oh *gods*.

But Filak didn't take more. Didn't sink deeper. And instead he settled both his warm hands to Daisy's bare, quaking thighs, and spread them wider apart. So he could better see this, oh gods, his marked cock just nudging into her, leaking his silvery nectar into her eager blossoming heat.

And Daisy shouldn't have allowed it. Shouldn't. Not with everything he'd done, everything he'd openly admitted to. He didn't own her, he had no right to her, to trap her and mark her and destroy her property and break into her apartment like this. He was an intruder, a cheat, a wraith, a magic-wielding monster...

But gods, she wanted it. Needed it. And she nodded, saying, *yes, more, please*, as he finally, finally eased forward. That smooth, leaking head not just tasting, now, but prodding, pushing, pressing. Spreading Daisy's slick spasming heat wide around him, stretching her open for him, demanding she take him, accommodate him, enclose him. Claiming her as his own, his to fuck and fill and keep as he pleased.

It was appalling, it was risky and reckless and utterly *unconscionable*, and if Daisy had possessed any remnants of sense whatsoever, she should have still argued it. Should have kicked, shouted, escaped. Made it clear that she wasn't his property, he couldn't just do whatever he wanted with her, she could leave anytime she wanted.

And Filak would allow it, if she tried. Wouldn't he? He hadn't forced her the night before, he'd let her leave this morning...

But Daisy still didn't move. Didn't make the slightest attempt. And when Filak's glinting eyes found her own, his black brows raised as his invading cock pushed through the last of her resistance, and sank to the hilt inside her—she could only gasp, and nod, and hold his glittering eyes.

Saying, again, yes. Yes. *Gods*, yes.

Filak's mouth quirked up again, into something almost like a smile, because of course he already knew it, just as well as she did. And even him doing it like this, so slow and deliberate and agonizing, on the messy table where she'd been drawing for Lew—maybe that was part of it, too. Him staking his claim, showing her how this stood, and what this meant.

It was a sweeping shuddering craving, or maybe even a relief, swarming Daisy with raw, dizzying power. Power that was echoed, amplified, by the orc plunged deep inside her quivering body, opening her, showing her. And now shuddering a little fuller against her, silently shouting his own ravenous hunger toward her, saying, *yes, yes, mine.*

And when he began drawing himself out, again moving with exquisite, unrelenting slowness, that was another lesson, another claim. His triumphant eyes feasting on her displeasure, on her ache and her need at the loss of him, her throat's low, plaintive whine as he fell fully free of her. Leaving her empty, bereft, enough that her desperate tingling hands finally clutched for him, gripping at his lean hips, needing him back, please.

But he again took his time, leisurely lining them up again, letting them both watch his marked, dripping, black-and-white cock settling against its home, tasting it, teasing it. And then slowly, deliberately easing back inside, smooth and perfect and devastating. While Daisy's body flared and arched, her teeth painfully biting her lip, fighting to hold back her moans, or her screams—

And then—a sound. A cough. From—the *bedroom.*

Daisy froze, her heartbeat skidding into a wild, piercing wail. *Lew.* Lew was here, Lew was *awake*—and she was sprawled on her back on the kitchen table, with an invading skeletal orc still feeding his huge tattooed cock deep between her spread legs, oh *gods*—

"Daisy?" called Lew's voice, hoarse with sleep. "Is that you?"

Daisy flinched and shuddered, cringing sideways, needing to escape, to run, to hurl herself out the window—but then, then, his hand. Filak's hand. Curving close and safe and reassuring around her neck, speaking silently of steadiness, of ease. And when Daisy's wild eyes met his, they were steady too, glinting with sharp, unwavering certainty.

Mine, they said, as that slowly sinking cock slowly sank home, anchored itself deep and full and pulsing inside. *Sólin mín.*

It was again utterly unthinkable, impossibly ludicrous. Lew could come out at any moment, and find this orc, with his clawed hand pinning Daisy by the neck to the table, and his marked, painted cock brazenly plunged all the way inside her, pumping out his seeping nectar into her—

But somehow, somehow, as ridiculous as it was, Daisy's wild pummelling heartbeat... softened. Steadied. Her breath exhaling heavy and slow, and inhaling again. *Sólin mín.*

"Yes, it's only me, Lew," she finally called back toward the bedroom, with only a faint tremor in her voice. "I'm just— still not feeling well."

A brief, unmistakable approval flared in Filak's shadowed eyes, that quirk again curling at his lips. And then, oh gods, he began smoothly easing himself back again, sliding out of her, away, *no*. And even worse, Daisy could hear the sounds of it now, too, the slick slippery wetness of that torturous slow glide, followed by the soft squelch as he fell free of her, and then her own clenched breathless hiss—

"Well, keep it down, then," snapped Lew's irritable voice, as Filak's free hand slipped down to his gleaming, dripping length, his claws grasping it easy and familiar—and then he raised it up, and gave Daisy a firm, demanding little slap. Thudding it down heavy and audacious against her coarse dark hair, spattering her with clinging drops of luminous white. Saying, again, *mine*.

Daisy's whole body writhed, her eyes fluttering on the sight, and for an instant there was no Lew, no apartment, no fear, no future, no failure. Only that shocking, thrilling display, that marked gleaming length again raising up, thudding down with another firm, wet, demanding little smack. Saying, *mine. You pay attention to me.*

And yes, Daisy would do that, even as a grunt of displeasure filtered out from the bedroom. "Or better yet," came Lew's sharp voice, "stop sulking, and come to bed."

But Daisy scarcely heard it, because now Filak was slipping down again, and swiping himself slick and messy against Daisy's open, dripping heat. Not pressing in and filling her, no—but instead just watching himself play with her, prodding her and painting her with his fluid, even popping slightly in and out of her. All of it brazenly coaxing out those slick, squelching sounds between them, far too loud and dangerous, all of it again shouting, *mine.*

"Daisy?" demanded Lew's voice. "Did you hear me?"

Gods damn it. And even as Daisy drew in a shaky breath to reply, Filak finally settled closer against her, and plunged himself deep inside, far faster and smoother than before. Making her shudder and arch upon him, again doing it on purpose, teaching her another lesson, *mine, mine, mine...*

But amidst the swirling craving in Daisy's skull, the fear was finally chattering again, distant but insistent. If Lew walked out here and saw them, it could only mean devastation for both of them, maybe all of them. And there was a sudden, dizzying vision of Filak reaching a hand to the apartment's wall, closing his eyes, and...

Daisy hauled in another ragged breath, and then clutched her jittering hands at Filak's sharp hips, holding him tight. Holding him here, and clamping on him from inside, too, as her eyes held his, and her head jerked a sharp, shaky nod. Saying, *yes, yes, Filak, I know. Yours. Please.*

"Sorry, Lew," she called back toward the bedroom, still holding her gaze on Filak's intently watching eyes. "Maybe later. Sleep well."

There was another low, irritated harrumph from the bedroom, but then only Filak. Only Filak's blazing eyes,

Filak's hips drawing back from her grip—and then Filak's slick slamming strength, ramming into her again and again and again. Being as loud as he damn well wanted, sliding and slapping and squelching, teaching her another furious, shouting lesson. He didn't care what Lew saw or heard, he would gladly kill Lew before Daisy stepped foot back in that bedroom, he would punch a rock down Lew's throat or jam his talons into his eyes. And Daisy wouldn't do a damned thing about it, she would lie here and take it, welcome it, cling and nod and silently beg for it, as his hips ground and gouged deep, his invading cock straining and spasming, until...

He wrenched all over, his eyes flashing white—and Daisy juddered as he spewed out, flooding fierce molten heat sharp and deep inside her. Shuddering so hard that she shuddered too, wrenched up rigid and high and tight—and then it all crashed down again, ecstasy white and frenzied and blaring, her impaled invaded body milking him and caressing him and screaming back at him. Shouting, *yes, yours, yes, you shameless feral domineering fiend, yes.*

And Filak knew it, of course he did, and there was only triumph in the graceful arch of his lean body, in the hooded glittering intensity of his eyes. And for a brief, dazzling instant, as the sheer ferocious bliss kept reeling, there was an acute, crystalline comprehension, sparkling light and easy between them.

Daisy was his, yes, that was settled, now—but that also meant that Filak was hers. He was bound to her, entwined with her, and he'd had no choice but to come here and find her again. To... tend to her. To care for her, and rescue her. To sweep her away from Lew, from all this grim miserable darkness, off into the magic, into the bright shimmering dream.

And when Filak's gasping, sweaty body finally sank over Daisy on the table, his face nuzzling at her neck, the truth of it only swirled closer, settling quiet and deep. He was hers.

And it was right that his clawed hand should gently tip her face sideways, exposing her throat. Right, that his sharp teeth should settle against her skin, seeking and scraping, far harder and more purposeful than the night before. And right, painful, *perfect*, that those teeth should snap down decisive and deep, breaking the skin, piercing her with marks that would never, ever fade.

Daisy didn't even gasp, didn't whimper or shudder or flinch. Only exhaled, shaky and slow, as her trembling arms curled around Filak's rigid, sweaty back, and held him close. Even caressing him, telling him yes, she understood, yes, she wanted it too. Wanted his sharp teeth, those rapid greedy gulps of his throat. And yes, he could swell and shudder like that again inside her, readying himself to again pour back inside, to return the gift she was giving him. Because he was hers, he was fierce and wild and feral but he was hers, her own marked magical devil, come to whisk her deep into his thrall, his lair, his dream.

And when he poured out again, softly groaning into her broken skin as he quivered all over, Daisy only clung tighter, and again allowed him to sweep her along with him, into the beauty and the wonder. She was his, he was hers, and he'd come to rescue her, to carry her away...

And even before he asked, Daisy knew the answer. Even when he slowly, gently extracted his teeth from her skin, and rose up to look at her. Even when his mouth was stained with red, his long black tongue sweeping hungry against his wet lips...

"*Þú kemur með mér,*" he murmured, so soft. "*Ach, sólin mín?*"

You will come with me, it meant, even if the words themselves were still meaningless in Daisy's ears. *Yes, my sun?*

And Daisy nodded, urgent and fervent, her smile quivering soft and true. "Ach, my devil," she whispered, toward his skeletal watching face. "I'll come."

11

I t didn't take long for Daisy to pack up her life.

She'd had her large travelling satchel stashed by the door, and into it she stuffed her grubby cloak, a waterskin, some fruit, and some clothes she'd had drying by the window—and on top, a large sheaf of paper, and some pencils. All the while not thinking, not letting her brain linger on what she was doing, this wasn't a bad idea, it wasn't. It was an opportunity. An escape. Exactly what she'd desperately needed.

She could feel Filak watching her, the satisfaction almost radiating off his lean unmoving body. And when she shot him a brief look under her lashes, he was almost smiling at her, his hard mouth gone soft and approving, his eyes gleaming in the dark.

But then his gaze purposely angled toward the bedroom, and his black talons drummed on one of the scattered sheets of paper on the table. On a failed sketch of the *cascabela*, and Daisy blinked at it, and then at his face. He wasn't suggesting—what? That she take her sketches? That she keep working on Lew's project? Maybe even... maybe even publish it herself?

Something flipped in her belly, something between hope and terror—of course she couldn't do such a thing, she was only Lew's illustrator—and Filak's head tilted, his smile slightly fading, as he tapped on the paper again, and then jabbed his claw toward Lew's bedroom. As if...

Oh. He wanted Daisy to write a *note*. To tell Lew she was leaving, so he didn't run off and mount some kind of frantic search for her.

And yes, that made sense, of course, and Daisy shoved down the strange disappointment as she flipped the paper over, and scribbled a note across the back.

Sorry, Lew, but I'm leaving for good, and going home to the city. I'm not interested in existing to serve you anymore, while you save your affections and your secrets for other people. Goodbye.

She should have written something about the apartment back in the city, or about her possessions, her finished drawings, whatever payments should still be hers—but suddenly it was all too overwhelming, too alarming to even consider. She was leaving everything, her career, her art, her *life*, to run off alone with an orc. With this orc. The orc who'd trapped her in a cave and destroyed her ring and drawn a sun on her without permission, and—and—

She drew in a bracing breath, and glanced again toward Filak's face. Needing his certainty, his reassurance, his soft, approving smile. Or maybe even his warm steady touch, his murmurs of *sólin mín*—

But this time, Filak wasn't looking at her. Instead, he was still studying the papers on the table. Her papers, her drawings of the *cascabela*, and several other plants for Lew's next book. *Abrus precatorius, Aconitum napellus, Atropa belladonna.* And Filak seemed strangely intent as he looked, his long claws lightly tracing over the belladonna's bell-shaped flowers, and then skittering sideways to the next drawing, the *Ricinus communis.*

"*Hvað er þetta?*" he asked, his voice sudden and curt, his

claws tapping hard at the *ricinus*' spiny seed capsules. "*Ert þú með þetta hér?*"

Daisy blinked uneasily toward him—he wanted to know more about the *ricinus*? But Filak's eyes on hers were unblinking, demanding, his lip slightly curling—so she attempted a shrug, and lurched over to the nearby counter, where Lew kept his boxes of pressed specimens. The specimens were all stored carefully in folded paper, labelled in Lew's familiar neat script, and yes, here was the *ricinus*, right on top. And Daisy jumped at the sight of Filak's clawed hand, flipping the paper open, revealing the *ricinus*' flattened leaves and capsules beneath.

"*Átt þú þetta?*" he asked, his eyes suddenly hard and narrow on hers. "*Afhverju?*"

Daisy's heart skipped, and she shook her head, and shoved the specimen back into the box with slightly trembling hands. "It's just a plant," she said, though her voice wavered, too. "For Lew's research. His next book."

She nodded down toward Lew's ever-present notebook, which he'd left lying nearby on the counter, and Filak's nostrils flared as he snatched it up, and began flipping through pages. Almost as if he could *read* them, but of course he couldn't, right? Not even Daisy could understand Lew's notes, and gods knew she'd surreptitiously tried, especially when it had come to this top-secret project. But Lew's notes were full of his own messy shorthand, with random calculations and coordinates, and it was only the sketches that made sense to Daisy, far rougher and messier than her own.

But Filak's eyes went narrower and narrower as he read, and his jaw spasmed as he halted on a page full of incomprehensible calculations and sketches. One of which was a *ricinus* seed, and Filak's claw settled purposefully on the seed, and then on the unintelligible scrawl of notes beside it. Notes that extended onto the next page, and the next, and

Filak's claw twitched as he turned the pages faster and faster, and a low, steady growl hissed from his throat.

And when his eyes finally snapped back to Daisy's, there was something strange in them. Something disbelieving, something menacing, something... wrong. Something that flashed her flailing thoughts back to that moment when he'd crushed her diamond in his claws, and collapsed the tunnel between them...

An icy chill wrenched up Daisy's back, and she took an unsteady step backward, her hand gripping tight at the heavy packed satchel still slung over her shoulder. "What?" she said, her voice wavering. "It's just a notebook. That's all."

But Filak was still growling, his lips now pulled back to show all his sharp teeth. And his lean body twitched, enough to jerk the notebook in his hand, while his eyes flashed with more menace, more disbelief, more... rage?

Daisy staggered another step backwards, and her heart-beat was suddenly far too loud, drumming in her ears. "Um," she said thickly. "Y-you know, actually, maybe it would be better to... to..."

She dragged in a desperate, hitching breath, because she wasn't—refusing. Second-guessing. Was she? She *knew* Filak was like this, she knew he was chaotic and impulsive and unpredictable... right? And she'd still meant to run off with him anyway, to follow the hope and the dream, but...

But gods, the way he kept looking at her. Not only with that strange blazing anger, but with disgust, and contempt. And he again swept up the drawing, her drawing—he'd still had the drawing?—and stabbed his claw at the spiky cluster of seed capsules.

"*Átt þú þetta,*" he hissed, as the claw swivelled toward her. "*Ach, Daisy?*"

He was asking if she'd drawn it, surely, and Daisy warily nodded, even as her heartbeat thumped harder in her chest. He wasn't angry at her over a drawing, surely, but what else could it be? What else could he mean? And his claws extended out even longer, somehow, glinting with alarming brightness in the faint moonlight, just like his sharp bared teeth...

"*Nei,*" he snarled, his eyes flashing on hers. "*Nei, Daisy.*"

What? Daisy stumbled another step backwards, nearly staggering into the table, and almost dropping her satchel. What did he mean? What was he doing? What did he want her to say, to do?

He spoke again, swift and unintelligible, jabbing his claw at the drawing again, but of course it meant nothing, and Daisy's head was shaking, her breath catching in her throat. "I—I don't know what you mean," she stammered. "P-please, Filak."

But he just kept speaking, faster and louder, and gods he was going to wake Lew up, and maybe—maybe that wouldn't be the worst thing, would it? And Daisy even shot a helpless glance toward Lew's bedroom, as her heartbeat thundered even louder, and something stung behind her eyes. It didn't make sense, it was supposed to be an escape, hope and excitement and freedom...

And instead, it was just more of—of this. More fear and confusion, more words Daisy couldn't follow. Using her art, lying to her, collapsing the tunnel, crushing her diamond, marking her with his sun...

But Filak just kept talking, waving wildly at the notebook's open page, and Daisy dragged in a deep breath, and ventured a small step sideways. Toward Lew's room, oh gods, and was she really choosing Lew over this, maybe she was, her mouth opening, about to—

Filak flashed toward her in a blaze of white, a flare of claws and limbs and rage—and suddenly a hot hand clamped over her mouth, a sharp claw jabbing into the soft meat of her throat. Not gentle this time, not teasing or tantalizing, but hard and fierce and aggressive, as if—

As if Filak wanted to hurt her. As if he wanted to *kill* her.

"*Nei*," he spat, his teeth still bared, his eyes deep black hollows, full of menace and hatred. "*Nei. Komdu nú.*"

And with a powerful, painful yank at her arm, he wrenched Daisy bodily toward the door. So fast she couldn't refuse, couldn't resist, couldn't even think—

Until the apartment door thudded shut behind them, and Filak hauled her out into the darkness.

12

Filak dragged Daisy down Dusbury's empty streets, one strong hand still clamped to her arm, the other around the back of her neck. Her feet stumbling, her breath heaving, her eyes wildly straining and searching the moonlit street.

This wasn't happening. This couldn't be happening. Why was this happening?!

"Filak!" she gasped, against the screeching wheeling panic. "Why? What is this? What are you *doing*?!"

But there was no response, only his nostrils flaring, his head twitching back and forth—and then he yanked Daisy down a side street, into a dark narrow alley. Pulling her faster, harder, she couldn't see, couldn't think, could scarcely stay upright. He was taking her, kidnapping her, dragging her off to—to hurt her? And he couldn't, this was illegal, she needed to run, to escape, something, *please*—

She sucked down a deep breath, a gust of desperate courage—and then she hurled herself backwards. Snapping sharp, dangerous pain down her neck, Filak's grip wrenching, his claws dragging away. Just for an instant, just enough for her to stagger a step away, to reel in a harsh hitching breath.

"Help!" she called out, her voice strained, broken. "Orc! Kidnapping! *Help!*"

Filak's furious growl scraped against her ear, his hand again clamping hard and hot against her mouth. And wait, was that a *voice* down the alley, it was, a man hollering, please, *please*—

But then—the world tilted. Swept up hard and sideways. And then Daisy was somehow hurtling through the air, gasping and unmoored, because—Filak was carrying her. Carrying her like a child, tight and trapped in his arms, as he whirled around, and sprinted straight into the main open street. Running so fast the street was nothing but a blur of moonlit shapes and shadows, rushing and vanishing behind them, but with no people, no help in sight, no, no, no—

Daisy kicked and squirmed, but Filak's hold was sharp, painful, relentless. And when she opened her mouth to shout again, something shoved deep between her lips. Something hard and crumpling and uncompromising, something that tasted like—paper. Like one of her papers, he'd shoved a ball of *paper* into her mouth, one of her own damned drawings, oh gods. Why was this happening, what was happening, what had she done...

Daisy attempted in vain to spit out the paper, and then to bite down on it, to shout as loud as she could around it—but her voice only came out as a muffled groan. While the streets kept sweeping past, dark and silent, and growing increasingly wider, the buildings further and further apart. Because they were approaching the edge of town, Filak was carrying her back out into the woods, the wilderness, where he could do whatever he wanted with her, *no*...

Daisy kicked and flailed again, pushing and twisting against his hard uncompromising body, but his sharp hands only grasped her tighter, his long legs sprinting faster. Carrying her further and further away from the apartment, from Lew, from any other living soul who knew her, who could help her, or save her, oh gods.

But there was no escape, nothing but this, this ongoing horrifying nightmare. And finally Daisy just sank into the implacable grip of Filak's arms, and blinked up at his face. His pale, sharp-featured face, gleaming with sweat, rigid with tension and rage. His shadowed eyes fixed straight ahead on wherever he was taking her, whatever he was going to do to her...

"Filak," Daisy tried to say, but it was only more meaningless muffled noise, spoken against the increasingly soggy, vile-tasting ball of paper. "Please."

He didn't even look at her, though finally his pace was slowing, first into a jog, and then into a swift, rolling walk. They were fully out of town, now, beyond where anyone could help her, and they'd long ago left the road, too. And now there were only fields, and trees, and silver moonlight dappling Filak's hard angry face. The face that had looked at her only moments ago with such longing, such approval. Such... *understanding*.

And curse her, but Daisy had been so sure they'd understood one another, back there. So sure she'd been able to trust him. So sure he would take care of her.

But there was no care in his eyes now. No kindness, no affection. Only contempt, and coldness, and rage.

And finally Daisy turned her face away, and sagged heavier against his hard forbidding chest, still so warm, still with his heartbeat thudding beneath it. The orc who'd come to her, who was supposed to save her, supposed to protect her and rescue her and care for her...

Hurting her. Destroying her. Crushing the last of her hopes and dreams beneath his claws, beneath his horrible whims, just like he'd done since the first moment they'd met.

Of course he hadn't wanted her. Of course he hadn't cared about her art. Of course it was only good enough to use against her, to block her voice, to make her choke...

Gods, she was stupid. So, so stupid.

And with that bitter certainty screaming through her skull, Daisy closed her eyes, and wept.

13

When Filak finally set Daisy down, it was in darkness.

She felt muddled, hazy, achy and exhausted all over, and she swayed on her feet, staggering for balance. Her head was pounding, her mouth fuzzy and dry, and her memories of the night were blurry, a wash of inky confusing darkness.

Filak had kidnapped her. Carried her away through the streets. Run over fields, through forests, for what had felt like an eternity, while the moon had slowly slid across the sky.

And then—underground. With Daisy weak, tired, kicking and moaning, but Filak had just kept walking, amidst ominous crackles and crashes of stone. Into air that felt denser, deeper, a grunt of effort from his body, a hard clang of metal—and finally—

This. Here. Daisy on her feet, finally free of Filak's punishing grip, and instead trapped in this empty, horrifying darkness.

But he'd also released her hands, at least, and Daisy could finally yank the sodden, revolting ball of paper from her mouth. Spitting and gasping for air, wiping her mouth with cold tingling fingers, oh gods, oh *gods*.

"Filak," she gasped, as her shaky hands groped forward into the darkness, and found—him. His warm, sweaty, solid body, the body that had caressed her, made love to her, *kidnapped* her. "What the hell is this? *Why?*"

Filak's answer was rough and harsh and unintelligible, his hands clamping too strong and sharp against her shoulders. Saying something, something important, but there was no way whatsoever to follow it, and Daisy clung to him harder, as hot liquid escaped her blinking eyes, streaked down her cheeks.

"Please, don't," she choked. "Please stop, whatever this is. *Nei*, Filak. *Nei*."

Filak's body briefly stilled beneath her desperate clutching hands, and that might have been a shudder, rippling beneath his skin—so Daisy clung tighter, searched for where his face would be in the darkness. "I—I thought I was your *sól*," she croaked. "Your Daisy. Please, Filak."

He betrayed another unmistakable shudder, quivering brief against her hands—and then another low, harsh reply from his voice. More words Daisy couldn't understand, and she wildly shook her head, desperately sought to find his eyes in the darkness.

"Your Daisy," she gulped. "Filak's Daisy. Filak's *sól*. *Sólin mín*."

There was an instant's choked silence, a shiver of an exhale from Filak's breath, whispering across Daisy's clammy, sweaty skin. Enough to lurch her closer, her hands spreading against his warm chest, his rapidly thudding heartbeat. He needed to see, he had to see, this was all some kind of horrible mistake, please...

She almost sobbed at the feel of his hand, slipping up against her shoulder, stroking warm and firm over her collarbone, curving against her neck. Touching her like he was supposed to, caressing her with that strangely reassuring safety, and Daisy's breath choked out, her entire body tilting into his touch. He had to see, he would, and...

Something cold. Something metal, something hard and thin and uncompromising, curving against Daisy's throat. Tightening, encircling, and then...

A decisive, gut-churning little *snap*.

Daisy froze, her heart thundering, and her hands frantically scrabbled upwards, groping for her neck. And clutching against—

The *ring*. The hard, smooth metal ring, circled snug around her neck. Like... a choker. A *collar*.

"What the hell," Daisy gasped, as ice and horror plunged in her gut, her hands clutching in vain at the hard metal around her neck. "What the hell, Filak!"

But he wasn't touching her now, she couldn't see him, couldn't find him—and there was only more sheer, screeching horror, clawing in her chest. "Get it off," she gulped, one hand now wildly groping into the darkness before her, the other still yanking painfully at the steel ring. "*Nei*, Filak. *Nei!*"

But he didn't reply, he wasn't even here, his touch vanished into the darkness, his body somewhere she couldn't find, couldn't feel. And when she staggered forward, there was only empty air, empty space, bumps and cracks in the uneven floor beneath her feet. Enough that she tripped, skidded sideways, no, no, no—

And finally, oh gods, Filak was here again. Catching her with those warm, steady hands, holding her upright, as a low, exasperated groan hissed through the thick black air. Swirling up the visions of the other cave, of the way he'd soothed and guided her with his warm reassuring hands— and even now, there was a desperate, helpless lurch of hope.

Maybe now he would see, now he would explain, call her his Daisy, his *sól*...

But instead, something... jangled. Rippled. Tinkling soft and light, as if it were music, or a song. And Daisy jolted, listening, as it came closer, closer, and...

Another snap. Another click, firm and decisive against the ring around her neck. And when Daisy's tingling hands flailed up again, it was—a chain. A thin, fine metal chain, linked against the ring, and leading toward...

The wall. The cold, solid stone wall.

Daisy stood there for a long, sickening instant, her breaths rattling in her chest, her fingers shaking against where the chain sank deep into the wall. As if it was embedded in it, trapped in it, part of the stone itself.

Filak had chained her to a wall. With... with *magic*.

A strange sound gulped from Daisy's throat, because of course he could do that. Of course he would wield yet more dark orc magic against her. Of course he hadn't cared, of course it had all been a lie.

"Filak," Daisy croaked, a last, helpless, desperate plea. "Filak, please. Don't do this. I'm your Daisy. Your *sól*."

But she couldn't feel him now, he was lost to her now, he'd tricked her, trapped her, chained her. He hadn't wanted her, he hadn't cared about her, just like Lew, just like everyone.

A bitter sob wrenched from Daisy's throat, and she uselessly yanked against the chain, groped helplessly into the darkness, no, *please*...

"Please, Filak," she whispered. "*Nei*, Filak."

But she could feel him vanishing, slipping further and further away, betraying her, destroying her. And that might have been a breath, a faint skitter of stone, further and further away.

"*Nei, Daisy*," came his distant voice, hard, forbidding, plummeting in her belly. "*Nei. Vertu nú kyrr og bíddu.*"

And then—another exhale. Another crackle of stone. And the gritty sound of swift, decisive footsteps on loose stone, fading into the dark.

He was gone.

14

Daisy had never felt so lost, so panicked, so utterly, desperately terrified.

She didn't know how long she spent yanking at the collar, the wall, the slim tinkling links of the chain. The collar had multiple sharp-feeling raised ridges in it, but no other obvious weak points, while the chain was so fine, so delicate, it should have been easy to break—but it was somehow as strong as a wire, as a thick braided rope. And it wasn't until Daisy could smell the blood on her stinging hands that she finally stopped, gasping and trembling, licking at her sticky, shaky fingers. She couldn't risk some kind of infection down here, she needed her hands to draw, to earn her livelihood—

But even that thought wrenched the miserable panic deeper, because maybe—maybe she would never draw again. Maybe she would never see the light again, maybe she would die alone here in the darkness. Maybe she would starve, or waste away to thirst or cold, filthy and terrified and alone, oh gods, oh gods—

The sobs consumed her then, wringing through her with

staggering force, ripping her apart. She'd been so, so stupid. Again. *Again.*

It ended with her curled up on the cold filthy floor, her face buried in her raw, bleeding hands. What was she going to do? What could she do? There was no escape. No way out. No one who even knew that she'd gone, except for Lew—but then she'd written that damned note to Lew, at Filak's behest. And surely that had been part of it too, right? Filak making sure he'd left no trail, no questions, no connections. No one to follow or blame.

The sobs wrenched through her again, weaker now, tinged with bitterness and loathing and despair. She'd been so stupid. So foolish. She'd trusted an orc, an *orc*, in the face of all rational sense, in spite of every blaring warning. She'd walked away from her life, her connections, her entire damned career, after Filak had already imprisoned her once, imposed his will on her, tattooed her, taken her, *ruined* her.

Gods, it made Lew look like a rational choice by comparison, like a brilliant enlightened catch. And what did it matter if Lew had only wanted her art, if he made love to beautiful women in Daisy's bed, and told them his secrets...

But that only gouged the despair deeper, because it did matter, it did. It had ruined everything, all Daisy's longings, all her quiet, hopeful, pathetic little dreams. Dreams of belonging with a partner who cared, having a career that mattered, making something worthy, being something worthy. A real artist, a desirable creative, wanted, needed, valued.

And Filak—Filak had drilled directly into that too, hadn't he? He'd made Daisy feel wanted. Worthy. Important. *Daisy mín. Sólin mín.*

Daisy dragged her sticky hands down her wet face, as yet more gasping sobs ripped from her throat. So, so stupid. What was she going to do?

But then—a sound. A crackle of stone, and again, again. Almost like... *footsteps.*

Daisy's heart kicked, and her head lurched up, her sticky hands trembling against her face. Was it—was it Filak again? Or someone else? Someone who could help her, or... or hurt her? And maybe she should hide, curl up, pretend to be dead, fight back the panic, the terror, the desperate all-consuming need to know—

"Filak?" her voice croaked, on its own, into the empty darkness. "Is that you?"

The footsteps hesitated, and Daisy winced, shook her head, silently cursed herself. If anyone else was down here, it couldn't be good, it had to be some cruel associate of Filak's, maybe come to finish the job...

And now the footsteps were moving again, coming closer, faster and louder in her ears. And Daisy cowered, cringed back against the wall, bracing herself for—for—

"*Halló?*" asked a soft, unfamiliar voice, far too close. "Hello?"

Daisy flinched, and her eyes snapped up, blinking uselessly into the darkness. "Hello?" she asked back, her voice wavering. "Wh-who are you?"

There was an instant's shocked-feeling stillness, and then something that sounded like a low murmured curse. And then a harsh scrape, something clanging hard and metallic, flicking orange and bright—

And suddenly, there was light. Light, fire, blazing so bright Daisy had to cover her eyes. It was some kind of torch, the new person was *holding* it, and Daisy squinted through the dazzling light, desperately searching for the newcomer's face.

It was... it was...

Another *orc.*

Daisy's heartbeat blared in her ears, and her body scrabbled back against the wall, her hands frantically yanking at the chain, trapped, doomed. "Oh gods," she gasped, and she shouldn't be talking, she shouldn't, stupid, *stupid*. "P-please, please don't hurt me, I d-didn't do anything, I'm sorry, I'm sorry—"

For an instant, the new orc just stared at her, his eyes wide—and it vaguely occurred to Daisy's panicked brain that he didn't look like Filak at all. He was tall and slim, yes, and had the same pointed ears, and black claws where his fingernails should have been—but his unmarked skin was a silvery light grey, and he had a full head of straight black hair, pulled back into a neat braid. And he was dressed in a simple tunic and trousers, with slim leather boots, and a black cloak slung over one shoulder. He looked almost—handsome, and Daisy wasn't following, her eyes blinking hard, her head twitching back and forth. No. No. He was still an orc, he could still be here to hurt her, to kill her.

But the orc had backed a step away, his face looking almost as alarmed as Daisy felt—and then he groped sideways with his hand, and propped the torch into a bracket on the wall. Illuminating this small, stone room, with its low stone ceiling, with loose rocks and rubble scattered all over. And when he turned to face her again, both his hands were upraised, his claws somehow pulled back deep into his fingers.

"There is naught to fear, woman," he said, though his voice wavered, his eyes still very wide. "I shall not harm you. I swear to you."

Oh. Oh, gods. Daisy quivered all over, and she couldn't bite back her sob, weak with terror and relief and hope. "Filak," she gasped, as she glanced furtively beyond the new orc. Toward—toward the *steel grate* behind him, now propped slightly open, almost as if this was a dungeon. A *prison.*

"D-do you know Filak?" she choked, toward the orc. "What if he c-comes back, he—he might h-hurt me, he—"

Her teeth had begun chattering, her body shuddering, and the new orc's eyes snapped even wider, his skin paler than before. "*Filak* did this to you?" he asked, and his voice faltered, too. "B-but your scent, and the..."

His wide eyes flicked to Daisy's neck, and she winced and gripped her stinging hands at the metal collar, as another hoarse sob escaped her throat. "Filak—*kidnapped* me," she gulped. "He b-brought me here, and put this—this *chain* on me, and trapped me here, and then"—she dragged for air—"he *left!*"

It sounded like a cry, a wounded helpless wail, as if Filak leaving had been the worst part of all that. And somehow, curse her, maybe it had. She'd wanted him to stay, to touch her and comfort her and speak to her, to call her *sólin mín*, *Daisy mín...*

But there was no judgement in the new orc's eyes, only sympathy, and perhaps more confusion, too. "But," he said, his brow furrowing, as his hand waved toward Daisy's trembling body, toward her neck. "But are you not... Filak's mate?"

Filak's *mate*. Daisy stared at the orc, her heartbeat erratically skipping, and for an instant, there was the strangest urge to say... *yes*. Because yes, of course that was what it had all meant, right? Filak's stroking hands, his furious hunger, his body learning hers, subduing her to his will. Crushing her ring, marking her with his sun, coming back for her, claiming her on a kitchen table, making his meaning all too clear. *Mine, mine, mine...*

"Filak's... mate?" Daisy echoed, too late, her voice cracking. "W-what is that? Why—why would you think that?"

The orc blinked at her, and his mouth twisted into something bitter, maybe even sad. "You... bear Filak's fresh scent," he replied, with another wave of his hand toward her. "And his mating-bite. And his mark. And his *kraga*."

What? Daisy stared at the orc for a breath, and then clapped her shaky hand to her neck. Toward where yes, Filak had *bitten* her back in the apartment, and she'd entirely forgotten that, amidst everything else—but she could still feel it there, in her very skin. The place where his teeth had punctured her, and left a distinct set of faint indents behind. Not twinging even a little, as if the wounds had somehow already healed, and...

"What do you mean by—his mark?" Daisy asked, over that deeply unsettling thought. "And what—what's a *kraga*?"

The orc blinked at her again, his mouth twisting even tighter. "His mark," he said, as his hand skittered to his chest, spread over his tunic. "Written over your heart. For the Nor-ka-esh—Filak's kin—this holds great weight, and for him to sign you there, with his own mark, in his own ink, by his own hand, it is..."

His voice trailed away, and Daisy blinked downwards, toward where yes, that sun was still visible, drawn in thick black ink over her heart. Filak's *mark*? In his own ink, his own hand? And what the hell did *Nor-ka-esh* mean, why did this hold great weight...

Sólin mín. Daisy mín.

"And the *kraga*," the orc continued, his voice slightly hitching, as his hand slid up to trace against his own throat. "The jewel you wear, around your neck. It is our clan's deepest sign of fealty. It is"—his swallow was audible in the silence—"Filak's promise to care for you, and keep you safe and content and fulfilled, for all the rest of your days."

What? Daisy might have laughed, if not for the strange sadness in the orc's eyes, in his voice. The quiver of some-thing almost like—like grief, shuddering out around him.

But it didn't make sense, none of it made sense, and—Daisy's hand tugged helplessly at her throat, her *kraga*—whatever this orc was claiming, it was all surely a mistake. Or failing that, a mockery, or even a punishment. Filak hadn't wanted her, he certainly hadn't meant to care for her, let alone make her his *mate*. Stupid, stupid, *stupid*.

"Well," she said thickly, "there's obviously been some misunderstanding, because Filak—he kidnapped me. He trapped me here, left me here, alone. He stuffed my own art in my mouth, he wouldn't listen to me, he told me—"

Her mouth had begun wobbling, the water prickling painfully behind her eyes, and she drew in a shaky breath. She hadn't understood his words, no—but she'd understood *him*. Hadn't she?

"He told me—he was wrong," she croaked, between her gasping breaths. "He told me he didn't care about me. He told me my art was worthless. He told me... *I'm* worthless."

The sobs finally fully escaped again, tearing out of her convulsing throat, breaking her apart. While the orc just stared, his own throat bobbing, his eyes glimmering far too bright. As if he knew. As if he... understood.

"Will you help me," Daisy whispered, pleading, her hand over her heart, as if to hide away Filak's sun, his mark, his mistake. "Please?"

And the orc—nodded. Nodded, quick and fervent, his own hand over his heart, his eyes solemn and sad on hers.

"Ach, sister," he said. "I will."

15

It turned out that escaping Filak's prison wasn't as easy as Daisy might have hoped.

"I cannot release it," the orc gasped, once he'd alternated between picking at the chain, yanking at it, and sawing at it with a small steel knife he'd produced from his belt. "Filak would have had it custom made, with a latch only he can release. I shall need to fetch a smith."

A *smith*. He had to mean he was going to *leave* her here, and fetch another *orc*, and Daisy's heartbeat stuttered, her body swaying on her feet. "B-but," she whispered. "What if Filak—what if he comes back?"

The orc squared his shoulders, shot her a searching sideways look. "Whatever Filak told you, or whatever reasons he had for this," he said slowly, "he has yet claimed you as his mate. I cannot see that he would truly harm you."

Daisy barked a sharp, shaky laugh, and waved her trembling hand at her neck, the chain, the wall. "Really?" she demanded, her voice wavering. "Are we—are we talking about the same person? Pale? Gaunt? Cruel? Murderous?"

The orc grimaced, and dropped his eyes back to Daisy's neck. "Ach, I know Filak," he said, quiet. "He can be stubborn, decisive, demanding. Single-minded. Obsessive. But not cruel. Not... *murderous*."

Daisy swallowed, shook her head, because this orc didn't know, he couldn't—but that sadness again glimmered in his eyes, and he abruptly turned away. "And even if Filak does return before I do," he added, "he shall find my scent here—and you can also use my name, should you wish. I am Julian, of Clan Ka-esh, and he shall know he has much to explain to us."

Much to explain to us. He made it sound... personal, somehow, but even as Daisy opened her mouth to ask why, the orc—Julian—was already walking away, his head ducked low. "I shall soon return," he said, over his shoulder. "I shall leave the torch for you, and mayhap you can rest, or eat, or drink."

She could... what? Eat, or *drink*? Daisy blinked, and then glanced uncertainly around her. Finding only stone, and the steel grate, and... her satchel?

But yes, there was her satchel, the one she'd filled at the apartment, with the fruit, the clothes, the waterskin. And somehow it had been sitting propped right here against the wall beside her, well within her reach this entire time. And how the hell had she missed it? How had she not thought to at least do a proper search?

And had Filak—left it here? On purpose? For her?

Daisy drew in another breath, glanced toward this Julian—but he'd already vanished around the corner, his footsteps fading into the silence. Leaving her here alone again, chained to a wall in a dungeon.

But at least now she could see, and she carefully sank down to sit on the floor against the wall, and took a long, gulping drink from the waterskin. Fighting to breathe, to settle her still-shouting heartbeat, even as she glanced uneasily into the darkness beyond that heavy steel grate.

Filak could still return at any moment, right? And if he

did, what would he say? What would he *explain* to them? Would he really be able to smell that this Julian orc had been here? And what was his connection with Julian, anyway?

But no, damn it, no. Daisy needed to stop thinking about Filak. She needed to be finished with Filak. He'd kidnapped her, trapped her, chained her alone in a dark dungeon. She'd already been so, so stupid, and now she needed to focus on staying alive. On escaping, and that was all.

She repeated that to herself again and again, while time slipped past with excruciating slowness. Where had Julian gone, what was taking him so long, what if he just meant to abandon her here forever, too...

Until finally—a clatter. Footsteps. Voices. Multiple voices, and Daisy staggered up to her feet, straining to hear over her wildly thudding heartbeat. Was it Filak? Was it Julian again? Should she call out, should she hide, oh gods...

"What is this place?" demanded a high-pitched voice, carrying around the corner. "It isn't an actual *dungeon*, is it?"

Daisy froze, staring blankly toward the direction of the voice. Had that been a *woman's* voice? Surely not... right?

But then three figures strode around the corner, and into the torchlight. One of them was Julian, and he was flanked by a big bulky orc, and... yes, a woman. A real-life, honest-to-gods *woman*.

She was small and blonde and pert-looking, dressed in what appeared to be a long, belted men's tunic. And when she caught sight of Daisy, she startled for an instant, her mouth falling open—and then she yelped as she leapt forward, flailing her hands toward Daisy's chain.

"You didn't say he had her *chained up!*" she snapped toward Julian, her voice shrill. "And she's *bleeding!* Oh, good gods, are you all right?"

The genuine concern in her voice and her eyes wrenched something in Daisy's gut, and she desperately gulped for air, fought down the sobs suddenly bubbling in her throat. "I—I don't know," she stammered. "Filak k-kidnapped me, and t-trapped me here, and put this collar on me, and left me—"

She couldn't finish, biting her lip and shaking her head, while the woman's own lip wobbled, and her blonde head whipped back and forth. "I'm so sorry this has happened to you," she said firmly, her eyes glinting with surprising fierceness on Daisy's face. "We'll get you out of here at once, and you'll be quite all right, you'll see. Perfectly safe! And as for that enraging mercenary racketeer Filak, he'll be getting—"

She broke off there, because Julian had briefly put his hand to her sleeve, his eyes darting uneasily toward Daisy's neck. "Filak has... claimed her as his mate," he said, his voice low. "With his bite, and his mark. And... his *scent*."

The woman's brow furrowed, and her eyes snapped back to Daisy again. "So?" she demanded. "And is that supposed to somehow make this *better*? Leave it to Filak to finally find a woman who's willing to tolerate him, and then he kidnaps her, snaps a *kraga* on her, and locks her up alone in a horrible ancient dungeon?! What if it fell in on her head and *crushed* her?!"

Julian winced, and betrayed a wary glance around at the small, stone-walled room. "I am sure it is very safe," he replied, though his voice sounded uncertain. "Filak knows subterranean engineering better than any of us, and he would never wish to harm his mate."

The woman scoffed again, and folded both arms over her slim chest. "You give him far too much credit, Julian," she snapped back. "Just because *you* like it when Filak chains you up and has his way with you, that doesn't mean his newest unfortunate target is going to feel the same!"

Oh. Daisy froze in place, her aching hands clutching against the wall behind her, as something dipped and swayed in her gut. Wait. Was this woman saying—Filak had chained up this *Julian*, too? And—*had his way* with him? Not like this, surely, but with... with pleasure? And what did this woman mean, Daisy was just—just Filak's newest *target*?

Julian swiftly shook his head, and shot Daisy a hunted, wide-eyed look. As if he hadn't at all wanted her to know such things, but it was too late, and Daisy's stomach was crumpling again, her eyes dropping to the floor. Because she *knew* it hadn't meant anything. She knew Filak hadn't cared. She knew he would have preferred this lovely, handsome orc instead...

But no. *No.* Daisy had to stop being so stupid. She needed to stop caring what Filak had done, or what he wanted. She needed to be finished with him. To forget him. *Forever.*

"Sister, please forgive us," cut in a new, deeper voice— and when Daisy's wet eyes darted back up, it was the other new orc. The bigger, bulkier one who'd come down with Julian and the woman, and his dark eyes were kind, even sympathetic. "I ken we have all been caught by surprise with this, and thus have forgotten our manners. I am Gareth, of Clan Ka-esh, and this is my clan sister Rosa. And I ken you have met our brother Julian, ach?"

Daisy blinked, but then squared her shoulders, and drew in a shaky breath. "Y-yes, thank you," she said thickly. "And I'm—Daisy. I'm an—"

An artist, she'd been about to say, but she bit it off, shook her head. Was she even an artist anymore? Without Lew, without her work? And even Filak had rejected her work, and she wasn't going to weep again, she wasn't.

"We are most glad to meet you, Daisy," the orc— Gareth—said, while the woman Rosa fervently nodded behind him. "Now, should you wish it, I can release you from this chain, for it is one I forged myself, ach?"

Oh. This Gareth was—the smith Julian had mentioned. Right. And Daisy swallowed hard as she jerked a nod, and then fought to hold herself still as Gareth slowly stepped closer. And with gentle, careful movements, he caught the long dangling chain at Daisy's neck, and somehow—*broke it off*, with only a deft twist of his hand.

Daisy's breath caught, and she reeled away from the wall. She was finally free, oh thank all the gods, and she fought down the irrational urge to hurl her arms around this Gareth's neck. "Th-thank you so much, sir," she croaked. "And is it also possible to—"

She tugged at the metal ring around her neck, her eyes silently pleading on Gareth's face—but he winced, and rubbed his hand at his mouth. "I am sorry, but the *kraga* cannot be removed so easily," he said. "It is meant to be... permanent."

Permanent. Wait. Filak had given Daisy a *permanent* collar? One that couldn't be removed? Ever?!

Daisy gaped at Gareth, at all of them, but none of them argued this appalling claim. Though Julian had begun to look rather ill, and Rosa's hand fluttered, perhaps unconsciously, toward her own neck. Toward where—Daisy's body stilled—*she* had a ring around her neck, too. It was made of slim, gleaming gold, shining bright against the pale, scarred skin of her throat. Scars that looked like... like *teeth-marks*.

Daisy's hand snapped up to her own marked throat, feeling those distinct indents in her skin, the hard metal ring curving over them. "B-but there must be *something*," she stammered. "I—I mean, I'm sure Filak didn't intend it to be permanent in the least, he made his feelings toward me very clear, and..."

Her voice was rising, her eyes helplessly glancing between the three of them—she couldn't wear this forever, she *couldn't*—and thank the gods, Rosa drew herself taller, and twitched a decisive nod. "Of course we can do some-thing, can't we, Gary?" she said briskly. "*Kragas* can still be cut off, or melted, with no trouble at all, I'm sure. And our healer can certainly also do something about the bite-marks, and the tattoo. I'm quite sure the ink isn't permanent, is it, Julian?"

She'd shot a narrow glance toward Julian—as if he would know, as if Filak had perhaps marked *him*, too? And Daisy fought back the deeply irrational surge of bitter, miserable jealousy, while Julian rubbed his eyes, and shook his head.

"No, his inks themselves are not permanent," he replied, his voice thin. "But before we remove any of this, I ken we ought to first find Filak, and speak to him, ach? This is not—like him. I cannot follow why he would treat his new mate thus, or why…"

His voice faded, his eyes trailing to Daisy's collar, and beside him, Rosa loudly snorted. "You can't, Julian?" she demanded. "Are we talking about the same Filak here? Rude? Demanding? Unpredictable? Deeply aggressive?"

It was almost exactly what Daisy had said to Julian before, and she couldn't deny a rush of dizzying gratefulness toward this Rosa. Who had fully rounded on Julian, now, jabbing toward his chest with her pointy finger. "And," she continued sharply, "the Filak who refuses to learn common-tongue? The one who mocks our *extremely* generous offers to work as an engineer, and instead charges his own clanmates *extortionate* prices for his help, and his ill-gotten gems? The one who won't tell us a single *word* about why he left his home in the north, or why the hell he doesn't still live there, with people he doesn't hate?"

Daisy blinked at Rosa, her overwhelmed thoughts twisting and tumbling into more stark, shouting chaos. Because this was more information about Filak than she'd learned yet, right? And it couldn't all be—*true*, could it? Filak refused to learn common-tongue, or work as an engineer? He charged high prices for his help, and for *ill-gotten gems*? He was from the north? He hated people here? His own people?

But Julian's head was whipping back and forth, while

unmistakable unease flickered in his eyes. "Filak does not *hate* us," he countered. "He only has had... much to bear. And I know he has long wished for a mate, and for him to find one and claim her so fully thus, and then..."

He swept his hand toward Daisy's chain, and again shook his head. "We ought to speak with him," he said stubbornly. "Before all else."

Rosa huffed an exasperated sigh, and furiously waved at the stone-walled dungeon around them. "Well, I can agree that might be highly convenient," she snapped, "if Filak was actually here! In case you've already forgotten, he dragged his new mate down here to a dungeon, locked her up, and *left*!"

Her voice echoed against the stone, ringing eerily through the silence. A silence that suddenly felt strangely, uncomfortably taut, empty, except for...

The crackle. The faint, distinct sound of scraping rock. Grating again and again, growing louder and louder...

Footsteps. Coming closer.

Daisy backed against the wall, her heartbeat surging into her throat, ringing through her skull. Her wild eyes straining in the darkness, frantically seeking, searching, and finding...

Him. There. A pale, gleaming corpse, emerging from the shadows, with death and fury burning all over his skeletal face.

Filak had returned.

16

Filak strode out of the darkness with long, swift steps, his hands in fists at his sides, his shadowed eyes flashing with rage.

Daisy's heartbeat screamed in her ears, and she shoved closer against the wall behind her, scrabbling uselessly against it. Filak was here. He'd come back. And he looked even angrier than before, like a vengeful fiend come to devour, to destroy.

"*Nei,*" he snarled toward them, through bared white teeth. "*Daisy er mín.*"

Wait—what? Daisy was—his?

Daisy blinked, stared, not thinking, not breathing—while Rosa rounded toward Filak, her pointed chin raised. "*Daisy er ekki þín,*" she snapped back. "*Þú lokaðir hana inni í dýflissu!*"

The words again didn't make sense, but her contempt and anger were all too clear, and Filak growled back toward her in kind, with something that might have been a curse. But then his hard shadowed eyes flicked toward Daisy, and... held. Shifted. Changed.

And for a halting, dangling instant, caught in those deep glinting eyes, Daisy thought maybe—maybe he would apologize. Maybe he would come to her, stroke her with his warm steady hands, murmur soft meaningless words into her ear. And he would somehow explain all of it, explain the chain and the *kraga* and the kidnapping, explain Julian, call her his *sól...*

But then his eyes dropped downwards, narrowing on the broken chain still dangling from the wall beside her. And with a swift movement, he closed the distance between them, and snatched the chain into his long clawed fingers.

"*Nei, Daisy,*" he hissed, his voice harsh and low. "*Ég sagði þér að bíða.*"

Oh. It wasn't an apology, of course it wasn't, and Daisy's quivering hopefulness plummeted, cracking into fear and dread and despair. And too late she staggered backwards, shaking her head, raising her trembling hands between them. No, no, not again, what else would he do, please...

She only vaguely heard Gareth's low voice, heavy with warning, but Filak snapped something back, and lurched closer toward Daisy. His head tilting, his nostrils flaring, as his hand swiped for—her wrist. Closing tightly around it, yanking it up toward him, twisting her palm up, and showing—

Oh. Blood. Daisy's raw, bloody hand, scraped and broken from where she'd so desperately yanked at the chain, and fought to break free.

The sight of it heaved in her belly, and she tried to wrench her hand away, to hide, to escape—but Filak held it firm, his grip hard and uncompromising, his eyes glowering down toward it, as if it was a personal affront, somehow. And when he finally met her gaze again, the rage in his eyes flashed even sharper, his lips again curling back to show all those sharp white teeth.

"*Nei, Daisy,*" he snarled, with palpable menace. "*Þú mátt ekki skaða sjálfa þig svona.*"

It meant nothing but more anger, more of him saying no,

no, *no*, with that painfully familiar fury and disapproval again flashing in his eyes. As if he truly hated her, his teeth so hungry and vicious, his strong hand raising hers toward his mouth. He was going to bite her, he was going to hurt her again, maybe even kill her, *no*—

Daisy gulped and flailed backwards, as more bitter screeching panic careened through her chest, her skull. "*Nei*, Filak," she gasped. "*Nei*, please, please!"

But he only lunged for her again, sudden and close and horrifying. And Daisy didn't even feel his tongue, licking like that against her palm, because there was only pure terror now, wheeling and wailing, shuddering her all over, escaping in harsh, helpless gasps from her convulsing throat. Weeping, oh gods, she was weeping and cowering, fighting to cover her eyes, to escape, to disappear.

"Please," she gasped, between her hoarse, desperate sobs. "Please, Filak, *don't*. I know you hate me, I know you don't want me, but—but—"

But then—chaos. Voices shouting, bodies thudding and colliding, grunts and scrapes and curses. And Filak's touch was gone, his tongue was gone—and when Daisy risked a glance upwards, Julian and Gareth were dragging Filak backwards, Gareth's face hard and grim, Julian's shocked and pale. And Julian was muttering into Filak's ear, the words a low rapid garble, while Rosa's sharp voice rang over all the rest. Shouting in more harsh foreign words, laced with fury and disbelief.

For a breath, Filak's eyes held to Daisy's, looking even more terrifying than before, cruel black shadows ringed with vivid white—but then he growled back toward Rosa, and knocked off Julian's arm. And he began speaking too, his voice low and urgent, his teeth still bared, his sharp-taloned hand waving toward—

More people?

But yes, good gods, that was an entire group of new

people, rushing out of the darkness. Several new women, and—new *orcs*. Multiple new orcs, with harsh faces and huge hulking bodies, crowding and jostling into this too-small stone room. All of them staring straight at Daisy, some with furious frowns on their unfamiliar angry faces, and this wasn't happening, what was happening, had Filak done this, were they going to kill her, oh gods, oh gods—

Daisy couldn't find air, couldn't stand, couldn't think, and her wild, frantic eyes again caught on—Filak. Filak, looming there before all of them, his shoulders heaving, his eyes glinting on hers with strange, bleak intensity.

And for a brief, humiliating moment, holding those shadowed eyes, Daisy almost crumpled beneath the overpowering urge to run to him, to cling to him, to beg. To fall at his feet, to swear to do anything he asked, if only he would forgive her, free her from this sickening, horrifying nightmare. If only he would take her back, back to the magical moment when he'd caressed her, when he'd sworn to care for her, to keep her safe, to sweep her off into the dream...

Daisy mín. Sólin mín.

But no. No. Filak had done this to her. Filak had destroyed her entire life. Filak had trapped her here in this endless hell, with all these terrifying new strangers, all of them watching as Daisy cowered and whimpered and wept. And now they would—they would—

A woman. Breaking free from the throng, and stepping forward. Her pale face rippling and twisting through Daisy's wet eyes, her outstretched hand looking like a snake, ready to attack, to kill...

"I'm Jule, and this is my mate Grimarr, the captain of this mountain," the woman said, with a nod toward the huge, menacing figure close behind her. "And I'm sorry to meet you like this, Daisy, but I'm afraid we've had a very serious accusation against you."

A very serious accusation. It wasn't possible, this couldn't be happening, no, no, no…

"An accusation," the woman continued, quiet but certain, "that you've come to kill us all."

17

Daisy had come to kill them all.

Those impossible words rang and reeled through her screaming skull, as something crunched and seized deep in her belly, in her chest. Something like terror, like agony, like wild spiralling grief.

Filak had done this. Filak had trapped her. Tricked her. Taunted her. And now...

A serious accusation. Come to kill them all.

It kept thudding like a strike, like a juddering blow to Daisy's head. So dizzying that she could only stare at this woman, at her dark searching eyes, her tight grim mouth. This woman who... believed this. Come to kill them all.

Because *Filak* had told her this. *Filak* had done this.

Daisy's wet eyes somehow found his, still so shadowed and strange. He'd done this to her. He hadn't only wanted to hurt her and humiliate her. He'd truly wanted to... to destroy her. Maybe to have these people punish her, *kill* her, while he watched, and laughed.

Suddenly Daisy couldn't bear to look at him, at any of them, and she dropped her eyes, dropped her head. Her shaky hands groped at the wall behind her, rough against her fingers, but she couldn't feel any pain now, not even through the sharp scent of blood. Only the searing, agonizing misery, and the bitter dread of the waiting, as she stood here weak and exposed in this horrible empty silence.

Because they were all waiting for her to speak. To defend herself. Weren't they? Maybe to add to the entertainment, to Filak's enjoyment of her destruction. And Daisy would not give it, not now. Not after she'd already been so humiliated, so defeated, so *stupid*...

But she still couldn't stop the tears silently squeezing from her eyes, streaking down her cheeks, dripping off her chin. While her numb hands gripped tighter at the wall, what would they do now, how painful would it be, why wouldn't it just *stop*...

"This is absurd," cut in a shaky voice, and when Daisy raised her wet eyes, it was Julian, lurching away from Filak, coming to stand beside her. "Daisy cannot have done any such thing. She is an artist, and now she is a Ka-esh, also."

Daisy's dull, hitching thoughts couldn't follow—how did Julian know she was an artist? Had Filak told him, just now? And why would Julian call her a *Ka-esh*?

But then Rosa swept over to Daisy's other side, and squeezed a gentle hand against her arm. "Yes, precisely," she said flatly. "And we're certainly not about to take accusations from *Filak* as truth now, are we?"

She shot a dark, disapproving glare in Filak's direction, but Daisy still couldn't bear to look at him, could barely breathe over the grief still choking her throat. He'd wanted to hurt her. To destroy her.

"These *accusations* are not only from Filak," cut in the big menacing orc—the one the woman had called the captain, his voice deep and deliberate. "The reports from our scouts uphold Filak's claims, also."

What? That didn't make sense, of course it wasn't possible... right? But Daisy's horrified glance upwards found the orc looking grim, decisive, utterly certain, while several others nodded, including the woman beside him. All of them accusing Daisy, attacking her, soon about to hurt her, while Filak watched.

But Rosa pulled her small body taller, and gave Daisy's arm another reassuring squeeze. "Look, I'm sure this can all be explained," she said firmly. "Just be honest, Daisy, and we'll get this sorted out. And no matter what, Filak will *not* touch you again, and we can promise you that. Right, Jule?"

The woman—Jule—shot a brief look toward Filak's frowning face, but then she nodded, short and decisive. "Of course," she replied. "Now, Daisy, do you recognize these?"

She thrust something out between them, something that looked like a stack of rumpled paper. And it took Daisy far too long to focus, to find an answer in her churning miserable thoughts. The papers were—her art. Her drawings, the ones she'd been working on, for Lew's next book. The belladonna, the *cascabela*, the *ricinus*.

"Yes," she said, her voice barely a whisper. "They're mine."

And gods, she hadn't even seen Filak take them from the apartment, and had he somehow planned to use her art against her, all this time? Did he truly hate her work that much? Hate *her* that much?

"And you work closely with the botanist Lew Wallace, yes?" came Jule's next question. "He's your long-term research and publishing partner?"

Daisy's eyes darted up at that mention of Lew's name— how would they know Lew, why would they care?—but after another squeeze from Rosa to her arm, she somehow jerked a nod. "Yes," she said dully. "For four years now."

This Jule's eyes went even more forbidding, her breath exhaling harsh. "Then I'm sure you're aware," she continued, "how Lew Wallace is actively working to isolate and extract large quantities of powerful poison from these plants. Enough poison"—her voice hardened—"to kill every person in Orc Mountain. Every last orc, human, and *child*."

What? No. Daisy's body jolted, while the room slowly tilted around her. Lew? *Actively working?* Enough poison to kill *everyone* in Orc Mountain?

"N-no," she said blankly. "Of course not. That's—impossible."

Jule's brows rose, and her gaze dropped to the stack of Daisy's drawings still in her hand. "Is it?" she asked, colder now. "Even with all the deadliest known plants in the realm?"

Daisy blinked again, because—no. Of course they weren't. Well, the belladonna, perhaps, and the *cascabela*—the yellow oleander—and its deadly seeds. And... oh... the *ricinus*. With its highly poisonous castor beans, beans that Lew had once said could be processed into the most concentrated and versatile poison in the world. Poison that could be drunk, eaten, inhaled...

Daisy's head was shaking, her heartbeat skipping, her eyes darting back up to Jule's face. "I... I didn't," she croaked. "I'm not..."

But Jule's expression hardened further, and she thrust out something else toward Daisy. Again, something familiar. Lew's *notebook*.

And good gods, Filak had stolen Lew's *notebook*. And Lew used his notebooks every single day, they contained all his research, all his plans, drafts of everything he published. And now Lew would think Daisy had stolen it, damn it, *damn* it—

"I'm afraid it's all written out in detail here," Jule said, her voice clipped. "Methods for growing, harvesting, and extracting these poisons. Calculations about quantities and timelines. Locations near Dusbury where large fields have already been planted and harvested. And even detailed plans for dissemination into Orc Mountain. It looks as though"—her lip curled—"underground airborne delivery of the ricin was isolated as the most promising prospect. Choking us all to death in our own *home*."

What? No. *No*. It was impossible. Lew had come to Dusbury to do *research*, he'd only ever brought up poisons in the context of his next book, he'd mentioned the ricin's properties only that one time, but... but...

Daisy's head was beginning to pound, and she groped for a solution, some possible explanation. "There must—be some mistake," she managed. "You've—misread the notebook, maybe. I mean, Lew writes it in his own shorthand, I can't even understand it, I don't know how anyone else could..."

But her voice faded under Jule's hard, angry laugh. "It's not special shorthand, it's Kraitish," she snapped. "And Filak speaks Kraitish fluently, and was easily able to translate it for us."

No. No, that wasn't possible, it *wasn't*. But then again—Daisy's eyes briefly closed—Lew *had* mentioned Kraitish before, hadn't he? Something about studying it at the university, years ago?

Beside Daisy, Rosa huffed a strange sound, and reached forward to snatch the notebook from Jule's hand. "Oh," she said, after a moment's flipping through it. "Yes, it's all in Kraitish. It's so rarely spoken outside of the northwest, I'm sure it was a good way to..."

She didn't finish, angling an uncertain look up toward Daisy's face, and Daisy gazed blankly back at her, and then down at the notebook. The notebook Lew had lied to her about, the notebook that apparently included detailed plans about how to kill an entire *mountain* of people...

Daisy's head pounded louder, as a distant shrieking awareness finally forced its way into her thoughts. The *project*, gods damn it. The top-secret project. The mysterious eight weeks here in Dusbury, all the things Lew had refused to tell her, whatever he'd been doing with Sybil...

Had it really been… this? Poison? *Mass murder*?

"But… why?" Daisy finally asked, her voice cracking through the silence. "Why would Lew do such a thing? He's a scientist, a *scholar*, we research, we write *books*, that's *all*."

But it sounded weak even to her own ears, and pathetic, and foolish, and stupid. So, so stupid, oh gods, oh gods…

"Well, according to this notebook," Jule's cold voice went on, "this project has been going on for well over a year, and it's being funded by Lord Nash. I presume you know who he is?"

Lord Nash. Daisy blinked, but slowly nodded—Lord Nash was the most powerful lord in the northern province of Albajar, and over the past few years, he'd become an increasingly influential member of the realm's ruling Council. And Daisy had even met him at several scholarly events, a tall handsome man perhaps in his early fifties, who had seemed to take quite an interest in Lew's research…

Gods damn it, *damn* it, and Daisy's eyes squeezed shut, as more memories paraded through her reeling brain. Lew *had* met with Lord Nash at least a few times too, hadn't he? He'd always thought Nash a clever, cultured man, with intriguing ideas, who had ushered Albajar into a much-needed economic expansion, and…

"And Lord Nash," Jule's inexorable voice continued, "has offered you *extremely* generous compensation for a successful stealth attack on Orc Mountain. An attack that can be publicly proclaimed as a tragic self-inflicted accident, rather than an act of war straight from the realm's Council. In *flagrant* violation of the established peace-treaty between orcs and men!"

The fury shuddered through her voice, ringing against the stone all around them, and Daisy bowed her pounding head, rubbed a stinging sticky hand to her eyes. Gods curse Lew, because it did make sense, it did. The secrecy, the timing, the reason to even come to this backwater in the first place...

And if Lew had needed to keep everything secret, then including all those plants in his next book would be an obvious cover too, wouldn't it? Explaining why he'd been studying them, why he'd had samples and drawings—and perhaps capitalizing on any public interest in poisons after the attack, too. And even bringing Daisy here would have been part of his coverup, damn him, *damn* him.

Daisy barely heard Rosa speaking beside her, or the answer from Jule, followed by an unfamiliar deep voice—but then something moved before them. And when Daisy blinked up, it was one of the new orcs, broad and bare-chested, wearing multiple jewels and piercings, and watching Daisy with unblinking dark eyes.

"You scent... *surprised* by all this, woman," the orc said, his head tilting as he studied her. "Did you not know of this plan, and this attack upon us?"

Daisy would have shrunk away, covered her face, but Rosa's grip on her arm felt far too strong, the orc's eyes far too intent on hers. So intent she couldn't seem to find the strength to look away, and instead she could only shake her head, fight to speak over her thundering heartbeat.

"I didn't know—any of it," she croaked. "Lew wouldn't tell me what the project was, and I would have never thought it was—*this*. I would never condone something like this, I would never want to hurt anyone, or *kill* anyone."

But it again sounded so paltry, so pathetic, and Daisy shook her head, silently pleaded with the orc's watching eyes. "I swear to you, I didn't know," she gulped. "I swear. I— I'm just Lew's artist, just his illustrator. I'm not even very good, I'm barely even a real artist, he didn't—he didn't even *want* me."

And oh gods, why was she saying such things, telling such shameful truths to all these strangers? But she was already dragging in more breath, holding her prickling eyes to the orc's watching face. "I should have known," her strangled voice gulped. "I should have guessed. I was so, so stupid. Just like with Filak, I thought he liked me too, but—"

Her voice tripped, as more bitter, horrible comprehension crashed through her thoughts. Oh. Oh. Of course.

"But," she whispered, "it was only about this for Filak too, wasn't it? Only about him getting the information he wanted from me. Trapping me, and—*defeating* me."

And of course that was true, of course that explained everything—and suddenly the sobs tore out of Daisy's throat, harsh and helpless and humiliating. It had all been a lie, it had all been about Lew, about Lew's horrible plan to attack the orcs. The way Filak had found her, touched her, caressed her, taken her. *Daisy mín. Sólin mín.*

Daisy couldn't stop weeping, her hands trembling against her face, her ugly sobs echoing through this dank awful room. She should have known. So, so stupid.

The room's silence suddenly felt awkward now, tight and tense and strange, and finally Rosa loudly cleared her throat. "Well," she said. "Now that this is settled, can we please get Daisy up to the sickroom at once? And arrange to have that *kraga* removed as soon as possible?!"

There was another instant's uncomfortable silence, and then Jule stepped forward, her hand over her heart. "Of course," she said firmly. "We'll do whatever we can to make you comfortable, Daisy. And"—her voice dropped—"our deepest apologies for cornering you like this. I know it's not an excuse, but this has been—quite an upsetting discovery. We were certain you were helping Mr. Wallace, and doing— research. Reconnaissance."

Oh. They'd all really thought Daisy was an enemy. And— and maybe that should have been comforting, maybe it offered some paltry explanation for everything Filak had done...

But Daisy only felt numb. Cold. Empty. And when her eyes slid to Filak's face, she couldn't follow that twist on his mouth, the strange shifting look in his shadowed eyes.

But beside her, Julian moved. Or rather, Julian's hand moved, making swift, purposeful motions in midair. And Filak's eyes flicked to watch, his mouth twisting tighter, his swallow bobbing in his throat...

And then—he lurched forward. Forward, toward—*Daisy*. His clawed hand swiping out, his mouth speaking swift and hoarse and urgent. As if he still wanted to attack her, to hurt her, oh gods, oh gods...

Daisy yelped and cringed backwards, hurling both arms up over her face, as her heartbeat screamed in her ears. No, no, not again, please...

But—a shout. A thud. A scuffle of bodies and feet. And when Daisy risked a terrified glance up, Julian and the big jewelry-wearing orc were both gripping Filak's arms, dragging him backwards. While Filak just stared at Daisy, his eyes so hollowed and empty in his stark white face.

"Right, then," said Rosa, a little too brightly. "Let's get you up to the sickroom, sister, shall we?"

Daisy numbly nodded, and allowed Rosa to march her forward. Past Filak, past his glinting staring eyes. Strong enough to wrench a vicious shudder up her spine, but she kept her gaze straight ahead, her hands clutched tightly together.

No. No. Filak had kidnapped her, and trapped her in a dungeon. Filak had accused her of attempted *murder*. She needed to forget him, to be finished with him, forever.

But even so, she could still feel his eyes, prickling stark and powerful into the skin of her back. Sinking in almost as deep as that mark over her heart, like a vow, a promise, a threat.

Nei, Daisy, it said. *Mine.*

18

As Rosa had promised, she escorted Daisy toward the sickroom, deep in the heart of Orc Mountain.

Daisy should have found it shocking to walk through Orc Mountain. To realize that Filak had truly brought her all the way here, to this huge, underground maze of rock and rooms and tunnels. And on another day, in another life, she might have stared and wondered and marvelled at it, or frantically drawn it in her sketchbook, capturing as much of it as she could. The elegantly arched tunnels, the intricate wrought-iron lamps lining the walls, the craggy, curious orc faces passing by in the corridor, and peering out through darkened doorways.

But instead, it all seemed strangely distant. Muddled, faded, far away. Daisy only vaguely heard Rosa's chattering voice beside her, maybe offering explanations or asking questions—and it was only Rosa's firm hand on her arm that kept Daisy moving at all. Putting one foot in front of the other, her eyes held straight ahead, her vision occasionally blinking away into darkness.

Murder. Poison. Kraitish. Sybil. Lord Nash. Every last orc, human, and *child. Nei, Daisy. Mine.*

"Well, here we are, then!" cut in Rosa's too-cheery voice, as she guided Daisy into one of the rooms lining the corridor. A room that indeed appeared to be an actual sickroom, lined with rows of beds separated by tall dividers, all softly illuminated by a crackling fireplace. "Our healer will get you sorted out right away, I'm sure!"

The rising note of panic in Rosa's voice sliced through some of the fog in Daisy's thoughts, and up ahead, a tall nearby orc instantly whipped around, and frowned toward them. He was lean and handsome, his long black hair gleaming against the elegant jewels hanging from his ears, and around his neck. And Daisy's numb staring eyes seemed caught on his jewels, on the hazy awareness that she would have liked to draw them, if her hands weren't still bloody and aching, if her sketchbook wasn't lost forever, if she was a real artist...

Rosa and the handsome orc had begun speaking together, Rosa's voice still far too shrill, and soon Daisy found herself being guided down onto a nearby fur-covered bed, and gazing up at yet another tall, unfamiliar orc. This one with harsh, scarred features, and a large hand that came to hover over her face, lingering with strange, alarming purpose.

"It's just shock and sleep deprivation, and a few superficial lacerations," this orc's deep voice said, becoming louder, clearer, with every word. "She ought to be fine, with a bit of rest and healing. Does that feel better, Ka-esh?"

Oh. He was talking to *her*, Daisy realized, his dark eyes searching her face—and somehow she cleared her throat, drew in a shaky breath. "Er, m-maybe," she stammered. "I think?"

The orc nodded back, and gave her a brief but genuine-seeming smile. "Good," he said. "I'm Efterar, Orc Mountain's Chief Healer, and this"—he nodded toward the handsome orc with the jewelry, now standing close behind him—"is my mate Kesst, our Infirmarian. We'd like to keep you here in our sickroom for a few days, so you can rest and heal. Is that all fine with you? Do you have anyone we ought to send word to?"

Daisy twitched as Lew's face loomed behind her eyes— poison, *murder*—and then rapidly shook her aching head. "N-no," she replied, quiet, ashamed. "No one."

But there was no judgement on the orc's harsh face, and his still-hovering hand shifted downwards, now hesitating over one of Daisy's raw, stinging hands. And suddenly, she could feel the pain... prickling. Itching. And then... fading?

Daisy blinked down at her hand, where the broken skin on her palm somehow seemed—*healed*. Fully and entirely healed, and her mouth opened and closed, as a shocked, shivering certainty flared up her spine. This orc had... *magic*. Just like... like *Filak*.

But he'd helped her, he'd *healed* her—and his hand had already moved to her other palm, which was now prickling just like the first. And Daisy almost sobbed as she watched the broken skin smoothing, lightening, knitting itself back together. "Th-thank you, sir," she whispered. "This is—very kind."

But the orc—*Efterar*, he'd said—only waved it away, and cast another brief, assessing glance up and down her body on the bed. "Is there any other pain, or anything else you need?" he asked briskly. "Some pregnancy prevention, perhaps?"

What? Daisy blinked wide-eyed toward him—he could prevent *pregnancy*, too?!—and then shook her head, too quickly. She ought to be still well covered by that extra-strong contraceptive concoction Lew had foisted upon her— her last dose would be good for at least another few weeks— and after all this, there was no way she would ever go near Filak again. No way she would ever *speak* to him again. Right?

"N-no," her hoarse voice told Efterar, a beat too late. "I'm—fine."

Efterar's thick brows slightly rose, but then he shrugged and nodded. "Just let us know if you change your mind," he said. "Or if there's anything else you need. Otherwise, we'll check on you regularly, and I suggest you stay here for a while, and get some rest."

It was again very kind, and when Daisy stammered her thanks, Efterar waved it away, and then strode off around the divider. Leaving her still lying there on the bed, with a relieved-looking Rosa sitting beside her, and the handsome orc—Kesst—still standing nearby. But this Kesst looked rather stiff, now, his arms folding over his lean chest as he angled a narrow, meaningful look behind him, toward...

Toward *Filak*.

Daisy froze, her heart thudding loud and panicked in her chest. *Filak*. Filak had followed them, Filak was *here*. Only a few steps away, almost near enough to touch.

Daisy only distantly noticed Julian standing beside him, too, because her eyes were caught, trapped, on Filak's gaunt, pale face, his shadowed staring eyes. Eyes that glittered on hers with menace, with rage. With... murder.

Nei, Daisy. Mine.

Daisy's terror jolted louder, screaming through her skull, and she scrabbled backwards in the bed, shaking her head. "N-no," she gasped. "P-please, Filak. *Nei.*"

Filak's watching eyes flickered, and his jaw flexed, his hands clamping into tight fists at his sides. "*Ég vil bara fá að tala,*" he said, fast and clipped. "*Til að biðjast afsökunar.*"

Daisy shoved back further in the bed, shaking her head, wrapping her arms around her shivering chest. While beside her, Rosa loudly snorted, and snapped back toward Filak in those same tangled words, swift and angry and entirely incomprehensible. But Filak's expression only hardened, the rage flaring higher in his eyes. No, no, no...

"*Bíddu*," Julian cut in, lurching forward, his eyes darting wide and urgent between Daisy and Rosa. "Wait. Filak does not wish to hurt you, Daisy, or frighten you any further. He only wishes—to apologize."

What? To—apologize? Daisy blinked dully toward Julian, and then toward Filak's pale, staring face. *Now* he wanted to apologize? After—after—

"Look, Julian," Rosa cut in, her voice cold. "I realize that Filak has an unusual background, and that only exacerbates our existing cultural differences. But even *you* must realize that his behaviour in this"—she flapped her hand at Daisy—"is *beyond* appalling!"

Julian winced, and Rosa drew in a deep breath, her chest puffing out. "Filak *mated* Daisy," she continued sharply, "and then he kidnapped her, and pushed that *kraga* on her, and chained her up, and *left* her! Alone and bleeding in a *dungeon!*"

Julian winced again, while Filak just kept staring at Daisy, his head slowly shaking. Until this Kesst—who had still been standing there listening—let out a long, low whistle, and then a merry little laugh. "Did he, now?" he asked, his voice unnervingly light. "What a delightful way to treat one's lovely new mate. I'd like to say I'm surprised, but we would all know better, wouldn't we?"

A fierce chill raced up Daisy's trembling back—of course they'd all known Filak was a monster, of course—but Julian stepped closer, whipping his head back and forth. "Filak thought Daisy *tricked* him," he replied, though his voice wavered. "He thought his new mate sought to kill us all. He thought she had mated him with the sole purpose of destroying us. Destroying our home, our children, our culture, our skill, our history. Our entire *people!*"

Their entire people. It juddered into Daisy's chest, still far too shocking to be real—but this Kesst appeared entirely unmoved, and gave another tinkling little laugh. "And it turned out that Filak was mistaken in his assumption, I presume?" he asked smoothly. "I don't suppose he thought to actually *ask* his new mate if she was involved in such a dastardly plan?"

Julian sharply exhaled, his eyes narrow and flinty on Kesst's face. "He could not have asked her," he stiffly replied. "They do not—share a language."

Kesst's laugh was cold and brittle this time, and didn't at all reach his eyes. "Ah, of course," he drawled. "And faced with such a complicated conundrum, it didn't occur to Filak to fetch someone who *did* share his mate's language, and ask them to translate? Perhaps the oh-so-helpful Ka-esh who's been trailing worshipfully at his heels for the past two years, hmmm?"

There was something pointed in his voice, in his cool eyes on Julian's face, and suddenly Rosa's words from the dungeon stabbed into Daisy's thoughts, bright and painful. *Just because you like it when he chains you up and has his way with you,* she'd told Julian, *that doesn't mean his newest unfortunate target is going to feel the same.*

It meant—it meant Filak really did want Julian. Like— like *that*. It meant they were—*lovers*.

And blinking at Julian's flinching face, Daisy only felt a distant, sinking comprehension. She'd never been one to judge such relationships—they were common in artist circles, and she'd had several interests that way herself over the years. And there was no denying that Julian was very handsome, with his symmetrical, finely carved features, his supple mouth, his large, long-lashed eyes. He had the kind of face real artists loved to paint, the face they would give to faeries and angels—and of course Filak would want that too, just like Lew had wanted the beautiful Sybil. Neither of them had actually wanted Daisy, she should have known better, *stupid...*

"Filak and I are *friends*," Julian's strained voice finally said, slicing into the thick silence. "And this is *all*."

But Kesst laughed again, even sharper this time. "Oh, is that so?" he asked, his arched brows rising. "And the things Filak does to you down in that ghastly Ka-esh wing are just *friendly*, too?"

Daisy's stomach painfully churned—so stupid, so *stupid*—and Julian shot her a brief, hunted look. "Ach, this *is* only friendly," he snapped back toward Kesst, with surprising vehemence. "It *was*. Neither of us had a mate, so why should we not find relief together, as best pleases us both? With someone"—his eyes narrowed toward Kesst—"who shall not look upon us with mockery and judgement and contempt?!"

Kesst betrayed a grimace, while Julian's glare deepened, his jaw tight in his handsome face. "I ken you all think of Filak as some foolish foreign *fiend*, come from the north only to vex you," he hissed. "But he bears much weight, and upholds much honour. And he has always spoken truth to me of his longing to find a mate—and now that he has finally found one, he would *never* break his vows to her!"

His *vows* to her? Daisy blinked at Julian, and then at—at Filak. Who was still looking back at her, his bottomless black eyes glinting with something like frustration, or bitterness, or maybe... regret.

"Your loyalty is admirable, Julian," Kesst's clipped voice cut in. "Touching, even. But perhaps you might consider that Filak locking his new mate alone in a dark dungeon would be quite a severe violation of those precious matehood vows, hmmm? With all those pesky little promises about keeping one's partner safe and content?"

What? Filak hadn't sworn such things to Daisy... had he? But he was still looking at her like that, oh gods, while Julian's low groan scraped into her ears. "Filak left Daisy alone for not even *one night*," he countered. "Whilst he ran to find the people he knew could learn the truth! You ken he was fool enough to march her all through our mountain, when he thought she wished to learn its layout and ventilation systems, so she could help our enemies flood it full of poison gas, and choke us all to death?"

Kesst wrinkled his nose, while beside Daisy, Rosa drew in a deep breath. "Well, no matter what Filak thought," she cut in, "he still had no right to force a *kraga* on her! Or chain her to a wall, and *abandon* her!"

But now Julian rounded on Rosa, his eyes hard, his cheeks flushed. "Ach, so instead he should have let her run free?" he demanded. "Back to this *partner* of hers, mayhap? Even if Daisy knew naught of this man's plans against us, he could easily have yet forced all of this from her, and wielded it to our doom! This is a man, Filak says"—Julian's voice cracked—"who wrote, at length, in his *own hand*, of how much belladonna a newborn orcling would need to drink with its milk, to ensure its death!"

Oh, gods. Oh, gods. Lew would never have written something like that, and planned for something so horrible... would he? But mass murder, poison, Kraitish, Sybil, Lord Nash. *They ought to have gone extinct millennia ago. Nei, Daisy. Nei...*

Daisy shook her head, too fast and jerky, but it was all still here, crowding her, crushing her. Filak's regretful staring eyes, Julian's rigid body, the fear and fervour in his voice. And the way Kesst and Rosa had glanced at each other, and then at Daisy, with something new, something uncertain, flickering in their eyes.

"You ken a death from poison is easy, or quick, or kind?" Julian demanded, between heavy breaths. "You ken what it must wreak upon your body, to bring about your death? And you ken"—his inhale sounded more like a sob this time—"how oft poisons like these have been wielded against our

Ka-esh kin, in the north? Why they have gone so deep under-ground, and may never again come out?!"

His eyes were far too bright now, his clawed hand scrub-bing at his flushed face. "Filak is the first Nor-ka-esh to come home in our *lifetimes*," he hissed. "And if he had not come, and found Daisy, and seen this attack for what it is—we might all have been dead by the next *moon*. Our home lost, defeated, *forever*."

His voice thudded through the air, through the sudden ringing silence, clanging into Daisy's aching skull. No. No. She should have known, should have seen, stupid, stupid...

The room had slowly begun to spin before her eyes, the sobs jostling dangerously in her throat. She was going to weep, she was going to scream, she needed her lost sketch-book, needed to draw something stark and hideous, needed to run, to disappear deep into a cave, to vomit. Poison, mass murder, *nei, Daisy, nei...*

But even as the bile surged into her throat, the Efterar orc stalked over, and sharply waved his hand between them. "You're distressing my patient, all of you," he snapped. "It's time to leave her alone and let her *rest*. Perhaps I could help you to fall asleep, Daisy?"

Sleep. Yes. Sleep, please, gods, and Daisy fervently, desperately nodded. Anything, anything, to escape this endless hell, this nightmare. Lew, Filak, poison, murder, herself...

And finally, with a wave of Efterar's clawed hand, and a small shaky sigh, it all flickered into darkness.

19

Daisy couldn't have said how long she slept, or when she awoke.

But when her gritty eyes blinked open, she was still trapped in the exact same nightmare. In the same bed, in the same sickroom, with the same—

She squeezed her eyes shut, but the image of him was still there, etched in sharp relief behind her eyelids. Filak. Sitting close beside her bed, and staring at her with bottomless black eyes.

Daisy swallowed hard, hauled in a deep, shaky breath. Maybe she'd imagined him. Maybe she was still overtired, befuddled, wounded...

But nothing actually hurt, not her head or her hands, and when she warily blinked her eyes open again, Filak was still there. Sitting on something beside her bed—a bench of some kind—and leaning forward toward her, his elbows on his knees, his shadowed eyes searching her face.

"Daisy," he said, his voice a low rasp. "*Líður þér betur?*"

A sharp shiver rippled up Daisy's spine, and she darted a look toward the rest of the room—or rather, what she could see of it, around the dividers blocking off either side of the bed. But there was no one else in sight, she was alone with Filak, what would he do now, oh gods, oh gods...

"Daisy," Filak said again, snapping her eyes back toward him. To where he was leaning forward even more, his hands gripping tightly together, his long black talons digging into his pale skin. "I am... sorry."

What? Daisy stared blankly at him, as her heart skipped a beat in her chest. Had he said—surely he hadn't said—he couldn't speak common-tongue, he was—

"I am—sorry," he said again, harder this time, steadier, though the words sounded wrong in his voice, the accent jolting, the stress misplaced. "I am—sorry, Daisy. I am—sorry."

It spasmed into Daisy's chest, blared behind her staring eyes, and she could hear Filak's swallow, could see it bobbing in his throat. "I am—sorry," he said again. "*Sól—sólin mín.*"

His long-taloned hand jerked to touch his chest, skittering against the pale marked skin over his heart. And blinking toward it, Daisy caught something that most certainly hadn't been there before.

He now had a sun there, too. A matching sun, just like the one he'd drawn over Daisy's heart. *Sólin mín.*

Daisy's bottom lip quivered, and she had to force her eyes away, blink back the foolish wetness prickling behind them. Stupid. *Stupid.*

"*Nei*, Filak," she whispered, toward the bed, toward the heavy fur lying over her, which she hadn't even noticed until now. "You—you kidnapped me. You shouted at me. You chained me to a wall, you left me alone in a dungeon, you gagged me with my own *art*—"

Her voice broke, her head shaking, because of all the awful things Filak had done, that still somehow hurt the most. Him taking all her worst doubts and fears, taking the work she'd fought so hard for, her life's ruined calling, and shoving it down her throat. Using it to silence her. To defeat her. To crush all her foolish, silly dreams into stark, miserable truth.

Nei, Daisy. Nei.

"I am—sorry," came Filak's hoarse, halting reply. "I am—sorry, *Daisy mín. Sólin mín.*"

It lanced more pain through Daisy's chest, more tight stinging behind her eyes. "But you still did it," she whispered. "Just like all the other things you did without my permission, too. Trapping me in that cave, crushing my ring, tattooing me, breaking into my apartment. I was so stupid to trust you, to think I knew you, *understood* you, when you only ever..."

Her voice trailed off, and she rubbed hard at her eyes, digging her fingers so deep it hurt—until something caught her wrist. Something warm, strong, familiar, safe.

Daisy's heartbeat stuttered, and she froze in the bed, her eyes snapping to Filak's face. To how he was still looking at her with those dark, shadowed eyes, his mouth tight and sad. "*Ég veit að ég var grimmur,*" he said. "*Ég hefði átt að vera betri.*"

But Daisy couldn't understand it, just like Filak couldn't understand her, and his warm callused fingers spread a little wider against her skin, almost like a caress. "*Mig langar að biðjast afsökunar,*" he added, quieter, as his other hand rose, and drew a cross over that new sun on his heart. "*Mig langar að bæta þér þetta upp.*"

Again it meant nothing, nothing, and Daisy needed to remember the crash of falling stone, the sickening ball of wet paper in her mouth, the horror of the darkness, the click of cold metal around her neck. And her other hand twitched up to that metal, clutching tight against it, feeling those distinct ridges upon it, because of course it was still there. He'd still done that to her. He *had*.

Filak's eyes had followed her hand to her neck, and his

breath shuddered out heavy and slow, harsh enough that she felt it on her skin. "I am sorry," he said again, even lower. "*Þessi kraga átti að vera gjöf til þín. Ég hefði aldrei átt að nota hana svona gegn þér.*"

But it was more empty, meaningless words, rattling inside Daisy's head, even when Filak's hand slowly rose toward her, and stroked gently against her neck. His warm long fingers curving against both the metal ring and Daisy's skin, drawing up gooseflesh, firing a hard shiver down her back...

And together with his watching, glimmering eyes, it had to mean—he wanted it there. He'd wanted Daisy to have it, to wear it. And he hadn't meant it this way, he was...

"I am sorry," he said again, as his mouth twisted, contorting with something like grief. "I am sorry, *sólin mín.*"

And for a shuddering, hanging instant, Daisy desperately wanted to believe him. Wanted to nod, and clutch at him, and drag him over onto the bed. Wanted to feel his warm tall body over hers, his firm stroking hands, his hot tongue tasting her skin. Wanted to feel him speak the only language they both understood...

But—no. *No.* She couldn't. She'd already been so foolish, so unthinkably, pathetically stupid. With Lew, with Sybil. With the cave, the ring. The chain, the dungeon, the Kraitish, the poison, the mass murder...

No. She needed to forget Filak. She needed to be finished with Filak, forever. Needed to stop believing he cared, needed to stop indulging her stupid naive fantasies, stop believing all those tempting stupid lies. She wasn't desirable, she wasn't a real artist...

And maybe Filak saw the truth of it, his hand stilling on Daisy's neck, his eyes rapidly searching her face. His mouth opening, as if to say...

"Filak?" demanded a sharp, vaguely familiar voice. "How the *hell* did you get in here again?"

Daisy jolted to look, wrenching backwards out of Filak's grip, as her heart thundered into her throat. It was Kesst again, now looking rumpled and bleary-eyed, and jabbing a pointed claw toward the door. "Out," he snapped. "Daisy's here to *rest*. Not to put up with even more utterly atrocious behaviour from the likes of *you!*"

Filak's eyes narrowed dangerously toward Kesst, but he didn't move, and his hand had even found Daisy's neck again, stroking gently against it. The movements purposeful, possessive, blatantly defiant, and again there was that appalling overpowering urge to clutch back toward him, to yank him close, to forget everything.

"*Daisy er mín,*" Filak told Kesst, his lip curling. "*Mín.*"

Daisy is mine, it meant. *Mine.*

But no, no, no, Daisy had to forget him, *no*. And it took far too much effort for her to yank away from his touch again, to whip her head back and forth, drawing in the too-thin air...

"No," she croaked, perhaps to herself, or to Filak, or all of them. "No, please. *Nei*, Filak. *Nei.*"

Filak drew back and blinked at Daisy, his head tilting sideways. His eyes searching and intense and maybe even pleading as his mouth opened again, about to say, *Nei, Daisy, mín...*

"*Nei*, Filak," Daisy said, louder now, against it, against him, against herself. "*Nei*. I can't. I'm *not*. Please, just—just go."

There was an instant's silence, Filak's eyes still far too intent on hers—and then Kesst spoke again, snapping out more harsh words Daisy couldn't understand. But Filak surely did, and he betrayed a brief, visceral flinch, a low hiss in his throat.

"Daisy," he said again, as his hand again rose to his heart, drawing that cross over his sun. "*Gerðu það, Daisy.* I am sorry."

Kesst's scoff was loud and disbelieving, and he launched into more foreign snarled words, speaking faster and sharper now, and again jabbing his claw toward the door. Clearly telling Filak, *Get out. Now.*

Filak watched Kesst in silence, as cold, unmistakable contempt flared through his eyes, but then he glanced back at Daisy, his black brows raised. Asking, perhaps, *You truly mean this? You want me to go?*

And suddenly Daisy couldn't bear to look at him, couldn't bear to answer, couldn't bear for him to leave. But Kesst had already barked something else, the healer's name *Efterar* very clear within it, and after another moment's ringing silence, Filak exhaled a low growl, and rose to his feet. His body so impossibly tall, so pale and marked and gaunt, and Daisy wouldn't look, no...

"*Sofðu vel, sólin mín,*" came his hoarse voice. "*Ég mun vinna mér inn traust þitt aftur og endurheimta hjarta þitt sem mitt eigið. Ég sver það.*"

Daisy still didn't look up, but when Filak finally walked away, she could almost feel his footsteps, his increasing distance, deep in her gut. And there was the ridiculous, absurd temptation to call after him, to bring him back, to hear him call her *sólin mín* again...

But no. No. He was gone. He needed to be gone. She needed to forget him. No. *Nei.*

But even as Daisy silently repeated that—*nei, nei, nei*— her eyes darted up to Kesst, still standing near the end of her bed. "What..." she whispered, "what did he say?"

Kesst sighed, and shot a narrow, disgruntled look toward where Filak had gone. "Are you sure you want to know?" he asked flatly. "If you ask me, you'd be better off never knowing anything he says again."

Daisy couldn't hide her wince, her hands clutching compulsively at her fur. While above her, Kesst sighed, slow and heavy and resigned.

"He said," he replied, clipped, "he'll soon prove himself to you as your mate, and gain you as his own."

It twisted in Daisy's chest—*nei, nei, nei*—and Kesst sighed again, and met her eyes with something not unlike pity.

"And he said," he continued, his voice low with foreboding, "he'll be back."

20

F ilak would be back.

It should have been a frightening thought. A threat with enough power to keep Daisy awake and terrified, huddled under her fur, casting fearful glances toward the door.

But instead, she felt herself sinking into the bed, into its surprisingly comfortable warmth. The furs were so soft, the room so dim and cozy, and she could just think about that, only that...

She ended up sleeping again, for what felt like a considerable amount of time, and when she awoke, the room was brighter and busier than before, with multiple people in view. Two of them were Rosa and the woman from yesterday—Jule, her name had been—and they were both sitting on the bench beside Daisy's bed, and speaking together in low, urgent voices.

But upon catching Daisy's gaze, Rosa instantly broke off, and beamed toward her with a warm, relieved smile. "Oh, it's so good to see you awake, sister!" she exclaimed. "I hope you're feeling better this morning? And that you're beginning to recover from yesterday's deeply traumatic and *highly unnecessary* ordeal?"

She shot a baleful glance toward the door—toward what?—and Daisy's heart skipped, her hands clutching at the heavy fur still draped over her. "Er, yes, I think so," she replied, in a voice still scratchy with sleep. "Thank you so much for the bed, and the help."

Rosa waved it away with a dismissive flap of her hand, while beside her, Jule cleared her throat. "You're welcome to stay here as long as you like," she said, her eyes steady on Daisy's face. "And again, I want to apologize for yesterday, and for all the distress we caused you. We'd be honoured to do whatever we can to try to make amends to you."

Daisy swallowed, but twitched a shrug, and dropped her gaze toward her fur. Yesterday's mess hadn't been Jule's fault, had it? No, it had all been due to Filak, and Lew. And the mass murder, the poison, Sybil, Lord Nash, how much belladonna to feed a newborn...

It still churned up bile in Daisy's empty-feeling stomach, and twisted more bitter awareness into her thoughts. Gods, it was all so appalling, so utterly, unconscionably vile—and how had she missed it, all this time? How had she not seen it, or suspected it? Lew had often been selfish or casually cruel, yes, but he'd never been partial to violence, either. His primary goal had always been his work, his research, his renown as a scientist and a scholar, and now—now he was willing to commit mass murder? To poison innocent *children*?

"So how are you going to stop Lew's attack?" Daisy asked Jule, far too loud and abrupt—but suddenly she needed to know, needed it more than anything else. "Because—you *will* stop him, right? You'll find a way to keep your people safe? Your children?"

She didn't miss the surprise flickering through Jule's eyes, followed by something much like relief. "Yes, of course," she replied. "Preventing this attack is now our top priority. We've already sent our best scouts to follow Mr. Wallace, to determine who he's been working with, and the extent of the Council's involvement. We also have a timeline—it looks as though they're planning to begin their offensive by the end of the month. Just over two weeks from now."

Two weeks. Daisy's breath shuddered out, and she swiftly calculated a timeline. That would have given Lew enough time to not only prepare and oversee the attack, but also to stay and evaluate the results afterwards, too. To catalogue the outcomes, maybe do some drawings or dissections of the casualties...

Daisy shivered all over, and drew in a deep breath. "Right," she replied dully. "Two weeks from now would— make sense."

Jule nodded, and made a note in a small book Daisy hadn't noticed she'd been holding. "But on the positive side," she said, "as far as we can tell, Mr. Wallace and Lord Nash don't yet realize we're aware of their plan. Which gives us a much-needed tactical advantage."

Daisy should have given some kind of response, but her voice felt locked in her throat, her eyes trapped on that book in Jule's hands. A book that whipped up a sudden panicked vision of *Lew's* notebook, down in that dungeon.

"But—what about Lew's notebook?" she demanded, her voice shrill. "If he realizes it's gone missing, won't he immediately suspect that he's been compromised? That his horrible plan might be at risk, after all?"

But Jule shook her head, and gave Daisy a reassuring smile. "Yes, which is why we sent the notebook back to Dusbury as soon as we could last night," she replied. "It's now been replaced in your apartment, and with any luck, Mr. Wallace won't have even noticed it was touched. But our scouts are still keeping close watch over the situation, and they'll be bringing us regular reports, and helping to guide our strategy."

Oh. Well. That all sounded promising—right? As though

they'd thought of everything, and had it all well in hand. So why was Daisy's heartbeat still pattering in her chest, a low miserable dread still drumming through her thoughts. Maybe because she was still part of this, partly at fault for this. And she should be doing more, she should be offering...

"But—wouldn't it be better for you if I went back to Lew myself, though?" she asked, though it came out unsteady, uncertain. "If I go apologize to him, and make up some story about where I've been? And that way, if he notices anything unusual about the notebook, I can take responsibility for it. And more importantly"—she hauled in a shaky breath—"I can try to learn more about his plans for the attack, and report whatever I learn back to you directly."

But her voice was badly wavering now, her heartbeat erratically jangling against her ribs. If she really went back to Lew, she would have to touch him again, to pretend to want him again, to sleep in bed with a lying cheating *murderer*. And suddenly the visions of Filak were swirling through her thoughts too, Filak's hands, Filak's teeth, *sólin mín*...

"I'm sorry, but we'd really rather you didn't," came Jule's reply, clipped and certain. "We're told you left behind a note saying you were returning to the city, and if you suddenly reappear out of nowhere, that will certainly raise Mr. Wallace's suspicions more than anything else. And if he believes you've been compromised, or that you've learned about the attack, that puts all of us at risk."

Right. Daisy couldn't deny her stark, sinking relief, even as her heart kept unevenly thudding, building a distant nagging ache behind her eyes. She should still be doing something, anything, and it felt like she was missing something important, but she couldn't even think, *stupid*...

"And also," Rosa's voice cut in, a little too sharply. "We have a slight... problem."

They did? Daisy blinked up, frowning, and then followed Rosa's narrow, glinting gaze across the room. Toward...

Filak.

He was leaning against the end of the opposite divider, standing casually with his arms folded, as though he'd always been there. But he surely hadn't been there even a moment ago, he *hadn't*. Because now Daisy could *feel* the weight of his eyes, glittering hard and intent on hers. Strong enough to be a touch, a caress, shimmering heat low in her belly, flaring it into her cheeks.

"He refuses to leave you!" Rosa snapped, with an exasperated flail of her hand toward him. "Kesst has thrown him out multiple times now, but he somehow keeps sneaking back in! And just before you woke up, we tried to have him bodily removed, so he wouldn't upset you—but he accused us of cruel and unwarranted mistreatment against a favoured son of the Ka-esh, by keeping him away from his newly bonded mate! And *then*"—she took a deep breath, puffing out her chest—"he threatened to declare *war* against us, on behalf of his kin in the north!"

Her voice had risen to a wail, her eyes flashing dangerously on Filak's cold watching face. While beside her, Jule clapped a hand to her shoulder, and gave her a reassuring little shake. "He wouldn't," she said, though she aimed a sharp look toward Filak, too. "No single orc has that kind of authority, not even in the north."

"But you don't know that for certain, Jule," Rosa countered. "None of us know anything about him! He's been nothing but chaos since the first day he came here, and now here he is, kidnapping innocent women and locking them in *dungeons*, and threatening to launch these—these *inter-Ka-esh hostilities*, for the first time in our clan's entire *history!*"

Her outraged voice rang even louder, while Jule's mouth betrayed a faint twitch, and she gave another reassuring shake to Rosa's shoulder. "I'm sure it was an empty threat," she replied firmly. "But Filak does seem very... attached to

Daisy. And"—she shot Daisy a rueful glance—"highly concerned for your welfare."

Rosa's loud snort rather echoed Daisy's own tumbling thoughts—Filak had locked her in a *dungeon*—but now Filak's hands rose before him, snapping out sharp movements in midair. The same way he and Julian had done the day before, almost as if it was a manner of speaking—and in return, Rosa wrinkled her nose, her lip curling in distaste.

"Filak's also demanding to speak with you, Daisy," she said sourly. "He claims that it's very important. And you'll want to hear what he has to say."

Oh. Daisy's breath caught, and when she darted another look at Filak, he was still watching her with those intent, piercing eyes. While his hand now jerked up to his heart, his sun, drawing that cross over it with his claw, again and again.

I am sorry, Daisy. I am sorry.

It twisted painfully in Daisy's own heart, in her empty curdling stomach, and she grimaced, dropped her eyes. She didn't want to hear anything else he had to say... did she? She should be finished with him, forgetting him...

"But of course there's no obligation whatsoever, Daisy," cut in Jule's flat voice. "If you would prefer Filak leaves you alone—whether just for now, or forever—he *will* honour your wishes, I promise you."

She sounded very certain about that, and Daisy risked another brief, searching glance up toward Filak. Who was still studying her, still signing that cross at her, his shadowed eyes bleak, or even regretful. As if he would never hurt her. As if he would never lock her alone in a dungeon, never snap a permanent collar around her neck, never stuff her own art in her mouth...

Daisy should have looked away, shaken her head. Should have said, *nei, Filak, nei,* and demanded he go away at once, to somewhere she would never see him again, forever. But her voice felt locked in her throat, as something prickled strange and hot behind her eyes. And finally she twitched a shrug, and dropped her gaze back to the fur.

"Fine," she managed, in a voice that didn't sound like hers. "Just this once."

There was an instant's stillness, and then Daisy was vividly, powerfully aware of Filak's tall form striding over toward them. Coming closer and closer, his footsteps silent on the stone floor, his eyes raking like a touch over her skin.

And then, in a jerky movement, he fell to his knees. Sinking down beside the bed, his body suddenly, unnervingly close. His shadowed eyes catching hers, glimmering as they held, as his clawed hands thrust something up toward her...

"For you, *sólin mín*," he said, in stilted-sounding common-tongue. "I am sorry."

Daisy blinked at him, and then at the object in his hands—the chest. The small, square chest of polished wood, with a gleaming little latch on the front. It was beautifully carved, as if it was made to hold something important, something precious.

And as Daisy kept staring, not breathing, Filak's claw carefully flicked the latch, and popped the lid open. Revealing...

The jewels. The *fortune*.

21

Daisy's mouth fell open, her eyes frozen on the sight. On the impossible fortune in jewels, just sitting here in Filak's hands.

There were deep green emeralds. Clear blue sapphires. Bright dazzling red rubies. All of them beautifully cut, flashing with piercing brightness in the firelight. And all just piled into this little chest, as plentiful as if they'd been rocks on a shoreline.

They were so stunning it swallowed Daisy's breath, and as she stared, there was the desperate, dizzying urge to touch them. To spread them out across the fur, and draw them one by one. To commit them all to paper so she would remember them forever...

The longing flared so strong she couldn't breathe for an instant, and she could only hear her racing heart, a loud steady drumbeat in her ears. Was Filak—*giving* these to her? Offering her a fortune? An escape? A future?

It took far too much effort to drag her gaze back to Filak's face, to his black eyes still boring into hers. Seeing too much, knowing too much, and he nudged the box closer toward her, brushing it against her shaky hovering fingers...

"For you, Daisy," he said again, quieter than before. "*Ég mun gera hvað sem er til að halda þér, sólin mín. I am sorry.*"

Oh, gods. He really was trying to give these to her. Daisy's stomach pitched, and too late she snatched her trembling hand away, rubbed it at her hot face. What the hell was this? What the hell was she thinking? She didn't want this, she didn't want gifts from him, no matter how beautiful or expensive they were, *no*...

"No, Filak!" cut in a sharp, disbelieving voice, and when Daisy jerked to look, it was Rosa. And good gods, she'd entirely forgotten about Rosa and Jule, but they were both still sitting there watching this, both looking just as shocked as Daisy felt.

"No, Filak!" Rosa barked again, frantically flapping her hand toward the box of jewels. "You cannot *buy* Daisy! Absolutely not! *Nei!* We have *talked* about this—"

She broke off into the orcs' language again, her voice rapid and high-pitched and utterly incomprehensible, while Daisy stared blankly at her, and then at Filak. What did Rosa mean? Filak was trying to—to *buy* her?

But he wasn't denying it, and he wasn't even looking at Rosa, either. Instead, his shadowed eyes stayed firmly fixed on Daisy's face, and he again nudged the box of glittering jewels into her hand, against her shaking fingers.

"*Ég vil heyra, Daisy,*" he said, his voice hollow. "For you, *sólin mín. Sálugjald.*"

Sálugjald. It sounded... heavy, somehow, strange on his voice, and his eyes on Daisy's looked strange, too. Glittering sharp and bright, and almost... bleak. As if there was something more to this, as if it meant something else entirely...

Rosa huffed a harsh, exasperated groan, while Jule loudly cleared her throat. "Could you please translate for us, Rosa?" she asked. "What's a *sálugjald*? And what is Filak trying to do with it?"

Rosa grimaced and nodded, and dragged both hands

down her face. "Well, from what we've been able to gather," she began, "the *sálugjald*—or the *mate-price*—is an old practice of Filak's kin in the north. It's how they find women, and reproduce. They... *buy* them."

They buy them?! Daisy gaped at Rosa, and then at Filak. His people truly *bought* women, as if they were *property*? Permanently? And now he was trying to do it with her?!

But Filak just kept holding that box, staring back at Daisy, his eyes still so strange and bleak in his sharp pale face. Dredging up the sudden, incongruous memory of that morning after the cave, when she'd first seen him in the sunlight. When she'd left him behind in that tunnel, and he'd collapsed it down between them, crashing it into dust and rock and ruin.

"The northern orcs supposedly hunt and save the jewels for years," added Rosa's flat voice. "It's supposed to be enough to feed and clothe someone for a lifetime. And in exchange, the woman swears to bear the orc's sons, and stay with him for years, or even until death. I'm told"—she drew in a deep breath—"the payments usually go to the families, and the women are often counted as lost."

Counted as lost. Daisy's shocked disbelief roiled higher, and she clapped her trembling hand over her mouth. "You mean—those women never come back?" she demanded. "The orcs—trap them? Or *kill* them?!"

Oh gods, oh gods, because maybe that explained everything Filak had done. He had fully intended to kidnap her, to entrap her, to keep her in that dungeon forever—

"Well, no, not exactly," said Rosa's strained voice. "As far as we've been able to tell, the orcs don't confine their mates, and they certainly wouldn't *kill* them, either. But most of the northern Ka-esh live very deep underground, and there's often just... no way out."

No way out. Daisy stared at Rosa, at Filak, and then down at that box of stunning, glittering jewels. Those poor women, their poor families, trading their daughters to a dark orc underworld for priceless boxes of jewels. And here Filak was, trying to buy her too, offering her his own mate-price, paying her to stay. Maybe even trying to bribe her into another horrible dungeon, where she would never escape, never see the sun again...

But Filak was still watching Daisy closely, his brow furrowing—and suddenly his head was shaking, swift and urgent. "*Nei, Daisy,*" he said. "*Ég sver að ég hvorki meiði þig né held þér frá sólinni. Þú getur jafnvel notað þetta til að yfirgefa mig.*"

It again made no sense whatsoever, but Rosa heavily sighed, and shifted awkwardly on the bench. "Filak says—he swears not to hurt you, or confine you," she translated, with a grimace. "He also *says* you can even use his mate-price to leave him, if you wanted."

Really? Daisy could use the jewels to *leave* him? And though Rosa hadn't sounded at all convinced by that, Filak's eyes were still burning into Daisy's, his hands again nudging the box toward her. Maybe not offering to buy her after all, then, but offering her... freedom. Escape.

Daisy swallowed, blinking down at the box, and she only vaguely heard Jule's quiet harrumph. "Well, if that's the case," she said bracingly, "it sounds to me like the jewels are more of a mating-gift. And therefore, it's Daisy's decision to accept them, or not."

Daisy's decision. Her breath juddered out, and she again found Filak's face, searching his eyes. Seeing how they looked even bleaker than before, his mouth thinning, as he again nudged the box against her quivering fingers.

"For you," he said again, very quiet. "I am sorry, *sólin mín.*"

But Daisy still didn't take the box, couldn't take it, because—had Filak really been saving these jewels for *years*, like Rosa had said? Had he truly meant them as a payment for the woman who would disappear underground with him, *forever*? And was that why he looked like this, like every breath was pain, like he was drowning in grief and darkness...

It was too much, too overwhelming, clamping too tight in Daisy's gut, careening through her thoughts. She should take the jewels. She should accept the fortune Filak was offering her, and run back home to the city, forever. She could buy a little cottage with a garden, draw whatever the hell she wanted, maybe even make her own book someday...

But no. No. The grief in Filak's eyes, the careful polish on the box, the beautiful little latch. The hard ridges of his ribs, the sun over his heart, the faint tremble of his talons on the box. The poison, the belladonna, *dead within the next fortnight, come to kill us all...*

Daisy shook her head without even knowing it, and her numb fingers skittered over Filak's, and shoved the box back toward him. "*Nei*," she croaked. "*Nei*, Filak. It's yours. I don't want your bribes, or your gifts, or your mate-price. *Nei*."

Filak's throat convulsed, and he stared back at Daisy for a long, thudding moment, as something complicated passed through his shadowed eyes. Something... surprised, something relieved, something confused and bitter and uncertain.

"*Skilur hún þetta?*" he said, with a brief, searching glance toward Rosa. "*Hún veit að hún getur tekið þetta og farið?*"

Rosa sighed, and said something back that Daisy again couldn't follow. But it sounded like she was confirming Daisy's answer, and it again flared in Filak's eyes, shifted dark and confused and strange. His mouth twisting, his head tilting, his hand briefly flinching beneath Daisy's touch. And wait, how was she still touching him, why was she still touching him, why wasn't she pulling away...

But Filak wasn't pulling away, either. He only kept staring at her like that, as if she was an impenetrable, all-consuming mystery he couldn't begin to decipher. And maybe she was, stupid, foolish, gift, *sólin mín*, her fingers trembling against his warm skin...

And in a flash of movement, he was—*here*. His tall body leaning close and alive over Daisy, his warm steady hand spreading against her face, tilting it swift and certain up toward him. His eyes glinting on hers for a fraction of a breath, seeking permission, seeking his right, *yes*—

And when his lips crushed against hers, there was no refusing, no resistance. Only Daisy's mouth willingly opening for him, welcoming him in, with his warm lips and clever hot tongue. So good, so bright, so hot and raw and staggering, his scent his touch his taste. His *sól*, his light, and he was him again, hers again, he would sweep her off and away, into the reckless raging wonder...

"Filak!" cut in a shrill voice, very far away. "*Nei*, Filak! What the hell!"

But it didn't matter, it didn't, it was only this. Daisy drinking him up, gasping into his mouth, inhaling the beautiful scent of him. Needing more, more, *more*—

Until it snapped away. Gone, lost, and Daisy lurched forward after it, needing it, please...

But the voice was shouting again, Rosa's voice, and it took Daisy far too long to reorient it, to see the reality unfolding before her eyes. To see Filak, now with both Jule and Kesst gripping at his arms, dragging him backwards, away. But his eyes on Daisy were alight, blazing with hot, feral hunger, with triumph.

Daisy mín. Sólin mín.

Daisy only vaguely heard Rosa's impressively eloquent string of curses as her hands waved wildly at the door, urging them out. And Filak didn't resist it, letting Kesst and Jule drag him off toward the door, but his eyes kept blazing on Daisy's, so bright, almost jubilant. And then they flicked purposefully downward, toward her hand. Toward the...

The *ring* in her palm. The gold ring, set with a round, glittering yellow stone.

Daisy's breath choked, and she stared at the ring for an instant too long, its stone bright and dizzying against her skin. When had Filak even given her this? How had he done this? And she didn't want it, she'd told him no gifts, she should give it back, now—

But when she glanced up again, Filak was gone. Vanished. Leaving her sitting alone in the bed, with his ring in her hand, and the taste of his kiss on her lips.

22

After Filak left, Daisy only half-heard Rosa's enraged tirade about his appalling behaviour, or Jule's grim promises to keep him away until he learned to control himself.

It was very kind of them, and Daisy should have thanked them, and loudly reiterated her fervent agreement. She was supposed to be finished with Filak. She was supposed to forget Filak, forever.

But instead, she only gave them halfhearted nods and smiles, until they finally said farewell, and left her alone to rest. And then she carefully opened her palm, and stared down at the glittering ring in her hand.

Stupid, to look. Stupid, to care. Stupid to not have immediately thrown it back in Filak's face, just the way he deserved...

An odd lump was rising in her throat, and she carefully traced a finger against the bright yellow stone, following its perfectly cut facets. Gods, it was beautiful, the way it caught the light, the way it glittered and flared. Just like a light of its own. A *sól*.

Daisy swallowed hard, shook her head, squeezed her eyes

shut. No. *No.* She'd told Filak she didn't want his gifts, and then he'd given her the ring anyway. Ignoring her own stated wishes, again. And since she hadn't given the ring back, she should now only be thinking of how impossibly large the jewel was, and how much coin it might fetch at market. How she could still sell it and buy passage back home to the city, and escape Filak forever...

"Daisy?" asked a tentative, familiar voice, jolting her eyes open—and she twitched all over at the sight of Julian. He was standing beside her bed, smiling uncertainly toward her, and holding a large basket.

"I apologize if I awoke you, sister," he said. "Filak only wished to send you this. They have barred him from entering here again, so..."

His voice trailed off, but he offered Daisy another cautious smile, and settled the basket beside her on the bed. And when Daisy blinked down toward it, she found—food?

Her breath caught, her eyes widening, because yes, good gods, the basket was packed full of *food*. A truly shocking quantity of food, all looking fresh and tempting and impossibly delicious. Thick-cut buttered bread, flaky golden pastries, sliced cured meats, bright berries, and little brown mushrooms. And not one, but *two* bulging waterskins, along with what appeared to be a full bottle of fresh milk.

"This is—for me?" she asked, her voice disbelieving. "All of it?"

Julian's smile drew higher, and he nodded. "A gift from Filak," he said. "He has been arranging it since early this morn, and had meant to bring it himself—but for now he said to tell you he sends his regards. And he hopes you like his last gift, also."

His last gift. Julian's eyes flicked down toward that yellow ring, still glittering with appalling brightness in Daisy's palm, and she grimaced, clamped her fingers tightly around it. "Well, I told him I didn't want gifts," she said thinly. "And he ignored my wishes, and went ahead and did what *he* wanted. Again."

There was a moment's silence, in which Julian blinked back toward her, his head cocking sideways. "Ach, Filak said you refused his *sálugjald*," he replied. "But he would never have thought you wished for no gifts at all, ach? He yet now sees you as his mate, and thus, he would be remiss to not offer gifts to you. It is his sacred duty to tend to you, and care for you."

Daisy should have scoffed, or laughed, but instead her unhelpful thoughts snapped backwards, to that moment with Filak in Lew's apartment. When he'd looked into her eyes, and she'd been so, so certain what it had meant. That he was hers. That he was bound to tend to her, and care for her, for always...

"And I ken yellow topaz is the sign of Filak's close kin, ach?" Julian added, with a nod toward the ring in Daisy's hand. "It is only right for him to offer you this, whether you took his *sálugjald*, or no."

Oh. Yellow topaz. Like... a *sól*. A daisy.

Daisy's eyes dropped back toward the ring, watching the beautiful glint of the firelight within it. And her traitorous thoughts couldn't help comparing it to Lew's diamond ring, which she'd instantly thought clunky and heavy, with such an overlarge, ostentatious stone. The kind of ring that was meant to impress various friends and colleagues, rather than to actually complement the wearer, or express one's affections.

But this ring—Daisy swallowed, audible in her ears—this ring was different. Simpler. More subtle, more elegant. And though she had limited knowledge of jewelry-making, she could still see the impressive care and skill in the ring's forging, the delicate curve of the band, the tiny perfect prongs holding the stunning round stone. *Sólin mín.*

"So if Filak really wanted me to have this," Daisy finally

said, without at all meaning to, "then why didn't he want me to have that mate-price he offered me? He didn't want me to have it, did he?"

Her thoughts were swarming again with that bleakness in Filak's eyes, that strange, crushing sadness. No, he hadn't wanted her to take it, and he'd been glad when she'd refused it. Right?

"Was it just because he didn't want to give up the jewels?" Daisy pressed, searching Julian's face. "Or he didn't want to risk me using them to run away from him?"

Julian was looking rather harried, now, and he shot an uneasy glance toward the door. "No, not that, I ken," he said, with a grimace. "It is only... the *sálugjald* is... fraught, amongst Filak's kin. He always swore he would never grant one to a woman, for his mother..."

He grimaced again, clamping his mouth shut, even as Daisy straightened in the bed. What about Filak's mother? And he'd sworn never to give a *sálugjald* to a woman... and then he'd tried to do it anyway, with her?

But Julian sharply shook his head, as if trying to shake away that thought of Filak's mother. "But now that you have refused this," he said firmly, "Filak shall be glad to offer you other gifts instead. Like this ring, and this meal. You shall eat it, ach?"

He was clearly trying to direct Daisy away from any further questions, and she sighed, and followed his gaze back toward the basket. Which still looked wonderful, and smelled wonderful, too—and she felt a sudden rumble in her belly, strong enough that Julian surely heard it. But when she shot a chagrined glance toward him, he looked almost indulgent, his eyes surprisingly soft on her face.

"I ken we have all forgotten about feeding you properly, amidst all the rest of this mess," he said. "I am glad Filak thought of this."

Right. Daisy sighed again, but finally she picked up a

slice of the thick buttered bread, and took a careful bite. It was delicious, of course, and she couldn't deny a grudging appreciation toward Filak for sending it—and in truth, it had been lovely of Julian to bring it, too.

"You'll have some too, won't you?" she asked him, with an attempt at a smile. "I don't think I could eat all this in a week."

Julian hesitated, but then gave a small smile back, and sank down onto the bench beside her bed. "Ach, it is far more than most orcs would eat, also," he wryly replied, as he plucked up a slice of meat with his claws. "I ken Filak has long ago forgotten how much food most people eat in a meal."

That seemed... an odd statement, and Daisy's head tilted as she chewed another bite of the delicious bread. "Does Filak... not eat?" she asked, while visions of his gaunt body flared behind her eyes. "He's not... ill, is he?"

She didn't miss Julian's twitch, or how he was looking distinctly harassed again, aiming another alarmed glance toward the door. "Ach, no," he replied, too quickly. "He is quite well, I ken."

Daisy's stomach twisted, because Julian was again avoiding the question, wasn't he? Keeping secrets from her. But gods, why did she even care anyway? She was supposed to be forgetting Filak, finished with Filak—and what did it matter if Julian knew all these things about him? If Filak had chained Julian up, and taken pleasure with him, and maybe still would...

But then Julian loudly cleared his throat, drawing Daisy's eyes back toward him. "I only should not wish to speak for Filak, without his leave," he said slowly, as though he was carefully choosing his words. "But the Nor-ka-esh—his kin in the north—are oft deeply devout, and put great faith in their gods. And fasting is an important part of their prayers, most of all when an orc is seeking the gods' help or guidance."

Huh. So Filak was so gaunt because he was *fasting*? Praying? Seeking his gods' help and guidance? About what? It had to be something important... right? Something so important that he'd forgotten how most people *ate*?

But Julian was looking uneasy again, and swallowed his next bite of meat with an audible gulp. "The marking is oft part of their prayers, too," he added, perhaps in another bid to change the subject. "The inks are made from a northern fruit called the *blekávextir*, and whilst this means they are very safe to use, they are also not permanent, unless they are embedded into the skin. So the marks must oft be redone, mayhap every fortnight or so. It is a way to invoke the prayer, to speak it strong and unceasing, for all to see and know."

Oh. It was a relief to hear the inks were safe, at least, but the rest of it only dragged up more questions, because Filak was *covered* in those marks, right? And were they all prayers, too? What the hell was he praying for? And...

Daisy's eyes darted briefly downwards, toward her own tattooed sun, peeking up over the neckline of her grubby dress. And was that supposed to be a prayer, too? *Daisy mín. Sólin mín...*

Julian's gaze had followed Daisy's downwards, shifting with something she couldn't quite read. "And ach, a mark upon one's mate is sacred, also," he said, quieter. "It is a sign of favour and fealty, and a plea to the gods for skill and wisdom and protection."

Daisy's breath hitched, and her thoughts flicked back to that night in the cave, to the memory of Filak's hand tracing the sun on her skin, again and again in the dark. A prayer. A sacred plea. For skill, wisdom, protection...

"Has Filak ever marked *you*?" Daisy asked him, too abrupt, too shameful—but she couldn't seem to take it back, couldn't stop searching Julian's handsome face. Because the more she studied him, the more he looked almost... sad. Almost the way he'd looked down in that dungeon, when they'd first met, and he'd called her Filak's mate.

But Julian instantly straightened on the bench, his eyes glinting on Daisy's face. "No, Filak has not marked me," he said firmly. "And as I have said, neither of us wished for this. He has always longed for a woman for his mate, and I have always longed for..."

His voice trailed off, the spark in his eyes fading again, and he let out a heavy exhale. "For someone I once knew, long ago," he finally finished, with a jerky shrug. "From the north. Filak oft... reminds me of him, I ken."

Oh. His sadness felt almost strong enough to taste now, catching at the back of Daisy's throat. And tangling with some-thing damnably like relief, because of course Filak wouldn't stand for being someone else's replacement, for being a permanent second best. He would want to be the only one, he would want a mate who was only, always his. *Mín. Sólin mín...*

"I'm sorry," Daisy said finally, uselessly, into the thick silence. "About the loss of your... friend."

But Julian quickly waved it away, shaking his head. "Ach, Rurik is yet alive and well," he said, too brightly. "And living a good life with many lovers in the north, as far as I have heard. It is"—he grimaced, his face reddening—"foolish, to yet think of him thus, I ken."

Daisy swallowed, and suddenly there was only sympathy, or maybe even commiseration, clutching tight in her gut. "Well, I don't think it's foolish," she told him, hoarse. "At least, not compared to any of the appallingly stupid things I've done, these past few days."

She attempted a laugh, but it came out sounding harsh and bitter, enough that Julian's head cocked sideways, his brows furrowing. "You mean with this?" he asked, with a vague wave at the room, the bed, maybe the mountain. "I am sure you have done naught to regret. This was all only an unfortunate misunderstanding, over this attack."

Daisy couldn't choke back her laugh, scraping hard and loud from her mouth. "No, I mean with *Filak*," she bit out, before she could stop it. "Because even before he locked me in that dungeon, he was—dreadful. *Dangerous*. He trapped me in an underground cave in the dark. He destroyed my valuable property. He broke into my apartment. He acted as though he *owned* me, from the first moment we met. And instead of running away, or telling him to leave me alone, forever, I..."

She drew down a breath, let it out in another hoarse, shaky laugh. "I touched him," she gulped. "I let him touch me. I let myself believe I knew him, I trusted him, I *understood* him, even if I didn't know a single thing about him. Or a single damned word he said!"

Her face was burning, now, her voice pained and trembling, and she braced herself for Julian's disbelief, his mockery, his judgement. Because surely even an orc would see this for what it was, an utterly indefensible display of weakness, a shocking lack of judgement, *foolish and immature behaviour, appallingly unscientific, dangerous...*

But Julian didn't say any of those things. And instead, his eyes looked sympathetic, even encouraging, as he twitched a small, knowing smile toward her. "Ach, but Filak has never been one to hide who he is, or how he feels, or what he longs for," he replied, with a shrug. "I ken he would have made himself quite clear to you, ach? He would have sought to show you that you could trust him, and that he would care for you."

Daisy blinked, frowned, as more memories blurred behind her eyes. Filak carefully guiding her across that rubble-strewn room, showing her those fallen rocks, explaining about waiting for the morning. Filak licking her wounds, drawing a sun on her heart, his hands gripping her hips, his body quiet and close against her in the dark...

"Also, you are Ka-esh now," Julian added, with another shrug. "And Ka-esh are oft... curious. We wish to learn, and explore, and seek truth and worth and beauty. Even if others cannot see it, or understand."

Daisy blinked at Julian again, her swallow catching in her throat—and too late, she shook her head. "But I'm not really—Ka-esh," she said, though it didn't sound even slightly convincing. "I'm not actually—Filak's *mate.*"

Julian's eyes betrayed a brief, telltale glance downwards, catching on Daisy's metal collar, the inked mark on her heart, the yellow ring she was still holding—but then he shrugged again, and glanced away. "Ach, well, you are yet an artist, then," he replied. "And artists also must needs be curious, ach? You must seek beauty and worth where no others care to look. You must... *see.* You must learn, and know, for *yourself.*"

Oh. Daisy could only seem to keep staring at him, as a sudden, involuntary shiver rippled up her back, prickling gooseflesh across her skin. *You must... see. Learn, and know, for yourself...*

As if Julian was—absolving her. Accepting all her ridiculous choices, all her foolish unthinkable actions, without mockery or contempt. Without even the slightest judgement. *You are yet an artist.*

And it shouldn't have mattered. Shouldn't have felt like this. Like a sudden bracing breath of cool air, a field of wildflowers rippling in the sunlight, a tight hug from the mother she barely remembered...

"But—I'm not," Daisy whispered, even as it tightened painfully in her gut. "A real artist, I mean. I don't have a job anymore, I only ever..."

But she couldn't seem to finish, not with that twisting in her stomach, or that distinct confusion again flaring across

Julian's eyes. "Ach, you are an artist," he said blankly, as if this was the most obvious statement in the world. "I saw your work. Those plants you drew, the ones Jule showed us. You cannot think those were not *art*?"

Daisy's stomach twisted again, and she choked down a strange, sudden urge to laugh, or maybe sob. No, they weren't, or were they, and it had nothing to do with Filak, with her foolishness, and...

"I ken you are only weary and overwrought, sister," Julian said now, with a decisive set to his mouth. "You ought to rest more, ach? And mayhap I shall bring you some drawing tools, also. This shall help, I am sure, for no Ka-esh—or artist—ought to be kept from their calling."

He still sounded so certain, so utterly convinced, and Daisy couldn't find a way to argue it, even as Julian rose to his feet. "And also," he added, quieter, "in all Filak's time here, his own people have not sought to know him, or understand him, or trust him. That *you* could do this in one night, enough to gain his lifelong fealty as your mate"—he twitched her a sad smile—"this is art all of its own, ach? This is... *seeing*."

Daisy still couldn't seem to counter it, but perhaps Julian didn't expect her to, because he only gave her a wave good-bye, and then strode away. Abandoning her with the basket, the ring, and all those impossible, unthinkable claims.

You are yet an artist. Artists must needs be curious. You must learn, and know, for yourself.

It kept ringing around and around through Daisy's thoughts for the rest of the day, even as she attempted to doze, to snack on more of the basket, to nod and smile at Kesst and Efterar when they stopped by to check on her. A few more people stopped by to introduce themselves, too, including a shy, smiling orc named Eben—who was apparently a friend of Julian's, and a medic here in the sickroom— and then another medic named Salvi, who cheerfully claimed to be Rosa's favourite kin-brother. And then came a kind, dark-haired woman named Gwyn, who apparently served as the mountain's midwife.

But despite Daisy's attempts to smile and converse, and to listen to whatever they were saying, she was admittedly still far too distracted. Not only by all Julian's hints and claims—Filak's fasting, his praying, his mother—but also by the beautiful ring still in her fingers. And finally, most of all, by the steadily rising sounds and voices coming from the sickroom's door.

The sounds had been quiet and intermittent at first—a few urgent whispers, a low angry growl. But they slowly grew louder and more frequent, until they were echoing through the sickroom, scraping up Daisy's spine. There were several sharp bangs and shouts, and then a harsh, angry voice that sounded far too much like Filak's...

"Yes, of course it's Filak," Kesst told Daisy, when she caught him walking past. "But don't worry, he won't get in. We've put an entire band of guards on the door, and Jule says he can declare war as much as he wants, we're not budging. So you stay put, and stay *safe*."

A resentful satisfaction flared across his face, and he gave her a grim smile before flouncing off again. And Daisy swallowed as she stared after him, and fought back the sudden appalling urge to slip out of bed, maybe even to follow him toward the door...

But she gritted her teeth and forced herself to stay in bed, even as she kept twisting that beautiful gold ring on her finger. Because somehow it had gotten onto her finger, and she couldn't have even said when, or how. Or, even more unnerving, how Filak had known the right size for a ring in the first place...

Had it just been luck? Or had he maybe somehow noted it, when he'd crushed Lew's ring? And was that why he'd crushed that ring in the first place? Because he'd meant to give her a replacement, all that time?

Daisy mín. Sólin mín...

But no. *No.* She wasn't supposed to care. She was supposed to be forgetting Filak, forever. She would rest here for another day or two, like she'd promised, and then she would sell the ring, and return home to the city, and find a way to salvage her career. And that was all.

But it all made for a strange, unsettled afternoon, one that dragged for what felt like an eternity. And even when it seemed that night had finally fallen, quieting the room and dimming the fire to a low flicker, Daisy's attempts at sleeping were restless and broken, full of strange, half-remembered dreams. Dreams of Filak's glinting eyes, his warm steady hands. The mate-price he'd offered her, but clearly hadn't wanted her to take, the joy and relief in his kiss afterwards. *Gift, sólin mín,* only an unfortunate misunderstanding, how much belladonna, skill, wisdom, protection, mass murder, learn, know, see...

It was too hot, too uncomfortable, agitated and aching, alone and untouched. Pulsing in Daisy's belly, grating and scraping in her ears. Louder and sharper, coming closer, closer, shuddering through the room, until—

The fire winked out. Plunging the room into pure, all-encompassing blackness, just like the black of the cave, the tunnels, the dungeon...

Daisy's eyes snapped wide open, her heartbeat suddenly thundering, her body strained and still in the bed. Craning to see, to hear, her panic roiling, her mouth opening, about to call for help—

When a hot, powerful hand suddenly clapped over her mouth, and held her still in the dark.

23

The panic screeched pure and blistering, blaring white behind Daisy's unseeing eyes. What was this, she needed to fight, to run—

Until a second hand found her neck, and curled gently around it.

"*Róleg, sólin mín*," came a voice, close and hot in her ear, as sharp claws prodded into her throat. "*Þetta er bara ég.*"

It was *Filak*. Here. Touching her.

Daisy should still have screamed. She should have fought, panicked, pushed away. She should have shouted for any of the people in the room, for Kesst or Efterar, who were surely only sleeping nearby. And if those guards were still outside, they would hear it too, they would rush in, and drag Filak away, forever...

But she didn't scream. Didn't resist. Didn't even try. Not even when Filak dropped his hands from her mouth and her throat. Not even when those hands then snaked down her trembling body, and caught her wrists, and raised them over her head. Pinning them firmly to the bed with his strong, uncompromising grip.

He was... trapping her here. *Confining* her here.

And yes, yes, that was what this was, his full weight now sinking down onto the bed over her, kicking off her fur toward the floor. So there was only him above her now, only his warm lean body settling down heavy against hers, his strong legs thrusting her knees decisively apart...

Daisy shuddered all over, but she still didn't protest, or refuse. Just stayed there on the bed, gasping in the darkness, as Filak shifted both her wrists into one hand, freeing his other hand to reach downwards and yank up her skirts. Exposing her entire bottom half to the room's cool air, oh gods, while his thighs settled deeper between hers, and hitched them even wider apart. He was baring her for him, opening her up for him, he was doing this, he was really, really doing this, and she was allowing it, *wanting* it—

And oh fuck, yes, she was—because now that was his thick prodding cock. Seeking between Daisy's spread thighs, notching itself firm and certain against her slick, wide-open heat. While she writhed and hissed against it, opening even wider for it, needing more, *more*...

"*Ach*?" came Filak's hot whisper in her ear, so soft she almost couldn't hear it over her thudding heartbeat. "*Ach, sólin mín*?"

Daisy quaked all over, because curse him, he was again—*asking*. Holding himself like this and asking, damn him, because then she had to answer. And she didn't want to answer, she didn't want to say it, because it was so foolish, so stupid, so ridiculous. He'd kidnapped her and locked her in a *dungeon*, she was supposed to hate him, to forget him, to sell his beautiful ring and run away forever...

You must learn, and know, for yourself...

"*Ach*?" Filak asked again, so soft and hot in her ear. "*Sannlega, sólin mín.*"

It was the same thing he'd told her that first night in the

cave, and it again shuddered Daisy all over, clutched her slick hungry heat against that gentle touch of his blunt invading crown. Still just nudging there, just prodding slightly inside her, impossibly intimate, appallingly infuriating. Taunting her, inflaming her, knowing how much she needed this, please, gods, please...

Daisy squeezed her eyes shut, dragged in a deep breath—and then, somehow, she nodded. Nodded, short and brief and fervent, saying...

Yes. Curse her, yes. *Yes.*

But Filak still didn't move, though his jutting cock spasmed against Daisy's quivering heat—and oh, she could feel liquid now, trailing thick and obscene down her crease. While his warm clawed hand gently grasped at her bare hip, and then began caressing up her shivering body. Moving slow and purposeful, stroking over her breast, her heart, and then curving gentle around her gasping throat...

"*Ach, Daisy?*" he breathed. "*Segðu mér.*"

Segðu mér. And even if Daisy didn't know the words, she fully understood Filak's meaning, as strong as if he'd shouted it in plain common-tongue. He wanted her to say yes or no, out loud. He wanted to know it for certain, and maybe he wanted her to know it, too. Wanted to make it into shameful, undeniable truth between them...

You must learn, and know, for yourself.

Daisy gasped and writhed again, perhaps even seeking to drive her body downwards onto that prodding strength, to swallow it deeper anyway—but Filak's hand instantly tightened around her throat, even as his breath huffed a sound that might have been a laugh, indulgent and gentle.

"*Komdu, Daisy mín,*" he murmured, his head shifting upwards, and oh, that was a light, brief kiss of his lips to hers, so honeyed and tantalizing and sweet. "*Segðu mér.*"

Fuck. There was no resisting it now, no more lying to herself, to him. And finally Daisy twitched another brief, shameful nod, and raised her blinking eyes toward where she knew his face to be.

"Ach, Filak," she whispered. "Yes. *Yes.*"

His answering groan was hot and low, fraying through the darkness around them—and with a sudden sharp snap of his hips, he slammed himself hard and deep. Stabbing her full of him, shivering her all through with the strength of him, the utter shattering relief of his body finally sheathed inside her. So good, so smooth, so raw and reckless and alive, swelling and straining to fill her, to meet her, to make her his own.

Daisy mín. Sólin mín.

And suddenly Daisy just needed it, needed more of it, all of it—and Filak's hand still holding her wrists flexed, pinning them tighter, as his other hand curved closer around her throat. Around that collar, too, that *kraga* he'd put on her down in that dungeon. And that awareness should have brought Daisy back, should have been enough to make her remember, make her push him away...

But it wasn't, it was only writhing her harder beneath him, around him, clutching him, craving him. And maybe even silently begging him for more, because she so desperately needed him to take charge of this, to take away all her culpability in this, all her stupidity...

She hissed as he slowly drew out again, deliberate and agonizing—but then he plunged back in, while she gasped and squirmed beneath him. Fuck, it felt good, he felt so good, his lean body so strong and warm, his capable hands holding her so safe and certain. Pinning her here beneath him, right where he wanted her, so he could again drag himself out, and drive back in. And then again, and again, sinking into a fast, brutal rhythm, his heavy thrusts meeting her shuddering grinding hips, his hot breath gasping close into her ear.

Gods. It was like he'd broken open something inside Daisy, something wild and utterly depraved, and if he hadn't still been pinning her hands over her head like this, she would have frantically clutched at him, and urged him on faster. Needing him so much it burned and seethed in her belly, the hunger and the frenzy catching and coiling between their driving bodies, wringing them up higher, closer, please, please...

She almost shouted as it pitched off the edge, convulsing her all around him, the ecstasy blazing out in pulse after furious pulse. But Filak's warm safe hand had clapped over her mouth, keeping it inside, for just her, just them—and with two more sharp slams of his hips, he was gasping too, his cock plunging hard and almost painful as it spewed out deep inside. Flooding her with slick molten heat, raw and shameless and defiant, making her his, his, *his*.

And with the certainty and the bliss still shivering through her, Daisy scarcely even noticed Filak's deft hand tilting her face further sideways, or his sharp teeth, settling with decisive purpose against her throat, just above her *kraga*. And even when the pain flashed beneath those teeth, hot and stark, she didn't resist, didn't even flinch. Just breathed deep and felt it, felt the certainty of his strong body over her, filling her and marking her, tending to her, caring for her. Just as he'd sworn to do.

Afterwards he kissed at his bite, stroking it with soft lips and tongue, until she again felt that now-familiar prickle of her skin healing, knitting itself back together again. And then Filak's gentle mouth kissed up her neck, up her cheek, until he met her lips again. Tasting them softly at first, and then taking more, parting them with his tongue, drinking her firm and deep. Locking their mouths together, just as their bodies were still locked together too, his hard shaft still slightly shuddering inside her, squeezing out all he had to give.

Mín, it said, without a single word. *Daisy mín. Sólin mín.*

And he kept saying it, as he finally released her wrists

from above her head, and then gently drew her left hand toward his face. So he could see—oh. The ring.

Daisy's cheeks burned, and she halfheartedly attempted to tug her hand away—but Filak held it firm and safe. And then he brushed it with something warm and familiar, with... his lips. Kissing it, oh gods, whispering more silent, certain words deep into her skin. *Mín.*

But this, finally, was enough to wrench Daisy's awareness back in again, shouting too loud behind her eyes. Filak had kidnapped her. Locked her in a dungeon. Stuffed her own art in her mouth. And even if, like Julian had claimed, it had all only been an unfortunate misunderstanding—Filak had still done it. She still couldn't trust him. She needed to be finished with him...

She somehow found the will to squeeze her eyes shut, to twist her face away. To say, *nei,* without saying it at all—but she could feel Filak's awareness in the sudden stillness of his body over her, the slight slackening of his cock inside her. The prickle of his eyes searching her face, seeing through all her secrets in the dark...

And then in his harsh, ragged exhale. In his body sinking sudden and heavy down on top of hers. In his face ducking into her neck, dragging in a deep bracing breath against her skin...

"I am sorry, Daisy," he whispered, the words flaring like a touch against her skin. "*Ég mun vinna mér inn traust þitt aftur og endurheimta hjarta þitt sem mitt eigið.*"

And this time, the words were... familiar. Words he'd spoken before, when she'd first come to the sickroom, and Kesst had translated for him. *I will soon prove myself to you as your mate, and gain you as my own.*

And Daisy shouldn't believe him. She shouldn't. She shouldn't...

It took almost all her strength to shove at him, to push

away his warm body with cold, shaky fingers. To say, *Nei, Filak. Nei. Go.*

She half-expected him to protest, to argue—but instead, he instantly lurched backwards and away, as his slackened cock swept out of her, too. Leaving her sprawled and debauched on the bed, with hot thick fluid bubbling from inside her, oh gods. And for a horrible, hovering instant, Daisy wanted to clutch after him, to run and hide, to weep...

But then something soft slipped between her thighs—a rag?—and something heavy settled over her. The fur. And she twitched all over at the feel of a hand, Filak's hand, so steady and reassuring, stroking at her throat...

"*Róleg, sólin mín,*" he murmured, so soft. "*Sofðu vel.*"

And with that, his hand drew away again, and she could feel his body drawing away, too. Leaving her just as silently as he'd come, vanishing into the pure inky blackness.

And as Daisy gazed into the darkness after him, she clutched at that ring again, twisting it on her finger. He wanted to prove himself to her. To gain her as his own. He wanted to show her, he wanted her to see...

You must learn, and know, for yourself.

It was all so much, so overwhelming, tangled up with fear and hunger and longing. Filak had kidnapped her, he'd locked her in a dungeon, he'd snapped this ring around her neck, he'd stuffed her own art in her mouth...

But... he'd also repeatedly apologized. He'd offered her gifts. He'd spoken to her in common-tongue. He'd sent Julian and the basket of food. He'd stayed close by. And tonight he'd come to her, and—yes, as shameful as it was to admit—he'd given Daisy exactly what she'd wanted. Exactly what she'd maybe even craved, all that endless day.

So maybe... maybe she could try something else. Maybe, instead of being finished with Filak, forgetting Filak forever... maybe she could take a little more time. Maybe she could just watch him, observe him, even for a few days. Maybe she could learn who he was, where he'd come from, what he wanted. She could *see* Filak, for herself.

And maybe it was still foolish, stupid, ridiculous—but Daisy finally sighed and closed her eyes, and curled up on the bed. Sinking into something that almost felt like contentment, like peace.

She would learn. She would see.

24

Daisy awoke the next morning to the sound of Kesst's shout, ringing shrill and furious through the sickroom.

"What in all the gods' holy mountains is this?!" he shrieked. "*Filak!*"

Daisy shoved up in the bed, her heartbeat thundering in her ears—and she just caught sight of Efterar sprinting past her bed, toward the rear of the sickroom. "What is it, Sweet-Fang?" his deep voice bellowed. "Are you—"

But then he broke off into a harsh, exasperated groan, and a low curse. "That damned stubborn Ka-esh," he muttered. "I suppose we probably asked for it, by trying to keep him out."

"We did *not* ask for it!" came Kesst's reply, now almost a wail. "And now he's attacked our sickroom! Our lovely, innocent sickroom, finally made properly habitable after shocking amounts of thankless labour on my part—now with a giant hideous *hole* knocked into it!"

A *what?!* Daisy's heart was still hammering, and after another instant's staring, she lurched up, and out of bed.

Staggering toward the back of the room, following Kesst and Efterar's voices into the latrine, to where there was…

A *tunnel*. A narrow, brand-new tunnel, cut roughly into the corner of the latrine's flat polished floor, and surrounded with a chaotic mess of dust and rocks and rubble.

It most certainly hadn't been there before, and Daisy's mouth fell open as she stared. *Filak* had done that? When? How? Why hadn't anyone heard it, or noticed?

But then her thoughts flicked back to the night before, to that strange scraping sound she'd heard, before Filak had touched her in the darkness. She'd thought the sounds had been a dream, but had they been—this? What the *hell*?

Kesst was looking unusually dishevelled, and he whirled around to stare at Daisy, his nostrils flaring. "So Filak got to you after all, then?" he demanded. "Did he at least give you a choice in the matter?"

Daisy's cheeks flooded with sudden heat, and she winced, dropped her eyes to the rubble-strewn floor. "Er, yes," she said, her voice barely a whisper. "But I'm sorry, I had no idea he—"

She flailed her hand at the tunnel, and shot a chagrined glance between Kesst and Efterar. And while Efterar easily waved it away, Kesst was still viciously glowering—but now toward the door, rather than at Daisy.

"Oh, we all know it's not *your* fault, sweetheart," he said flatly. "That disastrous dungeon-dwelling ghoul has gone too far, this time. This is *war*!"

With that, he stalked off toward the door, his body very straight, his hands in fists. And Efterar's expression as he watched Kesst go was almost painfully fond, and a little amused, too.

"You're sure Filak didn't hurt you, or pressure you?" Efterar asked, with a searching glance toward Daisy's eyes. "We can incapacitate him, if need be."

Daisy rapidly shook her head, and her face again felt far too hot, too ashamed. Because yes, again, she had to admit that she *had* wanted Filak, last night. She'd wanted that weight of his body, that certainty of his touch, the softness of his kiss...

"It's all right," Efterar said, and he looked like he meant it, his gaze surprisingly mild on hers. "Mate-bonds between orcs and humans can be very strong, and you're looking much better today, at least. Are you feeling better, too?"

Daisy blinked—she and Filak surely didn't have a *mate-bond*?—and then made herself consider Efterar's question. Did she feel better? She did, didn't she? More rested, more alert, more clear-headed?

"Good," Efterar said, as if she'd answered the question aloud. "Though I'd still recommend getting some more rest here today, if you can. Eating would be good, too—I saw Julian brought you another basket, if that helps. And Rosa stopped by with some reading for you, too."

Really? Daisy opened her mouth to ask how, or when—but Efterar had already strode off again. And when she followed him back toward her bed, she indeed found a stack of books and pamphlets waiting for her, and a brand-new basket, too. Overflowing with yet more food and drinks, and also—paper? And pencils? And even a small *drawing board*?

Daisy's breath caught, and she rushed to pluck out the paper, smoothing her suddenly trembling fingers against it. Julian had brought her *paper*, just like he'd promised, gods bless him. And she could have sobbed at the sight of it, the feel of it, the dizzying relief of it. She had paper again. She could draw again.

She almost hurled herself back onto the bed, setting herself up cross-legged with the board and paper, and a fresh pencil. And even the feel of the pencil on the paper prickled sudden heat behind her eyes, and she drew a long, heavy line across the paper, and then another. Just sinking into it, feeling it curl up and settle, warm and whispering and alive.

She drew aimlessly at first, just lines and shades and curves, getting a feel for the pencil, for the tooth of the paper. But then her strokes slipped into the arch of the sickroom's ceiling, the lines of the dividers, the shape of the empty bed opposite hers. The shadow of Efterar's bulky form passing by, the texture of the fur on her bed. The way the firelight flickered and danced on the ceiling, the light of its warmth, the cozy shadows it cast across the stone floor...

She'd absently begun to eat as she drew, too, picking at the basket with one hand while drawing with the other. But she only half-tasted the admittedly delicious food, because her full focus was just on this. On being finally, blessedly free of all the confusion and regret, and lost in the stream, the magic, the sweet wheeling wonder...

It was only the sudden sound of yet another commotion outside the door that dragged her awareness back again, jerking her upright in the bed. Because yes, that was again Filak's voice, deep and harsh and demanding—and Kesst's voice, sharper and colder. Both of them again speaking in that foreign tangled language, their voices rising almost to shouts.

Without thinking, Daisy had already set down her pencil, about to slip out of bed—when the voices abruptly halted, and Kesst stalked back into view. He was still looking frazzled, his lip contemptuously curled, his hair even more unkempt than before. But in his hand, he was holding—flowers?

"For you," he snapped at Daisy, as he thrust the flowers toward her. "From your most devoted deranged admirer."

He didn't wait for her reply, just spun around and stalked off again, while Daisy stared blankly after him, and then down at the flowers now clutched in her hand.

And they were—delightful. Common flowers, yes, and some unconventional choices for a bouquet—but still beautiful, all clustered together like this, in a mass of riotous, chaotic colour. Lupins, and daylilies, and marigolds, and even a few dandelions. And there, in the middle—Daisy's breath stilled—were a handful of bright, cheerful daisies.

Daisy mín. Sólin mín.

Daisy swallowed down the sudden constriction in her throat, and then groped for the empty bottle from the basket—gods, she barely remembered drinking the milk it had held—and placed the flowers' stems into it. And then she dragged over the nearby bench, set the makeshift vase onto it, and flipped to a fresh sheet of paper.

And this—this was more shimmering wonder, more sweet shaky relief. Bringing the flowers' wild beauty to life on the page, closer and brighter with every stroke, every shade. Ensuring they would never die, never be forgotten, her own magic whipping and whirling around her, making life, making immortality...

And if there was another commotion at the door, she didn't hear it this time. Because it was only this, only the art, only the magic...

And only... him. Filak.

She couldn't have said how long he'd been there, or how he'd gotten there—but somehow, as she drew in the daisies' tiny central spikes, she'd begun feeling that distinct weight of his eyes, and their telltale prickling touch on her skin. Watching her, silent and intent. Waiting.

She made herself finish the daisies, but her previously easy strokes had become careful and uncertain, her hand clammy and stiff. And she braced herself as she finally raised her eyes, and found Filak's face.

He was standing near the end of her bed, and his thin body was very still, his eyes dark staring hollows in his harsh face. And as Daisy blinked back up toward him, it was almost impossible to believe she'd allowed him into her bed last night, let him touch her, kiss her, ravish her in the dark...

Daisy's face heated, and she dropped her eyes down

toward the flowers on the bench. "Um, thank you for these," she said, hoarse, as she reached out her suddenly shaky hand to brush at a marigold—and then she caught sight of that yellow ring, still glittering far too bright on her finger.

But curse it, Filak was looking at the ring too, and Daisy hurriedly dropped her hand, and clutched tightly at her pencil. Gods, what was she thinking? Even if she'd decided to see and learn him for herself, she still shouldn't be encouraging him, right? Shouldn't just let him believe it was already settled between them?

But Filak didn't actually look as though he thought it was settled, in this moment—and if anything, he looked... wary. Cautious. And his steps toward Daisy were slow, careful, quiet, as if he didn't want to make any sudden movements, didn't want to alarm or frighten her.

"*Þóknast þau þér?*" his low voice finally asked, as he carefully reached out a long black claw, and brushed it at the marigold, too. "*Gott?*"

Gott meant *good*, Daisy was almost sure of it—he was asking if she liked the flowers, right? So she attempted a nod, and took a slow, shaky breath. "*Gott,*" she replied, quiet. "I love plants. Especially messy colourful ones like this. Not that"—she huffed a sound almost like a laugh—"anyone would ever put them in real books, though."

There was no chance Filak had understood any of that, but perhaps he'd followed the ruefulness in her voice, or even the regret. And he was watching her with that careful intensity again, his head cocking sideways—and then his dark eyes slid down, toward the drawing board on Daisy's lap.

She'd had it on her upraised knees, angled toward her, meaning that Filak likely couldn't see what she'd been drawing. But he just kept standing there staring, again almost waiting, and finally Daisy took another deep breath, and turned the drawing toward him. Feeling her heartbeat kick up in her chest, because last time he'd seen her art, he'd raged at her, and kidnapped her, and accused her of planning a mass murder...

But this time, he just... looked. Looked, and looked, while his brow slowly furrowed, and something convulsed in his throat. And when he reached out his clawed hand toward the drawing, Daisy let him take it, watched with her heart still loudly thumping as he kept staring down toward it, and then sharply glanced over at the flowers. And then he looked back at the paper in his hand, and the flowers, and then—he stiffened—his eyes caught on the other drawing she'd done. The one of the sickroom, now lying visible and slightly skewed on her drawing board.

"*Daisy*," he said quietly, almost reproachfully, as he sank down to sit on the bench beside the bed, and leaned over to trace his sharp claw along the line of the ceiling she'd drawn. "*Átt þú þetta?*"

It was the same thing he'd said to her back at the apartment, just before he'd begun raging at her—asking her if the art was hers, right?—and Daisy shrank back in the bed, and darted an uneasy glance toward the door. "Um," she said, "yes. Ach. It's mine."

But this time, instead of yelling or raging, Filak kept blinking down at the drawing in her lap, gently tracing his claw against the lines of it. As if he was caught in it, entranced by it, and Daisy felt her heartbeat slightly slowing as she watched, still clutching the pencil tight in her fingers.

"I didn't finish Efterar, though," she said, a little thickly, as she impulsively straightened the paper on the board again, and began sketching in his braid, his scarred, harsh profile, the elegant arches of his pointed ears. "He has a very interesting face, don't you think?"

She could feel the intensity of Filak's watching eyes as she drew, her hand shifting quickly across the paper. And when she'd finished—leaving a distinct little Efterar walking past on the page—and then risked a glance back at Filak, he was indeed still staring, his expression contorting into something that might have been awe, or disbelief, or even—jealousy?

At that moment, Efterar himself strode by, not even sparing them a glance. But Filak's sudden glare toward him looked deeply malevolent, his lip curling, and he even growled, low and menacing in his throat. Almost as if he really was—jealous. Jealous of Efterar, just because Daisy had drawn him.

Daisy's mouth twitched into a quizzical smile, and she shook her head, opened her mouth—but just then, Kesst stalked by after Efterar. And Filak's malevolent glare instantly flipped into something cold and contemptuous as Kesst skidded to a halt at the end of the bed, and gaped back toward him with wide, goggling eyes.

"What—the—*fuck*," Kesst snarled, dragging both his hands through his rumpled hair. "You—enraging—irreclaimable—incorrigible—*barnacle*. How the *hell* did you get in here again?!"

Filak only gazed back, his sharp teeth now slightly bared, because of course he wouldn't have understood anything Kesst had said, would he? And perhaps Kesst had now realized that, because he wildly flailed his hand, and began speaking in more sharp, furious words that Daisy couldn't understand.

But Filak clearly did, because after staring at Kesst for another long moment, he smoothly rose to his feet, and then bent down, and pressed his lips to Daisy's forehead. "I am sorry, *sólin mín*," he murmured. "*Ég kem fljótlega aftur.*"

Daisy couldn't hide her brief, convulsive quiver, as Kesst made a loud, enraged sound from the end of the bed. "No, you will *not* return soon!" he spat. "*Nei*, Filak! Out!"

But Filak didn't even look at him, and instead gave an irritated roll of his eyes toward Daisy before turning and

stalking away. While Kesst reeled off after him, still sputtering, and yanking at his rumpled hair.

But Daisy's forehead was still tingling from Filak's kiss,
and her traitorous mouth quirked up as she smoothed out
her sketch of the sickroom on the board, and began drawing
again. This time adding in an enraged Kesst, his handsome
face angry and appalled, his arms flailing, his long hair flying
out in a chaotic tangle around his head.

"Oh, good *gods*," came a shocked, hushed voice, some
time later. "That isn't... *me*. Is it?"

Daisy nearly leapt out of the bed, and found herself
blinking up at none other than Kesst himself. Who was
standing stock-still beside her, and staring down at her
drawing with a thoroughly horrified look on his face.

"*Unthinkable*," he breathed, as he shuddered all over, and
snapped his hands up to gingerly stroke at his messy hair.
"What has that Ka-esh menace done to me?! I need an
extremely extensive bath. And grooming! *Now!*"

With that, he dashed off toward the door, leaving Daisy
gazing guiltily after him, and also fighting back the sudden,
almost overpowering urge to laugh. And after eating another
tasty snack from Filak's basket—while reading one of the
highly informative pamphlets Rosa had left her—she pulled
over a fresh sheet of paper, and began drawing again.

It was another sketch of Kesst, but this time she chose a
flattering three-quarter angle, and put considerable time into
his smile, and his striking bone structure, and his expressive
dark eyes. And his hair would look lovely in the wind like
this, and his lean body had a fair bit of muscle definition,
and...

"Daisy!" cut in a sharp, angry voice, and when Daisy
flinched to look, it was Filak again. Standing tall and pale
over her, glaring down at her, and holding...

Her *sketchbook*?!

Daisy's initial alarm collapsed into confused disbelief—

where the hell had Filak gotten her sketchbook? Had he somehow gone back to Dusbury, and stolen it from Lew's apartment, or—

Or—wait. Daisy had last had that sketchbook when she'd been drawing that first night in the cave, right? When the tunnel had collapsed? And she'd dropped it, and thought it was lost, forever.

But clearly Filak had taken it. Kept it. And now... now he'd brought it back.

Something lurched in Daisy's belly, and she took the sketchbook from Filak with careful, shaky hands, and clutched it tight to her chest. It hadn't been lost forever after all, oh gods—and the relief of it felt like a light in the darkness, like a warm crackling fire, like more shimmering sparkling magic. Hers.

"Thank you," she whispered to Filak, before she could stop it—and it was stupid, ridiculous, because he'd been the entire damned reason she'd lost the sketchbook in the first place. But the way he was watching her, his eyes flickering, his hand again drawing that cross over his heart. Saying, silently, *I am sorry.*

Daisy swallowed, and cradled her sketchbook even closer, while Filak shot a narrow, disapproving glare down toward her sketch of Kesst. And with a swift swipe of his hand, he plucked it entirely away, and set it face-down on the small table beside the bed.

"*Nóg af Kesst,*" he said, still with obvious disapproval in his voice. "*Þú verður að borða.*"

With that, he pulled over the mostly-full basket of food, and plunked it onto Daisy's lap. "*Borðaðu,*" he said firmly, and that had to mean *eat,* right? He wanted her to eat more?

And despite the fact that Daisy had already eaten, she still felt surprisingly hungry, so she picked up a slice of buttered bread, and took a bite. While Filak settled his long body down on the bench again, crossing his arms tightly over his chest, and staring at her. Clearly intending to sit there and watch her eat, without having any food whatsoever himself.

"You'll have some too, won't you?" Daisy asked him, as she plucked up a piece of dried meat, and held it out toward him. "It was lovely of you to send it, but it's still way too much for one person, and you—"

But she broke off there, too late, darting a wincing glance down toward Filak's too-visible ribs. Because damn it, what had Julian said about Filak and eating? *Fasting is an important part of their prayers, most of all when an orc is seeking the gods' help or guidance.*

And whatever Filak's reasons were for fasting like this, Daisy had no desire whatsoever to disrespect his faith, or his prayers. But even as she made to lower her hand, he sighed, snatched the dried meat from her fingers, and took a furtive little nibble.

And oh, that look on his face. The ravenous hunger, the pleasure, the relief. Flaring bright and vivid across his eyes, softening his harsh features as he swallowed...

But just as quickly, his expression darkened again. Twisting into something unmistakably like guilt as he squeezed his eyes shut, and clenched his jaw tight.

It hitched oddly in Daisy's chest, and without at all meaning to, she slipped a hand out toward him, and gripped at his bony knee over his trousers. "Everyone needs to eat sometimes, Filak," she said, softer than she meant. "Whatever you're praying for, I can't imagine your gods would begrudge you even a tiny bit of food now and then, would they?"

Filak's eyes snapped open again, first staring at Daisy's hand on his knee, and then at her face. And too late, she yanked her hand away, because this was sheer stupidity again, wasn't it? She was only supposed to be watching him, not involving herself in his personal affairs, right?

But Filak was still staring at her, with something she couldn't read flickering in his eyes. And then, holding his gaze on hers, he took another small, tentative bite of meat, while more of that palpable pleasure—or even relief— passed across his face.

It again lurched in Daisy's chest, and she couldn't help her small smile toward him. "*Gott*," she said, again without at all meaning to. "It's good, isn't it?"

Filak's eyes flickered again, betraying more of that relief, or maybe even gratefulness—but then they darkened again as his throat convulsed with his swallow. Suggesting that eating truly wasn't easy for him, even if he wanted to do it. And after another instant's watching him, Daisy impulsively reached toward the table beside the bed, and plucked up one of Rosa's books.

"Rosa brought these for me today," she told him. "And this one"—she flipped it open, showed him the first page— "is called *The Official Orc Mountain Guide to Introductory Aelakesh*. That's your language, right? *Aelakesh*?"

She pointed toward the first entry on the page, which included the word *Aelakesh* in common-tongue, followed by what was clearly the orcs' flowing, unfamiliar script. And below it, there was even a helpful phonetic guide, followed by a definition. *The spoken and written language of all five orc clans, since their arrival on this continent roughly two millennia ago.*

Filak's gaze had snapped down to the book, his mouth still frowning—but then the comprehension flashed across his eyes. "Ach," he said, jabbing his claw toward the page. "*Aelakesh.*"

His pronunciation was far different than Daisy's had been, and she took a breath, and attempted to mimic it. "*Aelakesh*," she said. "*Aelakesh.*"

Filak's eyes flickered again, this time with obvious

approval, and he slid his claw down to the next entry on the page. "*Orkafjall,*" he said. "*Þetta fjall.*"

He'd aimlessly waved his hand at the room around them, and even if Daisy hadn't just read the definition on the page, his meaning was all too clear. "*Orkafjall,*" she repeated, again attempting to mimic his pronunciation. "Orc Mountain."

Filak's mouth slightly curved up, and his next nibble of meat was almost easy, almost unconscious. "Orc Mountain," he repeated, in flat-sounding common-tongue, once he'd swallowed. "Orc Mountain."

Daisy couldn't resist her reflexive grin toward him, and then took a bite of her own meat, and moved to the next entry down the page. It was *ach*, for yes, and apparently they sometimes used *já*, too—and then *nei*. Which Daisy already knew all too well, and easily pronounced, while Filak half-grinned toward her, and took another bite of meat.

And then they moved to the next entry, and the next, and the next. Until they'd somehow gone through half a dozen pages together, talking and smiling and learning together—and still eating together, too. And while Filak had only taken small, tentative bites, at Daisy's urging he'd also tried the bread, and the berries. All of it flaring more hunger and relief and guilt across his eyes, and when Daisy nudged the pastry toward him, he actually groaned aloud as he ate, his eyes fluttering closed. Enough that Daisy couldn't hide her chuckle, and when he caught her eye again, he twitched a small, rueful smile, too.

It made for a surprisingly enjoyable morning, easy and companionable—and it was truly helpful, too. It turned out that *gott* did mean *good*, after all, and *biddu*—which Filak had said so often during their first night in the cave—meant *wait*. And *róleg* meant *peace*, and *borða* meant *eat*, and *typpi* meant—*cock*.

"*Typpi,*" Filak told her, a wicked grin now playing on his mouth, as his clawed hand blatantly palmed at his trousers—

which, curse him, looked impressively swollen in front. "*Typpi, sólin mín.*"

Daisy should not have stared like that, or betrayed that hard swallow in her throat, because Filak's grin broadened, and he leaned closer toward her, gazing at her through hungry, half-lidded eyes. "*Ach, sólin mín?*" he murmured. "*Viltu typpið?*"

Daisy's breath caught, her cheeks damnably heating—but at that highly inopportune moment, Kesst strode around the divider. He looked damp and refreshed, his long hair neatly hanging down his back—but upon catching sight of Filak, he flailed to a halt, as more shocked fury flashed across his eyes.

"What the hell, Filak!" he shouted. "The guards swore you hadn't come through, and I put some on the tunnel, too—but wait, did you dig out *somewhere else*? Out! *Out!*"

Filak's glare toward Kesst was pure, withering scorn, but he huffed a sharp exhale, and rose to his feet. Not bothering to hide the very obvious bulge in his straining trousers, and he took his time gripping Daisy's chin in his hand, and tilting her face up toward him. So he could leisurely bend down and kiss her on the mouth, oh gods, his lips soft and hungry, his tongue curling against hers...

"OUT!" came Kesst's distant holler, to which Filak growled softly against Daisy's lips, and drew away. Though he kept his hand on her cheek, his hooded eyes steady on hers.

"*Vertu sæll,*" he murmured. "*Sólin mín.*"

Thanks to their discussion, Daisy now knew that *vertu sæll* meant *goodbye*, and she couldn't hide her smile as she nodded back. "*Vertu sæll*, Filak."

The warmth flickered across his eyes, curved up his mouth—and it wasn't until another enraged sound emanated from Kesst that Filak rolled his eyes, and stalked out. And for a brief, bizarre instant, Daisy fought down the overpowering urge to leap up and follow him, to put her hands to his straight stiff back, to trace those black marks on his skin...

But she somehow held herself still, watching him go. And once Kesst had stormed off again, she reached for her sketchbook, and reverently stroked her hand across its familiar hard cover. Filak had eaten with her, spoken with her, spent time with her—and he'd even brought back her sketchbook. Something to ground her in all this mess, something that was only hers. Hers.

She took far too long flipping through the pages, mostly wincing at her various previous mistakes, but also lingering on the better drawings, and the memories behind them. When she'd climbed to the top of that dangerous ridge for the view. When she'd found a cave full of pink stalagmites. When she'd been stuck in a tedious university meeting with Lew, and had instead drawn the little sparrows hopping around outside the window.

And the last page, of course, was that cave. Filak's cave. With the beautiful arched ceiling, the checkered tile floor. The cave that had felt entirely unlike a cave at all, but more... purposeful. Intentional. Powerful.

Daisy studied the drawing for a long, silent moment, tracing a careful finger against the line of the cave's ceiling. What had that cave been? What had it meant? And why had Filak trapped her inside it? He *had* trapped her in there on purpose, right? With his... magic?

It all twisted and tangled with the rest, so many questions, so many things Daisy didn't know. So many things she wanted to learn, wanted to see for herself, to draw for herself. To keep making sense of all this mess, this mountain, this orc. To see them through fresh eyes on a blank new page...

And before she'd quite followed it, she snapped the sketchbook shut, and shoved out of the bed. Smoothing out the fur, slipping a pencil into her pocket, and clutching the sketchbook close. Not thinking, just drawing in a breath, heading for the door...

"Wait, are you *leaving*?" cut in a voice, Kesst's voice—and when Daisy turned toward him, he still looked frazzled and put-upon, his tired eyes glinting suspiciously on hers. "Did Eft actually release you?"

Daisy twitched, and glanced toward where Efterar was striding over, too. "It's all right," he told her, as he gave a brief caress to Kesst's stiff shoulder. "I'm sure you'll be fine now, Daisy."

But he looked unmistakably relieved, too—no wonder, given all the chaos Daisy's presence had brought them—and suddenly she felt almost dizzy with the sheer, shuddering gratefulness. They'd been so kind to her, so generous, and she had no way of paying them back, except...

"It was so lovely of you both to have me here," she told them, as she began fumbling through her sketchbook, and the papers she'd haphazardly stuffed inside it. "Again I'm sorry for the inconvenience, and—here. It's not much, but— thank you."

She'd thrust out her drawing of Kesst, which she hadn't quite finished—but she could admit that it had captured him well, and was a very flattering likeness, too. And she was gratified by the way Kesst's eyes snapped wide at the sight of it, while Efterar blinked, and then gave a low, appreciative whistle.

"Look at that, Sweet-Fang," he murmured, as he reached to take the drawing from Daisy's hand, and held it up before them. "It's you. Just as beautiful as always."

Kesst kept staring at it with wide, disbelieving eyes, his mouth fallen open. And then he slightly shook himself, and shot Daisy a searching, accusing look. "You... *drew* that?" he demanded. "And we can... *keep* it?"

Daisy twitched an uncertain smile, but nodded. "Yes, of

course," she replied. "I'd be happy to do another one too, if you like. Perhaps a portrait of the two of you together?"

Kesst's mouth snapped shut, and he shot a glance toward Efterar that looked almost pleading. And at Efterar's wry, indulgent half-smile back, Kesst fervently nodded, his eyes alight on Daisy's. "Yes, please," he breathed. "Good gods, it might almost be worth all this horrifying desecration of our precious sickroom."

Daisy didn't know whether to laugh, or perhaps to apologize again—but beside Kesst, Efterar was fondly grinning, and pressing a kiss to his hair. And if nothing else, Kesst looked far more relaxed than before, his outrage entirely vanished, his gaze lingering on Daisy's drawing with something not unlike reverence.

"Where are you going, then?" Kesst asked, sparing only a brief glance toward her. "Meeting up with Filak again, I presume?"

Even the thought of it tugged in Daisy's belly, but she squared her shoulders, and drew in a breath. Where was she going? What was she doing? Not meeting up with Filak again, no, but...

"I'm going to draw," she said, and she could have laughed with the brightness of it, the relief. "And I'm going to learn."

25

Drawing in Orc Mountain was delightful.

Daisy began just outside the sickroom, sketching the lovely arch of its door, the beautiful detail of the wrought-iron lamp embedded in the wall beside it. And then she drifted down the corridor, drawing the long line of the ceiling, and vaguely smiling at a bulky, bemused-looking orc who passed by.

But he didn't interrupt her, and neither did the next orc, or the next. And Daisy's courage grew as she went, and she began cautiously glancing into the various rooms as she passed. One was a large, well-outfitted kitchen, with multiple orcs and women cheerfully working inside it, and another was a beautiful empty room with several huge baths cut into the floor.

Daisy eagerly slipped inside, and flipped to a new page—and indeed, the baths turned out to be wonderful to draw, with their sharp angles and rising tendrils of steam. So much that she barely noticed when a pair of orcs strode past her, stripped off all their clothes, and dove into the water.

But Daisy didn't draw naked people without their permission, so she again wandered down the corridor, until she found a bright, bustling forge, with several big, sweaty orc smiths working over a rounded, stunningly designed furnace. And when the smiths shot wary, uncertain looks toward her, she again drew up her courage, and shyly asked if she could draw the beautiful furnace.

The request earned her several more odd looks, but once the smiths had agreed, they seemed increasingly fascinated by Daisy's drawing, casting frequent curious looks at her sketchbook. And when the bulkiest smith asked if she could draw people, too, she tossed off a quick sketch of him with the huge axe he was forging, his sharp-toothed grin beaming bright across his broad face.

"Ach, look at this!" the smith said, once she'd torn out the page, and handed it over toward him. "It is me, brothers! Look!"

The other orcs looked both amused and intrigued, several of them angling increasingly intent glances toward Daisy—at least, until someone new materialized beside her. It was Julian, looking rather pale as he glanced at the huge smiths, but Daisy couldn't help a bright smile toward him as she waved him into the room.

"Julian!" she exclaimed. "I found the most wonderful furnace. And these smiths have been so lovely, too."

Julian's smile back looked distinctly alarmed, but he gave the smiths a careful nod. "Thank you, brothers," he said. "And sister, should you wish, mayhap I could show you some other rooms, also?"

Daisy eagerly agreed, and waved goodbye to the friendly smiths, who all waved back. While Julian rapidly ushered her out into the corridor, and then ran both hands over his sweaty-looking face. "Good gods, sister," he said thickly. "The Bautul forge—ach. You are lucky Filak—"

But his voice faded, his mouth grimacing, and Daisy's smile faltered as she studied him. "What about Filak?" she carefully asked. "He's not... here, is he?"

She shot a searching glance around at the corridor, but it seemed otherwise unoccupied, and Julian huffed a wry laugh, and shook his head. "No, I ken he is digging again," he replied. "He would not have thought—ach. But, I am glad to see you are up and about, and"—he slightly straightened, and gave her a more genuine smile—"there is much more I can show you, if you come?"

Daisy nodded and grinned back toward him, and then accompanied him down the corridor. And it soon turned out that exploring Orc Mountain with Julian was even more delightful than before, because he indeed showed Daisy an astonishing variety of intriguing rooms, and gave her detailed explanations as they went.

And while Daisy had already learned some of Julian's information from Rosa's helpful publications, seeing it first-hand was another experience entirely. The mountain was impossibly large, and it was apparently divided into five distinct wings for the five clans of orcs, all with fascinating differences between them. The Bautul clan's wing felt bulky and solid—not unlike the Bautul orcs themselves—with many lovely rounded shapes like the furnace. While the Skai clan's orcs were generally taller and leaner, and their wing was dimmer and narrower, too, featuring multiple twisty winding tunnels that hid several truly wonderful rooms. Including a massive fighting arena, a rounded shrine with some stunning carvings, and a bath with a huge *waterfall* pouring out from the wall.

Daisy had already gone through almost a dozen pages in her sketchbook, and she'd become so absorbed with the waterfall that she didn't even notice the arrival of several new people in the room. But when she glanced up, there was Rosa, together with a tall, handsome, stern-faced orc, and several small, adorable orc children.

"Daisy!" Rosa exclaimed, with a surprised-looking grin, even as she shot an accusing glance toward Julian. "What are you doing here? When did you leave the sickroom? And wait, is Julian giving you the *tour*?!"

She sounded deeply, inexplicably scandalized by this, and beside Daisy, Julian betrayed a faint wince. "Daisy wished to see the mountain," he said quickly, "and I did not wish to leave her to do this alone. But we should be glad to have you join us, should you wish?"

Rosa's face brightened again, and she immediately agreed, and made a quick round of introductions. It turned out that the stern handsome orc was her mate John-Ka, who apparently served as the leader of the Ka-esh clan, and had held the official title of *Priest* for the past four years. While the two orc children were Rosa and John-Ka's young sons, who apparently both adored the Skai baths, and often wanted to come here to play and swim with other orclings.

"That waterfall is marvellous, isn't it?" Rosa said to Daisy, once they'd headed back out into the corridor with Julian, away from the sounds of happy squeals and splashes. "It's a stunning example of ancient Ka-esh engineering. Much of the skill has unfortunately been lost now, but the Ka-esh designed and built most of this mountain, and you can still see how they tried to reflect each clan in their respective wings. I'm sure Julian has explained the clans to you, or perhaps you might have read about them in the publication I left you? *The Orc Mountain Manual for Modern Mates*?"

The title instantly sounded familiar, and Daisy nodded, and smiled back. "Oh, yes, I did read all of that one this morning," she replied. "It was so informative, thank you. And the Aelakesh book was such a helpful reference, too."

Rosa's eyes flared with eagerness, and with something much like relief. "Oh, I'm so glad!" she exclaimed. "I've led language classes here for *years*, but I've been taking a break to focus on my sons, so I hoped my book would offer a helpful resource in the meantime! Do you think it'll be enough to get you started on learning Aelakesh, at least? Or maybe"—her mouth pursed—"maybe I should try to launch more classes after all?"

Daisy waved it away, as her thoughts flashed back to practicing with Filak, to how it had felt almost... *fun*. "No, I'm sure the book will be plenty for now, thank you," she said, with her most reassuring smile. "Although wait"—she blinked toward Rosa—"did you say it's *your* book? Did you write it?"

She was rewarded with a delighted, contagious grin from Rosa, who bobbed excitedly on her feet. "Yes, I wrote and published it all myself," she said breathlessly, "and all the others, too! I don't suppose you'd like to see where, for your next stop on your tour?"

That did sound highly intriguing, and soon Rosa was ushering Daisy and Julian into the official Orc Mountain Communications Office. It turned out to be a large room that carried the familiar scent of ink and paper, and was well stocked with printing supplies—sheaves of paper, huge jars of ink, several good quality hand-presses, and even a clever binding machine.

"This is incredible, Rosa," Daisy said, once Rosa had shown her around the room. "How many publications have you printed here? How many pages can your binder handle? And have you done illustrations, too?"

Rosa answered all Daisy's questions with relish, and beamed as she demonstrated how to use her hand-presses, and the binding machine, too. And once Daisy had effusively praised all of it, she flipped to the next page in her sketchbook, and began making a quick drawing of the hand-presses' mechanism for printing plates. It was a style she hadn't seen before, and it was very cleverly done—and when Rosa asked why she was interested in plates, Daisy distractedly answered as she drew, explaining how she'd sometimes done the plates for Lew's books, too.

It wasn't until she'd finished drawing that she realized Rosa was staring at her, with a decidedly feral glint in her blue eyes. "*Daisy*," she said, hushed. "I don't suppose—have you ever—would you consider—doing some work for our publications, while you're here? Paid, of course? I've just been managing all our illustrations myself, but I'm sure you can see that I'm not even slightly trained! And the plates take me forever, and it would just be *so helpful!*"

She clasped both hands to her heart, her wide blue eyes fixed beatifically on Daisy's face. A look that reminded Daisy far too strongly of tiny puppies, or hungry children, and she quickly smiled back. "Yes, of course, I'd be happy to," she replied, and she meant it. "What kinds of drawings would you like done?"

Rosa's squeal of delight rang through the room, and soon they were poring over Rosa's current publications together, taking notes and making lists. And then Daisy even did a few rough preliminary sketches, while Rosa gleefully bounced up and down beside her.

It was a thoroughly absorbing experience, enough that Daisy had almost entirely forgotten about their tour, and about Julian, too. At least, until he made a strange sound from the nearby counter, and dropped a sheaf of paper on the floor. Scattering loose sheets out all over the smooth stone, and when Daisy knelt to help clean up, she noticed that the papers all seemed to be innocuous-looking letters and notes. But Julian just kept standing there, gazing blankly at Daisy and Rosa as a strange splotchy redness rose in his cheeks.

"Are you all right, Julian?" Daisy asked, frowning as she held the papers back out toward him. "You're not feeling ill, are you?"

Julian twitched and shook his head, but he didn't take the papers from Daisy's hand, and instead shot a searching look at Rosa. "These are," he said stiffly, "from *Rurik*."

From Rurik. As if that was someone important. And wait, Rurik was the name of Julian's former lover, right? The one who was now *living a good life with many lovers in the north,* Julian had said.

But Rosa hadn't seemed to notice anything unusual about this, and she absently nodded, from where she was reorganizing her own stack of papers. "Yes, we've been in regular contact with Rurik lately," she replied, as she reached for Daisy's stack of papers, too. "We've been trying to learn more about the Nor-ka-esh, and though Rurik is Skai, he's the only orc in the area who seems willing to tell us anything about them."

Wait. Daisy's head tilted, and the question bubbled up before she could stop it. "You mean—this Rurik has been telling you about Filak's people?" she asked. "Or even about Filak himself?"

Rosa gave another distracted nod, and kept shuffling her papers. "That's our hope," she replied, "but even Rurik hasn't been able to tell us why Filak left the Nor-ka-esh to come here—or what the hell he wants from us. Or why he's apparently so desperate for a mate that he's been propositioning every woman in sight for the entire past *year!*"

Daisy froze, and a sharp, sudden chill wrenched up her back. Wait. What? Filak had been—*propositioning* women? Almost every woman in sight? For the entire past *year*?!

But Rosa didn't correct it, and instead she bit her lip and shot Daisy a furtive, mortified look. Suggesting that yes, yes, this was true. Filak had wanted—other women. *Any* woman.

Daisy's heartbeat had begun pounding, and she shot a searching, desperate glance toward Julian—had *he* known about this, too? But he was still standing there staring down at Rosa's stack of papers, his eyes strangely bright. And after another instant's awkward silence, Rosa groaned aloud, shoved the papers back toward Julian, and wildly flapped both her hands toward Daisy.

"Look, it's not as bad as it sounds!" she said, high-pitched. "I mean, yes, Filak has made multiple offers to multiple women over this past year. But the thing is"—she took a deep breath—"it's been quite obvious that he doesn't actually *want* any of them!"

Daisy blinked, not following, while Rosa took another deep breath. "Apart from *you*, Daisy," she continued, "he's barely *looked* at any of the women he's spoken to, let alone trying to learn their language, or their names, or anything else about them! It's almost like it's—like it's all some kind of bizarre secret test. Some kind of challenge, or even an *attack*!"

A test. A challenge. An attack. The ice was still scraping up Daisy's spine, and her scrambled thoughts were shouting now, screeching wild warnings through her skull. Because gods, it had so often felt that way with her too, hadn't it? Like Filak was testing her, challenging her... attacking her? Just like he apparently had with every other woman in his sights?

"But as usual," Rosa's rushed voice continued, "Filak won't tell us why! He won't tell us anything about his motives, or his goals here, or his home in the north! We would love to know, we would *love* to help, it's John-Ka's *job* to help—and it's been like talking to a boulder! A boulder who's just waiting for the most opportune moment to smash down and *crush* you!"

There was genuine hurt in her voice, enough to drag Daisy out of her own hurt, her own whirling confusion. Rosa had made genuine efforts with Filak, that was clear, and why had Filak so consistently refused? What was he doing here? What did he want? What was he hiding?

Daisy shot another searching look at Julian, but he still seemed thoroughly occupied with the papers, bringing them to his nose, and inhaling long and deep against them. As if he hadn't heard a single word of this—but surely he'd known about it, hadn't he? And he hadn't told her, either?

"Er, I'm sorry again, sister," Rosa's subdued voice said,

into the silence. "I'm sure once we learn what Filak's motives are, it will all make sense. Right?"

But she didn't sound even slightly convinced, and her smile toward Daisy looked more like a grimace. And though Daisy attempted a smile back, it also felt forced, and the questions were still shrieking through her skull, pounding with her heartbeat. What did Filak want? Had Daisy really been different for him, somehow, or was Rosa just trying to reassure her? And she needed to learn, needed to know...

"Is there... anything else, then?" Daisy finally asked, flatter than she meant. "Anything else about Filak I should know?"

Rosa winced, and glanced away—meaning that yes, damn it, there was. And Daisy waited, watching, as Rosa drew in a deep breath, and let it out.

"Well..." she began, tentative, "do you know about Filak's... abilities? His... magic?"

Daisy nodded, even as the truth of that sank deeper—Filak really could wield *magic*—but Rosa's expression didn't change, the agitation glimmering in her eyes. "Well, he uses his magic to find rare gems, like those ones he offered you," she continued, in a rush. "He specifically seeks out gems he knows will be in high demand here in the mountain, and sells them at extortionate prices. Enough that he's surely amassed a small fortune in coin by now—but he hasn't spent a single copper of it. We have no idea why he wants it, or what he's doing with it!"

Her voice was rising again, her hands wringing together, and Daisy kept waiting, feeling her heartbeat thunder even louder. Filak had a *fortune* in coin? In addition to all those gems? Why? Where? What did he want with it? Because he would want something... right?

"And he seems *obsessed* with digging," Rosa said, even faster. "Not in a helpful way, not on our own projects or repairs—but alone. Digging these long winding tunnels to random places, even if there aren't any gem deposits there, or any other obvious reasons to do it!"

Oh. Daisy's thoughts flashed back to the cave, to Filak leading her through the close narrow darkness—maybe through a tunnel he'd dug? While before her, Rosa looked even more agitated than before, rocking from side to side. As if there was even more, something even worse...

"And," Rosa continued, scrunching up her face, "when Filak first came here... he *reeked* of blood. Not his own, but— from other people. *Multiple* other people."

Blood. Not his own. Other people's. Multiple other people's.

Daisy couldn't stop staring at Rosa, as her heart blared even louder in her ears. Did Rosa mean—Filak had—*killed* people? Multiple people?

"Could you tell—who the people were?" Daisy croaked, her voice cracking. "Were they all—orcs?"

Rosa winced, and shook her head. "John-Ka said he could smell women, too," she whispered. "And one of the orcs' blood smelled like—Filak. Close enough to be a family member of some kind."

Oh, gods. That couldn't be possible. It couldn't. Right? Filak couldn't be a killer, especially not of his own family. He couldn't, he *couldn't*...

But how could Daisy possibly know such a thing? She still barely even knew Filak, of course she still couldn't trust him, why would she have ever thought otherwise...

Her blinking eyes darted down to that yellow ring, still glittering so bright and beautiful on her finger. The sight of it churning something dark and miserable in her gut, because how had she been so stupid, yet again...

"We've been trying to learn what happened up north, before Filak left," continued Rosa's strained voice. "But ever since he came here, even our best scouts haven't been able to find any sign of the Nor-ka-esh. Either they've gone deeper underground, or else..."

She didn't finish, but the words bloomed on their own through Daisy's thoughts, stark and sickening.

Or else... they're dead.

Daisy's shaky fingers were clutching at that ring, maybe about to pull it off, to throw it away—when something lurched close beside her, and gripped at her elbow. Julian, his eyes wide and reproachful as he glanced between Daisy and Rosa.

"Filak has not killed his kin," he said, his voice hoarse but firm. "He has *not*. If he had, why should he come here just after this, scenting thus? No. There is more to this."

Daisy swallowed and blinked at him, searching his face— but his gaze was intent on Rosa, who was frowning straight back toward him. "Then why hasn't he told *you* anything either, Julian?" she demanded. "He still hasn't, has he?"

Julian shook his head, his mouth tight and thin. "No, he has not," he said. "He will not speak of it. But when I have asked, he looks and scents only of... pain. Grief."

Oh. Daisy's screeching thoughts whirled backwards, to all the times she'd caught that grief on Filak, too. When she'd left him behind in the tunnel, when he'd offered her that mate-price, when he hadn't wanted to eat...

And the prayers. The marking. The feel of his ribs under his skin, the weight of his jewel on her finger, his sun on her heart...

Daisy's heart pounded even louder, a dizzying endless din thundering against her ribs, shouting behind her eyes. She was supposed to be learning, forgetting, running, anything, please...

"Um," she said, choked. "I don't suppose there might be a latrine around here I could use? Just for a moment?"

Rosa's expression flashed into regret, or maybe even guilt—but she rapidly nodded, and waved Daisy toward the door, pointing toward a room just down the corridor. And soon Daisy was staggering alone toward it, while the questions screamed louder and faster through her skull.

Who *was* Filak? What had he done? Had he killed people? Multiple people? *Why*? And why was he digging? Why was he hoarding coin? Why had he been propositioning other women, all that time? What had he wanted from them? What did he want from Daisy?

Daisy shook her head as she shoved through the curtained door, into the latrine. Barely noticing its smooth lamplit floors and walls, or the washbasin, the looking-glass, the covered privy...

Because there, standing in the middle of the room...

Filak was waiting.

26

Filak had been waiting for Daisy. In the *latrine*.

Daisy gaped at him for a long, frozen instant, and then whirled around to stare at the closed curtain behind her. "H-how?" she stammered, over the thudding in her ears. "Where—where the hell did you *come* from?"

But Filak was already striding toward her, his head cocking sideways, his clawed hand reaching toward her face. "Daisy," he murmured. "*Hvað er að?*"

Daisy's heart was still clamouring, and she recoiled backwards, away from his outstretched hand. "You," she croaked. "Did you—did you *kill* someone? Someone you knew?"

Filak's head tilted further, and his brow furrowed. Looking confused, uncertain, because of course he couldn't understand her—and a harsh, frustrated noise escaped Daisy's throat as she wildly waved down the corridor. "Rosa said," she began, frantically grasping for the few Aelakesh words she'd learned that day. "*Rosa sagði*—your Ka-esh kin—your *fólk*—that you—"

There was no word for it, nothing, and finally Daisy made a fist with her hand, and stabbed it toward Filak's heart, toward his own marked sun. As if she was holding a dagger, and gouging it into him again and again. Killing him.

Filak stared down at Daisy's stabbing hand for a long, unmoving instant—and when he glanced up again, his eyes were wide, his face paler than before. "*Hvað?*" he asked. "*Sagði Rosa þetta?*"

He was asking if Rosa had said that, surely—and Daisy swallowed, and jerked an erratic shrug, another wild wave of her hand. "Rosa doesn't know!" she countered, stupidly, because of course Filak couldn't understand that, either. "Apparently no one knows, not even Julian! And how the hell am I supposed to know, either, when we still can't even *talk* to each other!"

Filak's head tilted even more, as distinct frustration flashed across his eyes. "*Daisy,*" he said, almost reproachfully. "*Rosa veit ekkert. Þú getur trúað mér.*"

As he'd said Rosa's name, his hand had slashed sideways, saying *no, no Rosa. Rosa doesn't know*, perhaps. *Do not listen to her.*

And gods, Daisy wanted to believe it. So stupid, so ridiculous, standing here unmoving as Filak eased closer, his gaze flinty on her face. "*Róleg, sólin mín,*" he said, quieter. "*Treystu mér.*"

Róleg meant peace, Daisy vaguely recalled, and she shuddered out a slow, unsteady breath as Filak's hand rose again, settling warm against her cheek. And though she flinched beneath it, she didn't move, didn't run away. *Peace, my sun.*

"And the other women, too," Daisy blurted out. "Have you really been propositioning every single woman you met? For an entire *year*? Looking for another"—she waved her still-shaky hand at the mountain around them—"another mate? Another *sálufélagi?*"

Sálufélagi had been another word from the book, and Filak's head tilted again, his fingers spreading wider against her face. "*Ég vil sálufélaga,*" he said, as his eyes held to hers. "*Ég vil þig, Daisy. Daisy mín. Sólin mín.* You."

You. Yet another word they'd both learned that day, and the common-tongue again sounded flat and stilted on Filak's mouth. But his eyes were still hard and certain, his sharp thumb now stroking at her cheek. "You, *Daisy mín,*" he said, lower. "*Sólin mín.*"

His other hand slipped down to Daisy's heart, spreading wide against that sun he'd drawn on her skin—and brushing against her breast through her dress, too. And curse her, because Daisy's breath should not—*not*—have caught like that. She did not want that, she did not want him, not now, not after everything...

But Filak's dark lashes lowered, his hand purposefully slipping downwards, curving brazen and proprietary over her breast. Touching her, caressing her, so warm and certain and reassuring, and Daisy should be shoving him away, demanding he explain and tell her the truth—

And not—this. Not standing here, breathing hard, as Filak stepped even closer, and ducked his face into the crook of her shoulder. "*Róleg, Daisy mín,*" he murmured, and oh, she could feel his soft lips, kissing at her skin, at that damned metal *kraga* still around her throat. "*Þú ert sálufélagi minn. Stjarnan mín. Sólin mín.*"

You are my mate, it meant. *My star. My sun.*

Daisy shuddered all over, but oh, the feel of his steady safe hands, still stroking and caressing, even as they began purposefully guiding her backwards. Toward the wall behind her, its stone hard and cool against her back, Filak's tall warm body blocking her in, pinning her close. As his kisses to her neck sharpened, deepened, his teeth gently scraping...

"*Filak,*" Daisy choked, grimacing over his shoulder. "This was already bad enough, but now you could be a—a *murderer.*"

But Filak only made a low rumbling growl against her

throat, his teeth nipping a little sharper. And Daisy gasped, shuddering again, arching into his hand caressing her waist, her hip, her arse...

"You could have *killed* people," she gritted out. "Your own family! And then you left and came here, reeking of their *blood!*"

But Filak's growl sounded distinctly displeased this time, his claw-tipped hand tightening against her arse. "Daisy," he murmured, muffled into her throat. "*Róleg. Nóg um þetta.*"

The sound from Daisy's mouth might have been a groan, or a curse. "Or an—an extortioner!" she continued, high-pitched. "Or a thief! Or a—a philanderer! You could have already done this to dozens of women, to all those women you were propositioning, all that time. You could be just another lying cheat, just like Lew!"

And surely Filak recognized Lew's name, at least, because his head snapped up and back, his eyes narrowing sharply on hers. "*Nei, Daisy,*" he said, low and commanding. "*Nei Lew. Nei.*"

No Lew, it meant. *No.*

But it was something, something, and maybe Daisy needed to push it, needed to hear it. Needed to know, to learn, for herself...

"Just like Lew," Daisy snapped, harder than before, jabbing her finger into Filak's bony chest. "Lying to me. Keeping huge deadly secrets from me. And acting as though I'm something special to you, as though I'm your *sól,* your *sálufélagi*"—she gulped for air—"when in truth, the offer is apparently open to any woman who wanders across your path! *Just—like—Lew!*"

Filak's expression darkened as she spoke, his brow deeply furrowing. And in a sudden movement, his hands snatched away from her, and instead yanked at—his trousers. Tugging them downwards with a swift, impatient jerk, and releasing—

That. His thick, bobbing cock.

Damn. It was just as impossible as last time Daisy had seen it, covered all over with those same curling black marks, its hood painted a full, inky black. And from within it, the pearly white was already seeping, hanging from his cleft in a glossy, lengthening string...

But—wait. There. Something—new. Those twining black lines on his shaft had been there before, yes, but now, in the midst of them, was... a *sun.* With multiple new lines radiating out from it, painted with what almost looked like fresh wet ink. And the lines didn't end with Filak's shaft, but instead spiralled up and out over his lean hips and his hollow belly—and even down over his swollen bollocks, too. As if the sun was... growing. Spreading.

Daisy stared at it for an instant too long, her body unmoving, her breath choked off in her throat. Gods, it was a sight, it was bizarre, it was absurd, it was utterly ludicrous—

And it was—hers. Her mark, her prayer, her sun, radiating out all over Filak's groin, all over his swollen leaking cock.

Hers. *Sólin mín.*

Daisy swallowed, still staring, and suddenly there was the strangest, most overpowering urge to—draw it. To put this to paper, to keep it, to remember it forever, because it was—it was art. It was art, it was shocking and surreal and—and absolutely, utterly stunning. *Hers.*

Daisy's face felt far too hot, suddenly, her mouth opening and closing—and when her gaze snapped back upwards, Filak's eyes were hooded and glittering on hers. "For you, *sólin mín,*" he said, husky, as his hand dropped downwards, and blatantly traced a claw over his new sun. "*Filak og Daisy. Sálufélagar. Ach?*"

Daisy's head twitched, maybe shaking, maybe saying no, she didn't believe him, she couldn't—they still weren't *mates,* were they? But in return Filak's eyes flashed, his hand snapping up to grip her chin, tipping her face toward him. Wanting her to say it, but she couldn't, she couldn't trust him, he could be a lying cheating *murderer*...

A low growl burned from Filak's throat, his head tilting back in obvious frustration—and in a sharp, sudden movement, he shoved Daisy—downwards. Down onto her knees, here, trapped between him and the stone wall, in a gods-damned *latrine*.

But Daisy... didn't fight it. Didn't even try. Just blinked at that shocking sight of his cock now bobbing before her eyes, marked and swollen and leaking. *Hers.*

"Ach?" Filak demanded, with a light little slap of his hand to Daisy's hot cheek—and her gasp escaped on its own, her lashes fluttering as she blinked up toward his hard watching eyes. Because maybe she wanted to see this, maybe she'd wanted him to show her, help her to see, to learn...

"*Þú ert mín, Daisy,*" came Filak's clipped, unrepentant voice. "*Filak og Daisy. Daisy og Filak. Sálufélagar.* Ach?"

And as if to prove his point, he even swiped for Daisy's hand, drawing it up into his clawed fingers. Showing them both that beautiful yellow ring, still sparkling on her finger, betraying her. Maybe even saying... yes.

But Daisy wasn't saying it, or was she? Just kneeling like this before him, waiting, needing. Needing to learn, to know, to see what he would do next.

"Ach?" he demanded, with another light, thrilling slap to her cheek, followed by a gentle stroke of his fingers against his new black-painted sun. "*Þú ert mín, Daisy. Sólin mín.*"

You are mine, Daisy. My sun.

"*Mín,*" he insisted, a low hungry hiss in his throat, as he spread his hand before Daisy's eyes, showed her the black ink now smudged onto his pale fingertips. Showing her that it was fresh, it was new, it was *hers*. And—Daisy's tongue brushed her lips—the ink was also safe, right? Made from fruit, Julian had said...

And when Daisy still didn't move, Filak's hand slid to her mouth, and tugged her lips apart. Opening her up for him, oh gods, making his intent very clear. Giving her every opportunity to say no, to shove him away, to run, to escape him, to forget.

But instead, Daisy just... stayed there. Stayed there, kneeling, gasping, waiting, saying... yes. Yes, yes, *gods* yes, even as Filak opened her mouth wider, shifted his hips forward...

And then he slid himself inside. Slow, brazen, utterly calm, as if he had every right to put his cock in her mouth. Every right to fill her, to occupy her, to flood all her screeching senses with his marked sliding skin, his thick vibrating heft. And most shocking of all, his impossibly stunning sweetness, oozing out from inside him, painting itself over her tongue...

Daisy choked, betrayed a low, shaky moan—and then she was lost, utterly defeated, sucking hard and desperate against him. Drawing more of that decadent sweetness out from him, while he hissed a groan, and shuddered even fuller between her lips. His clawed hands lightly skittering against her hair, because he liked it, he wanted it, he wanted *her*. Only her.

And she wanted him, wanted this, so much it was a fierce blazing frenzy, whipping her forward. Sucking him deeper, harder, feeling him swell and spurt out more in return. Speaking to her, speaking this one clear language they both knew, and Daisy moaned again, her fluttering eyes briefly finding Filak's face. And then holding, catching, because oh, that look in his eyes, that vicious glittering triumph, his mouth curling up, his claws sinking deeper into her hair.

"*Mín*," he breathed, hot and menacing. "*Sjúgðu á mér typpið, sólin mín.*"

With that, he held Daisy's head firm and still as he slowly slid himself out, until his oozing blackened crown was just kissing at her lips—and then, with a deep, satisfied growl, he sank himself back inside. Faster this time, smoother, again as if he had every right to fill her mouth with him, to bury himself snug and shuddering against her convulsing throat.

But he did, he *did*, even when he began moving harder and faster, plundering her with swift, decisive purpose. Plunging deeper and deeper, until Daisy almost gagged on it—but then he drew backwards again, until he'd tugged himself free with a loud, obscene pop. So he could instead prod and paint his seeping black tip against her lips, watching her desperately slurp and lick and suckle at him, and even kiss at that beautiful new sun—*her* sun—on his skin.

And he liked that, oh gods, the wicked satisfaction blazing through his eyes as he smeared himself back and forth on her mouth—and then he plunged into her throat again. Holding himself deep with his firm, unyielding hands on her head, his claws scraping against her scalp, as he murmured low, fluent, silken words she couldn't understand.

It was ludicrous, outrageous, this appalling orc making himself utterly at home in her mouth, using her, ravaging her. Maybe even trapping her again, holding her here on her knees with his hard invading flesh, his sharp deadly claws...

But it didn't matter. None of it mattered. Only the frenzy and the craving, the wild screaming need for it. Needing Filak's commands, his certainty, his control. And his approval, too, maybe even his tenderness, that gentle scrape of his claws, the husky softness in his voice as he spoke. All at such bizarre, compelling odds with the greedy, shameless way he kept using her mouth, plunging into her throat, making her his, his, his...

"*Gott, sólin mín,*" he breathed, as his head arched back, his teeth bared, his eyes half-lidded and blazing. "*Þú ert svo falleg, svo þröng, ach—*"

His voice broke, his whole body jolting—and with a shout, he bore down, and burst out into Daisy's throat. Spewing out spurt after spurt of that succulent sweetness, hot and fervid and gushing, so thick it flooded her mouth, spilled out her lips. But it tasted so good, so fucking *good*, and she desperately gulped to swallow, as her own shaky hand slid to her groin, ground against it once, twice—

And then her own release shot through her, too. Sharp and bright and burning, everything, oh gods, *everything*—

It took all her focus to stay upright, to cling to it, to ride the crashing, careening waves of it. To feel the steady certainty of Filak's hands, stroking her again, trembling just a little against her hair. And he was speaking again, too, hushed, rushed, breathless words she still couldn't understand, but they still made perfect, exquisite sense as they dropped through her thoughts. Like magic, like a soft, shimmering dream.

Good, Daisy. Good, my sun. You are so pretty, so sweet, you are mine, mine, mine—

But it was that, perhaps, that finally flickered into Daisy's awareness. His. *His.* As if this was settled again, now, now that she—she'd done this. She'd eagerly knelt and sucked him, in a *latrine.*

Because—because why? Because Filak had wanted it? Because he hadn't actually answered a single one of Daisy's questions, had he? She still knew nothing about his past, his family, what he'd done, or why... right? Was she really that desperate, *foolish*, oh gods, oh gods...

And even as she shoved Filak away, away, it was too late. Not just for her own stupidity, but for—for—

"Filak!" yelped a voice, far too loud and shrill and familiar. "What the hell?"

And when Daisy wrenched to look toward it, it was—Rosa. Rosa, standing in the curtained doorway—and now Julian appeared over Rosa's shoulder, too. Both of them looking shocked and chagrined and maybe even furious.

They'd seen—*everything*.

27

The humiliation felt like a hammer, smashing Daisy straight in her hot, sweaty face.

They had seen—everything. *Everything.*

And gods damn it, they were still seeing it. Daisy here on her knees in a latrine, with Filak's wetness still smeared all over her lips—and Filak's half-hard cock still hovering before her face, and seeping a glossy string of white toward the floor.

For a horrible, crushing moment, no one moved, and Daisy fought back the sudden, overwhelming urge to weep—when Filak lurched to stand before her, half-blocking her from Rosa and Julian's view. "*Hvað er þetta?*" he snarled at them. "*Af hverju ertu hér?*"

Rosa's mouth opened and closed, while Julian shot a reproachful look sideways toward her. "I could have told you, Rosa!" he hissed, before switching into Aelakesh, and speaking rapidly to Filak. Whose mouth pursed as he listened, his eyes narrowing on Rosa's face.

"Look, I'm sorry!" Rosa cut in, as her hands swiftly signed toward Filak. "I was just worried about Daisy, and wanted to make sure she was all right! And"—she shifted her glare to

Julian—"I *did* ask you, and you were too busy mooning over Rurik's letters to hear me!"

Julian's face instantly flushed, but he glared back at Rosa, his bottom lip jutting out. While Filak began snarling something back toward both of them, not even seeming to notice that his trousers were still sagging around his hips, and his marked, softened wet cock was still fully on display, still dangling a long string of white toward the floor.

Too late, Daisy dragged her gaze away, and shoved herself up onto her shaky feet, wiping both hands at her hot, sweaty face. The shame still felt like a boiling, bubbling thing, festering in her belly, but at least none of them were looking at her now, witnessing her weakness, her stupidity. And instead, Rosa and Filak had escalated to shouting at each other in Aelakesh, their hands wildly flailing in the air, while Julian blinked unhappily between them.

Daisy watched for another endless, dangling moment, caught in the sheer fury blazing in Filak's eyes, the way his long talons seemed to lengthen, stabbing toward Rosa's slim, gold-encircled throat. Making him look like just the kind of orc who *would* kill someone, anyone, even his closest kin— and then trap them all underground, and leave. Run off somewhere else, where he could amass a fortune, and then try to start it all over again, deep in some isolated tunnel, with the first woman stupid enough to agree...

The fear had begun shimmering with the shame, and Daisy swallowed hard, edging toward the door—when all three of them whirled around to look at her. Julian's eyes shifting with concern, Rosa's with regret, and Filak's with something Daisy couldn't at all read. And she stared at him as she sidled away further, clutching at the wall behind her. *Foolish, dangerous...*

"Gods, Daisy, I'm so sorry about all this," Rosa said in a rush, rubbing her hand at her eyes. "I shouldn't have barged in on you like that. And I certainly shouldn't be losing my temper like this, either. I should know better by now than to let Filak—"

She snapped her mouth shut, wincing, and took a deep breath. "Would you prefer we leave you and Filak for now, then?" she asked, searching Daisy's eyes. "Or would you rather be alone for a while? Or we could continue our tour, or go for a meal? Whatever you like."

She looked genuinely contrite, and behind her Julian nodded, the regret twisting on his mouth, too. "Aught you wish for, sister," he added. "I ken Filak should wish for this, too."

But Daisy's glance at Filak still found him staring at her, his eyes blank hollows in his shadowed face. The sight enough to send the fear simmering again, and suddenly she couldn't bear the thought of being alone with him, or alone by herself, either. Because he was sure to reappear at any moment, ready to draw her into his thrall, to put her on her knees, to refuse to answer any of her questions...

Daisy took a ragged breath, and shook her head. "Um," she began. "Maybe we could continue—the tour? Just—with you two?"

She bobbed her head at Rosa and Julian, and after a brief exchanged glance, they both nodded. "Of course," Rosa said firmly. "We'd be very happy to, wouldn't we, Julian?"

Julian nodded again, even as his hands swiftly signed something toward Filak. Something that had Filak's head tilting sideways, his eyes glittering and intent on Daisy's face. And she couldn't look away, couldn't, even when he came a step closer, and the fear spiked sharper into her throat.

"Daisy," he murmured, hushed, maybe even hurt—but she shook her head, and clutched tighter at the cold wall behind her. No. No. *Foolish and immature behaviour, appallingly unscientific, stupid...*

Julian murmured something under his breath toward Filak, and finally Filak grimaced, jerked a sharp nod, and tucked himself back into his trousers. "*Fyrirgefðu mér, sólin mín*," he told Daisy, his voice hoarse. "*Takk fyrir.*"

Takk fyrir. That was another phrase from the book, and it meant—*thank you*. Right? He was—thanking her?

But he'd already spun and strode out the latrine's door, leaving the curtain fluttering behind him. While Daisy dragged in deep breaths, and Rosa flashed her a smile that didn't at all reach her eyes.

"Well, then," Rosa said, a little too brightly. "Let's keep going, shall we? You haven't seen the Ash-Kai wing yet, have you? And the schoolroom? Or the Bautul garden?"

Despite the miserable mess still coiling in her gut, Daisy slightly straightened at the word *garden*, and blinked at Rosa's face. "There's a garden?" she echoed dully. "Here?"

Rosa eagerly nodded, and beamed back with palpable relief. "Yes, and it's lovely!" she said, as she excitedly waved Daisy toward the curtain. "I'm sure you'll find plenty to draw there, and in the Ash-Kai wing too, and—"

"*Wait*," cut in Julian's voice, sharp and urgent—and when Daisy and Rosa both twisted to look at him, he was gesturing toward—Daisy's face? "But first, mayhap, Daisy might wish to..."

His mouth contorted, and he flapped his hand toward the small looking-glass over the latrine's washbasin. Clearly wanting Daisy to... go toward it. To look into it.

Daisy's alarm spiked again, but she nodded, and lurched over toward the looking-glass. And blinking at her familiar face in the lamplight, she found...

Oh. Oh, *gods*. It was Filak's *ink*. Filak's black ink, now painted dark and brazen across her lips. Announcing to all the world what she'd just done with him.

Daisy stared at it for a long, dreadful moment, her heartbeat kicking ominously against her ribs—and with a sudden desperate movement, she plunged her hand into the washbasin, and began scrubbing at her mouth. But it was only slightly working, oh gods, fading the darkest black ink into a deep pinkish-grey, oh gods, oh gods, *no*—

"Er, perhaps a washcloth?" came Rosa's bracing voice, as she pressed something into Daisy's hand. "And some soap?"

Daisy frantically obliged, almost clawing at the soap Rosa handed over, too. But even her harshest scrubbing only faded the ink a little more, while also flooding her mouth with the awful bitter taste of soap, made all the worse against the distinct flavour of Filak's lingering sweetness.

"You know, I really rather like it," came Rosa's voice, finally, into the ongoing sounds of Daisy's scrubbing. "It looks dramatic, don't you think? And very neatly applied, too. Almost as if you did it on purpose."

On purpose. Daisy froze in place, staring at her stained mouth in the looking-glass, as her thoughts ripped backwards to Filak rubbing himself against her lips. Painting her with him, slow and deliberate, while the triumph flashed through his eyes.

Daisy didn't miss Julian's grimace in the looking-glass, or the quelling look he shot toward Rosa. And oh fuck, it meant Filak had done it on purpose, he *had*—because that ink all over him *had* been fresh, hadn't it? And why hadn't Daisy considered that, why hadn't it even slightly occurred to her?

Rosa cursed under her breath, her eyes widening on Daisy's face. "Gods damn him, again," she hissed. "He didn't warn you it was fresh?"

But Daisy froze again, and her face visibly blanched in the looking-glass. Because curse it, Filak *had* warned her, hadn't he? He'd touched that new sun on his shaft, and then he'd shown her the ink on his fingers. And then...

Daisy groaned aloud, squeezing her eyes shut, and she braced herself for Rosa and Julian's judgement, or maybe even their mockery. How had she been so stupid, so foolish, again...

"Well," came Rosa's bracing voice, along with a gentle

squeeze to Daisy's arm. "If it helps, sister, I really don't think anyone will wonder at it. Orcs can always smell such things anyway, so in truth, they'd probably wonder more if you *didn't* smell like Filak, or carry some remnants of his ink on you."

Really? Daisy darted a dubious glance toward Rosa in the looking-glass, but she looked surprisingly sincere, her eyes kind and reassuring. "Orcs *love* showing off their conquests," she continued. "It's very typical behaviour around here. I mean, just this morning I saw Gary—Gareth, you know—piercing his lover's nose, and dragging him by a chain down the corridor! And"—her smile went impish in the looking-glass—"I could spend *weeks* telling you the shocking things John-Ka does to me down in our clan's pleasure-room. A bit of ink on my mouth would be a *very* quiet evening, I assure you."

It was enough that Daisy turned to fully stare toward Rosa—Gareth was that friendly smith who'd helped free her from Filak's dungeon, right? And wasn't Rosa's stern mate John-Ka the leader of the whole Ka-esh clan? The one who went by the title of *Priest*?

"You have... a pleasure-room?" Daisy echoed, in the apparent absence of anything else to say. "And you... *use* it?"

She shot a brief, accusing look at Julian, because wait, yes, Filak had apparently chained *him* up too, right? But Julian's smile back was rather sheepish, and he absently rubbed his hand at his neck. At what looked like... fresh marks? From a *whip*, perhaps? And those certainly hadn't been there on him yesterday, had they?

"Yes, of course," Rosa replied, in a surprisingly matter-of-fact voice. "Many Ka-esh enjoy such pleasures, and our plea-sure-room—our *dýflissa*—offers a safe, supportive place to explore them. Seeking knowledge and self-awareness is a fundamental principle of our clan, and we want to encourage that as much as possible. Knowledge is just so powerful, don't you think?"

Oh. It tugged at something in Daisy's chest, and her gaze again flicked toward Julian, because it was just like what he'd told her before, wasn't it? *You must... see. You must learn, and know, for yourself.*

"Also, there's nothing like it for releasing tension, right, Julian?" Rosa blithely continued, with a teasing glance toward him. "I'm sure we'll see you down there tonight, huffing Rurik's letters, and begging the tallest, meanest orc you can find to pummel you senseless."

Julian scoffed and blushed, and elbowed Rosa in the side—but she only let out a peal of cheerful laughter in return, and soon he was chuckling, too. As if this really was something they did, something that was... *normal* for them. For the Ka-esh. For exploring. For... learning.

"So are you ready, then, sister?" Rosa asked, with an encouraging smile. "Come be a Ka-esh, and explore with us?"

Be a Ka-esh, and explore with us. It was enough to make Daisy raise her chin, and take a deep, bracing breath. She could do this. She would explore with them. She would keep seeing, and learning, for herself.

"Yes," she said, with only a slight quiver in her voice. "Let's go."

28

For the rest of the afternoon, Daisy fought to focus on seeing, and drawing, and learning.

It helped that no one seemed to notice Daisy's ink-stained lips, just as Rosa had predicted—or if they did notice, they didn't comment. Instead, they greeted Daisy with surprising kindness, and joined Rosa and Julian in showing her their astonishing home. Including everything from cozy common-rooms, to a huge round fighting-pit, to an outdoor bluff with a spectacular view of the sunlit forests and fields all around. And the schoolroom Rosa had mentioned was delightful too, full of cheerful artwork and excited children—and it was apparently run by Kesst's debonair elder brother Rathgarr, and his mate, a stylish Eziran woman named Geva.

"Oh, you're Daisy Carlyle!" Geva said, as a stunning smile flashed across her brown face. "I've read several of your books, and we even have one here, don't we, Rathgarr?"

This Rathgarr—who bore a striking resemblance to Kesst, despite being noticeably larger—smiled and strode off toward a shelf, and returned with a familiar book. It was the one Daisy and Lew had published two years before, about edible plants from the eastern coast, and Daisy flushed and stammered as Geva and Rathgarr flipped through it together with Rosa and Julian, pointing out their favourite sections and illustrations.

"You have a wonderful gift," Geva told Daisy, with another smile. "If you'd ever be interested in speaking to our students, or even leading a few classes, please just let us know. Anytime."

Daisy again flushed and waved it away—she liked children, but teaching an entire class of excitable students sounded almost worse than being locked in a dungeon. And thankfully she was rescued by Rosa, who gave her a knowing smile, and a reassuring squeeze to her arm. "No obligation, of course," she said cheerfully. "Now let's go to the garden next, shall we?"

Daisy shot a relieved smile back, and willingly accompanied Rosa and Julian back down through the mountain. Until they reached a clever stone door in the wall, and once Julian had shoved it open, he waved Daisy and Rosa out into the fresh cool air. And into—Daisy's breath caught—a huge, spectacular garden.

"Oh my gods," Daisy gasped, as she hugged her sketchbook to her chest, and slowly spun to drink in the sight. The garden was tucked up against the mountain's south side, fully enclosed by tall, sturdy-looking stone walls—and within the walls, it was bursting with green. Bright, riotous, beautiful green, flooding every available corner, sprawling out of beds and boughs and even massive boulders.

And all amidst the green, there were splashes of other colours, too. Orange marigolds, red raspberries, purple lavender, yellow coneflower and feverfew. And there—Daisy jolted to stillness—there was a scattering of tall, cheerful daisies, lining the edges of a meandering stone-paved path.

Daisy blinked down toward the daisies, as something pricked behind her eyes. Daisies, here, in Orc Mountain's garden. And surely this was where Filak had gotten the daisies he'd given her, right? And the rest of those flowers, too?

It was one question answered, out of what felt like a hundred, and Daisy couldn't stop staring at the daisies, while more of those questions suddenly crowded through her thoughts. Why had Filak come here? Why had he propositioned those women? What had happened with his kin, the coin, the blood...

"Welcome to our garden," cut in a low, pleasing voice, and when Daisy twitched to look, it was a tall, handsome orc with deep grey skin. "I am Kalfr of Clan Bautul, one of our gardeners here. Is there aught I can help you with?"

Daisy still felt too distracted to properly answer, but Rosa hopped up beside her, and flashed this Kalfr an approving smile. "Yes, Daisy's new," she said, "and therefore, we need a proper garden tour!"

Kalfr didn't seem at all disconcerted by this demand, and instead smiled and waved them forward into the garden. And with effort, Daisy shoved all those Filak questions away, and attempted to focus on the stunning sights around them. On the astonishing variety of herbs, grasses, shrubs, and fruits— and even the full-grown trees lining the walls, some with ladders and clever wooden platforms built across the upper branches.

It was all highly intriguing, and once Daisy had opened her sketchbook, it was wonderful to draw, too, tempting her back into the beauty and the art. And she even climbed up after Kalfr onto one of the treetop platforms, barely noticing when her already-shabby skirt ripped on a sharp branch. "This is *incredible*," she told him, as she flipped to yet another fresh page in her sketchbook. "The lighting up here, it's just..."

There were no words to describe it, but Kalfr only smiled indulgently, and waited as Daisy rapidly sketched the broad leafy canopy above them, and the dappled light of the late-afternoon sun streaming through it. It was a truly stunning sight, and though her sketch didn't even begin to convey its true beauty, she could still almost feel the magic glimmering within her pencil, unfurling snippets of light and wonder onto her page.

"You are a very skilled artist," came Kalfr's voice, once Daisy had finished her sketch. "I once knew a woman who drew her own designs for weaving, and I well saw how much time and talent and toil this takes. I could never even attempt such work, ach?"

Daisy gave a grateful smile back toward him, because most people tended to assume art was easy—or worse, that they would instantly become professional artists themselves, if only they'd bothered to try. "Weavers are absolute paragons of patience and skill," she told him. "Does your friend take commissions? I'd love to commission a tapestry of my own someday."

But at that, Kalfr's gaze dropped, and he twitched a shrug. "I am... not certain," he said thickly. "We have not spoken in many summers. And ach"—he cleared his throat—"if you are finished for now, I ken you have been sent a gift."

A gift? Daisy blinked down the ladder, toward where Rosa and Julian were still waiting below, now together with a vaguely familiar dark-haired woman holding a large basket. And when the woman grinned and waved up toward her, Daisy belatedly placed her as Gwyn, the kind midwife who'd previously visited her in the sickroom.

Daisy smiled and waved back, but couldn't help another uncertain look toward Kalfr, who was looking increasingly morose, and rubbing at his nose. But upon catching Daisy's gaze, he attempted a smile, and waved her toward the ladder—so she belatedly nodded, and clambered down to join the others.

"This is for you, Daisy," Gwyn told her, with a rueful

smile. "From Filak. He caught me inside, and demanded I bring it out to you at once."

She thrust out the basket toward Daisy, and good gods, it was another one of those food baskets, overflowing with fresh treats and drinks—and also with a few perfectly sharpened pencils, poking out the top. And Daisy stared at it all for a few breaths too long, and then shot a brief, searching glance back toward the mountain, and that firmly closed door in the stone.

"Why?" she stupidly asked, before she could catch it. "Why didn't Filak..."

Why didn't Filak bring it himself, she might well have asked, which was ridiculous, because she'd told him to go away, hadn't she? She'd told him she hadn't wanted him. And then he'd sent her this basket anyway, making sure she wouldn't go hungry without him.

And damn it, Daisy *was* hungry, her hand instinctively clutching to her stomach, while Gwyn only gave her a too-knowing smile. "Well, with the sun still up, it's not as though Filak could bring it out to you himself, right?" she replied, with a purposeful nod toward the setting sun. "He's been begging us to fetch you food and flowers from the moment you arrived."

Wait, what? Daisy gaped at Gwyn for another swaying, stuttering instant, while she frantically pieced that together. Filak *couldn't* bring her the basket himself? He'd been begging them to fetch food and flowers? Because of... the sun?

"What do you mean?" Daisy finally demanded, too sharp. "Are you saying... Filak can't go out into the sun? At all? *Ever*?"

Her swirling thoughts flashed backwards, back to that first time she'd seen Filak, the morning after the cave. That moment when she'd asked him to come away with her.

When he'd looked at the sunlight, and refused, again and again.

Nei. Nei, Daisy.

"No, many Ka-esh cannot bear the sun," came Julian's low voice, and when Daisy glanced toward him, she realized that he had a hand over his eyes too, blocking out the sunlight. "Of all five clans, we live the deepest underground, and have thus learnt to live without it—the Nor-ka-esh most of all. I have heard tales"—he grimaced—"of Nor-ka-esh orcs meeting their death, beneath a bright noon sun."

Meeting their *death*? The sun could *kill* them?! And Daisy couldn't stop blinking at Julian, at the visible sheen of sweat on his grey face, while her thoughts kept jamming with that memory of Filak. Filak standing trapped inside that cave, stiff and staring and helpless, as those rocks had skittered around his feet.

Filak had... *wanted* to say yes to Daisy, that morning. He'd wanted to go away with her. He *had*.

And after that, what had he done? He'd taken Daisy's hand. He'd pulled off Lew's ring. And then he'd crushed the ring into dust, and told her... *mine. Sólin mín.*

As if he'd been trying to tell her. To show her. To convey that she was still his, even if he couldn't go out into the sun with her. And then, that very night, he'd come back to her again in the dark, and caressed her, and again said... *Sólin mín. Daisy mín.*

"Well, why don't you all come join us at our firepit for supper?" cut in Gwyn's bracing voice. "You can enjoy your basket there, Daisy, and eat anything else you like, too. And if Filak would like to join us, we also have a sun shelter there, especially for our Ka-esh guests."

Oh. Daisy shot another brief, searching glance back toward the mountain, because she didn't actually want Filak to come, right? Didn't want him to walk out of that door, to share the basket with her, to draw her into his arms and call her *sólin mín*...

Daisy couldn't even seem to reply to Gwyn's invitation, but Rosa eagerly accepted on their behalf, while thoroughly ignoring the part about inviting Filak. And then she steered Daisy off toward the firepit, which indeed had a large canvas shade overhead, along with multiple new people already sitting beneath it.

Daisy hesitated at the sight, but Rosa kept drawing her forward, and then made a cheerful round of introductions. The tall smirking orc was Gwyn's mate Joarr, and the toddler climbing a nearby tree was Joarr and Gwyn's son. And the huge scarred orc was named Elgr, the handsome human man cooking over the fire was his mate Thomas, and they also had a son together, a sandy-haired human boy who might have been nine or ten years old.

It took all Daisy's concentration to greet them all, and try to remember their names. But they all seemed friendly enough, and when Daisy began unpacking her basket of food, and tentatively offered some around, Thomas gladly accepted some meat and milk, and deftly folded them into the delicious-smelling stir-fry he was cooking over the fire.

"So you're with Filak, then, Daisy?" he asked her with a smile, as he swept some of his fry-up onto a plate, and passed it over toward her. "He's been a great help out at our camp, hasn't he, *elskan*?"

He'd aimed his smile toward the huge scarred orc Elgr, and then handed him not one, not two, but *three* full plates of food. All of which this Elgr eagerly accepted, beaming fondly back toward Thomas as he balanced the plates on his crossed legs. "Ach, Filak has done much for the Skai at our camp," he replied, in a deep, gravelly voice. "Digging rooms and tunnels, finding gems. He has even begun to teach our younglings at our new school, when he is nearby. *Geology*, I ken it is called."

He said the word very carefully, casting a doting glance at his son beside him, and then took a large bite from his fork. While Daisy only stared back toward him, her heartbeat thumping oddly in her chest. Filak had—*helped* these people? Digging rooms and tunnels? Finding gems? Teaching children? *Geology*?!

A sudden vision of Lew tumbled into Daisy's thoughts, because what would he say? *Unbelievable, Daisy. Not only an orc, but another geologist? This is ridiculous and immature behaviour, appallingly unscientific, foolish...*

But somehow, Daisy took a deep breath, and shoved Lew's voice away. Filak had wanted to come away with her. Filak had wanted to reassure her. Filak had helped these people, he was a geologist, he taught *children*...

And clearly Rosa had also been unaware of that fact, because she'd instantly begun pelting Elgr with questions about Filak's qualifications, curriculum, and teaching methods, and demanding why he'd never once offered to teach at Orc Mountain's school. To which Elgr looked increasingly bewildered, and continued stuffing his face with food to avoid answering.

"So how did you and Filak first meet, Daisy?" Thomas broke in, loud enough to carry over Rosa's voice. "I know he doesn't go above ground much, and he usually has a hard time around humans, too."

It again took Daisy's overwhelmed brain a moment to follow, because—Filak usually had a hard time around humans? But then again, of course he would, with his black marks and his bare head, his tall gaunt body and his pale angular face. Gods, he would probably cause chaos every time he stepped out in public, and suddenly Daisy felt almost defensive on his behalf, or perhaps even sad.

"No, we first met in a cave, in the dark," she replied, with an attempt at a smile toward Thomas. "But then, afterwards"—her smile faltered, as her hand reflexively rose to the metal *kraga* around her neck, brushing over those familiar raised ridges in it—"he took me as his prisoner, and locked me in a *dungeon*."

And gods, why had she said that, now? Why would she bring up such a thing with a perfect stranger? Someone who clearly respected Filak, and trusted him enough to allow him around *children*? Around his own son?

But maybe that was exactly why she'd said it, because Thomas' sandy brows rose in genuine-seeming surprise—but then he gave her a regretful smile, and shook his head. "It's been too often the way, with this war still so fresh between us," he said. "I was Elgr's prisoner at first, too. But we just needed time to get to know each other. To learn the truth for ourselves."

Oh. The words pitched in Daisy's chest, shouted loud and strange in her ears. They'd just needed time to learn. To see for themselves.

It shouldn't have helped, but somehow Daisy smiled back at Thomas, small but grateful, as she finally began eating her delicious dinner. Everyone else seemed to be similarly engrossed, too—except, perhaps, for Kalfr. Who hadn't seemed to touch his plate, and was glancing between Elgr and Thomas with distinct misery in his dark eyes.

"You are lucky your mate forgave you for this," he told Elgr, jerking his head toward Thomas. "Many humans would not forget such wrongs, and we ought not to expect this of them."

Kalfr had glanced toward Daisy as he spoke, the sadness still glimmering in his eyes. The sight flashing Daisy's thoughts back to that moment up in the tree, when he'd spoken of his weaver friend. As if he had regrets, too.

"Ach, this is truth," Elgr replied, as his bulky arm reached for Thomas, and clasped him firmly against his side. "I thank Skai-kesh each day for my mate's kind heart. And his sweet scent. And his—"

But he was interrupted by a mushroom, bouncing off his broad nose—apparently thrown by Gwyn's slyly grinning mate Joarr. And with a loud scoff, Elgr carefully set down his three plates, and then launched himself straight across the fire toward Joarr, swinging for his face.

But it all seemed to be in good fun—both Joarr and Elgr were laughing, while Gwyn and the children were loudly cheering, and Kalfr was reluctantly grinning, too. And even Julian and Rosa were both watching with obvious interest, and finally Daisy smiled and flipped open her sketchbook, and began sketching the proceedings, too.

It was a surprisingly lovely way to spend an evening, full of food and greenery and laughter. And soon Rosa's mate John-Ka and their sons joined them too, adding their adorable giggles and squeals into the fray. All of it distracting enough that Daisy almost—almost—forgot about Filak, and the mess still quietly simmering at the back of her thoughts. All the questions, the mysteries, the women, the blood.

At least, until darkness had finally fallen, and they all said a cheerful round of farewells. And as Daisy headed back toward the mountain with their little group of Ka-esh, she felt...

A prickle, against the nape of her neck. Something... familiar.

Daisy whipped around, peering back into the darkness of the garden, but there was no one in sight. No one with pale skin and shadowed eyes, watching, waiting...

Daisy hugged her sketchbook tighter, and rushed into the mountain after the others. But the feeling kept lingering, even after Rosa had shut the stone door behind them, and all those questions had again begun bubbling louder, too. Who was Filak? Why was he here? And where had he been all day? Was he watching her? Waiting?

"Now, Daisy," Rosa said brightly, "you're no longer staying in the sickroom, right? Would you like to come with us to the Ka-esh wing, and we can find you a cozy room to sleep in for the night?"

Oh. Daisy's thoughts flicked longingly back to that sickroom, to the steady safe reassurance of Kesst and Efterar's presence in the darkness. But she didn't want to impose any further on them, either, or subject them to any more of Filak's havoc... right? And if she was alone in the Ka-esh wing, then...

"Right," Daisy belatedly replied. "That sounds lovely, thank you."

Rosa smiled back, though her eyes looked a little careful, now. "And did you still want to have that *kraga* removed, too?" she asked. "The Ka-esh forge is always running, and I'm sure it would only take a few moments."

Damn it, the *kraga*. Daisy's steps faltered, her heartbeat stuttering, as her hand fluttered up to that solid ring around her neck. Which had almost begun to feel... normal, somehow. Familiar. Maybe—maybe even *reassuring*. And the way Filak touched it, the way he kissed her neck against it, it was...

Daisy clamped down against that thought, because damn it, this was the stupidity again, wasn't it? She'd decided to observe Filak and learn about him, not to indefinitely keep wearing his permanent steel collar, the one he'd used to chain her up in a dungeon. She'd already given him far too much latitude with the ring, with the food baskets and flowers, with his hands and his mouth. With him pushing her down to her knees in a latrine, and covering her lips with his ink, so everyone could see...

"Right," Daisy said again, over the constriction in her throat. "Yes, let's go remove it. Of course."

In reply, Rosa patted her shoulder and made approving noises, and then said goodbye to John-Ka and her sons, promising to meet them soon for bed. But Daisy barely heard any of it over the irrational pounding in her skull, or the strange stinging behind her eyes. She would have Filak's collar removed, for good. That was the logical, reasonable thing to do. Right?

But her heart kept pounding louder the further they went, down into the dark, quiet Ka-esh wing. She hadn't actually seen the Ka-esh wing yet, and according to Rosa's enthusiastic explanations, it was the deepest area of Orc Mountain, dug far below the earth's surface, and it apparently contained a laboratory, a shrine, a room dedicated to drafting and mathematics, and even a well-stocked library. All of which would usually have thoroughly sparked Daisy's interest, but she couldn't seem to muster more than a few nods and smiles toward Rosa, and the occasional glance over her shoulder into the darkness.

"Here we go!" cut in Rosa's cheerful voice, as she guided Daisy into a bright, heated forge, with several masked smiths working around a large furnace. "And there's Gary, too!"

One of the masked orcs had already turned toward them, and when he pulled off his mask, Daisy instantly recognized him as Gareth, the kind orc who'd helped rescue her from the dungeon. And perhaps he'd been expecting them, because he immediately smiled and waved them toward the back of the forge, into a small adjoining room. This room was dimmer and quieter, and it seemed to be a showroom of some kind, with an impressive quantity of tools, weapons, and jewelry lining the stone walls.

But again, Daisy couldn't seem to make herself notice any of it. Especially once Gareth had reached toward the wall, and picked up what appeared to be a huge, wickedly sharp pair of *pliers*.

"Removing the *kraga* shall only take a moment," he told Daisy, his eyes warm and reassuring on hers. "And it is very safe, also."

But the drumbeat in Daisy's chest thudded even louder, and she couldn't stop her quick, instinctive step backwards.

An action that Gareth clearly didn't miss, based on the way he hesitated, and slightly lowered the pliers.

"Are you sure you wish to have the *kraga* removed, sister?" he asked, searching her face. "It is fully your choice."

Her choice. Daisy swallowed, and forced her mouth into a smile. "Yes, of course I want to remove it," she said, over the racing thunder in her ears. "Keeping it would be... foolish. Ridiculous."

She dragged her thoughts back to that terrifying moment in the dungeon, to when Filak had snapped the *kraga* around her neck, and used it to chain her to the wall. And how she'd yanked at it until she'd bled, how she'd wept and screamed, trapped and lost and alone...

"Your choice in this would not be *foolish*, sister," came Gareth's voice, quieter now. "The *kraga* is your jewel now, and it was made with much cost and care. I should know this, ach?"

His mouth betrayed a rueful twitch, because wait, down in that dungeon—he'd said he had forged that chain himself, right? And did that mean—had he forged the *kraga*, too?

But yes, curse it, surely he had. And here Daisy was, asking Gareth to destroy his own work. His own... art. And even the thought of it curdled uncomfortably in her gut, and her hand flitted up to the *kraga* again, stroking uneasily against it.

"I'm sorry, I forgot it was yours," she told him, as her fingers followed the curve of it, felt the familiar smoothness of the metal, the slight raised ridges within it. "It feels like lovely work."

Gareth blinked toward her, and cocked his head sideways. "Have you not," he began, "yet... *seen* it?"

Daisy's stomach churned again, and she shook her head, and attempted another false-feeling smile. "I suppose—I haven't," she said thickly. "I did see a looking-glass earlier today, but it was small, and I was distracted, and..."

Her voice trailed off, her mouth grimacing, but the look in Gareth's eyes was patient, even sympathetic. "We ought to have thought of this," he told her. "Now come, and see."

He waved toward a nearby wall, where a large looking-glass hung over a jewel-strewn counter. So Daisy took a deep, bracing breath, and then went over to the glass, and looked.

And—oh. *Oh.* The *kraga* was—*gold.* Not just metal, not just steel, like she had assumed. No, it was a smooth, elegant circle of bright burnished gold, gleaming against her skin.

And those raised ridges Daisy had felt in it—she swallowed, stepped closer—they were *jewels.* Square, sparkling orange jewels, exactly like—like the one in her ring. *Yellow topaz,* Julian had called it. The sign of Filak's kin.

Daisy's hand snapped up, her fingers spreading wide, setting her ring against the *kraga.* And yes, oh gods, the two pieces were a perfect match, the orange glittering against the gleaming gold, dancing bright and dazzling in the lamplight.

Sólin mín.

Daisy belatedly winced, thrust her hand downwards, away—but that still left her blinking at that beautiful *kraga,* and her own shocked face. Her face with its soft sooty lips, its flushed cheeks, its halo of orangey mussed-up hair—all of it a strange complement to the glittering gold jewel around her throat, and even those distinct new bite-marks in her skin. And for a bizarre, jolting instant, it occurred to her that she looked like... something she would draw. Someone who would make her look twice.

She looked like... an artist. *Sólin mín. Daisy mín.*

An odd tightness clutched in her throat, prickled at the back of her neck—but when she lurched around, it was still only Gareth, and Rosa, and Julian. Though Julian had been eyeing the door too, and he squared his shoulders as he turned back toward her. "The *kraga* is a lovely jewel, sister," he told her. "And it looks well upon you, also, for Filak had Gareth make it just to suit you, ach?"

He had? Daisy blinked at Julian, and then at Gareth, because that—that wasn't possible, was it? Gods, even the timing of it, it had only been a single day between their first meeting, and then Filak kidnapping her and chaining her up in the dungeon... right?

But Gareth's smile was wry and warm, now, and he nodded. "Filak rushed in here early in the morn, reeking of need," he told her, "and demanded I halt all my work at once, and make him jewels to best befit a sun."

A sun. Daisy couldn't stop staring at Gareth, and her heartbeat was now wildly galloping, swerving against her ribs. Filak had done that? He'd done that after she'd left him that morning, after he'd crushed her ring. He'd run here, and ordered new jewels for her. *Jewels to best befit a sun.*

"He also brought me a band from an old ring you wore," Gareth continued, with another wry smile. "One that once held a glass stone. He raged that anyone would dare make such a travesty, let alone offer it to you to wear, and swore he would never see you arrayed thus again."

What? Daisy's heartbeat spiked even higher, her mouth falling open. Lew's diamond ring had been... fake? Made of *glass*?!

"Are you sure?" Daisy blurted toward Gareth, before she could stop it. "That the ring was glass? And not—diamond?"

Gareth blinked, but then nodded, a little wary, now. "Ach, there were yet fragments upon it," he replied, as visible distaste curled on his mouth. "No true diamond would shatter thus, ach?"

Oh. Oh, gods curse her. Of course. Of course it hadn't been a diamond. Of course Lew hadn't bought her anything so expensive. And of course Daisy had hated it on first sight. She'd... seen it. She'd *known*.

And it also meant... she couldn't have sold the ring, after all. She couldn't have used it to run away. And that memory of Filak glaring down toward the ring with such obvious contempt, and then crushing it with one fierce snap of his claws, was shifting and flickering into something else. Something that felt almost like vindication. Like... *gratitude.*

For a long, hovering moment, no one spoke—but then Gareth cleared his throat, and nodded down toward his pliers. "But we can yet remove this *kraga*, sister, should you wish," he said. "And you could yet keep the pieces, or repurpose them for aught else, or sell them."

But even the thought sent a sudden, repulsed shudder up Daisy's spine, because she couldn't possibly break this stunning work of art into *pieces*, oh gods. Pieces that could be repurposed, *sold*, made to fit something else, or someone else.

"No," Daisy's voice croaked, and the word was a refuge, an absurd unthinkable relief. "No. It shouldn't be broken."

She didn't miss the distinct flicker of relief in Gareth's eyes, and perhaps in Julian's, too. Only Rosa still looked uncertain, her gaze darting from Daisy's neck, to her face, and back again. "You're sure, sister?" she carefully asked. "You're really under no obligation, either way."

But Daisy was clinging to it now, clutching at the bizarre relief still rushing through her breaths. "No, I'm sure," she said, and curse her, she meant it. No matter how foolish it was, how ridiculous, how unscientific and irrational. *You must learn and know for yourself.*

The certainty of that statement kept ringing as Daisy thanked Gareth for his help, and then followed Rosa and Julian back out into the dark, empty corridor. And though Rosa began showing Daisy various empty rooms as they passed—apparently all options for her to sleep in—she again only half-listened, too often glancing over her shoulder into the darkness.

Daisy mín. Sólin mín.

"Are your own rooms near here?" Daisy finally asked

Rosa, with a glance toward Julian. "Perhaps I could just stay somewhere near one of you?"

Rosa looked decidedly pleased by this, and swiftly ushered them further up the corridor, into an area so dark Daisy could scarcely make out the shapes of the adjoining doorways. But it turned out that there was a small empty room here, just down the hall from Rosa, and right next door to Julian, too. And as Julian ran off to fetch some fresh furs and bedding, Daisy did her best to thank Rosa for such a lovely and informative day, and for all her help and generosity.

"Oh, but it was my pleasure, sister," Rosa said, her voice slightly cracking, as she pulled Daisy into a quick, impulsive hug. "I've been the only Ka-esh woman in the mountain for these past four *years*, and I can't tell you how wonderful it's been to have you here! No one else has *ever* read all my publications, or shown so much interest in my communications work—let alone offering to *help*. And no matter what you decide about Filak"—Rosa blinked, and betrayed a sniff—"I really hope you'll stay."

Oh. It caught in Daisy's throat, tangled with a sensation much like longing, and her stammered answer felt too paltry, too foolish. Rosa couldn't really mean all that, and she couldn't truly want Daisy to—stay, right? Permanently? She was only supposed to be here until... until...

"How many days are left, again?" she asked, too abrupt, into the silence. "Until—Lew's attack?"

Something she couldn't quite read passed across Rosa's eyes, but then she nodded at Daisy, and squared her shoulders. "Two weeks exactly, as of today," she replied. "You'll at least stay until then, won't you?"

Stay, until then. Wait here, in Orc Mountain, for Lew's attack to come. For all that looming death, Lord Nash, Sybil, feeding belladonna to children...

It was again too much, yet more chaos in Daisy's

overwhelmed exhausted brain. And she was deeply, distantly grateful when Rosa didn't press the question, and instead waved over Daisy's shoulder, toward where Julian was coming back up the corridor, now heavily laden with furs.

Between the three of them, it didn't take long to set up the room, and once it was finished, Daisy again found herself struck to stillness, too overcome to speak. The room was small, yes, but it also felt comfortable and cozy, with a large fur-covered bed, a simple wooden chair, and a tall candle-stick burning on a small table beside the bed. A table that now held her sketchbook and pencils, too.

"You'll be perfectly safe here," Rosa said firmly, "but just call for help if you need us. Anytime, about anything at all."

Daisy fervently smiled and nodded, and after another round of heartfelt thanks and farewells, she was left alone in her new room, in the dark, with all the day's overwhelming turmoil still jangling through her skull. Everything she'd learned, everything she'd seen, all the unanswered ques-tions, everything that still waited ahead. The *kraga*, the ring, the sun, the belladonna, two weeks...

It took all her remaining focus to strip down to her shift, and slide into her new bed between the soft furs. Her thoughts whirling even faster as she reached to snuff the candle, plunging the room into utter darkness. What was she supposed to do next, what did she want, she needed to see for herself...

And then—then—she felt it. The presence in the room. The movement in the air. The prickle of eyes, stroking across her skin. Closer, and closer, until...

A warm, powerful, familiar body sank down over her, and crushed her heavy to the bed.

Filak.

And in the already-raging chaos of Daisy's thoughts, there were more shouts, more stark jangling truths. Filak had still kidnapped her. He'd locked her in a dungeon. He'd still pushed her to her knees in a latrine, and painted his ink on her lips. He'd still trapped her with a permanent collar she couldn't bear to destroy...

But he'd also made the jewels just for her. He'd brought her food and flowers. He'd warned her about the ink. He'd wanted to follow her into the sun. He'd crushed Lew's ring, just like he would crush Lew, too...

You must learn, and know, for yourself.

And with a deep, shaky breath, Daisy clutched for Filak's face, drew him close, and kissed him.

29

Filak's groan into Daisy's mouth was harsh, hungry, relieved. His hot mouth crushing hers, his tongue thrusting between her lips, as his hips ground against her over the fur, and his sharp claws stroked at her gold-encircled throat.

Sólin mín.

He didn't say it, but Daisy could feel it in the urgency of his body, the craving of his kiss. And she was returning it with just as much desperation, her hips arching up to meet his, her hands stroking swift and greedy against his warm skin. Touching him, caressing over the sharp angles of his face, the elegant taper of his pointed ears, the faint stubble on his bare scalp. The long line of his neck, the silken skin of his shoulders, the way his muscles flexed as he moved, as he ravaged her mouth in the dark.

But it only whipped Daisy's hunger higher, careened her into a fierce irrational craving that trampled all the questions and hesitations beneath it. There was only this, only heat and fervour and magic, only gasping as Filak shifted his weight, and yanked away the fur between them. And then he yanked up Daisy's shift too, and pulled it off over her head with a distinct ripping sound, leaving her entirely naked beneath him—but it didn't matter, none of it mattered, only his warm bare body settling back down against hers, his heavy cock streaking wetness against her thigh. Suggesting he'd already been naked too, he'd *planned* to do this, oh gods, but Daisy still didn't care, and her hand even stroked down his long back, and gripped at his arse.

Filak's groan hitched ragged into her mouth, his body juddering over hers, and then—no, *no*—he drew backwards. Away. So sudden and disorienting that Daisy whimpered, groped for him again, fought to drag him back, please—

But that was a low, breathless chuckle above her, a brief caress of claws against her straining neck. "Stay, *sólin mín*," came his heated, husky voice, firing deep into her belly. "Peace."

Stay. Peace. More common-tongue words from Rosa's book, and Daisy shuddered all over, and obeyed. Staying, waiting, as she heard a faint clink of something—of wood, or glass?—and then felt Filak's hand slipping down her belly. Stroking warm and reverent, further and further, until it slipped between her thighs, and then guided them wide apart.

It left Daisy spread-eagled and fully bared on the bed, the cool air prickling against her skin. And even despite that protective cover of darkness, she again shivered all over, and fought the urge to hide her exposed, swollen-feeling crease, the way it was convulsing at nothing, needing to be filled...

But Filak wasn't filling it, was he? No, no, he was just... touching. And not stroking or caressing now, either, but instead making careful, purposeful movements with something pointed. With... his *claws*.

Daisy's distant shouting thoughts briefly broke through the maelstrom—he was using his claws on her, *there*, on her body's most sensitive, vulnerable places—but she somehow held herself still, waiting. Waiting, feeling, learning, because he was...

He was *drawing.*

Daisy shuddered again, her breath catching in her throat—and suddenly her full concentration was on this, on following those distinct strokes of Filak's claws. Just the same way he'd done that first night together, but this time, his strokes kept circling around her wet quivering heat, again and again, and then... radiating outwards.

He was drawing... a *sun. There.* A sun to match his own.

And wait, did that mean he was using *ink* on her again? He was marking her again?! And before Daisy could stop it, she groped in the dark for his other hand, for the one that wasn't touching her. Feeling down his forearm, his wrist, and finding... something solid, sitting in his palm. Something solid, and cool, and rounded, like a bowl, or a jar.

His ink.

Daisy stared blankly into the dark, up toward where Filak's face would be, and she could feel the distinct prickle of his eyes in return. Studying her, watching her response, as his claw moved to dip into the ink, and then brazenly stroked up her belly.

"*Sólin mín,*" came his voice, cooler and harder than before, almost like a challenge. "*Sálufélagi minn. Mín.*"

My sun. My mate. Mine.

And it was a challenge, or maybe even a test, just like what Rosa had accused him of with all those other women— but this test had Daisy split wide open in the dark, while he used his deadly claw to paint his ink between her legs. To again mark her as his own, in the most shockingly intimate of ways.

Daisy's thoughts were spinning now, reeling between the dungeon the latrine the blood, the flowers the sketchbook the sun. *It is a way to invoke the prayer, you must seek beauty and worth, jewels to best befit a sun...*

And instead of refusing, or raging, or running, like any rational person should have done, Daisy took a shaky breath, let it out. And then... she spread her legs even wider. Showing him more. Inviting him to do whatever he wanted with her, oh gods...

Filak's answering groan was low and raw, his claw skittering against her skin—and in a sudden movement, his body shifted over hers, and there was a distinct clink of glass against the table beside the bed. And then both his hands were here again, spreading warm and possessive against her thighs, pushing them even further apart. Opening her for... for...

A hiss of hot breath. A flutter against her coarse hair. And then, oh *fuck*—his *tongue*.

Daisy arched and cried out, staring wild and unseeing into the darkness—but yes, yes, it was Filak's tongue. Stroking slow and wet and purposeful up her spread crease, licking her, *tasting* her—and then plunging hot and deep.

Daisy shouted, because Filak's tongue was *inside* her, and it was *wondrous*. Long and sinuous and slithering, like a fat hungry snake seeking to burrow itself all the way inside, and Daisy writhed and convulsed against it, as another shocked shout rang through the room. And oh curse her, what if Rosa and Julian heard, would they come in again, would they walk in on Daisy freshly painted and spread-eagled on the bed, with Filak greedily feasting between her legs?!

But Filak only betrayed another satisfied laugh, rumbling deep into Daisy's very core—and then he plunged his tongue even deeper. This time hard enough that she could feel his sharp teeth, scraping against her sensitive swollen skin. More danger, more threat, something else she should be resisting or running from, but she only shouted again, and writhed and convulsed against it. Maybe even pressing further down onto it, wanting more of it, craving that perfect edge of pain threading through the pleasure. Gods, it was good, he was good, his tongue curling and stroking exactly where she wanted it—and then his sharp claws found her inner thigh, and scraped slow and deliberate against her skin.

Daisy writhed and shouted again, her head arching back, and oh, that was his other hand, in the same place on the other thigh. Scraping down in stunning, dizzying tandem now, surely hard enough to leave marks. But between his tongue and his teeth and his low vicious laugh, it only wrenched her closer, closer, please—

The ecstasy blazed and crashed, burning through her in a feral trammelling blast, breaking her apart. Smashing her into a thrashing, sputtering mess, even spurting hot fluid onto Filak's face, into his scraping gulping mouth. While the distant shame shouted and wailed, she hadn't done that in years, and what if he—what if he...

Kept licking. Tasting. Kissing. The sounds thick and sloppy now, rising loud and brazen and debauched between them, along with the distinct rumbling purr of his groan. As if... as if he'd wanted it. As if he'd planned for it. As if he'd coaxed it out of her, making it his.

And when he gave her one last, hungry lick, and then heaved himself upwards over her, Daisy was sprawled, wet, wide open, waiting. Needing it, desperate for it, as his straining cock found her slick open heat, and slammed itself fierce and deep inside.

There was no teasing or gentleness in it this time, only the raw hammering of his hips, the wet squelches of slapping skin, the frantic shouts from Daisy's mouth. The rhythm of his hard cock impaling her again and again, swiving and pumping her and using her, until—until—

He howled as he broke, as his body juddered and spasmed, and shot out harsh and furious inside. Flooding her with thick molten heat, rushing and pooling between them, and gushing out around his still-spurting cock. Painting them both in a surge of more hot fluid, pouring it out onto the fur, unfurling its musky sweet scent all through the room. His. *Hers.*

Daisy couldn't have said how long it lasted, or how long they stayed there afterwards, their wet spasming bodies still notched together, still clutching and quivering with the lingering pleasure. Feeling each other, learning each other, finding beauty and wonder in the darkness. And speaking, too, whispering back and forth in that one language they both knew.

And though there were no words in it, Daisy could almost feel the truth hovering behind it. She'd missed him, today. He'd missed her, too. He hadn't meant to upset her in the latrine. And she hadn't meant to accuse him of something he hadn't done, or compare him to Lew. He'd wanted to explain, but he'd been so unthinkably angry with Rosa, maybe even with all his kin, and he hadn't known how to find a way to tell Daisy what he meant.

And even this, tonight, just now—it had been part of it, too. Him again showing her, in the one way he had. Showing her she was his. Showing her they matched, they belonged. Placing his prayer on her skin, in her most intimate place. And then brazenly kissing it, licking it, as if...

Daisy's hand fluttered up, found his soft, still-wet mouth. His mouth that still felt a little sticky, too, tacky, the way drying ink might have felt...

The recognition flashed through her thoughts, widened her eyes on where his face would be—because he'd done to himself what he'd done to her. Painting her with that fresh ink, and then kissing her. Staining his lips. Showing the world what this was, again showing how they matched.

Sólin mín.

Daisy swallowed, hauled in a shaky breath—and with a lurch upwards, her lips found his. Kissing him again, oh gods, letting him put even more of that fresh ink on her mouth. And he did it, he wanted it, betraying a low, hoarse moan as his lips gently met hers, tasted hers, marked her again as his own...

When they finally drew apart again, Daisy felt trembly and strange all over, and increasingly cold and wet, too. But Filak's hand spread warm and reassuring against her face, and with a careful shift of movement, he sank down onto the fur beside her, and gathered her into his strong, capable arms. And then he pulled up the fur again, settling it heavy over them both, and fully ignoring the mess of sticky fluid still smeared all over them.

But the rest of it felt so warm, suddenly, so soft and cozy and safe, finally lying sated and boneless in her devil's arms in the dark. Just the way it was supposed to be, perhaps, and Daisy belatedly shoved aside that alarming thought, and burrowed closer into his side, into the sweet scent of his neck. Into that smooth steady caress of his hands, the brief kiss of his stained lips to her hair.

"*Sofðu, Daisy mín,*" he said, husky and soft, his meaning unfurling all too clear through Daisy's foggy thoughts. *Sleep, Daisy mine. Sleep.*

And on that strange, quiet certainty, Daisy finally closed her eyes, and slept.

30

When Daisy next blinked awake, she was still sprawled naked against Filak's warm body beneath the fur, with his strong arms still wrapped tightly around her.

It was the loveliest feeling, despite the sensation of sticky dried wetness now spread across her groin and thighs, and Daisy let herself sink back into the contentment of it, slipping in and out of a relaxed, easy sleep. Filak had come to her. Filak had stayed with her. Filak had perhaps—perhaps?—apologized.

She only fully awoke again at a distinct sound from the door, and when she twisted to look, blinking in the light of the already-lit candle, it was Julian. Standing framed in the open doorway, and flashing a sheepish smile toward her in the bed.

"Good morning, sister," he said. "I only wished to see if you slept well? Or if there is aught either of you might need?"

His eyes flicked beyond Daisy, and when she followed his gaze, she found that Filak was awake, too. His shadowed eyes lazily searching Daisy's face, his mouth slightly quirking—

and then Daisy was caught staring at his mouth, oh gods. At where it was indeed smeared with black, far messier than her own lips had been, because last night he had... he had...

His stained mouth quirked a little higher, and then he spoke something to Julian in Aelakesh. And in return, Julian easily nodded and strode forward into the room, sinking himself down onto the wooden chair beside the bed.

"If you are not opposed, sister," he told Daisy, "Filak has asked me to come in and translate for you both, so you can speak together for a spell."

So they could speak? Truly? Daisy shoved up onto her elbow beneath the fur, and eagerly nodded as she glanced between Filak and Julian. "Yes, *please*," she replied. "That's a brilliant idea, thank you."

Julian smiled and waved it away, and then signed something toward Filak, the movements swift and graceful. And in return, Filak drew out his hand and signed back, as his other hand stroked reassuringly against Daisy's bare hip.

"Filak says... he will seek to answer any questions you have," Julian said, his brows rising with obvious surprise. "Aught that you wish, sister."

Really? Anything? Daisy blinked at Filak, searching his shadowed eyes, but his stained mouth looked thin, now, and he twitched a nod. Saying... yes. She could ask anything.

And gods, there were still so many questions, all suddenly churning and jostling at once. Questions about Filak, about this, about his past, his home, his people. And after an instant's consideration, Daisy plucked up the closest question, the one that had perhaps burrowed the deepest of all...

"Did you... did you really *kill* people?" she asked him, her voice cracking. "Before you came here? Your own family?"

She only distantly heard Julian repeating the question in Aelakesh, but she didn't miss how Filak's mouth went even tighter, his chest rising and falling against her. Hesitating, already, and Daisy grimaced and dropped her eyes, as something plummeted in her gut. Of course he hadn't really meant it, he didn't want to tell her the truth, and...

And then he began speaking in Aelakesh, his voice rushed and hollow, his body gone oddly rigid. But when Daisy glanced up again, his eyes were glittering and intent on hers, speaking of misery, of pain—and when she darted a glance sideways, Julian looked strangely pale too, his gaze locked on Filak's face.

"He says," Julian began, hoarse, once Filak had finished, "just before he left, there was a rebellion in the north. A coup. Against his father."

A rebellion. A coup. Against Filak's... father? But—why? How? By who?

But Filak was gesturing toward Julian again—maybe saying, *keep going*—and Julian cleared his throat, and met Daisy's eyes. "Filak's forefathers have long been leaders and builders amongst the Ka-esh," he explained. "Many ages past, after they helped to build this mountain, they next dug out a deep Ka-esh stronghold to the north of it. This was called the *Skýli*, and it was meant to bring orcs closer to the women they might mate, and offer women a home nearer to their kin. Many Ka-esh welcomed this, and the *Skýli* soon became a large settlement of its own. Until... the war."

The war. The war between orcs and men, he surely meant. And Daisy nodded, waiting, until Julian inhaled, and kept speaking. "When the war arose in earnest, several centuries past, the *Skýli* was oft attacked, and faced many deaths. Until finally"—Julian shot a brief glance toward Filak—"Filak's forefathers chose to abandon the *Skýli*, and led their loyal Ka-esh kin far to the north. There, they dug a new home even deeper underground, and sought to live in peace and safety. And they have done this, for many, many summers now, until..."

His voice trailed off, his eyes again searching Filak's face. But Filak was still staring at Daisy, his throat bobbing, and when he began speaking again, it was quieter and emptier, as though every word was pain. And there were so many words, so much pain, and Daisy could only blink uneasily back toward him, spreading her hand against his thin, clammy-feeling chest, waiting until he finally stopped.

"Filak says," continued Julian's voice, "that during his own father's rule in the north, the Nor-ka-esh faced many attacks from humans—most oft poisons and gases in their tunnels. These attacks killed and wounded many Ka-esh, and drove many more to the surface, where they were weakened and killed by the sunlight, or by waiting men."

Oh, gods. The poison attacks. Killing the Ka-esh, forcing them to the surface, out into the sun, destroying them. And no wonder Filak had reacted the way he had to Lew's horrible plans, no wonder he'd been so furious, so desperate.

"The Nor-ka-esh did not have the strength to stop these attacks," Julian's low voice added. "And despite their pleas to their fellow Ka-esh here at Orc Mountain for help, they heard no answer. So to keep his kin safe, Filak's father dug them further and deeper underground, until no human could reach them without aid."

Daisy's heart was skipping erratically in her chest, her eyes fixed on Filak's bleak face, on the strange glassiness in his eyes as Julian spoke again. "But this affected the Nor-ka-esh women most of all. They missed the sun, and struggled to breathe and sleep and birth healthy sons. Before this, the Nor-ka-esh orcs had most oft used the *sálugjald* to find women, in a trade that ought to have brought gain to both sides—but when the women stopped returning to the surface, new women also became too afraid to accept the orcs' offers. They already feared the orcs, but now they feared their own deaths, too."

Gods, Daisy could so easily picture it, bright and clear

behind her eyes. A leader desperately fighting to save his isolated kin from death, digging them ever deeper into a dungeon they couldn't escape. And of course women wouldn't want to bear that, Daisy knew all too well, but then...

"And Filak's father," Daisy ventured, still searching Filak's bleak eyes, "he didn't relent? He wouldn't... let the women out?"

But curse it, she *knew* Filak, she knew how stubborn he was, how determined. And even without ever meeting this father of his, she could already imagine how it had gone, how it would have only grown worse and worse. The leader clinging to what he believed to be the greater good, while the settlement dwindled and weakened and splintered apart beneath him.

"No, he—did not," came Julian's halting voice. "Filak says his father only became more set in his ways, and would listen to no one. Not even his mate, or his own son. Not even when his mate—Filak's mother, who had sworn to stay for life, due to her own *sálugjald*—also fell to sickness, and perished."

Oh. Oh, gods. Filak's own *mother* had died to this, almost as sure as if Filak's father had trapped her underground, and killed her. And Filak's eyes were still so shadowed and bleak, now gazing blankly beyond Daisy's head, off into the darkness.

"Filak was not yet fully grown then," Julian's voice continued, "but he deeply grieved his mother, and sought to sway his father. But his father would not hear him, either, and oft ordered Filak away to dig, alone. For like many of his forefathers, Filak carries the great gift of stone-seeing—and thus, he was the one best suited to build the clan's ever-rising *sálugjöld*, to keep drawing women toward them."

Daisy blinked at Filak again, her head tilting, her stomach twisting in her gut. So not only had he been cursed with a controlling tyrant for a father, but after his mother had died, he'd been sent away digging, alone? Ordered to save the clan through his great gift of... *stone-seeing*?

It dragged up yet another memory, another question, and Daisy groped for Filak's hand, turned it over, and held it up to the candlelight. Revealing the sight of his pale lined palm, with that distinctive black *eye* still inked into it. As if his hand could truly... *see*.

Daisy carefully brushed her finger against the eye, watched his hand slightly convulse in return, twitching his long black claws toward her. Almost like the kind of claws Daisy might have drawn on a clever little mole, digging tunnels through the dirt.

It again twisted in her belly, and she exhaled as she lowered Filak's hand, and dragged her gaze back to Julian. "So what happened next?" she asked, though she had to force the question out. "The others finally... rose up against Filak's father?"

Julian sighed and nodded, and rubbed his hand against his face. "Filak says he scented the blood through the tunnels, almost a league away," he replied. "And by the time he reached home again, his father and many others were dead, and the Nor-ka-esh lost to chaos and fear and grief. Some wished to escape, some wished to punish the killers, some wished to run here to the mountain. And some wished"—Julian grimaced—"to charge above ground in the night and steal women away to keep, whilst there was no one strong enough to prevent this."

Daisy swallowed, her eyes again caught on Filak's face. On that bleakness, the misery, the grief, all glimmering in his shadowed eyes. "So what did Filak do?" she whispered. "He tried to fix it, right?"

She waited, unblinking, as Julian relayed the question to Filak, and Filak gave a flat, rasping reply. But that grief still flickered in his eyes, and his hand was now gripping Daisy's hip, his claws pricking almost painfully into her skin.

"Ach, Filak sought to address this," came Julian's quiet reply. "He confined the orcs who wished to steal the women, and sought to come to terms with the rest. But there were no easy terms, most of all for the son of the orc who had caused such grief and pain. And by the end of this, the Nor-ka-esh chose to cast *him* out, also."

Oh. Filak's own people had thrown him out. Thrown him away from his home, and his dead father. And gods, that look on Filak's face, that loss, so strong Daisy could taste it, bitter and thick on her mouth.

"But Filak yet grieved this, and feared for his people's fate," Julian continued, even quieter. "Many of them had never before walked above ground, nor courted a woman— and humans find the Nor-ka-esh even more frightful than they find most orcs, ach? The Nor-ka-esh also had no means of gaining gems for their *sálugjöld* without him. So Filak agreed to leave, even as he vowed…"

Julian took a shaky breath, his eyes glinting on Filak's face. "He says he vowed to pay for his father's failings," he continued. "He vowed to yet provide their gems. He vowed to again find the *Skýli,* which had long ago been lost, so that they might again return home to it. And"—another deep breath—"he vowed to find a new way with women, also. He swore to show them that he could gain a good mate's fealty without any *sálugjald.* He swore to grant them this… hope. This light in the darkness."

Light in the darkness. It rang and echoed through the small room, even as Julian switched back into Aelakesh, and began speaking rapidly to Filak. Sounding almost angry, somehow, while Filak gazed straight back toward him without speaking, his jaw tight and set. Defending his decision to offer such things, surely. To keep working and fighting for the people who had cast him away.

"*Ég brást fólkinu mínu,*" Filak finally said, hard but steady, once Julian had stopped speaking. "*Ég verð að hjálpa þeim.*"

Julian threw up his hands, glaring at Filak's face, and snapped something else. And though Filak answered, it felt as though he was biting out every word, and his claws were digging even harder into Daisy's skin, perhaps strong enough to pierce it. But it didn't matter, nothing mattered but that look in his eyes, and somehow Daisy had begun caressing him, smoothing her hand up and down over his taut, rigid chest.

"Filak says," Julian finally translated, his voice stiff, "that he failed his kin, and thus he is bound to help them in this, and guard their names and their sins and their honour, until he can keep his word to them, and return home again. It seems"—he shot Filak another narrow look—"he has indeed been sending gems and coin north to them through a few of our Skai scouts, and has paid them to silence. And though he has not yet found the *Skýli*, he has begun sending word urging his kin to come here to the mountain, where they can be safe."

Safe. But that was another strike, a sudden kick in Daisy's gut, because perhaps even Orc Mountain wasn't safe, after all. Orc Mountain was now facing the exact same kind of attack that had driven Filak's people so far underground. And Filak—Filak really had thought *Daisy* had been part of that attack. He'd thought she'd tricked him, and used him to wreak the same kind of suffering that had splintered apart his people, and killed his own mother.

And truly, no wonder he'd reacted the way he had. No wonder he'd panicked, and kidnapped her, and locked her in that dungeon. Even though he'd already made her those beautiful jewels. Even though he'd surely thought he'd gained himself that mate, after all, that light in the darkness for his kin. *Sólin mín.*

Daisy felt almost stricken, still caught staring at Filak's

pale face, at the sharp bones of his skull beneath it. Because... was this why he was fasting, too? Why he was praying? Why he'd marked himself all over, and called Daisy his sun, his light, his hope...

"And is that why," Daisy whispered toward him, "you kept... *propositioning* all those other women, too?"

She barely heard Julian's translation of the question, but Filak grimaced, and jerked a nod. And then said something else, something else that made Julian groan, rubbing at his face.

"Filak says he first sought out a mate in earnest, and in secret," he told her, with a sigh. "With letters, and promises, and gifts. But no woman would see beyond his form or his face, so he then began freely asking, and offering other trades. Pleasure, or sustenance, or freedom. But no woman wanted any of this from him, either, and he began to believe that mayhap his kin had spoken truth, and it was only his jewels that could ever gain him a mate. Until..."

His voice faded, but his hand waving toward Daisy spoke all too clearly. And something spasmed in Daisy's throat, stung behind her eyes, and she blinked at Filak, watched her own trembling hand slide up to caress at his hard face. Again speaking to him, saying far too much, without speaking at all. Telling him, perhaps, *I like your face. I like your form. I found you, and you found me.*

Except.

"So why did you trap me the way you did, that first night?" Daisy whispered, toward Filak's glimmering eyes. "You did do it on purpose, right?"

She was very certain of that now, and she didn't look away as Julian translated her question. But then Filak's eyes slid closed, his mouth contorting, as if he couldn't bear to answer.

But Daisy kept watching, kept caressing his hard face, kept waiting. Seeking the truth for herself. Until finally Filak bit out an answer, curt and bitter, and she waited with her heart pounding until he finished, and Julian drew in a low, hissing breath.

"Filak says," came Julian's blank reply, "that he found you in—part of the *Skýli*."

Wait. Truly? That cave Daisy had been drawing that day, the one that had felt so intriguing, so intentional—*that* had been the place Filak had been seeking, all this time? The place he'd been digging to? His kin's ancient lost home?!

Daisy had found his *Skýli*?

Julian looked just as shocked as Daisy felt, and he again spoke to Filak in rapid, urgent Aelakesh. To which Filak nodded, brief and decisive, and then spoke back, surely saying...

Yes. Yes, he was sure it was the *Skýli*. And Daisy had been the one to find it.

"He says it was your scent that led him to it," Julian continued, hushed. "That it had somehow been—hidden, from orcs. And he mayhap never would have found it, without you."

Oh. Daisy's stomach flipped, her eyes again searching Filak's face, his set mouth, his glinting eyes. And his hand still on her hip had seized a little, as if clamping her closer to him, refusing to let her go.

Sólin mín.

But. There was still—the question. The question he hadn't yet answered. Had he?

"So why did you trap me in there, then?" Daisy insisted, holding Filak's eyes. "Surely you could have found it again on your own, after that?"

Julian didn't translate the question, but maybe he didn't need to, because Filak grimaced again, and said something else. Something he knew Daisy wouldn't like, and based on Julian's groan, it was something he didn't like, either. But

Daisy just kept waiting, because she needed to know, needed to learn, needed to see...

"Filak says he knew," Julian whispered. "When he saw you there, in his forefathers' long-lost home, he knew you were his mate. And he would do whatever it took to bind you to him, and keep you as his own. *Forever.*"

31

Daisy's breath hissed through her teeth, and her head whipped back and forth, as if attempting to knock those appalling words away.

He knew you were his mate. He would do whatever it took to bind you to him. Forever.

And it was... true. It was true, just like the rest of it was true, too. Yes, Filak had suffered for his father, and for his kin, and for the actions of the horrible humans who had attacked and harmed them. He'd still tried to do the honourable thing, to help his people, to support them, to find them a new home, to grant them that light in the darkness.

And, gods curse him, Filak had also trapped Daisy in that cave, on purpose. He'd been fully prepared to do whatever it took. To lie to her, to draw on her, to make all those false promises about the morning...

He was still dangerous. Deadly. A devil.

And this, surely, was where Daisy should leap up, and run. This was where she should finally forget Filak, forget this whole mess, and stop being so damned stupid. *This is ridiculous and immature behaviour, appallingly unscientific, fool-ish, dangerous...*

But somehow, Daisy couldn't seem to stop staring at Filak. *Seeing* Filak. And then... frowning at Filak, while her hand gripped at his harsh pale face, and the anger and disbelief choked in her throat.

"*Nei*, Filak," she snapped at him, as she gave his face a sharp little shake. "If you want to prove something to your people, and freely gain yourself a mate, you cannot go around trapping women in caves, and lying to them! Making false promises about the *sól*! And *morgun!*"

Filak blinked at her, his face reddening beneath her hand's grip, and gods bless Julian, curse Julian, he was quietly translating what Daisy had said. While Filak's nostrils flared, and his lip curled, his face slightly twitching beneath her touch.

"*Þetta var ekki falskt loforð!*" he snapped back toward her. "*Ég verð að hafa sól til að sjá steininn!*"

Daisy blinked, and then shot a searching look toward Julian, who was looking distinctly pained. "Filak says this was not a false promise," he told her. "And he must have the sun, in order to see the stone. The stone-seeing is always strongest for him during the daylight, even if he is deep underground."

Really? Daisy blinked again, but then frowned back at Filak, and huffed an exasperated groan. "Well, you still trapped me in there!" she shot back. "And you pretended to be all concerned and solicitous, when in truth you were just trying to trick me, and *own* me!"

Filak's low growl rose as Julian translated, and then he again shook his head, and spoke more rapid Aelakesh. "It was not a trick," Julian's voice translated. "And Filak *was* concerned. He could not bear for you to be harmed, and he wished to gain your trust. He wished to be a good mate to you."

"He is *not* my mate!" Daisy countered. "*Nei*, Filak!"

But Filak didn't wait for Julian's translation this time, and his growl rumbled between them, his teeth bared. "*Þú ert mín, Daisy*," he said, as he raised his own hand, and roughly palmed at the *kraga* on her throat. "*Daisy mín. Sólin mín.*"

Daisy growled straight back, and shook her head. "You don't get a mate just because you've decided it, Filak!" she snapped. "And just because you've locked them in a cave for a night! I barely even *know* you! And you barely know *me*!"

Her voice rang far too loud through the room, through her own ears, and she barely heard Julian's low translation. But Filak growled again, harsh and deep and sustained, and in a swift, sudden movement, he pushed Daisy onto her back beneath the fur, and heaved himself over on top.

"*Ég þekki þig, Daisy*," he hissed. "*Ég sé þig.*"

I know you, he meant, *I see you*, and Daisy understood it even before Julian's quiet translation confirmed it. And she shook her head again, raised her chin, glared up toward him, so close...

"You do not," she countered. "Until this morning, we've barely had a single conversation together!"

Filak didn't even wait for Julian's translation, and again began rapidly speaking in Aelakesh, his eyes flashing on Daisy's face. His ragged breaths shuddering through his long bare body over hers, hot and heavy and bizarrely enraging, again speaking its own truth, even if she didn't want to hear it.

"Filak says he does know you," came Julian's quiet voice. "From the first instant he saw you had found the *Skýli*, and chosen to enter it, alone. He knew you were clever. He knew you were brave. He knew you would see much that others did not."

Clever. Brave. He knew you would see. It all caught and quivered in Daisy's chest, and she fought to shove it away— but Julian was still speaking, faster now. "And in that night with you, he also learned you were kind. You were eager and curious. You did not run from him or curse him, or reek of revulsion and fear. You welcomed his touch and his pleasure. You granted him great and shining joy. The light he had so long been seeking."

Daisy grimaced, glared harder, while Filak glowered straight back, and pinned her tighter to the bed. And why was she still here, why wasn't she finishing this, shoving him off and running away...

"You saw him, also," came Julian's soft, inexorable voice. "You knew his aims. You knew his hungers. You spoke oft and long together, and learned one another, without words or sight. You welcomed his care and his seed, and his mark, and his mating-bite, and the promise of his sun. You welcomed his vow as your mate."

His vow as your mate. Daisy's clamouring thoughts flashed backwards to that night in Lew's apartment, on her back on the kitchen table, with Filak thick and powerful between her legs, and beautiful in her eyes. When he'd spoken the way he had, and put his mark on her throat, and asked her to come away with him. Forever.

And she... she'd understood. She'd... *agreed.*

"W-well," Daisy stammered, toward Filak's watching, glinting eyes. "Then—then Filak kidnapped me! Locked me in a dungeon! Put a chain on my neck! Stuffed my own—my own *art* in my mouth!"

The hurt of that memory still rang through her voice, shuddered in her chest. And as Julian translated it, Filak's lips twisted, and he then drew in a breath, and spoke his own rushed, rasping reply in return.

"Filak says he ought never to have done this," Julian translated, with a sigh. "He shall regret this until the end of his days. He thought he had failed his kin again, and forever bound himself to their enemy. He did not wish to hurt you or grieve you or frighten you as he did, or to cast darkness upon your art. He did not know the strength of your art when you first met, but he has now seen that it is your own great gift. Your art shall be part of the sun you make together, bright with your beauty and your kindness. Your *seeing*."

Her own great gift. Part of her sun. Her beauty, her kindness, her seeing.

Daisy's mouth opened and closed, and she swallowed hard, took a deep, shaky breath. "But—it's not," she whispered. "I'm not. I'm just…"

Stupid, she'd been perhaps about to say, *foolish, not a real artist*—but Filak's hand clapped over her mouth, his lips curling back to bare all his sharp teeth.

"*Nei, Daisy*," he hissed. "*Mín. Daisy mín. Sólin mín.*"

Gods, not this again, but Daisy's groan was muffled against his hand, and even her attempt at rolling her eyes earned her another low, spitting growl from his throat. And with another firm, decisive movement of his tall body, Filak kicked aside the fur covering them, baring both their naked bodies to the open air, as his knees shoved up strong and purposeful beneath her sticky thighs.

"Filak!" Daisy hissed into his hand, her eyes snapping wide and panicked—and then darting sideways toward Julian, who was watching this development with unmistakable curiosity. "You—you—"

But Filak's growl burned deeper, his brows rising high on his forehead. And his legs shoved Daisy's even further apart, and then tilted her hips up and back, too. Opening her wide and exposed, baring her enough that anyone who walked by in the corridor could see, too…

"*Mín*," he breathed, hungry and hot, his eyes glittering on her face. "*Mín, Daisy. Artistinn mín.* Ach?"

And for a breath, Daisy could only blink up at him, at this powerful, dangerous, unpredictable orc, this stone-seer, this fallen son who had failed his kin, and been failed by them in return. The orc who'd seen her, given her his jewels, locked her in his dungeon, called her his sun, his artist.

His hand slid away from her mouth, caressing her cheek, wanting her to speak. Wanting her to see him, just as he saw her...

And he saw her as an artist. Beautiful. Her own great gift. Part of her sun. His. Hers. Her own marked magical devil, come to whisk her deep into his thrall, his hope, his dream...

And finally Daisy let out a breath, and... nodded. Saying... yes.

Yes.

Filak's eyes blazed with triumph, with feral dangerous glee—and with a sharp snap of his hips, his hard cock plunged deep inside her. The shock wrenching Daisy all over, escaping in a harsh little cry from her mouth, as her fluttering eyes glanced wild and alarmed toward Julian's watching face.

But Julian's expression was still only curiosity, and far stronger was Filak's rumbling growl, the caress of his strong hand around Daisy's throat. The touch snapping her eyes back to his face, to his bared teeth, to the silent words he might as well have shouted toward her. *You look at me while I fuck you, my sun.*

So Daisy looked, gasping and trembling and taking it, as Filak's swollen, demanding cock slammed in and out between her legs. Even harder and faster than the night before, fluid squelching and bollocks slapping and skin striking against skin. Because this wasn't lovemaking, this was Filak speaking to her, hollering at her, circling his hand close around her throat, wringing up pain and fear and shock and pleasure.

He was saying, *You are mine. Mine. Mine. You swore it, now see it. My sun. My light.*

And when he yanked himself fully out of her, and sprayed out of his pulsing, marked cock, spewing his thick white fluid brazen and messy all over her bare breasts and her belly and her brand-new bed—that was speaking, too. Spreading his very essence all over her, covering her, showing her, needing her to see...

And maybe Daisy should have been offended, or humiliated. Maybe she should have still leapt up and run away. She should most certainly not have grasped her hand at Filak's jutting tattooed hipbone, and guided him up and forward, closer, even as she drew herself up to meet him. To meet that oozing, dripping, softening cock, and then sucking it smooth and easy into her mouth. Speaking back to him with her tongue and lips and teeth, telling him yes, yes, she saw him, she understood.

And gods, the way he moaned. The way his soft cock shuddered between her lips, squeezing out yet more fresh sweetness, just for her. The way his claws skittered against her hair, stroking, caressing, marvelling. All of it speaking, a dozen urgent clamouring voices at once, and when Daisy met his eyes, they shouted even louder than the rest, caught wide and stricken and reverent on her face.

Daisy mín. Sólin mín. I need you. You grant me such hope. Such peace.

It was too strong, too much, and finally Daisy dropped her eyes, and drew away. Fighting not to look at Julian, but then doing it anyway—and he looked just as flushed as she felt, with a distinctive bulge in his trousers. But upon catching her eyes, he twitched a soft smile toward her, looking indulgent, or maybe even approving.

"I am glad this has helped," he told her. "It is clear you two needed to discuss this, ach? You ought to know the truth of your mate, and the sun he longs to grant you."

Your mate. A distant voice was shouting, chanting, waving at the back of Daisy's thudding skull, but she was too caught in that claim, or maybe even... that truth. *Your mate.*

And in this moment, somehow, she couldn't find the

falseness in it. She had said yes to Filak. Not only that time in the apartment, but many, many times. And she had seen what it meant for him. She'd known. And she'd still done it anyway.

Stupid, a distant voice chanted, but Daisy shoved it away, drew in a deep breath. She'd already seen so much here, learned so much. And what did she want now? What did she want to see next? What did she want to learn, for herself?

"Are mates... permanent?" she finally asked Julian, her voice surprisingly steady. "Can I set... a trial period with Filak, as his mate? To see what it's like for myself?"

Julian blinked, but repeated the question toward Filak. And oh, the way Filak's eyes lit up, the grin flashing sudden and stunning across his face. As if he wasn't at all insulted by such a request, but instead saw it as a challenge. As... hope. Light.

"*Ach, sólin mín,*" he told her, his voice low and reverent, as he swept up her hand, and brought it to his mouth. "*Ég mun vinna mér inn traust þitt aftur og endurheimta hjarta þitt sem mitt eigið.*"

The words were again familiar—that same pledge he'd made twice before, back in the sickroom. He would prove himself as Daisy's mate, and gain her as his own.

And blinking at his shining, hopeful eyes, at the worshipful kiss of his ink-stained lips to her trembling hand, Daisy's thoughts were scattering again, into longing and fear and need. She wanted to see it, wanted to follow him into the fantasy—but he was still dangerous, and she needed to not be foolish. Needed to put some kind of boundary on this, a time frame, something she wouldn't ignore or forget...

"Two weeks, then," she blurted out, before she could catch it. "We can be mates for—two weeks. And then I'll decide whether or not to stay."

Too late, the possible visions of Lew's impending attack blared behind her eyes—the gas, the belladonna, the danger—all in two weeks, too. But in truth, did Daisy even want to leave here before then? Did she want to be trying to run away to the city, knowing that Lew was still back here in Dusbury, plotting with Sybil to commit mass murder? Trying to hurt all these people who had been so kind to her? Trying to feed belladonna to their children?

No. No. Daisy wanted to know. She wanted to see. But after that... what?

"But after that, if I decide to leave," she said, slower, to Filak's watching eyes. "You—you'll let me go. You'll help me go north, back to the city. And"—she took a deep inhale, as her hand fluttered up to the *kraga* at her throat—"you'll let me keep these jewels, too. In case I... need them."

And curse her, maybe it was too greedy, too demanding, and Daisy held her breath as Julian translated it all for Filak. As Filak's head slowly tilted sideways, and something she couldn't read flickered through his shadowed eyes. Something dark, searching, uncertain...

But then, oh gods, he nodded. Slow, but certain, telling her... yes. Yes.

"*Ach, sólin mín,*" he told her, with a faint twitch of a smile. "*þú verður hér þangað til á morgun. Þangað til sólin kemur.*"

Daisy's heart skipped as Julian translated it, because it meant—she would stay until the morning. Until the sun. Just like back in the cave. And if she wanted it, Filak would again lead her to the sun, and let her go.

And if nothing else, he had shown her he could do that much, hadn't he? He could keep his word to her. He *would*. Right?

The relief simmered through Daisy's belly, and she smiled back at him, cautious but true. She'd made a plan. She would see.

"Ach, Filak," she said, hushed and maybe even hopeful. "Until the sun."

32

For Filak's first act as Daisy's short-term mate, he had apparently decided to... wash her.

He'd sent Julian off with a list of instructions in Aelakesh, and when Julian had returned, he'd been carrying water and a washbasin, and some clean washcloths, too. And as Filak carefully set it all out on the bed, he gave Julian an even longer list of instructions, all of which Julian accepted with surprising magnanimity before leaving again.

It left Daisy finally alone with Filak again, his eyes glinting on hers as he wrung out a washcloth in the basin. And too late, Daisy realized that she was still sprawled fully naked on the bed, with Filak's mess still smeared and sticky all over her skin. Her white-spattered nipples flushed and peaked, her legs still splayed wide, showing off everything between them, and—

Wait. Something black, radiating up out of her coarse dark hair. Something... *new*.

Daisy stilled and stared, her breath caught in her throat—because those were... *marks*. Filak's marks. The marks she'd felt him making the night before. All those long, waving rays of a sun, drawn in thick black ink, emanating out from her groin over her belly, her thighs, her…

Daisy's face flushed hot, her body betraying a hard little quake—while above her, Filak shifted back onto his heels between her thighs, and spread her legs further apart. So he could freely look his fill at the sun he'd drawn, his eyes brazenly lingering on the sight.

"*Sólin mín*," he murmured, with a brief, intent glance up toward Daisy's face. As if willing her to try and challenge that statement, or to condemn him for staking such an audacious claim upon her. For putting his sign on her most secret vulnerable places.

But curse her, Daisy had committed to this, and she wanted to keep seeing. Keep learning. And without at all meaning to, she even shoved up onto her elbows to look, too. To see the glimpses of that stark black circle, curving amidst her coarse hair, and all those rays extending out from it. The sight of it so bizarre, so obscene, and so… intriguing, somehow, especially once Filak lowered his wet washcloth, and used it to begin gently tracing those new marks. As if showing her each one, each part of the sun he'd given her.

Daisy shivered as he went, as his careful touches broadened into full-on strokes, now wiping away his sticky mess from her skin, leaving only the black sun behind. His movements slow, careful, almost reverent, his eyes hooded and intent on the sight. Saying, without speaking at all, that he would care for her. That he would prove this to her, and show himself a good mate.

And once he'd finished washing her, leaving her skin damp but clean, he set the cloth aside, and reached for something from beside the bed. A rounded glass jar, half-filled with something black and viscous. Something that looked like—ah. His *ink*.

Daisy's heart pitched in her chest—what did he want with more ink?—but she just kept watching, waiting, as Filak unstoppered the jar, and dipped his claw inside it. And after a brief, assessing glance up and down Daisy's bared body, he lowered his ink-dipped claw back to her belly, and began... writing. Making slow, careful movements as his claw gently scratched across her skin, forming those lovely, flowing strokes of Aelakesh script. But keeping them surprisingly neat, too, written in a straight horizontal line below Daisy's navel, and she stayed silent and still as he began a second line, just as straight and careful as the first.

And the more Filak wrote, the more it began to look like his own marks. His own neat lines of script, written dense and dark all over his body. All of them prayers, Julian had said, a way to speak them strong and unceasing, for all to see and know...

Filak was giving Daisy a prayer? To gods she didn't know, in a language she didn't understand?

And maybe this was where she should have stopped him, or at least questioned what he was doing, what he was writing. But then again, she'd agreed to this, right? She wanted to learn. Wanted to see for herself.

So she again held herself still, watching, wondering, until Filak finally drew back again, gazing down at his handiwork with intent lowered eyes. He'd written three even lines of equal length, all in that careful curling script—and on the bottom row, a few of the letters were even connected to the rising rays of her new sun. As if the prayer was part of the sun, or an expansion of it, deepening into something hushed, something sacred.

"What... what does it say?" Daisy finally asked, with a questioning look toward Filak's face. "*Hvað?*"

Hvað meant *what* in Aelakesh, another word they'd learned from Rosa's book, and Filak's glance upwards was furtive, maybe even shy. "*Það segir,*" he began, "*Ég mun fljótt vinna mér inn traust þitt aftur og endurheimta hjarta þitt sem mitt eigið.*"

Oh. It was that same pledge from before, its familiar words thudding strangely through Daisy's thoughts. *I will prove myself as your mate, and gain you as my own.*

But now, all of it was written black and clear on Daisy's skin, and as she blinked down toward it, she could almost feel the sudden, visceral power in it. The vow made into flesh, into reality, into something they would both often see and touch. Something that would always be there between them now, reminding them both of it, holding Filak to account, binding him to his promise.

But then—Daisy swallowed—the ink would fade. The sun, and the vow. Right? And how long had Julian said Filak's inks lasted for? A fortnight? Two weeks?

Daisy's eyes searched Filak's face—that surely wasn't a coincidence, right? And no, no, it wasn't, based on that look in his eyes, the slight twist on his mouth.

"Þangað til á morgun," he told her, with a wan smile toward her. "Þangað til sólin kemur."

Until the morning. Until the sun. Two weeks.

Daisy couldn't seem to speak, just blinking down toward those striking lovely marks on her skin. Feeling almost bereft, somehow, at the thought of them all fading away forever, just like his vow...

But no. No. *Foolish.* She was supposed to be careful about this. To not just whirl off into the dream, but to see, and learn, for herself. Right?

But the silence kept dangling between them, growing thicker with every breath—and Daisy was deeply grateful at the sudden sound of a rap at the door. It was Julian again, wryly smiling toward them, while also holding a familiar large basket in one arm, and a stack of equally familiar books and pamphlets in the other.

"The food you wished for," he told Filak, as he strode into the room, and set the basket on the bed. "And sister, Rosa asked me to be sure you had your reading from the sickroom, also."

It was again very generous of him, and Daisy gave him a wavering smile. "Thank you so much, Julian," she said. "You've just been so kind. Will you stay and eat with us?"

Julian hesitated, and it took Daisy an instant to realize that he was blinking down at her belly, at that powerful new promise Filak had written on her skin. "Ach, mayhap another time," he replied, with a smile that didn't look quite genuine. "I have imposed enough upon you, and you ought to enjoy your first meal together as mates, ach?"

Right. *Mates.* And amidst the way that word shivered and sang beneath her new marks, Daisy didn't miss that unhappy glimmer in Julian's eyes, or the quiver on his mouth. And in a jerky movement, he spun and strode back for the door, his head bowed, his hands clenched. As if he was jealous, or maybe even... hurt? By this? By... them?

Daisy shot a searching look at Filak, the uncertainty edging deeper through her already-floundering thoughts. Why would Julian still be jealous? Was there still something else she should know? Something else Filak hadn't told her?

But Filak was watching her closely, his head tilting—and then he abruptly reached over, and hauled her naked body over into his warm bare lap. "*Róleg, sólin mín,*" he murmured, as he stroked his hand at her back, and kissed her hair. "*Þetta er bara... Rurik.*"

Rurik. Julian's ex-lover, right? The one who'd sent those letters? And at Daisy's next questioning look up toward Filak, he sighed, and wrinkled his nose. "*Rurik var sálufélagi Julians,*" he said. "*Þangað til Rurik*—go."

Go was another word they'd learned in Rosa's book, and Filak confirmed it with a walking motion of his fingers, moving away. Meaning—what? Rurik had been Julian's *sálufélagi*? His mate? And then he'd left?

"Really?" Daisy demanded. "Rurik... Julian's *sálufélagi*?"

Filak grimly nodded, and patted at his new vow on Daisy's belly. "*Rurik fann aðra*," he said flatly, as his other hand pointed at what might have been various imaginary people. "*Gleymdu Julian.*"

Oh. It sounded like he meant that Rurik had found other lovers instead of Julian, and forgotten Julian—and Julian himself had said something to that effect too, hadn't he? And suddenly Daisy only felt a stark, sinking sympathy for Julian, and maybe a whisper of traitorous relief, too. "Can we help, somehow?" she asked Filak. "*Hjálpa* Julian?"

Hjálpa was help, another word from the book, and warmth flared in Filak's eyes, even as he huffed an exasperated-sounding sigh. "*Ég reyndi að hjálpa*," he said, with a meaningful wave between himself, and where Julian had gone—perhaps meaning that he'd already tried to help. "*En Julian vill bara Rurik. Rurik. Rurik!*"

He made a sudden, exaggerated frowning face, and dragged his claws down his cheeks in a clear pantomime of tears. And despite Daisy's still-surging sympathy toward Julian, the sight was so comically ridiculous that a choked laugh escaped her throat—and then Filak was laughing, too. His shoulders shaking, his grin broad and bright and contagious, and for a breath, Daisy felt almost dizzy, blinking toward him. Because she'd never once seen him laugh before, had she? And gods, it was stunning, it was something she wanted to draw and remember forever...

And simmering even stronger in the midst of it was the truth that Filak was again... trying. Showing her that he would be a good mate. Soothing her, sharing information with her, making her laugh. Keeping his word and his vow.

That awareness only deepened as Filak next reached for the basket of food Julian had brought, and began placing various delicious-smelling treats into Daisy's hands. And though it should have been awkward, eating breakfast while still naked and gathered in his lap like this, it felt surprisingly comfortable, and maybe even reassuring, too.

At least, until Daisy noticed that once again, Filak wasn't actually eating anything. And instead, he was watching her eat with wide, unblinking eyes, not unlike a lost puppy longing for his dinner.

"*Filak*," Daisy said, exasperated, as she picked up a slice of buttered bread from the basket, and nudged it against his chest. "As your mate, am I allowed to ask you to eat with me? Or at least to stop staring at me like that?"

Filak surely hadn't followed all that, but he sighed, and grimaced, and took the bread. And after a long moment's staring at it, he snatched a brief, furtive little nibble, as his eyes fluttered closed with obvious pleasure.

"Ach, that's better," Daisy told him, with a smile that felt almost fond. "It's good, isn't it? *Gott*?"

Filak half-smiled back, and took another furtive bite of the bread. "*Kannski*," he said, with a wishy-washy gesture that might have meant *maybe*. "*En guðirnir halda ekki.*"

Daisy hadn't understood any of that, but she could easily follow the wry reluctance in his voice, that too-hungry look in his eyes. "You deserve to have things you like, Filak," she replied. "And how are you going to help your people if you don't eat? *Nei borða, nei hjálpa.* Ach?"

Filak's smile pulled higher, and he took another bite of bread. "*Ef ég borða ekki, get ég ekki hjálpað*," he said, and it sounded like a correction, like him telling her the proper way to say it—maybe with *ekki* instead of *nei*?—but then he sighed, and took another bite. "*Kannski, sólin mín.*"

That definitely sounded like an acknowledgement, grudging as it was, so Daisy gently elbowed him, and passed him some berries. And though he nudged her back, he ate them too, and then told her something else. Something that felt like more grudging capitulation, so Daisy grinned, and thrust the meat toward him, too. And when he complained in Aelakesh, she cheerfully told him in common-tongue to stop complaining, earning what sounded like an irritable curse in return. But then Daisy laughed, and cursed him too, and somehow it led to them both just... talking. Trading words, sentences, entire conversations, back and forth in their own languages, but still mostly following each other. Understanding each other.

It helped that Daisy was already getting a sense of Aelakesh's rhythms and inflections, and that Filak was just so damned expressive, too. And when they finally did get fully stuck, they again pulled out Rosa's book, which also had a helpful alphabetical section, to help them translate. And then they worked through a few more pages together as they kept eating, practicing and laughing and teasing each other, until the basket of food was almost entirely empty.

It felt far too easy, like something real mates would do together, and afterwards, Daisy couldn't seem to stop smiling at Filak, or eyeing his lean naked body. Especially once he slipped out of bed and bent to pick up his trousers off the floor, giving her a vivid view of his firm arse, and his full bollocks hanging between his thighs.

"You like," he murmured in common-tongue—one of the new phrases he'd just learned—as he flashed her a sly, teasing grin over his shoulder, and yanked on his trousers. "Fuck after, ach? *Ríða á eftir?*"

Daisy couldn't deny the flush of warmth to her face, or to her groin, either. And she was still smiling at Filak when he plucked up her abandoned shift, and held it out toward her—but then he grimaced, and drew it back again.

"Ach," he muttered, more to himself than to her—and when Daisy shoved up to look, he was fingering at a large new tear in the shift that certainly hadn't been there before. "I am sorry, *sólin mín.*"

Right. Daisy had almost forgotten that Filak had torn it in bed the night before, but she shrugged, and waved it away.

She'd certainly worn far worse over the years, and it wasn't as if anyone else would see it, right? But next Filak reached for Daisy's grimy-looking dress, which she'd draped over the nearby chair, and he frowned toward it, too. "Daisy," he said, almost reproachfully. "*Hvar er restin?*"

He gave a purposeful wave toward the dress, and then around the room—asking where the rest of her clothes were, perhaps? And yes, Daisy had packed some clothes, and the satchel had been with her when Filak had locked her in the dungeon... and then what?

And surely Filak had followed that, because the look on his face went regretful, or maybe even guilty. "I am sorry, *sólin mín,*" he said again, as he passed over the dress toward her. "I fix."

I fix. Daisy blinked at him, not following, but he was smiling again, the hope glimmering in his eyes. Suggesting that maybe he truly would fix this, prove this, and she would see...

"Come," he told her. "We go—*shop.*"

33

They were going to... shop. Here. In Orc Mountain?

But once Daisy had put on her shabby clothes and accompanied Filak out into the mountain's corridors, she soon discovered that Orc Mountain indeed had a genuine, real-life shop. It was a large, bright room in the Grisk clan's wing, with a long counter across the front of it, and multiple shelves and aisles extending out behind, seemingly stocked full of clothes and goods.

"Uh, Filak," Daisy said, with an uncertain glance toward him. "I don't have any coin. *Nei* coin. *Nei* shop."

She tried to gesture along as she spoke, but in return Filak's brow furrowed, his head shaking. "*Þú ert sálufélagi minn,*" he said firmly, with a purposeful pat of his hand over Daisy's belly—over his new vow. "*Ég mun fljótt vinna mér inn traust þitt aftur.*"

Oh. It was a line from that vow again, the one still whispering too powerfully from beneath the fabric of Daisy's dress. Which meant... Filak was again saying that he would handle it. That he would clothe her, and care for her, and prove himself as her mate.

It quivered in Daisy's belly, strong enough that it took her far too long to notice the new woman, striding up one of the shop's aisles. She was small and pretty and dark-haired, dressed in a striking ensemble that flaunted not only her bare legs and soft exposed midriff, but an impressive quantity of beautiful jewelry, too.

"Welcome to the Great Grisk Showroom-Shop!" the woman said, with a dazzling grin toward Daisy—but upon catching sight of Filak, her steps faltered, and a distinct wariness crossed her face. "Uh... Filak?"

Filak's lip curled with distaste, but he jerked a nod, and said something toward the woman in Aelakesh. Speaking very slowly, enough that Daisy could pick out a few words she now knew—*mate, coin, gift*—along with her own name.

"Oh, yes, of course!" the woman replied, flashing her smile back toward Daisy, though it still looked surprised, and a little strained, too. "Welcome to our mountain, Daisy. I'm Kitty, our shopkeeper, and Filak says he'd like to purchase you some new clothes? Because he's just sworn vows to you as his *mate*?"

Her voice was incredulous, her eyes rapidly searching Daisy's face, as if desperately needing independent verification of Filak's claim. And though maybe Daisy should have explained all the various caveats around this—two weeks, he was proving himself, until the sun—it felt far easier to just nod back toward this Kitty's staring face.

"Er, yes," she replied. "Though I'm not entirely sure"—she glanced uneasily toward Filak—"what he had in mind? Something serviceable, and affordable, I'm sure?"

That two-week timeline was again ringing through her thoughts, but before her, Kitty loudly scoffed, and gave a dismissive flap of her hand. "He'll be glad to buy you whatever you please, of course," she said firmly. "Orcs take their responsibilities in such matters very seriously. Now"—her eyes sparkled with eagerness—"come in, come in, and let's get started! Do you have a particular style or type of clothing you prefer to wear?"

Daisy fought to consider the question as she followed Kitty around the counter, with Filak striding close and silent behind her. She'd always appreciated interesting ensembles on other people, but clothes had never been a high priority in her own life—mostly because she hadn't had the extra coin to waste, but also because of her work, too. Wearing pretty dresses while tromping around in fields and caves was an appealing image, but an absolute nuisance in real life, and working with paints or charcoals or printing plates was even worse.

"I'm... not sure," Daisy finally replied, with a helpless-feeling glance toward Filak beside her. As if expecting him to come to her rescue, and that was ridiculous, and...

"Daisy artist," he cut in unexpectedly, with a decisive nod, and a firm pat to her back. "*Ach, sólin mín?*"

He looked decidedly proud of that fact, while before them, Kitty's brows snapped up, her eyes widening. "Oh, how wonderful!" she exclaimed. "Now, a working artist *is* an exciting clothing challenge, isn't it? Can you tell me how you spend your days, Daisy? What kinds of work do you do, and where?"

It was a start, at least, and Daisy did her best to explain, while Kitty peppered her with follow-up questions, and waved them down one of the shop's long aisles. It was bursting with an astonishing quantity of clothes, not only stacked neatly on shelves, but hanging on tall racks, and piled into open chests and trunks. And Daisy was so busy blinking around at it all that she barely noticed the person standing up ahead in the aisle—who now looked distinctly familiar. Kesst, from the sickroom.

He'd been intently digging through a stack of trousers, but upon catching sight of Daisy and Filak, he snapped up straight, and fixed Filak with a sudden, furious glower. "You again?!" he snarled. "I can't escape you here, either? Even when I'm desperately trying to soothe my frazzled wits after the mess *you* made of my treasured *home*?!"

Daisy winced—gods, she'd completely forgotten about that hole Filak had dug in the sickroom—while Filak only glared back toward Kesst, and made an obscene-looking gesture with his clawed hand. Earning a vicious snarl from Kesst in return, and an eloquent-sounding string of curses in Aelakesh.

Daisy had already taken an uneasy step backwards, but beside her, Kitty loudly harrumphed, and lurched herself in between Filak and Kesst. "Enough, both of you," she snapped. "We're here for Daisy, and she needs some comfortable, durable clothes to support her art, and help her feel at home here. So Kesst"—she fixed her glare on his face—"you're our resident expert on leather trousers, so why don't you help me find Daisy some good options? And Filak can help her try them on, and see how they fit?"

She repeated the instructions toward Filak in Aelakesh, and to Daisy's surprise, he looked almost mollified as he nodded. And then he turned back toward Daisy and reached for her shabby dress, tugging it off over her head. Leaving her standing there in only her torn shift, in the middle of a public shop—but no one seemed to take any notice, and already Kitty was passing several pairs of trousers into Filak's arms.

It was unlike any shopping Daisy had ever done before, and she'd never properly worn trousers before, either. And though they did feel strange at first, she could easily see how they would be far easier to explore and romp around in, and much better for dealing with dust and paint and dirt, too.

"These ones are perfect on you," Kitty said decisively, in regards to a pair of slim brown trousers that felt buttery soft against Daisy's skin. "And these ones"—she thrust two more pairs toward Filak—"were good too. You'll take them all, won't you?"

Daisy hesitated, glancing doubtfully toward Filak—he surely hadn't meant to buy her *three* pairs of trousers? But he didn't appear even slightly perturbed by this, and instead seemed preoccupied with appreciatively eyeing Daisy's arse through her new trousers' tight-fitting leather.

"Yes, he'll take them all," Kesst cut in, with a chilly, poisonous smile toward Filak. "After everything he's done, it's the least he can do. In fact, I think you should take these, too."

He irritably shoved two more pairs of trousers toward Filak, but to Daisy's ever-rising surprise, Filak accepted them without a hint of protest, and tucked them into the growing stash under his arm. And then he plucked at Daisy's torn shift, which was currently bunched around her waist, and said something else in Aelakesh toward Kitty—something that she returned with a nod, and an approving smile.

"Yes, tops next," she said firmly. "Something easy to clean, I think, and close-fitting, so it doesn't get in the way. Do you have any preferences in terms of type, Daisy? Blouses, tunics, jackets?"

She waved Daisy further up the aisle, to where there again seemed to be an impossible variety of options—so many that choosing one felt like an utterly overwhelming task. And after blinking around for a moment, Daisy glanced back at Kitty, whose top half appeared to be covered by little more than a large silk triangle, tied over her breasts. But the silk was woven in a lovely pattern of bright colours, and had caught Daisy's eye from the first instant she'd seen it.

"What about something like that?" she tentatively asked. "If you don't think it's—inappropriate?"

She blushed even as she said it—had she just called Kitty's outfit inappropriate? But Kitty only beamed back in return, and beckoned Daisy over toward a pile of similar colourful fabrics. And again, Filak didn't argue this plan whatsoever, and once Kesst and Kitty had plucked out a few options, he even pulled off Daisy's torn shift entirely, and helped them tie multiple different kinds of fabric around her. A process that regularly left Daisy's upper body fully bared to the air, but no one except Filak seemed to notice. And if Daisy wasn't mistaken, he almost seemed to be enjoying this, studying various options with a critical eye, and looking her up and down with obvious admiration.

"Þetta er gott," he finally announced, about a wrap that was a beautiful red and yellow, and brazenly showed off both the sun over Daisy's heart, and that new vow he'd written on her belly. "Ach, sólin mín?"

Daisy had never publicly worn anything so revealing in her life, but she had to admit she liked the look of it with the trousers, liked the colours against her skin. "Ach, Filak," she murmured, without quite meaning to. "Þetta er gott."

He flashed her a swift, sharp-toothed grin in return, bright and broad and approving—while beside them, Kitty betrayed a sudden shocked gasp. And when Daisy glanced over, both Kitty and Kesst were staring blankly toward Filak, with clear disbelief in their eyes.

"I didn't know he *could* smile," Kesst muttered to Kitty, under his breath. "Is it possible that he might actually be *attractive*? Oh, gods, absolutely not. I have most certainly exceeded my limit of Ka-esh for today."

With that, he shuddered and rushed off, without even a wave goodbye—but then he paused at the end of the aisle, and frowned back toward them. "Spend as much of his coin as you can, Daisy," he snapped. "Someone needs to make him pay!"

Daisy chuckled despite herself, but it soon seemed as though Kitty was determined to carry out Kesst's directives. First fetching a huge basket to pile their items in, before ushering them toward an overwhelming selection of fur coats and capes and shawls, and then boots and belts and

bags. But Filak still followed along with surprising eagerness, and he insisted that Daisy take three fur shawls and
capes, two pairs of sturdy leather boots, and a lovely water-
proof shoulder satchel with pockets, perfectly suited for
her sketchbook. He even insisted that they buy her a set of
new pencils and brushes, and a tall oil lamp, with a convenient handle for carrying. And when Daisy finally asked if
he was going to buy anything for himself, he initially
resisted, but then plucked up a nearby coiled rope, hung it
on his belt, and then kept urging her further down the
aisle.

By the time they finished, their basket was overflowing
with items—which Kitty promised to have delivered to their
room—and Daisy was fully dressed in one of her brand-new
ensembles. Featuring the leather trousers and boots, the
revealing red and yellow silk wrap, and a brown fur cloak.
And when Kitty steered them toward a large looking-glass at
the rear of the room, Daisy willingly went, and then almost
tripped over her feet at the sight.

She looked... different. So different. Unlike anyone she'd
ever seen before. Not only with her new vivid black marks
clearly displayed on her skin—the sun over her heart, the
vow below her navel—but also with all the contrasts and
colours, too. The dark browns and soft textures of the leather
and fur, the patterned orange and yellow silk, the glinting
gold of her ring and her *kraga*. All those browns and yellows
and reds making her look like something she'd find growing
in a field, something warm and bright and alive.

And when Filak eased up behind her in the looking-
glass, and slid his long clawed fingers over that vow on her
belly, Daisy could thoroughly appreciate the sight of that,
too. His body so tall and stark and pale, all cold black and
white, while hers was shorter and softer, rich with colour and
warmth. And the longer she blinked between them, the more
dangerous Filak looked, like a proud, vengeful, deathly fallen

prince, ready to maim and crush and destroy. While she looked like...

An artist. A sun. A light to his darkness. Like the only one in the world who could bring that warmth to his eyes.

And maybe Filak saw it too, because he kissed the top of Daisy's head, and drew her body a little closer against him. "*Sólin mín*," he murmured, his eyes glimmering on hers in the glass. "*Artistinn mín. Sálufélagi minn.*"

My sun. My artist. My mate.

And for a hushed, hovering moment, the promise of it—the possibility of it—stole away Daisy's breath. His sun, his artist, his mate, here, standing in the glass before her very eyes, with her fierce orc's hand stroking reverently against his powerful black vow. Showing her. Proving this to her. Fusing it all together, and offering it up like a new shining star, tempting her away...

"*Þú kemur með mér,*" he said now, so soft, his eyes still shimmering on hers in the glass. "*Ach, sólin mín?*"

And those words were—familiar. They were the same words he'd said that fateful night at Lew's apartment. And he'd even looked at her this same way, with such hope and hunger in his eyes. *You will come with me, ach, my sun?*

And maybe it was still foolish—two weeks, and that was all—but Daisy... nodded. Agreed. Relented to the hope, the light, the bright shining dream...

So when Filak took her hand, and drew her toward the back of the room, she went. Not thinking, not hesitating, not even when he walked straight up to the solid stone wall, and spread his hand against it. And after a loud, scraping crunch, the wall... slid open. Revealing...

A *hole*. A huge, yawning hole, dark and jagged and terrifying. The sight catching Daisy's breath, streaking cold and alarming up her spine...

And with a jolt and a crash, Filak dragged Daisy forward, and plunged them both into darkness.

34

Daisy's scream rose in her throat, thick and close and sickening.

She'd trusted Filak for one damned morning, and he'd already done this again. Trapped her again. Dragged her off into terror and darkness, where she would never escape...

But then—a light. Blazing bright and dizzying before her blinking, prickling eyes. And when Daisy squinted to focus, she found... the lamp? Yes, it was the lamp they'd just purchased, and Filak was holding it aloft in his clawed hand, searching her face with wide, worried eyes.

"I am sorry, *sólin mín*," he said, with a regretful grimace, as he waved purposefully toward her eyes. "*Ég gleymdi að þú sérð ekki.*"

Most of that was unfamiliar, but his meaning was unmistakably clear—he'd forgotten Daisy couldn't see in the dark. And while her heart was still wildly thudding, her shoulders were slowly sagging, her breath exhaling. He hadn't meant to trap her, or frighten her. Right?

Filak's hand had found her back, rubbing up and down, smooth and steady and reassuring. Waiting for her, comforting her, proving himself to her—and Daisy took a deep breath, and relaxed a little heavier into his touch. Two weeks. She would see.

"What... what is this, then?" she asked, as she finally glanced around them. Thankfully, the new lamp they'd bought gave off an impressive amount of light, and she could already see that this wasn't a hole, or another room, like she'd perhaps first thought. No, it was a broad, high, roughly carved tunnel, extending straight ahead into the earth. And there, standing in the tunnel just up ahead, was some kind of... large square metal thing, with wheels. A cart?

"Come," Filak told her, with a hopeful little smile, as he nudged her toward the cart. "We go *norður*, ach? *Til Skýlis*."

Oh. He was taking her to—the Skýli? To that first cave they'd met in? His people's long-lost home?

Daisy blinked toward Filak, taking in that eager grin on his mouth, the excitement shining in his eyes. Because yes, he'd finally found the place he'd been searching for, all this time—and then... he'd left it again. After that first night, he'd been here at the mountain with Daisy ever since. And now, of course he wanted to go back to see the Skýli again, and share it with her. Show it to her. Just like a good mate would do.

Daisy was already nodding, a slow smile pulling across her mouth, because yes, she could admit, she wanted to see the Skýli again, too. She wanted to explore that beautiful ruined cave, and learn it for herself.

So she willingly accompanied Filak to the cart, and climbed up inside. It was large and open, surely meant for hauling goods to and from the shop, and there was a steering mechanism at the front of it. And once Filak handed her the lamp, Daisy could hear him doing something outside to the wheels, something sharp and scraping—and with a sudden jerk, the cart began to roll down the tunnel.

Daisy yelped, clutching to the cart's solid edge for

balance—but then Filak leapt up into it beside her, and flashed her another reassuring grin as he reached for the steering mechanism. Pulling it slightly to the side, and thereby keeping the rolling cart in the middle of the rocky tunnel all around them.

It was a fascinating system, and Daisy's alarm faded as she watched Filak pull the mechanism the other way, steering them around another curve. While the cart kept moving faster and faster, bumping and reeling its way down the tunnel. And though the motion and the speed flipped oddly in Daisy's stomach, it also felt... riveting. Maybe even exhilarating.

"You like?" Filak asked, angling a knowing grin toward her, and Daisy didn't even try to resist her smile back. Not even when his clawed hand purposefully gripped at the side of the cart, his eyes gone briefly distant—and then the cart began rolling even faster, the wheels rattling beneath them, the air whipping through Daisy's hair.

"Are... *you* doing that?" she demanded, high-pitched. "With your... magic?!"

Filak likely hadn't understood most of that, but he shot her another broad grin, and steered them around another corner. Meaning that yes, he was somehow doing this, controlling this. *Stone-seeing*, Julian had called it. His great gift.

Daisy's smile felt almost shy this time, and when Filak's arm reached for her, drawing her into his side, she relaxed against him, and just let herself... enjoy it. The swaying cart, the speed, the rocky tunnel flashing by, the rush of cool air on her face, the thrilling edge of danger in the jagged shadowy walls. And yes, the feel of Filak's warm body against her, the deftness of his hand as he steered, the utter fearlessness in his eyes.

She couldn't have said how long they travelled like that, but she was almost sorry when the cart finally slowed, and then trundled to a stop. But Filak's grin was even brighter than before, and once he'd lifted Daisy out of the cart, he again took the lamp in hand, and guided her toward a new, smaller opening, barely visible in the stone wall.

It was another tunnel, but this one was far rougher and rockier, with occasional piles of rubble scattered about, and various forks branching away into darkness. And the further they walked, the more Daisy began to notice all the natural beauty embedded in the tunnel around them. Craggy rock formations, stunning colourful layers in the walls, frilly white stalactites growing from the ceiling.

She kept slowing down to stare, delaying their progress considerably, but Filak didn't at all seem to mind. If anything, he almost seemed to approve of Daisy's distraction, first watching her with warm, indulgent eyes, and then even pointing out notable features in the stone, moving the lamp close so she could see all the details. Patterns in the rock faces, traces of glittering colour in various jutting stones, a hidden cluster of sparkling stalagmites behind a large boulder.

"Those are *fallegt*, Filak," Daisy told him, breathless—*fallegt* meant *beautiful*, another one of the words they'd studied that morning. "Gods, I wish I could draw them, but..."

She trailed off, grimacing, because she'd foolishly left her sketchbook back in her room, with her pencils, too—and she hadn't brought her new satchel, either. But beside her, Filak firmly nodded, and set down the lamp so he could rummage for something in his own satchel—and with a flourish, he thrust out Daisy's sketchbook toward her.

Daisy almost crowed with delight as she clasped it to her chest, beaming brightly toward Filak's face. And in return, he grinned back toward her, and then fished in his satchel again, and plucked out one of the new pencils he'd just bought at the shop, too. "Daisy draw," he told her, with satisfaction, as he swiftly sharpened the pencil to a perfect point with his claw. "*Artistinn mín.*"

It shivered through Daisy's chest, and she felt her face heating as she fumbled to flip the sketchbook open, finding a new page. This was still only supposed to be for two weeks, she was still only seeing, he was still dangerous, she needed to remember that...

But the thought seemed to fade away beneath the drawing, the lovely feeling of scraping her sharp new pencil over the page. Capturing the stalagmites' feathery shapes, the glittering edges, the bizarre shadows they cast on the wall in the lamplight...

And to his credit, Filak didn't interrupt, or hover over Daisy's shoulder, or betray any sign of impatience whatsoever. Instead, he only wandered around nearby, trailing his claws against the jagged walls, picking up rocks, stroking them, sniffing them. And sometimes even *licking* them, his nose wrinkling, his head thoughtfully cocked sideways.

"What are you doing?" Daisy finally asked him, as she closed her sketchbook again. "Is that... your magic? Your... stone-seeing?"

Filak shot her a bemused smile—surely not understanding her—and Daisy went to clasp his hand, turning it over so she could see his palm. "Seeing?" she asked him, tapping her finger against the inked eye in his skin. "Magic?"

The comprehension flared in Filak's eyes, and he nodded. "*Steinsjáandi,*" he said. "*Ég sé stein.*"

He patted the tunnel's stone wall as he said *stein*— meaning *stone*, surely. And when Daisy nodded and repeated it, he gave her another smile, and bent to swipe up a large rock from beneath their feet. "*Í þessum steini,*" he said slowly, "*sé ég ekkert. Nei.*"

He let her see his hand running over the rock, his palm stroking as his claws searched and scraped—and then, with a twist of his fingers, he somehow snapped the rock into two perfect halves. Showing her how it was all rock inside, too.

"*Ekkert*," he said again, as he tossed the rock away over his shoulder, and picked up a much larger one. Running his hand over it, too, but far more carefully this time. "*En þessi steinn*," he said, "*viltu sjá?*"

It was a question, maybe asking if Daisy wanted to see— and she again nodded, intrigued, as she watched him caress the rock. Stroking it with deliberate movements of his hands, rolling it forward and back, sweeping and scraping with his fingers. Slow enough that it took Daisy a moment to realize that he was shaving off layers of the stone, piece by careful piece. Cutting away the top, until she saw... something bright. Colourful. Shimmering.

And the more Filak's hands caressed it, the brighter it grew. It was a mass of gleaming crystals, reds and browns and yellows, all growing out of the stone in riotous clusters of colour. And for a halting, dizzying instant, it almost looked as though Filak was creating them, coaxing them to life from within the stone. Making... art. Beauty. Magic.

Daisy's breath was frozen in her throat, and when she caught Filak's eyes, they were warm and rueful on hers. "You like?" he murmured. "You... draw?"

Daisy fervently nodded, and again fumbled for her sketchbook, flipping it open to a new page. And then she drew the stone as carefully as she could, capturing all those facets, the shadows and the light. Making its beauty hers, to keep.

"Thank you, Filak," Daisy told him once she'd finished. "It's beautiful. *Fallegt*."

Filak waved it away, and said something in Aelakesh that sounded dismissive, perhaps that it wasn't a good stone, or wasn't worth very much—and he didn't seem inclined to keep any of it, either. But as they began walking again, there was a distinct flush spreading across his cheeks, and a small smile pulling at his lips. Suggesting that he'd appreciated the praise, all the same.

Daisy could readily relate to that—she so often felt the same way about her own art—and it made it even easier to keep walking with him, talking with him, exploring with him. Frequently pausing to admire or draw whatever captured her interest, much of it pointed out by Filak, while he seemed to focus more and more of his attention on touching the walls. Spreading his fingers wide, digging his claws into the stone again and again, almost as if he was searching for something.

"What are you doing now, then?" Daisy asked, with genuine curiosity, once she'd finished drawing a little bubbling stream of water he'd pointed out. "Are you looking for the Skýli? I thought you knew where it was now?"

The comprehension flickered across Filak's eyes, and he half-smiled, half-grimaced. "*Kannski*," he replied, making that familiar wishy-washy gesture, before launching into another stream of Aelakesh, still motioning with his hands as he spoke. And while his meaning wasn't fully clear, it was enough to suggest that yes, he was looking for the Skýli, and yes, he now knew where it was, too. But it wasn't yet connected to any of his current tunnels, and he was now searching for signs of it, a way to reach it from underground.

That made sense, especially given his difficulties with sunlight, so Daisy happily kept wandering and exploring with him, sketching as she went. Until finally Filak stopped by a particularly large craggy section, frowning toward it, while she took the opportunity to draw the layers in the wall beside it, curving up toward...

"Filak," she said, her voice sounding odd, as she plucked up the lamp, lurched closer to the wall, and studied the... the mark. The mark that at first just looked like another variation in the stone, but the longer she looked at it, the more it reminded her of...

She groped beside her for Filak's hand, and brought it up next to the mark. Turning it so his palm faced toward them, its black eye gazing out with eerie intensity—and there, beside it, in the wall, was its match. A set.

"*Daisy*," Filak breathed, hushed, his body rigid all over— and then he thrust both hands to the wall beneath the eye, his fingers splaying wide, his claws digging deep. And as Daisy watched, the stone beneath his fingers began to... crack. Breaking first into fine jagged lines, and then crumbling away into rock and sand, pooling down toward the ground below.

Daisy's breath choked, and she flipped to a new page in her sketchbook, capturing this as quickly as she could. The exquisite deepening cracks in the rock, the certainty of Filak's long strong fingers, his sharp black talons pushing and seeking, the stone melting away beneath the dizzying power of his touch.

Because this was art too, perhaps more than anything Daisy had seen in these tunnels yet. The care with which Filak broke the stone, sliding it away from the wall in slow, steady sheaves. The way it was surprisingly subtle and quiet, like a light gentle scraping, drawing up memories of the sounds she'd heard the other night in the sickroom. The way he used his booted feet, too, shoving the rubble back and to the sides, opening up the beginnings of a brand-new tunnel before them.

Daisy had already filled one page, and flipped to the next, and the next. Her hand flashing across the paper, furiously capturing images, impressions, the power of it, the progression, the stone, his hands commanding the very earth...

"*Fallegt*, Filak," Daisy breathed, before she could stop it— and when he glanced toward her, his face was covered with a sheen of sweat, his eyes warm and bright and maybe even incredulous. Again, as if he wasn't used to hearing such compliments, to having his work called beautiful—but it was, of course it was, it was one of the most stunning marvels Daisy had ever seen in her life.

And when she impulsively showed Filak her sketchbook, and the multiple rough drawings she'd already made of this—the neat sheaves of stone, the piles of rubble behind his feet, the wall cracking beneath his hands—he rapidly blinked as he stared, as he raised his dirt-streaked hand to the page. Spreading his fingers out alongside the version of his hand Daisy had drawn, and yes, she'd managed a good likeness, surely aided by how damned often she'd looked at his hands, these past days.

But Filak just kept staring, and blinking, his swallow bobbing in his throat. And when he finally glanced at Daisy, he looked touched, almost shy, his smile slow and uncertain, his cheeks flushing with pink. "You like?" he asked her, husky. "Daisy like draw Filak?"

It was perhaps the most complete common-tongue sentence he'd said yet, and Daisy's grin felt too swift and affectionate, and gods curse her, she impulsively leaned over, and pressed a quick kiss to his hard cheek. "Ach, Filak," she murmured. "I like."

There was another instant's stillness, hovering between them—and then, beneath Filak's other hand, the wall splintered and crunched and rumbled. Breaking apart into huge, jagged boulders, and Filak hissed as he clutched for Daisy, and dragged her backwards. Holding her close and safe as the boulders thudded and fell and slightly rolled away, revealing... something dark. Something... open.

Another... tunnel?

Filak and Daisy both stilled, not moving, not breathing—and then Filak muttered under his breath as he swiped up the lamp, and waved Daisy forward. Through that new hole in the wall, and into the new tunnel, hidden here deep beneath the earth.

It was surely too straight to have occurred naturally,

though the walls were rough and crumbling, with visible signs of age and water damage. And the tunnel only extended for a short distance before ending again, blocked off by another solid, rocky wall.

But Daisy had already noticed another black eye, tucked up into a nearby corner—and Filak shot her a grateful grin as he strode over, and spread his hands wide against the wall. And Daisy gasped as the wall again cracked and broke apart, this time crumbling into smaller stones and gravel, which Filak pooled away into a growing pile behind them.

"Is this it?" Daisy asked him, the excitement rising in her voice. "The way to the Skýli?"

The comprehension flicked across Filak's eyes, and he clasped her hand, and drew her through the broken wall into yet another tunnel. "*Kannski, sólin mín,*" he replied. "*Komdu og sjáðu.*"

Come and see, it might have meant, and Daisy's heartbeat quickened as she accompanied him through the tunnels with the lamp, watching him break down one wall after another. And the further they went, the more the tunnels seemed like a maze, a twisty confusing mess of corners and dead ends, meant to conceal something important behind them.

But they hadn't counted on Filak, on an orc who could command the very earth to obey him. And perhaps they hadn't counted on Daisy, either, because she kept looking for those eyes, finding them tucked behind stones, into corners, even in the floor. Until finally she found one that looked different, placed on its own stone, jutting slightly out from the wall.

"Ach," Filak breathed, as he swept over beside her, his body taut, his hand spreading slow and careful against the stone. And this time, after a long moment, he pressed it. Pressed the eye in his hand into the eye in the stone, his muscles straining with the effort, until the wall... opened.

Heaving itself inward just like a door, with a sharp, deafening scrape.

And behind the door, there was a staircase. Leading downwards, into inky, empty blackness.

Filak's breath hitched, and he gripped Daisy's hand, and drew her after him down into the staircase. Jogging down further, and further, until they reached another dead end, with another jutting eye in the stone wall.

But Filak pressed it with obvious impatience this time, as if he fully expected the wall to open. And it did, obeying him with another harsh, grating sound, revealing yet another long tunnel. But this one was wider, with a flat floor and polished stone walls, and Daisy sprinted together with Filak down the length of it, their hands tightly clasped, their feet pounding in unison on the stone floor.

Until Filak pressed one last eye, and the corridor... opened. Vanished. And before them was...

A room. A huge, empty, echoing room. It was shaped in a massive domed circle, and the walls were carved from pure white stone, gleaming in the light of Daisy's lamp. And the smooth floor was tiled with black and white, following the circle, radiating out from the...

The *eye*. The eye in the floor. The same eye that was on the walls, and on Filak's hands. And when Filak stared at it, and then at Daisy, his expression was pure shocked, sweeping disbelief.

"*Fokk, sólin mín*," he breathed, and his voice shook, trembled just like his fingers on hers. "*Það er...* Skýli?"

They'd found the Skýli.

35

For a long, hanging moment, Daisy could only stare at Filak, and then at the room before them. The... Skýli?

But this—this wasn't the first ruined cave they'd met in. It couldn't be. That cave had been large, yes, enough that it had felt like a grand open room—but this, this was...

This was *massive*. A room meant to hold hundreds, or even thousands, of people. Big enough to be an arena, or a ballroom, or maybe—maybe even a temple. A soaring, sacred temple, hidden here empty and waiting under the earth.

And the longer Daisy stared at it, the more impossible it became. Not just the shining white stone, or the elaborate tiled floor with that eye in the middle—but also the multiple arched alcoves studded around the walls, suggesting many more tunnels and rooms. And—Daisy blinked, and peered closer in the lamplight—there appeared to be tall metal mechanisms lining the white walls too, extending all the way up the huge rounded ceiling. As if reaching for the sky, embracing it, lashing together around what looked like...

Another *eye*. This one made of black steel, there at the

ceiling's highest peak. Looking down at the room below, at the black-and-white tiled floor, and the eye directly beneath it.

Daisy stared at the ceiling's eye for a long, hushed moment, her breath quivering in her throat—but this time, when she followed the eye's gaze back downward, she finally noticed something else.

The ruins. The devastation.

Because as beautiful as the room was, it was also suffering from severe decay and neglect. Several of the adjoining tunnels had collapsed, their stone rubble spilling out onto the tiled floor, and the ceiling's soaring buttresses had begun to splinter and crumble, leaving their white pieces smashed across the floor beneath. And as Daisy stared, a head-sized chunk of stone broke off the ceiling far above, and fell long and silent to the floor. Where it landed with a dizzying crash, and shattered into a thousand sliding tumbling pieces.

Beside Daisy, Filak hissed and lunged for the wall behind them, thrusting both hands against it, squeezing his eyes shut—and then the open door they'd come in through slammed itself shut again, the sound echoing through the huge room. And Daisy could almost feel the white walls quivering and settling in response, while Filak sagged against the closed door, and exhaled his shaky relief.

"*Heilleiki burðarvirkisins,*" he breathed toward Daisy, with a shaky wave of his other hand at the high vaulted ceiling. "*Ekki gott.*"

Not good, that last bit meant, and though Daisy hadn't understood the first part, his meaning was still unnervingly clear. The Skýli was all connected, of course it was, and by opening that door, they'd somehow affected the integrity of the entire structure. And gods, the look on Filak's face as he kept touching the closed door, and then the wall. His expression shifting between shock and bafflement and disbelief, all shouting that he hadn't expected this. He hadn't known about this. He'd expected... what?

"The first cave," Daisy said slowly, her head tilting. "You thought that first cave we met in was the Skýli. Right?"

She gestured along as she spoke, and they'd practiced a few of those words together, too—and in return, Filak nodded, even as his voice broke into a long tumbling stream of Aelakesh. Far too fast for Daisy to follow, but she could piece it together, from his tone and his gestures and his face. Yes, he'd thought that first cave had been the Skýli. But he hadn't taken time to explore it, perhaps because he hadn't wanted to leave Daisy to do it. And in coming here, he'd fully expected to find that first cave again, or maybe more tunnels and rooms around it...

But instead—*this*. This huge, magnificent, ruined room. His people's lost, forgotten home, built by his forefathers hundreds of years before. And surely that first cave was still part of it, but this—this—was the heart.

And Filak just kept looking at it like that, like it was still something he couldn't understand, something he'd never dared to imagine. His eyes so bright, his mouth quivering, and in a flailing movement, he again flattened his hand against the wall, and clasped his other hand over his heart. And then he bowed his head and spoke, more rapid tangled Aelakesh, words that sounded like prayer, like he might fall to his knees and weep.

And when Daisy instinctively eased back toward him, slipping her arm around him, he instantly drew her tight and close, his claws digging into the skin of her waist. His breaths heaving hard and ragged against her, enough that her hands began stroking, all on their own. Rubbing up and down his rigid trembling back, pressing him as much reassurance as she could muster. Just as he so often did to her.

But instead of making him softer, steadier, Daisy's touch seemed to wrench Filak tighter, his lean body almost vibrating beneath her touch. His claws digging harder, as a fierce, tremulous shudder rolled up his body—and then, in a sudden jerk of movement, he clutched for her, yanked off her fur shawl, and dragged her down to the stone floor beneath them.

Daisy's breath heaved from her lungs, her body jolting at the feel of the hard tiles beneath her back—but then, somehow, the stone... softened. Curved. Cradling around her, almost as if welcoming her, while Filak exhaled and shuddered over her. One hand's claws digging into the large white tile beside her head, while the other hand slid down between them, yanking, pulling, opening...

Daisy groaned at the feel of cool stone against her bare arse, her thighs, her calves—because Filak was kicking off her new trousers, baring her for him, for this ancient ruined room. And he was baring himself, too, shoving down his own trousers, and revealing the stunning sight of his pale marked cock. Hovering and juddering between them, dangling white from the tip, like a threat, a claim, a vow...

Daisy's thoughts flashed backwards to that morning, to the vow he'd written across her skin. The vow that was still there, shouting between them, and oh, he was looking at it too, his eyes fluttering as he watched his cock's liquid seeping down to pool against it. As if painting it, or even sealing it, somehow, saying something sacred for all this room's ghosts to see.

And once again, Daisy wasn't fighting it. Wasn't refusing it. Was just watching it, witnessing it, as her hands stroked down his long back, and found his firm arse. Saying something of her own, saying, *yes, please, now*—and Filak heard it too, his shadowed eyes finding hers, his low triumphant growl burning from his throat.

And with a single shared breath, his hips plunged forward, and that hot hard cock burrowed inside her. Digging itself deep, just as sure and certain as his hands had been against the stone. And just like the stone, Daisy could only splinter and shatter and obey beneath it, opening up wide for his strength, his command, his magic.

"Oh gods, Filak," she gasped, as the floor beneath her arse rose with his thrusts, helping him meet her, driving him deeper. "Fuck!"

Filak's ragged exhale sounded like a laugh, his sharp teeth nipping at her throat, his body moving deft and powerful above her. "*Fokk, sólin mín*," he breathed back. "*Daisy mín.*"

There was still no fighting it, only moaning and clutching him and needing him closer, shuddering all over as the stone kept shifting beneath her, as Filak kept delving, digging, drilling. Gouging himself deeper and deeper, ramming faster and harder, until the sounds were loud and wet and lurid, echoing through the huge empty room. But there still wasn't any pain, and the cool stone beneath Daisy's back now felt more like sand, like easy rippling softness that only urged them on faster, harder, closer. Please, more, please...

Daisy's relief flashed out with sudden, shocking intensity, quaking her all over, while Filak's eyes rolled back, and he drove himself even deeper—and then he was breaking, too. Shattering out into molten flooding bliss, shuddering them both into the floor, the room, the very earth itself.

Daisy could only gasp and quiver and cling to him, feeling his body seize and spasm inside her as he emptied out every last drop. Again speaking to her in that language they both knew, swearing he would fill her, he would show her his secrets, claim her here in the long-lost home of his forefathers.

When Filak finally drew away again, his face was flushed, and he blinked down at the sea of black and white sand around them with unmistakable awe in his eyes. Awe that only grew as he watched himself slowly pulling out of Daisy, as that surge of hot fluid bubbled and belched in his wake.

Pooling out onto all that fine sand, painting and feeding it, too, life pouring out from the sun he'd given her...

"*Gott, sólin mín,*" he murmured, as he slipped his hand down into that thick, wet-stained sand, and delved his fingers into it. And then, as Daisy's heart skipped, he brought up his dripping, sandy fingers, and then sucked them off, one by one. Clearly not caring in the slightest about the sand, or about the fact that he was tasting his own seed, or even about the bright red line one of his claws drew against his lip.

It felt quietly, bizarrely sacred, somehow, and when Filak dipped his hand again, and brought it to Daisy's mouth, she didn't refuse. And instead, she carefully sucked off one finger, and then the next, and the next. Tasting the sweetness of his seed, the thick grit of his sand, the ancient weight of this room, the sharp threat of his claws against her tongue. All of it so strangely intimate, like another silent, secret conversation between them. With her saying, *yes, I want you, yes, I want your magic and your danger and your Skýli, even if it's foreign, even if it's wrong...*

And in return, Filak was—again—promising to give it to her. To prove this to her. To draw her into his world and his thrall, to share this impossible place with her, to whisk her into the bright shimmering dream.

That awareness kept whispering as they drew apart, and as Filak carefully cleaned Daisy up with a rag. And then, his hand smoothed over the sand beneath them, and... sealed it. Flattened it. Made the floor's tile new again, but now— Daisy's cheeks heated—now with the black and white slightly swirling together, with the remnants of their own blended pleasure embedded deep within it. Making it... theirs. Making it... art.

Daisy's eyes caught Filak's, held for an instant—and without at all meaning to, she groped sideways for her abandoned sketchbook, and the lamp. And then, still a little breathless, she began sketching all of it. The swirled tile. The stunning room. The beautiful curves of the ceiling. The black metal rising up toward it. The alcoves and doors lining the rounded wall, all silent promises of unknown wonder.

And once she'd captured all of it, she flipped to a new page, and drew one more. Filak's long clawed hand, spread wide against the polished floor. Hers. *Theirs.*

Beside Daisy, Filak hadn't even moved, waiting in perfect stillness while she drew. But once she finished, he twitched a satisfied nod, and then helped her dress again, and drew her back to her feet. "*Skýli, sólin mín,*" he murmured, with a wry shake of his head, and a disbelieving laugh. "*Við fundum Skýli!*"

We found the Skýli, it surely meant, and Daisy grinned and nodded back, while Filak turned and stared up at it again, and dragged both hands down his face. As if he still couldn't believe it, as if he almost expected it to vanish at any moment.

But then, as they watched, another large chunk of stone broke away from the white ceiling above. Plummeting downward in stark, eerie silence, before smashing apart into a spray of sliding pieces on the floor.

Filak flinched all over, and he shot a sudden wide-eyed look at Daisy—and then he clutched her hand, swiped for the lamp, and yanked her back toward the wall. Where he slapped his hand furiously against the stone door until it opened, and then dragged her out into the tunnel, and slammed the door shut behind them. Just in time, apparently, as the sounds of yet more smashing rumbled ominously from behind the closed door.

"*Fokk,*" Filak hissed, his head tipped back in another silent prayer. "*Fokk, sólin mín.*"

Daisy's breath escaped in a shrill-sounding laugh, and she again eased into his side, rubbed her hand firmly against his back. "It's all right, Filak," she said, though she had no conception whether that was true or not. "It's stood there for hundreds of years, I'm sure we haven't broken it permanently, right?"

Filak groaned and heavily sagged into Daisy's touch, even as he launched into another incomprehensible tangle of Aelakesh. Maybe telling her about what was wrong with the room, and maybe something about an earthquake, and all the repairs that needed to be done. And then—she was positive she'd caught this part—he told her that since his magic was always weaker after nightfall, it wasn't safe to stay much longer.

"*Við komum fljótlega aftur*," he said, with a decisive nod, as he clasped her hand, and led her back through the tunnel again. "*Á morgun?*"

Daisy mostly followed that too, and nodded back toward him. They would come back again in the morning. And suddenly the prospect felt impossibly warm and bright, a shimmering tantalizing beacon. They would come back, and spend more time in this beautiful impossible place, and she could draw every last corner and cranny of it, while Filak fixed and fortified it, and then...

"And then," Daisy ventured, glancing toward Filak's profile in the lamplight. "And then you bring back your people? The Nor-ka-esh, to the Skýli?"

But yes, of course that was Filak's plan, and the warmth flashed across his eyes as he gave an approving pat to her arse. "*Ach, sólin mín*," he replied. "*Nor-ka-esh. Skýli. Heim.*"

Heim was *home*, Daisy knew, and Filak said it with a catch in his voice, a slight straightening of his spine. As if this was a genuine relief for him, a light in his darkness, kindling in his eyes, curving at his mouth.

"*Líka fyrir þig, sólin mín*," he told Daisy, with another pat to her arse. "*Daisy og Filak og sonur okkar. Heim.*"

Oh. Daisy couldn't quite follow all of that, but his meaning was again far too clear. The Skýli was for her, too. And if she agreed to stay, they would make it their home.

The weight of that swung and swayed in Daisy's belly, because beyond her first few years of childhood, she'd never once had a real home of her own. And now Filak was just... offering this. Giving it to her. The most beautiful place she'd ever seen in her life, here, *hers*. A home, a dream...

But the further they walked, the heavier it felt, because damn it, she shouldn't be going along with this so easily, right? She was still only supposed to be observing, learning, for the next two weeks. Not longing for Filak's home, or believing his promises, or allowing him to act as though he owned her, and had settled her fate, again. He was still dangerous, he'd still locked her in a dungeon...

It made for a long, quiet walk back through the tunnels, and even once they reached the cart again, the distance back to the mountain felt much further this time, too. And driving the cart seemed to take far more effort than before, and at several points Filak even got out and pushed it from behind, the sweat trickling down his face.

But finally the cart rolled to a stop, and Filak guided Daisy back out of the tunnel, and into the familiar shop again. Though the room was now eerily dark and silent, with no one else in sight, and Daisy fought the urge to draw closer to Filak, to feel his safe solid body against hers.

But then, once they stepped out into the corridor, there were—people. A loud, motley knot of people, all rushing straight toward them. "There they are," called a vaguely familiar voice. "Filak! Daisy!"

Daisy froze in place, and after an instant's confused staring, she caught sight of Rosa, and her mate John-Ka, and the tall sly orc from the garden. Joarr, his name had been. And several other orcs she didn't know, and wait, there was also Jule, and her big captain mate Grimarr, too.

They all tumbled to a stop before Daisy and Filak, Rosa in front, with a worried-looking smile on her face. "It's so good to see you!" she told Daisy, a little too brightly. "Where have you two been hiding, all this time?"

Daisy blinked, and shot another uneasy glance at the assembled group of people behind Rosa, but then took a deep breath. Rosa would love to hear about the Skýli, right? Surely all of them would? And maybe that was why they were here, why they looked like this?

"Well," Daisy began, with an attempt at a smile toward Rosa, "we went exploring, and then we—"

But her voice broke there, because Filak's hand had suddenly clenched hard against her back. And when Daisy glanced toward him, she found him looking starkly, viciously forbidding. His shoulders hunched, his jaw set, his eyes narrow and glinting and cold. Speaking his own answer, as clearly as if he'd shouted it aloud between them.

He didn't... want Rosa to know about the Skýli. Maybe he didn't want any of them to know.

The confusion whirled through Daisy's thoughts—why didn't he want them to know?—but she wasn't about to argue it now, so she took another breath, let it out. "And... we found so many interesting things to draw!" she continued, as steadily as she could. "Tunnels, and stalactites, and crystal deposits..."

But her voice trailed off again, because none of them actually wanted to hear it, did they? No, no, they were just glancing uneasily at each other, shifting on their feet. Until beside Daisy, Filak drew a little taller, and snapped out some kind of demand that she couldn't understand. But in return, Rosa and John-Ka both winced, Grimarr and Joarr frowned, and Jule squared her shoulders and stepped forward, holding out a folded sheet of paper.

"I'm afraid we have some important news for you, Daisy," Jule said, her voice low with foreboding. "Your partner wants you back."

36

Daisy blinked at Jule for a blank, bewildered moment, while her heartbeat kicked in her chest. Her partner wanted her back? *Who?!*

But then her shaking hand swiped for the outstretched letter in Jule's hand, and flipped it open. And there, scrawled across the page, was a mass of familiar handwriting. *Lew's* handwriting.

Dear Daisy, it began. *I was shocked and devastated to learn of your sudden departure, and your claim of dissatisfaction with our relationship. I am sorry to hear of your distress, and disappointed that you did not offer me a chance to address your concerns before taking such drastic action.*

While I support your right to make your own decisions, I cannot fathom how you mean to survive on your own without an income, or without my generous stability and support. I also cannot fathom your reckless decision to travel to the city alone, through dangerous orc country.

I have therefore gone to the considerable expense of hiring an experienced team of armed guards to locate you and escort you safely back to Dusbury. I expect you will offer these professionals your full cooperation and gratitude.

Upon your safe return, I will gladly renegotiate the terms of our personal and professional relationship to ensure our mutual satisfaction.

As always, my heart is forever yours. Lew.

Daisy stared at the letter for another long, endless moment, and she only vaguely noticed that her hand had begun shaking, her heartbeat thundering in her ears. "Wh-where did you get this?" her faint voice asked. "And how?"

"We intercepted it today on the way out of Dusbury," Jule said, with a curt nod toward Joarr beside her. "Mr. Wallace apparently sent several duplicates to places he expects you could be. But the regiment he hired to fetch you is currently marching northeast, toward the city."

The *regiment*? Daisy gaped at Jule again, and nearly lost her grip on the letter. "The *what*?" she demanded. "How many men?"

"About fifty," came Jule's grim reply. "All of them active military personnel, supposedly now off duty. It seems that Mr. Wallace—and possibly his lord handler—are considering you a serious security threat to their mission against us."

Oh. Oh, gods. Daisy's head was already beginning to ache, pulsing along with her racing heartbeat. Because damn it, that would be just like Lew, wouldn't it? To assume that Daisy running away from him hadn't had anything to do with the actual reason she'd given him, or the other women in his bed—but instead attributing it to the mission. The top-secret project. The project Lew had refused to tell her about, likely because he'd guessed how she would respond. And if Daisy *had* found out about the project, would she have run away like this, and taken Lew's secrets with her? Perhaps?

Daisy groaned aloud, and rubbed her hands at her eyes. "So what now?" she asked, her voice hitching. "What do we do next?"

But there was only silence in return, and when Daisy

blinked at the group before her, they were all watching *her*. As if they expected *her* to answer that question, somehow, and suddenly there was just raw blazing panic, juddering through her chest. What the hell was she supposed to do, or say? She was only supposed to be watching and learning for the next two weeks, while they dealt with Lew's horrible attack... right? But now, if Lew had truly sent an entire regiment of men after her, did that mean she would never be able to leave Orc Mountain again, ever? Unless she wanted to end up trapped back with Lew again?

Daisy's swimming eyes stared back down at the letter, at all those snide implications, those thinly veiled threats. *Shocked. Devastated. Disappointed. Drastic action. Reckless decision. I cannot fathom how you mean to survive.* Followed by that tepid promise of renegotiating their relationship, and then that too-familiar line, *My heart is forever yours*. Now feeling just how that fake ring had felt, like a shiny empty bauble tossed toward an annoying, misbehaving pet.

Daisy still couldn't speak, and a sudden quivering tightness spasmed across her throat. As if she was about to start weeping, right here in front of all these watching people, and her thoughts snapped back to that dungeon Filak had trapped her in, to the terror, to that unbreakable chain trapping her alone in the dark...

But then—a growl. A deep, rumbling, furious snarl, erupting from beside her. From... Filak. His eyes were flashing, his mouth contorting with rage—and without warning, he snatched for Lew's letter. Giving it one single contemptuous look, and then stabbing it with his claws, and dragging them downward. Shredding the letter into long, jagged strips, and then again, and again, and again. Until it was reduced to a tattered dangling tangle of ribbons, which he hurled to the floor, and then stomped on with his big muddy boot.

"*Nei*," he hissed, not toward Daisy, but toward—the rest of them? "*Nei. Daisy er mín. Daisy er sálufélagi minn. Daisy verður hjá mér!*"

It meant—No. Daisy was his. Daisy was his mate. Daisy was staying with him.

And damn it, but it shouldn't have felt like such a relief. Like hope, like refuge. Because of course Filak would protect her, he would guard her and keep her safe, and he would happily tear Lew to shreds before he allowed him—or his appalling regiment—to ever touch Daisy again.

And without at all meaning to, Daisy eased closer into Filak's side, into his strong solid certainty. Into the dizzying reassurance of his arm instantly circling around her, yanking her tighter against him. And now his hand was stroking her, too, warm and steady and firm, and it was everything, gods curse her, everything.

"Right, then," came Jule's reply, sounding distinctly relieved. "Well, if you're in agreement, Daisy, we'll let that regiment keep chasing your imaginary trail toward the city. And with any luck, they won't start guessing you're here until after we've dealt with their attack."

Wait. *They won't... start guessing.* Daisy blinked blankly toward Jule, and dragged in a thin, shaky breath. "But—why would they—guess I'm here?" she croaked. "Won't they just think I'm—somewhere else? Or dead, maybe?"

And truly, what had become of her, that she wanted Lew to think she was *dead*, so she could stay here at Orc Mountain—and the look Jule gave her was tolerant, or maybe even pitying. "I'm afraid not," Jule replied. "If those men can blame orcs for their difficulties, they inevitably will, even without a good reason. And"—she raised her brows toward Daisy—"can you be sure you didn't give Mr. Wallace any reason to suspect your connection with us? Or with Filak?"

Daisy took a breath, and began to dredge up a reply—of course she hadn't told Lew about Filak—but then Jule's too-knowing eyes flicked downward. Running over Daisy's neck and collarbone, lingering on—oh. Her tattoo. Her *sun*.

But no, no, Lew couldn't have suspected the sun was related to Filak... could he? Or could he, and too late, Daisy clapped her hand up to her neck, to the familiar gold of her *kraga*, and to... Filak's *bite-marks*. Those distinct, raised ridges on her skin. The ones Lew had looked at with such pure, scathing contempt, and said, *Those teeth-marks had better not scar, either. Gods, did you go find someone feral?*

Jule's expression looked rather foreboding now, and her smile didn't at all reach her eyes. "Well, we'd suggest you stay well hidden here until the attack," she said flatly. "And if you'd still like to leave after that, we can create some alternate plans then."

Right. Daisy swallowed and nodded—in truth, that was what she'd planned for anyway, wasn't it?—though now the visions of that looming attack were swarming with dizzying, sickening strength. The poison. The belladonna. The orclings. And she would be right here in the midst of it, even if it killed them all.

"Do you... still feel confident that you can prevent the attack, and protect the mountain?" Daisy's small voice asked, into the silence. "Have you found out anything else? Is there... anything I can do to help? Maybe I should just go back and..."

But her fear was rapidly rising again, because gods, she didn't want to have to see Lew again. She didn't want to think about Lew again. He'd lied to her, used her for her art, and then planned to brutally murder an entire mountain of people...

Beside Daisy, Filak was hissing a low steady growl, and after a brief glance toward him, Jule shook her head. "We appreciate the offer, Daisy, but it would be best if you just stay put while we handle this," she replied. "None of us want Mr. Wallace getting his hands on you, or deciding to make use of you."

Make use of you. Another cold wash of fear streaked up Daisy's spine, because—wait. Was that why Lew had sent the regiment, too? Not just to find Daisy, but... to *use* her? Again? Not just for her art, but for... the attack? For murder? For feeding belladonna to children?

But the look in Jule's eyes suggested that this was exactly what they were worried about. Lew capturing Daisy with his regiment, and forcing her to help him. And gods, hadn't Julian mentioned that as a possibility too, back at the start of this? As something Filak had feared? *You ken he was fool enough to march her all through our mountain, when he thought she wished to learn its layout and ventilation systems, so she could help our enemies flood it full of poison gas, and choke us all to death?*

But now... Filak *had* done all that. Daisy now knew enough about this mountain to present a true risk to them, right? And could Lew truly force her, use threats or pain or blackmail to drag the truth out of her? Use an entire regiment against her? Surely he wouldn't... or would he? He'd already lied to her, hadn't he? Used her for his gain and his coin? Betrayed her with another woman? And wait, how did Sybil fit into this, too? Was Lew still working with her? Would she help him destroy Daisy, too, and everyone here she cared about?

Filak's hand was stroking Daisy's back again, but she barely felt it through the shouting, shuddering clamour—and she couldn't hear Filak's sharp response back toward Jule, either. But in return, Jule smiled and raised both her hands, and said something that might have been meant to be comforting. Something that brought no comfort at all, because Lew had somehow become a monster, and he wanted to make Daisy into a monster, too. To force her to hurt all these people who'd been so kind to her, to be part of feeding belladonna to children...

Filak barked something else toward the group, and finally they filtered off again, heading back down the corridor. And though Rosa furtively smiled and waved goodbye over her shoulder, Daisy couldn't find a response, not even when Filak kept stroking her, tucking her closer into his side.

"*Róleg, sólin mín,*" he murmured, into her hair. "*Þú ert örugg hjá mér.*"

He was trying to reassure her, to remind her that she was safe with him. But Daisy wasn't supposed to be binding herself to this, to him, not yet. She couldn't let him use this to trap her here, she was supposed to be—she should be—something—*something*—

"Daisy," Filak said, firmer this time, but it sounded very far away, and much closer was the rising roar of Daisy's heartbeat. Booming louder and louder with every breath, blazing with fear and bitterness and regret. *I cannot fathom how you mean to survive...*

"*Daisy,*" came Filak's voice again, but it felt even further now, barely a whisper amidst the chaos. *I expect you will offer these professionals your full cooperation,* Lew had written, and it was just like another dungeon, wasn't it? Another chain around her neck, dragging her to someone else's will, trapping her in the dark...

Daisy couldn't hear Filak speaking now, couldn't feel the touch of his stroking hands. Couldn't follow his urgent-sounding questions, spoken in a halting blend of Aelakesh and common-tongue, something about bed or eat or sleep. Could barely even see his face, how he looked even paler than usual, his eyes searching and intent on hers...

But then—he was moving, and guiding Daisy along beside him. Leading her numb, stumbling feet down the corridor. Further and further, around twists and corners, taking her to—to—

A room. A new room. A new dark, deep cave, full of danger and weapons and cold merciless steel.

A dungeon.

37

Filak had brought Daisy to a dungeon.

Daisy jolted, stared, and for a dizzying desperate moment, she wanted to shout at him, to cling to him, to run. To demand what the hell he was doing, what he was thinking, this room was—it was—

Her eyes swept over it again, as more shock and disbelief screeched through her skull, drowning out her thundering heartbeat. Because yes, it was a dungeon, illuminated only by a large crackling fireplace, with whips and cuffs and chains lining the stone walls, and dangling from the ceiling. And along the opposite wall, there even stood what appeared to be several *cells*, made of thick steel bars.

But. In this dungeon, there were also... people. Orcs. Multiple orcs, of various shapes and sizes, but mostly in states of undress. Gasping, groaning, striking, biting. Pinning each other to walls and platforms and benches. Kneeling and sucking and begging. Many of the orcs had *kragas* around their necks, too, some of them with chains that were clipped to the stone walls, or wrapped around their lovers' hands...

Because yes, they were—*lovers*. Right? That orc was willingly clinging to that other one, his face buried in his shoulder. Another orc was bent over and begging, while his partner stroked his bared arse. And another one—Daisy froze, stared at his vaguely familiar face—was that soft-spoken orc who worked in the sickroom. Eben. Kneeling before a tall, handsome orc with knives in his hair, who was fondly smiling and murmuring praises as Eben greedily kissed and sucked his huge, scarred cock.

Daisy's flailing heart skipped a beat, while her eyes flicked down the wall, and caught on another familiar face. Gareth, the smith. Stripped to the waist, showing off his bulky chest and shoulders, as he bent a lean, sweaty orc over before him, and snapped a long, coiled *whip* through the air above his head. But the orc's eyes didn't betray even a trace of fear, only hunger, and need, and... pleasure.

And finally, Daisy's whirling thoughts caught on some-thing solid, something certain. Rosa had told her about this, hadn't she? The Ka-esh pleasure-room. The *dýflissa,* she'd called it. A safe place to explore pleasure together. To learn.

The truth of it felt almost dizzying, a bright light blasting behind Daisy's eyes. Strong enough to drown out the screaming in her head, even for a brief blessed instant. Because yes, if nothing else, she still wanted to learn. She needed to learn. It was the one goal she'd decided on, the one conviction that held true in all this mess. Something that was art, something that was safe, something that was hers.

So when Filak guided her forward, into the room, she didn't hesitate, didn't resist. Not even at the curious glances from the room's occupants, and not even when Filak gently grasped her shoulders, and set her back against a cool stone wall. Not even when he boxed her close into it, his forearms settling to the stone on either side of her head, his face ducking into her throat.

"*Ach, sólin mín?*" he murmured, his breath hot against her ear. "*Ríða?* Fuck? In *dýflissa?*"

A sharp shiver trembled up Daisy's back—he was really

asking if she wanted this, here. And it was ridiculous, preposterous, utterly unthinkable, but somehow she was... nodding. Clinging to him. Drawing him closer. Because yes, yes, it was still something, it was learning in the madness, it was how desperately she needed his touch, his command, his reassurance. She needed him to keep distracting her, directing her, dragging her away from the horror and the fear, even if it was this, especially if it was this...

"*Gott*," Filak breathed, and oh, those were his hands again, stroking her, caressing her, smoothing over her sides, her arms, her shoulders. Sinking Daisy heavier and heavier against the wall, easing her breaths slower and deeper, even when he unhooked the fur cloak she'd still been wearing, and tossed it onto a nearby stone bench. Leaving her dressed in only her silk wrap and her boots and trousers, but he liked that, he was looking her up and down with hazy hooded eyes, as if she was a painting, a stunning work of art all his own.

And when his warm steady hands kept caressing, smoothing against her waist, her breasts, slipping beneath her wrap and her trousers, Daisy only gasped and arched into it, into the sweet steady reassurance of his touch. His certainty amidst the fear and danger, his light in the darkness, his silent promise that no matter what happened around them, he would keep her safe...

He meant it even when the silk slipped downwards, exposing Daisy's bare breasts and peaked nipples to the room. He meant it when he eased down her trousers, showing his marks on her belly and groin, the skin of her thighs, the dark hair in between. And he even meant it when he knelt to pull off her boots and trousers entirely, his mouth skating over that hair at her groin, and then leaning in further to kiss at it. To lick and taste and tease her, to even lazily scrape her with his teeth, while his glittering eyes held hers, and spoke. *You look at me, while I taste you, and bare you for me.*

And though Daisy could again feel the room's other occupants watching, their eyes prickling all over her bare skin—and especially over that vow on her belly—Filak's eyes were stronger. Filak's hands were warmer. Filak's tongue was a hot slithering wonder, now kissing slowly up over her marked belly, tasting the black lines of his vow. And then he eased further up, and up, gently catching each peaked nipple, swirling it with his tongue—and then rising to her throat, her lips. Kissing her with such fervent, ardent care, even as his warm wandering hands found her arms, her wrists, and slowly raised them over her head. Pressing them against the stone wall, and then...

Circling something cold around them. A *chain*.

Daisy froze, her heartbeat suddenly screaming in her ears, her eyes catching wild on Filak's face. On where he was already looking at her, searching her, his eyes burning, his breath shuddering out from between his parted lips.

"*Nei?*" he gasped, his voice ragged. "*Stoppa?*"

Stoppa meant *stop*, Daisy knew—but now that she was facing the question, facing him, she couldn't seem to find the wherewithal to answer. To say, *nei*, because then he would take this away, and the rest of it would all rush back in again. Lew, Sybil, the belladonna, the regiment, the attack, the dungeon...

But *this* was the dungeon, this was danger, and it was all twisting and tangling together with Filak's blazing eyes, with the hungry flex of his hand on her wrists. Shouting now, without him speaking at all, that he liked this, he wanted this. He truly wanted to chain Daisy up in a dungeon, and trap her, and keep her.

The fear should have spiked again, choked out all the rest. Screamed that he was still dangerous too, this was a horrible ridiculous mistake, she'd only given this two weeks, what the hell was she doing, what was she allowing...

But instead there was something... else. Something like... understanding. Or maybe even... appreciation. Because Filak wasn't hiding it. He wasn't lying or pretending, like Lew had done. No, he was shouting his truth straight into her face, showing it to her, and giving her the freedom to choose. To see. To learn.

So somehow, impossible, *appalling*, Daisy raised her chin, and nodded. Saying... *yes. Yes, Filak. I see you. I want you.*

And gods, the look in his eyes. Like art, like rapture, like bright sweeping ecstasy. Like Daisy was again the most stunningly beautiful painting he'd ever seen, and he even said it, or something like it, his voice raw and rasping as he circled that chain closer around her wrists, and bound them together against the wall. Holding her there, pinning her up for him, so he could again caress both hands down her naked exposed body, look at her and touch her and worship her, treat her like a jewel on display, polish her and break her with his clever stroking hands.

It was unlike anything Daisy had ever known, pleasure and danger and surrender pooling all at once, turning her to pliant quaking rubble beneath his hands, his claws, his mouth. And with her arms bound up over her head like this, she couldn't even urge him on, couldn't shove down his trousers, couldn't drag his mouth to the one place that was now screaming for him, frantic for his tongue and his relief. No, she could only shudder and gasp and beg, her words an incomprehensible blur of common-tongue and Aelakesh, *please* and *typpi* and *ríða* and *more, please.*

But Filak wanted that too, wanted her undone and begging, laid bare for anyone to see. Though Daisy could feel him shuddering too now, could taste the effort in his heaving breaths against her skin, the hunger of his hands. The way his touch was rougher now, his claws leaving vivid red scrapes behind them, but that only whipped it higher and hotter, reducing her to gasping, pleading, almost weeping...

And it was that, finally, that brought Filak up again, kissing her mouth and comforting her with sharp stroking hands. And then he dropped a hand to shove down his own trousers, letting his thick leaking cock slap wet and heavy against Daisy's belly, and even that made her shout and beg more, writhing against the wall, against the restraints, needing him, all of him, please.

"Please, Filak," she gasped, not caring who saw, who heard. "Please. *Ríða* me. Please."

Filak's voice in her ear was a laugh, a groan, something raw and aggressive and powerful—and with a firm grip of his strong hands to her hips, he hoisted her up off the floor entirely, spreading her legs wide around him. So his hard, leaking cock could streak down her belly, and seek its way up beneath. Prodding itself into her crease, delving up into where Daisy was already so wet, so open and desperate, clutching at him, welcoming him inside...

"Please," Daisy gasped again, as her body arched, grinding them together, oh. "Please, *sálufélagi minn*."

My mate, it meant, and why had she said such a thing— but that was why, that answering flash across Filak's eyes, raw and aggressive and victorious. And with a fierce snap of his hips, he plunged up swift and deep, encasing himself in her slick spasming heat. Pinning her trembling body tight against the wall, trussing her up in a dungeon—but this time Daisy wanted it, she needed every last breath of it, she would be destroyed if he stopped it, please...

"Please, Filak," she begged again, as he hoisted her higher, and gave an experimental little thrust, out and in. "Please. More. *Ach*."

Her voice was still badly wavering, perhaps hitching at the painful wonderful scrape of the stone wall against her bare back. But Filak swiped sideways for something—her fur cloak—and deftly maneuvered it back over her shoulders, between her and the wall. "*Róleg, sólin mín,*" he murmured, so soft, so soothing. "*Ríðum bráðum, ach? Róleg. Gott.*"

Daisy nodded and shivered all over, needing him to keep going, keep talking, yes, and his smile toward her was swift, approving, as he kept speaking. Murmuring that stream of soft reassuring words in Aelakesh, as his hips canted back toward her, and buried his spasming cock deeper inside her.

"*Almáttugur,*" he gasped, his lashes fluttering—and oh, yes, this was it, his body finally moving, plunging in and out of her with fast, urgent strokes. Jolting her back against the wall with every thudding thrust, pinioning her there, trapping her with his body, his chain, his eyes. Like a jailer with his hostage, a hunter with his prey, using her, consuming her, doing with her whatever he pleased...

But again, there was no fear. No resistance. Just the trammelling need for more of it, more of him, yes, gods, yes. And Daisy was even shouting it now, begging it, yanking against the beautiful bite of the chain on her wrists, wanting to feel it, to embody it, to be his quarry, his captive, his muse his mate his artist—

She screamed as the bliss thundered through her, striking her in reckless dizzying jerks. Her trapped body wrenching and thrashing against its bonds, clamping around Filak's cock buried inside her. Milking him and pumping him, demanding more, more, more—and yes, now he was crumpling too, his body juddering against her and inside her, his head tipping back, his shout hot and reverent. Undone by her, conquered by her, even like this, with his chains and his cock, his claws and his eyes and his teeth.

And that was part of it too, Daisy's distant thoughts pointed out, as she fought to find her breath again. The give and take of it. The way it always was with an artist and a subject, or the art and the viewer. The challenge, the learning, the trading back and forth. Just like they had earlier in the Skýli. Making a new experience, together. *Seeing* together.

And this—felt like that. Even when Filak's hand curved against Daisy's *kraga*, and then tilted her neck sideways. So his sharp teeth could scrape against her skin, hard enough to leave more marks—and then those teeth bit down, deep, as his softening cock slipped out of her still-spasming body, and released a shocking gushing stream of molten fluid from between her spread legs, spewing it down to the floor beneath them. And maybe it was foolish, flagrant, shameful... but it still felt like art, too. Like making something new.

Daisy couldn't have said how long they stayed there, shivering, riding through it together. But at some point, Filak carefully released her hands, and set her feet down onto the floor again. Drawing that fur shawl closer around her, covering her again, before snatching up the rest of her clothes, and guiding her past all those watching eyes out into the corridor. And though Daisy's feet slightly staggered, Filak's arm was firm and safe around her, his voice still murmuring purrs and praises against her hair.

She only vaguely noticed the people they passed in the corridor, or the way Filak guided her into a darkened door. And when he lit the candle, the sight of her new little room felt hazy and distant too, the feel of the bed's fur hot and strange against her tingling skin. But now Filak was here again, settling beside her on the bed, stroking her bare, trembling body with his warm steady hands.

"*Gott, sólin mín,*" he said, so husky and soft. "*Þú ert svo falleg. Svo sæt. Svo fullkominn sálufélagi.*"

Daisy shivered and curled closer against him, breathing in the rich familiar scent of him, the certainty of his strong caress. "You chained me up in a dungeon," she managed, through her thick throat. "Again."

But Filak only kissed her hair, and gave a gentle tweak of

his claw against her nipple. "Ach," he murmured back. "*Daisy mín. Sálufélagi minn. Þú ert örugg hjá mér.*"

It was the same thing he'd said back in the corridor, about Lew—and though the thought of Lew still shot ice up Daisy's spine, it felt far fainter, less potent, than before. And surely that was because of Filak, because of what he'd done, back there in that *dýflissa*. Showing her that she would be safe, with him. Safe, even in a dungeon. *Safe*, shouted so loudly she couldn't ignore it, couldn't unlearn it.

And in the midst of it, he'd made art with her, too. Just like he had in the tunnels, and with the Skýli. And now, lying here sprawled and sated on this bed, with this dangerous devil in her arms, Daisy could almost see it, almost believe it...

"Do you think I'm a real artist, Filak?" she asked, foolishly, into the close silence. "Daisy artist?"

She mimicked drawing in midair with her hand, and Filak's glance down toward her in the candlelight was bemused, and almost fond. "*Ach, sólin mín,*" he said. "Daisy artist."

He said it with such simple, decisive certainty, as though the matter had never been in question. And his eyes on hers were so certain too, just as sure as he'd been back in the *dýflissa*, just as sure as when he'd stomped Lew's tattered letter under his boot.

"Daisy artist," he said, with a soft kiss to her forehead. "*Artistinn minn. Sálufélagi minn. Heim.*"

Heim. Home. It shuddered against the distant nagging voice, still echoing through Daisy's thoughts—he was still dangerous, he'd locked her in a dungeon, and she was only supposed to be watching, right? *Ridiculous and immature behaviour, appallingly unscientific, foolish...*

"But... what about Lew?" Daisy croaked, wincing, into the silence. "And the regiment? The attack?"

But Filak's scoff was harsh and thick with derision, his

claws reflexively prodding against her shoulder. "*Nei Lew*," he snapped. "*Nei, sólin mín.* Lew is naught. Forget Lew."

The certainty of his voice shuddered her all over, another too-tempting beacon in the dark. No Lew. Forget Lew. Just like she'd tried to forget Filak, but he was still here, and far stronger than before. Drawing his vows on her skin, chaining her in a dungeon, sharing his long-lost home with her...

"Forget Lew, Daisy," Filak said again, even firmer than before, as his hand slid up to her neck, and curled close and tight around it. Letting his claws dig in, hard and almost painful, almost like a threat—and oh, then he bent his head down, too. Spreading his mouth wide and deliberate against the delicate skin of her throat, letting her feel all those sharp deadly teeth...

It truly was a threat, a show of his power, and his control. If she didn't obey, he could snap her and break her, tear her apart, leave her here to bleed out alone on the bed...

But instead of the fear Daisy should have felt, or maybe the shocked affronted rage, there was only a shaky, heavy exhale, and something almost like relief. Like... affection. Because just like in the *dýflissa*, this was just Filak trying to protect her, and help her, and comfort her, right? He wouldn't actually ever hurt her, or trap her again... would he?

"*Nei Lew*," he breathed again, hot and menacing and wonderful against her skin. "Forget Lew. Ach?"

And in this breath, this quivering waiting moment, it was everything Daisy wanted, everything she'd ever wanted for her own. A dream, a dark dangerous devil, a dungeon, an artist, a home...

"Ach, Filak," she whispered, as she drew him closer, and arched up into his teeth, his menace, his promise. "I'll try."

38

When Daisy awoke the next morning, she felt relaxed, refreshed, and strangely at peace.

She would forget Lew. She would focus on art, and learning, and seeing. She was an artist. She was.

That certainty settled deeper as she blinked toward Filak beside her in the bed, and found him already awake, watching her with warm, glimmering eyes. His tall lean body was still fully naked, his pale skin luminous in the light of the already-lit candle, and at his groin—Daisy's breath shuddered out—he was hard again, his cock long and glossy and thick, oozing a bead of shimmering white at its blackened tip.

Damn, he was a sight, and instead of speaking aloud, Daisy groped behind her for her sketchbook and pencils, which had still been tucked into Filak's satchel on the floor. And then she sat up on the bed, flipped to a new page, and began drawing.

And just as she'd fully expected, Filak was lovely to draw. The lines of him so smooth and lean, the black marks adding texture and drama to his pale skin. And the sharp angles of his face, the shadowy depths of his dark speaking eyes, the elegant tips of his pointed ears. And next the long cords of his neck, the rows of his ribs—perhaps a little fainter than they'd been before?—and then, his cock. His long, swollen, heavily marked cock, lying both innocuous and powerful against his hip, with Daisy's sun still brazenly drawn upon it. Silently shouting of whose it was, where it belonged, who it would be fucking and filling next.

Filak had lain almost perfectly still as Daisy had drawn, showing himself an excellent subject, too. And in return, she found herself taking extra time, extra care, adding as many details as she pleased. The dark hair peeking from under his armpit, the perfect little dip of his navel, the long claws he apparently had on his toes, too...

When she finally finished, she could admit that it was a very good likeness, and perhaps Filak thought so too, gazing down toward it with strangely intent eyes. "Daisy draw Filak," he murmured, as he lifted a finger, and stroked his claw against the page. "You like?"

He looked almost shy, suddenly, glancing up toward her under his lashes, and Daisy couldn't help her impulsive nod, her swift smile back. And in return, Filak's head slowly tilted, as if considering something—and then he reached his long arm over her toward the table beside the bed, and came back holding that jar of black ink.

"Daisy mark Filak?" he asked, as his hand gently dropped to caress against that vow he'd written on her belly. "Art Filak?"

Oh. He wanted her to—draw on him. To mark him, like he'd done to her. And maybe Daisy should have refused such a proposal, because Filak's marks were meant to be prayers to his gods, right? And they clearly carried considerable weight for him, and she was still only supposed to be learning, two weeks...

But Filak was still looking at her like that, so shy and serious and hopeful, and he again reached over her, and this time came back holding a handful of brushes. The brushes he'd bought her at the shop yesterday. All of them brand-new and untouched, just waiting for an artist to use them. Waiting for her.

The longing swelled in Daisy's chest, too powerful to resist—and after studying the brushes for an instant, she chose the smallest, finest one, and set the others aside. And then she prepared the brush, smoothing it to a fine pointed tip, before dipping it carefully into the jar of ink Filak was still holding.

"You're sure?" she asked him, hesitating, searching his watching eyes. "And what do you want? And where?"

She couldn't understand his reply, but she could easily follow the careless wave of his hand, the way he eagerly sank down onto his back on the bed. As if he didn't care what she did, what it said, or where she put it. As long as she did it.

And maybe that did give this too much meaning, too much power—a way to speak strong and unceasing, Julian had called it. But as Daisy's eyes ran up and down Filak's lean waiting body, she could almost see the appeal in that, could feel the longing to say something, to make a claim...

Her gaze caught on a bare spot above his sharp hipbone, beside where his still-hard cock was now lying on his belly, and weeping white fluid from its slit. And after a deep breath, Daisy carefully lowered her hand to that spot on his hip, and grazed the wet brush-tip against his pale skin.

The ink was dense and satisfyingly dark, without any running or fading, so she touched the brush again, more certain this time. Watching her hand draw a familiar ring of tiny little spikes, and then a long ray floret...

Filak's cock spasmed upwards, sputtering a thick streak of white against his belly, but Daisy fought to focus on her ray, on tracing the lines inside it, on the delicate ragged edge of its pointed tip. And then, once she was satisfied, she dipped the brush again, and then drew another ray, and another. Painting... a daisy.

And gods, it was probably so foolish, so juvenile, like a child scrawling her name all over her favourite toy—but Daisy twitched her head, shoved that thought away. Filak wanted her to do this, and she loved drawing flowers. She was damned good at drawing flowers. She was an artist.

And if she wanted to draw a long, stylized stem, she would. If she wanted to connect it to one of the thick black rays of the sun extending across his groin—just like he'd done with her vow—she would. If she wanted to shade the daisy's spiked disc, so it looked more and more like an eye, she would—and she would even turn over Filak's slack hand on the bed, and use the eye on his palm as reference. Making them match, giving him a daisy that could see, a daisy that was entirely unlike any of his other marks, but still felt like him. Still belonged to him. Just like the eyes in the Skýli, in his home.

Filak again didn't move as she painted, holding himself perfectly still, but for the erratic, sustained shudders of his swollen cock. There was now an entire glossy pool of white on his belly, connecting to his slit in a thick oozing string, and in a sudden, bizarre burst of daring, Daisy reached and dipped her brush into that string, and brought it back to the daisy. Painting in the rays with it, slightly smudging the black ink beneath its glossy strokes—but gods, maybe she liked that too. Liked the shade of it, the depth it gave it against his pale skin.

So she dipped the brush into it again, fighting to ignore the way his cock flexed and spasmed, and dribbled out more. Wanting her to do this, wanting to help her do this, and Daisy's mouth felt oddly dry as she kept going, and going. Painting in each ray, one by one, blending the ink with his seed, making art, together.

When she finally sat back on her heels and studied her

new daisy, she could admit that it looked—good. It looked strong, decisive, yet delicate, even exquisite. The way it grew out of his sun, like a daisy should, and that eye in its middle looked surprisingly vivid, unnerving, as if it might blink at any moment. And it did match the one on his palm quite well, enough that Daisy again spread Filak's hand beside it, to see both eyes looking at her, just like in the Skýli. Again, like... something new. Like art. Together.

And when Daisy finally risked a glance up at Filak's face, he was staring at it, too—and then his gaze flashed up to hers, and something was shouting, blazing in his eyes. So strong that Daisy didn't even twitch when his hand snapped to her neck, circling her *kraga* hot and certain, and then guiding her face down toward his spasming leaking cock.

"*Sjúgðu mig,*" he gasped, as his other hand grasped his swollen shaft, pointed it up, as he brought Daisy's mouth down. And yes, this was just what she needed too, Filak's fat succulent crown parting her lips, spreading her wide around him, so he could plunge up smooth and deep inside. So he could mark her, and paint her, just as she'd painted him.

His thrusts were fast and hard and rough, but his hands caressed her face with astonishing care, and he was again murmuring praises, so soft and reverent in his hoarse voice. Calling her his daisy, his sun, his artist, and a dozen other things she couldn't understand—but gods, it was so good, impossibly good, like a beautiful pitch-perfect harmony of pain and power and affection and worship and gratitude.

He arched and cursed as he sprayed out down her throat, flooding her with sweet jets of heat. His eyes burning on hers, his hands trembling on her face, keeping her there, wanting to see her swallow every last drop. And Daisy willingly did, holding his gaze, revelling in that look on his face, that quiver on his mouth. Again, as if this had meant far more than she'd intended, and now...

He moaned as his hands gripped her shoulders, and

dragged her upwards. All the way up his body, over his chest, until she was straddling—his *face*. With her swollen exposed heat blatantly spread, convulsing before his hungry watching eyes.

Daisy shuddered, stared, fought the sudden urge to draw away, to hide—but oh, he just kept looking at her like that, with such bright, awestruck yearning in his eyes. And with a firm, purposeful tug of his hands, he drew her downwards. Bringing her down further and further, toward where his long black tongue was waiting, sweeping against his lips.

Daisy gasped and froze again, but Filak growled, low and hungry, and tugged her closer. While that long tongue slithered straight up to meet her, flashing her full of sudden shouting sensation—and then, oh gods, it began seeking up *inside* her. While his strong hands kept pulling her downwards, guiding her right down where he wanted her, onto his open waiting mouth. Until his warm lips met hers, kissing her sloppy and fervent, while his tongue anchored itself hot and triumphant inside.

"Filak!" Daisy choked, writhing all over at the feel of it, the shocked staggering pleasure—and oh, hell, the way he laughed, vibrating it all through his tongue, rumbling it into her grasping opened core. Fuck, it felt so good, nothing had ever felt so good, and when he pulled her down harder she didn't fight it this time, sinking heavy and obscene onto his glorious taunting mouth. Not caring, for the moment, what this looked like, what she was doing, grinding helpless and greedy against an orc's face, smearing her slickness all over his skin. Just needing more of him, all of him, please, gods, please...

Her release was a careening clutching furor, reducing her to wild desperation, a blaze of staggering ecstasy. Her voice shouting, her body quaking, fluid leaking and lips frantically kissing at the hungry mouth beneath them. Feeling that mouth kiss back just as hard, just as hungry and brazen, as if it needed this just as much as she did...

As if it was, again... art. As if it was Daisy again painting him, marking him, claiming him as her own. Seeing him.

She was still trembling when she finally drew back again, revealing Filak's flushed, slick-streaked face, his swollen wet lips. But his expression was hazy and sated, his breath exhaling in a low, satisfied sigh. And in a swift movement, he furled himself up, clasped Daisy's face, and met her lips with his. Again kissing her, tasting her, drinking her with such raw, frantic abandon, as if he wanted to swallow her whole. And maybe Daisy wanted to swallow him, too, wanted to taste herself all over his lips, to again feel the wonder of that clever delving tongue.

"*Ach, sólin mín,*" Filak breathed, once he finally drew away again, his face still shiny with Daisy's mess. "*Daisy mín.*"

He cast a glance down to the new daisy on his hip, and again he looked almost awed, almost reverent. "Artist *mín,*" he murmured, hushed, as he dropped his finger to carefully stroke at one of the shaded florets—and Daisy had just enough awareness to be grateful that it didn't streak, that it stayed just the way she'd painted it. Her art. Her orc. *Hers.*

The strength of that thought was deeply alarming, and too late, Daisy squeezed her eyes shut, and gulped down a shaky breath. Damn it, she wasn't supposed to be getting so lost in this. She was still supposed to be watching, and seeing, and learning. Not committing to this yet, not even if Filak had let her paint a daisy on him. Not even if he loved it. Not even if he'd thanked her by painting her all over his face, too.

She attempted to keep repeating that thought, even as Filak next cleaned them both up with a cloth, his touches soft on her skin. And then he passed her his waterskin, and followed it by slipping a plump tart berry between her lips— apparently from a new basket of food that had somehow emerged in the night. And then he fed her another berry, and another, and gods, now he was *feeding* her, and she should be arguing this, she should.

"You're eating too, right?" she finally asked, with a twitch of a half-smile toward his face. "Filak *borða*?"

Filak betrayed a faint grimace, but that was unmistakable warmth in his eyes, too—and he swiped for a small piece of meat from the basket, and tossed it into his mouth. "Ach, ach," he said, his voice surprisingly mild, as he plucked up another piece of meat, and popped it into Daisy's mouth. "*Gott, sólin mín?*"

Daisy's smile drew higher, and she picked up a far larger piece of meat, and poked it between his lips. And though he playfully snapped at her fingers with his teeth, he also gulped down the meat, and then slowly smiled at her, still with that warmth shimmering in his eyes.

It made it too easy to keep eating with him, passing food back and forth, and when Filak again pulled over Rosa's language book, it was too easy to talk back and forth over it, too. Practicing words and pronunciations as they ate, correcting each other, laughing at each other's mistakes. And at some point, Filak had apparently even written his own list into the book, with a variety of Aelakesh words Rosa had missed. Including everything from innocuous terms like *húðflúr*—their inked prayers—all the way to words like *refsa* for *punish*, *heiðra* for *honour*, *biðja* for *beg*.

"Are these all supposed to be a hint?" Daisy asked him, with far too much warmth in her voice, and she didn't even twitch at Filak's wicked grin, the teasing tickle of his claws at her back. Suggesting that maybe they really would use those words together, and he wanted to be sure she understood them. Wanted to be sure she was safe.

She was almost disappointed when they finally finished eating, and put the book away—but then Filak went and picked up a large crate she hadn't noticed before. And when he set it onto the bed beside her, it turned out that it was full of *clothes*. All the lovely new clothes they'd bought at the shop yesterday, which Kitty must have had delivered, just as she'd promised. And Daisy watched with rising bemusement as Filak carefully sorted through the clothes, sniffing and stroking at them, setting various items aside, and even holding some up against Daisy's still-bared body.

"*Gott*," he said, more to himself than her—and then, without preamble, he tugged her up to her feet, and began *dressing* her. As if it was his right to do such a thing, or even his responsibility. And while Daisy probably should have argued, she could admit that it was a relief not to need to decide for herself, and she also liked the colours he'd chosen, the bright orange silk wrap top, the tawny buttery trousers. And his hands as he dressed her were warm and approving, stroking over her skin, smoothing out the fabric against her, making sure her black marks—her *húðflúr*—stayed visible for all to see.

Once he'd finished, he stepped back, and gave her an assessing look up and down. And then he reached for his satchel, and plucked out—something new. Something gold, something beautiful, glittering with familiar bright stones...

It was—a cuff. A thick gold cuff, set with yellow stones, made to match Daisy's ring, and her *kraga*.

Daisy's breath hitched, and she stared down at it, and then up at Filak's face. At how a slight flush was creeping up his cheeks, how his eyes looked almost nervous. "For you, *sólin mín*," he told her, as he carefully slipped the cuff over her hand, and then guided it up onto her upper arm. "You like?"

Daisy swallowed as she blinked at it, at the perfect smooth gleam of the gold, the sparkle of the beautifully cut stones embedded within it. And again, she should be refusing this, telling him no gifts, two weeks...

"Ach, Filak," she said, her voice hitching. "I like. It's beautiful. *Fallegt.* Thank you."

His smile was bright and dazzling, the flush deepening in his cheeks, and he promptly eased around behind Daisy, and began carding his claws through her tangled hair. While also speaking again in Aelakesh, telling her something about how he would have had it for her sooner, but Gareth had been too occupied punishing his wayward pet in the *dýflissa.*

Daisy chuckled and stroked her hand appreciatively at her stunning new cuff, even as she leaned closer into Filak's touch. Into the tantalizing feeling of his claws gently scraping against her scalp, combing her hair back, and then tying it together with something that felt like a ribbon. All of it too easy, too tempting, even if he'd apparently decided he had the right to decide her hairstyle, too. And she should be arguing it, saying something, anything...

"Can you grow hair?" her unhelpful voice asked instead, as she turned around to face Filak again. And at his quizzical expression, she reached and stroked her hand at his bare head, which—now that she was paying attention—betrayed a noticeable burr of stubble, and she could see the faint shadow of it, too. "Or do you cut it?"

The comprehension flared across Filak's eyes, and he went for his satchel, and drew something out of it—a sharp, gleaming blade. "*Ég klippti,*" he told her, as he mimed running the blade up over his scalp, before tossing it back into his satchel again. "Cut. For *húðflúr.*"

For *húðflúr.* For prayers. And of course that made sense, didn't it? He cut his hair as part of his worship, his marks. Giving him more of a canvas to work with, perhaps.

And Daisy could admit that it suited him, that he would look almost wrong otherwise—and now her traitorous eyes were again running up and down his tall marked body, and then catching on the too-compelling sight of that new daisy, *her* daisy, growing up onto his hip over the waist of his trousers. Making itself one of those prayers, making her claim on him very clear. Even just for the next two weeks, until it would fade forever...

"Are any of your prayers ever permanent?" Daisy asked, again without at all meaning to. "*Húðflúr*... last? *Endast*?"

Her face was already heating at the too-obvious implications in that question—she surely wouldn't want to mark anyone permanently, right? But she couldn't seem to take it back, either, because hadn't Julian said, back in the sickroom, about some of the marks being *embedded*, somehow? Beyond just the ink?

Something flickered in Filak's eyes, something almost like longing—but then he stepped closer, and brushed his hand against that vow he'd written on Daisy's belly. "*Bara heitin*," he told her. "Only... vows. These are... great power."

Vows. Great power. More new words they'd learned from the book, and Daisy's heart skipped as she glanced downwards. Because yes, he'd given her a vow, and she had to be misunderstanding him, because he certainly hadn't made it permanent... right?

But when she met Filak's eyes again, they were intent and far too knowing on hers. "No yet," he told her, in more careful common-tongue. "If you stay, I make vow... forever."

Forever. The word flared strangely in Daisy's belly, especially when Filak mimed again writing the vow with his claw, but more forceful this time. As if... as if he would cut the vow into her. With blood and ink. Permanently.

And Daisy didn't want that... did she? She should be running again, or maybe demanding why he hadn't told her this before, or why Julian hadn't, either. She should definitely not be imagining what that would feel like, to have Filak's art and his vow part of her, forever.

And most of all, she shouldn't be frowning back at Filak, again sweeping her eyes up and down his lean body, lingering on that new daisy. Because did that mean—surely it meant—that if that happened, she could mark *him* permanently, too. Give him a vow—or maybe some art—that would never fade. And would she want to keep the daisy, or draw something else, or both, and...

A low growl hissed from Filak's throat, and when Daisy's eyes darted up to his, he was watching her too closely, his nostrils flaring, his tongue brushing his lips. As if he knew just what Daisy had been thinking. As if he wanted it, too. And when he eased even closer, scraping his claws against her belly, there was the alarming awareness that maybe she wouldn't refuse, either...

"Er, are we ready to go, then?" her voice asked, too loud, over that dangerous impulse. "We're still going back to the Skýli, right?"

Filak's eyes flickered, as if he'd followed her thoughts all too easily. But he didn't argue, and even twitched her a small, indulgent smile before turning to swipe for his satchel, slinging it over his shoulder. "Ach," he said firmly. "*Við förum í Skýlið.*"

Daisy smiled back, and went for her own satchel, too— but then she remembered something she'd almost forgotten from the night before. "So why didn't you want to tell the rest of them about the *Skýli*, last night?" she asked. "Jule, and Rosa, and John-Ka? *Nei Skýli?*"

There was an instant's stillness, and then Filak grimaced, as genuine displeasure flared across his face. "*Nei,*" he snapped. "*Nei* Ash-Kai. *Nei* Ka-esh. *Nei* Rosa!"

There was surprising menace in his voice, enough that Daisy flinched slightly away—and Filak sighed, and grimaced again. "*Nei* trust them, *sólin mín,*" he said flatly. "Never trust them, ach?"

Right. Daisy winced, and her memories skipped backwards, back to everything Filak and Julian had told her about that. How the Nor-ka-esh had been suffering, dwindling, under attack. How they'd repeatedly sent to Orc Mountain—

to their own clan—for help. And how they'd received only silence in return.

"But that was... during the war, right?" Daisy asked, tentative. "Before Rosa came here? I just know she would love to see the *Skýli*, and I'm sure we can trust her, and I promised her I would..."

But Filak cut her off with a swipe of his hand, the anger flashing through his eyes. "*Skýli* is for Nor-ka-esh," he insisted, his voice hard. "Only Nor-ka-esh! *Ekki Rosa! Nei Rosa!*"

Oh. Daisy couldn't deny a sharp twinge of hurt, her gaze dropping—but then Filak's hand curved against her waist again, and when she glanced up, his eyes were worried, even apologetic. "*Fokk, sólin mín,*" he said, lower. "I am sorry. You wish... see Rosa today? *Nei Filak, nei Skýli?*"

Daisy blinked—he thought she wanted to spend the day with Rosa, instead of him? But yes, surely that was what he meant, his eyes now intently searching hers. "You go now?" he said, with a jerk of his head toward the door. "See Rosa?"

Daisy couldn't stop blinking at him, because he didn't actually *want* her to leave him and go off with Rosa, right? But no, no, he didn't, based on that tightness on his mouth, the deepening regret in his eyes. And the longer she gazed at him, the more dejected he looked, his shoulders heavily sagging. "I am sorry," he said again, with a sigh. "I take you to Rosa."

But Daisy held herself still, and kept searching his eyes. Because even though he clearly wasn't changing his mind about the Ka-esh and the Skýli, he was still... apologizing. Admitting defeat. And also... giving her the choice. Allowing her to decide how to spend her day, even if it was without him.

And suddenly, that felt... important. Like a crucial counterbalance to his refusal, and to how he'd decided her clothes and her hair and the gift, too. It felt like... something a good mate would offer.

But then it twisted around, turned inside out, because maybe... maybe to Filak, those were *all* things a good mate would offer. Clothes, gifts, grooming, washing, food, care. Time. Freedom. And maybe... maybe even permanent marks on his mate's skin. Something to prove his promises, to bind him to his vows forever. *Great power*, he'd said.

Daisy swallowed down the sudden lump in her throat, and before she could catch it, she slid her arms around his stiff waist. Squeezing him as tightly as she could, while something shifted and settled in her belly. Something that felt almost affectionate. Grateful. Maybe even... possessive.

"Thank you, Filak," she told him, as she ran both hands up and down his back, feeling him slowly relax beneath her touch. "*Takk fyrir*. But I still want to go see the Skýli again with you. Just you. *Daisy og Filak*."

And oh, the way his mouth softened, the light flickering through his eyes. Like relief, like gratefulness, like something too strong for Daisy to name...

"So will you come with me?" Daisy asked him, with her brightest, most hopeful smile. "*Kemur með mér, Filak minn*?"

Filak mine. Like he was infecting her, making her say things she should never, ever say—but yes, she wanted to see him blinking at her like that, with that awe shining in his eyes. Wanted to see him smile, slow and so impossibly stunning. Wanted to bring her orc to life like a painting, like a sparkling priceless jewel beneath her stroking hands.

"*Ach, sólin mín*," he whispered. "I come."

39

Returning to the Skýli with Filak was delightful.

They travelled there in the cart again, and now that Daisy knew what to expect, it was far easier to just relax and enjoy it. To revel in the air in her face, the stone walls sweeping by in the lamplight, the charge and the thrill of hurtling around sharp corners in the dark.

And once they stopped, in a place that felt deeper than last time, Filak led her to the Skýli in a different way. Through tunnels that were even rockier and rougher than before, but they also held even more new and fascinating sights—beautiful stalactites, jagged rock formations, stunning patterns in the walls. And though Daisy must have stopped a half-dozen times to draw, Filak again showed no signs of impatience, and even occasionally came over to hold the lamp close for her, or sharpen her pencil with his claws. And when he grinned and broke apart a wall, showing Daisy the wonderful little waterfall bubbling behind, it occurred to her that he'd brought her this way on purpose. He'd wanted to give her something new to draw, wanted to see it through her eyes.

And maybe he'd meant to do the same with the Skýli

itself, because this time, once he'd cut through several more thick stone walls, he led Daisy to a new tunnel. One made of smooth grey stone, with multiple rounded doors lining its walls—almost reminiscent of the corridors back in Orc Mountain.

"*Hellir*," Filak said, his eyes dancing, as he clasped Daisy's hand, and pulled her down the corridor. "Skýli... rooms, ach?"

Rooms. His excitement felt contagious, and Daisy eagerly accompanied him down the long corridor, exploring the rooms together as they went. Many of them were in a significant state of decay, with crooked floors and crumbling walls, but some were still intact, enough to suggest that this part of the Skýli had been focused on work, or perhaps schooling. There were multiple rooms with stone desks and tables, and one room had clearly been a workshop, still with a few rusty tools hanging on the walls. And next was a huge, empty forge, with a tall, beautifully preserved furnace rising up in the middle of it.

As they went, Daisy again captured as much of it as she could in her sketchbook, filling up page after page. Surely taking far too much time, but Filak still didn't complain, or betray the slightest hint of impatience. And instead, he only took his time exploring the rooms, too, spreading and scraping his hands against the walls, sniffing at rocks and holes and debris.

"You're sure you're not bored?" Daisy asked, once she'd finished a detailed rendering of what might have once been a set of baths. "Filak... *leiðist*? Gods, I've been drawing enough to fill an entire book."

But Filak only gave a dismissive flourish of his hand, and then came over and stood behind her, studying her drawing of the baths with unmistakable awe in his eyes. "*Gott*," he murmured, as he reached and carefully turned back a page with his claw, and then another. "Art. Book. Daisy draw. Daisy make book."

Daisy make book? Daisy blinked, and then huffed a bitter little laugh, shaking her head. It was foolish to think she would ever write another book again, especially now that she'd gone and made Lew a genuine enemy—but damn it, she was supposed to be forgetting Lew, right? And behind her, Filak's hand gave her arse a light little slap, followed by a gentle, reassuring squeeze. "Make book," he said again, firmer this time. "Draw."

Draw. Daisy couldn't recall him even learning that word, and again it was far too easy to just agree, and obey. Accompanying him further down the corridors, drawing anything and everything that caught her eye, taking as much time as she pleased. And when Filak hesitated by one particular crumbling wall, spreading his hands against it, she took her time drawing him, too, doing her best to capture the focused awareness in his lean body, the concentration in his eyes.

"Come see," he told her, with a swift grin over his shoulder, as he leapt up onto a tiny, almost imperceptible ledge in the wall, and peered up toward the ceiling. And when Daisy lurched over to look, holding up the lamp, she found a huge, gaping chasm up above, extending tall and narrow up into the blackness.

It was impossible to tell where it went, but Filak reached for his belt, where he'd again hung that rope they'd bought at the shop. And though Daisy hadn't seen him use it before, he handled it with surprising ease, whirling it out around him, and then tossing it up the wall. To where there appeared to be some kind of ledge, jutting out from above, and Filak crowed aloud as the rope caught on the ledge, dangling down toward them.

"You're not... *climbing* up there?" Daisy asked, while Filak hooked their lamp onto his satchel, still slung over his shoulder. And then, with a surprisingly graceful movement, he leapt onto the rope, and climbed up it with astonishing speed. His body growing smaller and smaller, the lamp's light dimmer and dimmer, until he swung off the rope and... disappeared.

"Filak!" Daisy gasped, nearly dropping her sketchbook, but then his familiar face peered down over the top, his grin bright and eager. And with a purposeful movement, he tugged at the rope, making it sway and bounce before Daisy's blinking eyes.

"Come," he told her, and then he gestured at his foot, and waved toward the bottom of the rope. Suggesting that—oh. He wanted her to put her foot in the loop, hanging there at the end of the rope. He wanted to drag her up through a mysterious rocky hole, and if she fell, or he dropped her, surely it would be her doom.

"*Komdu, sólin mín,*" he said, softer. "Safe. Ach?"

Well. And maybe it was foolish, dangerous, but Daisy squared her shoulders, and stuffed her sketchbook in her satchel. And then, on a deep breath, she tentatively slipped her boot into the rope's loop, and eased her weight onto it. Blinking up to where Filak grinned again, and then began hauling her up.

Daisy gasped at the feel of it—swaying on the rope, rising smooth and silent through the rocky dangerous chasm, while above her, Filak's straining body leaned heavily backwards, one hand's claws digging deep into the rope, winding it around his forearm again and again. And as Daisy rose nearer to the top, she could see that he was bracing himself against a ledge of stone, using his impossible magic to help. And for a breath, as she kept floating up through this stunning lost ruin in the darkness, this felt like magic, too. Like... art.

"*Gott, sólin mín,*" Filak said with a grunt and another grin, as he hauled Daisy up over the top, and into his safe sweaty arms. "You like, ach?"

There was no denying it, suddenly, and Daisy grinned back toward him, and fought to catch her breath. And then, finally, she glanced around toward the tunnel he'd brought her to—or rather, the room. The large, ruined room, with a domed ceiling, and a familiar-looking tiled floor...

"The cave!" she exclaimed, as her eyes met Filak's sparkling gaze. "Filak, you found the first cave again!"

He beamed and nodded, and then waved her further into it, raising the lamp high so she could see. And yes, this was it, the exact same room he'd trapped her in, that first night they'd met—but the awareness of that felt distant, somehow, blunted beneath Daisy's rising, clamouring curiosity. Despite the ruins, it still was a beautiful cave, with its rounded shape, its tiled patterned floor, its smooth, high stone ceiling. And those random rocks and boulders scattered about now looked more like benches, or maybe even beds...

And the longer Daisy blinked around at it, especially at the floor and the ceiling, the more it reminded her of that huge white room far below, with its beautiful domed ceiling, its eye in the floor. Except that this cave was noticeably smaller, and more damaged, and obviously much higher up, closer to the surface.

"What is it?" Daisy asked, hushed. "Do you know?"

Filak had already begun roaming around the room, trailing his hands at the boulders, and his smile over his shoulder toward Daisy looked wry, or maybe even sad. "*Ég held...* it is... for humans," he said slowly. "Skýli Ka-esh— meet humans here. Court mates. Speak, and fuck."

Oh. Ohhhh. Of course that made sense, so much sense. A place near the surface where orcs and humans could meet, a place that would offer a vivid example of the orcs' home deep below. Proving to their potential mates that they didn't live in tiny dank tunnels, but instead in large, dry, well-appointed rooms, where humans could still be happy and safe.

And Filak had... met Daisy here. Found her here. Found the entire Skýli, because of this. And gods, no wonder he'd taken it as a sign from his gods, and Daisy swallowed as her eyes settled on the largest flat boulder, in the middle of the room. The place, surely, where she'd spent the night with Filak. The place where he'd drawn that sun on her heart.

"It would have been a beautiful room," Daisy finally said, her voice thick—and then she fumbled to pull out her sketchbook again. Flipping it to a new page, and then glancing around the room again, fighting to imagine it how it must have once been. An open, airy space, with plenty of room for moving or eating or dancing, talking or playing or making love. A room meant as a promise, a pledge to their human mates, that even underground, they wouldn't be trapped alone in the dark...

Daisy's hand was rapidly moving over the page, envisioning it as clearly as she could, and Filak had come over to watch, his eyes intent on the sight. Watching as her hand hesitated, hovering at the top of the domed ceiling she'd drawn, where it reached its full height. Where—her head tilted as she glanced up again—it almost looked like another one of those eyes. But an eye that was closed, as if...

"Did it... open?" Daisy asked, high-pitched. "The eye? *Sól*?"

Filak blinked at her, once, and frowned up at the ceiling. And then, with jerky steps, he strode over to look straight up at it, while Daisy's hand sketched out what the room might look like, if that eye was open. If it allowed sun into this beautiful ancient room, maybe just enough to help and reassure humans, and to grow some plants and mushrooms—but not enough light to hurt the Ka-esh orcs, either. And what would it look like, that seemingly small stream of light reflecting off those black-and-white tiles in the floor, and maybe these walls had once been white, too. Just like... just like...

Daisy gasped just as Filak did, their eyes meeting, speaking, shouting—and when Filak rushed toward her, Daisy clasped his hand, and stumbled with him back toward the chasm they'd come up through. And with his help, she half-climbed, half-slid down the rope—far easier than she'd expected, thanks to her leather trousers—and then gripped his hand again before racing together through the corridors, taking a different turn than how they'd come in. Until Filak slammed his palm against another eye in the wall, and they burst out into...

The white room. The huge, domed temple, deep beneath the earth. A room that now looked so familiar, so similar to the room up above, especially with that closed eye embedded in the ceiling—and Filak set aside the lamp with a clatter, and sprinted over to the nearest wall. To one of the tall black metal contraptions that lined it, arching all the way up to circle around that eye. And those hadn't made sense, or had they, because Filak was now picking at something new in it, something like a lever. And when he drew the lever down, there was a harsh, echoing creak, and then...

Light. *Light.* From above.

Daisy gasped and squinted up toward it, shielding her eyes with her hand—but yes, oh gods, the eye was open. Just a tiny sliver, but still enough to illuminate the entire room, far brighter than the lamp. Reflecting beautifully off all the white stone, but also lighting strongest in the very middle of the room. So someone who wanted the light could go stand directly beneath it, while someone who didn't want it could stay against the walls, or even—more recognition flashed through Daisy's thoughts—stay safely tucked into one of the many darkened alcoves lining the walls.

It was a room for orcs, *and* for humans. A room where

Daisy and Filak could be together, and share the light and the darkness.

And even now, this very moment, Filak was standing in the dark against the wall, while Daisy had already drifted toward the light in the middle of the room. And she exhaled as she stepped into the full force of it, and then gave Filak a silly little wave, while something oddly pricked behind her eyes.

"How... how is this even possible?" she asked, her voice echoing across the room. "*Hvernig*? We're so far underground, there's no way..."

She attempted to gesture along as she spoke, and Filak's shoulders rose and fell before he answered in swift, jerky Aelakesh. But he gestured as he spoke, too, and it was enough to suggest that the sun was coming in through some kind of very long, very elaborate tunnel, likely built with more reflective stone, or maybe even mirrors. A tunnel that reached all the way to the surface, but had somehow remained hidden, for all these centuries.

"Must be... in hard place," he said, as his hands mimicked a tall mountain, a deep hole, a sharp dropping angle—a cliff, maybe. "No safe."

Of course that made sense, and Daisy nodded, blinking up toward the eye again, while a sparkling shiver rippled over her skin. It was a marvel, a stunning beautiful wonder, and suddenly she needed to see it opened all the way, needed to see this room bathed in light—

And surely Filak felt it, too, spinning back toward the lever in the wall, yanking harder against it—but then, something caught. Scraped, with a painful grating sound. And up near the light, the black metal quivered—and around it, Daisy could see the white ceiling... cracking. The jagged lines crawling out from the black metal, a spiderweb that kept growing, darkening...

Filak cursed and whirled back to the wall, gripping at the

lever with one hand, and furiously waving Daisy toward him with the other. But she was already sprinting over to join him, slipping her arm tight around his waist. Feeling the effort in his lean body, the way every muscle was straining, his skin beading with sweat. Trying to stabilize this, surely, to save his newfound home.

But then he flinched, hissed, yanked backwards. And with another low curse, he swiped up the lamp, grabbed Daisy's arm, and—ran. Sprinting at full speed out of the room and down the corridor, while the tunnel ominously heaved and shuddered around them.

It speared pure sharp terror through Daisy's chest, and she stumbled to keep up, to stay upright on the shifting roiling earth. But her breath was already panting, her feet staggering, Filak was too fast, the rumbling too close, the panic screaming screeching blazing behind her eyes—

And then—Filak wrenched sideways. Dragging her through another door, into another darkened room, as his hand slammed into the wall, his claws digging deep...

And as Daisy stared, the terror flashing wild and white, the door behind him... Fell. Crashed. *Collapsed,* into pure, utter blackness, beneath a thundering crush of stone.

40

Daisy screamed.

The sound was shrill and scraping, far too loud in the sudden dusty darkness. And for a fraying, frantic instant, Daisy was sure time had spun backwards, hurled her back into that cave, that horrifying dungeon, with—with—

"Daisy!" hissed a voice, that voice—and Daisy flailed all over at the feel of hands. His hands. Touching her, holding her, running warm and steady up and down her back. So dizzying, so familiar, and she gulped desperately for breath, for her shattered shaking awareness. She was—she was—

The words wouldn't come, wouldn't focus, but the hands were still here, still stroking solid and safe. Caressing over the gooseflesh still shivering across her skin, and... speaking to her. Shouting, in that language they both knew so well.

You are safe, his hands said. *I am here. You are mine. My sun. Safe.*

Filak.

The certainty came with a shaky, shuddering exhale, sagging Daisy's shoulders, sinking her forward into his solid weight. Filak was here. She was... safe.

"*Ach, sólin mín,*" came his voice, so low and soft, a flickering light in the darkness. "You are—safe. I swear this."

Oh. And despite the choking darkness, the wheeling echo of being trapped again, Daisy felt herself nodding—nodding!—and sinking heavier into Filak's warmth and his touch. Believing him. *Trusting* him.

"Wh-what happened?" she finally asked, between her still-broken breaths. "Where—where are we? Can we get out?"

Filak's hands kept stroking, and she could feel his nod, close against her head. "Ach," he said firmly. "I... make this. Make safe."

Wait. He meant—*he* had done this? Made the room collapse? He'd trapped them in here... on purpose?

Daisy's heartbeat spiked again, but Filak kept stroking her, and then carefully guided her forward in the darkness. So he could bend and reach for something—and suddenly the darkness blazed with light. Revealing the sight of Filak, dusty but unharmed, standing amidst a wash of stony rubble, and holding out their familiar lamp toward her.

Daisy let out another relieved breath, and she clutched the lamp tight, glancing toward the room around them. Another one of those ancient stone-walled rooms, but now with what looked like several huge, jagged stone pillars jutting between the floor and the ceiling.

"Safe," Filak told her again, patting one of the pillars with his hand. And wait, he was saying *he'd* done that, he'd put those there—and at Daisy's disbelieving stare, he launched into a swift stream of Aelakesh, while gesturing and walking around the small room, and kicking his boot at various walls.

And though Daisy couldn't understand all of it, she could catch enough to follow what he meant. The Skýli was already unstable, particularly that huge white domed room, and when he'd opened the eye in the ceiling, it had compromised the room's structure, and maybe even this entire side of the Skýli. So he'd calculated the nearest safe area—this room, apparently—and fortified it, and blocked them in.

"Safe, *sólin mín*," he said again, with a reassuring smile toward her, as he strode toward one of the room's original walls, and spread his hands against it. "I dig, ach? You draw."

Oh. Drawing. Right. Daisy groped for her sketchbook with a sudden, sweeping gratefulness, nearly tearing a page as she yanked it open. But yes, oh gods, it was already helping, even with her hand trembling like that on the paper, making a mess of that line of the pillar. But also turning her terror into lines and shapes, into art, into... seeing.

And the more she drew, the more she realized—this room was different than the others they'd seen so far. This room almost looked like a bedroom, or maybe even... a home. And despite the ruins of it, she could still make out what appeared to be a pair of bunks carved into the stone wall behind her, and over there was a rounded stone table, still with a few items scattered across its top. A rusted knife, a small stone bowl, and what might have been the remnants of an actual *book*, shrivelled and stained with mildew.

By the time Daisy finished the sketch, the fear had faded entirely, and in its place, there was only a quiet, slowly growing sadness. The disconcerting awareness of all the living, breathing people who had once lived here in the Skýli, and abandoned it hundreds of years before. The people who were now only ghosts, living only in memory, in the things they'd left behind.

That feeling kept lingering as Daisy closed her sketchbook, and went over to where Filak had already broken through most of the wall, his hands stroking against the stone with surprising care. Almost as if he felt it too, as if he couldn't bear to break this room any more than he already had.

But he was still doing it, still doing his best to help Daisy, to keep her safe. Because he wouldn't trap her in the dark again, he wouldn't—right?—and when the wall broke away to reveal yet another tunnel, open and untouched, she couldn't stop her relieved smile toward him, or her impulsive squeeze to his lean sweaty waist.

"*Fallegt*, Filak," she breathed, into his shoulder. "Thank you."

He dismissed it with an easy wave of his dusty hand, and then guided her out through the wall, and into the winding tunnel behind it. Which had yet more new rooms radiating out from it, and when Daisy peeked inside, holding out her lamp, she found they were again... that kind of room. Bedrooms. Homes. Some large, some smaller, some with fireplaces and chimneys, others with baths and drains. And most of them still had stone furniture, too, tables and bunks and platforms, along with more rusted, ruined items scattered across them. Tools and weapons, pottery and utensils, a few more books, and even some frayed, rotted textiles.

But again, the damage throughout these rooms was far too evident, too. Many of them had sagging walls and crumbling corners, collapsed doors and cracked splintering ceilings. And they all carried a distinct scent of mildew and decay, and one entire area was fully flooded, with unidentifiable rotting things floating in the water.

Daisy didn't miss Filak glancing around at it too, his frown deepening with every step—and she could feel his full-body flinch when they reached a section that was almost entirely rubble, with a huge gaping rift in the midst of it. And at one point, he whirled around mid-step, waving both hands over Daisy's head—and she shivered all over at the sight of rock spattering out around them, skipping across the stone floor. Because... Filak had broken it apart. The rock that had been about to fall on Daisy's head, and *kill* her.

After that, she joined him in jogging the rest of the way out, until they finally reached a familiar-looking tunnel—the one they'd come in through the day before, with all the broken walls. But now Filak was eyeing those piles of rubble with misgiving, too, almost as if he regretted breaking them, and opening a path to such a beautiful, devastating place. To the place that was supposed to be his home.

"So... you can fix it, right?" Daisy asked into the silence as they walked. "Filak fix Skýli?"

Filak's mouth twisted into a grimace, and he jerked a sharp shrug of his shoulder. As if... he wasn't certain. After all that work and effort, all that time finding the Skýli... he wasn't certain?

Daisy blinked toward him, frowning, and then impulsively squeezed at his arm, drew him to a stop. "You'll fix the Skýli," she said again. "You will... stone-see. *Steinsjáandi.* Magic."

But Filak's reply was all swift, incomprehensible Aelakesh, his other hand wildly waving behind them. Surely referring to all that devastation, the sheer daunting scale of it. So many rooms, so much danger, and he was only one orc, and gods only knew how long it would take for him to make it safe enough to bring his people here.

And the longer Daisy listened to him, the more it all pitched and churned in her belly. He wasn't supposed to be giving up, not already. He couldn't abandon the Skýli. It was his ancestors' home, maybe even their long-lost gift to their descendants—and it was so important to Filak, to everything he longed for. He needed his kin. He needed a home. He couldn't abandon this. He *couldn't.*

"Then maybe we'll have to ask for help, after all," Daisy said, quiet but steady, once Filak had finished speaking. "For *hjálpa.* From Orc Mountain. From the Ka-esh."

But Filak's body instantly recoiled, and his sideways glance toward her was viciously sharp and disapproving. Snapping her thoughts backwards to that morning, to how adamant he'd been about not telling anyone about the Skýli—especially the Ka-esh, and Rosa.

"*Nei, Daisy,*" he hissed now, his lips curling back to bare his sharp teeth. "*Nei.* We no trust them. Ka-esh never help. *Orkafjall* never help."

It was the same thing he'd said that morning, and Daisy's thoughts again flipped backwards, to how hurt he'd been by the Ka-esh, and Orc Mountain. How they'd all abandoned the Nor-ka-esh, and failed them, and forgotten them.

"I know," Daisy said, as she leaned into Filak's side, and squeezed him tight. "The Ka-esh failed you, and that was vile of them. *Hræðilegt.* But"—she took a deep breath, gathered her courage—"*núna?*"

Now? it meant, and Daisy drew back to wave up the tunnel, toward the mountain far ahead. "You're not at war anymore, Filak," she said. "All that was years ago. Before Rosa and John-Ka. And if we ask, I'm sure they will help. They want to be"—she searched for the word—"*vinir.* Friends."

But Filak's scoff was loud and mocking, his reply rushed and harsh and angry. And though Daisy again couldn't follow all of it, she recognized enough words to get the general sense of it—*sálugjald, women, blood, dead.* All the accusations the Ka-esh had thrown upon him, perhaps. All the ways his own clan had judged him, and mistrusted him, and shunned him.

And then something else, something that seemed to make him even angrier, punctuated with a purposeful wave toward Daisy, and a stab of his hand toward his heart. As if—oh. The murder accusation. How Rosa had told Daisy about the blood on Filak's scent, when he'd first come to the mountain. How they'd truly believed he had attacked his own people, his own family, and then abandoned them.

"Ka-esh—forsake me," Filak said, his voice cracking. "They cast me away. Just as—my kin. My father. My *gods.*"

He flailed his hand at his marks, and then upwards, toward the sky, maybe even the sun. "I pray, I pray, I pray," he added, the words heaving through his chest. "I seek. I work. I try. But it is only—no. Always no. No, no, no!"

It was the most he'd ever said at once in common-tongue, and every word was like a heavy thudding drum, striking against Daisy's chest. Each blow sinking the comprehension deeper, dark and wretched and sad.

Filak had been so alone. He'd lost his family, his kin, his home—and he'd truly believed even his gods had abandoned him, too. And—and *that* had to be why he was so covered in his prayers, right? And why he'd stopped eating, too? And maybe even why he'd shaved his head? He'd been desperately trying to please his gods, to win back their favour, to finally stop being rejected and alone.

Daisy couldn't stop blinking at him, her eyes prickling. "Ach, Filak," she whispered. "*Ég sé*. I see. But—you're not alone. *Nei* alone. *Ekki einn*."

Filak's eyes shifted on hers, speaking of surprise, or longing, or maybe even hope—and curse her, what was Daisy saying with this, and she took a deep breath, let it out. "It seems to me that your gods *have* heard you, and blessed you," she said thickly. "You found the Skýli. You kept your promise to your people, and found their lost home. You found a place for Ka-esh and humans to be together. To share the sun. And I think"—she took another breath—"I *know* the Ka-esh would care about that. They would want to help you."

She couldn't say how much of that Filak had understood, staring at her with those strange shifting eyes—but then he scoffed and drew away from her, and stomped off down the tunnel, alone. Leaving Daisy behind with the lamp, her heartbeat spiking as she watched him go. Would he truly leave her, and disappear off into the darkness...

But he hadn't even gone ten steps before he halted and exhaled, and glanced back at Daisy over his shoulder. And the look in his eyes was so bleak, so lost, or maybe even hurt—and Daisy's thoughts snapped back to what Julian had told her, back in the sickroom. *In all Filak's time here, his own people have not sought to know him, or understand him, or trust him.*

And based on that hurt in Filak's eyes, he'd wanted his new clanmates to trust him. He'd run away from something truly horrible—his father had just been killed, he'd been thrown out of his own home—and he'd wanted the Ka-esh here to try to understand, to respect his obligations and his griefs, to give him the benefit of the doubt. And instead, they'd judged him, and suspected him, and shunned him. Surely in part due to his gaunt body, and his shaved head, and all his copious marks. To all the ways he'd so fervently been trying to please his gods, and gain their favour, too.

Daisy's throat spasmed, and her body pitched back toward Filak, her hand again finding his stiff back, stroking up and down. Again speaking that silent language they both knew, shouting that she understood, she was sorry, she knew far too well how it felt. To work so hard, to care and create so deeply, only to be dismissed, underestimated, ignored. *Unbelievable. Irrational. Ridiculous and immature behaviour, appallingly unscientific, foolish, dangerous...*

Filak didn't reply aloud, but his glance toward her was grateful, and he pressed a brief, furtive kiss to her hair before again clasping her hand, and drawing her back down the corridor. But he didn't speak again, and the silence seemed to grow between them, as more chaos juddered and chattered through Daisy's thoughts.

Filak needed this. He needed his home. He needed to offer the Skýli's refuge to his people. He needed to give them a place to meet the women they longed for, to build the families they craved. And he needed to keep them safe from all those attacks, safe from the humans' poisons, safe from the likes of Lew...

But no, damn it, Daisy was not thinking about Lew, not

now. She was thinking about Filak, and watching Filak, and... *seeing* Filak. Seeing that slump in his shoulders, the tension on his jaw, the bitter misery in his eyes. Still speaking to her, shouting to her, screaming with darkness and pain.

He was... afraid. Afraid of losing the Skýli. Afraid of failing his gods and his people. Afraid of asking for help. Afraid of being judged and rejected, abandoned and forgotten. Left to face it all alone, again.

And with a sudden twitch, Daisy's memories flicked back to the night before, to the chain in the *dýflissa*. To the way he'd pinned her, cornered her, pressed her beneath his weight. And in truth, he'd done it so often before that too, hadn't he? Trapping her, confining her, keeping her where he wanted her. Where he could trust she would... stay. So he wouldn't be alone.

And gods, what if Daisy didn't stay? Even if the thought of it churned unsettlingly in her stomach, she was still watching, right? Still... seeing. Deciding. Two weeks. And if she wasn't here, who would Filak have left? Would he be forever alone, forever afraid, until he became a ghost, too? Another forgotten echo in an abandoned underground room, rotting apart into dust?

No. No. The certainty was so strong it was dizzying, shouting through Daisy's skull. No. Absolutely not.

So once they finally reached the corridor into Orc Mountain again, Daisy clasped for both Filak's stiff shoulders, and turned him to look at her. Flaring more of that unease through his shadowed eyes, but she held herself tall and straight, and took a deep breath.

"I want to go see Rosa," she told him, with as much certainty as she could muster. "Now."

Daisy walked through the mountain's corridors with Filak in silence, her heartbeat skipping erratically in her ears.

Filak hadn't refused her request, and he hadn't protested, either.

But Daisy could almost feel his grim unease, the silent shouting question in his eyes glancing toward her. But she wasn't meeting it, or answering it, because he needed this. His people needed this.

And also... she was an artist, and she wanted to... learn. Wanted to see this, for herself.

So she kept walking, following Filak down into the Ka-esh wing. Around this corner, then that one, toward a vaguely familiar opening in the wall.

The *dýflissa*.

Daisy hesitated outside the door, darting Filak a searching look—why was he bringing her to the pleasure-room again?—but he nodded, and then hung up the lamp and their satchels beside the door, and waved her forward. And Daisy was seeing this, she was, so she took a breath, and stepped into the firelit room.

It was just as shocking as it had been the night before, full of orcs taking heated hungry pleasure together—and there seemed to be even more of them this time, too. That medic Eben again, with the same handsome dagger-haired orc, and Gareth again, now working over his lean gasping orc with a big wooden paddle in his hand. And wait, that was even *Julian*, sagging against a wall with his face buried in the crook of his arm, while a tall, unfamiliar orc grunted and pumped his hips behind him.

But Filak didn't spare them even a glance, and he ushered Daisy past them, deeper into the room. Toward a tucked-away nook she hadn't noticed before, where—she hesitated again—a tall, fully clothed orc had a pale, pretty woman kneeling before him. She was wearing only a gold collar, but attached to it was a long *leash*, its thick gold chain wrapped casually around the orc's clawed hand. And as Daisy stared, the orc tugged the leash upwards, making the woman look at him, as his other hand slowly, deliberately opened his trousers. Revealing himself for her, showing her his long, scarred grey cock, wanting her to look at it, to beg for it...

And at the sound of the woman's voice, the room screeched to stillness, because it was—*Rosa*. Yes, of course it was Rosa, and the orc was her stern, buttoned-up mate John-Ka. The Priest of the Ka-esh. Who was now coolly feeding his scarred cock into Rosa's mouth, wrapping the chain tighter around his hand, using it to draw her closer...

Daisy truly could not look away, and for an instant, the Skýli utterly vanished from her thoughts. Replaced only by the bizarre, unspeakable urge to yank out her sketchbook, to draw this to keep, so she could look at it after for as long as she pleased.

She twitched at the feel of Filak's hand, tickling at her back—and when she glanced up, he was eyeing her intently, his brows raised. And then he gave a questioning jerk of his head toward the bare wall behind him, which had multiple chains hanging against it.

Daisy's groin convulsively clenched, but she took a shaky breath, and shook her head. This was important, damn it. He needed help, and she needed to give it. And still simmering alongside that, stubborn and strange, was that compulsive need to see it, to know, to learn.

Because—Filak had claimed Daisy as his mate, for these next two weeks. He'd given her that vow. He'd sworn to prove himself to her. He'd told her the Skýli was her home, too. And now, what would he do, if she displeased him? Disobeyed him? If she prodded at the places that hurt him the most? How dangerous would he be?

So Daisy raised her chin, and fought down the whisper of guilt, or maybe even fear—and then she strode straight over to Rosa and John-Ka, and waited until they'd both glanced toward her. John-Ka with distinct displeasure in his eyes, Rosa with her typical bright curiosity.

"Daisy!" Rosa exclaimed, once she'd drawn backwards enough to free her mouth, leaving John-Ka's scarred cock bobbing and dripping before her face. "What is it? Is everything all right?"

Daisy took another fortifying breath—Rosa was willingly on her knees, wearing a *leash*—and somehow managed a nod. And though she held her gaze on Rosa's watching face, she could feel Filak's full focus on her, his suspicion, his surely rising displeasure.

"You said to let you know if I needed anything," Daisy said, in a rush. "And we need your help. Both of us."

Rosa's brows snapped up, her eyes darting curiously toward Filak's face. To where he was looking highly forbidding now, folding his arms across his chest, and angling Daisy a narrow, disbelieving look.

But he didn't interrupt, so Daisy took another shaky

breath, and forced her gaze back to Rosa. She had to do this, and see this. She had to help him.

"We found something very important to your people," she told Rosa, between rapid breaths. "It's called—the Skýli."

She didn't miss Filak's deep growl beside her, but she kept her eyes on Rosa's face, and launched into possibly the most bizarre conversation she'd ever had in her life. Telling Rosa all about the spectacular ruined Skýli, and the eyes that reached all the way to the sun, and all the extensive repairs it needed. And though Rosa listened with increasing intensity, she also kept kneeling before John-Ka, stroking his waiting cock, and occasionally tilting her head to kiss and suck at the thick stream of white steadily pulsing out from its glossy crown.

"But I really thought the Skýli was just a myth!" Rosa exclaimed once Daisy had finished, with a scandalized glance up at John-Ka's inscrutable face. "Some sort of escha-tological reward upon death, or whatever. Not an actual *place*, just sitting there falling to ruin for all these years!"

So Daisy rapidly explained what she knew of that, too. How Filak's forefathers had built and abandoned the Skýli hundreds of years ago, and how he'd come here in part to search for it, and bring his people back to it. While Rosa's eyes went wider and wider, and Filak went stiffer and stiffer, his jaw grinding in his cheek.

"So why *was* Filak looking for the Skýli in the first place?" Rosa demanded, darting another searching look toward Filak's face. "And why does he want to move the Nor-ka-esh to live there?"

Daisy hesitated, the guilt shouting louder now—she didn't want to betray Filak's own secrets, right?—and her hand reflexively found his stiff back, stroking up and down. "That's... not my story to tell," she told Rosa. "But maybe"— she squared her shoulders—"maybe if you're willing to help

Filak with this, you can try to earn his trust, and see, and...
learn. Together."

Rosa was already nodding, looking genuinely delighted
by this plan, while John-Ka cast a narrow impenetrable
glance toward Filak's viciously glowering face. "*Viltu þetta?*"
he asked, even as he again tugged on Rosa's chain, and
brazenly sank his cock between her lips. "*Hjálp okkar við að
laga Skýlið?*"

He had to be asking if Filak really wanted this, right? And
though Filak's mouth was pursed, his arms still folded taut
and forbidding against his chest, Daisy kept rubbing her
hand at his back, and watched. Waited. Learned.

And then—Filak nodded. It was sharp, short, and angry,
but it meant—yes. *Yes.* He would accept their help. And
Daisy would have crowed with relief, would have maybe even
hugged or thanked him, if not for...

For this. His body whirling away from Rosa and John-Ka,
his arm circling swift and powerful around Daisy's waist, and
then hauling her toward the nearest section of bare stone
wall. Pinning her there by the wrists, as his breaths heaved
through his chest, and his eyes blazed hard and furious on
hers.

"Daisy," he hissed, his voice a low threat in his throat. "*Af
hverju gerðir þú þetta?*"

Why have you done this, it might have meant, and Daisy
held his eyes, and raised her chin. "*Þú þarf hjálp,*" she replied,
as smoothly as she could. "*Vinir.*"

You need help, it meant. *Friends.* And though she surely
hadn't said it all correctly, it still earned a furious, disapproving growl from Filak, along with a hungry flex of his
hand on her wrists. And maybe even a brief betraying spasm
in his trousers, too, jutting against her hip...

But Daisy didn't even flinch. Because maybe—she'd
expected this response from him. Maybe she'd seen it, from
the moment they'd walked into this heated, tantalizing room.

And she was an artist, she wanted to keep seeing it, sparking it, learning more of Filak's truth. How would he react to her displeasing him, and disobeying him? What would he do next?

And this was a safe place to learn, Rosa had said—and somehow it did feel safe, despite the sounds of slaps and cries filtering through the room. Rosa and John-Ka were here, Julian was here, Gareth was here. No matter what Filak did, she had witnesses. She had help.

And most of all, Filak had sworn she would be safe with him. He'd sworn to prove himself as a good mate. He'd promised.

"*Nei*," Filak snarled, a low shivering scrape up her spine. "*Nei, Daisy. Ég þarf enga hjálp. Engir vinir.*"

I need no help, it might have meant. *No friends*. And Daisy didn't try to suppress her sudden answering laugh, cold and mocking in Filak's face. Letting him see her contempt, her refusal, her disobedience.

"*Nei*, Filak," she snapped back. "You do need help. You've been doing so much alone, carrying all the burdens of your entire people, trying to save their lives and their future! Surely you can try to share the load even a little?"

Filak's lip curled up, baring all his sharp white teeth, and he snarled something back, all rapid incomprehensible Aelakesh. But Daisy understood that resistance, that rage, simmering brighter in his eyes...

"I don't care," she shot back, raising her chin even higher. "I'm helping you! *Ég hjálpa!*"

Filak snarled again, his lean body now pressing her tighter to the wall, and one of his hands slipped down to her collared throat, curving hot and hungry against it. "*Nei, Daisy*," he hissed. "*Nei!*"

But Daisy shook her head against his hand, and attempted a cold smile toward his furious face. "Yes, Filak," she replied, her voice rising. "And look, you wanted a mate.

A *sálufélagi*. And it's your *sálufélagi*'s job to help you! *Sálufélagi hjálpa*, Filak!"

Filak's lip curled higher—he did *not* like that point—and his tall body pressed her even closer to the wall. "*Sálufélagi* fuck," he snapped. "*Sálufélagi* sun. Artist. *Sálufélagi* come and hear. *Sálufélagi* no mock and scorn!"

But Daisy held his eyes, and shook her head. "*Nei*, Filak," she said. "*Nei, nei, nei*. I will disagree with you, I will disobey you, I will say and do whatever the hell I want, and you don't get to control me!"

Filak's snarl was deep and furious this time, and his narrow eyes flicked up to the wall above Daisy's head. As if he wanted to chain her up again, pinning her here, where he could do whatever the hell he wanted with her. But—a strange disappointment dropped in her belly—there was no chain on this wall, so what would he do now, and she wanted to see it, wanted to learn...

"So what are you going to do?" she demanded, with a taunting arch of her chin toward him. "How will Filak handle a disobedient *sálufélagi*?"

Filak stared back for a long moment, his eyes glittering, his breaths heaving. And then his hands gripped powerfully at Daisy's hips, and spun her around, facing away from him, toward—a platform. A small, fur-covered stone platform, about as high as Daisy's waist. And with another swift movement, he bent her forward onto it, pinning both her wrists to the fur over her head with one hand. While his other hand brought up something else, hovering it before Daisy's blinking eyes. His... his *rope*.

Oh gods, yes, and Daisy couldn't bite back her moan as Filak looped it around her wrists, and drew it snug. Leaving her bound and bent over on the platform, with her still-clothed bottom half facing out toward him, and toward the rest of the room, too. So anyone could see his hand now gripping against her arse like this, brazen and possessive—

and then his hand drew back, and gave her a light, stinging slap.

"*Ég refsa þér,*" he hissed from behind her, hot and menacing. "*Ég heyri þig biðja.*"

Oh, hell. They were words he'd taught her just that morning, and Daisy quaked all over, and nearly choked on her breath. *I punish you. I hear you beg.*

But yes, it was so right, it was so fucking good, it was suddenly everything Daisy wanted from him right now, *please.* But wait, now his hand was just caressing again, and he leaned down over her, his breath hot and ragged in her ear.

"Ach?" he whispered. "You wish, Daisy *mín*?"
You wish.

And together with the firing craving, it was relief, it was light, it was a dangerous swerving affection. Because Filak was still asking, still waiting, and that meant—Daisy was still safe. She could push him, and disobey him, even if it hurt him—and he would still keep his word, and be a good mate. He would still care for her, and offer her pleasure, offer to make art with her. Offer to use their disagreement to whirl out new magic between them, to sweep them both into the dream...

"*Ach, Daisy mín?*" he murmured, with another gentle stroke of his hand against her. "Ach, or *nei*? Stop?"

Daisy's breath swelled through her chest, and she leaned back into him, arched her body into his safe certain touch. "Ach," she gasped. "Please, Filak. Don't stop."

His exhale was heavy, hungry, his body rising tall again behind her—and then his hand drew back, and landed in another firm, decisive slap against her arse. "*Ach, sólin mín,*" he said, and it was harder now, with a cold ringing command that shot straight to her groin. "*Ég refsa þér. Ég ríð þér. Ég læt þig biðja.*"

Daisy gasped and quivered all over, and turned her head

to see his bared teeth, his blazing black eyes. "Gods, you are such a *fiend*," she breathed. "Such a demanding, bossy, belligerent *sálufélagi*—"

Her voice was drowned out by Filak's deep, disapproving growl, and then the shocking, exhilarating feeling of his hand deftly slipping around her front, and unfastening her trousers. Yanking them downwards, exposing her arse to the entire room, oh gods—and then, for good measure, he yanked off the fur cloak she'd been wearing, too. Leaving her only in her flimsy silk top, and the trousers now sagging around her knees.

"*Nei, Daisy,*" came his low hiss, as his clawed hand roughly palmed at her bare arse. "*Heiðra mig. Heiðra sálufélaga þinn.*"

Heiðra meant *honour,* another word from that morning, and Daisy made her best attempt at a laugh, a disdainful glance toward him over her shoulder. "*Eg nei heiðra,*" she snapped back, and though the grammar was surely wrong, the comprehension still flashed through Filak's eyes. "*Ekki heiðra, Filak! Þú ert—*"

But it was broken by Filak's firm slap to her bare arse, thrilling her all over, and she arched up for more, even as she rolled her eyes back toward him. "Is that all you can do?" she demanded. "*Er þetta allt, Filak?*"

His growl was harsh and vicious, even as something much like appreciation flared across his face. And his next strike was even harder, all stinging surging heat driving from his palm into her bare skin, her swollen seizing groin.

But it was still so good, so damned enthralling, so Daisy kept taunting him, cursing him, using both common-tongue and every Aelakesh word she could muster, while his slaps came harder, first with teasing brushes of his claws, and then with gripping painful scrapes. Striking both her arse-cheeks, now, and surely leaving marks all over her inflamed skin— but Daisy truly did not care. Didn't care what it looked like, or who might be watching Filak do this to her, exposing her and punishing her and humiliating her in public. She just needed more, more, please, please...

"*Gott*?" Filak finally demanded in her ear, and he sounded breathless too. "Enough, *sálufélagi minn*?"

But even as he said it, his clawed hand squeezed her arse again, its sharp thumb now slipping dangerously close into her exposed crease. Enough to make Daisy gasp and arch back again, her entire body just one bright vibrating craving, needing that dark hungry chuckle behind her, that slow tantalizing scrape of his claw over her most vulnerable places...

"*Ach, sólin mín*," he hissed behind her, triumphant, as his other hand spread her a little further apart, maybe so he could watch, oh gods. "*Þú þarft meira.*"

You need more, it meant, a statement, a question, a promise. A place for Daisy to decide to leave, or refuse... but instead she shoved further back toward his touch, jerky enough to feel his claw scrape her skin. Not much, but enough that he hissed at her, and gave her another firm, ringing slap.

"Ach," he growled, and oh, he was moving, doing something behind her—and then, a touch. A rounded, familiar, slick-tipped touch... his smooth slippery crown, oh gods. Not delving into her wet heat down below, where her legs were still clamped together by the trousers around her knees—but instead, further up. Closer to where he'd been slapping her. And fuck, the heat of it, the size of it, the inflamed stinging shame of it, of having her arse publicly spanked and punished, and then brazenly plundered like this, endangered like this, where anyone could see...

But suddenly Daisy needed it, enough that it ached. Needed to see it, to learn, to know. Needed to offer up everything, to lose herself entirely to Filak's control, his command, his care.

"Ach?" he asked again, soft again, making sure again, and Daisy fervently, frantically nodded, and shoved back harder. Saying, *yes. Yes. Yes.*

She could feel Filak shuddering in return, sputtering out his fluid heat into her crease—but he still didn't push. Didn't rush. And instead, his hands caressed her stinging arse-cheeks, and drew her apart wider. So his leaking crown could nudge and stroke, deepening the pressure, and then softening it again. The sounds already slick and humiliating, but of course he liked that, and maybe he was even doing it on purpose. Jutting in, popping out, stroking, circling, smearing his slippery seed up and down, prodding inside again. Perhaps going a little deeper each time, oh gods, and Daisy could only moan and shudder and feel it, welcome it, babble and beg for more.

But Filak kept taking his time, taunting her, playing with her, easing in more and more. Flaunting her and using her however he pleased, until Daisy felt more spread out, more exposed and vulnerable, than she'd ever felt in her life. Quivering all over as her wet opened body clutched and gaped and dripped for him, putting on a show for him, begging for the rest of him, all of him, please...

And when he finally, finally kept pressing, easing himself long and slow into her frantic clutching grip, all the whirling heat caught, shuddered, held—and then blared up into a great battering inferno. Shouting and scorching everything it touched, and Daisy was shouting too, her vision flashing with tones of coral and crimson, orange and ruby and scarlet. All flushed and blazing together, just like Filak's shuddering, sun-painted body finally burning all the way inside her—and then he was flashing and flaring too, erupting with arcs of white, painting her darkest places with white dizzying light.

It ebbed in shaky spurts, in sparkling shimmers behind Daisy's eyes, in the roughness of the rope against her bound, trembling hands. And then in the smooth, reassuring strokes of Filak's hands as he drew himself back out of her, just as slow and careful as when he'd gone in, waiting for her to adjust, to capture all his radiance inside.

Daisy only vaguely noticed him releasing her wrists, and pulling up her trousers again. But when those firm hands drew her up and around again, she leaned into his touch, his solid steady safety. Allowing him to guide her away, past a cheerfully waving, satisfied-looking Rosa, and then a distant-looking Julian. And then out the door into the dark corridor, now lit mostly by the sparks still flickering behind Daisy's eyes. But it was beautiful, a glimmering echo of the art they'd made together, still twisting her into the bright dazzling dream.

The dream kept simmering as Filak drew her into their dark room, and undressed her with careful clawed hands. And then he guided her bared body down face-first onto the soft furs of their bed, so he could crouch between her legs behind her, and... *lick* her. Not just the raw-feeling scrapes and scratches on her arse-cheeks, but everything up in between, too. Something that surely should have been shameful, but instead felt like more of the dream, like warm flickering wonder, like... care. Like affection. Like trust.

"So... you're not actually angry?" Daisy's voice asked, cutting into the haze. "*Reiður*? About what I did? Asking the Ka-esh for help? I know how much you didn't want..."

Her voice trailed off, and she could feel Filak's hesitation, the weight of his attention in the dark. "*Nei*, I no like," he said, finally, as his claws absently drummed against Daisy's back. "But... you are *sálufélagi*. Thus, I... uphold you. Stand with you. Trust you."

Oh. It was more shivery warmth up Daisy's spine, especially when those drumming claws pricked a little harder, just at the perfect edge of pain. "But also—my right to punish you, *sólin mín*," he murmured, as he gently kissed his way up her back. "Trap you. Rule you. Break you."

What? It sliced through the darkness, choked in Daisy's breath, because Filak truly believed he had the right to do those things? To trap her, rule her, break her? And of course he had no right to do such things, especially after how this had all begun, and when had he even learned how to say all that, and...

And then, as if to make his point, Filak deliberately drew his hand back, and gave her arse a light but purposeful slap. Driving a deep, betraying shiver all through Daisy's body, and a helpless moan from her mouth. Again shouting in that language they both knew too well, and he huffed a low, contented chuckle behind her, and nuzzled into the back of her neck. "You like, *sólin mín*," he murmured. "I see."

I see. Words that cut even deeper than the rest, because... oh. He was... seeing her, too. Seeing into the deepest, most shameful parts of her, the parts that even artists weren't supposed to have. The parts that were *ridiculous, immature, foolish, dangerous...*

But it was Lew's voice again, and Daisy was forgetting Lew, right? Filak had said no Lew, and Filak was here, seeing her, ruling her, trapping her, breaking her. Making her his, making art with her, in all these shameless shocking ways. Even though Daisy had pushed him and ignored his wishes, and probably hurt him, too, and did he really believe he had a *right* to rule over her in return? And it was all whirling and tangling together, too dense to break apart...

"I like, also," Filak breathed, hot into her ear, as his hand gave another firm, thrilling slap to her arse. "Like break you. Rule you. Keep you. *Mín.*"

Mín. Mine. The words again thudding through Daisy's body, strong enough to wash away the hesitation, the shame, the fear. And even enough to smother that distant chanting awareness from earlier that day, the certainty that he was afraid of being alone. He craved the power to trap her and keep her, maybe just like his father had done to his mother, trapping her ever deeper underground until she died…

But in this moment, there was only this. Only being caught against the bed and the art and the seeing, with her mate's strong body now decisively flipping her over, and spreading her legs wide with his knees. Holding her, splitting her apart, making her leak his hot fresh spunk out onto their bed…

"*Min*," he hissed again, and Daisy wasn't arguing it. Not the danger or the threat, the darkness or the unknown, the familiar beckoning call of the dream. Her devil was here, ruling and commanding, and she was still following. Following him deeper and deeper into the whirling, pitch-black fantasy, one where his hand on her wrists meant safety, his claws on her throat meant seduction, his legs between hers meant sanctuary. And his hungry body was pure blissful salvation, prodding slick and demanding back into where she was already wet and raw, used and broken from his punishment.

So she nodded, and gasped, and opened up wide. Embraced her dangerous, deadly devil in the darkness, and begged him for more.

42

When morning came, Daisy couldn't seem to look at Filak. Couldn't even touch at the memories of last night, of how he'd plundered her again and again, pouring her full of pain and fear and pleasure. And in return, she'd only begged him for more, begged him to mark her and choke her and drink her, to use her wherever and however he damn well pleased.

But now, in the bright light of the lamp, there was no avoiding it. No avoiding the sticky mess all over Daisy's belly and thighs, or the plentiful new red claw-marks on her pale skin. Or, oh gods, the brand-new lines of black ink he'd painted down both her thighs, in between bouts of feasting furiously between them.

Daisy grimaced, and touched a shaky finger to one of the new marks—but the ink was warm, dry, sunk deep into her skin. And gods, she didn't even know what they said, and what had she been thinking, it had been madness, surely...

But now—a claw. Gently following her finger down the mark, tracing its lines one by one. "*Daisy mín,*" Filak's low voice murmured, as if it was a translation—and then his claw slipped to the other side, and traced down it, too. "*Og hér—sólin mín.*"

Oh. And at the bottom of that one—she squinted, blinked—there was even an eye. A matching eye, just like the eyes in Filak's palms. Just like the one she'd painted on him the day before. Just like the ones in the Skýli.

And it was that, somehow, that snapped Daisy's eyes up to Filak's face. To where he was watching her, solemn and searching, his hand slipping up to tentatively stroke at the *kraga* around her neck. "*Gott?*" he murmured. "You like?"

And in return, there was only the heavy exhale of Daisy's breath, and the nod of her head. Because—yes. She liked it. She'd wanted it. She'd willingly followed him into the darkness and the danger, and he'd again kept his word, and kept her safe. Shown her his care. Made art with her.

Unbelievable, a distant voice nattered, very far away. *He publicly punished you. Told you he has the right to trap you and rule you. Irrational, foolish, dangerous...*

But Daisy again shoved it away, and reached her hand for Filak's stubbled bare scalp, and brought his head down toward her. So she could meet his mouth with hers, taste the tangy remnants of her own pleasure on his lips.

"*Gott*, Filak," she murmured, into the gentle scrape of his teeth. "I like."

He smiled against her lips, gave her a light little nip, even as his hand softly caressed her cheek. Silently speaking back to her again, telling her he liked it too, he liked her, he liked this. He liked being her mate.

It was enough that Daisy didn't resist when Filak nudged her out of bed, or when he swung her fur cloak around her wobbly, sticky body. Or when he plucked up the lamp and guided her out the bedroom door entirely, and then down the empty corridor, around a corner, and down a long, spiralling staircase.

It wasn't until they'd reached the rough stone floor at the

bottom of the staircase that Daisy realized Filak was still fully naked—and still streaked with his own mess, too. But he didn't seem slightly bothered by this, and he slipped his arm around her waist as he led her across the broad, low-ceilinged room, toward where several large, rounded stone basins stood along the opposite wall. They were perhaps as wide as Daisy was tall, and they were full of water, with billows of steam wafting away over them. As if... they were heated?

"*Bat*," Filak said, with a satisfied smile toward Daisy, as he drew her after him into the nearest basin. "Bath, *sólin mín*."

Oh, gods. A bath. A hot bath, just waiting here for them under Orc Mountain like this, and Daisy sank into the water with fervent, genuine relief. It was indeed hot, and clean-looking, and *wonderful*, enough that she betrayed a shocked, shaky laugh, and an astonished grin toward Filak's watching face.

He easily grinned back, and then produced a clean cloth from beside the basin, and began carefully washing her all over. Starting with her face, then moving to her neck, her breasts, her belly, her groin. Taking extra care with anywhere he'd broken the skin the night before, searching her face as he went, perhaps seeking any hints of pain.

But it was still wonderful, all of it, and Daisy felt dazed and boneless under his touch, and all too willing to spread wide for him, to welcome the familiar prodding touch of his hard cock beneath the water. Because after all they'd done last night, making love in a bath felt like the easiest, most natural thing in the world, like a quiet morning stroll under a sunny sky.

And maybe Filak felt it too, his cock easily stroking through the water into her clutching grip, his smile slow and approving, his hands moving lazily beneath the water, tweaking at her nipples, scratching gently against her belly and her thighs. And at Daisy's guiding, one of those clever hands rubbed against where she wanted it most, while his cock stabbed and swelled beneath—and when Daisy's release flashed through her, it was like a warm whispering wave, flooding her inside and out. Until Filak gasped and flooded her, too, his head arching back, his molten seed surging into her, and melting out into the water around them.

Afterwards, they didn't seem to need words, just smiling and touching each other as they dried off and dressed again. Or, rather, Daisy put on her fur cloak again, while Filak wrapped his hips with a flimsy little towel that still showed off far too much, including her own distinct black daisy rising up over his hip.

It was a lovely view, Daisy could admit, and she couldn't help eyeing him as they headed back to their room together. He still looked a little less gaunt than before, his ribs less visible, his arms bulkier. Making his marks look almost smoother somehow, or—Daisy frowned and peered closer as they walked—or maybe they were also fading a little, especially on his shoulder. The formerly stark black ink was now lighter, more of a deep cloudy grey. And when she glanced down toward her sun, just visible above her cloak, she was strangely disconcerted to see that it had slightly faded, too.

"Do you need your marks redone?" she asked Filak, over that unsettling thought. "Make *húðflúr* new again? *Nýtt*?"

Filak blinked, twisting to look at where Daisy's finger was brushing his shoulder, and then he nodded and grimaced. Saying that yes, he needed to repaint them—but perhaps he wasn't eager to do it, either. Flashing Daisy's thoughts back to the tunnel the day before, to how he'd despaired over his gods, how he'd thought they'd left him behind.

"Do you... actually *need* to repaint them?" she carefully asked, as Filak ushered her into their bedroom. "Can you just... let them go? Let them fade, and pray in other ways?"

She'd gestured as she spoke, motioning at washing the

marks away, and Filak's expression was suddenly aghast, his head shaking. "*Nei, nei!*" he replied. "Prayers are for gods, ach, but also... me. My prayer. My... art."

Right. Of course Daisy could understand that, enough that it flipped deep in her belly—but it still wasn't fully making sense, either. If Filak wanted the marks, then why did he seem reluctant about redoing them?

"I suppose... it must not be easy to do?" she ventured, as she mimicked holding a brush, and attempted to twist herself enough to draw on her own shoulder. "Can you even see them properly?"

Filak grimaced again, but then he reached for his nearby satchel, and plucked something out of it. A small, gleaming looking-glass. And while that would help, it certainly still wouldn't be an efficient process, especially with how perfect the marks were, how tiny and detailed and exquisite. And suddenly there was only the sad, sinking vision of it, Filak twisting and struggling to paint himself in the dark, to still make his own careful painstaking art, even if his gods had forgotten him.

"Can I help, then?" Daisy asked, without at all meaning to. "*Hjálpa*? Pray for you?"

Filak stilled all over, his swallow bobbing in his throat— but then he gave a slow, wary nod. And when Daisy guided him down to the bed, he easily went, sitting on it with his shoulder facing out toward her. Waiting patiently while she first cleaned her brush—which she'd forgotten to do the day before—and then while she plucked up his jar of ink from the table beside the bed, and set to work. Carefully tracing over the first few strokes of faded ink on his shoulder, following them as closely as she could.

"What does this prayer mean?" she asked, as she dipped her brush again, and brought it back to his skin. "*Hvað er þetta?*"

Filak's shoulder slightly rose and fell, and he cast a brief, unreadable glance toward it. "It asks for... strong," he said. "For... brave. *Hugrekki.*"

Right. And Daisy wanted that for him too, enough that she silently repeated it to herself as she painted, writing out line after careful line. Strength. Bravery. Courage. To face his past, his loneliness, his fear. To overcome all that darkness, and still seek the hope, the art, the light.

It felt strangely soothing, even contemplative, and the more Daisy painted, the more she could almost appreciate this as a form of prayer. The steady pattern and rhythm of it, intentions and longings slowly turned into something visible and tactile, into a promise of reality. Into art.

She exhaled as she finished re-inking his shoulder, leaving it all freshly painted in deep black. The sight of it almost as compelling as her daisy had been, her own prayers come to life against her mate's skin.

And if she wasn't mistaken, Filak liked it, too. His shoulder had steadily relaxed as she'd painted, his head slowly bowing, as if in a prayer of his own. As if this was a relief, or even a gift.

So without at all meaning to, Daisy dipped her brush again, and moved her hand up to his scalp. Feeling how the stubble was thicker now, a satisfying rasp beneath her fingers, enough that she hesitated—should she paint it anyway? But then Filak twisted sideways to grope for his satchel, snatching out his blade, and passing it into Daisy's hand. And after a deep breath, she carefully set the blade against the nape of his neck, and drew it up, slicing off the stubble beneath it.

But Filak's breath shuddered out, heavy and contented, so Daisy kept going, easing her way around his head, cutting until all the stubble was gone. And then she traded the blade for her brush, and began painting again. Tracing over all those marks on his scalp, even though they were far less faded than his shoulder had been. But again, Filak didn't at all seem to mind, and his head willingly tilted back toward her, angling into her touch.

"What do these ones mean?" she asked, as she gently gripped his sharp jaw, and tilted his head further to finish the last few lines over his temple. "The prayers? The *húðflúr*?"

Filak let out another shuddery exhale, and he angled a brief, hazy glance up toward her. "For... wise," he said, husky, as he tapped a claw at his forehead. "Clever. See."

Right. So the prayers on his shoulder had been for strength, and the ones on his head were for intelligence and wisdom and sight. And the eyes on his palms obviously were for sight, too, and the sun over his heart was for—for her. Right? And then...

Daisy's traitorous eyes darted down Filak's front, toward that damned towel still wrapped around his hips, and he twitched a wicked little grin as he followed her gaze. "*Ach, sólin mín,*" he murmured, brazenly cupping his clawed hand against the obvious bulge beneath the towel. "For good fucking. Good strong seed."

Daisy laughed and rolled her eyes, but her gaze couldn't stop lingering on that bulge, as a bizarre temptation whispered too strong and close. Would he allow her to paint it, too, maybe to add more to it, and then...

But that intriguing thought was broken by—a commotion. A blaze of loud voices and clanking metal and stomping feet, just outside the door.

Daisy's eyes met Filak's, the alarm blaring bright between them—and then Filak leapt off the bed, and swiped for his trousers. Yanking them on as he lurched for the door, his displeasure vibrating all through his body, his eyes darting longingly back toward Daisy and her brush. As if he would very much have liked her to keep going, too, but the commotion sounded even louder, closer, with a familiar voice ringing through it.

Filak halted at the door and groaned aloud, while Daisy

fumbled to set aside the ink, and then rushed over to join him. And there, clustered together in the corridor outside their room, was a large group of orcs, and at the head of them was... Rosa?

"Good morning!" Rosa told them, with a bright, dazzling grin. "I'm here to introduce our newest project. The Official Alliance for Skýli Restoration, Refurbishment, and Renovation!"

43

Rosa had brought... a what? An *Official Alliance for Skýli Restoration, Refurbishment, and Renovation*?

Daisy couldn't seem to reply, blinking stunned toward Rosa's excited face, and then toward the dozen-odd people clustered around her—including John-Ka, Gareth, and a few other vaguely familiar faces. While beside Daisy, Filak was glowering with pure glittering malevolence in his eyes, because of course he hadn't understood any of what Rosa had said, right?

The truth of that snapped Daisy's awareness back again, and she reflexively slipped her arm around Filak's back, taking care to avoid her fresh ink. "Ka-esh *hjálpa*," she murmured toward him. "Fix Skýli."

The comprehension flashed through Filak's eyes, and then, thank the gods, John-Ka cleared his throat, and began curtly speaking in Aelakesh. Translating for Rosa, and then elaborating further, gesturing in turn toward the various orcs behind him. And as Daisy again studied their faces, she recognized Elgr, the big hungry orc from the garden, and his human mate Thomas, who was looking decidedly orc-like in his leathers and furs, with a pickaxe swung over his shoulder. And the tall orc beside Gareth was the same one from the *dýflissa*, though the orc was now stubbornly glowering away from Gareth, his arms crossed over his chest.

Filak still didn't look happy either, his frown deepening as he listened to John-Ka speak, but even so, his shoulders had slightly sagged, and his eyes glinted on the last orc John-Ka had pointed toward. A tall, handsome fellow with pulled-back hair, and—Daisy blinked—a shocking quantity of scars all over his bare grey chest.

"Þekkir þú neðanjarðarhvelfingar?" Filak demanded toward the orc, his voice sharp. "Og burðarlínur?"

The orc nodded and spoke something back, while making a smooth arching motion with his clawed hands. And then he slung his arm around the shorter, severe-looking orc beside him, who was holding several books, and several complicated-looking metal tools, as well.

"William is one of our best stonemasons," Rosa said firmly, perhaps for Daisy's benefit, with a nod toward the tall scarred orc. "And his mate Soren is a brilliant surveyor and engineer. Along with Tvalli and Ronan and Orval, too."

She gestured toward three of the other orcs, all of them carrying a variety of books and papers and tools, and all eyeing Filak with similar uneasy expressions. "And of course Gary is our best metalsmith," Rosa added, with a proud nod toward Gareth, and then toward the pouting orc beside him. "And he's brought his... *friend* Hallr to help, too. And Elgr and Thomas also volunteered to come, because their son is attending school here at the mountain this week, and they think the Skýli must be close to the Skai camp where they live—and apparently they've also worked with Filak on digging there before?"

She shot another dubious look toward Filak, who was now eyeing Thomas and Elgr with what might have been reluctant approval. And when Elgr said something cheerfully toward Filak in Aelakesh, Filak twitched a wry, grudging smile in return, and even a small nod of his head.

"So we're settled, then?" Rosa asked, raising her brows toward Filak. "*Kemur þú?*"

Filak's shoulders rose and fell, his bottom lip jutting out, and for a brief, sinking instant, Daisy was sure he would still refuse. Would shake his head, and tell them he didn't need their help, and he would do this all alone...

But before he could say it, Daisy's hand slipped up his back, and briefly caressed against his shoulder, at one of the new marks she'd made. Her prayers for him, for strength, for courage.

The ink was still slightly tacky, and maybe she was streaking it, ruining it—but Filak's sideways glance toward her was knowing, maybe even resigned. And as Daisy held his eyes, his words from the night before rose up between them, too. *I uphold you. Stand with you. Trust you.*

"Ach," he finally said, to the watching, waiting group before them. "*Ég kem.*"

I come. It flared warmth all through Daisy's body, and she squeezed him tight, and beamed up toward his face. He would accept their help. He would work with his kin, and save his home.

His smile back toward her was slow and rueful, the fondness glinting in his eyes—but then he grimaced and glanced back toward John-Ka again, and muttered something in Aelakesh. Something that made John-Ka stiffen, casting a sharp look toward Rosa beside him.

"According to Filak, the Skýli is not yet safe," John-Ka said flatly. "Most of all for our human mates. You and Daisy ought to stay here today, Rosa-Ka, until we can be sure to secure this."

Rosa instantly bristled, protesting back in swift, fluent Aelakesh, and Daisy felt half-inclined to agree, darting a betrayed glance up toward Filak's face. But he was already looking regretful, his hand stroking her back. "I am sorry, *sólin mín*," he murmured. "I need you safe, ach?"

Right. Daisy's thoughts flicked back to the collapsed room, the crumbling corridors, the stone that had nearly fallen on her head. To how Filak could protect her, surely—but how he needed to focus on fixing the Skýli, too. He needed this. Needed his people and his home.

"I understand," Daisy told him, with an attempt at a smile. "And I promised Rosa we would spend some time working together on her projects anyway, right?"

Rosa's eyes betrayed a reluctant spark of interest, and Daisy didn't miss John-Ka's brief, grateful glance over Rosa's head toward her. "Ach, Rosa-Ka, you have much Daisy can help you with today," he said firmly. "And we shall return before nightfall, and spend the evening in the *dýflissa* together."

Rosa's eyes sparked even brighter, and Daisy was vaguely surprised to see Filak nodding too, his eyes intent on her own face. "Return before nightfall," he told her, carefully repeating John-Ka's words to Rosa. "And spend evening in *dýflissa* together. Ach, *sólin mín*?"

Well. Daisy couldn't argue with that, and she smiled up toward him, and then accompanied him back into their room to dress and pack for the day together. And Filak didn't even protest when Daisy packed him most of the food from the new basket he'd apparently had delivered, and then he took his time kissing her goodbye, stroking her again and again, as if he already regretted deciding to leave her.

"It's all right, Filak," Daisy said, caressing her own hand against his warm solid chest. "*Gott*. And—stay safe, ach? *Öruggur*?"

She couldn't deny the genuine concern in her voice, as visions of that collapsing room again swarmed through her thoughts. But Filak's grin was soft and amused, his head twitching back and forth. "No rock harm me," he replied. "I die of shame first, *sólin mín*."

There were again a few more new words in there—had he been studying overnight, somehow?—and Daisy grinned back toward him, and gave him one last kiss goodbye. And as she watched him walk away with the others, his new ink stark and clear on his back, there was a strange, swerving twist in her gut, something between affection and fear. What if he still ended up hurt somehow? What if he didn't come back? What would she do then?

But thankfully, Rosa was still bright and confident beside her, and once the group had gone out of sight, she gave an exaggerated sigh, and a roll of her eyes toward Daisy. "There's no convincing them when they think you're in danger," she said irritably. "I swear, it's like living with an obsessive overwrought *dragon*. Now, where to first? The communications office?"

Daisy readily agreed, and soon they were heading up through the mountain together, greeting various acquaintances as they went. And once again, Rosa's cheerful chatter was so easy to smile and laugh at, so easy to slip into—and it turned out that her current communications projects were just as intriguing, too. Comprising everything from flyers and advertisements promoting Orc Mountain, to a new edition of her *Manual for Modern Mates*, to a brand-new in-progress publication entitled *An Authoritative Guide to Orcish Anatomy*.

"I think that one will be *very* popular with humans, don't you?" Rosa asked, with a wink. "And since Filak is our only Nor-ka-esh here, do you think he might volunteer to pose for a few illustrations?"

Daisy barked a laugh, and easily nodded. "Oh, I'm sure he would," she said. "Although, he might not be so happy about me drawing anyone else."

She was thinking about Filak's reaction to her drawings of Kesst and Efterar, but Rosa's grin was impish, her brows waggling. "All the better," she replied, "because then he'll just have to punish you in the *dýflissa* afterwards, right?"

Daisy laughed again, even as her face prickled with heat, and with something almost like gratefulness. Because there was again no judgement whatsoever in Rosa's eyes, only easy accepting amusement. As if taunting one's orc in order to earn a humiliating public punishment was perfectly normal and understandable behaviour, barely deserving of a passing mention.

"Oh, and I also wanted to say," Rosa added, quieter now, "thank you for that last night, in the *dýflissa*. We all know Filak would never come to us and ask for help of his own volition. Let alone telling us about something as incredible as finding a long-lost Ka-esh ruin."

There was a distinct tinge of hurt in her voice, enough that Daisy hesitated, and studied her face. Her expression looked hurt, too, and resentful, and maybe still a little angry. Snapping Daisy's thoughts backwards, to Julian's claim about Filak's own people not understanding him—and then to Filak's own anger over this, too. To how he didn't trust the Ka-esh, or anyone in this mountain. How he'd resented and feared them.

And Daisy was still watching, seeing, learning, and she took a deep breath. "You were hurt," she said slowly, more of a statement than a question. "That Filak didn't tell you about the Skýli, or anything else about his past, or the Nor-ka-esh."

Rosa let out a shuddering exhale, a sudden spark flashing through her eyes. "Yes, of course!" she replied. "Sharing and deepening knowledge is a crucial foundational principle for the entire Ka-esh clan! And I mean"—she winced, glanced away—"obviously I understand if Filak didn't want to tell *me*, but *John-Ka*? He's worked so hard, Daisy, he's given up so much to help and protect the Ka-esh, and Filak has always just—ignored him. Dismissed him. Behaved as though John-Ka was his mortal enemy. As if Filak might even want to—to *attack* John-Ka! *Replace* him!"

That was true fear, now, lacing through Rosa's eyes and her voice—and curse it, that did make sense, didn't it? Filak had arrived at Orc Mountain furious, reeking of blood, hoarding wealth, refusing to speak of his past, or to acknowledge his clan's established leadership. Of course they'd seen him as a risk, or even a threat. And in truth, perhaps it was a testament to John-Ka's leadership that he hadn't had Filak forcibly questioned, or imprisoned, or worse.

"That must have been so difficult for you both," Daisy finally said. "But for what it's worth, Filak has no interest whatsoever in replacing John-Ka. He's just been... very hurt, by your clan. He just needs time. Patience. He needs you to... see him, as he is, without any judgement."

Her voice sounded so steady, so certain, as if Filak himself were there, speaking the words to her, stroking his safe warm hands over her skin. Of course Filak didn't want to replace anyone. Of course he didn't want to attack anyone. His goal was helping his people, and that was all.

And in return, Rosa visibly sagged, and gave Daisy a wan, grateful smile. "That's... really helpful to hear," she said thickly. "Thank you, sister."

Daisy waved it away, and then pulled Rosa into a quick, impulsive hug. Squeezing her perhaps too tightly, but Rosa instantly squeezed her back, and made a laughing sniffing sound into her shoulder. "Now, some flyers?" Rosa's wavering voice asked. "Or maybe some orc pricks?"

Daisy chuckled and nodded, and joined Rosa in returning to the flyers. And with that last bit of tension out between them, it felt even easier than before to laugh and sketch and plan with her, and then to sit down side by side to work together. As if they'd been friends for years, rather than only a few days.

By midway through the morning, Daisy had drawn three

new inked illustrations for Rosa's flyers—a simple depiction of the mountain, a smiling orc with his arm around a pretty human woman, and a plump-faced, wide-eyed orc baby. And Rosa's glee upon seeing them was truly contagious, enough that she dashed out into the corridor, apparently to show them off to random passersby, and then returned with—Julian?

"He was skulking alone out there!" Rosa exclaimed, wagging a teasing finger toward him. "Spying on us!"

Julian's smile was sheepish, his face flushed. "I did not wish to interrupt," he said, with a wincing glance toward Daisy, "but Filak charged me to watch over you whilst he is gone today, ach?"

This prompted another affronted but amused tirade from Rosa about overprotective Ka-esh mates, even as she steered Julian toward the desk beside Daisy. "Well, come make yourself useful, at least," she said firmly, plucking up a familiar-looking letter, and waving it toward him. "We're overdue for a letter back to Rurik, and he'd love to hear from you, don't you think?"

Julian sputtered and flushed even deeper, while Rosa flashed him a playful grin, and then set him up writing text for her new flyers instead. And it turned out that Julian's day-to-day profession was actually as a scribe and record keeper, and he had the most beautiful lettering Daisy had ever seen.

The rest of the morning passed with astonishing speed, and for lunch, they picked up Rosa's two adorable sons from the nearby nursery, and headed out into the garden. Where they chatted easily to Kalfr and Gwyn and Joarr, while Rosa nursed her youngest, and Daisy happily drew the surrounding snapdragons, and the holly bushes, and the unfamiliar stringy moss growing on a nearby rock.

"This moss is *stunning*," she said eagerly, to a bemused-looking Kalfr beside her. "Do you know what it is?"

Kalfr gave a wry shake of his head, and shot a

questioning glance over toward Gwyn and Joarr—but they both shook their heads, too. "No idea," Gwyn replied cheerfully. "Maybe it's in a book somewhere?"

But Daisy had read most of the published botanical books, and couldn't ever recall seeing it before—and as she carefully drew the moss, jotting down a few notes beside it, she couldn't help thinking that it really should be in a book. And what had Filak told her, back in the tunnel? *Daisy make book*, he'd said. *Daisy draw.*

The idea still felt preposterous, impossible, especially without Lew—but then again, Rosa did have all that printing equipment here, right? And Daisy had an impressive collection of new art now, too. Art from the mountain, the garden, the tunnels, the Skýli—not to mention all her drawings of Filak and various other orcs. So much that she'd gone through dozens of pages in her sketchbook, and... could it really be a book, somehow? A book of her own?

She was still considering that when they headed back inside, and then made a brief stop into the sickroom, so Rosa could check in on something with Kesst. But at the sight of the sickroom, Daisy was jolted out of her thoughts, because it turned out that Filak's huge gaping hole was still just sitting there wide open in the floor, waiting for some poor unsuspecting patient to fall into it.

"Yes, we were *supposed* to have a Ka-esh repair team today," Kesst irritably snapped, with a narrow, accusing glance toward Rosa and Julian. "But instead, they apparently all took off on some mysterious urgent expedition! Leaving us here to suffer this appalling, abhorrent, utterly *unconscionable* travesty here in our own *home*! And leaving Eft with the unpleasant prospect of denying our patients the care they desperately need, in order to heal anyone who's mortally wounded by falling into this highly hazardous *hole*!"

Julian had begun uneasily backing away toward the door, while Rosa squared her shoulders, and launched into an apologetic explanation about the Skýli—but this only seemed to raise Kesst's ire higher. "They abandoned us for *Filak*?!" he shrilly demanded. "For a decrepit old *ruin*?!"

Rosa winced again, and one of her wide-eyed sons clutched to her leg, while the other dashed over to join Julian at the door. And without at all meaning to, Daisy leapt in between Kesst and Rosa, and pulled herself as straight as possible.

"Filak will fix the hole," she said firmly. "Tonight. As soon as he returns. Also"—she brandished her sketchbook toward Kesst—"I almost forgot, but before I left here last time, I promised you a new portrait, didn't I? You and Efterar together?"

Kesst's disgruntled frown slightly faded, and despite his dubious glance toward Rosa, he irritably waved Efterar over. And after only a bit of fussing, he even allowed Daisy to pose them together, with Efterar standing close behind Kesst, both his bulky arms slung around Kesst's lean waist. And when Efterar pressed a brief, affectionate kiss to Kesst's cheek, Daisy quickly asked him to stay there, and then drew them as well as she could. Taking special care to capture Kesst's handsome features, and also his soft sidelong glance toward his doting mate, who was wearing a look of pure reverence on his harsh face.

Afterwards, once Daisy had passed the drawing over, Kesst blinked at it for a long, silent moment, his swallow bobbing in his throat. "Oh," he said. "Well. This earns Filak a reprieve, I suppose. *For now.*"

Daisy shot him a relieved smile, and beside Kesst, Efterar looked distinctly relieved, too. "We'll handle it until tonight, right, Sweet-Fang?" he said, with another kiss to Kesst's cheek. "Thank you, Daisy."

Daisy waved it away, and then accompanied Julian and Rosa and her sons back to the communications office, where they were soon joined by two of Rosa's close clan brothers—

the tall cheerful medic Salvi, who Daisy had previously met during her stay in the sickroom, and his mate Tristan. Tristan was slim, handsome, and soft-spoken, and it turned out that he also worked as a scribe, and was therefore good friends with Julian. Enough that he picked up the letter from Rurik off the counter, and then cast Julian a searching, worried look.

"You are not... *writing* Rurik, brother," he said warily. "Are you?"

Julian grimaced and shook his head, while Salvi winked toward Tristan, and elbowed him in the side. "We saw Rurik a while back, didn't we, *sæti*?" he said lightly. "He was *not* happy to be reminded of you, Julian."

Daisy darted a curious glance up—this Rurik still had feelings about Julian, too?—but Julian huffed a surprisingly bitter scoff, and glared down at his writing. "Ach, I heard," he said coldly. "And did Rurik not take a woman to bed soon after this? And did he not scent of several other women, also?"

Salvi wrinkled his nose, but then gripped Julian's shoulder, and gave him a reassuring little shake. "Mayhap," he admitted. "But you like women too, do you not, Julian? Mayhap you and Rurik could come to terms upon this."

But Julian's shoulder stiffened beneath Salvi's grip, and a blotchy flush had begun to creep up his neck. "Ach, just as you did with Tristan and *your* woman?" he shot back. "This worked well for you, did it not?"

Salvi visibly blanched, and shot a brief, hunted look toward where Tristan's gaze was now very intent on the counter. "Ach, no, it was a mess," Salvi said, raising both his hands, as his mouth pulled into a smile that didn't reach his eyes. "But I ken you are far wiser than I am, brother."

Julian's shoulders sagged, but for a long, awkward moment, no one spoke or moved. At least, until Rosa's elder son Thorin sidled over to Daisy, and cast a careful, curious look at the sketch she was drawing.

"How you do this?" he asked shyly. "Look like magic."

Like magic. It shimmered oddly in Daisy's gut, but it was clearly a much-needed diversion—so she handed Thorin a pencil and a blank sheet of paper, and guided him through drawing a simple orc face. A process which he followed with surprising dedication, and his result was easily identifiable as an orc, too. "Papa Tristan," he said proudly, holding up the sketch beside Tristan's still-silent form. "Papa Tristan, look! You!"

Tristan turned around with a wan smile, but it brightened into genuine warmth at the sight of Thorin and his portrait. And his praise for Thorin's efforts sounded genuine too, if still slightly choked—so after another moment's watching them, Daisy handed Thorin another blank sheet of paper, and suggested they try drawing Papa Salvi next.

This earned her grateful glances from everyone else in the room, Rosa included—and once Daisy was settled with Thorin again, she was surprised to discover that she was again thoroughly enjoying herself. Thorin was an attentive, curious child, and his approach to drawing was both simple and refreshing, showing her a new perspective she hadn't considered before. Another way of seeing, perhaps.

It made for a lovely afternoon, especially once the earlier conflict seemed to have been fully forgotten, in favour of cheerfully chatting and working together, and exclaiming over portraits. By the end of the day, Daisy and Thorin had drawn everyone in the room—including each other—and they were giggling together on the floor when someone new showed up at the door. Someone tall and pale and silent, with torn trousers, two broken claws, and dust up to his elbows.

Filak.

Daisy's heart skipped, and for an instant she could only

stare at him, her face heating, her eyes running up and down his lean, sweaty, dirt-streaked body. He was back, he was safe, just as he'd promised—and with a strange, breathless gasp, Daisy leapt to her feet, and hurled herself across the room toward him. Not caring how dirty or dusty he was, just desperately needing to touch him, to throw her arms around his waist, to bury her face into his warm sweaty chest.

For a breath, Filak stood very still against her, enough that Daisy twitched, made to back away—but then, oh gods, his arms snapped around her, and dragged her close. Crushing her against him, while he inhaled deep and ragged against her neck, and murmured low, hoarse words she couldn't understand.

It was pure, shuddering relief, and Daisy pulled back to beam at him, to search his eyes. "How did it go?" she demanded. "How was the Restoration Team? How much progress did you make? And how"—she groped for Filak's hand, brought it up between them—"how did you break not one claw, but *two*?!"

Filak's laugh was warm and affectionate, and he waved Julian over, and spoke in rapid, incomprehensible Aelakesh. But then Julian translated it just as quickly, and it turned out that the day had gone even better than Filak had hoped. The team had secured the large domed room—the *cathedral*, Julian called it—as well as the main tunnel in and out. Gareth had also taken detailed measurements of the eye-opening apparatus—the *sólarsýn*, or *sun-seer*, apparently—so the Ka-esh smiths could forge parts to repair it, while the rest of the team had worked on clearing the worst of the debris, and calculating the extent of the Skýli's size and sprawl and damage. They'd even dug a tunnel up to the nearby Skai camp—the *Wolf-Camp*—and had recruited some extra help there, too.

Filak's eyes danced as he spoke, his words escaping in a long eager stream, and Daisy grinned back at him as she listened, and as Julian translated it all beside her. Gods, it was good to see him, and hear him, and even to see the tolerant roll of his eyes when she again raised up his hand, and gave a purposeful questioning stare at his broken claws.

"Filak says he only pushed too far digging," Julian said, with a wry smile toward Daisy. "And they will grow back soon. And until then, you shall enjoy them."

As Julian spoke, Filak gave a teasing tickle of his now-blunt fingers to Daisy's bare belly, enough to make her gasp, and then cast a furtive glance toward the children behind her. But she hadn't noticed that John-Ka had returned, too, and he was currently being attacked by his two small squealing sons, while laughing and pulling Rosa close.

"You survived, then?" Rosa was asking him with a smile, her voice just loud enough for Daisy to hear it. "It wasn't a total disaster?"

"No, it was not," John-Ka murmured back, as he pressed a kiss to her hair. "And this Skýli was—ach. You must come tomorrow to see it, Rosa-Ka."

Rosa's squeal of delight was just as shrill as her sons', and she hopped up and down in John-Ka's arms. And when Daisy glanced back toward Filak, she found him watching this with surprising tolerance in his eyes, and his glance back toward her was even warmer. "You must come tomorrow," he told her, carefully echoing John-Ka's words. "*Ach, sólin mín?*"

And now Daisy was squealing too, and squeezing him tight, while he softly chuckled against her, and caressed his hands up and down her back. "Now *dýflissa*?" he murmured, soft. "Fuck me, *sólin mín*?"

The longing lurched in Daisy's belly with shocking strength, and she'd already begun to nod—but then she twitched and drew back, shaking her head. "But first," she began, with a grimace, "I promised Kesst you would fix the sickroom. Sorry."

Julian quietly translated beside her, while Filak's brows

snapped up, his lip curling with clear distaste. "*Kesst*?" he demanded. "Over *dýflissa*?"

Daisy grimaced again, while Filak's lip curled even higher, and a low growl burned from his throat. "*Nei, Daisy*," he hissed, as something dangerous flickered behind his eyes. "*Ekki Kesst.*"

A shiver ran up Daisy's spine, but she drew herself straighter, and held his gaze. "*Nei*, Filak," she snapped back. "Kesst. Now."

And yes, yes, she hadn't imagined that flare in Filak's eyes, or the heat in his slowly deepening growl. "Bad Daisy," he breathed, baring his teeth toward her. "*Þú veist að þú munt gjalda fyrir þetta.*"

Julian quickly translated that one—*you know you will pay for this*, it meant—and it fired another hot, glorious shiver up Daisy's back. "Oh, really?" she asked, as coolly as she could. "And what do you think *you* can do to me?"

And curse it, but Julian translated that too, and in return, Filak leaned in, and snapped his teeth with vicious, delicious menace against Daisy's ear. "You pay," he growled, in common-tongue. "You beg."

Gods. Daisy could barely hold her chin up, but she somehow rolled her eyes at him, snatched up her sketch-book, and flounced out of the room. Leaving Filak to prowl along behind her, his steps utterly silent—but she could still feel the hot weight of his eyes, could almost feel his claws on her throat.

"Filak's come to fix the hole," she announced toward Kesst, as she rushed into the sickroom. "Do you want another portrait while he does it, maybe?"

It was sheer desperation already, a frantic need to occupy herself, rather than either running away from Filak, or hurling herself at his feet. Because the feel of him behind her was still crackling with heat, with danger, with dark twisted promise, so strong she could scarcely bear it.

Perhaps Kesst had caught Daisy's heightened state, because he smirked coldly toward Filak, and imperiously waved him away toward the back of the room. And once Filak had stomped off, the thwarted fury radiating from his stiff body, Kesst went and collected Efterar, and drew him down onto a nearby bed. Where Kesst first draped himself over Efterar's bulky body, and then—Daisy's breath choked—he yanked down Efterar's trousers, and pulled out a hard, shockingly gigantic cock.

Daisy stared for an instant too long, her hand hovering over the blank sketchbook page—gods, it was too huge to be *real*—but Kesst only smirked again, and then began brazenly wrapping his fingers against it, stroking it up and down. Pumping it even longer and fuller, oh gods, while Efterar's hips arched up, his eyes fluttering, his head tipping back.

And truly, it *was* a sight worth capturing, so Daisy took a deep breath, and began drawing. Not only that vivid extremity at Efterar's groin, but also the hazy pleasure in his eyes, the hungry possessive triumph on Kesst's face. And the way their tall bodies so easily curled into each other, the way the trust and affection between them felt strong enough to taste.

It was so absorbing that Daisy almost—almost—forgot about Filak, and the distinct sounds of crunching and thudding and scraping at the back of the room. At least, until something loomed up tall and menacing beside her, its deep growl crawling beneath her skin.

"Daisy!" Filak snarled, and his sharp hand caught her elbow, gripping far too tight. "*Hvað er þetta?*"

The dark crackling heat was bubbling again, throbbing and needy in Daisy's belly, and she glanced toward Filak with as much courage as she could muster. "Art," she told him, archly, as her trembling hand brazenly added in the string of glossy white now seeping from the head of Efterar's gargantuan cock. "Daisy artist."

Filak's fierce, ominous growl burned into her belly, his sharp-tipped hand clutching tighter at Daisy's arm. And with a sudden wild flare of movement, he tore the page from her sketchbook, hurled it toward a smug-looking Kesst, and yanked Daisy away, toward the back of the room. Her feet tripping, her body trembling, her protests caught wordless in her throat. And she only vaguely heard Kesst's disbelieving curse behind her, because Filak was hauling her toward where there was still a small crack in the floor, and then...

He dragged her down into it. Into the deep gaping maw, rough and rocky and terrifying—and with a furious wave of his hand, it swallowed them whole into the darkness.

44

For a breath, Daisy's terror flared and flailed, as her heartbeat hammered in her ears. Filak was stealing her away, trapping her, crushing her into darkness, where she would never, ever escape...

But twisting with the fear and the darkness, this time, there was still the hunger. The craving. The rising, whispering, undeniable truth that she still... wanted this. Maybe even... welcomed this. Welcomed being trapped in the close confining darkness with a deadly furious orc she couldn't see, whose language she couldn't understand.

Because, like always, she could still understand *him*. The heated jealous fury in his growling voice. The disapproving scrape of his sharp claws against her skin. The urgent demanding jut of his hips against her, and that thick commanding ridge beneath his trousers. All of it shouting that she was his, he would take her where he wanted her, he would rule her and use her and make her pay. He could destroy her and bury her in this hole forever, he could ruin everything, take everything, the wild unpredictable devil of her nightmares...

"*Min*," he hissed, as his sharp clawed hand caressed

hungrily around Daisy's throat, and his other hand shoved down at her trousers, her boots. Stripping her, making her bare and even more vulnerable than before, now with only her fur cloak between her and the rough stone of the tunnel behind her. "Ach?"

And again, Daisy... welcomed it. Wanted it. Wanted his strong clawed hand on her throat. Wanted him to box her in closer to the wall. Wanted him to raise her knee sideways, to prop her bare thigh on what felt like a new stone peg, jutting out from the wall. Wanted him to do the same on the other side, and then beneath her arse, leaving her propped up and spread-eagled for him on the wall, at just the perfect height. So he could scrape one hand's claws down her side, and use the other to palm possessively at her opened, clutching heat.

"*Mín, Daisy*," he hissed again, as two of those fingers— the ones with the broken claws—broke away from the others, sliding up slow and proprietary inside her. "*Sólin mín*."

His other hand had begun tracing the sun he'd drawn down there, the sun he was also now penetrating with his long fingers, and Daisy nodded and gasped and writhed beneath it, heating all over at the feel of it, the danger of it, the slick brazen sounds from his plunging fingers. And the undeniable truth that he'd trapped her in a dark isolated tunnel, propped her up for his display and his use...

But she still didn't want to escape. Didn't want to escape the fear, the uncertainty, the darkness. Didn't care if Filak played with her until she was dripping wet, or if he yanked out his fingers and then *slapped* her there, gentle but purposeful, wrenching her all over. Didn't care if he next thrust those slick fingers into her gasping mouth instead, so he could line up his hard, spasming cock with her open waiting heat...

And with a snap of his hips, he plunged up deep and demanding inside. The sudden invading shock of it quaking Daisy all over, convulsing her around him, drawing up a broken moan from her throat. But she still needed more, more, please...

"*Mín*," Filak hissed again, gouging even deeper, and then he drew out, and slammed back in. Making her jolt all over again, utterly at his mercy, so good, oh gods—and he did it again, and again. Until he was ramming himself in and out of her, fucking her with furious feral abandon, hips thudding, teeth scraping. One hand's fingers still shoved into her mouth, the other alternating between clawing and caressing her, pinching her peaked nipples, slapping at her arse and her hot face, thumbing at the top of her crease.

It was sheer screaming chaos, borne of euphoria and pain and merciless blistering craving—and beneath it all was the awareness, ringing distant but certain, that Filak was shouting truth again, louder than he'd ever shouted yet. Showing her what he was truly capable of, what he would want from her, what he could take. That he could wield this much power over her, with his strength and his magic, and maybe he really was the devil, and maybe she should be afraid, maybe she should run...

But still, there was only hunger. Acceptance. *Seeing*. And when Filak finally slowed his thrusts, slipped his fingers out of her mouth, and gripped her chin, Daisy knew exactly what he wanted, exactly what he meant...

"Ach, Filak," she gasped, between juddering breaths. "*Minn. Filak minn. Myrkrið mitt.*"

It meant, *Mine. My Filak. My darkness.*

And oh, the way he shuddered. His groan so deep and breathless in his throat, the shock and disbelief spilling through his trembling hands against her skin. Saying, she couldn't still want it, she couldn't truly think so—and for an instant, Daisy could almost taste his fear again, bitter and pungent in the air. Fear of her leaving, if she knew his truth. If she knew the depths of what he wanted from her.

But of course she knew, maybe she'd known from their

very first night together, and she drew in a deep, ragged breath. "*Filak mín*," she said again. "*Myrkrið mitt*."

He shuddered again, both inside her and all against her, and maybe even the rock behind her shuddered, too. His inhale so slow and fragile, as if he might break—and then he was here, everywhere, his mouth desperately plundering hers, his hips furiously slamming, his cock burying itself again and again with thoughtless, reckless need. And one hand was back on her throat, clutching that *kraga* like it was his salvation, while the other was grinding his knuckles just where she craved it, wrenching her tighter and higher, shrill and bright and keening—

She broke on the screaming crest of it, shot into bliss and blinding light—and with a jerk and a shudder, Filak broke too, gasping into her ear as his swiving cock gouged deep, and poured her full of his slick molten relief. His body straining and shivering against her, hot and helpless and close, and she could only gasp and beg and take it, meet it, welcome it, revel in it.

It took a long time for the quivers to fade, and at some point, Daisy had begun stroking him, caressing him, easing the shudders away. But she couldn't seem to speak, and Filak didn't, either, not even through his body or his hands—and for perhaps the first time in this, she wished there was light, enough to see his face.

"*Gott*, Filak?" she finally asked, into the darkness, and he betrayed a brief, visceral-feeling twitch. Enough that his cock fell from between her legs, releasing a sharp stream of hot fluid in its wake—but whatever humiliation Daisy might have felt was blunted by the awareness of his hand slipping down into it, caressing her as it flowed through his fingers. And then he slipped that wet hand up her front, over her bare belly and her breasts, so he could again brush his wet fingers between her lips, make her taste what they'd made together.

"*Gott, sólin mín,*" he murmured, as she sucked his fingers, trailed her tongue carefully against his broken claws. "*Ach. Þú ert...*"

His breath caught, and she could hear his swallow, could feel the tremble of his other hand against her belly. "*Mín,*" he whispered. "*Sólin mín. Blómið mitt. Og bráðum, sonur minn.*"

Daisy didn't understand the last bit, but she could feel the reverence in his voice, the longing. Or maybe even the relief, because surely he'd thought this would be too much. This would make her leave. And somehow, instead, it almost seemed to draw her closer, binding her tighter against him. She'd again defied him, angered him, challenged him—and again, he'd given her only pleasure in return. He'd shown her she could trust him, even if he ruled over her. Right?

So she sank heavier against him, drank up his strength and his relief, his soft rapid words in her ear. Speaking of suns and safety and home, in common-tongue and Aelakesh both, and Daisy nodded, breathing in the sweet scent of his sweaty skin. She could trust him, she could see him even in the darkness, he was hers.

"*En ekki Kesst,*" Filak was saying now, his voice clipped. "Not Kesst. No Efterar monster prick."

Daisy huffed a shaky laugh, and patted at Filak's face. "It's only art, Filak," she replied. "Just drawing. It doesn't mean anything, and it's not fair of you to try to control my friends over it. Kesst and Efterar are—*eru*—my *vinir.*"

She wasn't sure how much of that Filak had understood, but he harrumphed, and slightly sagged against her. "Then—no Efterar prick," he snapped. "I no like."

Daisy chuckled again, but nodded. "Ach, then," she said. "No Efterar prick. But either way"—she patted his cheek again—"you know I like yours best. Daisy like Filak prick."

She could feel his smile curving across his face, his head tilting into the touch of her hand. "*Gott,*" he said, sounding almost shy, now. "Daisy draw Filak prick. Daisy draw—*sálufélagi þinn. Myrkrið þitt.*"

Oh. *Your mate*, it meant. *Your darkness.* Using that name she'd called him in the midst of that, as if he liked it, or maybe even wanted confirmation of it. Wanted to be sure, after all he'd done just now—and maybe there was still a flicker of fear in it, too. Fear that she would see him, see all the darkest parts of him, and then... leave. Leave him alone, like everyone else.

It tightened in Daisy's throat, because in truth, she was still supposed to be watching, wasn't she? Still learning, still deciding this. She'd committed to staying until Lew started his horrible attacks, and that would be—what, twelve days from now? Or wait, eleven?

But gods, the taste of that fear in the air, not only Filak's, but maybe her own, too—and with effort, she shoved it all away, into the darkness around them. *Nei Lew.* No Lew. She still had plenty of time, and right now, Filak was here, so warm and so bright she could almost see the glint in his eyes.

"Ach, I'll draw you, *myrkrið mitt*," she whispered. "*Sálufélagi minn.*"

My mate. Filak shuddered again, his hands finding her face, drawing her in toward him. And as Daisy met his kiss, tasted all the longing and the promise within it, she could almost—almost—believe it was true.

45

For the next few days, Daisy focused on drawing. On learning. And, perhaps most importantly, on forgetting about Lew, and his regiment, and his attack.

The first day began with a trip back to the Skýli with Filak and the Restoration Team, seeing all the progress they'd made so far. The huge white cathedral no longer dropped stones on anyone, nothing shook or rumbled, and the team all seemed to be working well together, too, following Filak's orders without obvious complaints. Surveying and levelling walls and floors, cutting stone and laying tile, and even, it turned out, etching new designs into the cathedral's white stone walls wherever they had been replaced.

"We need patterns for here, here, and here," the serious-looking surveyor Soren told Daisy, as he gestured toward the smooth new walls. "Filak says you are a skilled artist, and could mayhap draw these for us."

Daisy flushed and glanced toward Filak beside her, but he proudly smiled and nodded, patting her back. While Rosa—who had been nearby, excitedly exploring the Skýli with her sons—snapped her head up, and beamed toward them. "Yes, Soren, she's brilliant!" she exclaimed. "Have you seen the new flyers she drew for me? Or her botanical drawings, or her portraits? You should go see Kesst's newest portrait, he's already framed it!"

Filak grimaced at the mention of Kesst, while Soren's mate William laughed from down the wall. "Ach, I saw this," he cut in, with an impish grin toward Daisy. "And I salute your skill, sister, but I never wish to see this again."

And perhaps Filak had understood more of that than Daisy might have thought, because he shot a reluctantly grateful look toward William, and nudged Daisy toward the wall. "No draw for Kesst," he said firmly. "Draw for book. For Skýli."

Draw for book. For Skýli. And as Daisy's gaze travelled up the high, smooth white wall, the weight of it seized in her belly, prickled behind her eyes. Filak still thought she was good enough to make that book, and now he also wanted her to draw something to carve in stone. Something that would last possibly hundreds of years, in this place that was so important to him. His home.

So Daisy squeezed him tight, and then happily spent the rest of the day studying the walls' existing patterns, and sketching drafts of her own to match. And when Soren asked if she could also illustrate a floor plan he'd drafted for the ruined kitchen, she made her best attempt at that too, enough that Soren consulted it repeatedly afterwards—and then, later that day, he asked if she ever took commissions, and if she might be willing to consider a sketch of his mate William for him to keep, too.

Daisy readily agreed, and once they'd finished working for the day, she sat down with William in the cathedral and drew his handsome face, while Filak brooded restlessly around the room, poking at rocks, and casting dark looks over his shoulder. But afterwards, Soren seemed so pleased with the portrait that even Filak looked mollified, especially when Soren dropped a large, heavy coin into Daisy's hand.

"Oh, that's too much," Daisy protested, shaking her head. "I couldn't possibly—"

But Filak jerked a decisive nod, and tucked the coin into Daisy's satchel. And once they'd returned to the mountain again, he presented her with a beautiful, familiar-looking carved chest. The same chest he'd used to offer her the *sálug-jald*—but now it was empty, except for her brand-new coin.

"For Daisy gold," he told her. "Keep safe."

Oh. It was a stark contrast to how things had always worked with Lew, but Daisy could easily see the merit in managing her own coin, especially if she decided to leave. But no, damn it, she wasn't thinking about that, or about Lew, she still had ten days...

"*Takk fyrir*, Filak," she said, a little too late, with a smile toward him. "Now, maybe supper? And then I draw you?"

It was almost comical to see the mingled displeasure and eagerness on Filak's face—he'd already eaten breakfast and a large lunch together with the rest of the team at the Skýli— but as Daisy had expected, the promise of drawing was an excellent bribe. And once they'd picked up a basket of supper from the lovely cooks in Orc Mountain's kitchen and returned to their room, Filak allowed Daisy to nudge him onto his back on the bed, with the basket close beside him. And when she gestured for him to eat, he grimaced and obliged, despite the telltale pleasure fluttering his eyes.

But maybe this was exactly what Daisy wanted, with the glower and the pleasure, the dangerous glint of his sharp teeth as he bit into his meat. And once she'd drawn and eaten a bit, too, she let her free hand wander over the distinct bulge in his trousers, stroking and squeezing. And yes, that was even better, and Daisy captured it as thoroughly as she could. The insolent arch of his chin, the hunger and command glittering in his eyes.

It ended with Daisy kneeling between his sprawled thighs, pumping and milking him, until that glossy white seed spewed out all over his belly and chest. And gods, that was a sight, so she drew it too, in elaborate and obscene detail. Until her mouth had gone bone-dry, and Filak brazenly guided her head down, and ordered her in cool, clipped Aelakesh to clean up her mess.

Daisy enthusiastically obliged, and afterwards, Filak drew her up beside him, and again used those still-blunt claws on her. Teasing her and playing with her until she was boneless and quivering, and begging for release. And once he'd finally granted it to her, she heavily collapsed into his warm willing safety, and fell into a deep, contented sleep.

The next day, they did it all over again, except that this time Daisy got to see Soren carving one of her intricate floral designs into the wall with his sharp, glittering steel tools. And it was Thomas who asked for a portrait instead, at his mate Elgr's request, and Filak only slightly frowned this time, and again popped the proffered coin into Daisy's satchel. And after lunch, Daisy drew more of the Skýli's rooms, and some intriguing rock formations she'd found, and then she and Rosa ended up discussing Rosa's new orc anatomy publication, and working on some sketches together.

It was again a truly delightful day, and the restoration team seemed to be making excellent progress, too—at least, until there was a piercing shout from a nearby corridor. And then Rosa's brother Salvi burst into the cathedral, dripping wet, with an alarming rush of water racing at his heels. "The floor!" he hollered. "I poked it, and—it *exploded*! Turned into a *river*!"

Filak viciously cursed and shouted, and ordered everyone away to higher ground, even as he sprinted off toward the surging water. And after a moment's glancing around, Daisy shoved her sketchbook into Rosa's arms, swiped up her lamp, and chased off after him. Not thinking, not having any help to offer, just needing to be with him—and though Filak cursed at her, too, he didn't send her back, either. And once they'd reached the room with the torrent of pouring water, Filak dragged out a shelf of stone from the wall with a furious wave of his hand, and propped Daisy up onto it. And from there, she watched, her hands clapped over her mouth, as Filak dove into the water again and again, his lean body flashing white in the darkness, until the water began to rapidly pool away around him.

"*Fokk*," he breathed, once he rose to his feet again, the water streaming off his bare head and shoulders. "*Fokking Salvi, hvers vegna er hann hér—*"

He kept going, speaking far too quickly for Daisy to follow, but when she scrambled down to join him, he snarled toward her, and demanded why she hadn't gone with the others. But there was something about the edge in his voice, the whisper of fear in the air—so Daisy imperiously informed him that she could go wherever the hell she wanted, and there was nothing he could do to stop her.

As she'd expected—or even hoped—this led to Filak bending her over a nearby dripping-wet stone table, where he yanked down her trousers, and proceeded to give her a fierce, dizzying punishment. Leaving her arse-cheeks raw and stinging, but gods, it was worth it, especially when he flipped her over and shoved her legs up, so he could keep slapping her, while also furiously pounding himself into her slick hungry heat, too.

But afterwards, he was relaxed and easy again, his eyes wry and tolerant on her face. And when they went out to meet the others again, he only gave Salvi a halfhearted reprimand, and told them all that anyone non-essential needed to stay safe at the mountain tomorrow, so the rest of the team could focus on clearing and checking the drains, and making a thorough assessment of needed repairs.

Daisy joined the others in protesting at this, but Filak was thoroughly unmoved, and once they returned to the mountain that night, he took Daisy down to the *dýflissa*, and made his point again. This time binding both her hands and feet to the stone wall, and then—at her continued goading—he brought down a slim black item from the wall. A *whip*, oh gods, with multiple long leather strips dangling from its handle.

Daisy gasped and stared, while Filak coolly carded through the strips with his claws, and raised his brows toward her. "*Ach, sólin mín?*" he asked. "*Ertu stillt núna?*"

Now you behave, it meant, and it was all Daisy could do to keep cursing him, to make him bring that tantalizing leather closer. Until he was trailing it against her skin, watching with distinct satisfaction as she quaked all over, as gooseflesh rippled out in its wake...

"Please, Filak," Daisy finally gasped, as stark, feral glee flashed through his eyes—and at the whip's first gentle, teasing, thrilling strike, she arched and shouted, and again begged for more.

It was another step into darkness, into her devil's dangerous embrace, trembling and pleading and flinching beneath his command, his correction, his pure merciless dominance. And then beneath his hard, brutal taking, too, his hips punching a rapid rhythm against hers, gouging her into the stone wall behind her, until he stiffened and hissed, and spewed her full of his hot wet hunger.

Afterwards, as Daisy sagged against the wall, a familiar trickle of unease finally edged into her sated swaying thoughts. This was still risky, maybe even dangerous. Filak still thought he had the right to rule her, to break her. And maybe he'd just proven that, maybe she should still be terrified of that, *irrational, foolish...*

But once Filak had released Daisy from the wall, he carried her off to bed, and then licked over every mark and scrape with intent, focused care. And when morning came, he knelt between her legs and checked her all over again, kissing sweetly at the already-faded whip-marks, and murmuring soft wonderful praises against her skin. Shoving away all the doubts, all of Lew's awful nagging voice. Eight days.

"Can I come with you today?" Daisy asked once he finished, as her hands traced her own black marks on his lightly stubbled scalp. "To the Skýli? Please, *myrkrið mitt*?"

But Filak still shook his head, his eyes mild on her face. "*Nei, sólin mín*," he said. "You stay. Safe."

Daisy pouted at him, but he only twitched a half-grin back, and pressed a soft kiss to the vow on her belly, its ink now faded to a soft grey. "Mayhap next time," he murmured, "you obey."

His common-tongue was getting to be far too good—Daisy was now almost certain that he studied while she slept—and when she kept pouting at him, his smile drew higher, and he eased down to kiss between her legs. The feel of it firing a deep shiver all the way up her spine, and the way it looked was just as thrilling—enough that she groped sideways for her sketchbook, and began drawing it, as well as she could with her increasingly unsteady hand. Filak kneeling between her legs, his shadowy eyes hooded and affectionate beneath his lashes as he watched her, as his lips and tongue and teeth teased her and lavished her. Deeper and harder and hotter, until she had to drop the sketchbook entirely, in favour of gripping at his shoulders, and breaking apart on his mouth.

Afterwards, Daisy stared at the sketch for far longer than she meant—it really had turned out to be a very compelling piece—and Filak clearly liked it too, nipping at her neck as he eyed it over her shoulder. "Put in book," he told her, with a wicked grin. "You make with Rosa, ach?"

Make with Rosa. Daisy hadn't yet told Rosa about the book idea—maybe because that would make it too real, somehow, too impossible to ignore. But once she'd said goodbye to Filak, and met up with Rosa in the communications office, she took a deep breath, and drew up her courage.

"I've been thinking," she began, "once we finish your projects—maybe I could try—making a book of—my own. With art. And other things."

Rosa twitched beside Daisy, blinking at her with wide, piercing blue eyes, and Daisy took a breath, and soldiered on. "I mean—I only ever published with Lew—with my ex— and it was all botanical and very scientific, and I'm sure no publisher would want me without him, especially on a different topic, but"—she gulped for air—"but I would really like—to try."

For an instant, Rosa only kept staring at her, and Daisy desperately wished she could take it all back, pretend she'd never even thought such a preposterous thing—but then Rosa crowed aloud, and hurled her arms around Daisy's shoulders. "Yes!" she squealed. "Yes, of course! You have no *conception* how much I've been wanting to pitch the idea to you, but I didn't want to run you off! We've researched you, you know, and you *must* realize your books are some of the best-selling botanical books in the *realm*, and your name is just as well-known as your ex's, if not more! You know it would be such a communications *coup* to have you publish and distribute a book from Orc Mountain!"

She hadn't once stopped for breath, her eyes dancing with sheer delight, and Daisy suddenly felt dizzy, blinking at Rosa's flushed face. Rosa truly—thought such things? She'd *researched* Daisy? When? Why? And most importantly, she really wanted Daisy to distribute a book from here? She really wanted to be Daisy's publisher?

But Rosa was now bobbing excitedly on her feet, and a sudden, fervent hopefulness bubbled up in Daisy's chest. It would be wonderful to make a book with Rosa, and if it was even mildly successful, maybe then Daisy could look into other options to take it further, could maybe even look into a partnership with a publisher in the city...

But—wait. This was all a process that would take many, many months, and Daisy still hadn't even decided to stay, had she? And there was still Lew's attack, in—in eight days, right? And she'd heard so little about that attack these past days, she hadn't heard a thing about armies or evacuation plans, or any updates on Sybil or the regiment, either. And she should ask, she should be worried...

But no. No. She still had time, and she was forgetting about Lew. And she... she trusted Filak. Right? Trusted Filak, and Rosa, and everyone here, though she hadn't seen Jule in almost a week now, and...

"What kind of book were you thinking, then?" Rosa's excited voice cut in. "Did you have something specific in mind?"

Daisy took a breath, and glanced down at the sketchbook in her hands. "Well," she began, feeling her way as she spoke. "I'd like it to be—something I'm interested in. Something I'd want to read myself. I do love plants, of course, and I'd still want to include some, but I think broadening the scope would be more... widely appealing. Something with more to it, maybe something like"—she gulped down another breath—"*The Spectacular Sights and Secrets of the Orcish Underworld*."

Gods, it sounded so stupid out loud, the kind of book Lew would instantly call pedestrian, lowbrow, *foolish*—but Rosa's hands clasped to her heart, her eyes blazing with alarming brightness. "*Yes*," she breathed. "Oh, gods, *yes*, sister. It will be a marvel. A masterpiece. A true towering Ka-esh triumph!"

Daisy couldn't help her high-pitched laugh, but it was laced with relief, and gratefulness, and more rising hope, too. Maybe—maybe she could try this. Maybe she really could make this work. Eight days.

She and Rosa spent the rest of the morning discussing ideas, making sketches, and flipping through Daisy's sketchbook, which now was almost full of drawings from her time here. And if Rosa was shocked by any of Daisy's more graphic artwork of Filak, she certainly didn't show it. Instead, they debated the merits and pitfalls of including adult content in the book, and ultimately decided to leave it to Rosa's anatomy book, so Daisy's could be accessible to all ages.

"I do like the idea of the book being... a welcome," Daisy said, as her thoughts flashed back to that first cave where she'd met Filak—the cave that had been meant as a place to meet and share with humans, to prove that there would still be sun below. "A kind of... light, into the unknown."

Rosa's enthusiastic agreement prickled oddly behind Daisy's eyes, and together they began working through a detailed list of what to include. What outsiders might most like to see and learn about, what might put people most at ease. How Daisy could guide them with her art. Her... seeing.

The rest of the day passed with dizzying speed, and when a dusty-looking Filak appeared at the door, Daisy first gasped with surprise, and then nearly tripped as she rushed over toward him. "Rosa is helping me make a book!" she told him, once he'd drawn her into his safe steady arms. "With plants, and rocks, and tunnels, and just—interesting things. Things I saw, and liked, that might help other people, too."

It again sounded so lacklustre, but Filak's grin was slow and delighted, showing all his sharp teeth. "*Gott, sólin mín,*" he told her, with a firm kiss to her forehead. "Good. I am glad."

He even angled an approving glance over Daisy's head toward Rosa, unexpected enough that Rosa blinked and twitched, and cleared her throat. "Yes, it's all very exciting!" she said. "Also, Filak, I've been wanting to ask"—she squared her shoulders—"would you like to pose for my anatomy book? Your features are very compelling, you know, and humans—and orcs, too—really ought to learn more about the Nor-ka-esh."

She gestured along as she spoke, making sure he understood all that common-tongue, and now it was Filak's turn to blink and stare, as a faint flush rose up his cheeks. But then he shrugged and nodded, and pressed another kiss to the top of Daisy's head. "If my Daisy wish," he said decisively. "And draw this, also."

Daisy shot him a warm, grateful smile, while Rosa straightened, and a calculating gleam flashed across her eyes. "That's wonderful, thank you," she told Filak. "And also, while I'm asking, how would you feel about teaching a geology class at the school here, too? I'm sure it would be an excellent treat for the students. And"—her gaze flicked back toward Daisy—"Daisy could even join you, if you like? But no obligation on teaching yourself, sister, if you'd still rather not."

Daisy indeed still held very little interest in teaching, but she would happily observe—and though Filak viciously frowned at Rosa, he didn't actually refuse the request, either. Instead, he groaned and rolled his eyes, and steered Daisy around toward the door. A response that felt like a truce, almost, like a cautious but genuine step forward between him and the Ka-esh—just like the Skýli, and the Restoration Team, and the *dýflissa*. And when he kept marching Daisy toward the *dýflissa*, she gratefully went, and then lost herself in his claws and his control, his magic and his darkness.

For the next few days, Daisy happily divided her time between the Skýli and the communications office, and spent a few delightful afternoons reading books and studying Aelakesh in Rosa's well-stocked library, too. And of course, she also spent at least some time every day out in the garden, seeking out intriguing sights to include in her new book. She'd met multiple helpful gardeners now, but the tall, charcoal-skinned Kalfr had continued to be her most frequent guide, supporting her quest for unique flora with his typical quiet kindness.

"You have not yet seen Joarr's underground garden, have you?" he asked late one afternoon, when Daisy had returned from the Skýli early to fit in some drawing. "This shall please you, I ken, and your readers also."

Of course, Daisy was highly intrigued, and she eagerly fetched her lamp, and then followed Kalfr back into the mountain, and down into a long, twisting tunnel she hadn't seen before. And at the end of the tunnel, Kalfr led her into a room full of... mushrooms?

Daisy gasped, clapping both hands over her mouth, dropping her lamp in a clatter at her feet. There were mushrooms carpeting the floor. Mushrooms climbing the walls. Mushrooms tucked into little cliffs and boulders, growing out of logs and branches, mushrooms that even glowed pale and greenish in the dark. Because wait, Daisy's lamp had gone out, and she could still *see in the dark*, and she frantically fumbled for her sketchbook, and flipped it to a fresh new page.

"This is *wonderful*, Kalfr," she breathed, as she began sketching the outlines of the room. "Absolutely spectacular, and perfect for the book. Gods, it could be an entire book all on its own! *Thank* you."

But Kalfr only chuckled indulgently, and waved it away. "I am glad," he replied. "I ken there are many outside the mountain who should wish to see this. Mayhap it could urge them to come visit, someday."

There was a distinct wistful tone in his voice, one that Daisy had noticed on him multiple times now, and she angled him a brief, searching look—but just then, someone new stalked into the room behind them. Filak.

"Filak!" Daisy exclaimed, with a grin toward him. "Did you know about this—"

But her voice was drowned out by the sudden sound of Filak's growl, deep and furious. Because wait, he was glaring furiously at Kalfr, and striding toward him with long, menacing steps. "*Nei, Bautul,*" he hissed. "*Daisy er mín. Artistinn mín. Sálufélagi minn!*"

It sent a flare of that whispering unease up Daisy's spine—Filak was jealous of Kalfr, Filak still thought he *owned* her—and even as she opened her mouth to protest, Kalfr raised both his hands, and began speaking in rapid, apologetic Aelakesh. Something about only helping Daisy with her book, because he wanted to—to send a copy to someone? To maybe... his *son*?

Filak blinked at Kalfr, looking just as nonplussed as Daisy felt—Kalfr had a son?—and then he leaned in closer to Kalfr, and took a deep inhale. "Ach," he said, wrinkling his nose. "*Hvar er sonur þinn?*"

Where is your son, it must have meant, and Kalfr's Aelakesh was slow and halting this time. Explaining how he and his son's mother had bitterly quarrelled years ago, and how she'd barred him from his young son's life ever since. And how his son had therefore never stepped foot in Orc Mountain, and how—Kalfr's breath was heaving at this point—maybe a book like Daisy's would spark his interest, and encourage him to come visit some day.

It was all fitting together far too clearly, flashing Daisy's thoughts back to how Kalfr had spoken about his weaver "friend", and how sad he often seemed. And now there was only sympathy, churning in Daisy's gut, and she lurched between Filak and Kalfr, gripping Filak's hand, while giving Kalfr a firm nod.

"I really hope it helps, too," she told him. "It's been very good of you to help me so much. I'll be glad to also credit you in the book, and perhaps your son will see that, too."

Kalfr blinked, but gave her a wan, grateful smile, followed by a brief bow toward her and Filak both. And then he spun and strode out, leaving Daisy watching worriedly after him, while Filak irritably muttered in Aelakesh beside her. Something about Kalfr needing to tend his own garden, and stop being a terrible father to his son, and give up trying to steal away other orcs' mates by showing them good caves.

"Filak," Daisy said, with an exasperated smile toward him, as she slid both hands up against his warm chest. "It sounds like Kalfr cares a lot about his son. And he's not going to steal me away from you with good caves, either."

Filak didn't look convinced, glowering resentfully around at the room of mushrooms—and then, with a meaningful flick of his hand, he unfurled his rope from his belt. "*Nei, sólin mín,*" he breathed, his eyes glittering with sudden, tantalizing menace. "You are mine. You learn this. You honour me. *Mín.*"

It spiked up a distinct twitch of unease, but far stronger was the thrill and the danger, the hunger coiling hot in Daisy's belly. So she willingly goaded him, pushed and prodded and protested, until he dragged her to the ground, yanked off her trousers, and then began... tying her up. With the *rope.*

"*Ach, sólin mín?*" he hissed, searching her eyes. Asking, the way he always did. "You wish?"

Gods, yes, and Daisy fervently nodded, and strained against that beautiful bite of the rope against her bare skin. "Ach, Filak," she gulped. "Please. Show me. Use me."

It was yet another step into darkness, into a depravity Daisy hadn't once imagined herself wanting. But her hunger only burned hotter as Filak kept wrapping the rope around her, taking his time, using a strange combination of knots and weaving. And then—Daisy gasped—he swung the long end of the rope around a craggy rock up above, so he could haul her up off the ground entirely. Leaving her bodily dangling from the ceiling, caught and bound and at his mercy, the web of ropes gently biting into her skin.

"You learn now, *sólin mín*?" he asked, as he swung her around to fully face him. Showing her his glittering eyes, his flushed cheeks, his hand smoothly unfastening his trousers, and sliding them downwards. Revealing the sight of his long rigid cock, ready and waiting—and then his hands reached for Daisy's bare knees, spreading them wide apart. Revealing her open empty heat, on a perfect level with his jutting cock...

"Gods, yes," Daisy gasped, the craving pulsing and flaring, flooding her with sheer desperate need. "Please, *myrkrið mitt*."

And yes, that was it, Filak's groan low and guttural, his black tongue brushing his lips. And then, with a single fluid movement, he swung Daisy fully forward onto his waiting jabbing cock, sheathing himself whole in one long, smooth, devastating stroke. So swift and shocking that Daisy shouted and quaked all over, bound and impaled and trapped upon him.

"*Mín*," Filak hissed, as he swung her off again, leaving her dangling, wide-open, empty, impossibly far away. "You beg for more. *Mín*."

Fuck, yes, it was so good, the darkness whirling wild and hot and heady around her, and Daisy begged and pleaded, revelling in that perfect sting of the ropes, that cold dangerous gleam in Filak's eyes. While he sank them into a slow, maddening rhythm, skewering her on his waiting cock again and again, watching with smug triumph as she juddered and keened, her pierced body helplessly convulsing against his invasion.

"You learn?" he asked her, so calm and unaffected, apart from the faint flush creeping up his cheeks. "You like, *sólin mín*?"

There was no denying it now, especially when he sped up the pace, the sight and the sounds now slick and messy and obscene. But he liked that, he wanted that, wanted Daisy utterly at his mercy, under his control, his head tilting back, his body spasming inside her—

His groan was dark and guttural as he poured himself deep, flooding her with pulse after pulse of thick liquid heat. Filling her almost painfully full of him, sparking her own pleasure closer, too, almost to the edge...

But then, with another dangerous glint of his eyes, Filak swung Daisy off him again, pushing her back and away, and swiftly stepping aside. So he could coolly stand there and watch her helplessly swinging back and forth, while her bared pulsing body spewed out his fresh white seed in brazen spraying arcs. Painting it all over the floor, and all over the beautiful mushrooms, too.

It was quite possibly the most debauched thing they'd done yet, and Daisy's face burned as she watched, as her body's spewing stream slowly decreased, and finally faded to a steady oozing trickle. And only then did Filak step in again, catching Daisy's knees, drawing her to a halt.

"Filak," she gasped, between her heaving breaths. "I can't believe you—you—"

That unease was whispering again, flitting from Filak's unapologetic jealousy, to the ropes, to the shocking shameless mess. To him saying he had the right to trap her, to rule her, to own her...

But his hands were so gentle as he untied her, his soft kisses skating over her skin. And his eyes in the pale glowing light almost looked like they glowed, too, running over her with such warmth, such reverence.

"Thank you, *sólin mín*," he murmured, husky. "Make such good art with me, in good cave."

His eyes angled down toward the mess, and for the first time, Daisy studied it, too. How in the mushrooms' pale green light, those spatters of white across the cave seemed to glimmer and shine. How they looked like sparkles, like crystals, like bright fallen snow, lighting up the darkness.

"Oh," Daisy said numbly, holding out her shaky hand, closing her fingers on the sketchbook Filak silently passed into it. And then he guided her down onto his lap and touched her while she drew, stroking her all over, teasing his blunt fingers into the still-dripping softness between her legs. Until her pleasure whirled and sang up alongside the art, leaving her dazed and boneless in Filak's arms, lost in the beauty all around her, inside her.

"We should plant mushrooms in the Skýli," she murmured afterwards, once he'd carried her off to bed. "Maybe Kalfr could help? Invite his son?"

Filak harrumphed, but didn't argue, and tucked her closer against him. Suggesting that maybe the jealousy had just been part of the pleasure, too, part of the art they made together. And it was enough to shove the unease away again, to sink into the warmth and the relief, the safety and the dark.

When morning came, Daisy stirred awake to more warm hazy coziness, and to a vaguely familiar sensation—the feel of Filak's claw, tracing against her skin. Moving soft and purposeful on her lower belly, almost as if he was... marking her again.

Daisy twitched up to look, her heartbeat skipping—but no, no, there was no ink this time. It was just his claw, skating lightly against the vow he'd made. The vow that—along with the other marks he'd given her—had kept fading more with every passing day. Until those three lines of curling script were now a very light grey, barely legible against her skin.

And his touch like this, so tentative and gentle against that vow in the morning's shimmering quiet, almost felt like a nudge, like a question. Like a countdown of those ever-decreasing days, a warning of that looming attack—and most of all, a reminder of Filak's pledge to her. His promise to prove himself, and gain her trust, before the ink faded.

Daisy couldn't meet his eyes, suddenly, and her voice felt

frozen, locked in her throat. She was running out of time. They should be talking about this. She should be seeking out Jule, and asking about Lew, about the attack, about plans and contingencies. Three days...

But she was rescued by a cheerful-sounding rap from the door, and when Daisy jerked around to look, it was Rosa. Beaming brightly toward them, with an apologetic-looking Julian in tow.

"Are you ready to teach your geology class at the school, brother?" Rosa asked Filak, with a dangerous glint in her eyes. "They're expecting you this morning. The children are very excited!"

Filak's mouth dropped open, the fury and disbelief flashing in his eyes, but Rosa had already flounced off again, while Julian grimaced, and rubbed at his mouth. "I tried," he said, with a sigh. "Shall I tell them you wish to cancel?"

Filak's face twisted with distaste, but then he huffed an irritated growl, and waved it away. And when Julian turned to go, revealing a surprising mass of red marks on his back, Filak's frown only deepened, and he abruptly called out something after Julian. Something about how he needed to make sure he was getting enough rest, and seeing a healer if he needed it.

But Julian's brief flinch was the only indication that he'd heard, and he stalked away with stiff steps, his shoulders hunched. While Filak made a face at Daisy, and began muttering in Aelakesh about typical stubborn uncooperative ungrateful Ka-esh, who all ought to be tied up and taught some lessons.

Daisy's laugh was bright and incredulous, and she couldn't help a teasing swat at Filak's shoulder. "Really?" she demanded. "As if you aren't worse than them all!"

Filak replied with a much firmer swat to her flank, and a playful snap of his teeth toward her—but then they were grinning at each other, and climbing out of bed. And as they dressed and then headed out into the corridor together, Daisy could almost forget that silent question he'd asked, that fading vow on her skin. Three days.

Filak didn't bring it up again either, and once they reached Geva and Rathgarr's classroom full of wide-eyed children, he squared his shoulders and launched into his lesson, without hesitation or complaint. And instead of talking about types of rocks, or demonstrating his stone-seeing, as Daisy might have expected, he walked around the classroom, and pointed out various features of its stone walls and floors. Showing them the lines of the layers, the foundations, the places that bore weight.

The children listened with surprising attention, though some kept warily eyeing Filak's shaved head and his marks. But when he asked them to follow him down through the mountain, they all scampered after him, until they reached a dead-end corridor Daisy hadn't seen before. Where Filak announced, in easy-sounding Aelakesh, that he needed their help finding a hidden door.

It led to a frantic excited search around the corridor, and then a chorus of delighted shouts as the students found a tiny vertical crack in the wall. It indeed turned out to be a door, and when Filak pulled it open, it revealed another tunnel, with yet another hidden door waiting to be found.

This one was trickier, but Filak again showed the students how to study the layers of rock in the walls, and explained how the layers had first gotten there, many ages past. And again, the children shouted with glee as they finally found the next door, and Filak revealed yet another secret passage to explore behind it.

"I'm so glad he agreed to do this," Rosa murmured to Daisy and Geva as they followed along together, Daisy sketching while they went. "How did he ever find these tunnels? And who knew he would be so good with children?"

Daisy couldn't seem to answer, but an unmistakable

pride was bubbling in her chest, along with a whispering, dangerous affection. Of course Filak would know every secret passage in this mountain, and of course children would love him, too. He was always so... *himself*, somehow, so expressive and immediate, so true to what he felt, and what he wanted. And the more Daisy watched him, the more she could feel his enjoyment of this, too. His relief at being seen, and respected for his expertise, even if it was by a group of shouting excitable children.

That night, Daisy felt almost shy as they undressed for bed together, as she ran her eyes up and down Filak's lithe naked body. She could barely even see his ribs, now, and the muscles in his arms and shoulders looked noticeably smoother and bulkier than they once had, too. Gods, even his cock looked fatter than before, and her throat convulsed as she looked at it, and reached out a hand to carefully stroke down its velvety length. Smoothing her fingers over all his black marks, over that distinct blazing sun. The sun that was also fading, its ink even paler than her vow.

She eyed it for an instant too long, as something dipped in her gut, and Filak's silent question from that morning again flared through her thoughts. She'd had almost two weeks to see this, to learn for herself. To decide whether to stay here, as Filak's mate. To let him write that vow on her belly in blood and ink, to shout his ownership of her forever.

"These *húðflúr* need to be redone, right?" she asked him, too quickly, over that disconcerting thought. "Can I paint them for you? Pray for you, *myrkrið mitt*?"

She'd repainted a few of his other marks now, too, including the prayers down his arms, and the eyes on his palms, and even the sun on his heart. And just like the other times, Filak instantly nodded, the warmth flaring in his eyes. Because yes, of course he liked her painting him, praying for him—and in truth, Daisy liked it, too. Liked being part of his identity, his art, his connection to his gods. A connection that had almost begun to feel like it belonged to her, too.

So she shot him a grateful smile, and then readied her brush and ink, and got him settled. It took her a while to sort out the best way to do it, but she ended up propping his bare arse on the edge of the bed, his legs sprawled wide. So his jutting cock was a clear waiting canvas, accessible from all sides, wide open for her touch and her prayers.

But it meant kneeling before him, close between his sprawled legs, with the inkpot on the floor beside her. And as Daisy gently gripped his warm smooth shaft, and touched her brush to the marks circling its base, the painting suddenly felt even more intimate, more vulnerable, than before. Especially with her here on the floor before him, her head bent low, her brush carefully stroking his silken skin. And though Filak hadn't moved or spoken, his cock was already shuddering and bobbing in her hand, enough that she had to hold it tighter, fight to steady her own strangely trembling fingers.

"What do these ones say again?" she asked, her voice thick, once she'd worked halfway down his shaft. "What am I praying for, this time?"

She risked a glance up toward his watching face, his eyes shadowed and inscrutable in the lamplight. "For strength," he told her, his voice careful on the words. "For fire and sight and plenty. For strong fucking, and good seed. For"—he took a breath—"good filling of my sun."

His claw dropped down to trace against that faded sun he'd painted on his shaft, the sun that marked this as hers, and Daisy swallowed hard as she blinked at it, and moved her brush to stroke at it. To repaint her sun on his most intimate, revealing place, to again claim it as her own. To pray for it, for its fire and vigour and plenty, for its strong seed, for its good filling of her belly...

Her hand was trembling even more than before, and she

swallowed again, took a deep breath. And fought to keep praying, keep focusing, draw the circle of the sun, the light, the familiar seeing eye...

It wasn't until she heard Filak's low hiss that she blinked at it, and realized what she'd done. She'd put an *eye* on the sun. On her sun, on his *cock*. And that certainly hadn't been there before, and he hadn't asked her to do it, and would he mind, maybe she should paint over it?

But when she darted another glance up at Filak's face, he looked... stunned. Awed. His eyes glittering strangely on hers, his length shuddering hard in her fingers. And oh, he was leaking now, too, pooling it down warm onto her wrist, speaking without speaking at all.

"You like?" Daisy whispered, breathless, the brush hovering over him, and he nodded as he exhaled, and sputtered more liquid heat against her skin. Saying... saying...

"Ach," he whispered back. "I like, *sólin mín*. I love."

I love. Daisy's belly hitched, her eyes searching his face. Searching all the things he was saying, so close and heavy and powerful, so strong she almost couldn't bear it. And suddenly she was again far, far too aware of her own fading marks, of his vow, of that waiting shouting question. Did she want to stay? To be his mate? Forever?

But the answer still wouldn't come, choked off tight and painful in her throat, and with effort she dropped her eyes, and gripped tighter at her brush. And then just... kept painting. Kept speaking, in her own silent brushstrokes, her own shaky whispers.

I'm not sure, they might have said. *I'm not... ready. I've seen so much, these past weeks, but I still... I don't know.*

But gods, why didn't she know? Why did it still feel so difficult to tell the difference between the light and the darkness, the dungeon and the dream? Between Lew and his control over her, Filak and his right to punish her, to rule her,

to own her. So different in so many ways, but still, maybe...
an echo. The same painting in different lights.

*I love. I have right to rule over you. My heart is forever yours.
Mín. Foolish. Sólin mín. Nei. You are an artist.* Feeding
belladonna to children. Forgetting Lew, forgetting Sybil,
forgetting the attack, three more days...

Daisy was painting so slowly now, so carefully, as if she
couldn't bear for it to end. Gently moving Filak's warm cock
up and down and sideways, now, making sure to get everything beneath, too, and then, finally, the head. That silken,
fully black-painted hood, now peeking back to reveal that
glossy pale tip, the deep slit with the pearly fluid still seeping
from within. Still speaking back to her, even now. Still saying,
perhaps, *I still want you. I still... love.*

And was Daisy saying it back, maybe, maybe, as she
painted that hood as carefully as she could, covering all the
faded grey with thick dark black. With her own care, her own
affection, her own...

She still couldn't say it, couldn't even paint it, but without
at all meaning to, she leaned forward, and... kissed it. Kissed
that fresh black ink, full with her lips, slipping her tongue up
beneath. Painting it on herself, too, doing it on purpose this
time, gathering her courage, holding her hand out to the
darkness and the dream. Saying... saying...

Filak's groan was low and harsh, his cock vibrating hard
against her lips, spurting out hot flares of sweetness into her
mouth. Saying, again, he wanted her, he saw her, he understood. He... loved her.

And when Daisy drew away, Filak's warm mouth was
there, here, waiting. Meeting hers with such soft eagerness,
such affection, as his safe steady hands drew her up, and
spread her out on the bed beside him. Touching her, kissing
her, coaxing her to fire and light beneath his hands. And
then guiding her legs apart, opening her fading sun wide, so

his hot alive body could settle down over her, cover her with his safety.

"*Sólin mín*," he whispered, hoarse and pleading in her ear, as his freshly painted crown stroked up against her sun, delved into its light. And then eased itself inside, one smooth slow steady plunge, one sun meeting another, seeing another, finding its mate, its home.

Daisy gasped as he sank all the way, locked full and heavy within her, hers—but then Filak swallowed her gasp into his own mouth, into the sweetness of his lips on hers. His tongue slipping in so soft and gentle, whispering of how he could so easily plunder and consume her, but how he could also treasure her and heal her, make her warm and safe. Just like his familiar hands touching her, his hips gently rocking against her, his marked cock filling her, seeing deep inside her. Seeing all that fear, all that lingering shame, *foolish, stupid, ridiculous*. The deep lurking terror of being alone again, of being wrong again, of losing herself to the tempting deadly darkness...

A strange, hoarse little sob escaped from Daisy's throat, but Filak only kissed that too, saw it, accepted it. Saw her for who she was, inside and out—and he'd still wanted her, still cared for her, still shared his skill and his secrets and his life with her. And now he was showing her, making love to her in a way he never once had before, and maybe that was the seeing too, the eye in the dark, for strength and vigour and plenty. *I love*, he'd said, *I love*...

"Do you mean it," Daisy choked, against his soft kissing lips. "That you love me."

But she knew his answer, even before he nodded, before his body flexed and spasmed inside her. Because he was showing her, he was shouting it to her, just like he had ever since the first night they'd met.

"*Ach, sólin mín*," he whispered, with a faint break in his voice. "I love you. *Ég elska þig.*"

Oh, gods. Oh, please. And suddenly Daisy was breaking apart, crumpling and shuddering and blazing alive beneath his kiss and his touch. Flaring into white dizzying bliss, into raging roaring ecstasy, while Filak's hips juddered, his groan low and desperate, a prayer of its own—and then he poured out into her, flooding her with light and safety, with hope and heat and plenty. Just like they'd both prayed for, just like they'd both needed.

Daisy didn't know how long she clung to him afterwards, trembling in his arms, gasping with the lingering bursts of pleasure. But she couldn't bear to let him go, and maybe he knew that too, his long arms and legs wrapping tight around her, his claws prodding sharp and certain into her skin. Even as his breaths came fast and shallow, his heartbeat thudding against hers. All of it still saying, so clearly now, *I love you. You are safe with me. Sólin mín.*

"I prove this to you, ach?" he breathed, close into her ear. "You stay, *sólin mín*?"

You stay. Daisy's breath dragged in and out, because of course that was the question, the one he'd still been shouting over all the rest. Had he proven this to her? Would she stay? Follow him into the darkness, into the danger and the dream...

"Yes, Filak," she whispered. "I'll stay."

46

It was a hungry, heated night.

Daisy only slept in spurts and spells, slipping off and then awakening again, gasping and arching and clinging to Filak's lean moving body in the dark. Opening her legs wide for him, meeting his filthy kisses, sucking his long sharp fingers into her mouth. Fervently sucking his swollen sputtering cock, too, and then even pulling away to draw it in all its obscene beauty, hard and glossy and dripping, drenched in both their fluids, and greedy for more.

It was all the dream now, all the dark dangerous fantasy, lost in his beauty and his thrall. Lost in her mate, her *sálufélagi*, because she was staying with him, she was, she was. Even if he wanted to control her, to own her, to keep her forever. Even if it was *foolish, stupid, dangerous...*

She loved Filak. She loved this life here with him. She loved his danger and his passion and his art. She wanted to stay.

It was enough to shove down the last of Lew's whining nattering voice, and to lock it away in the haze. So she could sink deeper into the danger and the craving, into the truth of her mate—her mate!—making more new art with her, vicious and triumphant. Growling into her ears. Sinking his teeth into her throat. Dragging his claws against her collarbone, her hips, her arse—and then, when she pressed closer against those sharp claw-tips, he scored them all the way from her arse around to her thigh, drawing their long curving lines deep into her skin. Hard enough that Daisy felt the skin burn and break, the pain flashing bright. Marking her, permanently, on purpose.

And when Filak then bent down, touched those new marks with his soft seeking tongue, meaning to lick her, heal her, Daisy shoved his face away. Refusing his healing, defying it, and she could feel the relief in his exhale, even as he growled, low and harsh against her skin. And it was right, that he should next slap her arse, and nip at her throat, her aching nipples. Right, that he should flip her over, hold her down by the *kraga*, and furiously pummel himself into her, until she was boneless and incoherent and begging. And right, after, how he kissed and caressed her, folding her into his warm safe arms. Whispering again and again how much he loved her, how he would always cherish her, and care for her, and keep her safe.

And then, as she'd slipped off to sleep in the dark, Daisy had felt his claw tracing that sun on her heart. Just the way he had their first night together. Making it fresh and clear, inking it with their new, shimmering truth. She would stay. She was his.

When she finally blinked awake again, it felt like a long time had passed, and Filak had already lit the candle, filling the room with its bright glow. Showing her the sight of his tall beautiful body lying beside her on the bed, still fully naked, with her vivid new eye marked on his half-hard cock. Hers.

"You love?" he murmured, tentative, and when Daisy glanced up, he was watching her, his eyes glittering in the light. "Daisy love Filak?"

Daisy swallowed, and her face flushed as she held his gaze. Had she really marked him, and then sworn to be his mate? To stay? Forever? And then...

Her eyes darted downwards, to the vivid new black sun he'd painted over her heart, and then those five new long, curving white lines, etched deep into the skin of her hip and thigh. And her breath caught as she blinked toward them, because this had clearly been a test on his part, a taste of what was to come...

Daisy's hand slid down toward those claw-marks, following the line of them, feeling how there wasn't even a twinge of pain at the touch. Meaning that he'd still tended them while she'd slept, making sure they would heal, but also that they would stay. That they would forever speak of this night, of the art and the love they'd made together.

Daisy took a deep breath, raised her hand to Filak's face. And then she drew him down for a slow, reverent kiss, for the answer he would know, even before she spoke it. "Ach, Filak," she whispered, once she drew away again. "I love you, *myrkrið mitt. Sálufélagi minn.*"

Filak betrayed a brief, full-body shudder, a shaky exhale that could only be relief. And then he swung himself up over her, straddling her thighs, spreading his hand against her belly. Against... his vow.

It was almost entirely faded now, lost forever into her skin, and Filak let out another ragged breath as he studied it, and then gently set his sharp claw against the first line. Holding it there for a long, quivering moment, and then... pressing.

The pain flashed and burned, but Daisy took deep breaths, and fought to hold herself still. Watching, with a strange shaky unreality, as Filak slowly drew that claw downwards. Scraping out more sparks of pain, drawing up beads of red, carving his vow into her skin.

"This vow... new," he told her, hushed, as his gaze briefly met hers. "Vow of mates, for Nor-ka-esh."

Oh. Daisy swallowed and nodded, and Filak nodded too, and kept carving it into her skin. The feeling sharp and exquisitely painful, hushed and raw and dangerous, her mate swearing his care through her blood and her pain, through this silent shouting ownership. And Daisy had agreed to this, she wanted this, so why was her heart thudding like this, her breath heaving fast and unsteady beneath his carefully carving claw. And why was his breath heaving too, his eyes blinking hard, his claw hovering at the end of that first finished line, drawn deep and red and irrevocable into her skin.

Permanent. *Forever*.

The air felt dangerously thin, suddenly, the room slowly tilting behind him, and the unreality shuddered higher, darker behind Daisy's eyes. She wanted this. He wanted this. He had to keep going, even if his hand was visibly shaking now, even if a single tear streaked down his cheek.

"Daisy," he whispered, snapping her eyes up to his, swallowing her breath. Because that was a look she'd never seen on his face before, something unguarded and overcome. Something strong enough to streak another tear down his cheek, dripping off his jaw, falling hot and stinging onto his half-carved vow...

"What?" Daisy finally asked, her voice a jagged croak. "What is it, Filak? What's wrong?"

But he was shaking his head, and that might have been a twitch of a smile, small and wavering on his mouth. As if it wasn't something wrong, but...

"The sun," he whispered, hoarse, as his shaky claws spread against Daisy's lower belly, below that new red line of his vow. "Our sun, *sólin mín*."

Their sun. Daisy wasn't following, glancing uncertainly at the sun on his heart, and then the matching one on hers.

And maybe he meant he would make that permanent too, and...

But Filak shook his head again, and another tear slipped down his cheek, another shaky smile pulling at his mouth. "Our sun," he said again, with an intent glance down at his hand, still spreading like that, trembling like that, against Daisy's lower belly. "*Sonur minn.*"

Sonur minn. Daisy blinked, frowned, because that wasn't right. He'd meant *sólin mín. Sólin mín. Sól.* Sun. Right?

But her heartbeat was thumping erratically now, her wide eyes staring at his face. At his slowly tilting head, his furrowing brow...

"Not *sól, sólin mín*," he said, low in his throat. "*Sonur.*"

Sonur. Daisy's heartbeat thudded louder, because she'd learned that word, hadn't she? It had been in the book, and Rosa had used it when talking about—about—

Filak's eyes glimmered, and he angled a purposeful glance downwards, to his clawed hand still spread wide against Daisy's belly, just below her vow. As if guarding something precious, protecting it, marking it as his own...

"*Sonur minn,*" he whispered, into the whirling dizzying darkness. "We have made... my son."

47

y son.
   His *son.*
   Daisy was... pregnant? *Pregnant*?!

Daisy's mouth fell open, and something began roaring in her ears, even louder than her screeching heartbeat. She was pregnant? With Filak's *son*?!

A choked noise escaped her throat, and she yanked back from Filak on the bed, clapping both her tingling hands to her lower belly. As if she could feel something, know something, *see* something—but nothing looked different, nothing felt different. And how—how would Filak even know? And she'd still been on Lew's intensive concoction, it was good for a month, it had worked for years and *years*...

But Filak was still staring at her, the furrow still cut deep in his brow. "I... scent this, *sólin mín*," he said, and as if to demonstrate, to make it extra clear, he slowly bent down, and inhaled deep against her skin, against that fresh red line of his vow. "Scent him in... your blood."

In her blood. No, no, that couldn't be possible, Daisy couldn't be pregnant, she couldn't. She'd felt nothing, seen nothing, *nothing*...

"But," she croaked at him. "That doesn't make sense, Filak. I wasn't supposed to be able to get pregnant, not yet, my protection was supposed to be good for a month! And our agreement, it's only been two weeks! And I was definitely not supposed to..."

But her voice faded, because a horrible new suspicion was rising, festering, screaming through her skull. Had this been... on purpose? A plot? A plan to trap her here with him, forever? Even if she decided to leave?!

But Filak only blinked at her, and something bobbed in his throat. "Two weeks... for mate," he said, hoarse. "For see... *me*. Not... our *son*."

What? Wait, did he mean—did he think a son had been—*separate* from that two-week agreement, somehow? Exempt?! Something Daisy would want from him, even if she didn't want... him? Even if they weren't together?

But oh gods, oh no, that look in Filak's eyes, the rising confusion, the stubbornness, the disbelief. Dragging up visions of that terrifying night in Lew's apartment, *nei, Daisy, nei...*

"Why would you think that?" Daisy asked, as her body edged further backwards on the bed, away from him. "Why would I have still wanted to have a *son* with you, even if I *left* you?!"

It came out sounding far too shrill, like an accusation, or maybe a curse. Harsh enough that Filak flinched beneath it, and his face had gone very pale, his marks looking almost mottled against his white skin.

"Son is... gift," he said thickly. "Son is art. Son is... light. Blessing from gods, beyond price."

The chaos roared higher in Daisy's ears, pummelling against her ribs, because... he believed that. He really, really believed that. He wanted that. All this time, Filak had wanted a *son*. With *her*.

"But," Daisy gulped, her voice sounding very far away. "You never—you never said! You should have told me!"

The words echoed through the room, striking against the stone walls, against Filak's pale face. "I... tell you," he whispered, though his voice wavered. "Ach, *sólin mín*, I tell you."

What? No. He hadn't. Of course he hadn't. Not once. Right?

But the way he was staring at her again, as if Daisy was an unfathomable foreign enigma, a painful confusing mistake. "I tell you," he said again, harder this time, waving his claw between her vow, and the empty chair beside their bed. "I tell you, before I make vow! Julian sit here, and tell you in common-tongue, how I wish to grant you son!"

His voice sounded strained and wounded now, as if he was on the verge of weeping, and it took a long thudding moment for those words to settle, to sink through the screeching in Daisy's skull. Filak had told her. Before he'd made the vow. That morning when Julian had sat here, and translated for them, and said...

You welcomed the promise of his son. Your art shall be part of the son you make together. You ought to know the truth of your mate, and the son he longs to grant you.

Oh, gods. Oh, fuck. He *had* said it. And Daisy had thought... she'd heard...

"I thought you meant—sun," she whispered, raising her jittery hand to her heart, drawing the familiar shape against her skin. "The kind of sun in the sky. With clouds. Stars."

She attempted a wretched little smile, but Filak only kept staring at her, and she felt the smile falter and fade, twisting into something almost like a sob. Stupid. Foolish. Ridiculous...

"*Nei*," came Filak's voice, thin and scraping in her ears. "*Nei, Daisy.* We speak of son after, also. We learn this in book. We speak it in Skýli. Ach, we speak of Kalfr son, just two days past! You know *sonur* is *son*. You *know*."

Daisy flinched further back against the bed, yanking her knees up against her chest, wrapping her shaking arms tightly around them. "I didn't know," she croaked. "I mean, I suppose I did know *sonur*, but I didn't"—she gasped for air—"I didn't connect it, I didn't know you wanted it, I didn't think it was a risk!"

It came out in a wail, and Filak just kept staring at her, again as if she was something foreign, something wrong. "But... you *know* risk, Daisy," he said, halting now. "I send midwife to you. Gwyn. She tell you. I send Eben to you. He tell you. Even Efterar say he offer this to you, keep my son away from you—and you say no!"

What? Daisy gaped at Filak again, the protests whirling up hot and urgent. Of course that hadn't all happened, right? And yes, maybe she could remember Efterar offering her pregnancy prevention, and she hadn't thought she'd needed it—but when had Gwyn come to her, or Eben? Gods, she'd only met Eben a few times, in the *dýflissa* and back in the sickroom, and...

The memory swirled up into the chaos, the vision of Eben earnestly talking to her in the sickroom, just like... just like the way Gwyn had, too. Both of them had come to see her, droning on about tedious facts and probabilities and options, but Daisy had only half-listened, caught instead in the threat and the thrill of Filak, so close outside that sickroom, and still so far away.

And now Filak was here, near enough to touch, but he was all disappointment and disbelief, his bleak eyes searching her face. "You pray for this, Daisy," he whispered now, as his hand dropped to his groin, to the soft hanging length of his cock. "Last eve. I tell you all these prayers. For strong seed and fucking. For plenty. For good filling of my son."

No. *No.* Daisy squeezed her eyes shut, shook her head, but Filak's impossible words just kept dangling there, the conviction ringing through his voice. He'd said that, yes, he'd thought she'd understood it too, and then...

And then Daisy had knelt and painted him so slowly, so carefully. She'd given him that eye. She'd even kissed the fresh ink, marked it all over her lips. As though it really had all been a prayer, an urgent heartfelt plea to the gods, and then...

"Gods hear you," came Filak's hushed, halting voice. "They no hear my prayers, but they hear you. They *see* you, *sólin mín.*"

They heard her, they saw her, his gods answering her prayers, giving her a son. Giving her a gift, art, light, a blessing beyond price...

And for a breath, as Daisy's prickling eyes caught on Filak's pale watching face, she could almost see it, almost believe it. She could... stay. She could be Filak's mate, and they could live in the Skýli together, and raise a son. A small, dark-eyed orc son, who might grasp his tiny clawed hands at rocks, or pencils, or both. Who would be raised by parents who loved him, and maybe by all Filak's Nor-ka-esh kin, too, in a safe place, a *home*, free of danger and attacks and darkness...

But no, no, the vision was already fading away, breaking into the darkness. Because the darkness was so close now, maybe it always had been, creeping and curling around them...

Because no matter what else Filak had tried to tell Daisy, he'd still agreed to those two weeks. He'd promised to give her that time and space to choose. And the entire time, he'd also been trying to spawn his son upon her. Trying to trap her in a way that was far worse than the dungeon, than the chain on her neck in the dark. In a way that was permanent, forever, impossible to escape.

Daisy's stomach churned, the ache pulsing behind her eyes, because—because Filak still *had* told her that part of it, hadn't he? He'd told her again and again, without shame, without hesitation or remorse.

I rule you. I trap you. I break you. Mine. Mine, mine, mine.

And Daisy had kept ignoring it. She'd kept looking away, pretending she hadn't heard, trying not to see...

She'd been a fool. Such a stupid, stupid fool.

And before she could shatter apart beneath it, she shoved off the bed, groped for her clothes, and ran.

48

Daisy ended up in the garden, pacing frantic and unseeing down the familiar winding paths. She was pregnant. Pregnant. Pregnant.

Gods, she'd been so stupid. To again ignore all those doubts and whispers and warnings, all silently shouting and waving at her. So she could keep traipsing along into the darkness, into the forbidden dangerous ecstasy, the whirling dizzying dream.

Just like... just like with Lew.

Daisy's breath choked out in a loud, broken groan, earning her a worried sidelong glance from a nearby bulky gardener—and she rubbed at her face, and lurched down another path. Gods, how had she done all this again? How had she fallen for it again? How had she been so damned *stupid*?

She shook her head, dragged both hands down her wet cheeks. She should have known. She should have seen. She should have listened to all those warnings, all those hidden dangerous words. *Sonur.* Son.

But now—now it was too late. And she was trapped.

Pregnant. *Pregnant.* Just like Filak had wanted. Just like he'd planned.

"Daisy?" came a familiar voice, a woman's voice—and when Daisy whirled around, her heartbeat lurching, it was... Gwyn. The midwife.

"Is something wrong?" Gwyn asked, searching Daisy's face with worried eyes. "Is there anything I can help you with?"

A shrill laugh escaped Daisy's mouth, and she again wiped at her wet face, dragged in a deep breath. "Did you tell me?" she demanded, before she could stop it. "Back in the sickroom? That I might be pregnant? With—with Filak's *son*?"

Her voice cracked on the word, on the impossible swaying weight of it, and Gwyn blinked at her, and then nodded. "I did tell you that the likelihood of pregnancy was high, without any further precautions," she replied, as if she was carefully weighing each word. "Orc-seed is very strong, and beyond physical interventions from a healer like Efterar, we currently don't have any reliable protections against it."

Gods curse it, curse Daisy and her gods-damned stupidity, and she hauled in another breath, let out something too close to a sob. "But my ex was one of the best botanists in the realm," she gulped. "The herbs he gave me worked for *years,* and he said they could even terminate pregnancies, too. They were the best available, the latest science from the city, known only to acclaimed botanists like him!"

It sounded so pleading, so pathetic, and gods, it sounded just like something Lew would say, too. All of it scraping horribly up Daisy's back, no, no, she wanted to forget Lew, escape Lew, forever, two days...

But Gwyn's expression was regretful now, her head shaking. "I'm sorry, Daisy," she said. "But whatever those herbs were, they still weren't likely to have any effect on a pregnancy with an orc, especially with regular ongoing intercourse. At best, those herbs might have gained you a little extra time."

A little extra time. As if maybe Daisy could have escaped unscathed after that first night with Filak in the cave... and then she'd gone and agreed to two more weeks. Two full weeks, bedding Filak every day and maybe more, without any kind of protection whatsoever. Fuck. *Fuck.*

Daisy couldn't choke back her sob this time, and she dug her palms painfully into her eyes. "So that's it, then?" she demanded, too harsh. "I'm just trapped, forever? Just like Filak wanted? Just like he *planned*?!"

There was an instant's silence, an audible intake of breath—but when Daisy blinked her wet eyes open, Gwyn still looked perfectly calm, her gaze steady. "Of course not," she said firmly. "If you'd rather not proceed with the pregnancy, Efterar can certainly still help you. Or if you'd like to explore other options, or maybe a safe place to stay while you decide, we'll gladly help you with that, too."

Oh. Daisy stared at Gwyn, at the cool certainty in her eyes, while something flipped deep in her belly. She could still—choose *not* to be pregnant? She could still—walk away, and forget Filak, forever?

A sudden taste of bile burned in her throat, and Daisy took a swaying step backwards, twisting her clammy hands tightly together. No, no, she couldn't walk away from here, because there was still Lew, and still—the bile churned higher—still that awful regiment Lew had sent after her. And she'd fought so hard to ignore it, to lose it in Filak's whirling darkness, but it was still there, still real, still closing in like a chain around her neck, trapping her in a dungeon...

Daisy rapidly shook her head, and mumbled a hoarse unintelligible apology as she stumbled away from Gwyn, off into the garden again. Just needing to be alone, to escape, to forget. To forget about chains and dungeons, about Lew and regiments, about Filak and his son. The son who was here, now, with her, *inside* her.

She kept shaking her head as she staggered further and further, shoving it all away. Burying it in the same place she'd buried her dead mother, her unknown father, all the years she'd spent scrimping and striving, sleeping on friends' couches and floors, scraping by on underpaid art. Until that magical day Lew had come, but now that was all tainted too, Lew using her for her art, giving her fake jewelry, fucking other women in her bed. Hiring regiments and planning secret attacks, feeding belladonna to children, two days, two days...

No. No. Daisy didn't want it. She couldn't bear it. She needed it to go away, away, please, please...

But it still kept clamouring closer, no matter how fast she ran through the garden, no matter how she scrubbed the tears from her eyes. The fear, the terror, the danger, the son, Lew, Sybil...

Sybil. Daisy's breath choked, and she jolted to a juddering stop, gaping at the path up ahead. At the...

The woman, standing there beneath a tree. The tall, beautiful, dark-haired woman. A woman Daisy would recognize anywhere, even with those shabby homespun clothes, the simple unassuming braid in her hair...

Sybil. Sybil? The woman Lew had fucked in Daisy's bed? Was *here*? At Orc Mountain?

Daisy blinked, twitched, shook her head. No. No. It wasn't possible, she was seeing things, she was so lost in the darkness and the chaos that she was—she was—

"Kalfr!" she gasped, in shaky desperate relief, because he was there too, walking out from behind the tree. "What are you..."

But her voice faded, broke, as Sybil reached out, and... took Kalfr's hand in hers. And then she drew him over beside her, as if she had every right to do that, to touch him like that...

And Kalfr... wasn't fighting it. Wasn't protesting. And instead he turned toward Daisy, and... *smiled*.

"Please come, sister," he said toward her. "And meet my new mate."

49

Sybil was Kalfr's… mate?!

No. No. It wasn't possible, there was no realm in which this made sense, and Daisy blankly stared between Kalfr and Sybil, while her heartbeat wailed in her ears. Impossible. *Impossible.*

"It's so lovely to meet you," Sybil said, striding toward Daisy with her hand outstretched, and a bright smile on her face. "I'm Margaret, and Kalfr and I only met the other night. But"—she angled her smile up toward Kalfr beside her—"we had an instant connection, didn't we, love?"

Margaret. *Margaret*?! Daisy was one breath away from shouting, exploding, demanding what the fuck Sybil was playing at, what the hell she was doing—but then Daisy's eyes caught on Kalfr's face. On the strange stubborn set to his mouth, the intent unmistakable look in his eyes. The look that might have been… *longing.*

Kalfr… *wanted* Sybil? He wanted her as his *mate*?

"But what about—your son?" Daisy's sharp voice demanded toward Kalfr, in a horribly invasive question that was still preferable to the rest of the mess now screaming through her skull. "And your weaver ex? I thought you wanted to reconcile with her!"

The pain flashed bright and vivid through Kalfr's eyes, while beside him, Sybil patted his arm, and shot a reassuring smile up toward him. "Well, it's been a long time now, hasn't it?" she said bracingly. "At some point, you just need to accept your lot in life, and move on."

Kalfr didn't even argue this statement, aiming a wan little smile back down toward Sybil's face. While Daisy kept staring between them, her thoughts screaming, her heartbeat galloping in her chest. What the hell. What the *fuck.*

And—wait. Why in the gods' names wasn't Sybil calling out Daisy, too? She should be bringing up their meeting back in the apartment, demanding why Lew's illustrator was here at Orc Mountain, and then sending word off so Lew could call his horrid regiment at once...

But Sybil was smiling back at Daisy again, still without even a trace of recognition in her eyes—and too late, Daisy shot a brief glance down her own body. Down at her leather trousers and bare midriff—still with that one fresh red line of Filak's vow, oh gods—and suddenly her gold jewelry felt very distinct, too, heavy against her skin. Her cuff, her ring, the *kraga* around her neck.

Oh. Of course Sybil didn't recognize her, or remember her. Daisy hadn't actually introduced herself by name just now, and Kalfr hadn't yet used her name either, right? And maybe most crucial of all, Daisy had only ever been an unremarkable illustrator to Sybil, a mild curiosity at best, rather than a beautiful threatening enemy who'd been fucking her partner in her bed.

That awareness scraped at something important in the back of Daisy's thoughts—an enemy, a *threat*—and somehow, somehow, she bit back all the shouts still jostling in her throat, and took a deep, shaky breath. "Right, of course," she said, in a voice not at all her own. "I wish you both—all the best."

And before she could betray anything else, she whirled off, and staggered into the trees. Not looking, not thinking, but just needing to escape, needing to run, needing to shove it all away and forget and forget and forget...

But then, there, just up ahead, was—a figure. A figure that might have been death itself, tall and looming and cloaked in black. And for a flaring terrifying breath, Daisy thought it was Lew's regiment somehow, they'd gotten in, they would drag her back to Lew and trap her forever—

When the figure... held something out. Something so familiar it clanged through Daisy's screaming brain, choked tight around her chest.

Her sketchbook.

She stared at it, and then up at the—oh. That harsh angular face, its shadows even deeper beneath its heavy cloak. Or rather, what appeared to be multiple cloaks, draped over every part of his pale body.

It was Filak.

50

Filak didn't speak, or try to defend himself, or bring up their son.

Instead, he just kept standing there in all those black layers, holding out the sketchbook, waiting. His hand's pale skin looking almost translucent in the sunlight, but for the distinct red blotches already creeping over his fingers.

"You shouldn't be out here," Daisy finally croaked, even as she belatedly snatched for the sketchbook, and clutched it to her chest. Gods, she needed it right now, needed it so much it ached. And curse her, but maybe—maybe she needed Filak too. Even after all he'd done, after all he might still do, in this moment she just needed the familiar stubborn certainty of his presence, his solidness, his safety.

So she didn't argue with him, either. Didn't tell him to go. And instead she gripped his arm through his cloak, and dragged him away, over into the deepest shade beside the mountain. Where she sagged against the wall of stone, felt its cool reassuring strength behind her, just as solid and stubborn as Filak beside her.

"Did you bring a pencil, too?" she croaked, as her shaky hands flipped the sketchbook open—but yes, he was already holding one out, its tip freshly sharpened. And Daisy blinked at that for a brief, stuttering moment, and then smoothed out the page, and began to draw.

And it wasn't even... anything. It was just the pencil digging into the page, leaving behind angry lines and shapes, black barriers and blank forbidding walls. All the confusion and terror and chaos, all blocking her and closing her in, trapping her in a deep dark dungeon. With no freedom, no hope, no light. No art. No... seeing.

But she still kept going, jabbing with the pencil again and again, until the page was full with it, scarred and trampled and ruined with it. Showing her everything screaming its way through her, etched out and made real before her blinking, leaking eyes. Darkness. Loneliness. Fear. *Stupid.*

She sniffled as she stared at it, wiped at the wetness streaking down her cheek. Because that was so much of it, wasn't it? *Stupid, irrational, foolish, dangerous.* All those vicious black strikes from Lew against her, meant to make her cower and hide, and cover her eyes. Meant to... trap her. Chain her. Keep her locked alone in the dark.

She couldn't bear to keep looking at it, suddenly, couldn't stop the water from streaking down her cheeks. And her hand wouldn't even seem to turn the page, fumbling at the edges, her fingers sweaty and clammy, and...

And then, Filak's long black claw. Curving under all that darkness, sweeping it up with swift, easy purpose, and turning the page. Confronting Daisy with that fresh clean expanse of white, waiting and ready to reveal something pure and new.

Daisy's breath rushed in, and she slowly, carefully, set her pencil back to the page. Drawing, for maybe the first time ever, herself.

The strokes were thin and pale and ragged at first, as if seeing through a cracked clouded glass. But the more she drew, the more she could see the weight of it, the shape of it.

The small, thin woman, dressed in tatters, crouching in the corner, holding her hands over her eyes.

And there, much bigger and clearer, was the figure emerging out of the shadows, and standing over her. The tall, lean figure, with vicious claws and teeth. And he was holding something small, something helpless and wide-eyed and innocent...

A child. A helpless tiny child, held in the monster's arms.

Daisy only vaguely noticed Filak's sharp flinch beside her, the choking hitch from his breath. Because she was too caught in drawing this, in finally seeing it, desperately scrubbing through the cloudy glass. Seeing the child's small features, the familiar angle of his nose and chin. And the tall monster's handsome face was familiar too, and so were those herbs in his hand...

It was... *Lew*. Lew, standing over Daisy's cowering body, feeding belladonna to her son.

Daisy's eyes squeezed shut, but the vision of it was still there, shouting behind her eyelids. Lew, towering over her. Lew, threatening her. Lew, killing her son. Attacking, destroying. Doing everything she'd feared so much, all this time.

And... and yet, still Lew, with a child in his arms.

Daisy blinked her wet eyes open again, stared dully back down at the page. At the strange distant tug in her chest, still strong enough that it was almost an ache, a loss. A... grief.

Had she... had she *wanted* a child? With Lew?

Something like a laugh bubbled in her throat, or maybe it was another sob, because of course she hadn't... right? She'd never once been allowed to even consider such a thing. Lew had always been so adamantly against having children, so focused on his work and his career and his fame. It had never, ever been an option, and Daisy had long ago accepted that...

Or... had she? Had some quiet, hidden part of her still wanted it? A child? A little family of her own? A home?

The image of it was still here, still shouting so clearly in front of Daisy's eyes, and another choked sound escaped her mouth. Gods curse her, maybe she *had* wanted it. Because she still couldn't look away from the sight of it, the possibility of it, the... hope.

And how long had that hope been waiting there, hiding safe and secret, just out of sight? And how much—Daisy's wet eyes blinked toward Filak's silent form beside her—how much of it had been hiding here with Filak, too? How much of it had she been ignoring, shoving away, forgetting?

But maybe she already knew the answer, her pencil whispering once more against the page. Filling in the rest of it, finally coming clear before her eyes. The child's tiny pointed ears. His long sharp claws. The small perfect sun, marked over his heart.

Beside her, Filak's hand rose to his eyes, his breath shuddering out, and Daisy was breathing hard too, her other hand slipping down to her waist, spreading wide against it. As if... as if...

She'd known, somewhere deep down in the darkness. She'd *known.*

She shook her head, tried to question it, shove it away— but it kept shouting, louder and clearer before her eyes. Even if it had only been part of her, hidden and afraid, she'd still... *seen.* She'd still heard those risks of pregnancy, and chosen to ignore them. She'd still met all these adorable orc children. She'd caught sight of that future, opening up before her, and she'd still just kept walking forward. She'd called it a test. An experiment, for two weeks. A dream.

And—she closed her eyes, sank heavier against the solid stone behind her—Filak had seen it, too. Filak had known. Just like he'd seen so much of all the rest of it.

Son is gift. Son is art. Son is light. Blessing from gods, beyond price.

Stupid, that distant voice wailed, more angry black marks on a page, but Daisy felt the solid stone wall behind her, the earth beneath her feet, the warmth of the orc beside her.

No. No. She'd been alone. She'd been wounded and afraid. She'd longed for something she'd never believed she could have. A child. A family. A home.

And now? Daisy blinked back at the page, at that unflinching painful art before her. And finally she just made herself look at it, at all the terrifying truth she could no longer deny.

She was under attack. Her son was under attack. Her friends and kin were under attack. And she'd cowered and covered her eyes, and allowed Lew to make her part of it. Allowed herself to ignore Lew's own stupidity. His own weakness. His selfish, short-sighted, *ridiculous* foolishness.

And there was no more escaping it. No more hiding. And Daisy took a shaky breath as she slowly stood straight, closed the sketchbook, and turned to look at her son's father beside her.

"I need to see this," she said. "And I need you to take me to Jule. Now."

51

Filak didn't hesitate, or question Daisy's request. Instead he only nodded beneath his cloak, and then clasped her hand, and guided her back into the mountain.

As if... as if he still wasn't even angry with her. Not over Lew, or her fear, or the way she'd responded to the news of their son. The way she'd left.

But he didn't say anything else, and maybe Daisy couldn't either, not with everything else still shouting behind her eyes. All the things she hadn't seen, all the knowledge she'd ignored. All the truth she needed to finally learn.

They found Jule in a meeting-room high in the mountain, together with her mate Grimarr and a half-dozen familiar-looking others, including Joarr, and John-Ka, and Rosa. And upon catching sight of Daisy at the door, Rosa's expression went from surprised, to relieved, to... triumphant?

"I told you she would come!" she said to Jule, her voice loud and decisive. "I told you she had nothing to do with it!"

Jule betrayed an obvious wince, while Daisy blinked at her, and back at Rosa. Rosa had thought Daisy had had nothing to do with it? With what? With... Sybil?

"I... presume you all know, then?" Daisy asked them, her voice tentative beneath all the watching eyes. "That Kalfr's new mate 'Margaret' isn't who she claims to be?"

Jule winced again, and cleared her throat. "Yes, we're aware," she replied. "Lew Wallace's attack against us includes multiple women like her. The women's goals are to ally themselves with orcs, and build close relationships with them, in order to gain access to our mountain. And then..."

Her voice faded, but Daisy's eyes briefly closed, as the answer rose thick and bitter in her throat. "And then, the *women* will launch the attack," she whispered. "The *women* will spread those poisons, and try to kill us all."

There was an instant's silence, but no one argued it—and when Daisy met Jule's eyes again, the confirmation was there, stark and clear. Of course that was the plan. Of course that had been the plan, this entire damned time.

Sybil was part of Lew's attack. She was here to trick the orcs, and gain their trust, and *murder* them.

Daisy had to haul in a deep breath, force her whirling brain to pull it all together, alongside everything else she'd learned out in the garden. Sybil's involvement in Lew's awful project had never made sense, on its face. She hadn't been a botanist, or a scientist. She certainly hadn't seemed like part of the military. And what, exactly, had she actually been doing, there in Lew's apartment that day? Enthusiastically fucking a man, proving what she could do.

And gods, Daisy should have seen it. If not back then, at least at some point during her weeks here, once she'd finally noticed that there seemed to be no drills, no military efforts, no obvious attempts at evacuations or fortifications. And she especially should have seen it once Lew had hired that off-duty regiment to follow her, and thereby forcibly reminded her that he didn't actually have any soldiers or spies or infiltrators waiting at his command. Lew wasn't a soldier, or a captain. He was a scientist.

So the plan had been... something else. And now, that plan was finally clear, here in front of Daisy's face.

The plan had always been to use women. Spies. Infiltrators.

And *that* had been the beginning of the attack. That had been the two weeks Jule had given her. And gods, had Daisy even counted it properly, because Sybil's arrival had probably been right on schedule.

"How many women is Lew working with?" Daisy's hollow voice asked. "As part of the attack?"

Jule sighed again, but she only looked resigned, now. "About a dozen," she replied. "All of them instructed to seek out lone orcs, in isolated locations away from the mountain. Thereby seeking to reduce any suspicion from our side, while ensuring that mate-bonds between the women and their targets could be formed at length, without interference."

Daisy's head had begun distantly pounding, and her whirling thoughts flashed back to Kalfr in the garden. To that look in his eyes. That... longing. A *mate-bond*.

"And do the orcs—know?" Daisy demanded. "Does Kalfr know his lovely new mate is being *paid* to try to *murder* him?"

There was an instant's awful silence, filled only by that rising thunder in Daisy's ears—but then Jule sighed again, and nodded. "Yes, they all know," she said. "We've been sending orcs out to meet the women, with a goal of continuing the charade until we can stop the attack. We didn't like sending Kalfr, but"—she exchanged a glance with another bulky orc down the table—"since he already has two strong mate-bonds, with both an orc and a woman, he's much less likely to become permanently bonded to someone new."

Wait. Daisy blinked at Jule, the relief tangling up with confusion, with even more scraping unease. Kalfr already had *two* mate-bonds? With a woman and an orc? *Who*? And was that why he'd looked like that, with such longing in his eyes...

"And how long is Kalfr supposed to keep up this farce?" Daisy's sharp voice asked. "When is the actual attacking and poisoning supposed to start?"

"Not for another few weeks," Jule replied, with another sigh. "Their plan is to first put all the women in place, and then to have them send back detailed interior plans of the mountain, and as much information as they could find about exits and vents. Then, once that was assessed, the women would be given the poisons, along with detailed instructions on how and when to activate them, and escape."

Daisy fought down a sudden bizarre urge to laugh, because it was all so absurd, and so fucking *stupid*. As if all those women would ever escape something like that. And the bastards in charge—Lew and Lord Nash and gods knew who else—would sit back and watch, and wait for those poor women to do all their dirty work for them. Not even sending a single damned soldier.

"I hope they paid the women in advance, at least?" Daisy asked, clipped. "And warned them that they might never come home again?"

Her spinning thoughts snapped back to Filak's *sálugjald*, to the way his people had also paid their women to move underground, without any promise of coming home. But now, in comparison to this, it almost seemed like a fair bargain. An honest agreement on all sides.

"Of course they didn't warn the women," Jule replied, with a hard little laugh. "And they only offered them a quarter of the payment up front. A nice little ploy to keep costs down, likely with the full expectation that most of the women would conveniently poison themselves in the process."

Gods, it was so vile, so unbelievably horrifying, and Daisy

had to choke down the bile rising in her throat. "So what the hell are you actually doing, then?" she demanded, before she could catch it. "You've known about this plan for weeks, you said you were dealing with it! Why haven't you put a stop to it yet? Why are you making poor Kalfr walk around pretending as though he's found a new mate? Isn't he trying to reconcile with—with one of the first ones? What if they find out about it?!"

Beside Jule, Grimarr had betrayed a low, menacing growl, perhaps in response to Daisy's tone—but Jule put her hand to his arm, and held Daisy's eyes. "I assure you, we've been trying," she said, and suddenly she just looked exhausted, and frustrated, and sad. "But you must see the other side of it, can't you? What will happen next if we try to retaliate? If we try to stop these women, question them, lock them into dungeons?"

She shot Daisy a bitter little smile, and Daisy stared back at her, fought to shove aside that familiar stab of fear in her chest. No, no, the orcs couldn't lock the women in dungeons. Because unlike when she'd first come here, these women would all have people monitoring them. Waiting for them. Expecting reports and information. And if the women suddenly disappeared, what would Lew and Lord Nash do next? Attack? Launch another full-on war?

"Can't you just—refuse the women entry, and tell them you know everything?" Daisy asked, her voice plaintive. "Or—or bribe them, somehow? Make them an offer?"

She was thinking of the *sálugjald* again, but Jule again shook her head, looking even wearier than before. "And then what?" she asked. "The women stay here, so Lord Nash can still claim we've unjustly kidnapped them? Or we let them run back to our enemies, looking for the payment they've been promised? You can't think these men haven't considered those outcomes? That they don't have a convenient alternative ready and waiting?"

Daisy's heartbeat was thundering through her skull now, drumming with fear and dread, and Jule gave her another wan, empty smile. "According to our intelligence, they'll still offer to pay the women if they're sent back empty-handed," she continued flatly. "But only on one condition. If the women will loudly and publicly proclaim their vile mistreatment at Orc Mountain, in clear violation of our peace-treaty. An excellent way to rile up the masses, and gain an easy justification for another war."

What? Surely a dozen women wouldn't help do such a horrible thing... or would they? Gods, they'd already agreed to come here and poison innocent people, right? And it would only take some of them, or even a few, or maybe... maybe even one good instigator. Someone beautiful and articulate, perhaps, and...

"And that so-called *Margaret*, out there with Kalfr right now?" Jule went on. "She's not just any woman off the street. She's Lord Nash's favourite long-term *mistress*. Sent all the way here to help Lew Wallace implement this project, and lead the charge against us."

No. No, Sybil couldn't be, or could she—because damn it, *damn* it, of course it made sense. Of course that was the rest of it, curse Lew and his greed and his stupidity. And there had to still be a way through this, there had to be...

But it was all tangling together now, dark and cloudy and confounding, too thick and dense in Daisy's scrambled thoughts. Lew, Sybil, women, war, attacks, sons. All the things she'd avoided for so long, all of them still here, even stronger than before. And one more unanswered question, still maybe strongest of all...

"Why did you hide all this from me?" Daisy asked Jule, her voice strained and empty. "Why didn't you tell me, all this time?"

But even before Jule answered, Daisy knew. She knew from the look in Jule's eyes, from the betraying wince from

Rosa down the table. And most of all, from the telltale twitch from Filak's body behind her, a silent shrieking reminder of the chain, the dungeon, the darkness...

"You still thought... I was one of those women," Daisy whispered. "You still thought I'd come to kill you all."

52

They thought Daisy had come to kill them all. Again.

A sudden laugh grated from Daisy's throat, because of course she should have seen that, too. She should have paid attention. She should have realized that they'd been keeping information from her, keeping her quiet and placated in the dark, all this time.

"I'm sorry, Daisy," Jule said, and she did look sorry, the regret tightening her mouth. "We hoped you weren't still involved, but... you must see what it looked like. You were living with Lew Wallace, working very closely with him for years. And then you go spend time alone in that isolated cave, until Filak finds you there, and then you two..."

She grimaced, but gave a meaningful flap of her hand, suggesting that—oh. Of course. Daisy had... *mated* with Filak, without hesitation, that very first night they'd met. Just as if she'd been ordered to go off and do it. As if she'd been trying to—what had Jule said?—build the *mate-bond* between them.

"And what is a mate-bond, again?" Daisy asked, halting now—and that was losing the point, surely, but she couldn't seem to take it back. Because it did sound familiar, didn't it? Like something someone had said before...

There was an instant's empty silence, but then down the table, Rosa cleared her throat. "It's a biological connection between orcs and their mates," she replied. "It's not *coercive*—it doesn't override your free will—but it often increases your attraction and satisfaction in the relationship, especially over time. I know Gwyn and Efterar usually try to mention it to anyone new, but it was really chaotic when you arrived, so..."

She left it hanging there, giving Daisy that escape, just like a good friend would. But both of them knew it was rubbish, because of course Gwyn and Efterar had probably mentioned it to Daisy—and of course she'd ignored it, again. Just like she'd ignored what they'd said about pregnancy. And just like she'd ignored those other whispering hints from Rosa, too. *We've researched you. Where have you two been hiding, all this time?* And even what she'd just said, when Daisy had first come into this very room...

I knew she would come. I told you she had nothing to do with it.

It dragged Daisy's thoughts back to the point, to yet more of the sinking miserable truth. Because it meant—it meant *Rosa* had known about all of this too, since the very start. And even if Rosa hadn't believed Daisy was a murderer, she'd still hidden the truth from her. On purpose. For weeks. And they were supposed to be friends, they *were* friends, and Daisy couldn't deny the hurt plummeting in her gut, the sudden sharp stinging behind her eyes.

"I'm so sorry, Daisy," Rosa said, in a rush, and her eyes suddenly looked bright, too. "You have no idea how desperately I wanted to tell you, but I vowed to Jule and Grimarr when you first came that I wouldn't! It's been such a horrible vexing mess, and none of us knew what to think, or who was involved, and—"

Her voice broke off there, her head shaking back and forth, but her glimmering eyes had darted beyond Daisy, to something behind her. To—to *Filak*.

As if... as if... they'd suspected *him*, too?

Daisy whipped around, stared at Filak's eyes beneath his cloak. But yes, he'd understood exactly what Rosa had just said—and no, he didn't even look surprised. If anything, that look on his face was just anger, and frustration, and resignation.

Because—he'd fully expected something like this. He hadn't trusted them, from the very start. *Nei trust them*, he'd told her. *Never trust them.*

But—for them to believe Filak capable of such a thing? Of conspiring with his enemies, the people who had already destroyed his life in the north, so he could kill more of his own people here, too?

"You honestly thought *Filak* was part of this awful attack?" Daisy demanded toward the table, and for some reason, the anger was finally stirring, deep and hot in her chest. "You thought Filak would conspire with Lew and me to kill you? *Really*?!"

No one answered, and Daisy's eyes swept over them all, the anger hitching higher. "When Filak found out what Lew was doing," she snarled, "he *kidnapped* me. He locked his new mate in a *dungeon*. And then he came here and *told you* about it!"

There were multiple grimaces around the table, and Rosa was wringing her hands together, looking genuinely aghast. "Look, we didn't know for sure," she gulped. "It's just—Filak didn't ever tell us *anything*, before that! And once he brought *you* here, he constantly went to such great lengths to be with you, to make sure we never spoke to you alone! And you kept taking off alone together too, disappearing for gods knew how long, hiding things from us, and given everything else we knew at the time—"

She shot Daisy another helpless, miserable look, and too late, the rest of it was rushing in, too. How Filak had first come here reeking of blood. How he'd kept hoarding gems and coins. How he'd refused to tell anyone here about his family, or the Skýli, or where he was going, or what he was doing.

"And that was still enough for you to suspect us both of *murder*?" Daisy asked, her voice still sharp. "To believe we were both pretending, all that time? Even when you came and questioned me in the dungeon? When you released me? When Filak tried to give me the *sálugjald*? When you told me to stay here safe with you until the attack?"

Rosa's face crumpled, and she shook her head. "We didn't know!" she cried, high-pitched. "We just didn't *know*, you said all the right things, even our—our *experts* thought you were telling the truth, but you also kept offering to go back to Lew, and it didn't make *sense* that you wouldn't know anything about your own long-term partner's project! But then he sent that regiment after you in the wrong direction, and we learned about the Skýli, and you've just been so lovely, and—"

She paused to gulp for air, wiping at her eyes with her sleeve. "I know it's no consolation now, but"—she dragged in another deep breath—"I didn't really ever believe it, sister. Especially once I got to know you. You're so open-minded and empathetic, so accepting and welcoming of other people, there's no *way* you would ever support something like that. And also, you're just so focused on your art, and on creating and experiencing it, that you shut out everything else. I mean, you still haven't even noticed that you're *famous*."

She choked a little sob-laugh, the sound twisting bitterly in Daisy's gut—was Rosa mocking her? But no, no, that look in her eyes was something else, something between admiration and regret.

"It's absolutely brilliant, sister," she continued. "*You're* brilliant. Like you have a pure shining light you share with us all. And of course your awful ex saw that too, and of course he would do whatever the hell he could to hide all his mess from you. To keep your light all for himself."

It shuddered deep in Daisy's belly, echoed fierce and strange against all the rest, and for a brief, desperate breath, she wanted to run over and embrace Rosa, to weep into her arms. To shout at her, and grieve with her, and tell her everything she'd seen about Lew, and Filak, and her son.

But—no. No. They'd lied to her. They'd suspected her. They'd conspired against her. She couldn't trust them.

Filak had been right, all along.

And without another word, another look toward them, Daisy staggered around, and escaped into the darkness.

53

Daisy rushed through Orc Mountain's corridors without thinking, her sketchbook tightly clutched to her chest. Just needing to run, to escape, to forget...

But even as she sprinted down a long spiral staircase, lurched into a dark unfamiliar corridor, she knew there was no escaping it now. No forgetting. Not even down here, further and deeper, into a part of the mountain she'd never seen before. With rough broken walls, and twisty narrow corridors, and only a few dark jagged doorways...

But maybe she'd somehow learned to read the stone after all, from all that exploring and drawing with Filak, because she ducked behind a tall crevice in the wall, and found— another tunnel. Another deeper, darker passage through the stone, another door, leading into a small, unfamiliar, unremarkable stone room.

But it felt good, it felt safe, even with the too-distinct feeling of Filak striding into it behind her, snapping his hand to the wall. And with a loud, grating crunch, the door was gone, replaced with a solid, unmovable wall of stone. Leaving

Daisy... trapped. Caught in this dank little dungeon, alone, with him.

And maybe—maybe that felt right, too. Maybe even... a relief. Knowing they were alone together, safe together, where they could do and say whatever the hell they wanted. And as Filak angrily began prowling around the walls, thudding more stone down to reinforce them, to trap Daisy in deeper with him, she almost felt—grateful.

"What the hell was all that?" she finally demanded at him, through her still-choked throat. "*Hvað var þetta*? What the *fokk*!"

Filak's snarl back was just as angry, and he slammed down another sheet of rock with satisfying force. "I tell you we no trust them," he hissed. "I *never* trust them!"

Daisy jerked a nod, and began pacing too, clutching her sketchbook tighter to her chest. "I know," she gulped. "I thought—I hoped—ach. I never dreamt they would think we were *murderers*, all this time!"

Filak scoffed and slammed down another sheet of rock, and then launched into a swift, furious stream of Aelakesh. Something about selfish short-sighted top-dwellers, and Ash-Kai finding schemes behind every rock, and so-called scholarly Ka-esh being too stupid to see the truth shouting in front of their faces.

That wrenched at something in Daisy's belly, but Filak was still slamming down rocks, his eyes blazing on Daisy's face. "We leave them," he snarled. "We forget them. We go to Skýli, we keep them out, forever!"

It caught Daisy's breath for an instant—he wanted to leave with her, forever? But yes, wait, that was exactly what he was doing. He was blocking off this room, making it so no one could ever follow, and—Daisy's eyes followed the lines of the stone—he would start digging, there on that wall he hadn't yet touched. He would dig them straight to the Skýli, and block it off with endless walls of stone, and they would never, ever need to see anyone here again.

Daisy's agreement was already rising, almost escaping— yes, that was exactly what they should do—but then it caught. Quivered. Held. And her eyes dropped to the sketchbook still in her hands, to all the people and art and promises it held. All the... seeing.

"But what about... the rest of them?" she asked, thick in her throat. "Everyone else who's still back there, who wasn't involved in this?"

But Filak furiously shook his head, and waved them all away with a swipe of his claws, so sharp that rocks clattered across the room. "Forget them," he spat. "We no need them!"

Daisy blinked back down at her sketchbook, and then her numb fingers flipped it open. Skipping through pages, until she reached all her drawings from these past few weeks. The cave. Orc Mountain's sickroom. Efterar, and Kesst. The Bautul forge. The tunnels she'd explored with Filak. The Skýli. The garden. Rosa. Rosa's sons. Rosa's brothers. Julian.

The portrait of Julian was the one Daisy had drawn in Rosa's communications office, the day they'd all been laughing and drawing each other, and it was a good angle, a good likeness. Capturing that familiar wry smile on Julian's handsome face, and also that ever-present sadness, whispering in his eyes. And the longer Daisy blinked at it, the more it clutched in her chest, prickled behind her eyes. Gods, Julian had been so kind to them. So generous. And whatever he'd known about the attack, he surely hadn't suspected them. He'd defended them both from the start. From that first moment in the dungeon, when he'd promised Daisy his help.

And maybe Filak had caught that, glancing over his shoulder from where he was slamming down another rock. "We write Julian, after," he told her, his voice flat. "Send him to come to Skýli."

Daisy twitched a nod, but she kept blinking down at Julian's face, at that sadness in his eyes. Because Julian wouldn't really want to come live with them alone in the Skýli, would he? He wouldn't want to be blocked off from the rest of the world forever—and therefore, from any chance of seeing Rurik again, either. No, Julian deserved better, and gods, so did Kalfr, and Efterar and Kesst, and Rosa and John-Ka and their brothers and sons. And all the people who'd helped with the Skýli, and all the rest of the Ka-esh, and all that damned mountain.

All the people Lew still wanted to kill. Poison. War. Death. Feeding belladonna to *children*. To Daisy's own son.

And Daisy had sworn to stop hiding. She'd sworn to stop escaping and forgetting. No matter how terrifying it was, no matter how much it hurt.

She needed to see.

"Filak," Daisy whispered, tight in her throat. "We can't leave. Not yet. *Nei*."

Filak wrenched around again, his eyes wild and disbelieving on her face, and Daisy drew in a deep breath, pulled herself straight. "We can't leave yet," she repeated, steadier this time. "They were wrong, to suspect us like that. They were wrong to keep secrets from us. They were wrong to judge you for no reason, *again*."

Filak didn't speak, his eyes still glittering on hers, and Daisy blinked back down at her sketchbook, dragged in another breath. "But they also—helped us. They let us stay, even after we damaged their sickroom. They healed me, and kept me safe from Lew. They gave me freedom to wander all over the mountain, and draw whatever I wanted. They welcomed my art, and encouraged it, and—they even offered to help me publish a book."

But Filak's head was shaking, and he slammed down another slab of stone behind him without even looking.

"They do this for *them*," he hissed. "They wish to use you. Keep you."

Use you. Keep you. It was another clutch in Daisy's belly, bitter and daunting and far too raw, and she gulped down another breath, and shook her head. "Not all of them, Filak," she said thickly. "They paid me for my work. They helped me. They helped *us*."

Filak kept shaking his head, a growl rumbling from his mouth, but Daisy kept going. "And now—now they're under attack," she whispered. "And I want to help them."

Filak's growl deepened, and he broke into another stream of harsh, angry Aelakesh. Insisting that Daisy had already done enough for them, she owed them nothing, they could fix their own damned problems.

"But," Daisy cut in, between deep breaths. "I was Lew's partner for four *years*, Filak. I—I supported him, and helped him, and I didn't—I didn't even see what he was doing, with this attack. I did *nothing* to stop him. And I know his actions aren't my responsibility, but"—she dragged down more air— "I still think I can help. I want to help. I want to try."

She didn't know how much of that Filak had understood, but he came a slow step toward her, his hands in fists at his sides. "*Nei, Daisy*," he said, a hoarse, menacing snarl. "*Nei Lew*. Forget Lew."

It was another wrench in Daisy's gut, another whirling truth in the mess, because yes, Filak wanted to forget, too. And that wasn't new, was it? No, Filak had always wanted her to forget with him, to escape with him, to run away into the dark with him. And she'd been all too willing, but...

"I can't, Filak," she croaked at him, even as he came another slow, purposeful step toward her. "I can't forget Lew. It didn't work. It only let him keep doing this without inter-ference, getting that much further with his horrible plan! I need to—to face him, Filak. I need to *see* him."

Filak's eyes widened, his nostrils flaring, and too late,

Daisy heard what she'd just said. She needed to face Lew. To see him. *See* him.

And yes, that was what she needed to do. It was the only way...

"I need to see Lew, Filak," Daisy whispered, holding his flashing eyes. "I need to go back."

She needed to go back.

The words kept hovering, echoing, while Filak stared at Daisy with those wide, unblinking eyes. As if he was considering it, as if he might even allow it...

And then—something cracked, loud and jagged and thunderous. The—floor. The floor was breaking beneath them, because Filak was roaring, his eyes burning, his body a sharp furious torrent of wild shouting rage.

"*Nei, Daisy,*" he spat, as he surged toward her. "*Nei Lew. Þú ert mín.* Mine!"

She was his. His. And before Daisy could open her mouth, Filak crowded her back against the wall behind her, and yanked something out from his belt.

A... chain. A familiar, beautifully forged gold chain, shimmering and tinkling as it pooled through his long clawed fingers...

It was *that* chain. The chain he'd used to trap her in the dungeon. And why did he still have it, had he still had it this entire time, oh gods, oh *gods*—

But there was nothing Daisy could do. Nowhere to run. And she could only watch, waiting and trembling and terrified, as Filak swung the chain up, and snapped it to her throat.

54

Filak had chained Daisy to a wall in a dungeon. Again.

The panic spiked and blistered, gouging deep into Daisy's darkest memories, dragging her back down into that horrifying blackness of the first dungeon. To when he'd hurt and rejected her, trapped her there in the dark, and left.

But now—Daisy's thoughts hitched, jolting and frantic— now Filak was still here. Still here with her, even if he was now furiously jabbing the chain's other end into the wall behind her, folding it deep into the stone with an ominous grating crunch.

"*Mín*," he snarled at her, as his hand slipped back down to her throat, and gripped both the chain and the *kraga* beneath his strong fingers. "*Daisy mín. Sólin mín. Mín!*"

It rumbled through his hand, shook the wall behind her, and Daisy should have kicked and screamed, and fought for her life. Clawed out his eyes, or elbowed him in the gut, or kneed him in the groin. He had no right, she wasn't his property, he didn't own her, he *didn't*—

But suddenly, swarming behind Daisy's eyes, were all those memories, all those uneasy whispering fears. Filak trapping her in that cave. Filak drawing on her in the dark. Filak destroying Lew's ring. Filak breaking through the sick-room floor, cornering her in the latrine, spreading fresh ink on her lips...

He's always wanted to rule you, a voice whispered, distant and triumphant. *He told you he wanted to trap you, and break you. Foolish. Stupid. Dangerous...*

But no, no, Daisy knew that voice now, could see it for what it was—and the truth of it skipped, twisted, spun back around again. And this time—Filak licking her hands. Filak guiding her across the rubble-strewn room. Filak kneeling beside her bed, offering her that valuable *sálugjald*, refusing to leave her alone with the people he didn't trust. Filak giving her that beautiful jewelry, giving her his mark and his safety. Filak patiently waiting as she drew, Filak sharpening her pencils, Filak telling her to write a book. Filak keeping her safe in the collapsing Skýli, Filak obsessively inspecting her after their sessions in the *dýflissa*, Filak trying to tell her again and again about the possibility of a son...

And even now, this moment. Not with Filak suspecting her, trapping her, and leaving her, like he had before—but instead, defending her. Protecting her. Blocking her in this room with him, promising to take her away to safety, refusing to let Lew try to destroy her, again. Because—because—

He'd sworn it to her. He'd promised it, in that vow he'd made. *I will prove myself as your mate, and gain you as my own.*

Daisy's eyes blinked down to her heaving belly, to that first line of his matehood vow, now scored forever into her skin—and then she again found Filak's face. His rigid, contorted, furious face, a face that should have been terrifying, dangerous, the face of the devil himself...

But suddenly it was clear, it was bright blazing sight from Daisy's blinking eyes. No. No. Filak wasn't dangerous. Not to her. Not ever.

He was—*hers*. Her devil. Her mate. The father of her son.

And she knew it, she was sure of it, she *was*—but she still wanted to see it. Wanted to see the worth and the beauty in it. The art. The dream.

"Then prove it," she whispered, holding his burning eyes. "Show me, *myrkrið mitt*."

And yes, he needed it too, the hunger and relief flashing stark across his face. And in a sudden movement, his tall body boxed her in tighter against the stone wall, his strong hands clutching her wrists, snapping them up to the stone above her head. To where—Daisy shuddered all over—she could feel the cool stone curving out, wrapping around her wrists, trapping her there, oh gods.

But she needed this, needed to see everything he could possibly show her—and she shuddered again as Filak yanked off her fur cloak, and then her boots and leather trousers, too. Leaving her fully bared against the wall, but for the flimsy silk wrap tied over her breasts.

But then, in another swift movement, he swept that off, too. And instead of tossing it away, he held it before Daisy's wide staring eyes, let her watch him crushing it into a tight little ball—and then, slow and deliberate, he brought it to her lips, and gently shoved it into her *mouth*.

It flashed up more memories, more dark visceral fear, visions of him kidnapping her, carrying her away with that ball of paper stuffed into her mouth. But she wanted him to show her, show her everything—and as she blinked at his glittering eyes, she knew this was part of it, too. This was him calling back to that dark night, reminding her what he'd done, what he was capable of—but now, he was showing her something else. Proving it.

And also—more awareness flashed through Daisy's trammelling thoughts—without her voice, he would need to prove it even more. He needed to show he could watch her, and scent her. Prove he could please her. And—Daisy gasped into her gag as his hand slipped around behind her, between her and the stone wall—he needed to prove he could still protect her. Even from himself.

But now—this was something different. Something... new. It was the stone behind her... *moving*. Not unlike the time he'd taken her under the sickroom, when he'd used his magic to lift her off the floor—but this time, the stone beneath his hands wasn't only lifting. It was... *embracing*. Easing out cool and solid from the wall, circling around her ankles, her calves, her thighs. Curving up over her shoulders, around her hips. Spreading her wide, raising her up, putting her naked body fully on display, oh gods...

She quivered all over, breathing hard, watching as Filak drew his hand back again, and then eased down his own trousers. Revealing his hard, dripping length, and then he began stroking it even fuller, squeezing out a thickening string of shining fluid. A string that he then caught in his fingers, coating his hand all over, before sliding it around behind her again. To where yet more stone had begun nudging up against her, easing slow and slick and purposeful against... her *arse*.

Daisy gasped and quivered again, feeling that slick stone seeking up against her, into her already-open cleft... and then, oh gods, it slipped up *inside* her. Only a cool slippery tendril at first, a light teasing touch—but then it shifted. Changed. Thickening. Lengthening. Invading.

Daisy quaked and moaned, biting down on the silk in her mouth, because yes, Filak was doing this. Binding her bared, chained, gagged body to a wall with solid stone, and now... impaling her there, from behind. As if he was hooking her, hanging her, skewering her, trapping her and spreading her and owning her in every possible way.

Except—for this. His hand slipping around her again, down her front, between her split legs. To where her dripping-wet heat was still wide open and waiting, clutching back against him, meeting him, needing him with such wild fervent desperation.

"*Mín*," Filak breathed, as the challenge and the triumph burned through his eyes. "*Ach? Gott?*"

Gott. Still asking, always asking, even now, and Daisy distantly cast through her body, felt all that stone around her, and jutted up deep inside her. Piercing her with over-whelming power, binding her bodily to the wall, to this room, to his command. And she would never escape this on her own, not ever...

But still, somehow, there was no fear. No unease or alarm. Because Filak was still here, he would always be here, and even in this—trussed up and pinned to a wall with solid rock—there wasn't yet a twinge of pain. If anything, the rock all felt impossibly silken and smooth, and of course he knew that, of course he'd done that, he was hers.

But he was still watching, scenting her, the way he always did, and Daisy moaned and nodded, trembled beneath his eyes and his touch. While he kept studying her, his eyes shifting—and with a gentle flick of his fingers he plucked out the gag, and pressed a soft, searching kiss to her lips.

"*Gott*?" he whispered. "You like?"

Daisy could only moan and nod again, kissing him back with frantic abandon, needing his tongue and his teeth. And of course he gave that, too, flashing out the beautiful pain against the soft succulent warmth, while his hand kept stroking hungry and possessive against her slick open heat.

"*Gott*," he murmured, as he drew away again, his eyes flickering with something warmer, now, something almost fond—and then he thrust the gag back in, half-smiling at Daisy's exasperated moan. And then, oh gods, there was more, more of the stone circling around her, spreading her legs, more of the cool hardness inside her. All of it slightly shifting her upwards, lifting her off the floor entirely, splaying her out for Filak like a feast on a platter, skewered and exposed and shockingly obscene.

But it was just what he wanted, his eyes raking up and down, both hands now stroking and scraping over Daisy's trapped body. Pinching her peaked nipples, curling around her *kraga*, caressing her sun and her half-finished vow. And for a breath, Daisy urgently wanted him to finish that vow, to carve it into her here and now, but no, no, he wouldn't, not like this, not when he couldn't be sure…

And instead, there was—Filak's cock. His bulging, weeping, ink-tipped cock, jutting out fuller than Daisy had ever seen it—and now nudging up against her slick convulsing heat. Making her gasp and writhe against it, the sounds from her wet body loud and brazen, begging him to keep delving into her, deep into the bright burning core of her…

Filak was gasping too, his eyes hooded and hungry on the sight—and then he finally eased forward. Pressing. Invading. Filling that last empty part of her, slow and certain and powerful. His body so warm and throbbing and alive, so unlike that hard jutting stone still filling her from behind. The contrast stark and stunning, both of them rubbing up together inside her, stretching her to the brink. And Daisy never wanted to escape it, never wanted to forget it, the thrill and the risk and the trust of it, the dizzying power of her deadly beautiful devil, guiding her into the dark, into the dream. Right where they both wanted to be, together.

They moaned together as Filak sank all the way, as far as he could go. So good, so bright and brutal and glorious, and Daisy was fervently nodding, needing more, more, please—

And again, Filak saw it, he knew it. And with a gasp and a shudder, he finally let himself go, let the last of the hunger charge out between them. His hard body plunging in again and again, his head arching back, his howl burning from his throat. While the ecstasy spun and juddered, closer and closer, a dazzling light in the darkness—

Daisy screamed as it charged through her, crushing her beneath its sheer blistering euphoria, clamping her against Filak's invading strength. Shouting and demanding at him, *now*, and he could only nod, and tremble, and obey. Blasting her full of his hot liquid pleasure, answering her and honouring her with all his strength, and for a breath it was suddenly Daisy in charge, Daisy needing it and commanding it, while Filak gasped and shook and gave.

He was hers. *Hers.*

When the pleasure finally faded, ebbing away into wrenching little quivers, Filak's tall sweaty body collapsed against Daisy, his face buried hot in her throat. "*Mín*," he whispered, a prayer, a plea—and Daisy shivered and nodded, and then gasped into her gag as his teeth sank deep. The brief flash of pain and pleasure so right, so perfect, one more way he would trap her, and honour her, and show her. Hers.

Daisy couldn't have said how long they stayed there, breathing and shivering together, but at some point, Filak carefully drew away his teeth, and then the gag, and then that jutting stone inside her, too. And then the wall slowly shifted her backwards and down again, freeing her legs and her feet, and Filak's strong hands held and caressed her as she staggered back to standing again, found the steadiness in the solid floor beneath her.

But Filak hadn't yet released her hands, or the chain on her neck, and Daisy drew in a deep breath, and searched his face. His flushed sweaty cheeks, his red-stained lips, his pleading, glittering eyes.

"*Mín*," he whispered, his mouth twisting. "*Sólin mín*. I show you, ach?"

I show you. And yes, yes, he had. He'd shown Daisy— again—that she could trust him. She could trust him with her body, her life, her son. He wasn't dangerous. He was hers.

Daisy's nod came soft and easy, her eyes warm on his face. "Ach, Filak," she murmured. "You show me."

Filak's shoulders heavily sagged, and his gaze dropped to Daisy's belly, to that unfinished vow. "*Gott*," he said, hoarse, almost like a prayer. "So now—you come. We escape. We forget."

We escape. We forget.

And maybe it was the still-simmering pleasure, or the whispering vision of the art they'd just made, the trust they'd just built together. But for the first time, blinking at her mate's pleading eyes, Daisy suddenly saw the rest. The last quiet secret, hidden and cowering behind Filak's eyes.

He'd been running too, all this time. Trying to hide. To escape. To forget.

He'd run from his father's failures. He'd run from his people's mutiny. He'd run from his kin, and his home.

And even if it hadn't been all his fault, and he'd made them all those promises—to send gems, to find the Skýli, to bring them to a new home—he still hadn't tried to go back, had he? No, no, he'd stayed here, keeping himself closed off and safe, separate from his own clan. Blocking out all the fear and pain, keeping out anyone who could hurt him again.

And maybe—maybe he'd recognized that in Daisy, too. Maybe they'd seen it in each other, lonely hungry artists trying to escape into the darkness. Hurling themselves into danger and pleasure, anything strong enough to make them forget.

But amidst it all, Filak had still let Daisy in. He'd trusted her. He'd given her his care, his vow, his home. And now...

"*Ach, sólin mín?*" Filak asked, the longing cracking his voice, glinting in his eyes. "We leave. We forget. We have each other. We have Skýli. We have art. We have *son*."

It quivered Daisy's lip, stung behind her blinking eyes, because yes, she wanted that. She wanted it so damned much. She wanted him, she wanted the Skýli, she wanted art—and yes, she wanted their son. She wanted a family, wanted a home, wanted the dream in the darkness.

But—she couldn't. She couldn't run. She couldn't forget. She couldn't stop seeing, not now, no matter how much it hurt.

"I'm so sorry, Filak," she whispered. "But I need you to let me go."

55

Filak stared at Daisy for a silent, broken instant, his swallow bobbing in his throat.

"*Nei, Daisy,*" he rasped. "*Nei.* You come. You stay."

But Daisy couldn't, she couldn't, and even as she shook her head, the water was stinging behind her eyes. "*Nei,* Filak," she whispered back. "I can't. Not yet. I need to go back to Lew."

Filak swallowed again, and something flared across his eyes, bitter and bright. "*Nei Lew,*" he croaked. "*Ekki Lew.* Lew hurt you, *sólin mín.* Lew *danger.*"

Daisy couldn't argue it, her heartbeat spiking in her chest, and as if to prove his point, Filak swiped up her sketchbook from a nearby rock, and wrenched it open. Flipping through until he found that page she'd drawn in the garden, the one with Lew. Lew standing over her crouched form, feeding belladonna to her son. To *their* son.

"I—I know," Daisy gulped, between breaths. "Lew *is* dangerous. He *did* hurt me. And now—now he wants to do it to everyone else here. He wants to kill them all, and all their sons. And if he succeeds"—she took another ragged breath—"how can we hide in the Skýli and pretend? How could we ever forget?"

Filak grimaced, shook his head, but his eyes were glassy and distant now, speaking of loss and pain. Of his home in the north, maybe. And Daisy didn't want to hurt him, but she saw him, she knew him...

"We can't forget, Filak," she said, her voice hitching. "We can't escape. It will just—keep following us, keep haunting us. We need to try to face it, and I think—if I go see Lew—I think I can help."

The certainty settled low in her voice, raised her chin, but Filak was still shaking his head, the pain flashing brighter in his eyes. "Then send—one of *them*," he replied, with a flail of his hand up at the ceiling, at the mountain above them. "You no risk *you. Sólin mín. Sonur minn.*"

It sounded pleading, anguished, plummeting in Daisy's chest, but she swallowed hard, blinked back the wetness now pooling behind her eyes. "I'm sorry, Filak," she whispered. "But I *know* Lew. I'm the only person here who knows him. I can get him alone and talking. I can see for certain what's behind all this, and make him face it, and find a way out. I can help."

But Filak kept shaking his head, that fear and pain and grief so stark in his eyes, quivering on his mouth. And in another jolt of movement, he lurched for—his satchel. His satchel that Daisy hadn't even noticed until now, propped there against a wall, and he frantically pawed through it, and then brought something out. A small leather bag, clinking heavy and strange...

"You stay," he breathed, as he staggered back toward Daisy, releasing her still-captured wrists with a furious swipe of his hand. So he could hold the bag out toward her, fold her trembling fingers around it.

"You stay," he repeated, harder. "You keep."

You keep. Daisy blinked at him, and then at the bag, at his claw tugging the top of it open. Revealing... jewels. A mass of bright, sparkling, beautiful jewels, all clinking and tumbling together. The sight so stunning it swallowed her breath, and there was a sudden, desperate urge to clutch the bag close, to rush off to a corner and marvel at the jewels one by one, to keep them for her own forever.

But—but—no. She couldn't. And this was—it was—

"The mate-price?" she whispered, searching his eyes. "The *sálugjald*? The one you tried to give me, back in the sick-room? But I thought..."

She'd thought he'd meant it as a gift. As an apology, a reassurance. A way to leave him, if she wanted to.

But Filak clearly didn't mean that now, and he again folded Daisy's fingers around the bag, his eyes glittering on hers. "I buy," he said, his voice cracking. "I give great fortune. Greatest *sálugjald* of all Nor-ka-esh. Thus, you stay. *Mín.*"

Thus, you stay. Mín. Something wrenched in Daisy's throat—now Filak wanted to *buy* her, to treat her like property? When Julian had said Filak didn't even like the *sálug-jalds*, he'd never wanted to use one, after his own mother's death...

But oh, gods, that desperation in his eyes. The need and the terror, the agony and the loss. Of course he didn't want to buy Daisy, he hated the very thought of it—but he hated the thought of Lew more. He hated the thought of losing her, forever.

And Daisy hated it too. Hated shaking her head, and thrusting the *sálugjald* back toward him. Hated seeing that shock and hurt and despair, flashing through her mate's eyes.

"But—I need you, *sólin mín*," he whispered, hoarse. "I need your light. I love you."

It was more quaking misery, wrenching through Daisy's chest, and the water finally escaped her eyes, streaking down her cheeks. "I need you too, Filak," she whispered back. "I love you too. I want to stay with you. I still want to be your mate. But I"—courage, seeing, please—"I still need to do this. To try to fix this, and save them all. *Please*."

Filak stared at her for another empty, jolting breath—and then he spun around from her, away, his hand snapping up to his face. And suddenly his shoulders were shaking, his breaths heaving in deep dragging gasps, because he was—

He was *weeping*.

"*Fokk*, Daisy," he gulped, his voice a raw strangled croak. "I pray and I pray and I pray. I pray you no leave. I seek. I work. I try. I show. I prove. I gain your love for me! But it is only—no. Always no. No, no, no!"

Every word was pain, a sickening strike straight through Daisy's heart, because it was more of Filak's deepest fear, his deepest darkest loss. Being alone, rejected, forsaken. By his people, his clan, his gods. By her.

And with her, he *had* still been brave. He'd still faced his fears, just like she had. They'd danced together into the dark. And now she was hurting him too, making all his greatest fears into horrifying truth, and she couldn't even comfort him, try to ease the pain away. Because—she didn't know if this would work. She didn't know if she would ever escape Lew again. She didn't know if Lew would hurt her, trap her, kill her.

She would need to see. For herself.

"I'm so sorry, Filak," she whispered, into the grief, the regret. But there was nothing else to say, no way to salvage it. Only waiting, and weeping, and watching, as her hurt, devastated mate finally wiped his eyes, and turned back toward her. Showing her his red-rimmed eyes, his quivering mouth, and his—his resignation. His agreement. His love.

He was proving it to her, the way he always had. Even now.

"*Ach, sólin mín*," he said, as he reached for her neck, and gently stroked against the *kraga*. Blinking down toward it, his lashes wet and low over his watching eyes. As if he was drinking in the sight for one last time, one more deep shuddering breath, as his hand stuttered, and he—

He broke the *kraga* in two.

Its pieces fell to the floor with a clatter, its gold chain dangling empty and harmless against the stone wall. And it was all Daisy could do not to rush and scrabble for the broken pieces, to clasp them close, to beg for him to put them back, please...

But she couldn't. She couldn't. And all she had was Filak's brief, anguished kiss, shouting of grief and pain and loss.

"As you wish, *sólin mín*," he whispered, all his promises brought to bitter, miserable life between them. "You shall go."

56

Daisy's trip back to Dusbury was a muddled, miserable haze. With a horribly slow cart, bumping and creaking through an endless tedious tunnel, and what felt like dozens of eyes watching her, expecting some kind of miracle.

"You really think you can sway Lew Wallace?" Jule had demanded, once Daisy had somehow found her and Rosa again, in yet another meeting-room. "You can just convince him to stop implementing a powerful lord's elaborate and costly attack against us? Why? How? What will you do?"

But Daisy hadn't been able to answer it, wringing her hands together, shaking her head. She couldn't explain it, she couldn't just conjure up a neatly organized list, like Rosa might have done. It was all still swirling, slowly becoming clearer and clearer, and she needed time to think, to see...

But then Rosa had rushed over to stand beside Daisy, gripping her arm with decisive purpose. "Daisy knows Lew Wallace better than any of us," she'd said firmly, "and probably better than anyone else in the realm, too. If she's really willing to try this for us, after everything else"—she'd shot

Daisy a wavering little smile—"then of course we'll support it, won't we?"

It had still led to an argument, to Jule demanding how they would ever prevent Lew from just capturing Daisy, and sending her north to Lord Nash for questioning and imprisonment. But Rosa had fiercely counter-argued, and at some point John-Ka had appeared, and begun casting Jule disdainful glances, and finally coldly announced that henceforth, the Ka-esh would address this as an internal clan matter. And then he'd marched Rosa and Daisy off, and made various arrangements, and fetched what seemed like a dozen other Ka-esh to help.

And now—this. Daisy with her fur cloak wrapped tightly around her, and trapped in this horrible slow cart full of orcs. All while steadily sinking into the creeping miserable fear, and the harrowing aching visions of Filak alone at the mountain, weeping in that room in the dark.

"Are you all right, sister?" Rosa's tentative voice asked, from where she was seated beside Daisy in the cart. "How about a new pencil?"

She offered Daisy what seemed to be an entire handful of freshly sharpened pencils, along with a hopeful little smile. The sight of it hitching in Daisy's chest, and she made herself take a pencil, even though she couldn't begin to attempt a smile in return.

"Thank you," she said dully, and she again glanced around them, at the tunnel's endless droning stone walls. "Are we almost there? Why are we moving so slowly?"

Rosa blinked at her, and then looked up toward the front of the cart, where a vaguely familiar orc—Soren—was steering them around a corner. "I don't think it's possible to go any faster," she said uncertainly. "John-Ka says the cart is already at risk of tipping, even at this speed."

Daisy bit back her sigh, as her thoughts swarmed with the visions of Filak at the front of the cart, grinning toward her as he careened them around corners, the wind whipping in their faces...

"Maybe you could draw something while we wait?" Rosa asked, tentative again. "I could turn up the lamp."

Daisy glanced down at the already-bright lamp sitting beside Rosa's feet in the cart, and then shook her head, even as she blinked down at her sketchbook. She hadn't even remembered bringing the sketchbook, or the satchel she'd carried it here in, but it was a distant whispering comfort, a twinge of clarity in the muddle. And instead of drawing—she couldn't draw, not now—she slowly opened the sketchbook, and flipped through the pages. Seeing all her art of the mountain, all those people, and—Filak.

And maybe this was what she'd needed to see, amidst all this mess. Filak lying naked on their bed, watching her with warm, insolent eyes. Filak's long clawed fingers, breaking a rock apart. Filak kneeling between her thighs, feasting between her legs. Filak grinning at her over his shoulder in the Skýli, his eyes bright with teasing, glittering affection.

Daisy couldn't hide the helpless little sniff from her nose, and beside her, Rosa gave a reassuring squeeze to her arm. "Just think," she said bracingly, "how many punishments you'll get for this afterwards. I hope you're ready to beg, sister."

It was enough to snap Daisy's wet eyes up, catching on Rosa's rueful, impish smile. "I mean, you can't think he's going to just *forget* all this, can you?" Rosa added, her voice light. "You went and mated a Ka-esh, sister. They *never* forget."

They never forget. Daisy swallowed, and her hand reflexively slipped up, rubbed against her throat. Where without the familiar encircling weight of the *kraga*, it felt so bare, so empty and untouched and almost—unprotected, somehow. Dangerous. What if Lew tried to choke her? What if he swung a knife at her neck?

"But I—I left him," she whispered, down toward Filak's warm watching eyes on the page. "I made him break my *kraga*, and let me go. I—I *ran*."

And gods, she might have laughed, if she hadn't felt so broken. She'd wanted to stop running, stop escaping and forgetting, and she'd urged Filak to do the same—and now here she was, doing it all again. Running away from Filak, escaping him, while desperately hoping he wouldn't stop her, or forget her, or decide to run away forever, too.

"I don't think you need to worry, sister," Rosa said, quiet but decisive. "If you want Filak, he'll be there. And even if you don't still have your *kraga*, you still have his other gifts, don't you?"

His other gifts. Daisy blinked, because yes, she was still wearing her familiar clothes, and the gold cuff on her arm, and that beautiful ring still on her finger. And no, Filak hadn't taken any of it back, or broken anything else, had he? When he so easily could have, just like Lew's ring. Just like the *kraga*.

"And all his marks, too," Rosa added, with a meaningful nod toward the glimpse of Daisy's bare midriff, just visible through her fur cloak. "I mean, he went and wrote his mate-hood vows on you, right?"

Daisy let out a shaky exhale, and then slid her hand toward her belly, spreading her fingers over where she could still feel the pulsing strength of that new vow, embedded into her skin. And though he'd only carved the first line, it was still hers, still written by Filak's own hand with such earnest, purposeful care. Sworn over the promise of their son.

"And also, even without any of that," came Rosa's firm voice, "just look at him, sister. He's never looked at *anyone* like that, except you."

She huffed a laugh as she waved at Filak's smiling face still looking up from the open sketchbook, and Daisy's eyes dropped back toward it, studying it, seeing it. That affectionate glint in his eyes. The slight flush on his sharp cheekbones. The hint of softness in his grin, of warmth and light and danger and promise.

Her mate. Her home. *Hers.*

Something quivered in Daisy's throat, and she gently stroked her finger against Filak's smiling mouth, his jaw, his tall pointed ear. Against the truth of her beautiful familiar mate, looking back at her. Knowing her. Seeing her.

I know you, Daisy, he'd told her in fierce, stubborn Aelakesh, what felt like months ago. *I see you.*

And maybe—a tiny ripple of hope whispered in Daisy's chest—maybe Filak would see her in this, too. Maybe he would see that this—this was the only way she would find the light, for herself. The only way to make a safe home for their son. The only way they could truly be mates, and make a future together.

Daisy's hand slipped back down to her waist, spreading over that vow in her skin, and she took a deep breath, let it out. If nothing else, she would try to show him. She would prove it. He would see.

She only vaguely heard one of the orcs calling something out, but Rosa straightened beside her, and gave a reassuring pat to her shoulder. "We're almost there," she said. "And like we promised, we'll stay well out of the way, unless you signal for us. Believe it or not"—her eyes twinkled—"we've done this once or twice before, so you're in good Ka-esh hands, ach?"

Daisy twitched a wan smile back, because at this point, she really had no choice but to trust them, and see. To give them a chance to prove themselves, too.

"Is there anything else?" Rosa asked now, searching Daisy's eyes. "Just in case?"

Just in case. In case Daisy never came back, maybe, and she blinked back down at her sketchbook, and then flipped a few pages forward. To that portrait she'd done of Julian, with his wry little smile, his sad lonely eyes.

"Yes, actually," Daisy replied, with sudden decision, as she carefully tore out the page, and thrust it into Rosa's hand. "I want you to send this north to that arsehole Rurik, with your next letter. I want you to tell him to come back, and face what he's done."

Rosa blinked, once, but then nodded, and a slow, wicked smile curved on her mouth. "Oh, I will, sister," she said. "And we'll thoroughly enjoy seeing it, won't we?"

We. As if Daisy would still be part of this. As if they would get through this, together. And it was enough to make her lift her chin, and wipe away the wetness from her eyes. She would see this through. She would.

"Here we are," William's voice called, as the cart grated to a halt. "Dusbury ought to be just above, if we can find the—"

But Daisy had already seen it, and she stuffed her sketchbook into her satchel, and swung herself down out of the cart. Aiming straight for that typical vertical ridge in the wall, with the tunnel hidden just behind.

She would do this. She would see Lew, and save them all.

57

By the time Daisy finally reached Lew's apartment in Dusbury, the sun had set, and her heartbeat was jangling in her ears.

She had to do this. She had to try.

But her feet still dragged as she climbed up the stairs, and the mingled dread and determination simmered ominously in her gut. Maybe Lew wouldn't be home. Maybe he would be off with some other woman. Maybe there would be another new woman in his bed...

But when Daisy swung the door open, Lew was there. Sitting at the familiar kitchen table, writing in his notebook by the light of the single bright lamp beside him. And when he glanced up toward Daisy at the door, there was an instant's blank confusion in his eyes, as if he didn't even recognize her.

"What the—" he began, squinting toward the door. "*Daisy*?!"

Daisy raised her chin, and shut the door behind her. "Yes, it's me," she replied, as steadily as she could. "Lovely to see you again too, Lew."

Lew stared at her for another frozen instant, and then he

leapt to his feet, and stalked over toward her. "Where the hell did you come from?" he demanded. "Where the hell have you been? And"—his disbelieving gaze dropped downwards—"what the *fuck* are you wearing?!"

Daisy followed Lew's gaze, down toward where her fur cloak had fallen open, revealing everything beneath. The colourful wrap top, the jewelry, the sturdy boots and trousers—and most revealing of all, her bare belly, still with Filak's vow half-cut into it.

Lew stared at it for far too long, and then his narrow eyes darted over the rest of it, too. The black sun peeking up over Daisy's heart. Her lips, likely still stained with black. The distinct mess of bite-marks on her neck. The gold cuff on her arm. And finally, Filak's beautiful topaz ring, which suddenly felt very present, very powerful, in the place where Lew's garish fake diamond had once been.

"I'm an artist, Lew," Daisy said, the quiet conviction resonating through her voice. "I can wear whatever I want."

Lew sharply scoffed, but then he glanced away, over Daisy's shoulder. "Well, where the hell have you been, all this time?" he demanded. "Do you have any *conception* how much strain I've been under, these past weeks? How much time and coin and effort I've wasted searching for you?!"

Daisy took a deep breath, squared her shoulders. And then she took her time looking straight back toward Lew, studying the dark circles under his eyes, the way he looked slightly thinner than before, his trousers sagging on his hips. As if he truly was under strain, though all of it was his own damned fault.

"I left you a note, Lew," Daisy told him, her voice still surprisingly steady. "But, if you really must know where I've been, all this time"—she took a breath—"I've been staying at Orc Mountain."

Lew's mouth dropped open, his eyes flaring with disbelief, and Daisy could see him frantically weighing her words, working it through. Was she lying? Her appearance suggested not, right? And if she really had been at Orc Mountain, how much had she seen? How much did she know about his top-secret project? Had she gone there because of him?

Daisy let him wonder for a few more breaths, and then she even managed a cool little smile toward him. "And yes, now I know all about your horrible top-secret project," she told him, clipped. "You might even say that I've been *helping* you."

The disbelief flared brighter in Lew's eyes, followed by something stubborn, something contemptuous. And Daisy knew that look too, could almost predict what would come out of his mouth next.

"I have no idea what you're talking about, Daisy," Lew snapped back, a beat too late, with a familiar condescending curl of his lip. "You're clearly imagining things, again. And if you really ran off alone to Orc Mountain as some kind of petty revenge against me, that is ridiculous and immature behaviour, and appallingly dangerous! What if those inhuman parasites had *killed* you? Or worse, spawned their vile *offspring* on you?"

Daisy barked an empty little laugh, and her smile felt bitter this time, maybe even vicious. "Too late for that, I'm afraid," she replied, as she dropped her hand to her waist, and let her exposed belly round out beneath her touch. "How do you feel about raising a son, Lew?"

Lew's gasp was harsh and choked, the dismay flashing stark and genuine across his face—and Daisy laughed again, harder this time. "Don't worry, I wouldn't subject my son to that," she said flatly. "I know how much you despised the idea of a child or family obligations affecting your precious career. Although"—she raised her brows—"you still played your part very well, didn't you? Pretended to care about me, let me believe you were committed. While also giving me fake jewelry, fucking other women in my bed, and keeping me on a steady dose of the strongest pregnancy prevention herbs in the *realm*."

Daisy could see Lew's thoughts racing again, calculating, his breaths gone shallow in his chest. "I don't know what the hell you're raving about, Daisy," he finally replied, his voice thin. "If you really were foolish enough to run off to Orc Mountain, and allow those bastards to rut their degenerate spawn upon you, then—"

"Then what?" Daisy cut in, sharp and cold. "Then I deserve it? Then I'm a stupid, irrational fool, falling prey to my emotions, mistaking silly anecdotal hunches for actual proven science?"

Lew's eyes flickered, narrowed, surely recognizing his own voice in Daisy's words, and she smiled again, brittle and furious. "But it's *you*, Lew," she hissed. "It's *you*. You're the one who sent all those women to Orc Mountain. You're the one who's put them—and yourself—at risk. You're the one who's been stupid and irrational, falling prey to your emotions, mistaking them for actual proven science!"

Her voice carried through the room, and before Lew could try to argue it, she took a breath, and lurched a step closer toward him. "Tell me, Lew. Of those women involved in your project, how many of them did you sleep with? How many of them got to prove themselves to you? And how many of them did you send off to Orc Mountain, taking your rubbish herbs, that *don't fucking work*?!"

Lew's breath caught, his eyes gaping with new awareness down at Daisy's belly—so she snapped her hand back down to her waist, let him look, let him see. "Did you even test the herbs against orcs?" she demanded. "Did you even think to try? And did it not occur to such a brilliant scientist"—her voice deepened—"what will happen next, once all those women become pregnant, too? Do you really think they'll still go ahead and *kill* their sons' fathers, and leave themselves trapped and pregnant and alone?!"

Lew's throat bobbed, the alarm now rapidly rising in his eyes, and Daisy's mouth pulled into another cold smile. "Or… *wait*," she drawled, tapping with mock thoughtfulness at her chin. "Those women *won't* be alone, will they? Because they can still come to *you*. They'll come to the man who sent them on this mission. The man who gave them the useless herbs. The last human man who could have possibly fathered those children!"

Lew betrayed a faint but visceral flinch this time, but Daisy still wasn't done. "They'll give you sons, Lew," she snarled. "They'll give you the family you've always fucking *wanted*!"

The words hung there between them, brutal and uncompromising, and Lew was cringing now, cowering beneath them. Because yes, he'd done all that, and yes, he'd been such a damned fool. He'd fucked all those women, and then fed them all rubbish herbs, and sent them off to Orc Mountain. Where they were sure to become pregnant, and destroy everything he'd worked for.

"No matter what, Lew," Daisy snapped, "your precious project is done. *Finished*. And you can only pray that it doesn't end with a dozen pregnant women raging on your doorstep, or trying to murder you in your sleep!"

Lew flinched again, but then he took a deep breath, and squared his shoulders. Still attempting to collect himself, to fight it, even now. "This—this is ridiculous, Daisy," he said, though his voice wavered. "You have no proof whatsoever for these baseless and preposterous accusations. This is all a figment of your foolish, flighty imagination!"

"Oh, really?" Daisy shot back. "So if I trot off back to Orc Mountain, and bring Sybil here with me, she'll be a figment of my flighty imagination too, will she? I bet she'll *love* to hear the herbs don't work. I bet she'll laugh all the way home to Lord Nash!"

Lew's flinch was unmistakable this time, and that was finally a look of pure horror, flashing through his eyes. "You talked to Sybil?" he asked, hard and furious. "You *told* her all this, about our project?!"

And yes, there it was. The irrational cowardly confession. The short-sighted, immature selfishness. The foolishness.

"I haven't told Sybil *yet*," Daisy said, raising her chin. "But even if I don't, you must see how risky this already is for you? How foolish you were, to risk getting involved with a rich, powerful, ruthless man like Lord Nash? How easily he can *destroy* you?"

The fear held, quivered in Lew's eyes, because yes, even he must have realized that much. He must have realized how much was riding on this project. Because even with Lew's coin and his renown, he was no match whatsoever for a lord of the realm, with unlimited wealth and power and influence at his call...

"When this project fails, Lew," Daisy hissed, "Lord Nash will blame *you*. And even if he still uses this to start his war, *you'll* still be the scientist who made him false promises, and wasted all his coin. You'll be the one who knocked up his favourite mistress with an orc. You'll be the one who's left with all the consequences, and all the *failure*!"

Lew grimaced, glancing away, and Daisy stepped closer, took another deep breath. "Not to mention, even if by some miracle your horrid attack is still somehow successful," she went on, "you can still say goodbye to your reputation as a brilliant scientist. Instead"—she jabbed her finger toward him—"you'll be a *murderer*. The man responsible for murdering hundreds, or maybe even thousands, of people. Not just orcs, but women, and innocent *children*! The great botanist Lewis Wallace, reduced to slaughtering helpless *babies*!"

She accompanied it with an elaborate sweep of both hands through the air, as if painting the vision across the sky for all to see. And though Lew was shaking his head now, his jaw tightly clenched, Daisy could still see him, she *knew* him. And this—this was something else she'd ignored, something else that hadn't made sense. Something she hadn't seen until she'd drawn that vision of Lew, poisoning her son.

Lew didn't *want* to be a murderer. He didn't like being the villain. He never had, and he'd so clearly demonstrated that when Daisy had found him in bed with Sybil that day. He'd resorted to blame, justifications, science, enlightenment, *lies*. He'd done whatever he could to escape the responsibility for his actions. To hide, and forget. Just the way he always had.

So when Lew had agreed to do this project for Lord Nash, it hadn't been out of cruelty, or maliciousness. No, he'd wanted to show off to a powerful lord. He'd wanted praise, and accolades, and fame. He'd wanted to be the enlightened brilliant scientist. The hero.

"You won't be the hero, Lew," Daisy said now, flat and certain. "No matter how this ends. You'll never escape the damage this will do to your reputation, and your life's work. What will your colleagues think of you? What will your readers say? Will your publishers ever work with you again?"

Daisy could see the questions hitting Lew, striking him where it hurt most—and on a sudden impulse, she twisted and fumbled into her satchel. Yanking out her sketchbook, and then flipping open pages, shoving it toward him. "What will they say," she demanded, "when they see eyewitness accounts like *this*, strewn all across the realm?"

It was the sketch from the garden, the one she'd drawn of Lew. Lew, holding the tiny orc cradled in his arm, and the belladonna in his hand. Lew, feeding poison to an innocent child.

But also—another angle of what Daisy had seen, back there in the garden—it was still Lew, with an orc son. With one of the sons he would inadvertently spawn, on all those women. With all his stupidity, and his short-sightedness, and his greed.

And Lew was seeing it too, his eyes stunned and disbelieving, his throat working. And though his mouth opened, nothing came out, because there was nothing he could say. He'd been a stupid reckless fool, chasing off after a dream of fame and acclaim, and instead he'd caught himself a devil. A monster.

"Oh, and one more thing," Daisy said, with another cold smile toward him. "About your good friend Lord Nash. I assume you know he's already been doing this to orcs, up in the north? Poisoning them in their tunnels?"

The flicker in Lew's eyes said he did know that, and maybe it was even part of what had convinced him to do this—a project with proven success, an easy victory. But he didn't answer, and Daisy turned her sketchbook back around, flipped through more pages.

"The problem is, though," she continued, "the orcs here are now allied with the clan in the north. And now that they know the risk"—she turned the sketchbook back toward him—"they're restoring an alternative. A hidden place deep underground. A place large enough to safely accommodate *everyone* in that entire mountain."

The place, of course, was the Skýli. And the page in Daisy's sketchbook was the beautiful arching cathedral, with its light and its space and its air. Its safety.

And while Daisy didn't actually know if the Ka-esh had seen the Skýli's potential as a sanctuary, she was seeing it now, as clear as if she'd drawn it on the page. If Orc Mountain couldn't find a way to peacefully prevent the attacks, they could still evacuate to the Skýli. They could leave in advance, and stay as long as they needed. And while it might not save everyone, it would still help. It would keep Lew from feeding belladonna to their children.

And again, Lew was at least intelligent enough to see it. His eyes bulging as he stared at the page, his hands closing to tight fists at his sides.

"You're lying, Daisy," he finally hissed, his voice thin. "We've researched. We've *seen*. The orcs have *nothing* like that."

Daisy's lip curled, and she made a mental note to tell Jule to look for spies already in their midst, perhaps more so-called mates. "No, the orcs *didn't* have anything like that," she told Lew, her voice curt. "But they do now. And it's *very* well hidden, so don't expect you'll ever find it."

Lew's face had gone pale, his eyes still frozen on the page, his shoulders slowly slumping. And for an instant, gazing at her former partner of four entire years, Daisy almost felt... sorry for him. Sorry for his failures, his weaknesses, his loss. For all the dreams she was destroying, plunging him into the dark.

"So I'm here to make you a deal, Lew," she said, softer than she meant. "A way out of all this."

Lew didn't move or speak, just studying Daisy with uneasy eyes, and she took a breath, and again reached for her satchel. Pulling out a small, heavy bag this time. The same bag Filak had given her, down in that dark fortified room.

The jewels. The mate-price. The *sálugjald*.

"You take this," Daisy said, as she held it out toward him. "And then you'll go underground, and disappear. *Forever*."

58

Lew gaped at Daisy for another long, silent moment, his eyes wide and blank on her face. While Daisy kept holding out the bag, waiting, her heartbeat pattering against her ribs.

"It's a fortune, Lew," she said. "It's enough to support you for the rest of your life. Enough for you to sail across the sea and disappear, where Lord Nash will never find you again."

Lew's wide eyes blinked, once, and then glanced down at the bag. Where the top had slightly opened, showing the glint of rubies and sapphires and emeralds inside. Daisy's own priceless *sálugjald*, offered up to her selfish, foolish partner.

But it would be worth it. It would be worth it to stop this attack for good. To keep all those people and children safe. And maybe—maybe to show Filak, too. To show him she truly hadn't wanted the *sálugjald*. To show him that she would only use it to protect him, and all his people.

And for a hovering, hopeful instant, Daisy thought Lew would take it. He would see the wisdom in it, the freedom, the generosity. He would see how Daisy was offering him far more than he deserved, yet again.

And yes, yes, he was reaching out his hand, as if he was about to take it, please...

And then he swiped for—Daisy's *sketchbook*.

Daisy yelped and flailed toward him, but Lew swerved away around the kitchen table, hurling a chair into her path. "Don't even try, Daisy," he hissed, with a purposeful grip of his hand at the sketchbook's cover. "Or I'll rip it all into pieces, until there's nothing left!"

Daisy's breath heaved, her heartbeat surging into her ears, and she wildly shook her head. "Lew, it's *mine*," she shot back. "It's private. You do *not* want to see it!"

"Oh, yes, I do," Lew retorted. "You're *lying*, Daisy. You're lying about every damned word of this, and I guarantee you, this"—he brandished the sketchbook toward her—"will prove it!"

Daisy shook her head again, groped across the table for the sketchbook, but Lew easily wrenched away again, and began flipping through pages. "I *know* you, Daisy," he snarled. "I know you can't help but waste your time endlessly documenting every random meaningless detail you come across! If we *really* want to know how you spent these last weeks, this will..."

But then his voice thinned, faded, as he flipped past those ugly flowers she'd drawn at this very table, and then found... the cave. The cave she'd drawn before that first night with Filak. The Skýli's welcome chamber, its elegant beauty still all too apparent beneath the ruins.

Lew's mouth tightened as he looked at it, for an instant too long—but then he kept going. To Daisy's first drawings of Orc Mountain, after Filak had brought back her sketchbook. The wrought-iron lamp, the baths, the Bautul forge, the twisty Skai corridors, the beautiful garden...

Lew's expression kept darkening as he flipped pages, faster and faster, and Daisy again swiped uselessly toward him. "That's enough, Lew," she said, her voice hitching. "You have *no right!*"

But Lew fully ignored her, and kept going. Now onto that day when Filak had first taken Daisy to the Skýli, when she'd drawn all the rocks and crystals and stalagmites in the tunnels. And then—Daisy's breath stilled—the first glimpse of Filak. His long clawed fingers, spread against the stone in the tunnel, breaking it apart.

Lew stared at it for a long, silent moment, his jaw flexing in his cheek, but then he kept going. Moving slower now, flipping through more sketches of Filak's digging, his stone, his deft clawed hands spreading, working magic.

And then, the Skýli itself. The beautiful breathtaking cathedral, with its soaring rounded ceiling, its dark watching eye. And once again, Filak's hand, this time spread against the tiled floor, over where he'd embedded the proof of their pleasure into it.

"*Enough*, Lew," Daisy said, almost pleading now, because she knew what came next, she *knew*. But curse Lew, he just turned the page, and found...

Filak, lying naked in bed. His tall bare body shamelessly on display, showing all his marks, all his lean hard muscle. And—most vivid of all—his swollen, marked cock, propped long and innocuous against his hip, with Daisy's sun brazenly marked upon it.

Lew stared at it without speaking, his mouth slack—and then he shot a narrow, accusing glance at Daisy's chest. At where her own matching sun was still very visible, dense and black over her heart.

A low, angry hiss escaped Lew's throat, but then his hand began turning pages again. Flipping past many more drawings of the Skýli and Orc Mountain, as if he'd barely seen them—and then hesitating on another page. The one—Daisy's face heated—of Filak lying coolly back on the bed, flaunting his daisy tattoo, and all the vivid droplets of his own glossy white seed, spattered all over his belly and chest.

Lew stared at the daisy tattoo for an instant too long, surely recognizing Daisy's work—and then he shot another narrow, disbelieving look toward her, and then back at the page. As if he was stunned by it, as if he couldn't believe she had done such a thing.

"You had no right, Daisy," he finally said, his voice cracking. "We had an *agreement*."

Daisy's laugh escaped all on its own, too loud and harsh. "Really, Lew?" she demanded. "The agreement *you* wanted, where we were both free to see other people? And the agreement *you* broke when you fucked Sybil in my bed?!"

Lew's mouth spasmed, his eyes glittering, and then he roughly flipped to the next page, and the next. Finding yet more shameless artwork of Filak, including a view of his firm arse, with his bollocks a tempting hanging shadow between his thighs—and then the one of Daisy's own naked parted legs, and Filak feasting between them, his eyes bright and devilish on her face.

And finally, most graphic of all, was that detailed close-up she'd drawn of Filak's marked hard cock, just the night before. With its black hood peeled back, its shiny head still dripping with Daisy's juices, its deep slit oozing a long string of shining wet seed. As if it was just waiting to be kissed, suckled, worshipped.

"Gods, Daisy," Lew hissed as he stared at it, shaking his head. "What the *fuck*."

But Daisy didn't justify it with an answer, because Lew was the one who'd started this. He was the one who'd insisted on looking. And he was the one who'd recklessly plotted to hurt desperate women, murder innocent children, and start another *war*.

"Well, you can stop looking anytime, Lew," Daisy

snapped. "Or are you enjoying this too much? My mate *is* very striking, don't you think?"

Lew's gaze darted up to Daisy again, and he finally slammed the sketchbook shut, and hurled it down onto the table. "That outrageous orc is *not* your mate," he growled. "You are *my* partner, Daisy! *My* artist! And"—he flailed his hand toward her—"as per the terms of our agreement, I'm forbidding you from ever seeing that orc again!"

He was *what*? Daisy stared at Lew for a stunned, incredulous breath, and then barked another harsh, disbelieving laugh. "Like hell you are," she shot back. "You lost your artist when you broke our agreement. When you gave me a fake ring. When you sent a regiment after me, and threatened me. When you dragged me into this stupid, ridiculous project that will end up *destroying* you, and all the good work we've done together! Now"—she hauled in a deep breath—"take the extremely generous offer I'm giving you, and get the hell out!"

But Lew's eyes were blazing now, and he shook his head as he stalked around the table toward her. "Oh, I'll go, Daisy," he breathed. "But you're coming with me."

The room jolted all around her, while those impossible words pulsed, shuddered, flared in Lew's vicious dangerous eyes. *You're coming with me.* And suddenly there was a true flare of dark, visceral fear, streaking up Daisy's spine. Lew didn't actually mean that, or could he...

"You—you don't want me, Lew," she sputtered, taking a step backwards, raising her hands. "You want nothing to do with me!"

But Lew kept coming toward her, slow and purposeful. "We had a good life together, Daisy," he said, his voice hard. "I supported you, I gave you a career, I made you famous! You would have had *nothing* without me, not even this stupid fling with that hideous orc! The least you can do is come with me, and repay me!"

And as Daisy kept backing away, searching Lew's menacing eyes, there was... something else. Something else she hadn't seen, until this very moment.

Lew *did* want her. He wanted her work and her art. He wanted her knowledge and her collaboration. He wanted her ready to follow him across the realm, and ready to give him all the power, too. Ready to downplay her own hard-earned accomplishments, her own skill—and yes, maybe even her own fame—in favour of his.

But that wasn't all, was it? No, no, because he was still prowling toward her, looking her up and down, now with a familiar greedy glint in his eyes. A look Daisy knew too well, one she'd seen on him so many times before...

Lew still wanted *her*, too. He wanted all those heated nights they'd shared in bed together. He wanted her to draw him like she'd drawn Filak. He wanted to be the only one to give her that kind of inspiration, that kind of pleasure.

Lew was... *jealous.*

Daisy stumbled back further, shaking her head, but Lew kept coming closer, his eyes still flashing with jealousy, with greed, with rage. And damn it, Filak had been right all along, Lew was dangerous, but now there was no forgetting, no pretending...

Daisy glanced behind her for the apartment's door, and fumbled backwards for the latch—but then Lew leapt forward. Charging across the room toward her, his strong hands clamping tightly at her arms, and shoving her back against the solid door behind her.

"Let me go!" Daisy yelped, as she jerked and thrashed against him, and desperately fought to kick him as hard as she could. But he was too close, too strong, even the smell of him churning in her stomach—

"You're *mine*, Daisy," Lew snarled, loud and sickening in her ear. "And you'll never escape me again!"

No. No. He couldn't. And Daisy could only shake her

head, groping desperately behind her, all around her. "*Nei*," she gasped. "*Nei*, Lew! *Nei, nei, nei!*"

But Lew only laughed. Shoved her further back. Leaned in close, his hot breath and blunt teeth skating against her throat. Like a mockery of Filak, a mockery of his kiss, a twisted terrifying nightmare she couldn't escape...

And then, in a breath, the entire room went black.

59

Daisy froze all over, and blinked into the sudden, utter darkness.

The lamp. The lamp had gone out.

Before her, Lew froze too, his grip slightly slackening on her shoulders. And in the hushed hanging stillness, Daisy's frantic hands... found something, in her trouser pocket.

A pencil. The new sharpened pencil Rosa had given her, back in the cart.

Daisy's breath choked, her heartbeat surging—and in a desperate lurch of movement, she stabbed the pencil up, deep against the delicate skin of Lew's throat.

"Let me go, you fool," she hissed. "And don't move. Or I'll give you some marks that will never, *ever* fade!"

Lew quivered, clutched wild and unseeing for his neck—but it meant he'd released his hold on Daisy, and she ducked out from under his arm, and whirled around to face him. "Don't you *dare* try that again," she said, between her heaving breaths. "I am *not* yours, and I never, ever will be!"

Lew's face twisted, and he swung his arm out toward her, as if to grab her again. But Daisy reeled back out of his way, and Lew's arm only found empty air, his body staggering sideways, almost careening into the wall behind him.

Daisy took another careful step backwards, while Lew's eyes frantically darted from side to side, searching for her in the dark. But not settling, not seeing her, even though she was standing right here in front of him. And even when she waved the pencil again, his eyes didn't change, didn't focus— and as Daisy stared back toward him, a sudden astonished awareness flashed through her thoughts.

Lew couldn't see her, but... she could see *him*.

She could see him. In the *dark*.

Daisy's heart skipped, and she glanced down at her hands, her feet, the floor, the ceiling. Gods above, she could... *see*. Not just Lew, but... *everything*. Not bright, and not in colour, but... still there. Still clear. Despite there being no lamplight in this room, no fire, not a single pinprick of light.

But—how? *When*? She certainly hadn't been able to see a damned thing back when she'd first met Filak in that pitch-black cave, or when he'd locked her in the dungeon, either. And when the Skýli had fallen in, and Filak had trapped them in that room, that had been dark too, right? And then when he'd trapped her under the sickroom...

But under the sickroom—the memory flashed stark and vivid—Daisy had thought she'd caught a glimpse of Filak's eyes, glittering in the dark. Hadn't she? And then after that, the mushroom cave, which had felt so bright, so easy to see. Or that day with the schoolchildren, they hadn't taken lamps down into those tunnels, had they? And just multiple moments around the mountain, when Daisy hadn't always remembered her lamp, when there hadn't always been lamps in the corridors, either.

And then—that fight she'd had today with Filak, down in that room deep underground. She hadn't taken a lamp down there, or through any of those corridors... right? She'd been in full darkness, that entire time.

But—how? How was such a thing possible? And even as the disbelief shivered and swayed, Daisy glanced over her shoulder, back toward the table, where Lew's lamp had been. Where she somehow knew exactly who she would see there...

Filak. *Magic.*

He was standing casually beside the table, his arms folded over his chest, as though he'd always been there. And his eyes on Daisy were glimmering in the dark, whispering of hunger and pleasure and pride.

He'd come. He'd followed her.

For a choked, breathless instant, Daisy could only blink back at him, drinking up the sight of him, of everything he was silently saying in the dark. He hadn't abandoned her, or rejected her, even though she'd hurt him, even though she'd left. She was his mate, and maybe she always had been, since that first night in the cave. *Sólin mín.*

And even now, even as Filak was here, helping her—he was still letting her take the lead. Letting her decide how to handle this, what to do next. Trusting her, and her judgement.

You are my mate. I uphold you, before all else. Stand with you. Trust you.

It swayed and shuddered in Daisy's chest, and with a shaky little smile toward him, she raised her hand to the sun over her heart. Saying, just as strong, *You have my heart. I love you.*

Filak's throat convulsed, the slow smile twitching across his lips, and he raised his own hand to his heart, too. To his sun. *Sólin mín.*

The warmth unfurled low in Daisy's belly, shone with the truth of her vow and her son, her mate and her home. Her dream. *Hers.*

And with that safety, that peace, there was enough strength to draw in a breath, and square her shoulders. She'd come here, she'd faced Lew, and now she needed to finish it. She needed to defend her mate, her son, and her home.

But when she glanced back toward Lew, his body was already edging away from her, his arm groping out toward the door. As if he still thought he could run away from this, the utter infuriating bastard.

"I *said*, don't move, Lew," Daisy ordered, her voice loud and decisive in the silence. "You do *not* want to run into what's out there. Or what's waiting over by your lamp, either."

Lew jolted to stillness again, his unseeing eyes frantically darting back and forth, his breaths panting rapid and shallow. And that might have been a slowly growing awareness in his eyes, a reluctant realization that he wasn't escaping now. That Daisy hadn't come here alone, and now, she would decide his fate.

"So here's what we're going to do, Lew," she continued flatly. "Since you've shown yourself highly untrustworthy—*again*—I'm changing the terms of that offer I made you. You can still have the jewels, but only half of them—and only *after* you help us fix the mess you've made. After you prove to us you've done it."

Lew grimaced, but he didn't try to argue, so Daisy took a breath, thought it through. "You'll write letters to both Sybil and Lord Nash, tonight," she said. "You'll tell them that you've learned new information that renders the project unworkable. You'll tell them about the herbs, and the inevitable pregnancies. You'll also tell them that your security has been compromised by the orcs, and for your own safety, you'll be going into hiding for the foreseeable future."

Lew was far worse at concealing his expressions in the dark, and his eyes flickered with a grudging recognition, or maybe even relief. Suggesting that this wasn't a terrible plan, and maybe it was even the route he might have chosen himself—though likely with more blame and insults toward Daisy thrown in.

"You'll also write to all those women you hired," Daisy added. "You'll tell them about the herbs, and the cancellation of the project. I'll then deliver the letters myself, under the guise of still being your partner, and therefore personally involved in the project. And I'll offer them other options, including termination of any unwanted pregnancies."

That was another unmistakable flare of relief in Lew's eyes—he *really* hadn't wanted those sons—and Daisy shot a reflexive, grateful glance over toward Filak, still silently watching from the corner. "And while we wait for their responses, and any possible countermeasures from Lord Nash," she continued, "you'll stay under our guard. You'll make any appearances necessary, to make sure you haven't been impersonated or kidnapped or killed. And—"

But Lew's scoff cut her off, his eyes goggling toward her in the darkness. "But—you *are* kidnapping me," he said, his voice shrill. "Aren't you? If you're planning to put me under guard, by orcs?!"

"Yes, exactly," Daisy replied, without sympathy. "And if you're well behaved, maybe they won't chain you, or lock you in a dark dungeon. Gods, Lew, I made you a very generous offer, and"—her voice sharpened—"you still tried to *kidnap* me! Did you really think you'd still get to wander around free, so you can try to ruin everything, and kill us all? Again?!"

Kill us all, again—as if she was part of them, as if she herself had been under attack, too. But she was, she would have been, because Orc Mountain was part of her home now, too. And maybe she'd always wanted it to be, even from the start.

"Well, will you still draw for me, at least?" Lew's voice asked, plaintive now. "We can still publish together, right?"

Good gods, this selfish ridiculous man, and Daisy's

exasperated groan came out sounding more like a roar. "*Nei,* Lew!" she snapped. "No, we can't! I'm publishing my own book, without you!"

And it was that, finally, that sagged Lew's shoulders, and shot the petulant defeat through his eyes. "I can't believe you, Daisy," he muttered. "After everything I've given you."

It took all Daisy's restraint not to stab him with her pencil after all, and she stalked away from him, toward Filak by the table. And it was sheer, sweeping relief to see his slow approving grin, to feel his strong arms yanking her close, his familiar hands running up and down her back. She was his. *His.*

"Daisy?" Lew's grating voice demanded, even as he began shuffling sideways in the darkness toward the door, *again.* And with another loud, irritated groan, Daisy reluctantly broke away from Filak, and strode around Lew to the apartment door. First yanking it open, and then rapidly flapping her hand in the darkness outside it.

It wasn't an elaborate signal, but it was good enough, because multiple people instantly rushed around the corner—Rosa and John-Ka, Soren and William, Gareth and Hallr. All of them bursting forward into the room at once, while back by the table, Filak suddenly lit the lamp again, illuminating the entire scene for Lew's eyes.

Lew yelped and staggered backwards, gaping open-mouthed toward the group at the door—but then his eyes darted sideways, and caught, held, on Filak. On where Filak was still coolly standing beside the kitchen table, drumming his long deadly claws against his bicep, and giving Lew a vicious, murderous smile.

"Oh, do you recognize him?" Daisy said toward Lew, as sweetly as she could. "He's my mate Filak, of Clan Nor-ka-esh. The father of my son, and an artist, too. He's also a spectacular geologist, aren't you, *myrkrið mitt?*"

Filak's eyes glinted on hers with dizzying warmth, while

Lew's mouth dropped open, and yet more petulant disbelief shot through his eyes. "Another geologist?" he muttered. "Really, Daisy?"

Daisy kept sweetly smiling back toward him, and then waved toward the group by the door. "And several of my friends are excellent geologists, too," she added. "They'll be helping to keep an eye on you, for these next few weeks."

Despite the confidence in her voice, she couldn't help a beseeching glance toward them—would they mind her unilateral change of plans? But Rosa was already nodding and grinning back, with a dangerous glint in her blue eyes.

"Yes, indeed, we expected it might come to this," she said, as she whipped out a sheaf of paper and several more sharpened pencils. "Let's get started writing then, Mr. Wallace. If you cooperate, we might not even chain you to your chair."

Lew's voice came out in an enraged squeak, but Rosa's grin only broadened as she waved the other orcs forward. And suddenly they all looked impossibly large and dangerous, crowding in a tight circle around Lew's much shorter and slimmer body. William and Gareth were both wearing disapproving frowns, while Soren's glower was scathing, and John-Ka's eyes glittered with cold danger. While Hallr plucked out a shining dagger from his belt, and began lightly tossing it from hand to hand.

And when Daisy glanced back toward Filak, there was something new, flickering through his eyes. His own still-seething anger, yes, enough that Daisy was certain he would still gladly murder Lew where he stood—but also, something like surprise, or even relief. Maybe because he didn't actually need to do that murdering after all, now that his Ka-esh kin were here. Supporting him, taking his side, defending his mate and his home.

"What are you waiting for, human?" cut in Hallr's cold voice, his eyes contemptuous on Lew's face. "For a geologist to begin digging in your trousers, mayhap?"

Lew blanched and glared up at Hallr, but even he wasn't fool enough to try to argue, and finally he sighed, and went and sank down at the table. Where Rosa plunked down the paper and pencils before him, while the rest of the orcs all closed in around him.

Daisy's breath heavily exhaled, because this meant—it meant they'd done it. Right? Oh, gods, they'd done it. She'd done it.

She'd faced Lew. She'd seen the truth, and she'd found a solution to this mess. She'd helped the mountain, she'd saved all her new friends, she'd spared Kalfr from a miserable charade with a woman he didn't want. She'd done it.

She could see it in Filak's eyes too, in the approving softness in his grin toward her—and then he strode over toward her. Slipping his strong, safe arm around her waist, drawing her in beside him, and then... pulling her away. Not toward the apartment door, no, but toward... the bedroom?

"What are you..." Daisy began, with an uneasy glance back toward where Lew was studying them, his lip curling. But Filak's grin only drew higher, and he brazenly palmed his clawed hand at Daisy's arse as he ushered her through the door, and into the room she'd once shared with Lew. The room where Lew had loudly and blatantly fucked Sybil, breaking his agreement with Daisy, while she'd sat at that table and listened.

And suddenly Daisy knew what this was, what it meant, and when Filak slammed the door shut, and then eased Daisy back onto the bed, there wasn't a single thought of resisting. Lew had done what he'd wanted in their bed, so why couldn't she do the same?

She sank down onto her back with desperate eagerness, kicking off her boots, shoving down her trousers. While Filak guided her legs wide, stepped in between, and thrust down his own trousers, too. Revealing his marked beautiful cock, hard and hungry and ready, lining itself up with smooth, familiar ease...

And then, with a firm, decisive snap of his hips, he buried himself deep inside her. The sudden sensation so shocking, so thrilling, that Daisy's breath shot out in a yelp, her body quaking all over upon his stark stabbing strength.

"*Fokk*, Filak," she gasped, earning an insolent, dangerous grin in return—and then a slow, agonizing draw out, and another fierce slam inside. While Daisy writhed and moaned, her frantic hands yanking him tighter, needing more, more—and yes, he was already moving faster, sinking into his favourite furious rhythm, the slick slapping sounds ringing through the air, surely even beyond that closed door.

But Lew had done it too, and then he'd tried to *kill* her, and Daisy was finally finished with him, forever. And instead, she had this stunning, shameless orc, with his beautiful body, his demanding possessive pleasure, his breathtaking art. And even all the sounds felt like art too, the slick messy squelching, the sucking and slapping, slippery and obscene. Their bodies coming together, meeting each other with frenzied abandon, driving each other higher and higher—

"*Fokk*, Filak!" Daisy gasped, clutching his firm arse, yanking him harder. "Oh gods, yes, give me your good orc seed, fuck me full of it, please!"

And yes, please, that was it, her fierce feral mate obeying, and honouring her. Pleasing her. Offering up all he had for her, just like he had since the first day they'd met. While Daisy arched and begged for it, welcomed it with all her strength, as her own release washed over her, flooding her with pleasure, and with peace.

And in the quiet afterwards, the peace kept unfolding, radiating out between them, soft and bright and new. Like something certain, something finally settled, warm and content in her mate's beautiful eyes.

"*Þú kemur með mér*," Filak murmured, so soft, with a slight catch in his voice. "*Ach, sólin mín?*"

You will come with me, it meant. The same words he'd spoken in this same apartment, all those weeks before. *Yes, my sun?*

And Daisy nodded, intent and fervent, her smile quivering soft and true. "*Ach, myrkrið mitt*," she whispered. "*Ég kem.*"

60

They ended up back in the Skýli, gathered together in the beautiful, familiar cathedral.

It felt like a celebration, especially since John-Ka had already handed Lew over to a group of waiting Skai guards he'd organized, and he'd sent off Lew's letters to Sybil and Lord Nash, too. He'd also arranged for multiple baskets of food to be delivered—hauled in by a wryly smiling Julian—and he'd even brought in Efterar and Kesst, in case there had been any injuries.

"No, I'm really fine," Daisy told Efterar, who was running his hand up and down her torso, his brow deeply furrowed. "It all went as well as it could have, right, *myrkrið mitt*?"

Beside her, Filak firmly nodded, though he also kept frowning at Efterar, and casting disapproving glances down toward the front of Efterar's trousers. "Ach, *sólin mín*," he replied. "You were magnificent."

He said the word carefully, accenting every syllable, and Daisy shot him a warm, surprised grin, because that one definitely hadn't been in the book, right? While before them, Efterar harrumphed, and hovered his hand over that half-carved vow on Daisy's belly. "Well, you still should have come to see me about this tattoo," he said, though his voice was mild. "And I assume you know about your son?"

Daisy nodded, and angled another warm glance up at Filak's face. "Yes, thank you," she replied. "It's something we both wanted, and we're very excited."

Filak's eyes on hers had slightly widened, a slow, stunning smile drawing at his mouth—and in a jerky movement, he tugged her tightly into his side, and pressed a fervent kiss to her hair. "Ach, very excited," he repeated, husky. "Our son shall be greatest Nor-ka-esh artist in realm."

Daisy beamed back toward him, and only half-noticed Efterar's preoccupied nod. "Well, it all looks good," he said. "You'll need to start coming by the sickroom for regular visits, especially if you do any more of *this*."

He waved his hand toward that carved vow, which now seemed to be fully healed and embedded in Daisy's skin, written in a pale perfect white. And she seemed strangely caught on the sight, blinking down toward it, and Filak softly caressed his hand over it, too.

"This is *gott*," he told Efterar, with a grudging little smile. "*Við erum þakklát.*"

We are thankful, it meant, and Efterar easily waved it away, and turned to go—but then found himself blocked by Kesst, who had stalked over to join them, wearing a suspiciously innocent smile.

"Yes, and if you'd ever like to return the favour, you can draw us more portraits," Kesst said toward Daisy, his voice light. "I have a few fabulous ideas, and I'd love to hear if you ever do inking? Or paints?"

Daisy opened her mouth to agree, but then she was interrupted by Filak's loud, vicious growl beside her. "*Nei*, Kesst," he snarled. "Daisy is *mine*. Daisy make art of *me*. Daisy colour *my* prick!"

Daisy half-laughed, half-grimaced, and lightly patted Filak's arm. "Of course I'll colour your prick, *myrkrið mitt*," she said bracingly. "As much as you like. And how about we'll talk about the rest later?"

Filak shot her a narrow, dubious look, while Kesst's grin was bright and stunning, and surprisingly grateful, too. "Thank you, sister," he replied. "And also, this Skýli really is quite something, isn't it? Have you arranged for any proper decorating, or furnishing? It could use some help from someone with an excellent eye for style, don't you think?"

He didn't wait for a reply, and instead just grasped Efterar's arm and steered him off, flashing a satisfied smile back toward them over his shoulder. Leaving Filak furiously glowering after them, and muttering to himself about meddling Ash-Kai and their infuriating good taste, and how he might need to dig a special soundproof dungeon, just for Kesst.

"*Nei*, Filak," Daisy cut in, with a teasing grin toward him. "He'll do a fantastic job of decorating, and you know it. And also"—she raised her brows—"you are mine, *myrkrið mitt*. You make *dýflissa* for *me*!"

Filak's chuckle was bright and amused, the approval glimmering in his eyes, and he gave a tantalizing squeeze to Daisy's arse. "Ach, *sólin mín*?" he murmured. "We make good *dýflissa* here for us?"

Daisy shyly nodded, leaning closer into his touch—but before it could go any further, they were joined by John-Ka and Rosa, and all the rest of the orcs who'd helped them with Lew. And the warmth bubbled higher in Daisy's belly as Filak nodded toward them, a genuine smile on his mouth— and then he even bowed his head toward John-Ka, and raised his hand to his heart.

"*Þakka þér fyrir, bróðir*," Filak said. "*Fyrir að hjálpa Daisy, og koma okkur aftur saman.*"

Thank you, brother, it meant. *For helping Daisy, and bringing us back together.*

It took an instant for Daisy to digest that—*John-Ka* had

brought them back together? But glancing back and forth between them, Daisy belatedly realized that of course John-Ka had helped to manage that, too. He'd surely sent for Filak, and kept him informed on their plans, and included him. Just like a good leader would.

But John-Ka didn't seem to expect any accolades for this, because he only curtly nodded, and then began speaking in calm, steady Aelakesh. Telling Filak that it was his honour to be of service, and that he hoped to continue supporting Filak and the Skýli, and rebuilding the mountain's relationship with the Nor-ka-esh.

"Also, brother," John-Ka said, switching to common-tongue, "if you agree, I wish to grant you a new title, on behalf of all the Ka-esh. Henceforth, you shall be known as"—he took a breath—"the *Verndari* of the Skýli."

The... *Verndari*? Daisy shot an uncertain glance toward Filak, who had snapped to sudden, curious stillness, his eyes wide and unblinking on John-Ka's face. While beside John-Ka, Rosa cleared her throat, and smiled encouragingly toward Daisy. "The *Verndari* used to be the keeper of the Skýli," she explained. "The guardian, you could say, or the warden. We found it in one of the old books here, and it was a position that was originally granted by the Priest of the Ka-esh, toward an orc who had demonstrated great commitment and self-sacrifice toward the Skýli, for the gain of all the clan."

Oh. And surely Filak had already known all that, and that was why he still looked so astonished, his swallow bobbing in his throat. As if he would have never expected such an appointment from John-Ka, or maybe—the certainty flicked through Daisy's thoughts—he'd expected John-Ka to take all the credit for the Skýli, or even to assume such a prestigious position for himself.

"*Þú heiðrar mig, Prestur*," Filak finally said, hoarse, raising his hand to his heart. "*Ég þigg það með glöðu geði, ef sálufélagi minn samþykkir það.*"

You honour me, Priest, it might have meant. *I am glad to accept, if my mate agrees.*

It unfurled bright and bubbly in Daisy's belly, and she nodded and smiled up toward him. "Ach, Filak," she murmured. "Of course I agree."

Filak slowly smiled back, squeezing her closer into his side, and Daisy could almost feel the new title settling upon him, relaxing his shoulders, warming his eyes. He was no longer an outcast, running afraid and alone. He had friends, and a clan, and a mate, and a home—and even a title that sounded like him, like art. The *Verndari of the Skýli.*

Filak's eyes were blinking hard now, and he squared his shoulders, and glanced up at the other orcs still gathered around them. Julian, and William and Soren, and Gareth and Hallr, even Kesst, who had dragged Efterar back over to observe the goings-on.

"I... thank you all," Filak said toward them, in slow, careful common-tongue. "You helped me regain my mate, my son, and my home. I shall no forget this. I hope"—he drew in a shaky breath—"you shall come here to Skýli as oft as you wish. Make Skýli your retreat, or your home."

The assembled orcs nodded and smiled back, and several of them—especially Soren and William—looked as though they might be seriously considering it. While Filak kept rapidly blinking, as if he was still thoroughly overcome by this, and Daisy stroked his back as she drew in a deep breath. "And also, maybe the Skýli can be a refuge for all of Orc Mountain, too, whenever you need a safe place," she added, with a hopeful glance up toward Filak's face. "As long as you don't mind, *myrkrið mitt.*"

Filak shot a small, wavering smile down toward her, as if they'd already agreed on this, long before Daisy had gone off and announced it to Lew. As if this had always been part of their plan for the Skýli, and maybe—maybe it really had been, all along.

"Yes, we would be very grateful," cut in a familiar voice, a woman's voice—and Daisy twitched at the sudden sight of Jule, walking across the cathedral toward them, together with Grimarr and two adorable orclings. "It's a truly spectacular place, and a great asset to us all. Thank you for offering to share it with us."

Filak's lip slightly curled as he gazed back at Jule, but then he eyed her orclings, and sighed, and nodded. "You send more orcs for digging," he told her, his voice flat. "Many strong hale orcs. With no mistrust, and no secrets, and no schemes!"

Jule wryly smiled and nodded, raising both her hands in clear capitulation. To which Filak curtly nodded back, and made to guide Daisy away—but then he hesitated again as another orc stepped forward. Julian, with a soft smile on his mouth, and a full food basket in his hands.

"May the gods bless you both, and your son," Julian told them, as he held out the basket toward Daisy. "I am so glad you have found one another, ach?"

Daisy's eyes prickled, and she nodded and clutched the basket, and gave Julian a weepy, grateful smile. While Filak lurched forward, and clasped Julian's slim body into his arms. "*Ach, bróðir,*" he replied, hoarse. "*Þú hefur hjálpað okkur svo mikið. Þú ert gimsteinn.*"

You have helped us so much, it meant. *You are a jewel.* And Daisy nodded and sniffled as she kept smiling toward Julian, and wiping away the tears streaking down her cheeks. Julian had vowed to help her, that first night they'd met, and he'd kept his word ever since.

"Yes, you've been so good to us, Julian," she said, once Filak had drawn back again. "You know we'd love to have you here anytime, and we'll do our best to return all your kindness."

But Julian only shook his head, and waved it away. "Ach, there is no need," he replied, though his voice slightly wavered. "You have both granted me much hope, and helped me forget."

Helped him forget. It again spasmed in Daisy's throat, but before she could speak, Julian gave them another sad little smile, and walked away. And Daisy's glance up toward Filak found him looking just as stubborn as she suddenly felt, his brow creased with deep disapproval.

"We find Rurik, and lock him in new *dýflissa*," he said flatly. "Swarm him with hungry vermin. Feed him mouldy mushrooms. Taunt him with pretty jewels, just out of reach."

Daisy couldn't help her bright laugh—of course Filak would consider that the worst kind of torture—and she willingly leaned into his side as he steered her toward the door. But then she hesitated and glanced backwards, toward Rosa and John-Ka. "One more question, Rosa," she said. "How... how did I start to see in the dark? Is it really just... magic?"

Rosa's eyes instantly sharpened, and her darting glance toward Filak looked almost impressed. "Already?" she demanded. "Really? That is most definitely a new record, it took me *years*! I wonder if there's something in the Nor-ka-esh genetics, somehow? That would be a highly beneficial adaptation for their women, and a very important note for my anatomy book, too..."

She fumbled into her satchel for some paper, frowning as she began taking notes, while beside her, John-Ka fondly smiled, and then cast a too-aware glance toward Daisy. "This is oft an effect of orc-seed upon humans, over time," he told her. "We have only begun to fully study this, but it seems that of all the clans, Ka-esh seed oft tends to grant night vision the strongest—though never before in a matter of weeks."

His gaze on Filak had begun to look rather assessing, too, while Filak gave a bemused smile back, and a reassuring squeeze to Daisy's side. "We pray, ach, *sólin mín*?" he said, with satisfaction, as his free hand firmly patted at the front of his trousers. "Pray for good seeing, and strong fucking. Gods hear us, and grant this."

He sounded so certain, so decisively pleased, and Daisy's thoughts flashed back to that eye she'd painted there, that night she'd promised to stay. Almost as if she had known, or maybe the gods had even shown her the way...

"Ach, Filak," she replied, with a grateful smile up toward him. "We prayed, and the gods heard us. Both of us."

She didn't miss John-Ka and Rosa exchanging a deeply dubious glance, and Rosa had stopped writing down notes—but thankfully, they didn't argue. And when Filak began steering Daisy away again, she cheerfully waved goodbye, and then sank heavier into Filak's touch and his certainty. Into the truth of her magical powerful mate, reconciled to his clan and his home—and to his gods, too.

"So what were you doing all this time, after I left?" she asked lightly, glancing up at his face. "And did I tell you about the portrait Rosa is sending to Rurik for me?"

Filak shot her a curious look, pulling her tighter into his side, drawing her toward the door. And as they walked through the Skýli's familiar corridors together, Daisy told him all about her plan with Rosa and the portrait, and in return, Filak told her everything he'd done after she'd left Orc Mountain. Which had apparently included him commandeering a second cart from the shop, and racing after them toward Dusbury.

They kept talking and laughing together as they climbed up a now-repaired staircase, and through multiple thick doors only Filak could enter—and then, finally, into the cave. The first cave, the welcome cave, their cave. It hadn't yet been fully restored, but all the rubble was now cleared away, and the shape of it was beautifully clear, with the rounded walls, the arched ceiling, the protective watching eyes in the floor and the ceiling.

It felt so familiar now, so safe, their own refuge from everything else, and Daisy settled beside Filak on that same large flat rock, and joined him in digging into the basket of food Julian had given them. As always, it was full of delicious-smelling treats—cured meats, fresh breads, nuts and berries—and Daisy was surprised to see Filak's eagerness as he instantly began eating, munching away with astonishing speed and ease.

"Uh, are you feeling all right?" she asked him, wryly smiling around her own mouthful of meat. "Did you finally realize how much you love food?"

Filak shot a sheepish grimace toward her, even as he popped a handful of berries into his mouth. "*Nei, sólin mín,*" he told her, once he'd swallowed. "It is only—the gods. They now answer the greatest of all my prayers, ach?"

The greatest of all his prayers. As if Filak had still really been praying, all this time? Still fasting? Maybe praying for the Skýli's restoration? Or his son? Or the reconciliation with the Ka-esh?

"The gods grant me *you, sólin mín,*" Filak added, softer, with a brush of his claws to her cheek. "My sun. My artist. The one who sees me."

Daisy swallowed, searched his eyes, but he truly meant it, his gaze steady and certain on hers. "You choose me," he said, even quieter. "You choose to stay, and share your light with me. This is all I pray for, all these days and nights."

It was a quiet quivering wonder, blossoming in Daisy's chest, and she leaned into the touch of his hand, the familiar light scrape of his claws on her skin. And when he set the basket aside, and closed the space between them, Daisy sank deeper into his hands and his kiss, the gentle weight of his body guiding her downwards. Until she was lying on her back on the hard flat stone, with Filak's body long and warm beside her, his lips hot and hungry against hers.

It whirled up a memory of another long-ago night in this

room, another blaze of burning colours in the dark—but this time, it wasn't a distant dream, a sparkling far-off fantasy. No, no, it was hers, it was real and alive and true, and Daisy welcomed it, opened for it, bloomed all over beneath the sheer aching joy of it. Filak was hers. Her mate.

And when his caressing hand began undressing her, revealing her to the darkness, Daisy welcomed that, too. The freedom, the art, the familiar wonderful contrast of his warm skin and strong fingers and sharp claws. And in return, her own tingling hands shoved down his trousers, and she shivered all over at the heavy, tantalizing weight of his velvety cock on her hip, already streaking its sweetness against her skin.

But Filak didn't rush, didn't push. Only kept drawing her deeper into him, into his strength and his need and his intensity. His body easing up over her now, his kisses still filling her mouth, his knees spreading hers wide apart. And then his hand found her throat, curving around it with such careful gentleness, close and dangerous...

But Daisy trusted him now. She saw him, she knew him, she wanted everything about him—and when Filak reached down, and brought up the two halves of her broken *kraga*, it was more stunning art, more stark beautiful truth. And—her breath caught—it was even written there on the *kraga*, etched into both curved inside edges, in elegant curling Aelakesh. A vow. A new vow.

"I honour you, and cherish you," Filak murmured, translating, as he traced his claw against the script. "I keep you safe and whole and fulfilled, so long as I live."

Daisy met Filak's eyes, drank up the undeniable weight of that vow—a vow that had surely been written there on the *kraga*, this entire time. It had always been part of this, and he had always, always meant it, even in their darkest nights.

But it was right, now, that Filak let her look at the vow, let her wonder at it, bring up her finger to stroke against it. And then right, too, that his knees should spread her thighs wider, so his hot delving cock could nestle against her wet willing warmth, find its flower, its home. And then right, glorious, perfect, that he should ease in slow and deep, fill her and quake her all over, while his warm hands spanned the cool *kraga* around her throat, and closed it with a soft, decisive snap.

Mine, it meant, loud and unshakeable, defiant in his eyes. *Mine, mine, mine.*

And yes, that was exactly what Daisy wanted, her fierce stunning mate staking his claim, swearing his vow, locking and guarding her throat—and now, with a sudden stuttering snap of his body, he was fucking her, too. Pumping in and out, slamming hard and fast and possessive, driving as deep as he could go. Shouting, screaming it to all the world, *mine, mine, mine.*

But Daisy was shouting it too, clamping her arms and legs tight around him, digging her fingernails into his skin. Dragging him harder, hotter, closer, demanding he shout it louder, show her with everything he had. His hips thudding, his bollocks slapping, his cock plunging in and out with staggering strength. The sounds slick and wet and shameless, rising with their gasps and cries, urging them closer and closer—

And then it caught, shivered, held—and blazed up into a raw, shuddering euphoria. Spinning them both up into its wild whipping thrall, shouting and clinging together, pouring out their pleasure and wonder. And Daisy had never felt so pure, so real and alive and powerful, cradled tight between Filak and the stone, while he pummelled her full of his hot surging seed, and sank his sharp teeth deep into her gold-encircled throat.

Daisy couldn't have said how long they stayed locked together, the truth and the power still juddering out between them. But when Filak finally drew back, his eyes were bright, his face wet, his reddened mouth slightly quivering. And Daisy might have been weeping too, stroking both her hands at his wet cheeks. Her mate. *Hers.*

He smiled back at her with such warm, shining affection in his eyes, and then, with a brief glance downwards, he sank backwards out of her, onto his knees between her legs. Releasing a sudden surge of molten heat from deep within her, spilling it all over the stone beneath them.

But that was part of the art, too, just like the way he leaned down and gently kissed her belly, where the bottom two lines of his vow had almost fully faded. And then he brought down his claw, brushed it carefully at her skin, and searched her blinking eyes. Asking, *Do you still want this, from me?*

But yes, Daisy still wanted it, and Filak saw it, he knew it. Nodding back toward her, giving her another wavering little smile, before slowly strengthening the pressure of that claw, sinking it deep enough to leave the first careful mark on her skin.

And maybe it was the still-radiating pleasure, or his other hand still gently stroking her hip, but the pain was only a distant shimmering prickle, another colour in the joy. In the truth of her mate finally finishing this, marking her with firm, deliberate strokes, moving slow and reverent across her skin. Making her his own. Making it forever.

When he finished, those three equal lines of his vow were finally there, complete, together. And Daisy blinked down toward them again and again, while a sudden tightness caught in her throat. Filak had sworn it. Embedded it forever into her skin, and her heart.

"*Ég mun virða og dá þig,*" Filak murmured, as his eyes glimmered on hers. "*Ég mun veita þér öryggi, kærleika og lífshamingju svo lengi sem ég lifi.*"

And it was the same vow as the one on the *kraga*, the

same truth. *I will honour you, and adore you. I will keep you safe and loved and fulfilled, so long as I live.*

For an instant, Daisy could only feel the strength of it, shuddering all through her—and then she hurled herself up, and into her mate's waiting arms. Squeezing him as tightly as she could, feeling his heartbeat race against her skin. Feeling how much this had meant to him, and now—now—

"Can I do one too?" she whispered, pulling back, searching his eyes. "Mark you, *myrkrið mitt*?"

Filak's eyes widened, flared with warmth and longing, and then he glanced downwards. Toward—oh. That daisy she'd drawn on his hip, its ink now faded too, worn to a pale grey.

He jerked a fervent nod, and Daisy guided him down onto his back. Feeling how easily he went, how he shivered as he settled against the stone, how much he wanted this. And he even offered up his hand toward her, giving her a hopeful little half-smile. Suggesting that—oh. She could use his own hand, his own claws.

It would be the most unusual medium Daisy had ever used for drawing, but suddenly it felt just as right as all the rest. Just him, and them, and their art. And she shot him another shy, grateful smile as she carefully gripped his long clawed finger, and guided it downwards, toward the eye in the middle of the daisy.

She'd meant to scratch lightly, maybe just deep enough to sink through, but Filak's claw pressed down with surprising force, instantly bringing red to the surface. And Daisy's shocked glance up toward his eyes found them warm and glinting, sharp with stubborn certainty. Wanting this. Wanting it to stay.

So they did it together, drawing together line by line, stroke by stroke. Marking Filak forever with Daisy's hand, Daisy's sign, Daisy's art. And as raw and strange as it was, it also again felt like a prayer, stronger than any of the rest.

Speaking her vow, showing her care, pleading for his partnership, his seeing, his home.

By the end of it, she felt almost dazed with it, lost in the overwhelming intensity of it—but it was still real. Still here. Still alive and warm and true, her wondrous mate now wearing her mark in bright vivid red, and blinking at her with utter devotion in his eyes. His mouth opening and closing, silent and helpless, as if he couldn't find words to speak.

But it didn't matter. It had never mattered. They had always known, always understood, always seen. And when Daisy knelt down over her beautiful bonded mate, they shouted it together with their kiss, their hands, their art.

Mine, they said, promised, in perfect accord, in every language in the realm. *Mine, mine, mine.*

EPILOGUE

I t was the night of the Skýli's first-ever *gleðskapur*, and Daisy couldn't remember the last time she'd seen her mate so agitated.

"*Vertu kyrr, myrkrið mitt,*" she said lightly, gripping his chin, tilting his head slightly sideways. "Almost done, ach?"

Filak wrinkled his nose, but otherwise obliged, holding himself rigid and still while Daisy finished repainting the *húðflúr* down his jaw. It was a fairly recent one, one he'd asked her to paint just last week, praying for wisdom as he spoke on behalf of his kin—but Daisy knew how much he wanted to face the *gleðskapur* with all his *húðflúr* dark and new, made fresh for his kin.

"There," she said firmly, as she drew back, and ran her eyes up and down Filak's familiar form. He hadn't dressed yet, giving her a marvellous view of all his smooth pale skin, and his newly shaven head, and all his fresh black marks. Some of them the same as he'd always had, but some of them extended, or changed, or new. Daisy was especially partial to the elaborate sun she'd carved into his chest, and the intricate inked flowers rising up on both his shoulders. And, of course, the promises on his thighs, the tantalizing rings on his bollocks, the prayers of adoration and bounty all over his hanging half-hard cock.

That cock gave a hopeful little twitch as Daisy eyed it, but she reluctantly shook her head, and angled a wry smile at Filak's face. "You didn't want to be late, remember?" she said. "But after, ach? *Ríða í dýflissu?*"

Filak's eyes flickered with warmth, and then he slid his arm around Daisy's back, and drew her close. "Ach, please, *sólin mín,*" he murmured, into her hair. "Thank you, for bearing me today."

Daisy huffed a laugh and waved it away, because these days, even Filak's grumpiest moods were surprisingly mild, and usually targeted at understandable subjects. Like the other day, when Kesst had brought in a massive, monstrous carved bed, apparently meant for posing in. Or when Rosa had signed Filak up to teach weekly classes at Orc Mountain's school, without actually consulting him first—in addition to his regular teaching at the nearby Skai Wolf-Camp, too.

But of course Filak had agreed to the extra teaching, after a considerable amount of muttering and complaining. And Daisy always thoroughly enjoyed their weekly overnight trips back to Orc Mountain, especially now that Filak and the Ka-esh had designed a new cart, which ran with satisfying speed on clever steel rails through the tunnels. It made visits far easier than before, and it meant that there was usually a steady stream of people back and forth between Orc Mountain and the Skýli, visiting friends and working on restorations and making trips to Dusbury and the Wolf-Camp.

And tonight, they had multiple guests on the way for the *gleðskapur*—a Nor-ka-esh tradition, Daisy now knew, to honour the longest day of the year. The eye in the cathedral—its *sólarsýn*—had been wide open all day, pouring the room full of dizzying sunlight, so bright Filak had only been able to look at it from afar. But now that the sun had set, they would gather and celebrate it, and dance together in the dark.

And as the Skýli's vaunted *Verndari*, Filak would serve as the night's host, and he even had a prescribed outfit to wear, too. A short black leather kilt, and one of those long hooded cloaks Daisy remembered him wearing out to the garden—but now it hung off his shoulders behind him, showing off all his marks, and his tall muscled body. Which, thanks to all his constant eating, had filled out an astonishing amount these past few months—to the point where Daisy couldn't see a single rib, and his upper arms were thicker around than her head.

"Must be strong and hale, to guard mate and new son," he'd firmly told her, when Daisy had first mentioned it. "You no like?"

But of course Daisy liked it, just as much as she'd liked the previous slimmer version of him, too—which would likely reappear someday, if he ever had something important to pray for. And he was still her absolute favourite subject to draw, his body a work of art in so many ways, and Daisy still took a strange, visceral thrill in capturing it on the page, especially her own marks that were now forever embedded into his skin. She'd marked him, she'd claimed him, he was *hers*.

And she was also his, and once she'd helped him finish dressing, Filak guided her over to stand before him, and began dressing her, too. Not in the leather trousers these days—her pregnant waist was far too full for that now—but instead in a new black kilt and cloak of her own, ordered from Orc Mountain's shop just for the party. And then he chose jewels for her, too, all her beautiful pieces of yellow topaz—though he'd given her many other splendid jewels these past months, too. Jewels made of deep red rubies, bright orange amber, even pale yellow diamonds. All of them gems Filak had carefully sourced and dug himself, and then cut and polished into brilliant facets, and given to Gareth for forging. Filak's own stunning art, created just for her.

But the yellow topaz jewels were still Daisy's favourites, and maybe Filak's, too. And she loved the way he was looking at her in them, his eyes proud and hungry and admiring all at once, his hands spreading wide and possessive against the bare round swell of her belly.

"Beautiful, *sólin mín*," he murmured, husky. "Mayhap one more prayer, before *gleðskapur*?"

He was tracing his claw down some of the last remaining unmarked skin on Daisy's belly—he'd done an admirable job of covering it all over with his prayers, these past months—and she smiled up at him, slid her arms around his neck. "You know I would love that," she murmured back. "But you're still going to be late, *myrkrið mitt*."

Filak made a face, and shot a longing glance toward the nearby jar of ink—and then he swiped for it anyway, and dipped his claw in with quick, decisive purpose. "Ach, only a small one," he said. "Mayhap... here?"

He gently tapped his claw at Daisy's cheek, his eyes searching hers. Still uneasy about marking her face, even though they'd done it a few times now—a small prayer for wisdom on her temple, one for intelligence along her hairline, one for pleasure down the side of her neck.

But Daisy could almost taste his longing for it, his hunger to so clearly mark her as his own, before all his kin. And despite all the other marks that already claimed it, Daisy always still wanted more, too. Wanted that pride and possession made truth, wanted it shouted fresh and clear for all to see.

So she nodded, her heart skipping in her chest, as Filak stepped close, and raised his ink-dipped claw to her cheek. And then, with soft, gentle strokes, he wrote the prayer all the way down her cheek, from the corner of her eye to her jaw.

"Pray for seeing," he told her, hushed. "For art."

For seeing. For art. It prickled behind Daisy's eyes, drew her mouth into a slow smile—and when Filak guided her over toward the wall, toward the perfectly smooth looking-glass he'd embedded into it, she eagerly went and drank up the sight. The new prayer so stark and vivid on her skin, a strangely powerful anchor for the others all over her. For seeing. For art.

Behind her, Filak looked like art, too, tall and striking and marked all over. The prayers on his head now thick enough to look like hair from a distance, the sun on his chest so compelling and intricate, and—Daisy could admit—some of her best work. And between their marks, and their matching black ensembles, and the sight of Filak's clawed hands now circling around her, stroking possessively at her swollen belly, it was a sight Daisy wanted to commit to memory, to revel in for as long as she pleased.

"*Gott*, ach?" she murmured toward him, meeting his glittering eyes in the glass. "Like we belong. Together. And here, too."

She'd cast a brief, appreciative glance at the room around them, which she always loved looking at, too. Filak had worked intensively on it for weeks and weeks, first in choosing the location—just beside and below the *forsalur*, the Skýli's greeting-room, so he could be easily available in case of emergency. And then he'd cut the room out of the stone himself, and carved all the surfaces with painstaking care. The floor was all smooth black tile, as soft as velvet beneath Daisy's feet, and the rounded walls were far rougher, an intriguing mix of natural stone and glittering colour. And of course, the colour was all from stunning gems Filak had unearthed himself—many from Daisy's *sálugjald*—and then he'd embedded them into the stone in clever and complicated ways. So there was always something new to discover, an intriguing angle to study and see.

And best of all, hidden in one of those walls, was the secret door to Daisy's studio. A door only she and Filak knew how to open, and which led to a large, white-walled room, full of paper and paints and canvases and notebooks and sketchbooks and pressed flowers and stones. Many of the paints were made from stone sourced by Filak himself—iron ochre for orange and yellows, lapis lazuli for blues, celadonite for greens—and to protect Daisy from the fumes, he had also installed excellent ventilation, too. And for the finishing touch, embedded high in the studio's ceiling, there was an impressive new *sólarsýn*, running up through multiple layers of rock, so Daisy could draw and paint below its bright beaming light.

"*Ach, sólin mín,*" Filak murmured now, husky into her ear. "Mates. Artists. Home."

Daisy exhaled and nodded, drank it all up for one more deep, satisfying breath. It was here, it was real, it was *hers*.

And when Filak gently clasped her hand, drew her toward the door, she eagerly went. Waiting while he closed off the stone door to their room, shutting it so that it appeared to vanish into the wall itself. And then he stopped to briefly consult with Thomas and Elgr, who were guarding the nearby exit from the *forsalur*. But apparently all the confirmed guests from Dusbury had now arrived, so Filak also closed off that door, and thanked Thomas and Elgr before waving them off to the party, too.

The sounds from the cathedral rose as they approached, the excited voices and laughter carrying between the heavy, propulsive drumbeats. Stirring up Daisy's own excitement too, thrumming with her heartbeat. They would honour the sun, and all their kin, here in their newfound home.

When they reached the cathedral's familiar main entrance, Daisy had to pause and take a breath, drink up the spectacular sight before them. The huge room had been fully restored, its walls pure white and gleaming, carved all over with beautiful matching patterns. While the floor's tiles followed their own black-and-white pattern, spiralling in a perfect circle toward the middle of the room—with only one slight variation, where Filak had blended the stone with the proof of their lovemaking. And high above, the *sólarsýn* in the ceiling was still wide open, its iris a deep watching black, reflecting the night sky far above.

And instead of being bare and empty and broken, like the way they'd first found it, the cathedral was full of life and energy and warmth. Kesst had done an admittedly impressive job with the decorating, creating multiple distinct areas for sitting and gathering, full of durable, comfortable furnishings. There was also a dedicated space for music and art and dancing—currently occupied by multiple Ash-Kai drummers—and all the alcoves surrounding the room were covered with colourful silks, offering privacy or extra sun protection as needed. And scattered throughout the room were large rounded planters, bursting with food and flowers grown in the light of the sun, while one of the alcoves hid a delightful mushroom garden, too.

But most wonderful of all were all the people. All Daisy and Filak's familiar friends from Orc Mountain, chattering and laughing and dancing together, along with a large contingent from the nearby Wolf-Camp, too. And of course, most of the mountain's Ka-esh seemed to be in attendance— and mingling all amongst them, their pale marked bodies gleaming in the lamplight, were the Nor-ka-esh. Filak's kin.

They'd begun arriving months before, soon after Filak and Daisy had taken their first trip north together. It had been a long, tiring journey, but Filak had known the route well, and all the best places to camp underground along the way. And when they'd finally arrived at the twisty, impossibly deep warrens the Nor-ka-esh had dug for themselves, Daisy and Filak been greeted with unease and confusion, and a significant amount of suspicion, too.

But the Nor-ka-esh hadn't been actively hostile, either, and Daisy hadn't missed how gaunt and pale they'd been, including the small group of silent, shadow-eyed women. And though some of the Nor-ka-esh orcs had hair, most of them did not, suggesting they'd all been intensively praying, too, surely for help and food and safety. And upon seeing Filak, several of the orcs had greeted him with genuine-seeming excitement, and even eagerly demanded—in heavily accented Aelakesh—that he give them a thorough account of all he had done, since he'd left.

Filak had switched into the same accent with easy famil-iarity, and he'd then told them the entire tale of how he'd spent the past few years—even the parts of how he'd strug-gled to gain a mate, and mistrusted the other Ka-esh at Orc Mountain. And when he'd reached the part about finding the Skýli, the Nor-ka-esh had gasped and stared, and several of them had loudly protested, and insisted he show them proof at once.

But Filak had anticipated that, and he'd produced multiple artifacts from the Skýli for them to touch and scent. But it turned out that the strongest proof of all had been Daisy's sketchbook, and all her detailed illustrations of the Skýli—from their first discovery of its ruined state, all the way to the restorations they'd recently completed.

After that, the Nor-ka-esh had finally agreed to send a small band south to investigate, led by a bulky, unsmiling, heavily marked orc named Krusa. Daisy had initially been uncertain about travelling back with Krusa and the others, but she'd quickly come to know and appreciate them, and their many commonalities with Filak. She'd especially enjoyed seeing Filak interact with them, excitedly debating about stones or gems or digging, or telling tales of days long past, or exploring underground with astonishing ease. Filak seemed particularly close to this Krusa—apparently they'd grown up together—and Daisy had been highly entertained by how Filak would rant and gripe at Krusa about some insignificant topic or another, growing more and more expressive and eloquent with every breath, until Krusa's stern demeanour would finally break into deep, earth-rumbling laughter.

And when they'd finally reached the Skýli again, it had been Krusa who had been most enraptured by it. First just staring at the cathedral for an entire afternoon, and then wandering endlessly around the corridors, and eagerly discussing repairs with the Ka-esh from the mountain. And it had only taken a few days before Krusa had begun disappearing with various Ka-esh orcs into dark corridors, too, to which Filak had rolled his eyes, and irritably complained to Daisy that they could have saved themselves all this effort just by sending a few portraits north instead.

But in the end, Krusa had returned north to his kin, and had fiercely advocated for Filak's full restoration to the clan, and a return to the Skýli. And several weeks later, he had come back leading a group of about a dozen Nor-ka-esh—multiple orcs, a few women, and even two small, wide-eyed orclings. And Daisy would never forget the moment when the Nor-ka-esh first stepped into the Skýli's brightly sunlit cathedral, gasping and clutching each other, gazing around at the stunning white room with shock and wonder and longing.

Since then, the Nor-ka-esh had devoted themselves to the restoration efforts, working closely alongside their new Ka-esh kin, and freely sharing their significant knowledge of ancient Ka-esh building methods. And though the transition hadn't always been seamless—mostly due to various cultural differences around food, language, and sunlight prefer-ences—they'd so far managed to settle any conflicts peacefully, with heavy reliance on their shared Ka-esh commitment to knowledge, curiosity, and exploration.

But a crucial part of it, Daisy also knew, had been Filak. Since his kin's arrival, he'd worked tirelessly to support them, explaining customs and rationales, providing food and ink and furs, and freely offering his stone-seeing skills whenever needed. He'd also arranged regular group tours south to Orc Mountain, made dozens of personal introductions, and fiercely advocated for the Nor-ka-esh with John-Ka and the rest of the mountain. Showing himself a truly excellent *Verndari* of the Skýli, just as Daisy had known he would be.

And while Filak hadn't yet received any formal apologies from the Nor-ka-esh for their treatment of him in the north, he hadn't seemed bothered by that fact, either. And when Daisy had asked him about it, he'd only shaken his head, and wryly smiled toward her. "Ach, they show their truth, *sólin mín*," he'd told her. "They follow me, and honour me, and heed my words. They know I have earned this right amongst them, and the more I show them kindness in this, without seeking their penance or pain, the more they will honour it, and bring the rest of our kin here to be safe with us."

It had shimmered in Daisy's belly—her formerly angry, lonely mate, now trusting his kin, freely offering them patience and forgiveness, and earning their trust in return. And he hadn't been wrong, either, because now—Daisy's eyes ran over the assembled guests in the cathedral—there were dozens of Nor-ka-esh making their homes here. Dozens of orcs, women, and children, all living peacefully with their fellow Ka-esh, and working to restore all they'd lost, and to build a new future together.

And there, striding over toward them, was none other than Krusa himself, giving them a curt nod. "*Góður gleðskapur*," he said, with a wave of his clawed hand toward the hubbub behind him. "*Og góð húðflúr.*"

Good party, it meant, *and good prayer*—and he'd directed that last bit toward Daisy, and that distinct new mark Filak had drawn down her cheek. And Daisy could feel Filak preening beside her, a satisfied smile pulling at his mouth. "*Ach, þú líka*," he replied, with a nod toward an intricate new prayer running down Krusa's bulky shoulder. "*Er eitthvað að grafa?*"

Is there anything to dig, it meant, a Nor-ka-esh phrase that essentially meant, *what's new*? And as usual, Krusa puffed out his broad chest, and launched into a grave-sounding list of various concerns, including everything from a new crack in the ceiling to a disappointing lack of biscuits at the refreshment table.

But Daisy's attention had already begun to wander, her eyes drifting off toward the drummers, and beside her, Filak gave a light slap to her arse, and a brief kiss to her hair. "Go see and draw, *sólin mín*," he murmured. "Find you soon, ach?"

Daisy shot him a swift, grateful smile, because while she loved Filak's commitment to all the facets of his new calling, she herself could still muster very little interest in managing tedious administrative tasks. A fact which Filak had never held against her, and instead he always encouraged her to live and work in her own way. To focus on drawing, and learning, and seeing.

So Daisy kissed Filak's cheek goodbye, and then happily wandered off toward the party. Where she first chatted briefly with William and Soren, and then admired Geva's beautiful new dress, and spent some time with a few of the Nor-ka-esh women, all of whom seemed far happier and healthier than before. And then she spoke with Jule for a while, too, and got a new update on Lew and Sybil, and the entire situation with Lord Nash.

But it was all still proceeding to plan, as well as they could have hoped. Lew had kept his word and shut down the entire project, and then he'd used his half of Daisy's *sálugjald* to run off to Mirkandos, across the western sea—where, Jule informed Daisy with a roll of her eyes, he was apparently already writing a new book, and seeking to capitalize on his status as a foreign celebrity. As for Sybil, after learning of the project's cancellation, she had instantly abandoned Kalfr and gone back north to Lord Nash, where she'd only been seen a few times since.

"Nash certainly isn't pleased with her, or the outcome of this mess," Jule said, with a grimace. "But he hasn't mentioned any of it in public, and we haven't yet been able to learn what his next plans are, either. But"—a dangerous glint flashed through her eyes—"we're putting multiple measures in place, and we will find a way to *crush* that warmongering scum, don't you worry."

Daisy didn't have any doubts about that whatsoever, and she smiled fondly back toward Jule, and thanked her for all her help. And then, once Jule had run off after her sons, Daisy drifted toward the nearby drummers, first listening to their propulsive thudding rhythms for a while, and then settling down to sketch them, too.

"Your music is wonderful," she told one of them, a bulky handsome Ash-Kai whose name she vaguely recalled was Othan. "Would you mind if I drew a close-up of your drum?"

Othan readily obliged, and he soon proved to be an excellent subject, with his easygoing patience and broad, dazzling grin. And once Daisy had finished multiple sketches of his drum, he bashfully rubbed the back of his neck, and glanced meaningfully down at her sketchbook.

"Do you ken you might put this in your next book about our mountain?" he asked shyly. "I have read your first one a dozen times, I ken."

Really? Daisy blinked, but then couldn't help her own delighted grin back toward him. Her new book had only been published a few months before, but *The Spectacular Sights and Secrets of the Orcish Underworld* had already proven to be a surprising success, both in and out of Orc Mountain.

Everyone in the mountain had wanted to read it, especially if they or their friends were included, and—as Rosa had repeatedly predicted—many humans outside the mountain had shown themselves to be desperately curious about what scandalous secrets the orcs might be hiding.

Of course, many of those secrets had been not-so-scandalous caves and mushrooms and flowers, but Daisy had done her best to include compelling scenes and sights from all around the mountain, and from the Skýli, too. The forges, the cathedral, the schoolroom and cisterns and waterfalls—along with plenty of orcs of all ages, enjoying a variety of typical orcish activities. And while she hadn't included anything too suggestive, she'd also slipped in a few hints here and there—the spattering of Filak's seed across the mushroom garden, his clawed hand digging possessively into something soft, a detailed depiction of some of his most intriguing marks. And of course, she'd drawn him in all his naked glory for Rosa's orc anatomy book, which they'd promoted as a companion to her own—and which had also seen record sales, much to Rosa's delight.

"I'm so glad you liked my book," Daisy belatedly told Othan, with another grateful smile. "And yes, I've been working on a sequel. I'm not sure what I'll include yet, but right now I'm gathering as much as I can, so thank you for your help."

Othan's smile beamed even brighter, his eyes shining hopefully on hers, and after an instant's considering it—and a quick request for permission—Daisy began drawing a close portrait of his smiling face, too. He really was an excessively striking orc, one that her readers would likely enjoy seeing, and...

"Oh good gods," came an exasperated voice from beside them—Kesst's voice—and without warning, he snatched Daisy's pencil from her fingers, and jabbed it toward Othan's face. "Do you have a death wish, brother? Have you *met* her mate?"

Daisy shot a surprised glance upwards, and then followed Kesst's eyes toward—oh. Filak, frowning across the room toward them, with a vicious deadly glint in his eyes. And though Daisy gave him a cheerful wave, his expression didn't change, now glowering dangerously toward Othan's handsome face.

Daisy chuckled and fondly shook her head, because while Filak had grown more tolerant of her drawing most orcs—even Kesst and Efterar—he still highly mistrusted orcs he didn't know well, and especially handsome ones without mates. Even so, Daisy knew Filak was unlikely to actually do anything about it—except delightfully punish her in the *dýflissa*, perhaps—but Othan kept eyeing him with deep trepidation, and then darted Kesst a grateful look.

"Ach, brother, I have no wish to have my bollocks crushed," he told Kesst under his breath, before tucking his drum under his arm, and leaping to his feet. "Wait, but"—he hesitated, glanced back toward Daisy—"if you do include me, sister, shall you sign it for me?"

Daisy smiled and nodded, while Kesst rolled his eyes, and shooed Othan away. "Typical vain Ash-Kai," he told Daisy, with a twist of a smile toward her. "But really, if you do want to include some of us"—his eyes twinkled—"you *will* pick me and Eft, won't you? Maybe we could try a few more poses?"

Daisy half-laughed, half-groaned, about to remind Kesst that she'd given him a half-dozen new portraits this year, including a detailed, full-colour illustration of him and Efterar together in the baths, with Kesst worshipfully kissing at his mate's massive cock. But Kesst's eyes had suddenly narrowed on something behind her, his lip sharply curling. "What the..." he said, under his breath. "What the hell is *he* doing here?"

Daisy twisted around to look, and found herself blinking at a tall, unfamiliar orc, striding gracefully into the room. He was startlingly handsome, with his long black hair and pale grey eyes, but his expression was cold and disdainful, and he didn't spare a single glance toward anyone in the room. Instead, he seemed fully focused on stalking straight ahead, aiming toward—Daisy followed his gaze—toward *Julian*?

Julian had been standing not far from the drums, talking to Tristan and Salvi, and he looked particularly handsome tonight, wearing a white tunic that contrasted beautifully with his grey skin. But now his eyes had snapped up toward the new orc too, holding on his face with strange, sudden intensity.

"*Rurik*?" Julian gasped, his voice barely audible—and oh, gods, of course this orc was Rurik. And Julian's hands were visibly trembling now, his face flushing, his eyes shimmering with something between hope and longing and terror as Rurik swept to a halt before him.

"Julian of Clan Ka-esh," Rurik said, with a brief, fluid bow. "Shall you hear an offer from me?"

The conversations around them had begun to quiet, enough that Daisy could hear Julian's deep, ragged inhale. And though his mouth opened, nothing came out, and finally he jerked a short, shaky nod.

Rurik nodded too, and his cold expression shifted, into something Daisy couldn't read. "I cannot offer you a fortune, nor my favour, nor my fidelity," he told Julian, his low voice carrying through the room. "Nor shall you have any freedom to sway what I must next do. But should you yet wish for me"—his eyes shimmered on Julian's—"I yet wish to have you by my side. I will yet grant you my care, and my pleasure, and my safety. I shall make you *mine*, for as long as I live."

The last part sounded like a vow, like the words forever written across Daisy's belly, and on her *kraga*. And Julian clearly recognized them too, his body betraying a faint flinch, his shoulders rising and falling, while his bottom lip began quivering, as though he might weep.

"Ach, Rurik of Clan Skai," he finally whispered, soft and hoarse. "Yes. I wish."

For an instant, Rurik looked genuinely stunned, enough that his tall body slightly swayed in place, his lashes fluttering low. But he quickly recovered, and then squared his shoulders, and plucked out something from his trousers. A thick, solid gold circle, curving out bright and gleaming from his grey fingers. A... a *kraga*?

Julian's breath caught, his eyes frozen on the sight, and Rurik brought the *kraga* up between them, and snapped it open. And his black brows rose as he studied Julian, in a silent but very clear question. *Do you truly want this from me?*

Julian shuddered all over, his eyes briefly closing with palpable relief. And when his gaze met Rurik's again, he looked utterly calm, utterly certain—and then he took a smooth step forward, straight into the waiting touch of the *kraga*.

Rurik's eyes fluttered again, but then he slowly, carefully closed the *kraga* around Julian's throat, until it snapped shut with a decisive-sounding *click*. And in return, Julian again shuddered all over, hard enough that he lost his balance, tilting toward the floor—

But then Rurik surged forward, catching Julian's smaller body tightly in his arms. His hands running all up and down Julian's back, and then up to his shoulders, his head, his face, as if he desperately needed to touch him all over, while Julian trembled and gasped in his arms, and looked dangerously close to weeping.

"Come away with me, *elskan*," came Rurik's voice, muffled into Julian's hair. "I shall tend you, and treasure you, and seek to earn your trust again."

With that, he began guiding Julian away toward the door, without a single look back. And though Julian willingly went, he also cast a brief, wet-eyed glance over his shoulder, his eyes catching on—Daisy. And she could only beam tearfully toward him, giving a frantic wave goodbye with her pencil. To which he smiled back, slow and breathtakingly stunning, looking suddenly happier than she'd ever, ever seen him.

"I don't see what he has to be so happy about," Kesst muttered beside Daisy, once Rurik had dragged Julian out of the room. "That sounded like an absolutely rubbish offer to me, all of it to that smug Skai's benefit. No fidelity, and no say over what Rurik decides to do, and no coin, either? Julian should have at least bargained for..."

His voice trailed off as he shot a narrow, searching look toward Daisy, who was still sniffling and smiling and wiping her eyes, while also casting up a silent fervent prayer that Rurik would appreciate Julian properly, and treat him the way he deserved. But Julian knew what he wanted, and Daisy had a suspicion that Rurik might be in for a few surprises, too.

"Wait," cut in Kesst's sharp voice, his nostrils flaring. "Daisy. Did *you* have something to do with this?"

Daisy thought about denying it, but Kesst always had an uncanny ability to sniff out whatever gossip he wanted, and they were already attracting multiple glances, too. Especially from Rosa's brothers Tristan and Salvi, who had both still been standing nearby, Tristan with a stunned expression on his face, Salvi with an angry, disbelieving frown.

"Er, only a little, probably," Daisy said, with a half-smile, half-wince. "We just—sent Julian's portrait to Rurik, that's all."

Kesst stared at her for an instant too long, his brow slowly furrowing—and then he spun around, and flailed his hand toward his bulky brother Rathgarr. Who had been standing halfway across the crowded room, animatedly talking with a few other Ash-Kai, but he somehow instantly noticed Kesst's signal, and strode over to join them at once.

"What is it?" he asked Kesst. "Is aught amiss?"

"No, I've just had a revelation," Kesst said, with a wave toward Daisy. "She got Rurik to come back for Julian, with a *portrait*."

Rathgarr turned his intent gaze on Daisy, his brow furrowing to match Kesst's, and Daisy fought the sudden urge to open her sketchbook and draw the pair of them. "Um, is there something wrong with that?" she asked. "I mean, Julian *wanted* Rurik to come back, so..."

But now both Kesst and Rathgarr had shifted their matching frowns across the room, toward—oh. Kalfr. He had come to the party at Daisy's express invitation, together with a few other Bautul—but since the entire situation with Sybil, he'd been even quieter than before. There had been several weeks where he hadn't been seen in the garden at all, and even now, he was sitting alone on a bench beside the wall, staring blankly down at the tankard in his hands.

"We need a portrait," Kesst said flatly toward Daisy, while Rathgarr produced a large gold coin, and then plunked it into her hand. "Of Kalfr, looking excessively sad and handsome."

"Ach," Rathgarr added. "And with that lying murderous woman beside him, I ken. Simpering, mayhap? Or showing her teeth?"

"Both, I think," Kesst replied thoughtfully, tapping his claw imperiously on Daisy's sketchbook. "Ooooh, or maybe you could draw us multiple versions?"

Daisy should probably have protested, but she couldn't stop glancing over at Kalfr, either. She knew he'd sent a copy of her book to his son, but he'd avoided mentioning it ever since, and she'd hated the thought of him waiting alone, hoping his son had seen it, praying for a response that never came.

"Are you sending this portrait to Kalfr's weaver ex?" she

asked now, chewing doubtfully at her lip. "Do you really think that's going to help?"

"Ach, no, not *her*," Rathgarr replied firmly, with a dismissive wave of his hand. "This shall go to the other one. Gaelfr. It shall set him raging, I ken."

He looked darkly pleased by this, and beside him, Kesst was cackling, and drumming his claws together. "I only wish we could see it," he said gleefully. "I wonder if we should try to deliver it in person?"

This led to an intensive discussion on the merits and dangers of taking such a long trip, and whether this Gaelfr would be likely to murder whoever dared to deliver him such a portrait. While Daisy half-listened and focused on drawing, first sketching a tall, handsome, sad-eyed Kalfr, and then adding a beautiful, sharply smiling Sybil beside him, clutching tightly at his arm. As if she was about to open her mouth at any moment, and tell him to move on, and forget his son forever.

Daisy wasn't sure if it was actually an accurate likeness of Sybil—it had been a long time since she'd seen her—but once she'd finished, both Kesst and Rathgarr seemed thoroughly pleased, and Rathgarr even plunked another coin into Daisy's hand. "Thank you," he told her. "Your art is a great gift to us all."

It fizzled low and content in Daisy's belly, and after a few deep breaths, she finally returned to the party. Eating some of the delicious treats from the huge table of food, sketching some of the beautiful outfits their guests were wearing, and chatting to more familiar friends. Thomas and Elgr and their son, Kitty and her two doting mates, Tristan and Salvi and Rosa. Though Tristan and Salvi still seemed unusually quiet, Tristan looking withdrawn and morose, Salvi glancing repeatedly toward Tristan's bare neck. Until Rosa finally rolled her eyes toward them, and told them to stop ruining what was supposed to be a delightful Ka-esh party.

"Although," she said to Daisy, narrowing her eyes across the room, "are they *working*? Again? At their own party?!"

Daisy followed Rosa's gaze toward where Filak had barely moved from where they'd first come in, and was indeed deep in discussion with Krusa and John-Ka. Krusa even appeared to be taking notes, writing with his claw on a scroll of paper, while Filak and John-Ka nodded and gestured at each other, speaking back and forth in swift, intent Aelakesh.

"Gods, Ka-esh orcs are utterly *dreadful* at relaxing," Rosa groaned, as she promptly began steering Daisy across the room. "There's only one way to handle this, sister."

Daisy blinked, but followed along with rising bemusement, having long ago learned that Rosa's plans were always worth being involved in. Although they often ended in trouble, too, and Daisy didn't miss Rosa's wicked smile at the sight of both Filak and John-Ka glancing up toward them at once, wearing similar wary expressions on their faces.

"Daisy and I are bored with all your ceaseless working, while we're supposed to be having fun," Rosa announced, without preamble. "So we've decided to go off to the *dýflissa* together, to see if we can find some fun there instead."

She didn't wait for the answer, just steered Daisy back off toward the nearby curtained alcove that led to the new *dýflissa*. But Daisy could hear Filak's low, displeased growl behind them, could feel his sharp gaze raking up and down her back. Growing stronger and stronger with every breath, because of course he was following them, guarding what was his.

Daisy didn't dare look back as they wound their way down the corridor, but she could almost taste his rising disapproval, the anticipation simmering hot and restless in her belly. Especially once Rosa pressed the waiting eye in the wall, and thereby swung the *dýflissa*'s heavy stone door open.

Even now, months after the *dýflissa* had been built, Daisy's heart still skipped at the sight of it, at all the clever, thrilling ways the Ka-esh had devoted it to pleasure. Many of the room's elements were similar to the *dýflissa* at Orc Mountain—the fur-covered benches and platforms, the convenient drainage, the chains and cuffs and whips lining the walls, even the menacing steel cage in the middle of the room. But the Nor-ka-esh had also added their own aspects, too—ropes and swings from the ceiling, hoods and cloaks and blindfolds, large jars of ink, bulbous stone implements jutting out from benches and walls. And there were even several tiny adjoining rooms carved into the stone walls, just big enough to fit two people inside.

Daisy had spent considerable time in those rooms, blind-folded and begging for release, but when she finally risked a glance behind her toward Filak, she knew she wouldn't escape this that easily. No, not with his eyes blazing like that, his face flushed, his teeth bared. She'd publicly challenged him, walked away from him, and now she would pay.

But it was just what she'd wanted, and maybe what Filak had wanted, too, and Daisy quivered all over as he stalked forward, and caught her arm in a gentle but decisive grip. And then he marched her deeper into the room, straight past the various clusters of gasping writhing orcs, and toward that empty cage in the middle of the room.

"*Mín*," he hissed toward her, as he yanked open the steel bars of the cage door, and thrust her inside. "You wish to taunt me, and defy me? Then you stay where I put you, until you show me what is *mine*."

With that, he slammed the door shut with a ringing clang, and then stepped back, and coolly raised his brows toward her. "Ach, *sólin mín*?" he drawled. "Wish me to see?"

But it was again him asking, making sure, the way he still always did. And Daisy knew from experience that if she said no—or even slightly hesitated—he would instantly stop and comfort her, and seek to learn where he'd gone wrong, and how he could better anticipate it the next time.

But right now, Daisy wanted this, needed it with a sudden screaming desperation. Needed her mate's full attention, his full possession, his demands and his pleasure and his praise. So she fervently, urgently nodded, holding his glinting demanding gaze through the bars. "Ach, Filak," she gasped. "I'll show you."

Filak's brows arched higher, his arms folding over his chest, and he casually sank down to sprawl on a nearby bench, as if readying himself for a show. "Ach, will you?" he drawled. "When there is so much else here to tempt me?"

He waved his hand toward the room of gasping, grinding orcs—and a few women, too—and though he hadn't actually spared them a glance, the jealousy kicked and surged in Daisy's chest, choked in her breath. And she kept her eyes on Filak's face, willing him to keep looking back at her, as she slowly slipped off her long black cloak, and let it fall to the floor behind her. And then she did the same with the silk top beneath, and—she took a bracing breath—her short black kilt, too.

It left her fully bared behind the bars, clothed only in Filak's black marks, and she didn't miss his eyes flickering as he took them in, raking from her face down to her ankles. She had so many now, so many of his prayers and longings all over her, and she slowly caressed her hands over them, lingered on a few of her favourites. The sun on her heart. The intricate script on her neck. The deep claw-marks on her hip, the thick black proclamations on her thighs, the patterns on her heavy, bulging breasts. And of course, the marks all over her round pregnant belly, with the vow embedded deepest of them all.

And yes, Filak was watching, unmoving, his lips slightly parted, and Daisy stepped closer toward him, letting her firm belly rub against the cool steel bars. "You did this," she told him, her voice hitching. "You trapped me, and covered me with your marks, and filled me with your spawn. You made me *yours.*"

Filak just kept watching, gazing up at her through hooded eyes, and Daisy could feel other eyes on her too now, prickling into her skin. But she held her gaze on Filak, on the orc who'd done this, the orc who craved this. Who maybe would never stop craving this, his woman so thoroughly trapped for him, claimed by him, utterly unable to escape him—and still wanting him. Still wanting more.

"But I need more, *myrkrið mitt,*" Daisy breathed, as she palmed at her full breast, slipped her fingers down between her thighs. "I need you to give me more. Please, Filak."

He didn't move, but his gaze dropped downwards, glittering on her hand at her groin, so she eased her fingers in a little, let him watch her gasp as she scissored and stroked. And then she slowly drew her fingers out again, and let him see how wet they were, how that wetness looked when she trailed it up over her marked rounded belly. "Please, *myrkrið mitt,*" she gasped. "I need you. I need more of you."

Filak's lashes fluttered, but he otherwise still didn't move, so Daisy stroked her hand up higher, slipped her wet fingers between her lips. Sucking them slow and deliberate, tasting herself all over them, and desperately wishing they were something else, wishing they were him...

"Please, Filak," she begged. "I'm yours. You took me and trapped me and claimed me as yours, you filled my empty belly with your seed and your heir. You did this, *forever.*"

Her breaths were heaving now, her eyes holding Filak's, seeing those flickers of greed and triumph and guilt and relief. How this plucked at the deepest parts of him, at the still-present cravings they both knew he wasn't supposed to have. The constant, all-consuming need to make her his, his, *his.*

But Daisy wanted it too, wanted the power and the danger and the thrill of it, the bright strokes of art in it. And strongest of all, she still just wanted him in it, wanted him to see himself as she saw him. As a fierce, stubborn, relentlessly possessive orc, who would never doubt or abandon or betray her, who would sooner crush himself to dust than hurt her.

"You made me yours," Daisy breathed, holding his eyes. "And that means it's your job to take care of me. Your job to comfort me. Your job to give me what I need, and right now"—she took a shaky breath—"I need you, *myrkrið mitt.*"

She held his eyes for one last, dangling moment, and then, before she could think better of it, she twisted around away from him, and bared herself to him. Showing him her wet hungry crease, empty and untouched, and then—in another burst of desperate daring—she bent double and shoved her hips backwards, toward the bars. Feeling the cold rods of steel pressing into the soft skin of her thighs and arse, as her slick swollen heat waited, opened, exposed toward him.

Of all the shocking things Daisy had done in this *dýflissa*, it was quite possibly the most audacious yet—naked and on display in the middle of the room, brazenly grinding her wet open body back into the bars behind her, blatantly begging to be filled. Begging for someone to walk up to the bars behind her, to start fucking the wet waiting hole on offer, and oh gods, anyone could do it, any one of these orcs could just walk over and slide himself inside...

But they wouldn't, because it was Filak's. She was Filak's. She was Filak's mate, his property, the carrier of his son, and it was his right to sit there, and look his fill of what was his. His right to take as long as he pleased. His right to let her stand there, on display, waiting and begging for his touch and his favour...

His right, finally, and his responsibility, to at last shift up to his feet, and loosen his kilt. His right to ease up behind her, just on the other side of the bars, his breath a faint whisper on the bare skin of her back...

And then she felt it. That familiar nudge through the bars, smooth and wet and rounded—and then the press. The long, slow slide of his hard body sinking inside, taking the offer, filling her empty waiting spaces with hot pulsing possession. Until he was buried all the way, plunged deep inside her, with only those cool steel rods between them.

"*Mín*," he said, husky but clipped. "*Mín*."

He accompanied it with a gentle slap to her arse through the bars, and Daisy shuddered all over as she nodded, and pressed back harder. "Ach, Filak," she gasped. "Yours."

His groan was low and hungry, his body swelling fuller inside her—and then he drew backwards, slow and excruciating, making sure Daisy felt every bit of the loss. Until he fell fully free of her, leaving her empty and quivering again, grinding back against the cold steel.

"Please, Filak," she moaned. "Please, give me more, please!"

She didn't care who was watching now, how many eyes had lifted to see the *Verndari*'s naked, pregnant mate trapped and begging for him, shamelessly baring her most secret parts for him. While he again took his time looking, waiting, flaunting his power and his ownership.

But finally he took mercy on her, slowly carving his way inside again, burying himself to the base. Holding there for a few long breaths, while she writhed and moaned and thanked him—and then he slowly took it away again, until he fell free of her with a soft, wet squelch.

He was making a point, putting on a display, but Daisy gladly kept bearing it, begging for it, welcoming his slow, agonizing rhythm with rising desperate pleas. Because despite all the watching eyes, she knew, to the depths of her being, that this wasn't about them. It wasn't for any of them. No, as always, it was for her, and for Filak. It was both of them seeing each other, and meeting each other, and pushing each other even further. It was Filak saying, shouting, *This is how much I want you, this is how deeply I need to own you.* And in return, it was Daisy saying…

"Yes, Filak," she choked, shoving back harder against the bars, her body empty, dripping, fully on display. "Yours. Give me more. More. All your seed, all your strength, all your stone and your seed and your sons. All you want, all you can give me. Please, Filak, *please.*"

His growl behind her was raw and ragged, and his hips suddenly snapped forward, his cock punching in sharp and shocking and deep. And then again and again and again, jolting and juddering Daisy all over, her gasps rising to shouts, the room whirling bright and quivering and alive—

The ecstasy surged and swayed with staggering strength, wracking Daisy again and again, wrenching her invaded body against Filak's spasming, spewing cock buried inside her. Locking them together in perfect dizzying unity, even with those steel bars still between them—or were they, because suddenly Daisy couldn't even feel them, and it was all *him.* All her warm, shuddering mate, closing her tightly in his safe powerful arms, gasping into her shoulder, while his throbbing body kept squeezing out inside her, giving her all he could, all he had.

When the room finally stopped spinning, Daisy found herself sagging back against Filak's solid familiar strength, her skin hot and sweaty against his. And when her blinking, bewildered eyes glanced sideways, toward where the cage door had been, she saw that the bars had all been bent and broken, leaving a huge orc-shaped hole in the midst of them.

But Filak clearly didn't care, his hands now stroking Daisy all over, his mouth kissing up her shoulder, lingering against the rapid pulsing in her throat. "*Gott?*" he murmured. "Is aught amiss? Pain, or cramps, or faintness?"

He was always extra careful these days, due to the pregnancy, and Daisy shook her head, even as her still-spasming body sank back heavier into his solid weight. "All good," she murmured back. "*Takk fyrir, myrkrið mitt.*"

There was a low breathless catch in Filak's throat, and with a jerky shift of his hands, he swiped for Daisy's clothes, and then swept her up into his arms. Not seeming to even notice the mess, streaming down from her thighs, and instead just carrying her off toward the door. And she briefly caught sight of Rosa, naked and gasping beneath John-Ka's clawed hands, and still managing to flash Daisy a jaunty, satisfied little smile.

But then it was only the dark familiar corridors, the faint crunch of stone as Filak opened the door to their bedroom. And then Daisy was sinking down into the sweet softness of their bed, while Filak settled heavy and warm beside her, stroking a damp rag at her sweaty, sticky skin.

"*Gott, sólin mín,*" he murmured into her hair, his voice catching. "You are so kind. So brave, so beautiful. So good to me."

Daisy attempted to wave it away, but Filak caught her tingling hand in his, brought it to his lips. "So good, *sólin mín,*" he insisted, hoarse. "To see me, and welcome all this. To grant me all this."

He'd set the rag aside, his hand now stroking slow and reverent over Daisy's rounded belly. Over their son. Saying, again, how much he'd wanted this pregnancy with her. And how, maybe, it was part of the possession, too, even stronger than the ink and the *kraga.* Her body forever changing for him, forever marked by him, bearing him the son he'd put inside her. A kind of ownership that nothing else would ever match, not even a cage, or a dungeon in the dark.

"Someday, mayhap, you will yet regret this," he murmured now, quieter—and when she glanced up to his eyes, they were sober, maybe even sad. "Mayhap you will yet see the danger in the darkness, and run from me. Forsake me."

Forsake me. Daisy's throat convulsed, and in a jerky flailing movement, she shoved Filak over onto his back, and caught both his wrists in her hands. Pinning them to the bed above his head, the way he so often did to her. And he didn't even fight it, just gazed up at her beneath his lashes, his eyes shadowed and dark.

"*Nei*, Filak," Daisy said, firm and decisive. "No. I won't. Because"—she took a breath—"I do see you. I saw you from that first night we met. And I wanted it. I wanted it so damned much. All of it."

The emotion wavered in her voice, and she held his eyes, flexed her hands against his wrists. "You helped me learn how to be... *here*," she said, with a nod toward the room around them. "How to face what was real, what was in front of me. But you also"—her exhale shuddered out—"you also gave me the dream, *and* you made it—safe. A home."

It sounded like such a paltry word, but Daisy meant it, felt it so much it ached. "I want to be safe," she whispered. "I want to be guarded, and treasured, and looked after. I—I want to be able to focus on art, and on creating, without needing to think about all the tiresome little details. I *like* you managing things, and taking care of me."

It was something she'd only slowly realized these past months, something else she hadn't fully seen about her relationship with Lew. Lew had handled everything, in life and in finances and in bed, and if Daisy was honest with herself, it had been part of why she'd stayed so long, and tolerated so much. And since that first night she'd met Filak, he had fulfilled that same role, far more than she'd originally noticed. He'd arranged all those baskets of food, full of treats he'd thought she would like. He'd given her clothes and furs and jewels and art supplies. He'd practiced Aelakesh with her. He'd made sure she'd slept, and stayed with her at nights, even though she now knew he needed far less sleep than she did. And throughout it all, he'd constantly supported her art, encouraged her in it, and helped her make it.

And in the bedroom, in all those heady games they played, he'd helped her, too. Recreating that night he'd kidnapped her, replaying all those parts of it again and again, until there wasn't even a trickle of fear left behind. And now, he just kept reminding her, proving it to her, showing her again and again. She was safe, safe, always safe, no matter how dark or dangerous it was. He was hers, he was here, and he always, always would be. *Home.*

"I want it, Filak," Daisy said again, holding his eyes. "I want you. I want you to keep me, and own me, and take care of me. I want you to do whatever the hell you want with me."

Filak's lashes fluttered, his breath shuddering out in something that might have been hunger, or relief. And his body shuddered beneath her, too, his cock swelling and bobbing between her legs. Saying what he wanted from her, so Daisy shifted herself forward until she could catch its rounded head, ease it up slow and thrilling inside. "I want all of it, Filak," she whispered. "I want all of you."

His hips rocked up to meet hers, his eyes shifting, flickering, shadows and light and uncertainty. "Even if I might someday mark you all over?" he murmured back. "Or shave your hair to match me? Or dress you only in stone, or fuck you with floor in *dýflissa*? Embed my jewels in your skin?"

Daisy considered all that, her head tilting, as one of Filak's hands slipped out of her grip, slid down to stroke against her rounded belly. "Or," he continued, quieter, "fill you with another son, and another? Fuck you full of my brood, until you can no more bear them?"

He surely meant to frighten her, to scare her away—but he hadn't counted on the depths of Daisy's curiosity, or maybe her sheer and utter depravity. Because she was still considering all of those things he'd said, weighing each one, her body convulsively spasming against his throbbing strength inside her.

"How would that work with the floor, exactly?" she asked, chewing her lip. "Would I be *inside* the floor? Or would you just use the whole slab to—"

"*Daisy*," Filak said, with a smile that was both fond and exasperated, his hand rising to cup at her cheek. "You ought to say *nei*. Ought to be shocked and afraid. Ought to run screaming from me."

But his words were betrayed by the softness in his voice, the affection and concern in his eyes, the tenderness in his touch. All of it such a clear, powerful demonstration of why Daisy wouldn't run. Why she wasn't afraid. Because she knew, no matter what, that he would always ask, and she could always say no. He'd sworn to honour her, and care for her, and he'd shown it, again and again and again.

She saw her mate. She *knew*.

"You won't hurt me, *myrkrið mitt*," she told him, the certainty thudding through her voice. "You won't."

Filak's eyes kept shifting on hers, now glimmering with warmth and light and relief, because even he couldn't deny it. And Daisy bent down and kissed him, tasted him, met his twining tongue with hers. Silently speaking to him, showing him, in that language all their own. Saying, so clear and certain, *I trust you. I know you. Mine.*

"And whatever we end up doing," she added, as she drew away, "it'll be art worth making, don't you think?"

And oh, the way he smiled at her, so soft, so fond, showing all his sharp teeth. Her sweet, devoted, dangerous mate, with all his contrasts and contradictions, all his light and darkness and great, dazzling beauty. *Hers.*

"Ach, *sólin mín*," he whispered back. "It shall be art well worth making."

THE END

CODA: THE FIRST PORTRAIT

Rurik drew Julian's sleeping body closer into his side, and took a deep, dragging breath. Inhaling the sweet, dizzying scent of his *elskan*, after so, so long. A scent that spoke of peace, and comfort, and home...

And of his own great failure, also.

Rurik squeezed his eyes shut as he stroked Julian's warm familiar back, and inhaled another long, traitorous breath. He ought not to have done this. He ought to have been stronger. He ought to have better resisted the bond, the call, the ever-present visions and memories of his lost *elskan*, haunting his days and his dreams.

And ach, he had resisted for so long. Long enough to learn of the strife to come. Long enough to make all his plans. Long enough to find other lovers, to learn their bodies and their secrets. Long enough, even, to hunt down the most gifted hidden healer in the realm, and to bind him close with coin and promises, and to know the depth of their rare shared skill, and the danger in the longing.

And next, Rurik knew, he would gain *her*. The other one he had been hunting, all this time.

He took another deep desperate breath of Julian's hair,

and again bitterly cursed himself, and his weakness. He ought never to have drawn Julian into this. He ought to have held fast, and kept his eyes on his amends, and his fate. And not on that damned devastating portrait those enraging Ka-esh had sent, showing his *elskan*'s painfully familiar face, his slightly sunken cheeks, the sad smile that had not touched his hollowed eyes. All of it striking stark and vicious at Rurik's deepest weakness, his guilt, his grief.

Ach, he had missed Julian. He had craved Julian, night after night. He had needed with all his strength to tend Julian, to heal Julian, to cover Julian with his scent, to fuck Julian full to bursting with his good Skai seed. To again make Julian his own, to build the bond so deep he could never leave his side again...

Rurik cursed under his breath this time, and shook his head. And then felt his *elskan* shifting beside him, his body stirring awake, and Rurik fought down the compulsive urge to wield only a touch of magic, and put him back to sleep, so he could heal...

No. He would not abuse his power over Julian in this. Never again.

"What is it, *herra*?" came Julian's soft voice, even the sound of it striking straight to Rurik's prick, and he took another deep breath of Julian's scent, and mayhap his courage, as he blinked downwards, and found his *elskan*'s face. His perfect familiar face, even more beautiful than the portrait, but with even more signs of strain, too. Faint furrows on his brow, shadows beneath his eyes, sharpness in his bones, too close beneath his skin. Naught he should have ever needed to bear, if Rurik had been here, and now he would heal it all, and make Julian whole again. He would.

"Ach, it is naught, *elskan*," he murmured, even as his hand stroked reflexively down Julian's lovely face, until it found that shining new *kraga* around his slim throat. "I am only glad to hold you again. As if"—he swallowed—"as if all is right in the realm again, even for this one night."

Julian's smile was so soft and warm it ached in Rurik's chest, and he swallowed again as Julian nodded, and leaned closer into his touch. "It will all be right again now, *herra*," Julian said, with such impossible ease, such light, artless hope. "Will it not?"

Ach. Rurik's breath stilled, his fingers spasming on the strength of that *kraga*, for he would not harm Julian again. He would not abuse his power. He would not speak false, in order to gain Julian's trust, to keep him forever by his side...

"Ach, my sweet *elskan*," he said, with yet another bitter break in his heart. "It will."

CODA: THE SECOND PORTRAIT

Gaelfr halted in the midst of the street, and stared at the paper in his hand.

He had not known the human who had passed him the letter, and he had not even thought to mark the scent. For he had expected naught of the plain brown envelope, with no name or inscription upon it. An advertisement, mayhap. A scheme to gain coin or labour, or some such.

But then, within the envelope, he had found... this. A drawing. A portrait.

It was sketched in pencil, in lines and tones of grey. And though it was not detailed, with no earth nor sky to be seen, it was yet enough to show the skill of the artist, and the distinct faces of the portrait's two subjects. Two people. A human woman, and...

An orc. *Kalfr*.

Even now, after so many summers, the sight of Kalfr's face was yet enough to steal Gaelfr's breath, and stop him in the street. His *Ástvinur*—his bond-brother—had always been one of the fairest orcs amongst the Bautul, with his tall, hale form and his deep speaking eyes. And best of all, his clever hot mouth, a mouth that would laugh as easy as it moaned, that had always felt like heaven itself upon Gaelfr's neck and his prick.

But in this portrait, Kalfr was not smiling. In truth, he looked as though he had not smiled in some time. The upward quirk of his lips was gone, and there were faint lines etched around his mouth and his eyes, and furrowed deep in his brow. And even his form was slimmer, his stance weaker and smaller, and where was his axe, or his sword?

Someone bumped into Gaelfr from behind, but he only pulled his hood a little higher, and kept studying his long-lost *Ástvinur* in the portrait. Why did Kalfr look thus? What was amiss? And where—Gaelfr's eyes narrowed—where was their son?

His heart had begun loudly thumping, and finally he dragged his gaze to the second person in the portrait. The woman. Standing close beside Kalfr, clinging to his arm, digging her long human fingernails possessively into his skin.

And until this instant, Gaelfr had not deigned to even look upon the woman, for she yet mocked and haunted him in his dreams, even with all these years and an entire ocean between them. She was the woman who had stolen away his *Ástvinur*. The woman who had borne a son of Kalfr's loins, and driven Gaelfr deep into exile, away from his kin and his home.

Gaelfr's lip was already curling as he looked at her, the fury boiling in his belly—but then he startled, and near dropped the portrait in the street. For the woman was—*wrong*. She was not the plump, lush woman he remembered, with the thick dark curls, the full lips, the ample succulent breasts. The woman whose sweet scent upon Kalfr had not only swarmed Gaelfr with rage, but a deep resentful understanding, also. For she had been just the kind of woman he and Kalfr had both liked most, the kind of woman he had always expected they would seek and woo together, and share with joy between them. A goddess, just like the one they both faithfully worshipped.

But this—this was not that woman. This was not the mother of their son. No, this woman was tall and slim, with hard angular features, and arrow-straight hair. And her smile was cold and cruel, stark with possession and pride, in strange striking accord with those sharp fingernails yet digging into Kalfr's too-thin arm.

Gaelfr's eyes snapped back to Kalfr's face, to all those whispers of pain and grief upon it, and his own heartbeat thudded louder, and sweat began beading on his brow. Whilst before him, the portrait had begun to quiver, in time with the uncontrollable trembling of his hand.

This was *wrong*. It was dangerous. It was *obscene*. For this strange woman to be smiling thus, and touching his *Ástvinur* thus. For her to see that grief on Kalfr's face, that weakness all over his form, and to claim it. To *welcome* it. And mayhap to urge it on even further...

But how had this come about? Where was Kalfr's mate? Where was their *son*? Their son ought to be seven summers old now, not near old enough to be without either of his fathers, and why was he not here? *Where was he?!*

The fury and fear punched higher through Gaelfr's chest, pitched hard and bitter in his belly. For this was why he had left, was it not? He had left to help Kalfr. To help their son. To help Kalfr's mate, even as he had hated and envied her. For he had sworn thus to Kalfr with his vows as his *Ástvinur*, before their goddess' watching eye. And he had faithfully kept his vow for all these summers, keeping himself away from Kalfr and his mate. Fighting away the grief and the longing, and clinging to the surety that this was best for their son, and their son was what yet mattered most.

But now—this? Kalfr with no mate, and no son? And with this—this cruel repellent *harpy*, clinging to him thus, sucking out his lifeblood for her own?

No. *No.* Gaelfr would not stand for it. He would *not.*

He had already spun around in the street, striding north with long, certain steps, when he finally flipped the hideous drawing over, and saw the single line of text, written upon the back.

You need to come, it said, in graceful Aelakesh script. *Now.*

A harsh, ugly sound escaped Gaelfr's mouth, and he crumpled up the portrait as he stalked up the street, his cloak billowing out behind him.

He was going home, on the first ship north. And no matter the cost, he would save his *Ástvinur,* and their son.

And mayhap—his hand now clenched on his sword-hilt—he would even save their woman.

If he did not kill her first.

BONUS EPILOGUE

Filak strode toward his *hellir* with ever-quickening steps, the fervour flickering through his chest. It had been two days since he had last been home, since he had been called away to that curst collapsed tunnel. And he was finally so close he could taste it, could near drown in the glory of its scent. *Home.*

He opened the door to their *hellir* as quietly as he could, finding it empty and still—but after a deep inhale, a reverent glance toward the half-closed door to the right, he strode across the room to the open door of Daisy's studio. And there, standing with her back toward him, was his sweet, barefoot, paint-spattered mate, fully absorbed in her canvas, in stroking her brush against the petal of a bright orange flower.

Filak watched her for a few long, quiet breaths, marvelling at the truth of her, the familiar wondrous sight and scent of her. His Daisy, his mate, his bright stunning sun, yet here where he had left her, just where he wanted her. In his home, in his rooms, creating her wondrous art, smelling only of his scent and his seed. *His.*

And mayhap Daisy had felt it, or scented it, lowering her

brush, glancing over her shoulder—and amidst a choked breath, she rushed across the room toward him, and hurled herself into his arms. "Filak!" she gasped, before drawing back, and gifting him her swift, stunning smile. "How did it go? Did you fix it? You were gone for so *long!*"

Filak could not bite back his own helpless groan, and he again crushed her close, squeezing as tightly as he dared. "Ach, too long," he murmured, in common-tongue. "I missed you so, *sólin mín.*"

His mate shivered and sank deeper into his arms, exhaling a slow contented sigh, and Filak drank her up with his hands, let her feel the gentle bite of his claws. Ach, she was so sweet, she scented so good, he longed to drag her to their bed, to plunge her full of his prick and his ploughing, to make her beg and scream—

But then aught more clutched through his chest, and he glanced backwards, toward their bedroom. "And how is Fiallarr?" he asked, softer. "Has he granted you any sleep these past nights?"

Daisy's soft chuckle rippled through Filak's chest, her head shaking. "Not much," she said wryly. "But Krusa took him to the nursery this morning while I slept, and he's finally napping now."

Filak nodded, for he had scented that from all the way down the corridor, and when Daisy nudged him back toward their bedroom, he gladly went. Heading for that new door, the new room he'd so carefully cut into the stone, just for this.

For their son.

Fiallarr was yet asleep, his pale little body sprawled on his fur, his tiny black claws spasming as he slept. And for a breath, the sight of him swayed before Filak's eyes, and near staggered him on his feet. He had a son. He and Daisy had made a son. A son of his own loins and seed, a son that scented of him, and looked of him. Down to his pale little limbs, his short-shorn hair, and the small, careful prayers Filak and Daisy had painted upon him. Praying for Fiallarr's good health, his safety, his strength.

But the gods had well heard their prayers, for from the first day of his birth, Fiallarr had been bright and hale and curious, eager to explore and to learn. And it had only been a few short moons before he had begun grabbing at dirt and pebbles, merrily breaking them apart beneath his tiny claws. A stone-seer. His son.

Daisy's hand had begun stroking at Filak's back, and he blinked hard as he smiled down at her, and pressed a kiss to her hair. He well knew growing and nursing their son had not always been easy for his sweet Daisy, and had stolen away much time from her art, which then oft left her fretful and out of sorts. But Filak had always sought with all his strength to see this, and to fully share in their son's tending, and to grant his mate the time and peace she needed to find her art again.

And amidst it all, Daisy had shown herself a wondrous mother to their son, also. She was curious and playful, easy to accept Fiallarr's many moods and needs, always ready with a smile or a sketch or a game. And there was naught else in the realm like seeing Daisy and Fiallarr babble and cuddle and play together, their shared light so bright it near pained Filak's eyes.

His eyes kept stinging as he watched their son beginning to stir, mayhap scenting them so close—and when Fiallarr's dark little eyes blinked open, they first found Daisy, and flared with joy as he flailed his little limbs toward her. "Mama!" he exclaimed, and Daisy laughed as she drew him up into her arms. But turning him toward Filak as she did this, upon which Fiallarr's eyes flashed even brighter, and he launched his small body straight at Filak's face. "Papa! Papa home!"

Filak's own laugh wrenched through him, and he cradled

Fiallarr close, dragging in the sweet wondrous scent of his son, the unthinkable joy of this small squirming body, settling so easy into his arms. "Ach, I have missed you, my son," Filak murmured in Aelakesh, with a heavy catch in his voice. "I hope you have been good to your mother? And stayed well out of trouble?"

Fiallarr's answer was a long unfathomable babble, but Filak listened with close attention, his smile so broad it hurt his face. "*Gott*," he told Fiallarr. "Very good, my son."

Fiallarr gurgled with glee, and then scrambled down out of Filak's arms, over to the pile of rocks that had steadily been growing in the corner of the room. His own Ka-esh hoard, mayhap inspired by the ones his little Ash-Kai friends liked to make, and Filak gladly followed him to it, and then joined him in fussing over some new rocks he had found— beryl, agate, even malachite.

"Ach, malachite, my son," Filak told Fiallarr with genuine pride, as he stroked his claws over the stone. "This shall make a good paint for your mama, you ken."

He aimed a smile over his shoulder toward Daisy, and found that she had fetched her sketchbook, and had begun drawing them. And when her eyes caught Filak's, they were soft and sparkling, bright with affection and pride, and with... aught else. With something he could not fully follow, but it was yet there in her scent, also. Something... heavy. Something new.

Filak's head cocked, and he patted Fiallarr's head, and rose to his feet. "What is it, *sólin mín*?" he murmured, drawing her into his side again. "Are you weary? Unwell?"

Daisy smiled and waved it away, but Filak knew his mate, knew that too-easy gesture, that weight yet in her scent. And he darted a searching glance down at her page, at the beginnings of him and Fiallarr kneeling together, the lines clear and certain, with no wavering or darkness, naught angry or hidden that he could see.

"It's fine, Filak," Daisy said now, and when he met her eyes again, they were yet warm, and too knowing, also. "I just missed you, that's all. And..."

Her voice trailed away, and her hand had slipped, mayhap unknowingly, up to caress her *kraga*. A familiar gesture, one Filak had seen her do from their earliest days together, but just as back then, there was no fear in it, or regret. No, it was almost as if she was... soothing, mayhap. Longing. *Needing.*

Filak's mouth pursed, and after a firm pat to Daisy's back, he strode over to Fiallarr, and swept him up off the floor. And then he stalked for the door, where he had just caught scent of John-Ka, coming up from below with a few of their Ka-esh kin.

"Ach, brother," John-Ka said, upon catching sight of Filak in the corridor. "We had scented your return, and would welcome a quick report, so we can assign a team for the rest of the repair."

Filak nodded—he would have next sought out John-Ka for this himself, after he had seen Daisy and Fiallarr—and then told him all he needed to know, as swiftly as he could. And then, once John-Ka had sent the others off with their orders, Filak squared his shoulders, and plunked Fiallarr into his arms.

"I need help watching my son," he told John-Ka, "whilst I tend to my mate. Can you arrange this?"

Even one summer past, Filak would have never dared to make such a request of the busy, powerful Priest of the Ka-esh, let alone trust him with his precious son. But he had learnt much of John-Ka and the Ka-esh these past moons, and would have never fathomed how oft he would find himself in accord with John-Ka, or even considered him a brother, or a close friend. They had much in common, from their rigour in work to their tastes in the *dýflissa*, and Filak could even admit that he had come to tolerate—or mayhap even appreciate—John-Ka's yappy little mate Rosa. Though he had yet taken great satisfaction in introducing John-Ka to the joys of using gags in the *dýflissa*, and then watching him wield them upon Rosa to great effect.

"Ach, I am glad to help," John-Ka replied, with a brief but fond glance down toward Fiallarr. "Our sons shall be pleased to see him. But"—he raised his brows at Filak—"we shall yet need you at our meeting about the new northern passage, in the morn."

It sounded like an order, but Filak knew it was yet a gift. An offer to watch Fiallarr all the way to the morn, if Filak needed it, whilst also acknowledging his importance in the clan's ongoing work together. Honouring his skill as a stone-seer, and his rightful place as the *Verndari* of the Skýli.

"I shall be there, brother," Filak said, with a nod and a bow toward John-Ka. "I thank you."

John-Ka nodded back, and angled a brief glance over toward Filak's *hellir*, with Daisy still inside it. "I wish you much joy with your mate," he said, "and pray for great blessings upon you both."

Ach. Filak exhaled a slow breath, and could not hide his swift, grateful smile toward John-Ka's face. He yet knew that John-Ka did not himself honour the gods, or even believe them to be truth—but these past moons, John-Ka had sometimes begun to speak thus, toward Filak and the Nor-ka-esh. Knowing, now, that they believed their Priest's prayers yet held great power, and served as a great gift toward them all.

"I thank you," Filak said again, with a brief, grateful clasp to his Priest's shoulder. "And I pray for the gods' blessings upon you, also."

He knew it meant little to John-Ka, but John-Ka smiled back, all the same. And after a farewell to Fiallarr, and a kiss to his sweet-scented head, Filak strode back into his *hellir*, where his Daisy was waiting for him, now with a familiar simmering warmth in her eyes and her scent. And Filak knew just what she wanted, and ach, he wanted it too, so deep it burned in his loins, and in his heart.

"Now, my sun," he growled into Daisy's ear, as he reached for his trouser pocket, and brought out a long, tinkling chain. "You will come with me, and *obey*."

Daisy's breath contracted, her pupils widening, and Filak could scent the sudden sharp thrill of her craving, furling bright through the air. With not even a twinge of fear upon it, not even when he dangled the chain before her eyes, and then twined it slow and deadly around her slim gasping neck. The same chain he had used to bind her in the dungeon, all those moons ago—but even thus, as it curled closer around her throat, there was yet not a whisper of pain or alarm in her scent, not one lingering memory of that long-ago night.

But Filak was always yet sure to ask, and he raised his brows, and circled the chain a little tighter against her skin. "Ach, *sólin mín*?" he breathed, still watching her, seeking her truth. "You will come?"

Daisy's nod was rapid and instant, surging Filak's own hunger yet higher, and he clipped the chain to her *kraga*, and drew her across the room. Leading her like a pet on a leash, like his possession, his property—but again, there was not yet a trace of fear or reluctance upon her, and the truth of it only stirred Filak's own hunger hotter in his loins. After all he had done to her, his Daisy yet wanted this. She wanted *him*. And there was none other in the realm who held such power over her, who had earned such forgiveness and trust from her. She was *his*.

He took his time opening the little door on the opposite wall, letting her see it, letting the sight and sound of it stoke her own hunger yet brighter. He always revelled in her response to this, to this tiny secret room he had built just for them, with all their favourite toys tucked inside. Shackles, chains, gags, pricks made of stone and steel. And the walls were thickly lined with the most pliable gypsum Filak had been able to find, so he could easily bend it to his will, and use it to make Daisy bend, also.

The scent of her urgent need was now filling Filak's breath, blending beautifully with the distinct tang of her juices in the air, and he turned back toward her, drinking up the scents, the sight of her parted lips and flushed cheeks. And then he slowly began undressing her, first releasing her full breasts, and then easing downwards, and pulling off her trousers and boots. Skating his tongue over her skin as he went, feeling her quiver and quake beneath it, whilst her craving swelled even stronger between them.

But Filak meant to take his time, draw it out, and he slowly stood back to his feet, and allowed himself to assess his sweet mate's beautiful form. Running his gaze up and down, lingering on all her ink-marked skin, her full hips and breasts, and her rounded belly, now marked with lines of faint silver, also. Growing and birthing Filak's son had changed her, softening her and stretching her and swelling her all over, and Filak would never tire of seeing it, of knowing the stark, unshakeable truth of what he had done to her. His seed and his son had made her look thus, had forever altered her thus, and it was power and possession so great it could never be lost. She was his. *His.*

"Look at you, *sólin mín*," he told her in Aelakesh, as he trailed his hand down her front, and gave her full breast a brief squeeze. "So soft and plump and sweet for me. So full of my good scent and seed, and my sweet milk, also."

Daisy's breath heaved, and her face flushed even redder as she glanced downwards, toward the trickle of white already escaping from her breast. A tendency that had come soon after Fiallarr's birth, and at first it had alarmed and shamed her—but to Filak, it had been yet another dizzying gift from the gods, a strike of power and ravenous thirst. Not only had he fucked and marked Daisy, and bound his *kraga* around her throat, and filled her with his scent and his son, and altered her entire form for him—but now he had also done *this*. He had made his sweet mate's teats full and swollen, even more than their hungry son needed, so he could squeeze her and milk her, make her leak and trickle and spray for him. And then he could even taste and suckle at her own rich sweetness, just as she so oft did to him.

"Have you been behaving for me, *sólin mín*?" he murmured now, husky, as he gave her breast a slow reverent caress, and then a light, gentle slap. "Have you been making much good milk for me whilst I was away, as I asked?"

Daisy shuddered and nodded as her cheeks flamed brighter, and she even raised her own shaky hand to her breast, and squeezed out another trickle of white for him. And ach, the *sight* of that, and Filak's prick spasmed as he caught that sweet liquid on his fingers, and brought it to his mouth. Let his Daisy see him licking, swallowing, indulging in the succulent taste of her.

"*Gott, sólin mín*," he told her, giving her breast another approving squeeze, and then sliding his other hand downwards. "And have you been making your good nectar for me, also?"

He followed it with another soft slap, to the thick hair at her groin this time, and Daisy again shivered and nodded, and slipped her own hand down to join his. Easing her fingers up inside, and then bringing them out again, letting him see how they glistened with her arousal—and then she shuddered again as Filak drew up her hand and lazily sucked her wet fingers off, one by one. The tangy flavour blending so beautifully with her milk's lingering sweetness, enough that he bent down, and took a few sips straight from her breast, too. Drawing it out with his lips and tongue, urging out its sweetness, whilst Daisy moaned, and slightly staggered on her feet.

"*Nei, sólin mín*," Filak said, with genuine sharpness in his voice, as he drew back again, and gripped both her shoulders, holding her steady. "You must stay safe and upright whilst I taste you, and use you. Now come."

He caught her chain again, and then drew her at last toward that little open door, into its waiting temptation and its danger. And ach, that juddering throb from his mate's scent was just what he wanted, the relief and the need, the stark craving of her hunger.

"*Gott*," he breathed, as he slammed the door shut, trapping them both inside the tiny room, and then crowded Daisy's soft body back against his favourite wall. "Ach?"

He did not even truly need to ask, not with that burn of her need filling his breath, but upon seeing her frantic nod, he relaxed against her, all the same. His Daisy wanted him. She needed him. She was his.

He wasted no time in mounting her and spreading her, wielding the soft gypsum to bind her up against the wall in the way they both liked best. With both her arms clamped high over her head, her arse well supported, her legs spread wide. Showing the sweet tempting sight of her fully opened womb, swollen and leaking its nectar, at just the right height and angle for Filak's strong ploughing.

Ach, it was a sight, but Filak was not yet done, and next he kicked off his own trousers, and milked out a handful of his own slick seed. And then he watched his mate, drank up her flashing eyes and flushed cheeks, as he slipped both hands behind her, and carefully fed a slick jut of stone up inside her tight little rump. Only thin and small at first, but then spreading, widening. Filling her fuller and fuller, just to the edge of what Filak knew she could bear, whilst she gasped and shuddered and keened upon it.

It left his sweet mate fully trapped and bared and opened for him, fixed and skewered upon his stone. Her soft body heaving and trembling, again dripping from her open womb, and now from both her teats, also. And for the final gift, the final strike of beauty to Filak's eyes, he again grasped that chain at her throat, caressed it through his fingers, and then embedded it deep into the wall behind her.

Daisy was trapped, just where he wanted her. She would never move from here again, without his leave. She was *his*.

"*Gott, sólin mín?*" he murmured, as he leaned in, and pressed a slow, hungry kiss to her soft gasping mouth. "You like?"

But again, he had not even needed to ask, for she was already nodding and quaking, and her blunt little teeth bit at his lip with surprising strength. "Ach, Filak," she gasped. "Please, *myrkrið mitt*. Fuck me. *Now*."

Filak's growl burned from his throat, and he made himself draw away, and give her a light slap across the cheek. "*Nei, sólin mín*," he breathed. "You are mine, and I shall fuck you at my leave. Once you have shown me you deserve this."

Daisy groaned and writhed, just as he knew she would, and her eyes darkened, her open crease spasming again and again. "You are such a tyrant," she gasped at him. "Such an arrogant demanding *verndari*, such a vicious brutal *fiend*—"

Another bolt of hunger struck through Filak's body—it meant his sweet mate wanted more, so much more—and he groped at the wall close behind him, plucking up the gag from upon it. He had had it made just for her, with its gem-studded leather straps and leather-wrapped steel bar for her to bite upon, and she moaned at the sight of it, her lashes fluttering, her exposed crease yet pulsing so hard he could hear it.

"You will honour me, *sólin mín*," Filak purred, as he settled the leather straps around her head, and slipped the bar between her teeth. "Thus, you will be silent, until you learn."

She moaned again, biting at the gag, even as she cast a narrow, reproachful glance down at Filak's dripping prick, which had been lightly nudging against her slick open warmth whilst he had affixed the gag. And Filak raised his brows as he stepped backwards, and gave his hard shaft a long, luxurious stroke. "Ach, was this what you wished for, *sólin mín*?" he asked, as he stroked it again, squeezing out a growing string of its hot fluid. "You wished for your mate's good Ka-esh seed?"

Daisy fervently nodded, her moan thick around the gag in her mouth, so Filak pumped himself again and again, watching her eyes darken further, tasting the scent of her rampant craving in the air. "You wish me to empty myself for you?" he breathed, as he dropped his other hand, and cupped at his full bollocks, also. "You wish to see what I make for you?"

Daisy moaned and nodded again, her pupils so wide they now near filled her eyes, and Filak smiled as he kept stroking himself, smoother, faster. Feeling his prick swell even fuller at the sight of his Daisy's response, her red cheeks and dragging breaths, her jiggling leaking breasts, her exposed clutching womb, now leaking a clear string of fluid, also. All of her opened and inflamed and blooming for him, making her sweet milk and nectar for him, even as she stayed trapped and skewered for him, ach—

He moaned as the pressure caught, quivered, pitched over the edge—and then his seed broke free from him, spewing out his spasming prick in hard, juddering spurts. Aiming straight for his mate's trapped, trembling body, catching on her own leaking breasts, her opened womb, her soft belly and thighs. Painting his brilliant *artistinn* all over with him, with her, with them, until she was a soaked dripping mess of it, a beautiful painted canvas on display, all Filak's own, made just for his eyes.

But even as Daisy moaned and shuddered for it, her entire body arching beneath it, Filak could yet taste her displeasure, could see it in her eyes. And were she not gagged, she would now be cursing him, demanding why he would treat her so cruelly, and deny her the seed and the joy that was rightfully hers.

And in the wake of Filak's own joy, in the mingled whirling ease and relief—ach, and the dizzying sight of his sweet mate dripping all over with his fresh seed—he could no longer hold the posture, the game. And he rushed toward Daisy with desperate speed, gripping one hand at her *kraga*, the other at the slick quivering heat between her thighs.

"Do not doubt your mate, *sólin mín*," he hissed. "You shall yet have my strong ploughing, should you yet wish."

And ach, she yet wished, just as much as he did, for she was frantically nodding, and Filak was already fully hard again, and finally settling his aching crown to her womb's slick soft embrace. Feeling her flutter and kiss against him, craving and welcoming him, needing him. *His.*

He thrust in fast and hard, burying himself to the bollocks, and then quaking at the hot plush grip of her, the silken sweetness spasming all around him. Still the most wondrous thing he had ever felt, in all his days, and it was his, his, *his.*

"Mine," he snarled at her, needing to feel her spasm even harder, needing to see the matching flare in her eyes. "Mine, *sólin mín. Mine.*"

She again nodded with fervent force, her eyes helpless and pleading upon his, for yes, she was his. She was bound with his vows and his *kraga*, with his stone and his marks, with his gag and his chain, his power and his son. And she was yet squeezing him and milking him, begging with her eyes, needing more, needing him. This. Now.

The last of Filak's control snapped and shattered, and with a wild wrench of his body, he was fucking her. Pumping himself in and out of her, slapping their skin together, burying his greedy prick again and again and again. The sounds slick and slurping, pure music to his ears, and Daisy's muffled shouts were music too, just like her bouncing leaking breasts, her arched body, the pleasure and the craving in her eyes. And Filak dropped his hand to the top of her crease, just above where he was pounding into her, rubbing just where he knew she liked it, wringing her up closer and closer...

Daisy screamed as her ecstasy tore through her, her impaled body wracking Filak's straining prick with fierce milking shudders—*now*—and he could only crumple beneath it, and obey. Bursting open inside her, flooding her full of his hot gushing seed, pouring it where she wanted it, where it belonged. Deep inside her perfect body, painting her there with him too, his priceless work of art, flaunting his riches both inside and out.

When Filak was finally empty, he waited for a few more breaths, until his Daisy had stilled again—and then he drew backwards, out of her sweet enclosing heat. A loss that made him wince, but the gain was the stunning sight of this, the truth of his bright flushed flower, burst into bloom before his eyes. Her plump body pinned and sprawled and opened, her full teats streaming her sweet milk, her slack gaping womb spewing out a rushing spraying torrent of her own sweet nectar and his hot fresh seed. The sight and scents so stunning, so succulent, that Filak near felt drunk upon it, and he could not stop himself from reeling back toward her, touching and tasting and caressing her, drinking her up with all his strength.

She was his. His. *His.*

She again quivered and gasped beneath his touch, and then beneath his deep hungry bite to her throat, too—but there was only relief in her scent now, and ease, and a sweet shivering contentment. And when Filak finally tended the bite and drew back again, and then carefully pulled the gag from her mouth, she moaned as she leaned forward to kiss him, and again tasted only of nectar and sweetness.

"*Fokk*, Filak," she gasped once they parted, her eyes soft

and shining on his. "Ach, that was so good. Just what I needed."

Filak smiled and exhaled as he kissed her again, running both hands over her slick warm skin. Above even his own joy, he had wanted to grant her that, had needed to offer her his focus and his care. Had needed to wipe away that strange weight in her scent, and replace it only with pleasure, and with peace.

But as he drew away again, he could yet scent that whisper upon her, that weight. And beneath the soft sheen of warmth and pleasure, it now felt not like a threat, or a burden, but more like... a secret.

"What is it, *sólin mín*?" he asked, again drawing back to search her eyes—but she did not yet speak. Needing time to see it, mayhap, as she sometimes did, so Filak lightly patted her cheek, and then turned to the jug of water he kept in the corner, and the small basin, and the stack of fresh cloths. And then he began washing his sweet mate's sticky, dripping form, cleaning their shared pleasure away.

"You're not going to put me down?" Daisy asked now, but there was only yet warmth in her voice, and Filak quirked a smile toward her as he kept wiping, lingering against her opened heat.

"*Nei*," he murmured, and he followed it with another brief kiss to her lips. "Not until you tell me, *sólin mín*."

Daisy's chuckle was both scoffing and tolerant, not truly displeased, for Filak knew she liked being tended to, and liked being made to bear it, also. So she could not feel guilt or shame over it, and instead could only settle and welcome it. And he knew it helped her think, too, helped her see through the ever-whirling streams of colour behind her eyes.

So he kept stroking, wiping, wringing out his cloth again and again, and then wiping himself down, too. Until they were both clean and dry again, but for the still-present dribble of milk from her full teats—so Filak raised her up on the wall, and then leaned in, and gently took turns drinking from one, and then the other. Revelling in the sweet taste of his Daisy, filling his mouth and his belly, and he sank into the light and the joy of it, suckling until both sides were empty.

Daisy exhaled once he finished, and murmured her thanks. And Filak licked his lips and smiled back at her as he drew her down the wall again, until her eyes were level with his. "Now, *sólin mín*?" he murmured. "What is it?"

Daisy took a shaky breath, her hands flexing against where they were still caught in their stone binding, and Filak released them with a touch, and welcomed their wavering grip against his shoulders. Knowing that touching him helped her too, and it was a true honour that she drew up such strength from this, from him.

"It's..." Daisy began, and then drew in more breath. "I want you to give me another son."

Fokk. Filak stilled all over, staring at Daisy's face, as his heart skipped, and then roared in his chest. She wanted him to give her another son. Another *son*.

And ach, Filak wanted this. He had always, always wanted this. But he had also seen how Fiallarr had brought Daisy pain and weariness, and had kept her from her art and her sleep. So he had not raised this with her, not once since Fiallarr's birth, for his Daisy's health and peace and art was his greatest aim, his greatest need. She was his, he had ensured this in all the deepest ways, and thus he was bound to tend to her, and guard her, even if it was from his sons. From himself.

And this meant—he ought to at once reject this. To refute this. To keep his sweet Daisy safe. But even as he opened his mouth, her hands fluttered up to his face, spreading against his lips.

"*Nei*, Filak," she said. "Don't argue with me, or lie to me. I know you want it, too."

Filak's sigh felt heavy against her fingers, for no, he would not speak false to his Daisy, either. "I only must care for you, *sólin mín*," he murmured, with a faint break in his voice. "My own wishes are naught, in this."

But Daisy groaned and shook her head, and her bottom lip jutted into a pout. "*Nei*, Filak," she insisted. "We're mates. Partners. Equals. You already give up so much for me, and take such good care of me, and you've been such a good and devoted father, too. I want this for you, and for us. For both of us."

It yanked deep in Filak's belly, twisted upon his mouth—and as she so oft did, his Daisy saw too much, knew too much. "I'm not surrendering to your fear on this, Filak," she said flatly. "Whether it's your fear of losing me, or of failing me. Or of somehow taking things too far with me, and scaring me away for good."

Filak could not find his breath now, could not find an answer, for ach, those were yet all his greatest fears, spoken too sharp and clear in his wise mate's mouth. Fear of his own weakness and longing. Fear of losing all he loved. Fear, always, of being alone.

"You won't scare me away, *myrkrið mitt*," Daisy said, softer now. "I mean, just now you trapped me in a dark closet, bound me to a wall, jammed a huge rock up my arse, slapped me, milked me, bit me, and sprayed your spunk all over me. And"—her voice dropped—"I'm still here, aren't I?"

Filak's laugh sounded hoarse, bitter, and he stroked his claws down his Daisy's warm cheek. "Mayhap you have forgotten," he murmured back, "but you are yet trapped here, *sólin mín*. With my rock yet up your arse."

Daisy chuckled and shrugged, and leaned into the touch of Filak's hand on her skin. "But I like it, Filak," she replied. "I love it. I love you owning me, and worshipping me. I love how supportive you are, how proud you are of me. I love how much you still want me, no matter what my body looks like."

She cast a brief, wry glance down her front, lingering on her soft belly and her new silver marks, and Filak could not stop his hand from slipping down to caress her, stroking protectively against her skin. For ach, his mate was beautiful, and she had always longed for his own form also, whether it was strong or gaunt or aught in between.

"And," Daisy added, her eyes glinting, "if I told you to put me down, or to stop anything we do together, you would. In a heartbeat."

Filak's throat tightened, but he could not deny it. Could not refuse any true plea from his mate. He had only done it that once, that night when he had kidnapped and trapped her, and sometimes it yet haunted him, kept him afraid and awake in the night.

"And most importantly," Daisy went on, and there was again a twitch of that weight, that... secret, in her scent. "You won't be angry if I tell you—"

She hesitated, searching Filak's eyes, and he searched her in return, studying his Daisy's flushed cheeks, her jutting chin, the stubborn spark in her eyes. And he knew that look, it was her defiant look, the one that meant...

"I already did it," she whispered. "Yesterday. I went to Efterar, and asked him to remove my pregnancy protection."

Filak's stomach thudded, flipped, and he gaped at his mate in stunned, frozen silence. She had already done it. Yesterday. And that meant, what they had just done, just now, mayhap, mayhap...

His claws clutched against Daisy's soft belly, at where he had just poured her full of his best freshest seed—and in a jumble of swift frantic movements, he drew all the stone away from her, and carefully out of her rump, also. And then, finally, his mate was in his arms, her warm body locked in his tight desperate embrace, her heartbeat pattering against his own.

"You're sure you're not angry?" she whispered, even as

she squeezed him back just as tightly. "It's not too late to change it, you know, but I just wanted—"

She did not finish, but there was no need to, either, for Filak already knew it, he already knew *her*. And this had been a kindness, a way for her to prove her words, to make sure he saw the truth she had already seen for herself. He would not harm her. He would not rage at her. He would not overrule her own deeply held wishes, even for his fear.

"I do not deserve this, *sólin mín*," he croaked, into her hair. "You ought to yet fear me, in this."

But Daisy scoffed and shook her head, and may have even chuckled into his chest. "You do deserve it, Filak," she murmured back. "And what should I fear, exactly? You obsessing over my belly and my stretch marks, and over-feeding me delicious treats, and making damned sure I'm well cared for? Or maybe"—she drew back to fix him with a mock glare—"you being even more creative and compelling and commanding in bed, and giving me exactly what I want from you? What I *need* from you?"

Filak's groan was low and disapproving, but something swayed and settled in his chest, in his heart. His sweet mate wanted him. She needed him. And she wanted to make another son with him. *His*.

And when he reached for his Daisy's chain, and wrapped it around his palm, there was only trust in her eyes, only relief. And she willingly padded after him out of the little door, back into their bedroom, and over toward their fur-covered bed. Where Filak eased her down onto her back, and then sank himself down atop her, enclosing her beneath him. Trapping her by yet another means, but she welcomed this one also, arching up beneath him, twining her arms around his shoulders.

"Please, *myrkrið mitt*," she whispered, as her legs spread wide for him, tempting him back inside. "Please, fuck me.

Fill my empty womb with your strong Nor-ka-esh seed. Breed me, fill me with your spawn. Please."

Every word was a wonder, a bright blast of joy in Filak's chest, and already he was obeying. Plunging deep into his flower, rutting her and ploughing her with all his strength, all his abandon. Making her his, his, his, about to swell her and fill her and flood her with his seed, so close...

"Trap me, Filak," she gasped, as she spasmed back against him, spurring him higher. "Fill me so full of you I can never escape. Make me yours. *Yours.*"

And as Filak's prick burst open, granting his fearless fertile flower all that she wished, it was only surety, and rightness, and ease. The glory of his sweet blooming mate, his first and second and future sons, his Skýli, his kin, his home.

"Mine," he breathed, and it was truth, it was trust, it was bright blazing light, here before his eyes. "*Mine.*"

THANKS FOR READING

Thank you for joining me for this Ka-esh tale! I loved writing this book so much, and it's been such a joy to share it with you.

If you'd like to see even more of Daisy and Filak, I've also written five bonus chapters from throughout the book, especially for my Orc Sworn Patreon!

And for even more Ka-esh fun, you can find them in multiple books throughout my Orc Sworn series. In particular, Rosa first catches John-Ka's eye (and his punishment) in *The Librarian and the Orc*, and the sweet medic Eben earns a dangerous Skai's protection in *Tryggred by the Orc*. And of course, more Ka-esh stories will be coming in the future... I especially think Tristan and Salvi have some issues to resolve, and I definitely want to see more of Gary too!

As for what else is coming up... you may have noticed that I'm VERY invested in both Kalfr and Julian's stories, and I expect they'll be our next two full-length books! I've had such a blast writing about them so far, and I have so many plans for them. Stay tuned for more!

Finally, I'd love to see you on my mailing list, which has all kinds of free bonus content for you—including artwork from this book, and a free Orc Sworn story! Find it all at finleyfenn.com.

Thank you again for joining me on this journey, and may the Ka-esh gods grant you all their insight, cleverness, and pleasure. Hugs from Orc Mountain!

ACKNOWLEDGMENTS

Writing this book was another epic adventure, and I'm so thankful to all the incredible readers and friends who helped to make it possible!

First, I want to particularly thank all the generous members of my Orc Sworn Patreon. Your kindness and enthusiasm as I've written this book has meant so much to me, and it's such an honour to write for you. Thank you.

I also want to thank all the early beta readers who shared their insights on this book with me: Amy F., Amy G., Anne-Marie, Ari, Coco, Cookie, Erin, Judi Szabo, Karen Meeus, Lauren Mauchley, Lou M., Mary Lynne Nielsen, MK, Serena, Stacy, authors Jo Henny Wolf and Kahaula, and my proof-reader Emmy from @brabedrebelt. I'm also especially grateful to Goddess Ruby Dixon for all her advice and support, and to author Lillian Lark for being such a wise, generous, and inspiring friend. And special thanks to author and artist Eris Adderly/Octavia Hyde, who has once again served as this book's editor, and remains an absolute creative genius. (Please go read all these authors' awesome books!)

This book also included a lot of technical detail, and I'm so grateful to the informed subject matter specialists who advised me (though all remaining errors are fully my own!). A huge thank you to my botanical science and art consultant, Linda Ann Vorobik, PhD; to my mining and geological advisor, J. Calamy; to my additional artistic advisors Coco, Lillian, and Mr. Fenn; and to my Icelandic translator, Þórey H. When I decided on a whim years ago to use Icelandic as a stand-in for Aelakesh (in honour of my orcs' Viking inspirations), I had NO idea whatsoever what I was getting myself into... and gods bless her, Þórey has helped me with everything from tone and style to audiobook pronunciations to making up multiple new words entirely. Thank you, Þórey!

I also want to thank all my friends and collaborators who consistently share their help and Orc Sworn love with us. All my gratitude to my Bautul Enforcer Marykate, for the fierce friendship and for keeping everything running; to Amy, the best Skaibrarian in the realm; to Morning Dove, for the delightful writing and faithful Grisk fealty; to my fellow Canadian Anne-Marie, for the constant help, hype, and kindness; to Erin, fearless leader of the Skai Mafia PR team; to Vio and Clay for the Discord greetings that always brighten my day; to my audio publishers at Podium for making my audiobooks possible; to Katie at Romantically Inclined Reviews for all the hilarity and support; and to Stacy, Amy, and EJ for the fabulous Tales from the Orc Den podcast.

And in a book about artists, I especially want to honour and thank the many brilliant professional, amateur, and fan artists who I've had the pleasure of working with these past few years. Many of those artists helped to inspire Daisy, including Anna K., Coco, Erin, and Serene Yoshiko—who between them have created hundreds of pieces of stunning Orc Sworn artwork! But I also need to thank Elaine Ho, Katy Black, Chloe, Alexandra, Skemz, Amarna, Hexxart, Nsf-ko, Qaisan, my generous commissioner Elizabeth, my cover illustrators Skadior Art and Helena Nikulina, my cover designer Sylvia Frost, and so, so many more.

Together, these artists have truly brought Orc Sworn to life in a way I never could on my own. Their unique perspectives and astonishing skills have given us hilarious comics, clever graphics, thoughtful character and costume designs, spicy comparison charts (!), emotional scene illustrations, in-depth character studies, and beautiful, fully rendered paintings and prints. (You can see a variety of their work on my website at finleyfenn.com!) I've been so, so humbled and awed by their unbelievable insights and generosity. And in a time where artists' work has been horrifically undervalued and blatantly stolen to fund massive and soulless corporate gain, I hope we can all make a concerted effort to support our artists, and appreciate the invaluable gifts they offer to us all.

Finally, as always, all my deepest love and gratitude to my very own brilliant artist Mr. Fenn, who has given me untold amounts of his insight, laughter, loyalty, and inspiration. From your biggest superfan, I adore you, *myrkrið mitt*.

PRONUNCIATION GUIDE

Throughout the Orc Sworn series, Icelandic is used as a stand-in for Aelakesh, as a tribute to Orc Sworn's Viking inspirations.

Here are a few key pronunciations from this book:

eth (ð)
sounds like "th" in "they"

thorn (þ)
sounds like "th" in "thing"

***nei* (no)**
nay

***sól* (sun)**
sole

***sólin mín* (my sun)**
SOLE-in min

***morgun* (morning)**
MOR-gun

***stjarnan mín* (my star)**
STYAR-nan min

myrkrið mitt (my darkness)
   MEER-krith mitt

sálufélagi minn (my mate)
   SAL-oo-fyell-a-gee min

Skýli
   SKEE-lee

dýflissa (dungeon)
   DEE-fliss-a

takk fyrir (thank you)
   tak FEER-eer

borða (eat)
   BOR-tha

róleg (peace)
   ROLL-eg

hjálpa (help)
   HYAL-pa

fallegt (beautiful)
   FAHT-legt

Ég elska þig (I love you)
   yeg EL-ska thig

ABOUT THE AUTHOR

Finley Fenn is "the queen of dark orc romance" (Virgo Reader), and her ongoing Orc Sworn series has been praised as "sexy, romantic, angsty, and captivating ... utter brilliance" (Romantically Inclined Reviews).

When she's not obsessing over her stories, Finley loves reading, drooling over delicious orc artwork, and spending time with her incredible readers on Patreon, Discord, and Facebook. She lives in Canada with her beloved family, including her very own grumpy, gorgeous orc husband.

For free bonus stories and epilogues, special offers, and exclusive Orc Sworn artwork, sign up at www.finleyfenn.com.